TREASURY OF BEST-LOVED STORIES, POEMS, GAMES, AND RIDDLES FROM *ST. NICHOLAS* MAGAZINE

Said one bookworm to another, as they stopped one day to talk,
"I am getting so rheumatic, it is hard for me to walk;
But, in spite of close confinement, you are youthful, fresh, and gay.
Now what could cause the difference in our constitutions, pray?"
Answered then the youthful bookworm, "There's no need to feel
  so blue;
There was a period, long ago, when I was sickly too.
But for thirty years or more, since first it went to press,
My sole and daily diet has been St. Nicholas."

—By Miriam A. DeForde (Age 15)

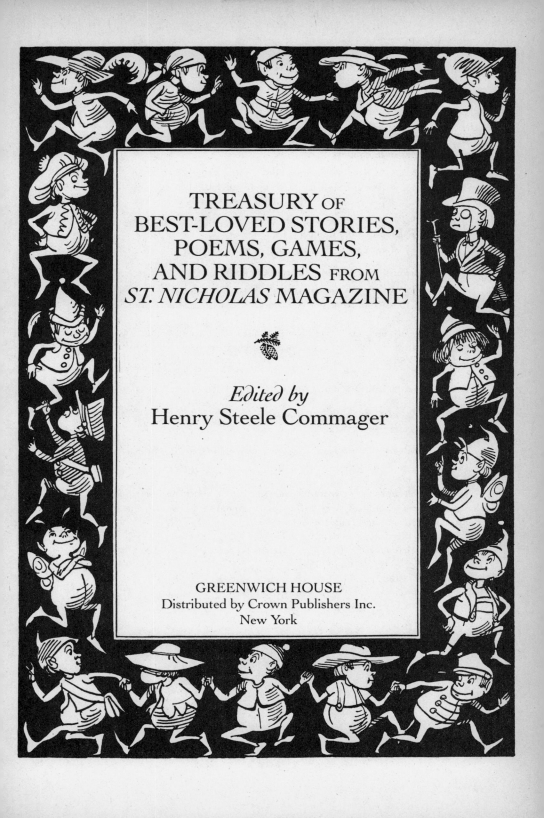

TREASURY OF BEST-LOVED STORIES, POEMS, GAMES, AND RIDDLES FROM *ST. NICHOLAS* MAGAZINE

Edited by
Henry Steele Commager

GREENWICH HOUSE
Distributed by Crown Publishers Inc.
New York

A Lou Reda Book

ACKNOWLEDGEMENT is here made for permission to reprint the copyrighted items in this volume.

Copyright 1895, 1897, 1898, 1899, 1900, 1902, 1903, 1905, 1906, 1909, 1911, 1912, 1913, 1914, 1915, 1916, 1917, 1918, 1919, 1921, 1922, 1923, 1924, 1925, 1926, 1927, 1928, 1929, 1931, 1933, by the Century Company.

Copyright, 1934, 1937, 1939, 1940, 1941, 1942, 1943, 1944, 1945, 1946, 1947, by D. Appleton-Century Company, Inc.

Copyright, 1949, 1950, by Appleton-Century-Crofts, Inc.

Reprinted by permission of Appleton-Century-Crofts, Inc.

Copyright, 1932, 1933, 1934, by Scholastic St. Nicholas Corporation. Reprinted by permission of Scholastic Magazines.

This 1984 edition is published by Greenwich House, a division of Arlington House, Inc. distributed by Crown Publishers, Inc. by arrangement with Lou Reda and Henry Steele Commager.

Manufactured in the United States of America

Library of Congress Cataloging in Publication Data
    Main entry under title:

    Treasury of best-loved stories, poems, games, and riddles from St. Nicholas magazine.
    "A Lou Reda book."
    Summary: Selections from a venerable magazine, now defunct, have been chosen from a period of many years. Includes such famous authors as Cornelia Meigs, Louisa Alcott, Bret Harte, and Mark Twain.
    1. Children's literature, American. [1. Literature—Collections]
I. Commager, Henry Steele, 1902-   II. St. Nicholas (New York, N.Y.)
PZ5.T745   1984   [Fic]   84-13536
ISBN: 0-517-448106
h g f e d c b a

*TO
LISA*

TABLE OF CONTENTS

THE ST. NICHOLAS LEAGUE

THE RIDDLE BOX

PREFACE

by Henry Steele Commager

THOSE of you who read the first *St. Nicholas Anthology* may recall—you won't, of course—a sentence from the preface. "Had we our own way," I wrote, "this anthology would probably have run to several volumes, and in our more ecstatic moments we talked of a second *St. Nicholas* anthology." Well, here it is, our wishes come true, just like in so many of the *St. Nicholas* stories—remember the street car that came in a stocking! The first *St. Nicholas Anthology* gave so much pleasure to so many people, including the editors, that it became more than just self-indulgence to prepare a second.

So here is another selection from the inexhaustible and enchanting volumes of *St. Nick.* Here are some of the old familiar names, and some newcomers. The list of contributors is, once more, a Hall of Fame, and not of juvenile literature alone. We have here old friends and favorites like Lucretia P. Hale of Peterkins fame, and Sophie Swett—we wanted to put in a half dozen of her wonderful stories—and Frank Stockton who wrote the best fairy tales (if you can call them that) of any one in our country, and Palmer Cox and his inimitable Brownies, and Ralph Henry Barbour of course—imagine *St. Nicholas* without Barbour! We have here the great names that turn out to be so simple and friendly, like Mark Twain and Louisa May Alcott

and Frances Hodgson Burnett and Joel Chandler Harris. And we have, too, those modern masters who are still, happily, with us, like Cornelia Meigs and Dorothy Canfield and Frank Dobie. The same illustrators, too, lend a hand: Reginald Birch, E. W. Kemble, Arthur Rackham, George Varian, Palmer Cox, and others.

In making this second anthology we have built, of course, upon our experience with its predecessor. We had a great mass of selections left over from that first one, but we weren't satisfied with that. Our judgment might have changed, or we might have missed something that was good. We had, too, a great many letters from *St. Nicholas* enthusiasts calling our attention to their particular favorites and invoking our interest in them. To all of these, and to the many, many others who wrote us, we are grateful. So we went back and started afresh, going through the volumes once again, making our choices all over again. We tried to keep pretty much the same recipe as before, too: mostly short stories, with a few long ones; a mixture of stories of family life, adventure, sailing, sports, history, and the like. We found room for a few—alas only a few—longer stories, like "Davy and the Goblins" and the "Two Biddicut Boys," everybody's first choice for the serial. We put in a few articles, interspersed the whole with poetry, spiced it with the League and the puzzles, and decorated it all with the best illustrations that any magazine ever had.

Like the original *St. Nicholas Anthology,* this one is a family enterprise; it wouldn't have been much fun any other way. Evan and I read everything, and agreed most of the time. Nell and Steele read everything, too, and their judgment was as sound as ever. But there is one important difference between this volume and its predecessor. When we compiled the first anthology Lisa was but an interested spectator. By the time we were ready to make this one she had graduated to a full partnership. No one read these stories more avidly than she and probably no one ever loved them better. It is only right that this second *St. Nicholas* anthology should be dedicated to her.

June, 1950

TREASURY OF
BEST-LOVED STORIES,
POEMS, GAMES,
AND RIDDLES FROM
ST. NICHOLAS MAGAZINE

THE PETERKINS' CHRISTMAS TREE

by Lucretia P. Hale

PRETTY early in the autumn the Peterkins began to prepare for their Christmas tree. Everything was done in great privacy, as it was to be a surprise to the neighbors, as well as to the rest of the family. Mr. Peterkin had been up to Mr. Bromwich's woodlot, and, with his consent, selected the tree. Agamemnon went to look at it occasionally after dark, and Solomon John made frequent visits to it, mornings, just after sunrise. Mr. Peterkin drove Elizabeth Eliza and her mother that way, and pointed furtively to it with his whip, but none of them ever spoke of it aloud to each other. It was suspected that the little boys had been to see it Wednesday and Saturday afternoons. But they came home with their pockets full of chestnuts, and said nothing about it.

At length Mr. Peterkin had it cut down, and brought secretly into the Larkins's barn. A week or two before Christmas, a measurement was made of it, with Elizabeth Eliza's yard measure. To Mr. Peterkin's great dismay, it was discovered that it was too high to stand in the back parlor. This fact was brought out at a secret council of Mr. and Mrs. Peterkin, Elizabeth Eliza, and Agamemnon.

Agamemnon suggested that it might be set up slanting, but Mrs. Peterkin was very sure it would make her dizzy, and the candles would drip.

But a brilliant idea came to Mr. Peterkin. He proposed that the ceiling of the parlor should be raised to make room for the top of the tree.

Elizabeth Eliza thought the space would need to be quite large. It must not be like a small box, or you could not see the tree.

"Yes," said Mr. Peterkin, "I should have the ceiling lifted all across the room; the effect would be finer."

Elizabeth Eliza objected to having the whole ceiling raised, because her room was over the back parlor, and she would have no floor while the alteration was going on, which would be very awkward. Besides, her room was not very high now, and if the floor were raised, perhaps she could not walk in it upright.

Mr. Peterkin explained that he didn't propose altering the whole ceiling, but to lift up a ridge across the room at the back part where the tree was to stand. This would make a hump, to be sure, in Elizabeth Eliza's room; but it would go across the whole room.

Elizabeth Eliza said she would not mind that. It would be like the cuddy thing that comes up on the deck of a ship, that you sit against, only here you would not have the seasickness. She thought she should like it for a rarity. She might use it for a divan.

Mrs. Peterkin thought it would come in the worn place of the carpet, and might be a convenience in making the carpet over.

Agamemnon was afraid there would be

trouble in keeping the matter secret, for it would be a long piece of work for a carpenter; but Mr. Peterkin proposed having the carpenter for a day or two, for a number of other jobs.

One of them was to make all the chairs in the house of the same height, for Mrs. Peterkin had nearly broken her spine, by sitting down in a chair that she had supposed was her own rocking-chair, and it had proved to be two inches lower. The little boys were now large enough to sit in any chair; so a medium was fixed upon to satisfy all the family, and the chairs were made uniformly of the same height.

On consulting the carpenter, however, he insisted that the tree could be cut off at the lower end to suit the height of the parlor, and demurred at so great a change as altering the ceiling. But Mr. Peterkin had set his mind upon the improvement, and Elizabeth Eliza had cut her carpet in preparation for it.

So the folding-doors into the back parlor were closed, and for nearly a fortnight before Christmas there was great litter of fallen plastering, and laths, and chips, and shavings; and Elizabeth Eliza's carpet was taken up, and the furniture had to be changed, and one night she had to sleep at the Bromwichs', for there was a long hole in her floor that might be dangerous.

All this delighted the little boys. They could not understand what was going on. Perhaps they suspected a Christmas tree, but they did not know why a Christmas tree should have so many chips, and were still more astonished at the hump that appeared in Elizabeth Eliza's room. It must be a Christmas present, or else the tree in a box.

Some aunts and uncles, too, arrived a day or two before Christmas, with some small cousins. These cousins occupied the attention of the little boys, and there was a great deal of whispering and mystery, behind doors, and under the stairs, and in the corners of the entry.

Solomon John was busy, privately making some candles for the tree. He had been collecting some bayberries, as he understood they made very nice candles, so that it would not be necessary to buy any.

The elders of the family never all went into the back parlor together, and all tried not to see what was going on. Mrs. Peterkin would go in with Solomon John, or Mr. Peterkin with Elizabeth Eliza, or Elizabeth Eliza and Agamemnon and Solomon John. The little boys and the small cousins were never allowed even to look inside the room.

Elizabeth Eliza meanwhile went into town a number of times. She wanted to consult Amanda as to how much ice-cream they should need, and whether they could make it at home, as they had cream and ice. She was pretty busy in her own room; the furniture had to be changed, and the carpet altered. The "hump" was higher than she had expected. There was danger of bumping her own head whenever she crossed it. She had to nail some padding on the ceiling for fear of accidents.

The afternoon before Christmas, Elizabeth Eliza, Solomon John, and their father, collected in the back parlor for a council. The carpenters had done their work, and the tree stood at its full height at the back of the room, the top stretching up into the space arranged for it. All the chips and shavings were cleared away, and it stood on a neat box.

But what were they to put upon the tree?

Solomon John had brought in his supply of candles, but they proved to be very "stringy" and very few of them. It was strange how many bayberries it took to make a few candles! The little boys had helped him, and he had gathered as much as a bushel of bayberries. He had put them in water, and skimmed off the wax, according to the directions, but there was so little wax!

Solomon John had given the little boys some of the bits sawed off from the legs of the chairs. He had suggested they should cover them with gilt paper, to answer for gilt apples, without telling them what they were for.

These apples, a little blunt at the end, and the candles, were all they had for the tree.

After all her trips into town, Elizabeth Eliza had forgotten to bring anything for it.

"I thought of candies and sugar plums," she said, "but I concluded if we made caramels ourselves we should not need them. But, then, we have not made caramels. The fact is, that day my head was full of my carpet. I had bumped it pretty badly, too."

Mr. Peterkin wished he had taken, instead of a fir tree, an apple tree he had seen in October, full of red fruit.

"But the leaves would have fallen off by this time," said Elizabeth Eliza.

"And the apples too," said Solomon John.

"It is odd I should have forgotten, that day I went in on purpose to get the things," said Elizabeth Eliza, musingly. "But I went from shop to shop, and didn't know exactly what to get. I saw a great many gilt things for Christmas trees, but I knew the little boys were making the gilt apples; there were plenty of candles in the shops, but I knew Solomon John was making the candles."

Mr. Peterkin thought it was quite natural.

Solomon John wondered if it were too late for them to go into town now.

Elizabeth Eliza could not go in the next morning, for there was to be a grand Christmas dinner, and Mr. Peterkin could not be spared, and Solomon John was sure he and Agamemnon would not know what to buy. Besides, they would want to try the candles tonight.

Mr. Peterkin asked if the presents everybody had been preparing would not answer? But Elizabeth Eliza knew they would be too heavy.

A gloom came over the room. There was only a flickering gleam from one of Solomon John's candles that he had lighted by way of trial.

Solomon John again proposed going into town. He lighted a match to examine the newspaper about the trains. There were plenty of trains coming out at that hour, but none going in except a very late one. That would not leave time to do anything and come back.

"We could go in, Elizabeth Eliza and I," said Solomon John, "but we should not have time to buy anything."

Agamemnon was summoned in. Mrs. Peterkin was entertaining the uncles and aunts in the front parlor. Agamemnon wished there was time to study up something about electric lights. If they could only have a calcium light! Solomon John's candle sputtered and went out.

At this moment there was a loud knocking at the front door. The little boys, and the small cousins, and the uncles and aunts, and Mrs. Peterkin, hastened to see what was the matter.

The uncles and aunts thought somebody's house must be on fire. The door was opened, and there was a man, white with flakes, for it was beginning to snow, and he was pulling in a large box.

Mrs. Peterkin supposed it contained some of Elizabeth Eliza's purchases, so she ordered it to be pushed into the back parlor, and hastily called back her guests and the little boys into the other room. The little boys and the small cousins were sure they had seen Santa Claus himself.

Mr. Peterkin lighted the gas. The box was addressed to Elizabeth Eliza. It was from the lady from Philadelphia! She had gathered a hint from Elizabeth Eliza's letters that there was to be a Christmas-tree, and had filled this box with all that would be needed.

It was opened directly. There was every kind of gilt hanging thing, from gilt-pods to butterflies on springs. There were shining flags and lanterns, and bird-cages, and nests with birds sitting on them, baskets of fruit, gilt apples and bunches of grapes, and, at the bottom of the whole, a large box of candles and a box of Philadelphia bonbons!

Elizabeth Eliza and Solomon John could scarcely keep from screaming. The little boys and the small cousins knocked on the folding-doors to ask what was the matter.

Hastily Mr. Peterkin and the rest took out the things and hung them on the tree, and put on the candles.

When all was done, it looked so well that Mr. Peterkin exclaimed:

"Let us light the candles now, and send to invite all the neighbors to-night, and have the tree on Christmas Eve!"

And so it was that the Peterkins had their Christmas tree the day before, and on Christmas night could go and visit their neighbors.

GUESTS IN THE SMOKEHOUSE

by Cornelia Meigs

THE broad lake at the foot of Mt. Neshobe had been swept by the bitter wind until it was bare of snow, a smooth expanse of blue ice which reached away northward, winding and turning among the rocky spurs of the Vermont hills were familiar and friendly and yet totally strange, since, although he had seen them every summer for nearly ten years, he had never before looked at their ridges and sharp summits in the winter, when their abrupt slopes were

mountain. For more than an hour Richard Kent could see it spread out below as the sleigh, with its two fast, big, jingling horses, swung down the road cut from the steep hillside. The boy had the feeling, as he looked about him, that the blanketed with hard-frozen snow instead of being shrouded in the abundant leafy green of the summer forests. The sky was gray behind the mountain tops, for it had snowed yesterday and would, in all probability, snow again before tomorrow. Rich-

7

ard burrowed a little deeper into the warm buffalo robes at the thought of it.

"We are lucky to find the way open," his Uncle Nathan observed, shifting his cold hands to get a new grip on the reins. "One more storm and the whole lake valley will be blocked."

Richard looked up at him, an erect, surprising figure with his tall, bell-crowned hat and close-fitting, caped greatcoat. He seemed curiously out of place, the boy thought vaguely, against that wild landscape of hill and snowdrift. Uncle Nathan Kent was always dressed just as a prosperous lawyer of the 1850's should be garbed, although just now he would have been more comfortable if he had buttoned himself into the old coat which Uncle Hiram Kent had sent along with the sleigh to meet the travelers, a coat which had belonged to a black bear before it had become Uncle Hiram's.

It was strange, also, Richard kept feeling, to be driving this last twenty miles of the accustomed journey without Uncle Hiram's cheerful presence, for it was his delighted face which they always saw first of all when they got down at the coaching station, stiff from the long ride up from Massachusetts. Travel was not easy in those days before the Civil War, but there was no difficulty too great to keep Richard from coming, summer after summer, to spend his vacation on the Vermont farm where his father and his two uncles had all grown up. Nathan and Thomas Kent, Richard's father, had long since made successful places for themselves in a Massachusetts manufacturing town and often wondered aloud how their elder brother could cling so stubbornly to those rocky acres above Neshobe Lake. Richard had wondered, too—until last summer. It was then that some inkling of an astonishing truth had suddenly burst upon him.

It had been a warm day, hot for Vermont, with brilliant sunshine everywhere, the most complete contrast to the present bleak afternoon. He and Selina had been picking summer apples, Selina being the lively granddaughter of that elderly cousin who kept house for Uncle Hiram. Selina lived the year round on the mountain farm; her cheerful company was always a taken-for-granted part of Richard's vacations. They were both tired on that afternoon, and a little dazzled by the bright sun. Richard, carrying the bushel basket of apples into the kitchen, was moved by a sudden fancy to seek the coolness of the dark cellar. He slipped down the stairs—groping, for he was quite blind in the dimness—and heard, all at once, under the vaulted arch of the farthest recess, the stirring of a big body, and a great voice sunk to a thick whisper saying:

"Is you coming to take me out of here, Mars'er Kent? Isn't you going to get me out of this pretty soon?"

He retreated abruptly, but stood for a long minute at the foot of the stairs, his heart hammering in his ears. Everything was still now, but Richard still thought that he could hear from that far, dusky corner a faint sound as of some great body trying to keep utterly silent, trying even to breathe as lightly as possible. Should he go forward boldly into the dark and demand who or what was there? Something kept him back, and it was not fear. This was Uncle Hiram's secret, and prying curiosity might bring disaster. He turned about and stumbled up the stairs. Out in the sunny orchard, Selina was still sitting, leaning against a twisted trunk with a yellow apple in her hand. Forbearance had its limits, nor could he have possibly helped putting that breathless question:

"Selina, what's—what's that in the cellar?"

Selina looked at him steadily. She was a year older than he; she had honest blue eyes which could, when she chose, be very determined in the guarding of secrets.

"I'm not to tell you," she answered. She set her lips resolutely, as though she were issuing the order to herself and not to him. "I—I only found out by accident, and Uncle Hiram knows I know, but we don't speak of it. My grandmother has never guessed, but I think Uncle Nathan has, and that he argues with Uncle Hiram about its being wrong."

This baffling statement was far from giving Richard satisfaction, but she told him no more, except to burst out a moment later, "Do you think, when your father and Uncle Nathan have done so much, away from here, that Uncle Hiram has stayed behind for nothing else than to grow hay and potatoes on this stony mountain? Did you ever think that he might be doing something special, too, that the others didn't even dare to think about?"

The time for Richard's departure came so soon after that day that he had little time to push the matter any further. He did slip into the cellar again, but realized from the very feel of the cool shadowy emptiness that there was now no presence there save his own. More than once he looked into Uncle Hiram's kind, sun-browned face and longed to frame a question, but went away without ever having found words for it.

D URING the next winter there was news that Uncle Hiram was less well than usual, crippled by rheumatism, an ancient and stoutly contested enemy. It was on an evening in early January that Uncle Nathan, immaculate in blue broadcloth and bright buttons, came to confer with Richard's father. Although it was still a number of years before the Civil War, the shadow of that great upheaval was already on the horizon, and the question of slavery was drawing closer and closer to the hearts and souls of all citizens of the United States. It was not surprising, therefore, that the two Kent brothers plunged immediately into discussing the new laws which had to do with runaway slaves. What was odd was that Uncle Nathan should say suddenly in the midst of the heated talk, "I'm going up to see Hiram. I can get there, even through the snow. I worry about him more every day. I wrote him, and I am starting next week."

A few days later there came, rather surprisingly, a letter to Richard from Selina. She wrote very seldom and only when she had something particular to say. "When Uncle Nathan comes up," she directed now, "ask to come with him. I believe Uncle Hiram needs you." She had signed her name with proper messages and then added: "Do you remember that secret about the cellar? If ever Uncle Hiram told anyone about it of his own will, I do believe, Richard, that it would be you."

Richard had never been to the farm in winter, but there proved to be little difficulty in getting permission to go. Uncle Nathan was glad to have company on the stage journey, and it was holiday time from school. So here were uncle and nephew, driving down the freshly plowed road, with old Silas, who had brought the sleigh to meet them, tucked up in the back seat. Uncle Nathan, in spite of his elaborate clothes and manners, had not been brought up on a Vermont farm for nothing. He could not bear to drive behind a good pair of horses unless he held the reins himself. It was he who had taught Richard to drive, so that the boy now could appreciate the adroit skill with which his uncle eased the big grays down abrupt drops in the road and around the high-banked curves.

At a narrow place the sound of bells coming toward them made them pull up suddenly. A smaller sleigh drew out to make room for them to pass, and one of the two men in it first hailed Uncle Nathan, and then got down, knee deep in the drifts, to come over to speak to him. Richard had seen that rough-hewn face before, and knew that this was John Halloway, a neighbor of Uncle Hiram's and the sheriff of that county.

"Coming up to see Hiram Kent, be ye?" he asked. When Uncle Nathan answered yes, he went on in a lowered voice: "Just you tell Hiram, from me, that I've had orders to watch him." He jerked his head toward the other man in the smaller sleigh, a stranger with a narrow face sunk deep into the warmth of his big coat. "That fellow there is from down southward, a slave owners' agent, sent up to try to get back runaway property. You see it's my place to show him around, whether I like it or not. It's beyond my duty to say much, but you ask Hiram Kent just to read over the text of the Fugitive Slave Law. That's all."

He turned about hastily, climbed into his sleigh and slapped the reins over the horses' backs. Uncle Nathan drove on, looking straight ahead and making no comment upon the message. Richard, after glancing back to observe, as he had expected, that Silas was napping in the rear seat, asked abruptly, "Uncle Nathan, just what is the Fugitive Slave Law?"

"It's a regulation put through Congress by the men who support slavery," his uncle returned. "It says that any person who finds a runaway slave must return him to his master, or help to do so, otherwise he will be liable to arrest and fines. The owners of plantations in the South are complaining loudly over the number of runaways who have been smuggled all the way north as far as Canada."

"Are they free when they get to Canada?" Richard asked.

"They are," answered his uncle, and concluded grimly, "The Canadian line, you may remember, is just forty miles from your Uncle Hiram's farm."

"Oh," was all that Richard could say, and was silent for a long time.

It had begun to snow when they drew up at the farm gate, but it was still light enough to see the row of buildings sheltered under the wall of the mountain— the big barns, the square brick smokehouse where the meat was cured for winter use, the long woodshed adjoining the broad, bright-windowed farmhouse itself. Selina was on the step to greet them and bring them in to the blazing fire.

"Uncle Hiram can't come down," she said, "and he wants you to have supper before you come up. You must be starving."

Selina and her grandmother had set forth a real banquet of country fare to which Richard did ample justice, but which seemed scarcely to tempt Uncle Nathan. He hurried through it and got up abruptly, just as Selina was bringing in the pumpkin pie. "I am going up to see my brother," he said. "You finish your supper, Richard, and come later when I call you."

THE bountiful meal had long been over and the dishes washed and put away before Richard heard Uncle Nathan's voice summoning him upstairs. Cousin Sarah, Selina's grandmother, had been in the room all the time, so that Selina had said nothing to him in private. But as he mounted the stair the words of her letter were burning within him—"Uncle Hiram needs you. If he ever tells anyone, of his own will, it would be you."

The eldest of the Kent brothers was sitting close to the narrow fireplace, which was all that gave warmth to the big, low-ceiled room. Hiram was taller than his brother Nathan, with a broader forehead and deeper, brighter eyes; with a general air of character and command which Nathan Kent, at that moment, seemed to lack. He stood behind his older brother and, in spite of his well-cut coat and his manner of ease and self-confidence, he was, very distinctly, less of a man than this crumpled giant who sat helpless in the great wooden chair. Hiram Kent sat looking at his nephew with twinkling gray eyes, but waited, obviously, for his brother to speak.

"You have surely guessed by now, Richard, what has brought me here—the fact that your Uncle Hiram has been smuggling slaves over the border into Canada, and the need of warning him that he is in danger. Such folly has to be stopped; he is under suspicion already. Even you can add a word. We can save him from his wrong-headed mistakes if we can make him listen to reason."

He walked toward the door, seeming to‧ grow of more consequence the farther he got from that strangely powerful presence beside the fire. "I have used every argument I can to you," he concluded. "Any sane man can see the danger and what the end will be. I have nothing more to say."

He went out, and Richard came forward to sit on the stool beside the fire. For some minutes the burning wood snapped and crackled and neither of the two spoke.

"Selina sent for you?" Uncle Hiram began at last. "Selina is a wise girl. It is quite true that someone must save me to-night; must save me—and two others.

This rheumatism has caught me at a bad moment. I can't leave my chair—and it's forty miles to Canada."

Richard had been sitting with his hands clasped between his knees and his eyes on the floor. He looked up startled; Uncle Hiram gave him the quick flash of a smile and went on, "I can't ask you to involve yourself, Richard. Your Uncle Nathan is sensible and cautious; you will have to stand on his side or mine. You can try to save me from what he calls my folly, or you can save me where I have given my promise that another shall get away to safety. It is our fault, every living American's fault, that anything so hideous as slavery exists. It will continue to be our fault until we find some way to be rid of it. Mine is not a good way, Richard, I admit that; but it is, so far, the best way open. Now think a little, and choose. Don't decide too—"

They were interrupted by a sudden disturbance below by voices in the lower hall, and, a moment later, by Uncle Nathan's bursting into the room. "It's as I told you," he cried, his voice high with excitement. "John Holloway gave you one warning; what he could not tell you was that he was on his way to the village to take out a search warrant. He's here now with the slave owners' agent, a fellow named Atkins. They have authority to search the farm for runaway slaves and they're going to do it."

"Let them," returned Uncle Hiram easily and quite unmoved. "Give them the freedom of the place and tell them to look anywhere they want. But ask Sarah to give them some hot supper and have Selina light the fire in the front bedroom. They'll have to stay the night, with it snowing the way it is. A lot of guests we have this evening, for a quiet place like Neshobe Mountain Farm!" As Richard went downstairs to carry the message to the women he heard Hiram Kent chuckling.

As he came into the big kitchen, he saw that John Holloway was just taking a lamp from the table. "We can't waste any time," Holloway was saying in an undertone to his companion, Atkins, "especially after what we heard in the village of what had been seen up here." He led the way down a dark passage. Richard, unforbidden, came after the two, and Selina followed behind.

They went thoroughly up and down the whole of the rambling old house, poked their heads into closets, tapped on walls, flashed the light into dark places behind stairs. Richard stayed behind when they pushed into Uncle Hiram's room, but he heard cheerful voices and saw that both the men were laughing as they came out. He held his breath as they descended into the cellar. Here were a hundred shadows and hidden places, but search revealed them all as empty. For the first time he saw the big, arched niche from which he had heard that whispered voice the summer before. Nothing was there now save sacks of apples and a row of golden squashes. They all came tramping up the stairs again, with the long shadows trailing behind them.

The men armed themselves with lanterns before they sallied out to examine the barns, Richard and Selina still bringing up the rear. There was little wind, but the snow was coming down in a smooth white curtain, with the air feeling soft and moist. The slave agent shivered and drew his big coat closer about him. "Hideous weather you have in this wilderness," he observed, but he followed stoutly as John Holloway led the way.

It was a long journey all through the great barns, past the stalls where cows were munching comfortably in the dark or where a startled horse, now and again,

stamped and rolled a bright eye in the lantern light. In the farthest corner of the loft, where Richard and Selina had played when they were smaller, the expedition came to a brief halt. A ladder reached up to the rafters—a rather tall one which neither of the men seemed anxious to climb.

"Just get up there, Richard," directed Holloway, "and flash the light into that space between the beams."

As the boy hesitated, hoping to exchange glances with Selina and get a signal as to whether he would betray some desperate hiding place, the agent, Atkins, cut in roughly, "What are you waiting for when you have your orders? Don't you know what the law says, that any citizen, anywhere, can be summoned by an officer to help recover a runaway slave? Get up there of yourself or we'll make you."

Sudden, blind fury seized Richard. The man had thrust the lantern into his hand, but he threw it down as he cried hotly, "I won't go. You can't force me to go." He turned about and swung toward the stairs.

"Gently, there, gently, young man," came the sheriff's big voice as he caught up the lantern. "You don't want to burn down Hiram Kent's barn, no matter who is in it. Well, since no one else will, I'll just climb up myself." Glancing over his shoulder, Richard saw the tall man go clambering up the ladder, saw him lift the lantern high to illuminate the dark space and saw, with a gasp of relief, that it was unoccupied. He did not wait, but flung himself down the narrow stair and out of the big door. He breathed deeply of the cold wet air, so different from the warm, hay-perfumed atmosphere within.

There had been some doubt in his mind as he listened to Uncle Nathan and Uncle

Hiram—a wonder as to who was right; whether Uncle Hiram was wrong in running his whole household into danger by giving shelter to fugitive slaves. Uncle Nathan was very plausible, but his words no longer carried weight with Richard—not in the face of a law which not only dragged an escaped slave back into captivity, but even haled every free man into taking part in such cruelty. He stood a minute, seeing only faintly the bulk of the buildings about him, knowing that those great familiar mountains were all around—watching him, he almost felt, through the curtain of the dark; watching to see his mettle tried and his courage tested. He would not fail; his mind was made up now; he would help Uncle Hiram to the utmost that was in him.

He turned and saw the lights bobbing toward him from the barn. Selina, wrapped in an old shawl, came to stand beside him while the men strode past through the snow. "Here's one place we haven't looked," Richard heard Atkins say as they passed the brick smokehouse a few yards from the kitchen steps.

The sheriff fumbled at the low oak door, opened it and let out the dull glow of a smoldering fire and the sharp smell of smoke. "No one could abide in that stifling place," he said decisively. "We can be certain there's nothing here, at least."

They went up the steps, opened the kitchen door, showing a stream of ruddy light, and closed it. Even in the shrouding darkness Richard did not dare speak above a whisper, close to Selina. "Whatever has to be done, I am going to do it."

He could just see that she nodded. "You'll have to help. There are two here, and Uncle Hiram can't stir from his chair. I know how to tell you just what to do. But oh, Richard, are you sure?"

"Yes," he answered resolutely. "I'm sure

—now." Whatever his Uncle Hiram had dared and accomplished, Richard Kent would do also.

Selina turned about, lifted the latch of the smokehouse door and opened it. She bent her head to the choking smoke within, but pushed forward into the blackness, Richard behind her. An inner door swung open under her hand, through which they stepped and closed quickly behind them. Nobody ever could have guessed that the square smokehouse contained not one room, but a second also, reached through the forbidding interior of the first. There must have been hidden slits at the edge of the roof; for there were no windows in the blank, brick walls, yet it was a comfortable place, spotlessly clean, with its own fireplace and burning logs upon the small hearth.

Richard had not known what to expect, but he was completely unprepared for what he saw—a tall, grave-faced man who seemed of the same sort as Uncle Hiram himself, and a neat little lady garbed in gray, whose thin white hands were busy with knitting as she sat beside the fire. They were Quakers from Pennsylvania, they explained to him, friends of Hiram Kent for years, but through correspondence only; for they, at their end, shared in that slave-smuggling traffic which history has called the Underground Railroad. These two, so quiet in their manner, so bold and flagrant in their defiance of injustice, had finally been under such suspicion that they were forced to flee, also, to escape imprisonment and prosecution.

"Thee understands that there was nothing more that we could do for the poor blacks," the little lady said gently, "so it has seemed best for us to go away into Canada while we could. Some day we will come back and begin again in another place. Good friends have seen us thus far on our journey, and it is almost ended."

"Uncle Hiram only just finished building this room last autumn," Selina told them, "and you are the first to hide in it. He laid the first bricks the day the Fugitive Slave Law was brought up in Congress."

She had slipped out and returned, her arms laden with coats and blankets. She held out to Richard Uncle Hiram's bearskin coat and put his fur cap into her cousin's hands. While the other two were making ready, the boy and girl emerged again into the snow and took their way toward the barn. She was giving rapid and detailed directions as they went.

"You will have to drive on the ice; the road is blocked. Get well out into the middle and then face north. Uncle Hiram has sent you down his compass and says you are to put a lantern under the buffalo robe. That will keep your feet warm, at least."

They came within the cavernous door of the barn. Richard knew at once which sleigh to take and understood now why Uncle Hiram kept that team of swift black horses, too light for farm work. He backed one out of its stall and Selina the other, and the two harnessed quickly, as they so often had done in the summer. Selina was continuing those directions which it was not safe to seek at first hand from Hiram Kent. "It's twenty miles you have to go, to Seth Bronson's house, on the shore beyond Goose Neck Point. You remember that we sailed there last summer and the summer before. You must bear in toward shore as you pass the point, and when you get near enough you will see two lights shining from Seth's house for a signal. He will take Uncle Hiram's friends the rest of the way. This is the hardest and most dangerous part of the journey, for it is the one the gov-

ernment men are watching, since they suspect Uncle Hiram."

So many times had they harnessed together that both finished at exactly the same moment. The sleigh runners grated on the board floor, then glided out across the snow. In the recessed door of the smokehouse stood the Quaker pair, muffled to the eyes. The bright windows of the main house showed where the two officials were settling to an evening by the fire, with no intention of leaving shelter again that night.

The little lady murmured a word or two as she got in. "Tell thy uncle—just bless him, that is all."

Richard was in his place, with Selina looking up at him through the veil of white flakes. At the last moment misgivings seemed to have seized her. "Are you sure you can find the way?" she asked desperately.

"Yes," he nodded answer. "I will find it." He could see the two big pines which marked the track that led down to the shore. The little black Morgan mare pawed with anxiety to be off, partaking, as horses love to do, in the excitement of the errand. The sleigh slipped between the pines and the house with all its cheerful lights disappeared from view behind the swirling curtain of snow.

A FROZEN lake makes a magnificent highroad. The horses tugged at the bits as they swung into their course northward. Now and then the two in the rear seat stirred—from this time on, their liberty and even their lives depended on what Richard could do. The team was galloping wildly; now their pace increased and it was almost as though they were running away, only in this vast emptiness there was little sense of speed; no feeling of danger at all. He knew he must hold the horses; that otherwise they would exhaust themselves long before the journey's end. He braced his feet, took an iron grasp of the reins and drew them down to a more reasonable pace, although they still plunged forward the moment his hold relaxed.

They went on for hours; for untold time, it seemed to Richard. Once the snowfall lightened a little and he caught sight of a wooded island just where he had thought it ought to be. The white blanket came down again—still without wind, but with a steady, merciless increase of cold. His feet ached, his hands were numb, his arms up to his elbows were stiff as stone. The smaller of his two passengers had slipped down, completely hidden under the blankets. He heard a despairing voice behind him.

"Are we nearly there? I know thee is doing all thee can, but my poor wife—she can bear little more."

"It's not far now." His lips were so rigid that he could hardly make the words. He looked down at the compass; the needle was just visible. Then the lantern went out; the oil was spent. From that time on he drove blindly, so cold and exhausted that he did not know, and seemed scarcely to care, whether the way was right or not. A dark line of trees rose up before him. This was Goose Neck Point, or else he was hopelessly lost. He bore away to one side, but the line of trees seemed to have no end. He was lost—he wasn't—he was—. Suddenly beyond the last tall tree there was an opening. He rounded into it and saw a pair of twinkling lights, Seth Bronson's signal.

It was the horses, who had been on that errand before, who found their own path up to the house and stopped before a snowdrifted door. It was thrown open

as Richard got down, a wooden thing without feeling or joints. He indicated the heap of robes in the back of the sleigh. "Carry her in," he said hoarsely, not knowing his own voice. "I will get the horses into the barn."

They know in Vermont how to revive half-frozen travelers; they have so often had need to do so. Richard, warmed, fed, assured of the well-being of his fellow travelers, slept the day out until late afternoon. The storm had cleared when he came out again, the cold had softened, the black team, sobered to reason, trotted steadily with the sure pull of horses going home. The stars rode high, then began to sink, and the yellow winter dawn was showing behind Neshobe Mountain when he came in sight of Hiram Kent's farm.

The dark gables of the house and the tall bare elms showed plainly against the white hillside. There was a light in one window, growing fainter as the day brightened. Was it Selina's lamp, set there to guide him home? No, this was the upper chamber, where Uncle Hiram sat crippled in his great chair. Suddenly it came to Richard that his part in the work had been small and Hiram Kent's infinitely great. All the responsibility, many times the risk, had been Uncle Hiram's in planning this thing which must be done and done again and again—"until we find some way to be rid of slavery." Instead of excitement and striving and the thrill of triumph to repay him for the danger, he must simply sit and wait in pain and straining anxiety, while his own safety and Richard's and that of the two whom he had promised to save were all thrust into totally inexperienced hands.

It was certain that Uncle Hiram had sat there by the fire through both nights of waiting, watching the lamp, trying to pierce the darkness beyond the window.

Richard could see now, even at this distance, that the front door opened and a small figure which must be Selina's stood upon the step. It disappeared instantly and a moment later the light in the window went out. The gold of the sky behind the mountains was so bright now that it was no longer needed; the messenger had come safely home and the task was finished.

Selina came out to him as he was unharnessing the horses in the dusk of the barn. "Uncle Nathan stormed at first, when he found where you had gone," she told him, "but I think finally he was glad. He sat and talked with John Holloway and the other man, and never let them suspect."

The horses were fed and bedded, and the two came out together into the white dooryard. Richard knew within himself that he was going to help Hiram Kent not this once, but many times, as long as there was need, until a great evil was brought to its end. The mountains, clear and white against a brilliant sky, were witnesses of how unshakable was his determination to bear his part in all that remained to be done.

HOW THE SHOES FITTED THE BABY

by Sophie Swett

SUCH a pair of feet as the baby had!—plump and dimpled and satiny, and there was a bewitching little crease for an ankle, and the toe-nails were like bits of the inside of a sea-shell. I don't suppose there ever were such feet before, or, in fact, such a baby, altogether; at least, that was the opinion of the baby's little brothers and sisters, and, indeed, of the big brothers and sisters, and, now I think of it, the father and mother thought so, too. And there were, besides, some uncles and aunts and cousins (who had no babies of their own), and they were of the same opinion. And as for grandma, who had had a good many babies and grandbabies, she was sure of it. So it must have been so.

"Bless the darling! I wish she had some shoes," said grandma.

"She ought to have some shoes," said the baby's father.

"It's a *pity* she can't have some shoes," said the baby's mother.

"It's a *shame* that she's never had any shoes," said the older children—all except Jacob Abimelech.

"Can't she have some shoes?" said the younger children.

"She *shall have* some shoes!" said Jacob Abimelech.

Then they all knew that the baby would have some shoes. When Jacob Abimelech said a thing should be done, it was just as sure as roast turkey at Thanksgiving.

Jacob Abimelech was "smart." It was whispered in Brimfield that he could "spell down" the schoolmaster, and he had beaten the minister at checkers.

If Jacob Abimelech had said that a lovely little pair of shoes, with buttons on them, that exactly fitted the baby, would presently come skipping up the garden path to the front door, all by themselves, the children would have rushed to the window fully expecting to see them. They had such faith in Jacob Abimelech. But he did not say anything of that kind, and it wasn't probable that the shoes would come in any such fairy-book way as that, though it would be very convenient to have them; very convenient, indeed, for the Sparrows were poor—so poor that they had had to

Shoe the horse, and shoe the mare,
And let the little colt go bare.

To think of the baby having been in the world almost two years without having had a pair of shoes to shelter those pinky toes! I think nobody could blame the children for saying that it was a shame.

A squaw, who was wandering about, had once given the baby a pair of moccasins, gaily embroidered with beads, but they were too large,—almost large enough for Hannah,—and the baby would not keep them on.

Grandma knitted plenty of good, warm

17

little socks to keep Jack Frost from nipping her toes, but she knitted them of homespun yarn, and, though nobody wanted to hurt grandma's feelings by saying so, they were very clumsy, and not pretty at all, and, moreover, the baby could pull them off just when she liked.

Now, Jacob Abimelech had never said before that the baby *should have* some shoes. He had been the only one who had said nothing. Jacob Abimelech was one of those very uncommon people who, when they have nothing to say, say nothing. But his pumpkin had just taken the prize at the fair, and he had ten dollars of his own to do what he liked with. Although he was almost seventeen, I don't think he had ever before had ten dollars of his own in his life. They were so very poor! Mr. Sparrow had the rheumatism, and half of the time he could not work at all, and the farm was mortgaged, and seasons that were too wet, or too dry, or too cold, or too hot, came very often and spoiled the crops. And there were so many children to clothe and feed! But they found the world worth living in, after all; because there are so many beautiful things that money cannot buy.

It was such a delightful happening that Jacob Abimelech raised the prize pumpkin! And yet, like a great many good things that are called happenings, it had taken a good deal of patient care and labor to bring it about. And if it was like anybody in the world to raise a prize pumpkin, it was like Jacob Abimelech! He had chosen a place to plant the seeds where pumpkin seeds were never planted before; but it was on a sunny slope, and he made the earth rich, and that did its best to help; and the rain came along and helped at just the right time; and the sun—oh, how the sun did shine on that pumpkin-vine! and, by and by, it seemed to send its very first beam in the morning,

and its very last beam at night, down on that particular pumpkin, so that it outstripped all the others, and grew and grew, until, one day, they stood the baby up beside it, and it reached to her shoulder, and a few weeks afterward they measured again, and it actually overtopped the baby's head!

You may believe that that *was* a pumpkin, and they were all very proud when Jacob Abimelech carried it to the fair, from Father Sparrow, who said he didn't know but Jacob Abimelech knew more about farming than he did, down to the baby, who understood more about it than they thought. And they were prouder still when he came home from the fair with the prize.

I have not space to tell you of the things that Jacob Abimelech had planned to buy with that ten dollars. He would have needed Aladdin's lamp, or Fortunatus's purse, to pay for them all, instead of only a ten-dollar bill. By retiring to the barn two or three times in a day, and making out a list of things he wanted most, and their probable prices, he had discovered how very few things he could have. He *did want* a gun. Jacob Abimelech was only a boy, if he was "smart." There was a fox that tried every night to get into the hen-coop; hawks and crows, too, that did great mischief. But then, there was the shawl that he wanted to get for his mother, the warm gloves for his father, and grandma's new spectacles—and the baby's shoes! He might waver a little about the shawl, and the gloves, and the spectacles,—that gun was such a temptation,—but the baby should have her shoes!

The next question was where they should be bought. There were no shoes worthy of such a baby as that in the one country store that Brimfield boasted, and at Mapleton, five miles away, where they did most of their shopping, there was a very small stock to choose from, and it was very doubtful whether there could be any found to fit her. Oh, if they could only get a pair from the city—the great city eighteen miles away, where there were shoes fit for a queen's baby—or for theirs!

"I'll tell you what!" said Jacob Abimelech, bring his hand down on his knee with great force, "Obadiah Cherrywinkle is going to the city to market to-morrow!"

"I wouldn't trust Obadiah to get them. He would never choose the right pair. They would be sure not to fit," said his mother.

"It's a pity we're so busy harvesting that one of us can't go," said Jacob Abimelech. "One of the children might go. There's James Albert; he isn't of much use at home, and he knows what's what, and is pretty sharp at a bargain."

"Oh, yes," cried all the children, in chorus. "Don't you remember the time when James Albert didn't let the tin-peddler cheat him?"

You could scarcely mention James Albert's name in that family without all the children shouting that out in chorus, it being considered one of the important events in the family history that James Albert, at the age of eight, had got the better of a tin-peddler, or, at least, had prevented the tin-peddler from getting the better of him.

"I don't know but James Albert might be trusted; he is such an old head," said his mother. "And we could measure the baby's foot exactly."

"I'll go right over and ask Obadiah if he'll take me," cried James Albert, seizing his hat.

He was back again in a very few minutes, and called out before he got the door open:

"He says *yes!* Obadiah says yes! And he says Hannah can go, too, as well as not!"

"Oh, James Albert, I'm awful sorry I told of you about the woodchuck, and you can have my bantam rooster to keep!" she exclaimed, in a gush of gratitude.

"Oh, pooh! who wants your old rooster? I just thought I'd take you for fear I'd be lonesome," replied James Albert, who did good by stealth and blushed to find it fame. "You'd better find out whether mother'll let you before you make such a fuss."

"It's a long ride. I'm afraid she'll be tired. And I suppose you'll have to be off by four o'clock in the morning. But if she wants to go, I don't know as it will do any harm," said their mother.

"It will do both the children good to see the world!" said grandma.

So it was settled, and Hannah dreamed, that night, that Jacob Abimelech's big pumpkin had turned into a coach, like Cinderella's fairy godmother's, and James Albert and she were going off to seek their fortunes in it. But they had hardly got started, it seemed to her, when James Albert was screaming "Spiders!" at her door. That was the only way they could wake Hannah, she was such a very sound sleeper. If she had not been terribly afraid of spiders I don't know what they would have done.

Jacob Abimelech had got up, and made a good hot fire in the kitchen stove, and put some potatoes in to bake, and they had a nice hot breakfast; and it seemed delightfully queer to be up eating breakfast in the night. Old Lion, who never approved of anything unusual, growled and barked; but Nebuchadnezzar got up and chased his tail as composedly as if he were in the habit of doing it at three o'clock in the morning.

There was scarcely a gleam of daylight when they heard Obadiah Cherrywinkle's heavy wagon creaking through the lane, and Obadiah's cheery voice called, "Halloo, youngsters!"

Obadiah was in a great hurry. "You have to get up early to get the start of them market fellers," he informed them. He hurried James Albert and Hannah into the wagon, cracked his whip over the horses' backs, and they were off.

James Albert had the money for the shoes, and a paper that was the exact measure of the baby's foot, carefully pinned into his jacket pocket, and Hannah had a bright new silver quarter, that Abimelech had given her, tied up in a corner of her pocket-handkerchief. And they would not have thought of changing places with the President or Queen Victoria!

They felt, too, a kind of proprietorship in the wagon that was very pleasant. The Cherrywinkles owned the largest farm in Brimfield, and the great wagon was filled with barrels of apples,—rosy-cheeked Hubbardstons, golden pippins, and little crimson-and-yellow snow apples, nicest of all, —barrels of golden squashes, and green and purple cabbages, a firkin of sweet, golden butter, and a big sage cheese; and hanging around the sides were rows of turkeys, poor things! that had strutted their last strut, and gobbled their last gobble in the pleasant Cherrywinkle farmyard. All these good things Obadiah was carrying to the unfortunate people who lived in the city, where nothing grew. James Albert and Hannah both felt that it would be the proudest day of their lives, even without that wonderful and delightful commission to buy the baby's shoes.

Obadiah fell fast asleep, and James Albert had the great privilege of driving the finest horses in Brimfield. It was a peculiarity of Obadiah's to fall asleep whenever he had to sit still; his father had tried to make a minister of him, and was forced to give it up because he could not keep awake. He did not wake until the wagon began to clatter over the pavements, and then he seized the reins from James Albert's hand, and said he was "beginnin' to feel kind of drowsy; guessed he should have come pooty nigh fallin' asleep if they hadn't got there pooty soon!" James Albert and Hannah thought it was not polite to say anything, but they had to make a great effort to smother their giggles.

But they were soon too much occupied with the delightful novelty of their surroundings to think of Obadiah. The streets were so queer, with houses "all hitched together in a row," as Hannah remarked, and so full of people that it seemed as if it must be the Fourth of July, or, at least, a circus day. When they reached the markets it looked as if all the farmers in the country had "got the start" of Obadiah. Vegetables, and fruit, and meat, and poultry seemed to have overflowed through all the doors and windows; the sidewalks were almost covered.

"Oh, Obadiah, we ought to have started the night before," cried Hannah, the tears coming into her eyes; she felt so sorry for Obadiah, who, she thought, might as well carry water to the well as to bring his wagon-load here.

But Obadiah only laughed. He was as wide awake now as a Yankee farmer ought to be. He jumped out of the wagon, and began to talk to men standing about on the sidewalk, and in a few minutes everything was sold, and they were driving gaily off, with an empty wagon, in search of the baby's shoes!

Hannah's heart beat fast when Obadiah lifted her down from the wagon in front of a large store whose plate-glass windows showed row after row of the most elegant boots and slippers imaginable. James Albert assumed a manly and assured bearing, but in truth he was almost as much frightened as Hannah. Inside they found the whole store, larger than the Brimfield meeting house, full of boots and shoes.

He walked up to a clerk as coolly as if it were an everyday occurrence for him to go shopping, and said:

"We want a pair of shoes for our baby."

The clerk did not seem to be struck with the importance of the occasion. He asked, carelessly, what kind and what size, and took a big box down from the shelf. Hannah was seized with violent admiration for a pair of dainty white kid slippers with white satin rosettes, but as they had been carefully enjoined to get shoes that would "wear well," she was forced to turn away from them. After many trials the clerk at last found a lovely little pair of black kid button boots that just fitted the measure, and James Albert put his hand into one of them as far as it would go, and decided that there was room enough,—the baby's feet were plump, if they were tiny,—and Hannah anxiously felt of the soles to be sure that they were not stiff enough to hurt the baby, and, after much deliberation and consultation, they decided to take them. The price was higher than they had expected to pay, but Jacob Abimelech had charged them to buy the best, and surely the best was not too good for such a baby as that!

They hurried out, impatient to show their purchase to Obadiah, but lo and behold! when they reached the sidewalk neither the wagon nor Obadiah was to be seen!

"We were so long he got tired, and went off and left us. Oh, James Albert, what shall we do?" exclaimed Hannah.

"I wouldn't have believed Obadiah would be so mean as that," said James Albert. And then he suddenly caught sight of a wagon that looked like Obadiah's going around a corner a few rods off, and started after it, Hannah following.

They followed it around three corners, and when at last they reached it, breathless, it was not Obadiah's at all, but an expressman's!

James Albert and Hannah looked at each other in dismay. Tears were running down Hannah's cheeks, and James Albert had a lump in his throat, but he suddenly remembered the tin-peddler, and the reputation for "smartness" which he had to maintain.

"We'll just go back to the shoe-store, and wait until Obadiah comes after us. He'll be sure to come. I suppose he just went off on an errand, and maybe he got lost. I don't think Obadiah is so very smart!"

It cheered Hannah very much to hear James Albert speak in this confident and easy manner, but, strange to say, when they reached the place where he thought the shoe-store ought to be, it wasn't there!

"Oh, James Albert, we're lost, we're lost!" cried Hannah.

"The shoe-store is lost, and Obadiah is lost, but we ain't, because here we are!" replied James Albert, stoutly.

This may have been very poor logic, but it made Hannah laugh.

"Let's go over there, and sit down, and get rested, and think it over," said James Albert, pointing to a large park with broad, shady walks, and a pond and a fountain shining through the trees.

Just inside the gate was a man with a Punch and Judy show, and they laughed at that until they almost forgot their trouble.

"Let's spend your quarter!" said James Albert, when they were tired of the show.

So they each had a glass of red lemonade which an old woman was dispensing from a large pail, and then James Albert advocated a "jawbreaker" apiece, because jawbreakers "lasted long." Hannah did not like them particularly, because they were flavored with cinnamon, but she deferred to James Albert's taste. Then both heartily agreed upon having a big paper bag full of peanuts, and with those and the "jawbreakers" they retired to a bench under a tree in a secluded corner.

The goodies were even more effective than the Punch and Judy show in helping them to forget Obadiah's mysterious disappearance, and they were laughing and making merry, just as if he might be

nah so much of grandma's drab parrot that it was quite startling; he had even the same way of holding his head on one side, and looking straight at one, with little sharp, beady eyes.

After he had looked at them long enough, he took off his hat, with a very polite bow, and remarked that it was a very fine day; to which remark the children responded, with their very best manners.

" 'I sell him to you sheap—so sheap as nozzing at all!'—said the ragman"

expected to drive up, all ready to carry them home, at any minute, when the queerest figure they had ever seen came hobbling along the walk, and stopped in front of them.

It was a little old man, with a huge bag of rags on his back, that bent him over nearly double. He had such a very long, large, hooked nose that his face looked all nose when you first saw him, and he had such a little bit of a chin that it was like having no chin at all. He reminded Han-

"You are all 'lone—all 'lone?" he inquired, looking cautiously around. "Zen I show you somezing bee-utiful! more bee-utiful as you evair have see!"

And setting his great bag of rags upon the ground, he drew from it a most beautiful doll. Hannah could hardly believe it was a doll. She had lovely blue eyes that opened and shut, golden hair that was "banged" in the most approved fashion, a pink silk dress trimmed with lace, and turquoise ear-rings in her ears. To be frank, her complexion was somewhat faded, and the tip of her nose was broken off, but those slight blemishes quite escaped Hannah's notice. Hannah, who had never in her life had any doll better than one made of a shawl, felt her heart yearn over this beautiful creature.

"I sell him to you sheap—so sheap as nozzing at all!" said the ragman.

There was only one cent left of Hannah's quarter. She held it out, saying mournfully, "That is all the money we have!"

"But vat is dis?" said the ragman, touching the package that was sticking out of James Albert's pocket.

"That is the baby's shoes," said James Albert, glad of an opportunity to display them.

The ragman looked at them, curling his lip and shaking his head contemptuously:

"No goot! no goot! Bad shoe! ver' bad shoe!" he said; and James Albert and Hannah felt their hearts sink within them, for of course he would not speak so confidently unless he were a judge of shoes!

"Poor shildern, I pity you! I mooch kind-heart man, and I pity you. I gif you ze doll, and I take ze shoe! No goot, but I take zem!"

And he stuffed the shoes hastily into his pocket, leaving the doll in Hannah's lap.

"Oh, we can't let you have the shoes; they're the baby's!" cried James Albert and Hannah, in chorus.

"You not gif doze bad shoe, good for nozzing at all, for dat bee-utiful doll wort' twenty dollar? You sell him for dozen pair shoe like dat, if you want!"

"It does seem a splendid bargain, James Albert!" said Hannah, hugging the doll.

It did seem so to James Albert, and he did want to have the credit of doing a fine stroke of business. If they *could* sell the doll for twenty dollars, he should distinguish himself even more than he had

done in that little affair with the tin-peddler.

While he was considering, with his forehead puckered into the deepest of frowns, the ragman was making off, with the baby's shoes.

Suddenly Hannah began to feel misgivings.

"Oh, James Albert, if we *couldn't* sell the doll, we should have to go home without the baby's shoes! And the tip of her nose is broken, and her dress isn't so very clean!"

"I'll run after him and get the shoes back. Give me the doll!" cried James Albert.

But not a trace of the ragman was to be seen. For an old man he must have walked very fast indeed after he turned the corner.

The children sat down again on the bench and looked at each other blankly, then they looked at the doll. It was astonishing to see how much worse her nose looked, and how much more soiled and disheveled she appeared, now that she belonged to them!

"We must go to a store and try to sell her right away," said James Albert. "But I am afraid nobody will buy her, she is so dirty!"

A young man was passing just then, and James Albert resolved to have the benefit of his opinion.

"Do you think this doll is worth twenty dollars, sir?" he asked.

"Twenty dollars! That old doll? Why, it isn't worth twenty cents," said the young man, with a laugh.

"And we have lost the baby's shoes! Oh, James Albert!" exclaimed Hannah, with a great sob.

"I just wish we had never seen the old doll! He was an awful bad man. He cheated us," said James Albert.

"He was worse than the tin-peddler, wasn't he? And you were not so smart as you were then, were you?"—which was somewhat aggravating to poor James Albert, although Hannah did not mean it to be so.

"It was awful wicked of us to do it, and I never should have thought of such a thing if it hadn't been for you. You wanted the horrid old doll so much!" he said, not very kindly.

Hannah's tears began to flow.

"It's no good to sit here and be a cry-baby!" said James Albert. "We'll go out into the street, and perhaps we shall come across Obadiah."

"I don't want to find Obadiah. I don't want to go home without the baby's shoes!" said Hannah. But as James Albert strode along crossly, with his hands in his pockets, she followed him, the tears rolling down her cheeks, and the doll tucked carelessly under her arm, a most melancholy picture.

As they were going through the park gates, one of a group of children playing near, under the care of what Hannah thought was a very queer-looking nurse, with a white cap on her head, came running up to Hannah, and seized the doll from under her arm, with a cry of delight.

"Oh, my own dear, sweet, darling Florabella!" she cried, hugging and kissing the doll. "I thought I never should see you again! Oh, dear, how she looks! The darling must have been through so much! But she would be my own darling Florabella if her nose were twice as bumped!"

And then the nurse came up, and asked Hannah, in a very severe manner, where she got the doll.

Before she had time to answer, James Albert constituted himself spokesman and told them all about it.

"Oh, what a wicked ragman!" cried the little girl, who was still hugging the doll. "Florabella fell out of the window onto the sidewalk; I ran down to pick her up,

but when I got there she was gone. You come home with us, and tell mama about it, and she'll give you something to pay for Florabella—for of course you can't have her!" And she gave the doll an extra hug at the thought.

"We don't want her!" said James Albert and Hannah, in concert, and, indeed, the doll had caused them so much grief that she didn't look pretty, even to Hannah. "We only want the baby's shoes!"

"Well, perhaps mama can get them back for you; she can do almost anything," said the little girl, confidently.

So, feeling a little cheered, James Albert and Hannah went home with the children.

They lived in a house that made Hannah think of the palaces in her fairy-book, and their mother was as lovely and kind as one of the good fairies. Hannah would not have been very much surprised to see her whisk out a wand, and tap three times, and there would be the baby's shoes!

And she did do something that was almost as good as that.

After she had given them a nice luncheon, she said it would never do in the world for them to go home without the baby's shoes. So she ordered her carriage, and drove, with James Albert and Hannah, and all the children, to a shoe-store. But when they got there James Albert suddenly remembered that he had left the measure of the baby's foot in the store where they had bought the shoes; and where that was he could not tell.

Then what did the lady do but buy three pairs, graduated in size, like the porringers of the three bears, one "great big" pair (comparatively), and one "middle-sized" pair, and one "little wee" pair. And they were lovely shoes, even nicer than the pair that the children had lost.

Then each one of the children wanted to buy a present for the baby, and one bought a beautiful little white dress, and another a dainty little bonnet with white ribbons, and another a rubber doll, that the baby could not break; and then, after a great deal of whispered consultation, they bought a big doll like Florabella for Hannah, and a jackknife with four blades for James Albert.

It was no wonder that Hannah thought they had got into fairyland!

In the meantime the good fairy had sent a messenger to all the station-houses in the neighborhood, to give information of the children's whereabouts, because she thought Obadiah would know that those were the places to look for lost children; and when they drove back to her house, there was the wagon, with Obadiah calmly seated in it, standing before the door!

He told his adventures only after much urging and in a shamefaced way. Poor Obadiah! While the children were in the shoe-store he fell asleep, and the horses, thinking they had stood long enough, wandered along. A policeman caught sight of Obadiah and his horses,—that did not trouble themselves to turn out for anything—and thought Obadiah had been drinking, and took him, team and all, to the station-house!

Obadiah said, "It beat all natur' that he should 'a' done it, for he wa'n't generally one o' the sleepy kind!"

Hannah and James Albert were too happy to blame him, and they tried hard not to laugh.

They had a very exciting time telling their adventures when they got home that night. James Albert would have preferred not to tell about the ragman, but of course it had to be done, and I am afraid that now the tin-peddler will never be mentioned without the ragman being brought up to offset him!

As for the baby's shoes, the great big pair were entirely too large for her, but would do nicely for her by and by; the middle-sized pair gave so much room to her toes that they might have pushed ahead too fast; but the little wee pair fitted her as perfectly as if her feet had been melted and poured into them!

THE DOG THAT RETURNED TO MEXICO

by Ellis Parker Butler

SAMUEL DAZZARD was a great friend of mine and when I was working in the garden he often came and leaned over the fence and told me how the peons made gardens in Mexico.

Indeed, he told me many things about Mexico, for he had been there, and had walked all the way back to Iowa carrying a Mexican carved leather saddle and a braided-hair bridle, which were all he had to show for a herder's outfit that he assured me was the finest a man ever owned. He had a dog, a coal black one, that he had brought from Mexico, but it was a surprisingly mixed breed of dog, and not at all the kind that he could trade for a horse.

As a money-maker Sam Dazzard was a failure, but he was a powerfully lively thinker and he had a mechanical bent that would have made him rich if it had turned toward anything useful, but it didn't.

Sam—we all called him Sam—was a lank man, with innocent blue eyes and light hair. He had always a faraway expression, as if he was thinking of Mexico, and he was the most deadly serious man I ever knew.

I could hardly believe my ears when Sam came to me one day and offered to trade me the braided-hair bridle for the old buck-board that we were letting rot to pieces in the barnyard. One wheel of the buck-board was badly dished, and it had been a cheap vehicle when new.

"Have you got a horse, Sam?" I asked.

"No," he said. "No, I wouldn't have a horse in this country if you gave me one. A horse is all right in Mexico, but up here they eat their heads off. It doesn't pay to keep horses in Iowa."

"Then what do you want the buck-board for?" I ventured to ask.

Sam shook the bottom of the buck-board to see how sound it was.

"Well," he said, slowly, "I'll tell you. I am going to make an automobile. An automobile is the thing to have in this country. What a man wants up here is speed. Horses are all right in Mexico, where everybody takes plenty of time, but up here we have to move about fast. You mark my word; in ten years there won't be a horse left in Iowa."

He sat down and studied the buck-board for a while, and we waited.

"How are you going to run it?" I asked, after a while.

"Gasoline," he said, simply. "I prefer gasoline. You get more speed with gasoline, and that's what I'm after. I've got as fine a little gasoline engine as you ever saw—as soon as I get it in shape."

"Why, I thought that engine blew up and wrecked the launch!" I said, surprised.

"Well, it did blow up some," Sam admitted, reluctantly. "It blew up some! But I can put it in good shape again in no time, and it was a mighty fine engine when it was new. Two-horsepower en-

26

gine. Why!" he said, enthusiastically, "one horse could run away with this buck-board and not know it had anything behind it; and when I get *two*-horsepower in it, it will fly! That's what I want—speed."

He paused, thoughtfully.

"Oh, yes," he continued, "I've got some ideas that I'm going to use that will sur-

some ingenuity, he seemed to have more patience than anything else.

It was no trick at all for him to rig up a steering gear, but it troubled him to connect the engine with the rear wheels of the buck-board. He explained to us what he needed, and it seemed to be nearly everything he didn't have and couldn't get, and he admitted it frankly

"The hind wheels of that buck-board revolved so rapidly you couldn't see the spokes"

prise some people. I do wish that hind wheel was a little better, but I guess I can fix it up. It's got to stand a lot of speed. Maybe," he said, dreamily, "I'll buy a new wheel if it doesn't cost too much."

We boys spent a great deal of our spare time for the next month or two at Sam's cabin watching the progress of the auto-mobile. It took no little ingenuity and a great amount of patience to patch up the gasoline engine, but, while Sam had

and said that if he just had a couple of good cog-wheels and a piece of endless chain he could do without the other things, but he didn't have the cog-wheels and chain either, and he finally rigged up a rope to drive the wheels.

He had the engine screwed to the floor slats of the buck-board and, for the test, he had the rear axle jacked up on a barrel so that the wheels were a foot or so above the ground, and there were almost tears in his eyes the first time he started the engine. The hind wheels of that buckboard revolved so rapidly you couldn't see the spokes. Sam said he figured they were going at the rate of at least one hundred miles an hour, but that he wouldn't drive the automobile that fast at first. He said it took some time to learn how to handle an automobile, and that until he learned he would not think of going over ten miles an hour, especially as he hadn't rigged up a brake yet. He explained that he could easily make a brake, if he had a few articles he didn't have, but there was no place to put it on the buck-board.

Sam's cabin was by the river bank, surrounded by brush and undergrowth, so we boys all lent a hand to carry the automobile to the road, which was not far. It was a good road for speeding an automobile, level as the top of a table—and we begged Sam to let the automobile go full speed, but he firmly refused. He said we might enjoy seeing him dashed to pieces, but that he was not going to trust himself at any hundred miles an hour until he learned to handle the machine properly.

He climbed in and braced himself firmly on the seat and turned on the power a little. The engine chugged and chugged away, as gasoline engines do, but nothing happened. Then Sam turned on more power, but the automobile sat still in the road and did not move. I could see that Sam was chagrined, but he said nothing. He turned the gasoline engine on at full power.

That engine certainly was a good one. It was full of life and vim, and it fairly jumped up and down on the buck-board, like a child romping on a spring bed, but the buck-board seemed frozen to the road. It did not move an inch.

Sam stopped the engine and got out and crawled under the buck-board, which was so much like what a man with a real automobile would have done that we all cheered. Then Sam got up and shook his head.

"It beats me!" he exclaimed, sadly. "I can't see what is wrong. I can't for a fact."

He leaned over the engine and turned on the power at the lowest notch and what do you think! The automobile moved! It did not run away; it did not dash off at a hundred miles an hour, but it moved. It went about as fast as a baby could creep.

Sam got in again and gave it the full power once more but the automobile would not budge. Then he got out and gave it half power and it started off so fast that he had to dog-trot to keep up with it, but the moment he got in, it stopped dead still. We found by experimenting that when Sam was in the automobile and the engine doing its best it was just an even balance. One of us boys could push the automobile along with one finger, but the moment we stopped pushing, the automobile stopped going. If the engine had been one fraction of a horse stronger the automobile would have run itself, or if Sam had been a couple of pounds lighter the engine would have been able to propel the automobile, but, as it was, it would not go alone. It would almost go, but not quite; but an automobile that will almost go is no better than one that will not go at all.

The first minute Muchito—that was the dog's name—heard the gasoline engine he crawled under Sam's cabin and refused to come out, and, when he found that Sam meant to keep the engine and make a sort of pet of it, Muchito took to going away during the day. He would come back to the cabin at night, with his coat full of burrs, but early the next morning he would run away again.

The next morning after that I was starting for a good day's fishing and had just got to the edge of the town when I heard a noise down the road like a steamboat trying to get off a sand-bar, and coming toward me I saw Sam in his automobile. He was holding to his steering bar with both hands and his hat pulled down over his ears to keep it from shaking off, and the engine was bouncing the bed of the buck-board so that Sam's teeth rattled like a stick drawn along a picket fence. Sam was jigging up and down on the seat like a man with the chills, and the whole outfit was palpitating as if it would be shaken to pieces the next minute. Everything was going at the rate of one hundred miles an hour except the wheels, and they were moving about as slowly as a tired turtle travels in the sun. I never saw so much noise and rattle and energy produce so little forward motion. I should say Sam was moving at the rate of about one mile an hour, but he was moving and his face showed his triumph.

I could walk so much faster than he could ride that I might say that I met him before he met me. He did not see me until I was right in front of him, for he was too busy being shaken, but the minute he saw me the automobile stopped.

Muchito saw me at the same moment, and jumped up on me, as a dog will. I never saw a dog so glad to see anyone as Muchito was to see me. We had always been good friends but not affectionate, but this time he wanted to love me to death. Sam had him fastened to the front axle of the automobile with a ten-foot rope.

"Hello, Sam," I said; "got the automobile so that it runs all right now, haven't you?"

"Yes! Oh, yes!" he said quickly. "She runs fine now. Not fast, but steady. That's what a man wants in an automobile— steadiness. This idea of speed is all wrong. You get too much speed and you run over people. It isn't safe. Steadiness is what a man wants in this country; a good, steady automobile that will go where he wants it to go. I was just going up to town," he added.

"You must have started pretty early," I ventured.

"Yes," he admitted, "pretty early. About four o'clock. I want to take my time. I want this machine to get down to good, steady work before I try any speed."

He looked anxiously over the front of the buck-board at Muchito, who was cowering close to my legs.

"Well," he said, "I guess I'll move on. I've got quite a way to go yet."

He turned on the power and the buck-board began to palpitate and bounce and jolt, but it did not move. Sam stood up and looked over at Muchito. Muchito was sitting on his tail looking sad and scared.

"Well, so long!" I shouted. "I want to get to the dam before the fish quit biting this morning."

I moved off down the road and Muchito followed me as far as the rope would allow. I looked back when I had gone a few yards and saw Sam get out of the automobile and take Muchito in his arms and carry him around to the front of the automobile and point him toward the city. Six times Sam carried Muchito to the front of the automobile and six times Muchito turned back and strained toward me at the end of the rope. Then Sam stood up and called to me.

"Hey!" he shouted. "Wait!"

I waited and saw Sam lift the rear wheels of the automobile around and straighten it out so that it was headed *away* from the city. Then he got in and turned on the power. Muchito was still straining toward me. The automobile moved toward me, slowly, but as Sam desired, steadily.

I understood Muchito was running away from the automobile, and if Muchito did not run neither did the automobile. His slight pull on the rope was all that was necessary to change the automobile from an inert but jolting buck-board into a slow but steady forward-moving vehicle.

"I guess I won't go to town today," chattered Sam, when he was near enough to make me hear; "I don't want to go to town much anyway. I enjoy riding one way as much as the other."

If he enjoyed being joggled I could admit it. I waited for him to come up with me, but as soon as Muchito reached me the dog sat down and the automobile stopped. Sam looked at me and at the dog.

"Suppose," he shouted, "suppose you walk on a little ahead. That dog—, I don't want to run over that dog. If you go on ahead he won't lag back. I wouldn't run over that dog for a good deal. That dog came from Mexico."

I started forward and whistled to Muchito. The dog jumped forward and the automobile moved, but the rope Sam had used was an old one and it snapped.

For one moment Muchito stood in surprise. The next moment Sam had jumped from his automobile and made a dash for Muchito, but the dog slipped quickly to one side, glanced once at the automobile which was moving rapidly into the fence at the side of the road, and then tucking his tail between his legs started down the road at a gallop. We saw him turn the bend in the road and we never saw him again. He was tired of being an assistant motor to an automobile and he was headed for Mexico, where there are peons and haciendas and rancheros, but no buck-board motor cars.

THE LAST MAN IN MARBLEHEAD

by Don C. Seitz

WE celebrate July 4, 1776, as the birthday of American Freedom because the Declaration of Independence was signed on that date; but its real anniversary is April 19, beginning with the year 1775, for then the battles of Concord and Lexington were fought, and armed conflicts continued thereafter between the forces of the colonies and those of the king.

Of course, there had long been friction and much hot oratory on this side of the ocean, but the War of the Revolution began with little real preparation on the part of the colonists. True, the direct clash arose because the British marched from Boston to seize munitions of the militia stored at Concord, but these supplies were scant; nor was there much to be found elsewhere; while upon the sea, where a deal of the fighting was to be done, the "rebels" had no ships fitted for war.

Soon a slender squadron put to sea, but the bulk of the work had to be done by privateers, and here our story begins.

Until 1907, when, by international agreement, the practice of fitting out private armed vessels to prey upon enemy commerce was ruled off the ocean, it was legal for nations to issue "letters of marque and reprisal," under which individuals or companies could fit out ships to seize merchant vessels, wherever found, and do with them as they would.

Great Britain was rich upon the sea. She numbered war-ships by the hundred, and trading vessels by the thousand. These soon fell in fat harvests to the bold Yankee privateers, sailing from Charleston,

Baltimore, Philadelphia, New York, New Haven, New London, Providence, and, above all, Salem, Newburyport, Gloucester, and Marblehead. Nor did they limit their operations to home waters, but pushed into all of the seven seas, some even making haven at the Isle of France (Mauritius), in the far-off Indian Ocean, while swarms of them hovered off the English and Irish coasts, even venturing into the channel between them and that separating England from the European shore.

Now one of the boldest and most successful of these rovers was the *Lion* of Marblehead, that sturdy seaport of Cape Ann, where even to this day they breed the boldest of seamen, who sail in their slight vessels to the Grand Banks of Newfoundland, seeking cod, halibut, and like important members of the finny tribes. It is with the *Lion* and one of her crew that this tale is concerned. Great-grandfather Nathan Clapp used to tell it as he sat beside the glowing fireplace in his Cape Ann home, and a grandson told it to me long ago. It is such a valorous yarn as all youngsters of spirit like to hear.

In the year one thousand, seven hundred and eighty-one, when he was but eighteen, Nathan had sailed from Salem on the brig *Lark* for Oporto, in Spain, to come back with a rich cargo of Spanish wares—silks, drums of figs, cork, and wine.

They had easily evaded the British cruisers congregated off the Bay of Biscay and were returning full laden, when at the dawn of day they ran into a great convoy of more than three hundred sail. This convoy, it must be explained, was a gathering of merchant ships proceeding, as nearly as they could, together for protection against raiding privateers. This great fleet of merchant craft was guarded by a dozen ships of war, the chief of

which was the *Royal George,* one of the biggest ships under the British flag and commanded by the master of the fleet, Admiral Sir Richard Kempenfelt. Several light cruisers were attached to the squadron, and two of these soon ran down the little *Lark.* Her captain, Josiah Lunt, surrendered at discretion, and because her barrels of port were taken to the flagship, the men went thither with them, while the *Lark,* under a prize crew, was sent into Portsmouth, so as not to encumber the convoy.

Some effort was made to make the Yankee seamen enlist in the English service, but none would join. They were well treated, however, and allowed to loiter about the ship while the convoy made its slow way toward Jamaica, whither it was bound, to scatter thence among the various islands of the West Indies belonging to the British.

The winds were baffling and the convoy made slow headway. It was difficult to keep them together, and the cruisers were always busy, like hens among their chicks, trying to herd their broods. One day a storm arose and the vessels were badly dispersed. The bulk of the convoy had to lie to, waiting for the others to come up. When nearly all were gathered, the Yankees on the *Royal George* were thrilled and startled to see a schooner heave in sight a league—three miles—away and pounce upon a luckless bark that was striving to beat up to the squadron. In almost a jiffy she was boarded and taken, the Stars and Stripes hoisted to her mizzen, and she was sailing away under guard of her captor.

Quite rudely, Nathan Clapp and his companions gave three cheers for the privateer, whoever she might be, for which they were clapped under hatches to cool off. The next day they were allowed up and saw the privateer repeat the performance. This time they were discreet enough to repress their joy.

But wasn't there a to-do on the king's ships! The admiral summoned all his captains and gave them a good dressing-down on the quarter-deck. Was the glory of England to be dimmed by a rascally Yankee but one degree removed from a pirate? He hinted grimly at courts-martial and losing numbers,—dreadful things to happen to naval gentlemen,—and the worthies departed to bestir themselves.

One of the smaller cruisers, the *Sprite,* captain the Honorable George Clowden, was hurriedly altered to look like a clumsy merchantman. With her ports painted out, her sails slack and gear loose, and straggling from the fleet, the *Sprite* became a well-baited trap. A few sailors in nondescript garb "worked" the ship. The others were kept below, lest some searching spy-glass might penetrate the disguise. On the morning of the third day that this trap was set, the sea became calm and a light mist obscured the view. Little puffs of wind rippled the water, and as it blew the mist away, a quarter of a mile to leeward lay the privateer. She spied the *Sprite,* and soon her long sweeps were out and brawny arms were propelling her toward the prospective prize. Clowden might have opened with a broadside, but he was not sure that he would not be outranged by the long pivot-gun of the privateer, which, in itself, carried heavier metal than any of his guns. He had set his heart on cutting her out by boarding and awaited events. In a quarter of an hour the *Lion* was alongside, bow to bow, the forward quarter almost touching, while the stern yawed off. The bulwarks of the privateer were lined with men ready to leap aboard the *Sprite,* on whose decks a dozen sailors in nondescript togs appeared to be listlessly resigned to their fate. A grappling-iron thrown from the bow of the *Lion* lodged forward on the *Sprite* and bound them together, but the grapple cast from the stern failed to land, dropping into the water with a splash. This mishap saved the privateer.

As the bows touched, a score of the *Lion's* seamen leaped to the deck of the *Sprite,* and the first one to find footing was a boy—a brown-haired, blue-eyed, sunny-faced lad, quick of limb and eye. He had no more than touched the deck when he saw the glint of cutlasses, a hatch covering slide back, and men crowding each other to come up from below. The vessels had drifted a little apart, though the grappling-line held. Instantly the lad cast off the grapple and shouted:

"Look alive! Sheer off! She's a Britisher. Don't mind us!"

The privateer lost no time in heeding the warning cry. The helmsman put his wheel hard down and a handy puff moved her sixty feet away in almost as many seconds. On board the *Sprite* a volley of pistol shots came from the mizzen hatch, and uniformed seamen swarmed to the deck. They ranged themselves at once against the privateersmen. These now rallied to defend themselves. Two fell under the pistol-fire and there ended their cruising. The others, cutlass and pistol in hand, sustained the assault. They were soon overpowered; but in the confusion, Clowden failed to use his guns. The ports were tightly closed, and gummed with the paint that hid them. By the time a few were opened, the privateer was yards away. The pivot-gun on the forecastle sent a heavy shot into the *Sprite's* stern-post and the vessel ceased to mind the helm. Another shot from a long 18-pounder smashed the binnacle and struck down the man at the wheel. Then, opportunely, the wind rose and the *Lion* took to her heels. She was no match for broadsides and a crew double her own. Her speed was three knots better than that of her opponent, even had the latter not been disabled. It was not the policy of privateers to fight full-fledged warships, except in case of necessity, when they usually got the worst of it. The captain of the *Lion* was prudent in his getaway.

You may be sure that Captain Clowden was a very angry man at this outcome, and he vented his spite on the prisoners by putting them in irons and clapping them in the hold.

Repairs were made to the rudder, and in another day the *Sprite* found the convoy. Her captain had a very bad half-hour with the admiral, which ended in his being ordered to send the prisoners to the flagship. Their irons were knocked off and they were taken in the long-boat to the *Royal George.* The story of the boy's valor had become known, and every man on board wished to see the hero.

The prisoners of the *Lark* were not hindered from joining the eager crowd of sailors that manned the shrouds and bulwarks as the captives came over the side, and their hearts glowed at the sight of their countrymen. These bore themselves bravely. They were ranged abaft the mast for the inspection of the admiral. The great man regarded them curiously. They were nondescript to look at, coatless, hatless, bloody and scarred, but all were stalwart and young. One of them was very young. Indeed, he was nothing but a bit of a boy. He looked fourteen, and across his forehead was a bloody bandage that hid a cutlass scratch.

"What did he do?" asked the admiral of Captain Clowden.

"Fought like a lion's cub," replied the commander. "It took two men and a be-laying-pin to subdue him."

The admiral looked at the boy kindly. "Come here, my lad," he said gently.

The youngster stepped out of the line of prisoners and stood before Kempenfelt.

"What is your name?" he asked.

"Nathaniel Libbey, sir."

"How old are you?"

"Fifteen, come next January." (It was then May.)

"Tell me," said the admiral, "how such a little fellow as you came to be in this mad adventure?"

"I was the last man in Marblehead," replied Nathaniel, proudly.

And indeed he was! The *Lion* had lacked one man to fill her hammocks, and the Widow Libbey gladly spared her only son to complete the company. There were no grown-ups left to go.

Well, the "last man in Marblehead" was soon a favorite aboard ship. The admiral even had him to dinner in the great cabin, and would much have liked to tempt him with a midshipman's cocked hat and dirk, but Nathaniel was too loyal to be led away from his flag.

When the fleet reached Jamaica they found there a cartel awaiting to exchange prisoners, and the admiral sent Nathaniel to his mother, with a couple of gold guineas jingling in his pockets so that he should not reach home poor. There was great rejoicing in Marblehead when he came back, and the owners of the *Lion* saw that he received more than a cub's share of prize-money.

Fate was unkind to the good admiral. Returning from his voyage, the *Royal George* was "careened" in Portsmouth Harbor that the dockmen might repair a leak below the water-line. It was a fair August day. Many visitors and nearly her entire crew of over seven hundred were on board. The admiral was writing in his cabin. A sudden squall struck the tilted ship and she careened still farther, until the water entering her ports, she went down with nearly all on board, including her commander.

JIMMY'S MADE-TO-ORDER STORIES

by Dorothy Canfield

"WHAT I like best about your stories," said Jimmy, "is that there isn't any moral to them."

"Nor any sense," said a grown-up.

"Yes, that *is* another nice thing about them," said Jimmy, and continued:

"Seems as though we hadn't had any made-to-order stories for quite a while, and I'm sort of hungry for one."

"All right," said I. "Have you settled yet what you want to have in it this time?"

Jimmy fell into deep thought. You might, perhaps, imagine from the jumbled-up things he puts together for his stories that he grabs up any idea that comes into his head. But you'd be mistaken, for he often takes a long time to make his choice.

"As you haven't told me one for three whole days, the things I want have piled up and *piled* up!"

"Let's hear what they are."

"A little boy and a ship's anchor and a library full of old books and a woodchuck and a spider and a bed and a door-knob."

"Not on your life!" said I. "That's three days' worth, not one. There are too many."

"All right, I'll leave out the spider," said Jimmy. "I didn't want him in so very much, anyhow. It would probably turn out that he spun his web over the mouth of a cave and saved the life of somebody hiding inside. And I'd hate that."

As I have said, Jimmy's choice of what to put in a story is not wild and haphazard as it seems. He has one fixed aim, to avoid certain stale old combinations that make him groan in printed stories. For instance, he never has put into a story either a millionaire or an orphan child; but if he did, I know that nothing could make him put them into the same story. He would be afraid that the orphan couldn't help turning out to be the long-lost child of the millionaire. To prevent such a vexing thing, he would, I am sure, put the millionaire in with a cake of soap and have the orphan child in the story with a hippopotamus.

In this case, I asked him indignantly what made him think me capable of getting out that old cave-and-web combination; but he persisted, "Well, if he didn't do that, I bet he'd tell all about how many joints he has in his front legs and what spiders eat in winter; and I'd hate that worse. No, we'll leave the spider out."

ANCHOR HOUSE

"WELL, without the spider, it is, of course, the story about the little boy whose brothers and sisters got the measles, and the family weren't sure whether he'd been exposed, so they sent him off to Anchor House, which was the name of his old uncle's house down by the seashore."

"Was it in school-time?" asked Jimmy.

"Yes, right in the first part of May."

"Didn't he have the luck!" commented Jimmy.

"Oh, I don't know. Anchor House was 'way out on a sandy point, with no children in any of the farm-houses around. His uncle was a retired sea-captain, pretty deaf and awfully fat, who only wanted to read his newspaper all day and snore all night. And the old cook who did for them was as cross as two sticks and hated little boys in the kitchen. So he had to invent games to play all by himself. Mostly he played with the books in the library. They had belonged to his uncle's wife's father, who'd been a minister, and they were all full of theological facts that aren't so any more, so nobody thought of reading them. The little boy played blocks with them. They were big and thick and made splendid walls to forts. His uncle didn't mind, and the old cook didn't know anything about it, because she never went into the wing of the house where the library was. It was a good way from the kitchen, and she had rheumatism in her knee.

Well, one night the little boy woke up and remembered that he had carried a lot of the books out on the porch of the wing to build a rampart there, and hadn't taken them back in. It was a nice clear night; but you never know for sure about the weather, so he thought he'd better go down and carry them back into the library, in case of rain.

It was lovely and warm, so he didn't need anything but his pajamas; and he'd been going barefoot daytimes, so he didn't stop for slippers. He trotted downstairs and along the hall that led to the wing, into the library and out on the porch that was back of the main part of the house. The books were a little damp, already, from the night air, so he was glad he had come down. He carried them into the library, armful after armful, dozens and dozens of armfuls, it seemed to him. It took him a long, long time, even though he didn't try to put them back on the shelves, but just piled them up anywhere. He was pretty tired when he finally got the last one in, and started back up the stairs.

He was yawning and stretching and thinking how nice it would be to get into bed and snuggle down and doze off, when he noticed that the door to his room stood open. This gave him rather a turn, for he was sure that he had shut it very carefully. But that was nothing compared to what he found when he stepped inside his room.

For his bed was gone!

Yes, just like that. The head-board was leaned up against the wall, and the foot-board lay on the floor, and the bedclothes were tossed over the back of a chair; but the springs and mattress had disappeared! Not a sign nor a smitch of them was to be seen.

Of course, the little boy knew at once that this couldn't be so. Whatever else might get carried away out of a house at night, it wouldn't be a *bed*.

So he went out into the hall, shut his door behind him, waited a minute, and then opened it quick, expecting surely to see his bed all there, just as he'd left it.

But it wasn't, only just the head-board leaned up against the wall, and the foot-board lying on the floor.

You can't imagine how *queer* the little boy felt. Not scared, for there wasn't anything to be scared of; but so queer-feeling that he sat down quick in a chair.

"Let me think," he said to himself. "Let me *think*." But every thought he tried to think was perfectly impossible. How *could* his bed be gone, and he away for only a few minutes from his room, and not a soul awake in the house? And anyhow, why would anybody *want his bed*? Burglars didn't steal beds, any more than they stole kitchen stoves.

At this he gave a start. Maybe they *had* stolen the kitchen stove. He ran down the stairs and into the kitchen. But no, there it stood, in the dim starlight, nicely blacked, the way old Mary always left it, with no more notion of stirring than the big anchor half buried in the lawn, that his Uncle Peter had brought there from his last ship.

Well, if the stove was still there, maybe his bed was. He ran back upstairs and dashed open the door. No, it wasn't!

Good gracious! Now he was really a little scared. He decided he would go and tell Uncle Peter and find out— Oh mercy! suppose that Uncle Peter had disappeared, too, like the bed! This did scare him, really and truly, so that he could barely stagger across the hall to his uncle's door and turn the knob.

Uncle Peter always kept a little night-light burning, and by its light the little boy could see him plainly. He was oh so beautifully, comfortably asleep, as only deaf people can sleep, and snoring so loudly and so enjoyingly as only old sea-captains can snore. It made the little boy all right again, just in a minute, only to look at him. Nothing much could be the matter with Uncle Peter hitting the pillow like that.

He drew a long breath, stepped out again into the hall, and shut the door behind him. It would be a sin to wake up anybody who was having such a sleep as that. But all the same, it didn't get him back his bed.

Then he had another idea, that explained everything perfectly. This was all a dream, and he'd wake up in the morning just as usual. That was the way all the stories in books ended. The best thing for him to do was to turn over, curl up, drop off to sleep more soundly, and—

But how could he do all that without any bed to do it in?

Mercy! This was getting worse and worse. He put his hand up to his head to see if it were still on his neck and in the right place. It was. But that was all the good it did him.

Of course, he could have wrapped the bedclothes around him and lain down on the floor; but although he wasn't scared,— not *really* scared,—he wouldn't have lain down between that head-board and foot-board, not for a million dollars. Suppose whatever it was that had carried off the bed should carry him off to the same place. Not, of course, you know, that he really believed for a minute that his bed was gone. How could it be?

He began to feel a little chilly and went in to get his blanket. The phosphorescent hands of his alarm-clock showed him that it was nearly three o'clock. It would soon be day. He had an idea. He'd take his blanket and go out of doors for the rest of the night. He'd never seen dawn begin, and all the nature-books said that the animals got out and played more and moved around more just at dawn than at any other time. He wrapped the blanket around him and started out of the front door to go down to a big rock by the brook. There were woodchucks in the field beyond. Maybe he'd see them out feeding when it got light. He was sure of *one* thing! He wouldn't miss them from dropping off to sleep. He felt as though he never, never would sleep again—if, as a matter of fact, he wasn't sound asleep all this whole time!

As he stepped down the front path he saw something white lying there. And what do you suppose it was? The knob of his door. He recognized it because it was cracked in a funny way, with lines that made a triangle. He stooped over it to make sure, but you'd better believe he didn't pick it up or touch it. No, sir! All this was too queer for *him*. He stepped wide around it, left it lying there, and kept turning his head over his shoulder as he went on down the path. It wouldn't have surprised him to see it begin to roll along after him. But he was pretty sure that he could run faster than a door-knob —although, of course, he had never tried.

It seemed awfully good to get away from the house altogether and out on the rock, where he lay down with his blanket. The rock was hard and humpy, but he loved all the humps. They felt so natural and real. In a few minutes, as his eyes got used to the light, he saw that dawn was almost there. The sky was lighter in the east and the trees and bushes began to look gray. A big maple tree stood over the rock, and he heard a bird rustling around in the leaves and by and by it said *"Queet! queet!"* in a sleepy little voice.

And then, right under where the little boy lay, not two feet from his face, he saw something move and come slowly out of

a hole. It was a woodchuck's head. It looked around an instant and then dodged back so quickly that the little boy was afraid he had moved and frightened it, though he had hardly breathed for fear of making a noise. But in a minute, out it came again and looked all around, very cautiously. Then the whole woodchuck came out, and, behind it, four baby wood-chucks, little soft, furry, gray things, all roly-poly and round. They toddled along after their mother for a few steps. Then, as she began to eat, they began to play— just like a family of puppies or kittens, rolling each other over and over, squeal-ing and running around, or standing up on their hind legs to push each other. The little boy could hardly keep back his laugh-ing, to see them, they were so jolly. After a while, their mother took them down to the brook for a drink, and he could hear them going on with their fun, pushing for the best place, falling into the water, squalling, and shaking themselves and starting another roughhouse the minute one was finished. They came racing back up the slope to the rock, bouncing along with their mother back of them. And now it was almost daylight, so the little boy could really see them. He had never seen wild animals close at hand before, when they were not frightened or angry, and he never forgot the gay look of fun on their bright little faces as they came scampering along toward him.

Something dreadful happened then. A shadow—or what the little boy had taken for a shadow—sprang up from beside the rock, pounced on the first of the baby woodchucks, and pinned it to the ground, with a horrid noise of snarling and craunching, like the noise a cat makes over a mouse. The mother woodchuck heard it too, and never hesitated an in-stant. The brave mother-thing made one great jump and landed on top of the animal, whatever it was,—weasel perhaps,—that had killed her baby. And then there was a frightful fight, a snarling, snapping, growling ball rolling over and over, with sharp yells when somebody got bitten, and a gnashing click-click of angry teeth snapping together that sounded to the little boy ever so much fiercer than the roaring of any lion at the zoo.

The little boy grabbed up a stick and stood over them, trying to see where to hit, for he didn't want to hurt the woodchuck. For a minute they didn't notice him, they were so set on tearing each other to pieces; but all of a sudden they must have caught a glimpse of him, for—whiz! flash! In a jiff, they had both vanished, the woodchuck back into the hole, and the weasel off into the bushes. There was the little boy, left alone, with the sun just up over the horizon, and the poor little woodchuck lying with its head bent under it, all limp.

He picked it up to be sorry for it, and thought he felt its heart still beating. Oh, perhaps he could save its life and have it for a pet! He left his blanket on the rock and ran back into the house to the kitchen. There was an old box there, with straw in it and wire netting on two sides, that somebody had brought a setting hen in, the day before. He lifted the top, laid the woodchuck in on the straw, and got a cup of water to sprinkle on its face, in case it had just fainted.

Old Mary came in as he was running back to the box, and when he told her about it, she advised him to try to see if they couldn't get a little milk down the poor thing's throat.

By the time they had some milk in a saucer, with a bit of cloth to let it drip from, the woodchuck had come to, had got up on his feet, and backed off into a corner. The little boy was so glad of this, and knelt down in front of the box to put his face close up to the netting to see how the new pet looked. The woodchuck sprang at him so savagely, clicking its teeth so horridly, that he pulled away in a hurry. It made him feel bad to have the little creature hate him so; but, of course, it didn't surprise him. Just caught and imprisoned, it couldn't know who was its friend. But he'd tame it; he'd be so good to it, it would have to learn to love him! That's what he told his uncle at the breakfast table, where he set the box with the little captive up beside him. His uncle said that he didn't think anybody ever *had* tamed a woodchuck; but the little boy was sure *he* could.

Well, he certainly tried his best. For the next two days he didn't think of another thing. He sat right beside the cage by the hour, so that the little wild thing would get used to him. He tried everything he could think of, to make it eat—from fresh clover, to angleworms and sugar. But it wouldn't even look at any of the foods, and snarled and jumped wickedly at his hand whenever he put something new into the box. And when he sat still and looked in lovingly at it, it would glare back at him, hating him so that the little boy could scarcely stand it.

Of course, not eating anything, it soon grew weak, and could barely stand on its feet. But even lying down and panting for breath, it still had strength enough to stare hatingly at the little boy if he came near.

The second night after he'd caught it, he couldn't sleep for thinking of it, and finally got up to light a candle and go to look at it again. It was crouched together in a corner, its fur every which way, looking miserably sick; but as the little boy came up with his candle, it staggered to its feet and made a feeble little spring toward him, gnashing its teeth and glaring its eyes. Then it fell over weakly on its side. But still it stretched its neck around to keep its hot eyes on the boy.

He remembered, then, how he had seen it playing and joking so happily with its brothers and sisters. He picked up the box in a great hurry and ran with all his might out to the big rock. There he opened the box, took the little woodchuck out, and laid it down on the ground in front of the hole. As soon as it felt the earth under it, it struggled up to its feet, and without once looking at the boy, it let itself slowly down into the hole. The last the little boy saw was a tiny black-striped hind leg, trembling with eagerness, as the little wild baby went home.

Jimmy drew a long breath. "I'm *glad* he let him go," he said softly, and fell into a dreaming silence.

I started to move away, but was recalled by an indignant yell from Jimmy, "But what about that *bed?*"

His eyes were fairly flashing fire.

"Oh," said I, "that turned out not to be interesting at all. One of the neighbors, going home late at night, had had an automobile accident around the turn of the road and his wife sprained her ankle. They came up to Uncle Peter's house to ask for a bedspring to carry her home on, and Uncle Peter stuck his head out of his door to say, sure, yes, they could have the one in the little bedroom on the right-hand side of the landing. They made a mistake and took the left-hand room. That was all.

"And as for the door-knob, that was loose and came off in the hand of one of the men, and he was so excited he didn't think about it till he got downstairs and out on the path."

DAVY AND THE GOBLIN

OR, WHAT FOLLOWED READING "ALICE'S ADVENTURES IN WONDERLAND"

by Charles Carryl

CHAPTER I

HOW THE GOBLIN CAME

IT happened one Christmas eve, when Davy was about eight years old, and this is the way it came about.

That particular Christmas eve was a snowy one and a blowy one, and one generally to be remembered. In the city, where Davy lived, the storm played all manner of pranks, swooping down upon unwary old gentlemen and turning their umbrellas wrong side out, and sometimes blowing their hats quite out of sight. And in the country, where Davy had come to pass Christmas with his dear old grandmother, things were not much better; but here people were very wise about the weather, and stayed indoors, huddled around great blazing wood fires; and the storm, finding no live game, buried up the roads and the fences, and such small-fry of houses as could readily be put out of sight, and howled and roared over the fields and through the trees in a fashion not to be forgotten.

Davy, being of the opinion that a snow-storm was a thing not to be wasted, had been out with his sled, trying to have a little fun with the weather; but presently, discovering that this particular storm was not friendly to little boys, he had retreated into the house, and having put his hat and his high shoes and his mittens by the kitchen fire to dry, he began to find his time hang heavily on his hands. He had wandered idly all over the house, and had tried how cold his nose could be made by holding it against the window-panes, and, I am sorry to say, had even been sliding down the balusters and teasing the cat; and at last, as evening was coming on, had curled himself up in the big easy-chair facing the fire, and had begun to read once more about the marvelous things that happened to little Alice in Wonderland. Then, as it grew darker, he laid aside the book and sat watching the blazing logs and listening to the solemn ticking of the high Dutch clock against the wall.

Then there stole in at the door a delicious odor of dinner cooking downstairs—an odor so suggestive of roast chickens and baked potatoes and gravy and pie as to make any little boy's mouth water; and presently Davy began softly telling himself what he would choose for his dinner. He had quite finished fancying the first part of his feast and was just coming, in his mind, to an extra-large slice of apple-pie well browned (staring meanwhile very hard at one of the brass knobs of the andirons to keep his thoughts from wandering), when he suddenly discovered a little man perched upon that identical knob and smiling at him with all his might.

This little man was a very curious-looking person indeed. He was only about a foot high, but his head was as big as a cocoanut, and he had great bulging eyes, like a frog, and a ridiculous turned-up nose. His legs were as slender as spindles, and he had long-pointed toes to his shoes, or rather to his stockings, or, for that matter, to his trousers,—for they were all of a piece—and bright scarlet in color, as were also his little coat and his high-pointed hat and a queer little cloak that hung over his shoulder. His mouth was so wide that when he smiled it seemed to go quite behind his ears, and there was no way of knowing where the smile ended, except by looking at it from behind—which Davy couldn't do without getting into the fire.

Now, there's no use in denying that Davy was frightened. The fact is, he was frightened almost out of his wits, particularly when he saw that the little man, still smiling furiously, was carefully picking the hottest and reddest embers out of the fire, and, after cracking them like nuts with his teeth, eating them with great relish. Davy watched this alarming meal, expecting every moment to see the little man burst into a blaze and disappear, but he finished his coals in safety, and then nodding cheerfully at Davy, said:

"I know you!"

"Do you?" said Davy faintly.

"Oh, yes!" said the little man. " I know you perfectly well. You are the little boy who doesn't believe in fairies, nor in giants, nor in goblins, nor in anything the story-books tell you."

Now, the truth was that Davy, having never met any giants when he was out walking, nor seen any fairies peeping out of the bushes, nor found any goblins about the house, had come to believe that all these kinds of people were purely imaginary beings, so that now he could do nothing but stare at the little man in a shamefaced sort of way and wonder what was coming next.

"Now all that," said the little man, shaking his finger at him in a reproving way, "all that is very foolish and very wrong. I'm a goblin myself,—a hob-goblin —and I've come to take you on a Believing Voyage."

"Oh, if you please, I can't go!" cried Davy, in great alarm at this proposal, "I can't, indeed. I haven't permission."

"Rubbish!" said the Goblin. "Ask the Colonel."

Now, the Colonel was nothing more nor less than a silly-looking little man made of lead that stood on the mantel shelf holding a clock in his arms. The clock never went, but, for that matter, the Colonel never went either, for he had been standing stock-still for years, and it seemed perfectly ridiculous to ask *him* anything about going anywhere, so Davy felt quite safe in looking up at him and asking permission to go on the Believing Voyage. To his dismay the Colonel nodded his head and cried out in a little cracked voice:

"Why, certainly!"

At this, the Goblin jumped down off the knob of the andiron, and skipping briskly across the room to the big Dutch clock, rapped sharply on the front of the case with his knuckles, when to Davy's amazement the great thing fell over on its face upon the floor as softly as if it had been a feather bed. Davy now saw that instead of being full of weights and brass wheels and curious works, as he had always supposed, the clock was really a sort of boat with a wide seat at each end; but before he had time to make any further discoveries, the Goblin, who had vanished for a moment, suddenly reappeared, carrying two large sponge-cakes in his arms. Now, Davy was perfectly sure that he had seen his grandmother putting those very sponge-cakes into the oven to bake, but before he could utter a word of remonstrance the Goblin clapped one into each seat, and scrambling into the clock sat down upon the smaller one, merely remarking:

"They make prime cushions, you know."

For a moment, Davy had a wild idea of rushing out of the room and calling for help; but the Goblin seemed so pleased with the arrangements he had made and, moreover, was smiling so good-naturedly that the little boy thought better of it, and after a moment's hesitation climbed into the clock and took his seat upon the other cake. It was as warm and springy and fragrant as a day in May. Then there was a whizzing sound, like a lot of wheels spinning around, and the clock rose from the floor and made a great swoop toward the window.

"I'll steer," shouted the Goblin, "and do you look out sharp for light-houses!"

Davy had just time to notice that the Colonel was hastily scrambling down from the mantel shelf with his beloved time-piece in his arms, when they, seated in the long Dutch clock, dashed through the window and out into the night.

CHAPTER II

THE BEGINNING OF THE BELIEVING VOYAGE

THE first thought that came into Davy's mind when he found himself out-of-doors was that he had started off on his journey without his hat, and he was therefore exceedingly pleased to find that it had stopped snowing and that the air was quite still and delightfully balmy and soft. The moon was shining brightly, and as he looked back at the house he was surprised to see that the window through which they had come, and which he was quite sure had always been a straight-up-and-down, old-fashioned window, was now a round affair with flaps running to a point in the center, like the holes the harlequin jumps through in the pantomime.

"How did that window ever get changed into a round hole?" he asked the Goblin, pointing to it in great astonishment.

"Oh," said the Goblin, carelessly, "that's one of the circular singumstances that happen on a Believing Voyage. It's nothing to what you'll see before we come back again. Ah!" he added, "there comes the Colonel!"

Sure enough, at this moment the Colonel's head appeared through the flaps. The clock was still in his arms, and he seemed to be having a great deal of trouble in getting it through, and his head kept coming into view and then disappearing again behind the flaps in so ridiculous a manner that Davy shouted with laughter, and the Goblin smiled harder than ever. Suddenly the poor little man made a desperate plunge and had almost made his way out when the flaps shut to with a loud snap and caught him about the waist. In his efforts to free himself, he dropped his clock to the ground outside, when it burst with a loud explosion and the house instantly disappeared.

This was so unexpected and seemed so serious a matter that Davy was much distressed, wondering what had become of his dear old grandmother and Mrs. Frump, the cook, and Mary Farina, the housemaid, and Solomon, the cat. However, before he had time to make any inquiries of the Goblin, his grandmother came dropping down through the air in her rocking-chair. She was quietly knitting, and her chair was gently rocking as she went by. Next came Mrs. Frump with her apron quite full of kettles and pots, and then Mary Farina, sitting on a step-ladder with the coal-scuttle in her lap. Solomon was nowhere to be seen. Davy, looking over the side of the clock, saw them disappear, one after the other, in a large tree on the lawn; and the Goblin informed him that they had fallen into the kitchen of a witch-hazel tree and would be well taken care of. Indeed, as the clock sailed over the tree, Davy saw that the trunk of it was hollow and that a bright light was shining far under-ground; and to make the matter quite sure, a smell of cooking was coming up through the hole. On one of the topmost boughs of the tree was a nest with two sparrows in it, and he was much astonished at discovering that they were lying side by side, fast asleep, with one of his mittens spread over them for a coverlet.

"I suppose my shoes are somewhere about," he said, sadly. "Perhaps the squirrels are filling them with nuts."

"You're quite right," replied the Goblin, cheerfully; "and there's a rabbit over by the hedge putting dried leaves into your hat; I rather fancy he's about moving into it for the winter."

Davy was about to complain against such liberties being taken with his property, when the clock began rolling over in the air, and he had just time to grasp the sides of it to keep himself from falling out.

"Don't be afraid!" cried the Goblin, "she's only rolling a little," and as he said this, the clock steadied itself and sailed serenely away past the spire of the village church and off over the fields.

Davy now noticed that the Goblin was glowing with a bright, rosy light, as though a number of candles were burning in his stomach and shining out through his scarlet clothes.

"That's the coals he had for his supper," thought Davy; but as the Goblin continued to smile complacently and seemed to be feeling quite comfortable, he did not venture to ask any questions, and went on with his thoughts. "I suppose he'll soon have smoke coming out of his nose, as if he were a stove. If it were a cold night I'd

The rabbit takes liberties with Davy's property

ask him to come and sit in my lap. I think he must be as warm as a piece of toast!" And the little boy was laughing softly to himself over this conceit, when the Goblin, who had been staring intently at the sky, suddenly ducked his head and cried "Barkers!"—and the next instant a shower of little blue woolly balls came tumbling into the clock. To Davy's alarm they proved to be alive, and immediately began scrambling about in all directions, and yelping so ferociously that he climbed up on his cake in dismay, while the Goblin, hastily pulling a large magnifying glass out of his hat, began attentively examining these strange visitors.

"Bless me!" cried the Goblin, turning

very pale, "they're Skye-terriers. The dog-star must have turned upside down."

"What shall we do?" said Davy, feeling that this was a very bad state of affairs.

"The first thing to do," said the Goblin, "is to get away from these fellows before the solar sisters come after them. Here, jump into my hat!"

So many wonderful things had happened already that this seemed to Davy quite a natural and proper thing to do, and as the Goblin had already seated himself upon the brim, he took his place opposite to him without hesitation. As they sailed away from the clock, it quietly rolled over once, spilling out the sponge-cakes and all the little dogs, and was then wafted off, gently rocking from side to side as it went.

Davy was much surprised at finding that the hat was as large as a clothes-hamper, with plenty of room for him to swing his legs about in the crown. It proved, however, to be a very unpleasant thing to travel in. It spun around like a top as it sailed through the air, until Davy began to feel uncomfortably dizzy, and the Goblin himself seemed to be far from well. He had stopped smiling, and the rosy light had all faded away, as though the candles inside of him had gone out. His clothes, too, had changed from bright scarlet to a dull ashen color, and he sat stupidly upon the brim of the hat as if he were going to sleep.

"If he goes to sleep, he will certainly fall overboard," thought Davy; and with a view to rousing the Goblin, he ventured to remark, "I had no idea your hat was so big."

"I can make it any size I please, from a thimble to a sentry-box," said the Goblin. "And speaking of sentry-boxes—" here he stopped and looked more stupid than ever.

"I verily believe he's absent-minded," said Davy to himself.

"I'm worse than that," said the Goblin, as if Davy had spoken aloud. "I'm absent-bodied," and with these words he fell out of the hat and instantly disappeared. Davy peered anxiously over the edge of the brim, but the Goblin was nowhere to be seen, and the little boy found himself quite alone.

Strange-looking birds now began to swoop up and chuckle at him, and others flew around him, as the hat spun along through the air, gravely staring him in the face for a while, and then sailed away, sadly bleating like sheep. Then a great creature with rumpled feathers perched

"I'm a Cockalorum," he softly murmured

upon the brim of the hat where the Goblin had been sitting, and after solemnly gazing at him for a few moments, softly murmured, "I'm a Cockalorum," and flew heavily away. All this was very sad and distressing, and Davy was mournfully wondering what would happen to him next, when it suddenly struck him that his legs were feeling very cold, and looking down at them he discovered to his great alarm that the crown of the Goblin's hat had entirely disappeared, leaving nothing but the brim upon which he was sitting. He hurriedly examined this and found that the hat was really nothing but an enormous skein of wool, which was rapidly unwinding as it spun along. Indeed, the brim was disappearing at such a rate that he had hardly made this alarming discovery before the end of the skein was whisked away and he found himself falling through the air.

He was on the point of screaming out in his terror, when he discovered that he was falling very slowly and gently swaying from side to side, like a toy balloon. The next moment he struck something hard, which gave way with a sound like breaking glass and let him through, and he had just time to notice that the air had suddenly become deliciously scented with vanilla, when he fell crashing into the branches of a large tree.

CHAPTER III

IN THE SUGAR-PLUM GARDEN

THE bough upon which Davy had fallen bent far down with his weight, then sprang back, then bent again, and in this way fell into a sort of delightful up-and-down dipping motion, which he found very soothing and agreeable. Indeed, he was so pleased and comforted at finding himself near the ground once more that he lay back in a crotch between two branches, enjoying the rocking of the bough and lazily wondering what had become of the Goblin, and whether this was the end of the Believing Voyage, and a great many other things, until he chanced to wonder where he was. Then he sat up on the branch in great astonishment, for he saw that the tree was in full leaf and loaded with plums, and it flashed across his mind that the winter

had disappeared very suddenly, and that he had fallen into a place where it was broad daylight.

The plum-tree was the most beautiful and wonderful thing he had ever seen, for the leaves were perfectly white, and the plums, which looked extremely delicious, were of every imaginable color.

Now, it immediately occurred to Davy that he had never in his whole life had all the plums he wanted at any one time. Here was a rare chance for a feast, and he carefully selected the largest and most luscious-looking plum he could find, to begin with. To his disappointment it proved to be quite hard and as solid and heavy as a stone. He was looking at it in great perplexity, and punching it with his thumbs in the hope of finding a soft place in it, when he heard a rustling sound among the leaves, and looking up, he saw the Cockalorum perched upon the bough beside him. It was gazing sadly at the plum, and its feathers were more rumpled than ever. Presently it gave a long sigh and said, in its low, murmuring voice: "Perhaps it's a sugar-plum," and then flew clumsily away as before.

"Perhaps it is!" exclaimed Davy joyfully, taking a great bite of the plum. To his surprise and disgust, he found his mouth full of very bad-tasting soap, and at the same moment the white leaves of the plum-tree suddenly turned over and showed the words "APRIL FOOL" printed very distinctly on their under sides. To make the matter worse, the Cockalorum came back and flew slowly around the branches, laughing softly to itself with a sort of a chuckling sound, until Davy, almost crying with disappointment and mortification, scrambled down from the tree to the ground.

He found himself in a large garden planted with plum-trees, like the one he had fallen into, and with walks winding about among them in every direction. These walks were beautifully paved with sugar-almonds and bordered by long rows of many-colored motto-papers neatly planted in the ground. He was too much distressed, however, by what had happened in the plum-tree to be interested or pleased with this discovery, and was about walking away along one of the paths in the hope of finding his way out of the garden, when he suddenly caught sight of a small figure standing a little distance from him.

He was the strangest-looking creature Davy had ever seen, not even excepting the Goblin. In the first place, he was as flat as a pancake, and about as thick as one; and in the second place, he was so transparent that Davy could see through his head and his arms and his legs almost as clearly as though he had been made of glass. This was so surprising in itself that when Davy presently discovered that he was made of beautiful, clear lemon-candy, it seemed the most natural thing in the world, as explaining his transparency. He was neatly dressed in a sort of tunic of writing-paper, with a cocked hat of the same material, and he had under his arm a large book with the words "HOLE-KEEP-ER's VACUUM" printed on the cover. This curious-looking creature was standing before an extremely high wall with his back to Davy, intently watching a large hole in the wall about a foot from the ground. There was nothing extraordinary about the appearance of the hole (except that the lower edge of it was curiously tied in a large bow-knot like a cravat), but Davy watched it carefully for a few moments, thinking that perhaps something marvelous would come out of it. Nothing appeared, however, and Davy, walking up close behind the candy man, said very politely, "If you please, sir, I dropped in here——"

Before he could finish the sentence the Hole-keeper said snappishly, "Well, drop out again—quick!"

"But," pleaded Davy, "you can't drop out of a place, you know, unless the place should happen to turn upside down."

"I *don't* know anything about it," replied the Hole-keeper, without moving. "I never saw anything drop—except once. Then I saw a gumdrop. Are you a gum?" he added, suddenly turning around and staring at Davy.

"Of course I'm not," said Davy, indignantly. "If you'll only listen to me, you'll understand exactly how it happened."

"Well, go on," said the Hole-keeper, impatiently, "and don't be tiresome."

"I fell down ever so far," said Davy, beginning his story over again, "and at last I broke through something——"

"That was the sky-light!" shrieked the Hole-keeper, dashing his book upon the ground in a fury. "That was the barley-sugar sky-light, and I shall certainly be boiled!"

This was such a shocking idea that Davy stood speechless, staring at the Hole-keeper, who rushed to and fro in a convulsion of distress.

"Now, see here," said the Hole-keeper, at length, coming up to him and speaking in a low, trembling voice. "This must be a private secret between us. Do you solemsy promilse?"

"I prolemse," said Davy, earnestly. This wasn't at all what he meant to say, and it sounded very ridiculous; but somehow the words *wouldn't* come straight. The Hole-keeper, however, seemed perfectly satisfied, and picking up his book, said: "Well, just wait till I can't find your name," and began hurriedly turning over the leaves.

Davy saw, to his astonishment, that there was nothing whatever in the book, all the leaves being perfectly blank, and he couldn't help saying, rather contemptuously:

"How do you expect to find my name in *that* book? There's nothing in it."

"Ah! that's just it, you see," said the Hole-keeper, exultingly; "I look in it for the names that ought to be out of it. It's the completest system that ever was invented. Oh! here you aren't!" he added, staring with great satisfaction at one of the blank pages. "Your name is Rupsy Frimbles."

"It's nothing of the sort," said Davy, indignantly.

"Tut! Tut!" said the Hole-keeper. "Don't stop to contradict or you'll be too late"; and Davy felt himself gently lifted off his feet and pushed head-foremost into the hole. It was quite dark and rather sticky, and smelt strongly of burnt sugar, and Davy had a most unpleasant time of it crawling through on his hands and knees. To add to his distress, when he came out at the further end, instead of being, as he had hoped, in the open country, he found himself in a large room fairly swarming with creatures very like the Hole-keeper in appearance, but somewhat darker and denser in the way of complexion. The instant Davy came out of the hole, a harsh voice called out:

"Bring Frungles this way," and the crowd gathered around him and began to rudely hustle him across the room.

"That's not my name!" cried Davy, struggling desperately to free himself. "It isn't even the name I came in with!"

"Tut! Tut!" said a trembling voice near him, and Davy caught sight of the Hole-keeper, also struggling in the midst of the crowd with his great book hugged tightly to his breast. The next moment he found himself before a low platform on which a crowned figure was sitting in a gorgeous tin chair, holding in his hand a long white wand with red lines running screw-wise around it, like a barber's pole.

"Who broke the barley-sugar sky-light?" said the figure, in a terrible voice.

The Hole-keeper began fumbling at the leaves of his book in great agitation, when the king, pointing at him with his wand, roared furiously: "Boil *him,* at all events!"

"Tut! Tut! your majesty——" began the Hole-keeper confusedly, with his stiff little tunic fairly rustling with fright; but before he could utter another word he was dragged away, screaming with terror.

"Don't you go with them!" shouted Davy, made really desperate by the Hole-keeper's danger. "They're nothing but a lot of molasses candy!"

At this the king gave a frightful shriek, and aiming a furious blow at Davy with his wand, rolled off the platform into the midst of the struggling crowd. The wand broke into a hundred pieces, and the air was instantly filled with a choking odor of peppermint; then everything was wrapped in darkness, and Davy felt himself being whirled along, heels over head, through the air. Then there came a confused sound of bells and voices, and he found himself running rapidly down a long street with the Goblin at his side.

CHAPTER IV

THE BUTTERSCOTCHMEN

BELLS were pealing and tolling in all directions, and the air was filled with the sound of distant shouts and cries.

"What were they?" asked Davy, breathlessly.

"Butterscotchmen," said the Goblin.

"And what makes you that color?" said Davy, suddenly noticing that the Goblin had changed his color to a beautiful blue.

"Trouble and worry," said the Goblin. "I always get blue when the Butterscotchmen are after me."

"Are they coming after us now?" inquired Davy in great alarm.

"Of course they are," said the Goblin. "But the best of it is, they can't run till they get warm, and they can't get warm without running, you see. But the worst of it is that *we* can't stop without sticking fast," he added, anxiously. "We must keep it up until we get to the Amuserum."

"What's that?" said Davy.

"It's a place they have to amuse themselves with," said the Goblin,—"curiosities, and all that sort of thing, you know. By the way, how much money have you? We have to pay to get in."

Davy began to feel in his pocket (which is a very difficult thing to do when you're running fast) and found, to his astonishment, that they were completely filled with a most extraordinary lot of rubbish. First, he pulled out what seemed to be an iron ball, but it proved to be a hard-boiled egg, without the shell, stuck full of small tacks. Then came two slices of toast firmly tied together with a green cord. Then came a curious little glass jar filled with large flies. As Davy took this out of his pocket, the cork came out with a loud "pop!" and the flies flew away in all directions. Then came, one after another, a tart filled with gravel, two chicken bones, a bird's nest with some pieces of brown soap in it, some mustard in a pillbox and a cake of beeswax stuck full of caraway seeds. Davy remembered afterward that as he threw these things away they arranged themselves in a long row on the curb-stone of the street. The Goblin looked on with great interest as Davy fished them up out of his pockets, and finally said, enviously: "That's a splendid collection; where did they all come from?"

"I'm sure *I* don't know," said Davy, in great bewilderment.

"And I'm sure *I* don't know," repeated the Goblin. "What else is there?"

Davy felt about in his pockets again and found what seemed to be a piece of money. On taking it out, however, he was mortified to find that it was nothing but an old button; but the Goblin exclaimed in a tone of great satisfaction, "Ah! hold on to that!" and ran on faster than ever.

The sound of the distant voices had grown fainter and fainter still, and Davy was just hoping that their long run was almost over, when the street came abruptly to an end at a brick wall, over the top of which he could see the branches of trees. There was a small round hole in the wall with the words "PAY HERE" printed above it, and the Goblin whispered to Davy to hand in the button through this hole. Davy did so, feeling very much ashamed of himself, when to his surprise instead of receiving tickets in return, he heard a loud exclamation behind the wall, followed by a confused sound of scuffling, and the hole suddenly disappeared. The next moment, a little bell tinkled and the wall rose slowly before them like a curtain, carrying the trees with it, apparently, and he and the Goblin were left standing in a large open space paved with stone.

Davy was exceedingly alarmed at seeing a dense mass of Butterscotchmen in the center of the square, pushing and crowding one another in a very quarrelsome manner, and chattering like a flock of magpies, and he was just about to propose a hasty retreat, when a figure came hurrying through the square, carrying on a pole a large placard bearing the words:

"JUST RECEIVED!
THE GREAT FRUNGLES THING!
ON EXHIBITION IN THE PLUM-GARDEN!"

At the sight of these words, the mob set up a terrific shout, and began streaming out of the square after the pole-bearer, like a flock of sheep, jostling and shoving one another as they went, and leaving Davy and the Goblin quite alone.

"I verily believe they're gone to look at my button," cried Davy, beginning to laugh in spite of his fears. "They called *me* Frungles, you know."

"That's rather a nice name," said the Goblin, who had begun smiling again. "It's better than Snubgraddle, at all events. Let's have a look at the curiosities"; and here he walked boldly into the center of the square.

Davy followed close at his heels, and found to his astonishment and disappointment that the curiosities were simply the things that he had fished out of his pockets but a few minutes before, placed on little pedestals and carefully protected by transparent sugar shades. He was on the point of laughing outright at this ridiculous exhibition, when he saw that the Goblin had taken a large telescope out of his pocket and was examining the different objects with the closest attention, and muttering to himself, "Wonderful! wonderful!" as if he had never seen anything like them before.

"Pooh!" said Davy, contemptuously. "The only wonderful thing about them is how they ever came *here.*"

At this remark the Goblin turned his telescope toward Davy and uttered a faint cry of surprise; and Davy, peering anxiously through the large end, saw him suddenly shrink to the size of a small

beetle and then disappear altogether. Davy hastily reached out with his hands to grasp the telescope; but it, too, disappeared.

The next moment he felt something spring upon his back. Before he could cry out in his terror, a head was thrust forward over his shoulder, and he found the Goblin, who was now of a bright purple color, staring him in the face and laughing with all his might.

CHAPTER V

THE GIANT BADORFUL

"GOBLIN," said Davy, very seriously, as the little man jumped down from off his back, "if you are going to play such tricks as *that* upon me, I should like to go home at once."

"Where's the harm?" said the Goblin, sitting down on the grass with his back against a wall and smiling contentedly.

"The harm is that I was frightened," said Davy, with great indignation. But as he spoke, a loud rumbling noise like distant thunder came from behind the wall against which the Goblin was leaning, followed by a tremendous sneeze that fairly shook the ground.

"What's that?" whispered Davy to the Goblin, in great alarm.

"It's only Badorful," said the Goblin, laughing. "He's always snoring and waking himself up, and I suppose it's sleeping on the ground that makes him sneeze. Let's have a look at him," and the Goblin led the way along the wall to a large grating.

Davy looked through the grating and was much alarmed at seeing a giant, at least twenty feet in height, sitting on the ground, with his legs crossed under him like a tailor. He was dressed in a shabby suit of red velveteen, with a great leathern belt about his waist and enormous boots, and Davy thought he looked terribly ferocious. On the grass beside him lay a huge club, thickly studded at one end with great iron knobs; but Davy noticed to his great relief that some little creeping vines were twining themselves among these knobs, and that moss was growing thickly upon one side of the club itself, as though it had been lying there untouched for a long time.

The giant was talking to himself in a low tone, and, after listening attentively at the grating for a moment, the Goblin shrieked:

"He's making poetry!" and throwing himself upon the ground kicked up his heels in a perfect ecstasy of delight.

"Oh, hush, hush!" cried Davy in terror. "Suppose he hears you!"

"Hears me!" said the Goblin, discontinuing his kicking and looking very much surprised. "What if he does?"

"Well, you know, he *might* not like being laughed at," said Davy, anxiously.

"There's something in that," said the Goblin, staring reflectively at the ground.

"And, you see," continued Davy, "a giant who doesn't like what's going on must be a dreadful creature."

"Oh! there's no fear of *him*," said the Goblin, contemptuously, motioning with his head toward the giant. "He's too old. Why, I must have known him, off and on, for nearly two hundred years. Come in and see him."

"Will he do anything?" said Davy, anxiously.

"Bless you, no!" said the Goblin. "He's a perfect old kitten"; and with these words he pushed open the grating and passed through with Davy following tremblingly

at his heels. Badorful looked up with a feeble smile, and merely said, "Just listen to this:"

My age is three hundred and seventy-two,
  And I think, with the deepest regret,
How I used to pick up and voraciously
    chew
    The dear little boys whom I met.

I've eaten them raw in their holiday suits,
  I've eaten them curried with rice,
I've eaten them baked in their jackets and
    boots,
    And found them exceedingly nice.

But now that my jaws are too weak for
    such fare,
  I think it excessively rude
To do such a thing, when I'm quite well
    aware
    Little boys do not like to be chewed.

And so I contentedly live upon eels,
  And try to do nothing amiss,
And I pass all the time I can spare from
    my meals
    In innocent slumber—like this.

Here Badorful rolled over upon his side, and was instantly fast asleep.

"You see," said the Goblin, picking up a large stone and thumping with it upon the giant's head, "you see, he's quite weak *here*. Otherwise, considering his age, he's a very capable giant."

At this moment a farmer with bright red hair thrust his head in at the grating, and calling out, "Look out, there!" disappeared again. Davy and the Goblin rushed out and were just in time to see something go by like a flash with a crowd of people, armed with pitchforks, in hot pursuit. Davy and the Goblin were just setting off on a run to join in the chase, when a voice said, "Ahem!" and looking up, they saw Badorful staring at them over the top of the wall.

"How does this strike you?" he said, addressing himself to Davy:

Although I am a giant of the exhibition size,
I've been nicely educated, and I notice with surprise,
That the simplest rules of etiquette you don't pretend to keep,
For you skurry off to races while a gentleman's asleep.

Don't reply that I was drowsy, for my nap was but a kind
Of dramatic illustration of a peaceful frame of mind;
And you really might have waited till I woke again, instead
Of indelicately pounding, with a stone, upon my head.

Very probably you'll argue that our views do not agree,—
I've often found that little boys have disagreed with me;—
But I'm properly entitled, on the compensation plan,
To three times as much politeness as an ordinary man.

Davy was greatly distressed at having these severe remarks addressed to him.

"If you please, sir," he said earnestly, "I didn't pound you."

At this the giant glared savagely at the Goblin and continued:

My remarks have been directed at the one who, I supposed,
Had been violently thumping on my person while I dozed:
By a simple calculation you will find that there is due
Just six times as much politeness from a little chap like you.

"Oh! you make me ill!" said the Goblin, flippantly. "Go to sleep."

Badorful stared at him for a moment, and then with a sickly smile, murmured: "Good afternoon," and disappeared behind the wall.

Davy and the Goblin now hurried off wildly to resume the chase, when the Goblin suddenly stopped, and by an ingenious twist of his body sat down on his long shoes or stockings, and began to rock to and fro like an animated little rocking-chair.

"Dear me!" exclaimed Davy, perfectly amazed, "I thought we were chasing something."

"Of course you did," said the Goblin, complacently; "but in this part of the world things very often turn out to be different from what they would have been if they hadn't been otherwise than as you expected they were going to be."

"But you thought so yourself——" began Davy, when to his distress the Goblin suddenly faded into a dull pinkish color, and then disappeared altogether. Davy looked about him and found that he was quite alone in a dense wood.

CHAPTER VI

THE MOVING FOREST

"OH, dear!" cried Davy, speaking aloud in his distress, "I do wish people and things wouldn't change about so! Just so soon as ever I get to a place, it goes away, and I'm somewhere else!" And the little boy's heart began to beat rapidly as he looked about him; for the wood was very dark and solemn and still.

Presently the trees and bushes directly before him moved silently apart and showed a broad path beautifully overgrown with soft turf; and as he stepped forward upon it, the trees and bushes beyond moved silently aside in their turn, and the path grew before him, as he walked along, like a green carpet slowly unrolling itself through the wood. It made him a little uneasy at first to find that the trees behind him came together again, quietly blotting out the path,—but then he thought:

"It really doesn't matter so long as I don't want to go back," and so he walked along very contentedly.

By and by, the path seemed to give itself a shake, and, turning abruptly around a large tree, brought Davy suddenly upon a little butcher's shop, snugly buried in the wood. There was a sign on the shop, reading, "ROBIN HOOD: VENISON," and Robin himself, wearing a clean white apron over his suit of Lincoln green, stood in the door-way, holding a knife and steel as though he were on the lookout for customers. As he caught sight of Davy, he said, "Steaks? Chops?" in an inquiring way, quite like an every-day butcher.

"Venison is deer, isn't it?" said Davy, looking up at the sign.

"Not at all," said Robin Hood, promptly. "It's the cheapest meat about here."

"Oh, I didn't mean that," replied Davy; "I meant that it comes off of a deer."

"Wrong again!" said Robin Hood, triumphantly. "It comes on a deer. I cut it off myself. Steaks? Chops?"

"No, I thank you," said Davy, giving up the argument. "I don't think I want anything to eat just now."

"Then what did you come here for?" said Robin Hood, peevishly. "What's the good, I'd like to know, of standing around and staring at an honest tradesman?"

"Well, you see," said Davy, beginning to feel frightened, "I didn't know you were this sort of person at all. I always thought you were an archer, like—like William Tell, you know."

"That's all a mistake about Tell," said Robin Hood, contemptuously. "He wasn't an archer. He was a crossbowman,—the crossest one that ever lived. By the way, you don't happen to want any steaks or chops today, do you?"

"No, not today, thank you," said Davy, very politely.

"Tomorrow?" inquired Robin Hood.

"No, I thank you," said Davy again.

"Will you want any yesterday?" inquired Robin Hood, rather doubtfully.

"I think not," said Davy, beginning to laugh.

Robin Hood stared at him for a moment with a puzzled expression, and then walked into his little shop and Davy turned away. As he did so, the path behind him began to unfold itself through the wood, and looking back over his shoulder, he saw the little shop swallowed up by the trees and bushes. Just as it disappeared from view, he caught a glimpse of a charming little girl peeping out of a latticed window beside the door. She wore a little red hood and looked wistfully after Davy as the shop went out of sight.

"I verily believe that was Little Red Riding Hood," said Davy to himself, "and I never knew before that Robin Hood was her father!" The thought of Red Riding Hood, however, brought the wolf to Davy's mind, and he began to anxiously watch the thickets on either side of the path, and even went so far as to whistle softly to himself, by way of showing that he wasn't in the least afraid. He went on and on, hoping the forest would soon come to an end, until the path shook itself, again disclosing to view a trim little brick shop in the densest part of the thicket. It had a neat little green door, with a bright brass knocker upon it, and a sign above it, bearing the words,

"SHAM-SHAM: BARGAINS IN WATCHES"

"Well!" exclaimed Davy in amazement. "Of all places to sell watches in, that's the preposterest!" But as he turned to walk away, he found the trees and bushes for the first time blocking his way, and refusing to move aside. This distressed him very much, until it suddenly occurred to him that this must mean that he was to go into the shop; and after a moment's hesitation he went up and knocked timidly at the door with the bright brass knocker. There was no response to the knock, and Davy cautiously pushed open the door and went in.

The place was so dark that at first he could see nothing, although he heard a rattling sound coming from the back part of the shop, but presently he discovered the figure of an old man, busily mixing something in a large iron pot. As Davy approached him, he saw that the pot was full of watches, which the old man was stirring about with a ladle. The old creature was very curiously dressed in a suit of rusty green velvet, with little silver buttons sewed over it, and he wore a pair of enormous yellow-leather boots; and Davy was quite alarmed at seeing that a broad leathern belt about his waist was stuck full of old-fashioned knives and pistols. Davy was about to retreat quickly from the shop, when the old man looked up and said, in a peevish voice:

"How many watches do you want?" and Davy saw that he was a very shocking-looking person, with wild, staring eyes, and with a skin as dark as mahogany, as if he had been soaked in something for ever so long.

"How many?" repeated the old man impatiently.

"If you please," said Davy, "I don't think I'll take any watches today. I'll call——"

"Drat 'em!" interrupted the old man, angrily beating the watches with his ladle, "I'll never get rid of 'em—never!"

"It seems to me—" began Davy, soothingly.

"Of course it does!" again interrupted the old man as crossly as before. "Of course it does! That's because you won't listen to the why of it."

"But I *will* listen," said Davy.

"Then sit down on the floor and hold up your ears," said the old man.

Davy did as he was told to do, so far as sitting down on the floor was concerned, and the old man pulled a paper out of one of his boots, and glaring at Davy over the top of it, said angrily:

"You're a pretty spectacle! I'm another. What does that make?"

"A pair of spectacles, I suppose," said Davy.

"Right!" said the old man. "Here they are." And pulling an enormous pair of spectacles out of the other boot he put them on, and began reading aloud from his paper:

"'My recollectest thoughts are those
    Which I remember yet;
And bearing on, as you'd suppose,
    The things I don't forget.

"'But my resemblest thoughts are less
    Alike than they should be;
A state of things, as you'll confess,
    You very seldom see.'"

"Clever, isn't it?" said the old man, peeping proudly over the top of the paper.

"Yes, I think it is," said Davy, rather doubtfully.

"Now comes the cream of the whole thing," said the old man. "Just listen to this:

" 'And yet the mostest thought I love
Is what no one believes—' "

Here the old man hastily crammed the paper into his boot again, and stared solemnly at Davy.

"What is it?" said Davy, after waiting a moment for him to complete the verse. The old man glanced suspiciously about the shop, and then added, in a hoarse whisper:

" 'That I'm the sole survivor of
The famous Forty Thieves!' "

"But I thought the Forty Thieves were all boiled to death," said Davy.

"All but me," said the old man, decidedly. "I was in the last jar, and when they came to me the oil was off the boil, or the boil was off the oil,—I forget which it was,—but it ruined my digestion and made me look like a ginger-bread man. What larks we used to have!" he continued, rocking himself back and forth and chuckling hoarsely. "Oh! we were a precious lot, we were! I'm Sham-Sham, you know. Then there was Anamanamona Mike—he was an Irishman from Hullaboo —and Barcelona Boner—he was a Spanish chap, and boned everything he could lay his hands on. Strike's real name was Gobang; but we called him Strike, because he was always asking for more pay. Hare Ware was a poacher, and used to catch Welsh rabbits in a trap; we called him 'Hardware' because he had so much *steal* about him. Good joke, wasn't it?"

"Oh, very!" said Davy, laughing.

"Frown Whack was a scowling fellow with a club," continued Sham-Sham. "My! how he could hit! And Harico and Barico were a couple of bad Society Islanders. Then there was Wee Wo; he was a little Chinese chap, and we used to send him down the chimneys to open front doors

for us. He used to say that sooted him to perfection. Wac——"

At this moment an extraordinary commotion began among the watches. There was no doubt about it, the pot was boiling. And Sham-Sham, angrily crying out "Don't tell *me* a watched pot never boils!" sprang to his feet, and pulling a pair of pistols from his belt, began firing at the watches, which were now bubbling over the side of the pot and rolling about the floor; while Davy, who had had quite enough of Sham-Sham by this time, ran out of the door.

To his great surprise, he found himself in a sort of underground passage lighted by grated openings overhead; but as he could still hear Sham-Sham, who now seemed to be firing all his pistols at once, he did not hesitate, but ran along the passage at the top of his speed.

Presently he came in sight of a figure hurrying toward him with a lighted candle, and as it approached he was perfectly astounded to see that it was Sham-Sham himself, dressed up in a neat calico frock and a dimity apron like a housekeeper, and with a bunch of keys hanging at his girdle. The old man seemed to be greatly agitated, and hurriedly whispering, "We thought you were *never* coming, sir!" led the way through the passage in great haste. Davy noticed that they were now in a sort of tunnel made of fine grass. The grass had a delightful fragrance, like new-mown hay, and was neatly wound around the tunnel like the inside of a bird's nest. The next moment they came out into an open space in the forest, where, to Davy's amazement, the Cockalorum was sitting bolt upright in an armchair, with its head wrapped up in flannel.

It seemed to be night, but the place was lighted up by a large chandelier that hung from the branches of a tree, and Davy saw that a number of odd-looking birds were roosting on the chandelier among the lights, gazing down upon the poor Cockalorum with a melancholy interest. As Sham-Sham made his appearance with Davy at his heels, there was a sudden commotion among the birds, and they all cried out together, "Here's the doctor!" Before Davy could reply, the Hole-keeper sud-

The Cockalorum is ill

denly made his appearance with his great book, and hurriedly turning over the leaves, said, pointing to Davy, *"He* isn't a doctor. His name is Gloopitch." At these words, there arose a long, wailing cry, the lights disappeared, and Davy found himself on a broad path in the forest with the Hole-keeper walking quietly beside him.

CHAPTER VII

SINDBAD THE SAILOR'S HOUSE

"**Y**ou had no right to tell those birds my name was Gloopitch!" said Davy, angrily. "That's the second time you've got it wrong."

"Well, it's of no consequence," said the Hole-keeper, complacently. "I'll make it something else the next time. By the way, you're not the postman, are you?"

"Of course I'm not," said Davy.

"I'm glad of that," said the Hole-keeper; "postmen are always so dreadfully busy. Would you mind delivering a letter for me?" he added, lowering his voice confidentially.

"Oh, no," answered Davy, rather reluctantly; "not if it will be in my way."

"It's sure to be in your way because it's so big," said the Hole-keeper; and taking the letter out of his pocket, he handed it to Davy. It certainly was a very large letter, curiously folded like a dinner-napkin and sealed in a great many places with red and white peppermint drops; and Davy was much pleased to see that it was addressed:

> *Captain Robinson Crusoe,*
> *Jeran Feranderperandamam,*
> > > *B. G.*

"What does B. G. stand for?" said Davy.

"Baldergong's Geography, of course," said the Hole-keeper.

"But why do you put *that* on the letter?" inquired Davy.

"Because you can't find Jeran Feranderperandamam anywhere else, stupid," said the Hole-keeper, impatiently. "But I can't stop to argue about it now," and saying this, he turned into a side path, and disappeared in the wood.

As Davy walked mournfully along, turning the big letter over and over in his hands, and feeling very confused by the Hole-keeper's last remark, he presently saw, lying on the walk before him, a small book beautifully bound in crimson morocco, and picking it up, he saw that it was marked on the cover:

"Perhaps this will tell me where to go," he thought as he opened it; but it proved to be far more confusing than the Holekeeper himself had been. The first page was headed "How to frill griddlepigs"; the second page, "Two ways of frumpling crumbles"; the third page, "The best snub for feastie spralls"; and so on, until Davy felt as if he were taking leave of his senses. He was just about to throw the book down in disgust, when it was suddenly snatched out of his hands; and turning hastily, he saw a savage glaring at him from the bushes.

Now Davy knew perfectly well, as all little boys should know, that when you meet a savage in the woods you must get behind a tree as quickly as possible; but he did this in such haste that he found to his dismay that he and the savage had chosen the same tree, and in the next instant the savage was after him. The tree was a very large one, and Davy in his fright went around it a number of times so rapidly that he presently caught sight of the back of the savage, and he was surprised to see that he was no bigger than a large monkey; and moreover, that he was gorgeously dressed in a beautiful blue coat, with brass buttons on the tail of it, and pink striped trousers. Davy had hardly made this discovery, when the savage suddenly disappeared through a door in a high paling of logs that began at the tree and extended in a straight line far out into the forest.

It was very puzzling to Davy when it occurred to him that, although he had been around the tree at least a dozen times, he had never seen this paling before. The door through which the savage had disappeared also bothered him; for, though it was quite an ordinary-looking door, it had no knob nor latch, nor indeed any way of being opened that he could perceive. On one side of it, in the paling, was a row of bell-pulls, marked:

> *Family*
> *Butcher*
> *Baker*
> *Police*
> *Candlestickmaker*

and on the door itself was a large knocker, marked:

> *Postman*

After examining all these, Davy decided that, as he had a letter in charge, he was more of a postman than anything else, and he therefore raised the knocker and rapped loudly. Immediately all the bell-pulls began flying in and out of their own accord, with a deafening clangor of bells behind the paling; and then the door swung slowly back upon its hinges.

Davy walked through the doorway and found himself in the oddest-looking little country place that could possibly be imagined. There was a little lawn laid out on which a sort of soft fur was growing instead of grass, and here and there about the lawn, in the place of flower-beds, little footstools, neatly covered with carpet, were growing out of the fur. The trees were simply large feather-dusters; but they seemed, nevertheless, to be growing in a very thriving manner. And on a little mound at the back of the lawn, stood a small house built entirely of big conchshells with their pink mouths turned outward. This gave the house a very cheerful appearance, as if it were constantly on a broad grin.

The savage was sitting in the shade of one of the dusters, complacently reading the little red book; and as Davy approached, he saw, to his astonishment, that he was the Goblin dressed up like an Ethiopian serenader.

"Oh! you dear, delicious old Goblin!" cried Davy, in an ecstasy of joy at again finding his traveling-companion. "And were you the savage that was chasing me just now?"

The Goblin nodded his head, and exclaiming, "My, how you did cut and run!" rolled over and over, kicking his heels about in a delirium of enjoyment.

"Goblin," said Davy, gravely, "I think we can have just as good a time without any such doings as that. And now tell me what place this is."

"Sindbad the Sailor's house," said the Goblin, sitting up again.

"Really and truly?" said the delighted Davy.

"Really and treally truly," said the Goblin. "And here he comes now!"

Davy looked around and saw an old man coming toward them across the lawn. He was dressed in a Turkish costume, and wore a large turban and red morocco slippers turned up at the toes like skates; and his white beard was so long that at every fourth step he trod upon it, and fell forward to the ground. He took no notice whatever of either Davy or the Goblin, and after falling down a number of times, took his seat upon one of the little carpet foot-stools. Taking off his turban, he began stirring about in it with a large wooden spoon. As he took off his turban, Davy saw that his head, which was perfectly bald, was neatly laid out in black and white squares like a chess-board.

"He's the most absent-minded story-teller that ever was born," said the Goblin, pointing with his thumb over his shoulder at Sindbad.

As Davy and the Goblin sat down beside him, Sindbad hastily put on his turban, and after scowling at Davy for a mo-

ment, said to the Goblin, "It's no use telling *him* anything; he's as deaf as a trunk."

"Then tell it to me," said the Goblin, with great presence of mind.

"All right," said Sindbad, "I'll give you a nautical one."

Here he rose for a moment, hitched up his big trousers like a sailor, cocked his turban on one side of his head, and sitting down again, began:

"A capital ship for an ocean trip,
   Was 'The Walloping Window Blind';
No gale that blew dismayed her crew
   Or troubled the captain's mind.
The man at the wheel was taught to feel
   Contempt for the wildest blow,
And it often appeared, when the weather
     had cleared,
   That he'd been in his bunk below.

"The boatswain's mate was very sedate,
   Yet fond of amusement, too;
And he played hop-scotch with the star-
     board watch,
   While the captain tickled the crew.
And the gunner we had was apparently
     mad,
   For he sat on the after-rail,
And fired salutes with the captain's boots,
   In the teeth of the booming gale.

"The captain sat in a commodore's hat
   And dined in a royal way
On toasted pigs and pickles and figs
   And gummery bread each day.
But the cook was Dutch and behaved as
     such;
   For the diet he gave the crew
Was a number of tons of hot-cross buns
   Prepared with sugar and glue.

"All nautical pride we laid aside,
   And we cast the vessel ashore
On the Gulliby Isles, where the Pooh-
     pooh smiles,

And the Rumbletumbunders roar.
And we sat on the edge of a sandy ledge
And shot at the whistling bee;
And the cinnamon-bats wore water-proof
*   hats*
As they danced in the sounding sea.

"*On rubgub bark, from dawn to dark,*
*   We fed, till we all had grown*
Uncommonly shrunk,—when a Chinese
*   junk*
Came by from the torriby zone.
She was stubby and square, but we didn't
*   much care,*
And we cheerily put to sea;
And we left the crew of the junk to chew
*   The bark of the rubgub-tree.*"

Here Sindbad stopped, and gazed solemnly at Davy and the Goblin.

"If you please, sir," said Davy, respectfully, "what is gummery bread?"

"It's bread stuffed with molasses," said Sindbad; "but I never saw it anywhere, except aboard of 'The Prodigal Pig.'"

"But," said Davy, in great surprise, "you said the name of your ship was——"

"So I did, and so it was," interrupted Sindbad, testily. "The name of a ship sticks to it like wax to a wig. You *can't* change it."

"Who gave it that name?" said the Goblin.

"What name?" said Sindbad, looking very much astonished.

"Why, 'The Cantering Soup Tureen,'" said the Goblin, winking at Davy.

"Oh, *that* name!" said Sindbad; "that was given to her when—— But speaking of soup-tureens—let's go and have some pie;" and rising to his feet, he gave one hand to Davy and the other to the Goblin, and they all walked off in a row toward the little shell house. This, however, proved to be a very troublesome arrangement, for Sindbad was constantly step-

ping on his long beard and falling down; and as he kept a firm hold of his companions' hands, they all went down in a heap together a great many times. At last Sindbad's turban fell off, and as he sat up on the grass and began stirring in it again with his wooden spoon, Davy saw that it was full of broken chessmen.

"It's a great improvement, isn't it?" said Sindbad.

"What is?" said Davy, very much puzzled.

"Why, this way of playing the game," said Sindbad, looking up at him complacently. "You see, you make all the moves at once."

"It must be a very easy way," said Davy.

"It's nothing of the sort," said Sindbad, sharply. "There are more moves in one of my games than in twenty ordinary games;" and here he stirred up the chessmen furiously for a moment, and then, triumphantly calling out "Check!" clapped the turban on his head.

As they set out again for the little house, Davy saw that it was slowly moving around the edge of the lawn, as if it were on a circular railway, and Sindbad followed it around, dragging Davy and the Goblin with him, but never getting any nearer to the house.

"Don't you think," said Davy, after a while, "that it would be a good plan to stand still and wait until the house came around to us?"

"Here, drop that!" exclaimed Sindbad, excitedly, "that's my idea. I was just about proposing it myself."

"So was I," said the Goblin to Sindbad. "Just leave my ideas alone, will you?"

"*Your* ideas!" retorted Sindbad, scornfully. "I didn't know you'd brought any with you."

"I had to," replied the Goblin, with great contempt, "otherwise there wouldn't have been any on the premises."

"Oh! come, I say!" cried Sindbad, "that's my sneer, you know. Don't go to putting the point of it the wrong way."

"Take it back, if it's the only one you have," retorted the Goblin, with another wink at Davy.

"Thank you, I believe I will," replied Sindbad, meekly; and as the little house came along just then, they all stepped in at the door as it went by. As they did so, to Davy's amazement Sindbad and the Goblin quietly vanished, and Davy, instead of being inside the house, found himself standing in a dusty road, quite alone.

CHAPTER VIII

LAYOVERS FOR MEDDLERS

As Davy stood in the road, in doubt which way to go, a Roc came around the corner of the house. She was a large bird, nearly six feet tall, and was comfortably dressed in a bonnet and a plaid shawl, and wore overshoes. About her neck was hung a covered basket and a door key, and Davy at once concluded that she was Sindbad's housekeeper.

"I didn't mean to keep you waiting," said the Roc, leading the way along the road; "but I declare that, what with combing that lawn every morning with a fine-tooth comb, and brushing those shells every evening with a fine tooth-brush, I don't get time for anything else, let alone feeding the animals."

"What animals?" said Davy, beginning to be interested.

"Why, *his,* of course," said the Roc, rattling on in her harsh voice. "There's an Emphasis and two Periodicals and a Spotted Disaster, all crawlin' and creepin' and screechin'——"

Here Davy, unable to control himself, burst into a fit of laughter, in which the Roc joined heartily, rolling her head from side to side and repeating "All crawlin' and creepin' and screechin' " over and over again, as if that were the cream of the joke. Suddenly she stopped laughing and said in a low voice, "You don't happen to have a beefsteak about you, do you?"

Davy confessed that he had not, and the Roc continued, "Then I must go back. Just hold my basket, like a good child." Here there was a scuffling sound in the basket and the Roc rapped on the cover with her hard beak and cried, "Hush!"

"What's in it?" said Davy, cautiously taking the basket.

"Layovers for meddlers," said the Roc, and hurrying back along the road, was soon out of sight.

"I wonder what they're like," said Davy to himself, getting down upon his hands and knees and listening curiously with his ear against the cover of the basket. The scuffling sound continued, mingled with little sneezes and squeaking sobs as if some very small kittens had bad colds and were crying about it.

"I think I'll take a peep," said Davy, looking cautiously about him. There was no one in sight, and he carefully raised the cover a little way and tried to look in. The scuffling sound and the sobs ceased, and the next instant the cover flew off the basket and out poured a swarm of little brown creatures like snuff-boxes with legs. As they scampered off in all directions, Davy made a frantic grab at one of them, when it instantly turned over on its back and blew a puff of smoke into his face, and he rolled over in the road almost stifled. When he was able to sit up again and look about him, the empty basket was lying on its side near him, and not a layover was to be seen. At that moment, the Roc came in sight, hurrying along the road with her shawl and her bonnet-strings fluttering behind her; and Davy, clapping the cover on the basket, took to his heels and ran for dear life.

CHAPTER IX

RIBSY

THE road was very dreary and dusty, and wound in and out in the most tiresome way until it seemed to have no end to it, and Davy ran on and on, half expecting at any moment to feel the Roc's great beak pecking at his back. Fortunately his legs carried him along so remarkably well that he felt he could run for a week; and indeed he might have done so if he had not, at a sharp turn in the road, come suddenly upon a horse and cab. The horse was fast asleep when Davy dashed against him, but he woke up with a start, and, after whistling like a locomotive once or twice in a very alarming manner, went to sleep again. He was a very frowsy-looking horse with great lumps at his knees and a long, crooked neck like a camel's; but what attracted Davy's attention particularly was the word "RIBSY" painted in whitewash on his side in large letters. He was looking at this and wondering if it were the horse's name, when the door of the cab flew open and a man fell out, and after rolling over in the dust, sat up in the middle of the road and began yawning. He was even a more ridiculous-looking object than the horse, being dressed in a clown's suit, with a morning gown over it by way of a top-coat, and a field marshal's cocked hat. In fact, if he had not had a whip in his hand no one would ever have taken him for a cabman. After yawning heartily, he looked up at Davy and said drowsily: "Where?"

"To B. G.," said Davy, hastily referring to the Hole-keeper's letter.

"All right," said the cabman, yawning again. "Climb in, and don't put your feet on the cushions."

Now, this was a ridiculous thing for him to say, for when Davy stepped inside he found the only seats were some three-legged stools huddled together in the back part of the cab, all the rest of the space being taken up by a large bathtub that ran across the front end of it. Davy turned on one of the faucets, but nothing came out except some dust and a few small bits of gravel, and he shut it off again, and sitting down on one of the little stools, waited patiently for the cab to start.

Just then the cabman put his head in at the window, and winking at him confidentially, said: "Can you tell me why this horse is like an umbrella?"

"No," said Davy.

"Because he's used *up*," said the cabman.

"I don't think that's a very good conundrum," said Davy.

"So do I," said the cabman. "But it's the best one I can make with this horse. Do you say N. B.?" he asked.

"No; I said B. G.," said Davy.

"All right," said the cabman again, and disappeared from the window. Presently there was a loud trampling overhead, and Davy, putting his head out at the window, saw that the cabman had climbed up on top of the cab and was throwing stones at the horse, which was still sleeping peacefully.

"Oh! don't do that," said Davy, anxiously. "I'd rather get out and walk."

"Well, I wish you would," said the cabman, in a tone of great relief. "This is a very valuable stand, and I don't care to lose my place on it;" and Davy accordingly jumped out of the cab and walked away.

Presently there was a clattering of hoofs behind him, and Ribsy came galloping along the road with nothing on him but his collar. He was holding his big head high in the air, like a giraffe, and gazing proudly about him as he ran. He stopped short when he saw the little boy, and giving a triumphant whistle, said cheerfully: "How are you again?"

It seemed rather strange to be spoken to by a cab-horse, but Davy answered that he was feeling quite well.

"So am I," said Ribsy. "The fact is, that when it comes to beating a horse about the head with a three-legged stool, if that horse is going to leave at all, it's time he was off."

"I should think it was," said Davy, earnestly.

"You'll observe, of course, that I've kept on my shoes and my collar," said Ribsy. "It isn't genteel to go barefoot, and nothing makes a fellow look so untidy as going about without a collar. The truth is"—he continued, sitting down in the road on his hind legs, "the truth is, I'm not an ordinary horse by any means. I have a history, and I've arranged it in a popular form in six canters—I mean cantos," he added, hastily correcting himself.

"I'd like to hear it, if you please," said Davy, politely.

"Well, I'm a little hoarse——" began Ribsy.

"I think you're a very big horse," said Davy, in great surprise.

"I'm referring to my voice," said Ribsy, haughtily. "Be good enough not to interrupt me again;" and giving two or three preliminary whistles to clear his throat, he began:

"It's very confining, this living in stables,
And passing one's time among wagons
and carts;

I much prefer dining at gentlemen's
tables,
And living on turkeys and cranberry
tarts."

"That's rather a high-toned idea," said Ribsy, proudly.

"Oh! yes, indeed," said Davy, laughing; and Ribsy continued:

"As spry as a kid and as trim as a spider
Was I in the days of the Turnip-top
Hunt,
When I used to get rid of the weight of
my rider
And canter contentedly in at the front."

"By the way, that trick led to my being sold to a circus," said Ribsy. "I suppose you've never been a circus-horse?"

"Never," said Davy.

"Then you don't know anything about it," said Ribsy. "Here we go again!"

"It made me a wreck, with no hope of im-
provement,
Too feeble to race with an invalid crab;
I'm wry in the neck, with a rickety move-
ment
Peculiarly suited for drawing a cab."

"I may as well say *here*," broke in Ribsy again, "that the price old Patsey Bolivar, the cabman, paid for me was simply ridiculous."

"I find with surprise that I'm constantly
sneezing;
I'm stiff in the legs, and I'm often for
sale;
And the blue-bottle flies, with their tire-
some teasing,
Are quite out of reach of my weary old
tail."

"I see them!" cried Davy eagerly.

"Thank you," said Ribsy, haughtily. "As the next verse is the last, you needn't trouble yourself to make any further observations.

*"I think my remarks will determine the
    question
Of why I am bony and thin as a rail;
I'm off for some larks to improve my digestion,
    And point the stern moral conveyed by
    my tail."*

Here Ribsy got upon his legs again, and after a refreshing fillip with his heels, cantered off along the road, whistling as he went. Two large blue-bottle flies were on his back, and his tail was flying around with an angry whisk like a pin-wheel; but as he disappeared in the distance, the flies were still sitting calmly on the ridge of his spine, apparently enjoying the scenery.

Davy was about to start out again on his journey, when he heard a voice shouting "Hi! Hi!" and looking back, he saw the poor cabman coming along the road on a brisk trot, dragging his cab after him. He had on Ribsy's harness, and seemed to be in a state of tremendous excitement.

As he came up with Davy, the door of the cab flew open again, and the three-legged stools came tumbling out, followed by a dense cloud of dust.

"Get in! Get in!" shouted the cabman, excitedly. "Never mind the dust; I've turned it on to make believe we're going tremendously fast."

Davy hastily scrambled in, and the cabman started off again. The dust was pouring out of both faucets, and a heavy shower of gravel was rattling into the bath-tub; and, to make matters worse, the cabman was now going along at such an astonishing speed that the cab rocked violently from side to side, like a boat in a stormy sea. Davy made a frantic attempt to shut off the dust, but it seemed to come faster and faster, until he was almost choked. At this moment the cab came suddenly to a stop, and Davy, rushing to the window, found himself staring into a farm-yard, where a red cow stood gazing up at him.

CHAPTER X

JACK AND THE BEANSTALK'S FARM

IT was quite an ordinary-looking farm-yard and quite an ordinary-looking cow, but she stared so earnestly up at Davy that he felt positively certain she had something to say to him. "Every creature I meet *does* have something to say," he thought, "and I should really like to hear a cow—" and just at this moment the cab door suddenly flew open and he pitched headforemost out upon a pile of hay in the farmyard and rolled from it off upon the ground. As he sat up, feeling exceedingly foolish, he looked anxiously at the cow, expecting to see her laughing at his misfortune, but she stood gazing at him with a very serious expression of countenance, solemnly chewing, and slowly swishing her tail from side to side. As Davy really didn't know how to begin a conversation with a cow, he waited for her to speak first, and there was consequently a long pause. Presently the Cow said, in a melancholy, lowing tone of voice:

"Are you a market-gardener?"

"No," said Davy. "Why?"

"Because," said the Cow, mournfully, "there's a feather-bed growing in the vegetable garden, and I thought you might explain how it came there."

"That's very curious," said Davy.

"Curious, but comfortable for the pig," said the Cow. "He's taken to sleeping there, lately. He calls it his quill pen."

"That's a capital name for it," said Davy, laughing. "What else is there in the garden?"

"Nothing but the beanstalk," said the Cow. "You've heard of 'Jack and the Beanstalk,' haven't you?"

"Oh, yes, indeed!" said Davy, beginning to be very much interested. "I should like to see the beanstalk."

"You can't *see* the beans talk," said the Cow, gravely. "You might *hear* them talk —that is, if they had anything to say, and you listened long enough. By the way, that's the house that Jack built. Pretty, isn't it?"

Davy turned and looked up at the house. It certainly was a very pretty house, built of bright red brick with little gables, and dormer windows in the roof, and with a trim little porch quite overgrown with climbing roses. But it had a very comical appearance, for all that, as the cab-door was standing wide open in the walk just a little above the porch. Suddenly an idea struck him, and he exclaimed:

"Then you must be the cow with the crumpled horn!"

"It's not crumpled," said the Cow with great dignity. "There's a slight crimp in it, to be sure, but nothing that can properly be called a crump. Then the story was all wrong about my tossing the dog. It was the cat that ate the malt. He was a Maltese cat, and his name was Flipmegilder."

"Did you toss *him?*" inquired Davy.

"Certainly not," said the Cow, indignantly. "Who ever heard of a cow tossing a cat? The fact is, I've never had a fair chance to toss *anything*. As for the dog, Mother Hubbard never permitted any liberties to be taken with *him*."

"I'd dearly love to see Mother Hubbard," said Davy, eagerly.

"Well, you can," said the Cow, indifferently. "She isn't much to see. If you'll look in at the kitchen window, you'll probably find her performing on the piano and singing a song. She's always at it."

Dave stole softly to the kitchen window and peeped in, and, as the Cow had said,

Mother Hubbard sings a song

Mother Hubbard was there, sitting at the piano and evidently just preparing to sing. The piano was very remarkable, and Davy could not remember ever having seen one like it before. The top of it was arranged with shelves on which stood all the kitchen crockery, and in the under part of it, at one end, was an oven with glass doors, through which he could see several pies baking.

Mother Hubbard was dressed, just as he expected, in a very ornamental flowered gown with high-heeled shoes and buckles, and wore a tall pointed hat over her nightcap. She was so like the pictures Davy had seen of her that he thought he would have recognized her anywhere. She sang in a high key with a very quavering voice, and this was the song:

"I had an educated pug,
  His name was Tommy Jones;
He lived upon the parlor rug
  Exclusively on bones.

"I went to a secluded room
  To get one from a shelf;
It wasn't there, and I presume
  He'd gone and helped himself.

"He had an entertaining trick
  Of feigning he was dead;
Then, with a reassuring kick,
  Would stand upon his head.

"I could not take the proper change
  And go to buy him shoes,
But what he'd sit upon the range
  And read the latest news.

"And when I ventured out one day
  To order him a coat,
I found him, in his artless way,
  Careering on a goat.

"I could not go to look at hats
  But that, with childish glee,
He'd ask in all the neighbors' cats
  To join him at his tea!"

While Mother Hubbard was singing this song, little handfuls of gravel were constantly thrown at her through one of the kitchen windows, and by the time the song was finished, her lap was quite full of it.

"I'd just like to know who is throwing that gravel," said Davy, indignantly.

"It's Gobobbles," said the Cow, calmly. "You'll find him around at the front of the house. By the way, have you any chewing-gum about you?"

"No," said Davy, greatly surprised at the question.

"So I supposed," said the Cow. "It's precisely what I should expect of a person who would fall out of a cab."

"But I couldn't help that," said Davy.

"Of course you couldn't," said the Cow, yawning indolently. "It's precisely what I should expect of a person who hadn't any chewing gum." And with this the Cow walked gravely away, just as Mother Hubbard made her appearance at the window.

"Boy," said Mother Hubbard, beaming mildly upon Davy through her spectacles, "you shouldn't throw gravel."

"I haven't thrown any," said Davy.

"Fie!" said Mother Hubbard, shaking her head; "always speak the truth."

"I am speaking the truth," said Davy, indignantly. "It was Gobobbles."

"So I supposed," said Mother Hubbard, gently shaking her head again. "It would have been far better if he had been cooked last Christmas instead of being left over. Stuffing him and then letting him go has made a very proud creature of him. You should never be proud."

"I'm not proud," replied Davy, provoked at being mixed up with Gobobbles in this way.

"You may define the word proud, and give a few examples," continued Mother Hubbard, and Davy was just noticing with astonishment that she was beginning to look exactly like old Miss Peggs, his school-teacher, when a thumping sound was heard, and the next moment Gobobbles came tearing around the corner of the house, and Mother Hubbard threw up her hands with a little shriek and disappeared from the window.

Gobobbles proved to be a large and very bold-mannered turkey, with all his feathers taken off except a frowsy tuft about his neck. He was pounding his chest with his wings in a very disagreeable manner, and altogether his appearance was so formidable that Davy was half inclined to take to his heels at once, but Gobobbles stopped short upon seeing him, and discontinuing his pounding, stared at him suspiciously for a moment, and then said:

"I can't abide boys!"

"Why not?" said Davy.

"Oh, they're so hungry!" said Gobobbles, passionately. "They're so everlastingly hungry. Now, don't deny that you're fond of turkey."

"Well, I *do* like turkey," said Davy, seeing no way out of the difficulty.

"Of course you do!" said Gobobbles, tossing his head. "Now, you might as well know," he continued, resuming his thumping with increased energy, "that I'm as hollow as a drum and as tough as a hatbox. Just mention that fact to any one you meet, will you? I suppose Christmas is coming, of course."

"Of course it is!" replied Davy.

"It's *always* coming!" said Gobobbles, angrily; and with this he strutted away, pounding himself like a bass-drum.

CHAPTER XI

ROBINSON CRUSOE'S ISLAND

"THIS is a very sloppy road," said Davy to himself, as he walked along in the direction taken by the turkey; and it was, indeed, a *very* sloppy road. The dust had quite disappeared, and the sloppiness soon changed to such a degree of wetness that Davy presently found himself in water up to his ankles. He turned to go back, and saw, to

his alarm, that the land in every direction seemed to be miles away, and the depth of the water increased so rapidly that, before he could make up his mind what to do, it had risen to his shoulders, and he was carried off his feet and found himself apparently drifting out to sea. The water, however, was warm and pleasant, and he discovered that instead of sinking he was floated gently along, slowly turning in the water like a float on a fishing-line. This was very agreeable, but he was, nevertheless, greatly relieved when a boat came in sight sailing toward him. As it came near, it proved to be the clock with a sail hoisted and the Goblin sitting complacently in the stern.

"How d'ye do, Gobsy?" said Davy.

"Prime!" said the Goblin, enthusiastically.

"Well, stop the clock," said Davy; "I want to get aboard."

"I haven't any board," said the Goblin, in great surprise.

"I mean I want to get into the clock," said Davy, laughing. "I don't think you're much of a sailor."

"I'm not," said the Goblin, as Davy climbed in. "I've been sailing one way for ever so long, because I don't know how to turn around. But there's a landing-place just ahead."

Davy looked over his shoulder and found that they were rapidly approaching a little wooden pier standing about a foot out of the water. Beyond it stretched a broad expanse of sandy beach.

"What place is it?" said Davy.

"It's called Hickory Dickory Dock," said the Goblin. "All the eight-day clocks stop here," and at this moment the clock struck against the timbers with a violent thump, and Davy was thrown out, heels over head, upon the dock. He scrambled upon his feet again as quickly as possible, and saw to his dismay that the clock had been turned completely around by the shock and was rapidly drifting out to sea again. The Goblin looked back despairingly, and Davy just caught the words, "I don't know how to turn around!" when the clock was carried out of hearing distance and soon disappeared on the horizon.

The beach was covered in every direction with little hills of sand, like haycocks, with scraggy bunches of sea-weed sticking out of the tops of them; and Davy was wondering how they came to be there, when he caught sight of a man walking along the edge of the water and now and then stopping and gazing earnestly out to sea. As the man drew nearer, Davy saw that he was dressed in a suit of brown leather and wore a high-peaked hat, and that a little procession, consisting of a dog, a cat, and a goat, was following patiently at his heels, while a parrot was perched upon his shoulder. They all wore large standing linen collars and black cravats, which gave them a very serious appearance.

Davy was morally certain that the man was Robinson Crusoe. He carried an enormous gun, which he loaded from time to time, and then, aiming carefully at the sea, fired. There was nothing very alarming about this, for the gun, when fired, only gave a faint squeak, and the bullet, which was about the size of a small orange, dropped out quietly upon the sand. Robinson, for it was really he, always seemed to be greatly astonished at this result, peering long and anxiously out to sea, after every shot. His animal companions, however, seemed to be greatly alarmed whenever he prepared to fire; and scampering off, hid behind the little hills of sand until the gun was discharged, when they would return, and after solemnly watching their master reload his piece, follow him along the beach as before. This was all so ridiculous that Davy had

great difficulty in keeping a serious expression on his face as he walked up to Robinson and handed him the Hole-keeper's letter. Robinson looked at him suspiciously as he took it, and the animals eyed him with evident distrust.

Robinson had some difficulty in opening the letter, which was sopping wet, and took a long time to read it, Davy meanwhile waiting patiently. Sometimes Robinson would scowl horribly as if puzzled, and then again he would chuckle to himself as if vastly amused with the contents; but as he turned the letter over in reading it, Davy could not help seeing that it was simply a blank sheet of paper with no writing whatever upon it except the address. This, however, was so like the Hole-keeper's way of doing things that Davy was not much surprised when Robinson remarked: "He has left out the greatest lot of comical things!" and stooping down, buried the letter in the sand. Then picking up his gun, he said: "You may walk about in the grove as long as you please, provided you don't pick anything."

"What grove?" said Davy, very much surprised.

"This one," said Robinson, proudly pointing out the tufts of sea-weed. "They're beach trees, you know; I planted 'em myself. I had to have some place to go shooting in, of course."

"Can you shoot with *that* gun?" said Davy.

"Shoot? Why, it's a splendid gun!" said Robinson, gazing at it proudly. "I made it myself—out of a spy-glass."

"It doesn't seem to go off," said Davy, doubtfully.

"That's the beauty of it!" exclaimed Robinson, with great enthusiasm. "Some guns go off, and you never see 'em again."

"But I mean that it doesn't make any noise," persisted Davy.

"Of course it doesn't," said Robinson.

"That's because I load it with tooth powder."

"But I don't see what you can shoot with
it," said Davy, feeling that he was somehow getting the worst of the argument.

Robinson stood gazing thoughtfully at
him for a moment, while the big bullet
rolled out of the gun with a rumbling
sound and fell into the sea. "I see what
you want," he said, at length. "You're after
my personal history. Just take a seat in
the family circle and I'll give it to you."

Davy looked around and saw that the
dog, the goat, and the cat were seated respectfully in a semicircle, with the parrot,
which had dismounted, sitting beside the
goat. He seated himself on the sand at
the other end of the line, and Robinson
began as follows:

"The night was thick and hazy
    When the 'Piccadilly Daisy'
Carried down the crew and captain in the
        sea;
    And I think the water drowned 'em,
    For they never, never found 'em,
And I know they didn't come ashore with
        me.

"Oh! 't was very sad and lonely
    When I found myself the only
Population on this cultivated shore;
    But I've made a little tavern
    In a rocky little cavern,
And I sit and watch for people at the door.

"I spent no time in looking
    For a girl to do my cooking,
As I'm quite a clever hand at making
        stews;
    But I had that fellow Friday,
    Just to keep the tavern tidy
And to put a Sunday polish on my shoes.

"I have a little garden
    That I'm cultivating lard in,

As the things I eat are rather tough and
        dry;
    For I live on toasted lizards,
    Prickly pears and parrot gizzards,
And I'm really very fond of beetle pie.

"The clothes I had were furry,
    And it made me fret and worry
When I found the moths were eating off
        the hair;
    And I had to scrape and sand 'em,
    And I boiled 'em and I tanned 'em,
'Till I got the fine morocco suit I wear.

"I sometimes seek diversion
    In a family excursion
With the few domestic animals you see;
    And we take along a carrot
    As refreshment for the parrot,
And a little can of jungleberry tea.

"Then we gather as we travel
    Bits of moss and dirty gravel,
And we chip off little specimens of stone;
    And we carry home as prizes
    Funny bugs of handy sizes,
Just to give the day a scientific tone.

"If the roads are wet and muddy,
    We remain at home and study,—
For the goat is very clever at a sum,—
    And the dog, instead of fighting,
    Studies ornamental writing,
While the cat is taking lessons on the
        drum.

"We retire at eleven,
    And we rise again at seven,
And I wish to call attention as I close
    To the fact that all the scholars
    Are correct about their collars
And particular in turning out their toes."

Here Robinson called out in a loud
voice, "First class in arithmetic!" but the

animals sat perfectly motionless, sedately staring at him.

"Oh! by the way," said Robinson, confidentially to Davy, "this *is* the first class in arithmetic. That's the reason they didn't move, you see. Now, then!" he continued sharply, addressing the class, "how many halves are there in a whole?"

There was a dead silence for a moment, and then the Cat said gravely, "What kind of a hole?"

"That has nothing to do with it," said Robinson, impatiently.

"Oh! hasn't it though!" exclaimed the Dog, scornfully. "I should think a big hole could have more halves in it than a little one."

"Well, *rather*," put in the Parrot, contemptuously.

Here the Goat, who apparently had been carefully thinking the matter over, said in a low, quavering voice: "Must all the halves be of the same size?"

"Certainly not," said Robinson, promptly; then nudging Davy with his elbow, he whispered, "He's bringing his mind to bear on it. He's prodigious when he gets started!"

"Who taught him arithmetic?" said Davy, who was beginning to think Robinson didn't know much about it himself.

"Well, the fact is," said Robinson, confidentially, "he picked it up from an old adder that he met in the woods."

Here the Goat, who evidently was not yet quite started, inquired, "Must all the halves be of the same shape?"

"Not at all," said Robinson, cheerfully. "Have 'em any shape you like."

"Then I give it up," said the Goat.

"Well!" exclaimed Davy, quite out of patience. "You are certainly the stupidest lot of creatures I ever saw."

At this, the animals stared mournfully at him for a moment, and then rose up and walked gravely away.

"Now you've spoiled the exercises," said Robinson, peevishly. "I'm sorry I gave 'em such a staggerer to begin with."

"Pooh!" said Davy, contemptuously. "If they couldn't do that sum, they couldn't do anything."

Robinson gazed at him admiringly for a moment, and then, looking cautiously about him to make sure that the procession was out of hearing, said coaxingly: "What's the right answer? Tell us, like a good fellow."

"Two, of course," said Davy.

"Is that all?" exclaimed Robinson, in a tone of great astonishment.

"Certainly," said Davy, who began to feel very proud of his learning. "Don't you know that when they divide a whole into four parts they call them fourths, and when they divide it into two parts they call them halves?"

"Why don't they call them tooths?" said Robinson, obstinately. "The fact is, they ought to call 'em teeth. That's what puzzled the Goat. Next time I'll say, 'How many teeth in a whole?'"

"Then the Cat will ask if it's a rat-hole," said Davy, laughing at the idea.

"You positively convulse me, you're so very humorous," said Robinson, without a vestige of a smile. "You're almost as droll as Friday was. He used to call the Goat 'Pat'; because he said he was a little butter. I told him that was altogether too funny for a lonely place like this, and he went away and joined the minstrels."

Here Robinson suddenly turned pale, and hastily reaching out for his gun, sprang to his feet.

Davy looked out to sea and saw that the clock, with the Goblin standing in the stern, had come in sight again, and was heading directly for the shore with tremendous speed. The poor Goblin, who had turned sea-green in color, was frantically waving his hands to and fro, as if motioning for the beach to get out of the way; and Davy watched his approach with the greatest anxiety. Meanwhile, the animals had mounted on four sand-hills, and were solemnly looking on, while Robinson, who seemed to have run out of tooth-powder, was hurriedly loading his gun with sand. The next moment the clock struck the beach with great force, and turning completely over on the sand, buried the Goblin beneath it. Robinson was just making a convulsive effort to fire off his gun when the clock began striking loudly, and he and the animals fled in all directions in the wildest dismay.

CHAPTER XII

A WHALE IN A WAISTCOAT

DAVY rushed up to the clock, and pulling open the little door in the front of it, looked inside. To his great disappointment, the Goblin had again disappeared, and there was a smooth round hole running down into the sand, as though he had gone directly through the beach. He was listening at this hole in the hope of hearing from the Goblin, when a voice said, "I suppose that's what they call going into the interior of the country," and looking up, he saw the Hole-keeper sitting on a little mound in the sand, with his great book in his lap.

His complexion had quite lost its beautiful transparency, and his jaunty little paper tunic was sadly rumpled, and, moreover, he had lost his cocked hat. All this, however, had not at all disturbed his complacent conceit; he was, if anything, more pompous than ever.

"How did *you* get here?" asked Davy in astonishment.

"I'm banished," said the Hole-keeper cheerfully. "That's better than being boiled, any day. Did you give Robinson my letter?"

"Yes, I did," said Davy, as they walked along the beach together; "but I got it very wet coming here."

"That was quite right," said the Hole-keeper. "There's nothing so tiresome as a dry letter. Well, I suppose Robinson is expecting me, by this time,—isn't he?"

"I don't know, I'm sure," said Davy. "He didn't say that he was expecting you."

"He *must* be," said the Hole-keeper, positively. "I never even mentioned it in my letter—so, of course, he'll know I'm coming. It strikes me the sun is very hot here," he added faintly.

The sun certainly was very hot, and Davy, looking at the Hole-keeper as he said this, saw that his face was gradually and very curiously losing its expression, and that his nose had almost entirely disappeared.

"What's the matter?" inquired Davy, anxiously.

"The matter is that I'm going back into the raw material," said the Hole-keeper, dropping his book and sitting down helplessly in the sand. "See here, Frinkles," he continued, beginning to speak very thickly. "Wrap me up in my shirt and mark the packish distingly. Take off shir quigly!" and Davy had just time to pull the poor creature's shirt over his head and spread it quickly on the beach, when the Hole-keeper fell down, rolled over upon the garment, and bubbling once or twice, as if he were boiling, melted away into a compact lump of brown sugar.

Davy was deeply affected by this sad incident, and though he had never really liked the Hole-keeper, he could hardly keep back his tears as he wrapped up the lump in the paper shirt and laid it carefully on the big book. In fact, he was so disturbed in his mind that he was on the point of going away without marking the package, when, looking over his shoulder, he suddenly caught sight of the Cockalorum standing close beside him, carefully holding an inkstand, with a pen in it, in one of his claws.

"Oh! thank you very much," said Davy, taking the pen and dipping it in the ink. "And will you please tell me his name?"

The Cockalorum, who still had his head done up in flannel and was looking rather ill, paused for a moment to reflect, and then murmured, "Mark him *'Confectionery.'*"

This struck Davy as being a very happy idea, and he accordingly printed "CONFEXIONRY" on the package in his very best manner. The Cockalorum, with his head turned critically on one side, carefully inspected the marking, and then, after earnestly gazing for a moment at the inkstand, gravely drank the rest of the ink and offered the empty inkstand to Davy.

"I don't want it, thank you," said Davy, stepping back.

"No more do I," murmured the Cockalorum, and tossing the inkstand into the sea, flew away in his usual clumsy fashion.

Davy, after a last mournful look at the package of brown sugar, turned away, and was setting off along the beach again, when he heard a gurgling sound coming from behind a great hummock of sand, and peeping cautiously around one end of it, he was startled at seeing an enormous Whale on the beach lazily basking in the sun. The creature was dressed in a huge white garment buttoned up in front, with a bunch of live seals flopping at one of the button-holes and a great chain cable leading from them to a pocket at one side. Before Davy could retreat, the Whale caught sight of him and called out in a tremendous voice, "How d'ye do, Bub?"

"I'm pretty well, I thank you," said Davy, with his usual politeness to man and beast. "How are you, sir?"

"Hearty!" thundered the Whale; "never felt better in all my life. But it's rather warm lying here in the sun."

"Why don't you take off your——," here Davy stopped, not knowing exactly what it was the Whale had on.

"Waistcoat," said the Whale, condescendingly. "It's a canvas-back-duck waistcoat. The front of it is made of wild duck, you see, and the back of it out of the foretop-sail of a brig."

"Is it nice, being a Whale?" inquired Davy curiously.

"Famous!" said the Whale, with an affable roar. "Great fun, I assure you! We have fish-balls every night, you know."

"Fish-balls at night!" exclaimed Davy. "Why, we always have ours for breakfast."

"Nonsense!" thundered the Whale, with a laugh that made the beach quake; "I don't mean anything to eat. I mean dancing parties."

"And do *you* dance?" said Davy, thinking that if he did, it must be a very extraordinary performance.

"Dance?" said the Whale with a reverberating chuckle. "Bless you! I'm as nimble as a six-pence. By the way, I'll show you the advantage of having a bit of whalebone in one's composition," and with these words the Whale curled himself up, then flattened out suddenly with a tremendous flop, and shooting through the air like a flying elephant, disappeared with a great splash in the sea.

Davy stood anxiously watching the spot where he went down, in the hope that

he would come up again; but instead of
this, the waves began tossing angrily, and
a roaring sound came from over the sea,
as though a storm were coming up. Then
a cloud of spray was dashed into his face,
and presently the air was filled with lobsters, eels, and wriggling fishes that were
being carried inshore by the gale. Suddenly, to Davy's astonishment, a dog
came sailing along. He was being helplessly blown about among the lobsters, uneasily jerking his tail from side to side to
keep it out of reach of their great claws,
and giving short, nervous barks from time
to time, as though he were firing signal-
guns of distress. In fact, he seemed to be
having such a hard time of it that Davy
caught him by the ear as he was going
by, and landed him in safety on the beach.
He proved to be a very shaggy, battered-
looking animal with a weather-beaten tar-
paulin hat jammed on the side of his
head, and a patch over one eye; and as he
had on an old pilot coat, Davy thought
he must be an old sea-dog, and so, indeed,
he proved to be. He stared doubtfully at
Davy for a moment, and then said in a
husky voice:

"What's *your* name?" as if he had just
mentioned his own.

"Davy,——" began the little boy, but
before he could say another word, the old
sea-dog growled:

"Right you are!" and handing him a
folded paper, trotted gravely away, swag-
gering as he went, like a sea-faring
man.

The paper was addressed to *"Davy
Jones,"* and was headed inside *"Binnacle
Bob: His Werses,"* and below these words
Davy found the following story:

"*To inactivity inclined
Was Captain Parker Pitch's mind;
In point of fact, 't was fitted for
An easy-going life ashore.*

"*His disposition, so to speak,
Was nautically soft and weak;
He feared the rolling ocean, and
He very much preferred the land.*

"*A stronger-minded man by far
Was gallant Captain Thompson Tar;
And (what was very wrong, I think,)
He marked himself with India ink.*

"*He boldly sailed 'The Soaking Sue'
When angry gales and tempests blew,
And even from the nor-nor-east
He didn't mind 'em in the least.*

"*Now Captain Parker Pitch's sloop
Was called 'The Cozy Chickencoop'—
A truly comfortable craft
With ample state-rooms fore and aft.*

"*No foolish customs of the deep,
Like 'watches,' robbed his crew of sleep;
That estimable lot of men
Were all in bed at half-past ten.*

"*At seven bells, one stormy day,
Bold Captain Tar came by that way,
And in a voice extremely coarse
He roared 'Ahoy!' till he was hoarse.*

"*Next morning of his own accord
This able seaman came aboard,
And made the following remark
Concerning Captain Pitch's bark:*

"*'Avast!' says he, 'Belay! What cheer!
How comes this little wessel here?
Come, tumble up your crew,' says he,
'And navigate a bit with me!'*

"*Says Captain Pitch, 'I can't refuse
To join you on a friendly cruise;
But you'll oblige me, Captain Tar,
By not a-taking of me far.'*

"*At this reply from Captain Pitch,
Bold Thompson gave himself a hitch;
It cut him to the heart to find
A seaman in this frame of mind.*

"'Avast!' says he; 'We'll bear away
For Madagascar and Bombay,
Then down the coast to Yucatan,
Kamchatka, Guinea, and Japan.

"'Stand off for Egypt, Turkey, Spain,
Australia, and the Spanish Main,
Then through the nor-west passage for
Van Diemen's Land and Labrador.'

"Says Captain Pitch: 'The ocean swell
Makes me exceedingly unwell,
And, Captain Tar, before we start,
Pray join me in a friendly tart.'

"And shall I go and take and hide
The sneaking trick that Parker tried?
Oh! no. I very much prefer
To state his actions as they were:

"With marmalade he first began
To tempt that bluff sea-faring man,
Then fed him all the afternoon
With custard in a table-spoon.

"No mariner, however tough,
Can thrive upon this kind of stuff;
And Thompson soon appeared to be
A feeble-minded child of three.

"He cried for cakes and lollipops—
He played with dolls and humming
tops—
He even ceased to roar 'I'm blowed!'
And shook a rattle, laughed, and
crowed.

"When Parker saw the seamen gaze
Upon the Captain's cunning ways,
Base envy thrilled him through and
through
And he became a child of two.

"Now, Thompson had in his employ
A mate, two seamen, and a boy;
The mate was fond as he could be
Of babies, and he says, says he,

"'Why, messmates, as we're all agreed
Sea-bathing is the thing they need;
Let's drop these hinfants off the quar-
ter!'
—(They did, in fourteen fathom water)."

Just as Davy finished these verses, he discovered to his alarm that he was sinking into the beach as though the sand were running down through an hourglass, and before he could make any effort to save himself, he had gone completely through and found himself lying flat on his back with tall grass waving about him.

CHAPTER XIII

THE END OF THE BELIEVING VOYAGE

WHEN Davy sat up and looked around him, he found himself in a beautiful meadow with the sun shining brightly on the grass and the wild-flowers. The air was filled with dainty colored insects darting about in the warm sunshine, and chirping cheerily as they flew, and at a little distance the Goblin was sitting on the grass attentively examining a great, struggling creature that he was holding down by its wings.

"I suppose,"—said the Goblin, as if Davy's sudden appearance was the most ordinary thing in the world,—"I suppose that this is about the funniest bug that flies."

"What is it?" said Davy, cautiously edging away.

"It's a cricket-bat," said the Goblin, rapping familiarly with his knuckles on its hard shell. "His body is like a boot-jack, and his wings are like a pair of umbrellas."

"But, you know, a cricket-bat is something to play with!" said Davy, surprised at the Goblin's ignorance.

"Well, *you* may play with it if you like. *I* don't want to!" said the Goblin, carelessly tossing the great creature over to Davy, and walking away.

The cricket-bat made a swoop at Davy, knocking him over like a feather, and then with a loud snort flew away across the meadow. It dashed here and there at flying things of every kind, and turning on its side, knocked them, one after another, quite out of sight, and finally, to Davy's great relief, disappeared in a distant wood.

"Come on! come on!" cried a voice; and Davy, looking across the meadow, saw the Goblin beckoning vigorously to him, apparently in great excitement.

"What's the matter?" cried Davy, pushing his way through the thick grass.

"Oh, my! oh, my!" shrieked the Goblin, who was almost bursting with laughter. "Here's that literary hack again!"

Davy peered through a clump of bushes and discovered a large red animal with white spots on its sides, clumsily rummaging about in the tall grass and weeds. Its appearance was so formidable that he was just about whispering to the Goblin, "Let's run!" when the monster raised its head and, after gazing about for an instant, gave a loud, triumphant whistle.

"Why, it's Ribsy!" cried Davy, running forward. "It's Ribsy, only he's grown enormously fat."

It was Ribsy, indeed, eating with all his might. The name on his side was twisted about beyond all hope of making it out, and his collar had quite disappeared in a deep crease about his neck. In fact, his whole appearance was so alarming that Davy anxiously inquired of him what he had been eating.

"Everything!" said Ribsy enthusiastically. "Grass, nuts, bugs, birds, and berries! All of 'em taste good. I could eat both of you, easily," he added, glaring hungrily down upon Davy and the Goblin.

"Try that fellow first," said the Goblin, pointing to a large round insect that went flying by, humming like a top. Ribsy snapped at it and swallowed it, and the next instant disappeared with a tremendous explosion in a great cloud of smoke.

"What was that?" said Davy, in a terrified whisper.

"A Hum Bug," said the Goblin calmly. "When a cab-horse on a vacation talks about eating you, a Hum Bug is a pretty good thing to take the conceit out of him. They're loaded, you see, and they go booming along as innocently as you please, but if you touch 'em—why, 'there you aren't!' as the Hole-keeper says."

"The Hole-keeper isn't himself any more," said Davy mournfully.

"Not altogether himself, but somewhat," said a voice; and Davy, looking around, was astonished to find the Hole-keeper standing beside him. He was a most extraordinary-looking object, being nothing but Davy's parcel marked, "CONFEXIONRY," with arms and legs and a head to it. At the sight of him the Goblin fell flat on his back, and covered his face with his hands.

"I'm quite aware that my appearance is not prepossessing," said the Hole-keeper, with a scornful look at the Goblin. "In fact, I'm nothing but a quarter of a pound of *'plain,'* and the price isn't worth mentioning."

"But how did you ever come to be alive again, at all?" said Davy.

"Well," said the Hole-keeper, "the truth of the matter is that after you went away, the Cockalorum fell to reading the *Vacuum;* and if you'll believe it, there wasn't a word in it about my going back into the raw material."

"I *do* believe that," said Davy; but the Hole-keeper, without noticing the interruption, went on:

"*Then,* of course, I got up and came away. Meanwhile, the Cockalorum is filling himself with information."

"I don't think he'll find much in your book," said Davy, laughing.

"Ah! but just think of the lots and lots of things he *won't* find," exclaimed the Hole-keeper. "Everything he doesn't find in it is something worth knowing. By the way, your friend seems to be having some sort of a fit. Give him some dubbygrums," and with this, the Hole-keeper stalked pompously away.

"The smell of sugar always gives me the craw-craws," said the Goblin, in a stifled voice, rolling on the ground, and keeping his hands over his face. "Get me some water."

"I haven't anything to get it in," said Davy, helplessly.

"There's a buttercup behind you," groaned the Goblin, and Davy, turning, saw a buttercup growing on a stem almost as tall as he was himself. He picked it, and hurried away across the meadow to look for water, the buttercup, meanwhile, growing in his hand in a surprising manner, until it became a full-sized tea-cup, with a handle conveniently growing on one side. Davy, however, had become so accustomed to this sort of thing that he would not have been greatly surprised if a saucer had also made its appearance.

Presently he came upon a sparkling little spring, gently bubbling up in a marshy place with high sedgy grass growing about it, and being a very neat little boy, he took off his shoes and stockings and carefully picked his way over the oozy ground to the edge of the spring itself. He was just bending over to dip the cup into the spring, when the ground under his feet began trembling like jelly, and then, giving itself a convulsive shake, threw him head-foremost into the water.

For a moment Davy had a very curious sensation as though his head and his arms and his legs were all trying to get inside of his jacket, and then he came sputtering to the top of the water and scrambled ashore. To his astonishment he saw that the spring had spread itself out into a little lake, and that the sedge-grass had grown to an enormous height and was waving far above his head. Then he was startled by a tremendous roar of laughter, and looking around, he saw the Goblin, who was now apparently at least twenty feet high, standing beside the spring.

"Oh, my!" cried the Goblin, in an uncontrollable fit of merriment. "Another minute and you wouldn't have been bigger than a peanut!"

"What's the matter with me?" said Davy, not knowing what to make of it all.

"Matter?" cried the Goblin. "Why, you've been and gone and fallen into an Elastic Spring, that's all. If you'd got in at stretch tide, early in the morning, you'd have been a perfect giraffe, but you got in at shrink tide and—oh, my! oh, my!" and here he went off into another fit of laughter.

"I don't think it's anything to laugh at," cried Davy, with the tears starting to his eyes, "and I'm sure I don't know what I'm going to do."

"Oh! don't worry," said the Goblin, good-naturedly. "I'll take a dip myself, just to be companionable, and to-morrow morning we can get back to any size you like."

"I wish you'd take these in with you," said Davy, pointing to his shoes and stockings. "They're big enough now for Badorful."

"All right!" cried the Goblin. "Here we go;" and taking the shoes and stockings in his hand he plunged into the spring, and a moment afterward scrambled out exactly Davy's size.

"Now, that's what I call a nice, tidy size," said the Goblin complacently, while Davy was squeezing his feet into his wet shoes. "What do you say to a ride on a field-mouse?"

"That will be glorious!" said Davy.

"Well, there goes the sun," said the Goblin; "it will be moonlight presently," and as he spoke, the sun went down with a boom like a distant gun and left them in the dark. The next moment a beautiful moon rose above the trees and beamed down pleasantly upon them, and the Goblin, taking Davy by the hand, led him into the wood.

*   *   *   *   *

"Freckles," said the Goblin, "what time is it?"

They were now in the densest part of the wood, where the moon was shining brightly on a little pool with rushes growing about it, and the Goblin was speaking to a large toad.

"Forty croaks," said the Toad, in a husky whisper; and then, as a frog croaked in the pool, he added: "That makes it forty-one. The Snoopers have come in, and Thimbletoes is shaking in his boots." And with these words the Toad coughed, and then hopped heavily away.

"What does he mean?" whispered Davy.

"He means that the Fairies are here, and *that* means that we won't get our ride," said the Goblin, rather sulkily.

"And who is Thimbletoes?" said Davy.

"He's the Prime Minister," said the Goblin. "You see, if any one of the Snoopers finds out something the Queen didn't know before, out goes the Prime Minister, and the Snooper pops into his boots. Thimbletoes doesn't fancy that, you know, because the Prime Minister has all the honey he wants, by way of a salary. Now,

here's the mouse-stable, and don't you speak a word, mind!"

As the Goblin said this, they came upon a little thatched building, about the size of a baby-house, standing just beyond the pool; and the Goblin, cautiously pushing open the door, stole noiselessly in, with Davy following at his heels, trembling with excitement.

The little building was curiously lighted up by a vast number of fire-flies, hung from the ceiling by loops of cobweb; and Davy could see several spiders hurrying about among them and stirring them up when the light grew dim. The field-mice were stabled in little stalls on either side, each one with his tail neatly tied in a bow-knot to a ring at one side; and at the farther end of the stable was a buzzing throng of fairies, with their shining clothes and gauzy wings sparkling beautifully in the soft light. Just beyond them Davy saw the Queen sitting on a raised throne, with a little mullen-stalk for a scepter, and beside her was the Prime Minister, in a terrible state of agitation.

"Now, here's this Bandybug," the Prime Minister was saying. "What does *he* know about untying the knots in a cord of wood?"

"Nothing!" said the Queen, positively. "Absolutely nothing."

"And then," continued the Prime Minister, "the idea of his presuming to tell your Gossamer Majesty that he can hear the bark of the dogwood trees——"

"Bosh!" cried the Queen. "Paint him with raspberry jam and put him to bed in a bee-hive. That'll make him smart, at all events."

Here the Prime Minister began dancing about in an ecstasy, until the Queen knocked him over with the mullen-stalk, and shouted, "Silence! and plenty of it, too. Bring in Berrylegs."

Berrylegs, who proved to be a wiry little

fairy, with a silver coat and tight, cherry-colored trousers, was immediately brought in. His little wings fairly bristled with defiance, and his manner, as he stood before the Queen, was so impudent that Davy felt morally certain there was going to be a scene.

"May it please your Transparent Highness—" began Berrylegs.

"Skip all that!" interrupted the Queen, flourishing her mullen-stalk.

"Skip, yourself!" said Berrylegs, boldly, in reply. "Don't you suppose I know how to talk to a queen!"

The Queen turned very pale, and after a hurried consultation with the Prime Minister, said, faintly, "Have it your own way," and Berrylegs began again.

"May it please your Transparent Highness, I've found out how the needles get into the hay-stacks."

As Berrylegs said this, a terrible commotion arose at once among the Fairies. The Prime Minister cried out, "Oh, come, I say! That's not fair, you know," and the Queen became so agitated that she began taking great bites off the end of the mullen-stalk in a dazed sort of way; and Davy noticed that the Goblin, in his excitement, was trying to climb up on one of the mouse-stalls so as to get a better view of what was going on. At last the Queen, whose mouth was now quite filled with bits of the mullen-stalk, mumbled, "Get to the point."

"It ought to be a sharp one, being about needles," said the Prime Minister, attempting a joke with a feeble laugh, but no one paid the slightest attention to him; and Berrylegs, who was now positively swelling with importance, called out in a loud voice: "It comes from using sewing machines when they sow the hay-seed!"

The Prime Minister gave a shriek and fell flat on his face, and the Queen began jumping frantically up and down and beating about on all sides of her with the end of the mullen-stalk, when suddenly a large cat walked into the stable and the Fairies fled in all directions. There was no mistaking the cat, and Davy, forgetting entirely the Goblin's caution, exclaimed, "Why! it's Solomon!"

The next instant the lights disappeared, and Davy found himself in total darkness, with Solomon's eyes shining at him like two balls of fire. There was a confused sound of sobs and cries and the squeaking of mice, among which could be heard the Goblin's voice crying, "Davy! Davy!" in a reproachful way; then the eyes disappeared, and a moment afterward the stable was lifted off the ground and violently shaken.

"That's Solomon, trying to get at the mice," thought Davy. "I wish the old thing had stayed away!" he added aloud, and as he said this the little stable was broken all to bits, and he found himself sitting on the ground in the forest.

The moon had disappeared, and snow was falling rapidly, and the sound of distant chimes reminded Davy that it must be past midnight, and that Christmas-day had come. Solomon's eyes were shining in the darkness like a pair of coach-lamps, and as Davy sat looking at them, a ruddy light began to glow between them, and presently the figure of the Goblin appeared dressed in scarlet, as when he had first come. The reddish light was shining through his stomach again, as though the coals had been fanned into life once more, and as Davy gazed at him it grew brighter and stronger, and finally burst into a blaze. Then Solomon's eyes gradually took the form of great brass balls, and presently the figure of the long-lost Colonel came into view just above them, affectionately hugging his clock. He was gazing mournfully down upon the poor Goblin, who was now blazing like a dry chip, and as the light of the fire grew brighter and stronger, the trees about slowly took the shape of an old-fashioned fire-place with a high mantel-shelf above it, and then Davy found himself curled up in the big easy-chair, with his dear old grandmother bending over him, and saying, gently, "Davy! Davy! Come and have some dinner, my dear."

In fact, the Believing Voyage was ended.

THE OWL, THE PUSSY-CAT, AND THE LITTLE BOY

By J. G. FRANCIS

THE Owl and the Pussy-Cat went to see
A Boy of diminutive size,
Who was full of contrition, remorse, and crust
From lemon and gooseberry pies.
They lifted him up, and they cast him down,
And rolled him over the floor,
And the Boy resolved, when they vanished away,
That he'd sleep after dinner no more.

UNDER COVER OF APOLOGIES

by Geoffrey Household

WHEN the draft of the naval pact was stolen from the archives of the Foreign Office in London, the American ambassador and the British officials despaired. They knew who had it—Cosmo Casals, the popular but unscrupulous first secretary of a foreign embassy—but they could not hope to get it back. Embassies may not be raided, and diplomats cannot be prosecuted.

In a Knightsbridge apartment two young men sat gloomily in front of an array of empty dishes, digesting their breakfast and reading their mail. They had every right to be gloomy, for the work of years had been undone by the daring coup of Mr. Casals. The owner of the apartment was Oscar Lund, an attaché of the American Embassy. All Lund's duties were obscure; nothing was expected of him except that he should have information on every subject when the ambassador wanted it. His guest was Lord Reginald Bathgate, a tall, hatchet-faced, monocled Englishman, who, so far as London society knew, did nothing at all for a living, and did it very gracefully. But on the continent of Europe various mysterious travelers knew him as Number 4X. He was one of the unsuspected chiefs of the British secret service.

"Casals is leaving for his own country today," said the American. "He'll carry a diplomatic mail bag, and the pact will be inside it. Can't you stage a hold-up, Bats?"

"I could, old chap," answered the Englishman, "but I daren't risk it. If Casals were a spy, I could do anything to him short of murder. If he were a criminal, I could set the police on him. But since he's a diplomat, his person is sacred."

"Oh, all right!" said Lund wearily, and went on reading his mail. He slit open a pale blue envelop and glanced through the enclosed letter.

"Just listen to this, Bats," he groaned, turning to his friend.

"Dear Mr. Lund: I *do* hate to trouble you again, but I know you will forgive me, as we are such *old* friends. My little Teddy is leaving London for his school in Switzerland, and I can't *bear* to think of him traveling alone. Would you send him in charge of one of your charming diplomatic friends, so that he doesn't get frightened and has no trouble with the customs? Please tell your friend to see that he has a glass of milk at eleven, and that he keeps his throat *well* covered up on the boat. . . .

"And two pages more of the same," said Lund. "But that's nothing. I once had to forward her Pekingese to a dog show!"

"Who is this mother's darling?" asked Bats.

"Teddy van Ness. The first time he was over here he ran away and joined a Paris circus. Then his tutor lost him in Constantinople, and he turned up as the Wonder Boy Drummer in a German cabaret.

He knows Europe better than I do, and I'm supposed to nurse him."

"Send him with Casals!" snorted Lord Reginald.

"That's an idea!" the American exclaimed.

Bats screwed his monocle well home and stared at his friend.

"Are you serious?" he asked.

"Sure! Listen here! If young Teddy steals the bag, nobody can say he's one of your agents. He'll be taken for a spoiled, mischievous child playing at being a gangster. You people over here believe anything of our American boys."

"But can he keep his mouth shut?"

"Can he?" answered Lund. "That kid could keep his mouth shut if he had a hot potato in it. I'll call him over and you can judge for yourself."

Lund telephoned Teddy at his hotel, and the boy promised to be right over. Then the attaché telephoned Cosmo Casals.

"Mayfair 1756, please. Hello, is that you, Cosmo? Sorry to call you so early, old man. . . . I hear you're leaving us today. . . . Isn't that just too bad! What's a London season without our Cosmo? I wonder if you'll do me a favor? Will you take a fifteen-year-old pet of the embassy as far as Lausanne with you? . . . That's fine! He won't give you any trouble. Momma says keep his throat well covered—he's that kind of boy."

Bats, who was seldom deceived by appearances, liked Teddy at first sight. There was a suggestion of a thoroughbred greyhound about Theodore van Ness. When he was bored he looked a pampered pet; but when he was aroused his pale face became keen and remarkably intelligent, and the sleek young muscles tautened all over his lanky body. Deep down in his eyes was a wicked sense of humor—unless

Teddy was suspected of wrongdoing, when they were blue, innocent, and appealing.

"Teddy," said Lund, "we've a job for you. Promise me on your honor that you will keep to yourself what I'm to tell you."

"On my honor," replied Teddy.

"In the event of any nation declaring war on another," Lund explained, "the United States and Great Britain have agreed to pool their naval and air forces to prevent it. The pact hasn't been ratified by the Senate or by Parliament, but it will be if we can choose our moment to get it passed. Other countries are pretty sure that the unofficial agreement exists, but they daren't say so unless they have an authentic copy of it. Teddy, Cosmo Casals has such a copy. He will show it to his government and then to the newspapers; the whole world will ring with it prematurely, and it will never be signed.

"Now, then! Mr. Casals, at your mother's request, has consented to escort you as far as Lausanne, and to give you your glass of milk at eleven."

Teddy grinned broadly.

"Be the nastiest kind of spoiled child you can imagine. Watch him closely. Note who talks to him. And keep your eyes on his mail bag."

"Shall I grab it if I can?" asked Teddy.

"This is where I chip in," interrupted Lord Reginald. "Get the bag if you can, and bring it to Mr. Lund. But remember —there would be a first-class international row if it were known that we were behind you. So if you're caught, you must pretend you did it for a lark."

"And if I succeed?" asked Teddy. He had grown serious.

"If you succeed," answered Lund, "I shall have to disown you, and apologize for you, and probably the ambassador will send you home in disgrace."

"Gee!" Teddy gasped. "Then I get it in the neck both ways."

"You do," admitted Lord Reginald. "That's why there are very few men in the world brave enough to be secret agents."

"I don't know about brave," said Teddy, "but I do love excitement. When do I start?"

"This morning," answered Lund, putting his hands on Teddy's shoulders. "Our men will be near you, though they can't help you much. If anyone addresses you as Mr. Thwaite, show no particular interest, but listen to what he has to say."

Teddy spent a frantically busy hour at his hotel and then returned to Lund's apartment, where he was handed over to the care of Casals, an exquisite young diplomat, dark, slim, and beautifully dressed.

When the diplomat saw Teddy he wished to Heaven that he had not been so obliging. The boy looked sulky, he was bad-mannered, he had an indecent quantity of baggage. Although it was a warm spring day, the fur collar of his overcoat was turned up to his ears.

"Well, well, my little man! So you're going back to school!" remarked Casals, as soon as they were settled on the gorgeous cherry-colored cushions of the boat train, and roaring smoothly from London to Dover.

"Don't want to!" replied Teddy, and started to kick the mahogany paneling.

"I wouldn't do that, if I were you," said the diplomat firmly.

"Why wouldn't you?" asked Teddy, continuing to kick.

There was a strained silence for some minutes. Then Teddy, pointing rudely at the small white mail sack with the arms of Mr. Casals' country stamped on the outside, asked, "What's in that bag?"

"Just letters and reports," said Casals politely.

"Huh!" Teddy grunted. "If it's got money in it, you'd better be careful I don't steal it!"

Mr. Casals, sighing at this crude boast, called the attendant, and ordered lunch for them both.

"Soup, sir?" the attendant asked, turning to the sulky boy.

"No," said Teddy. "I want a big cream puff. Right away!"

"That isn't very good for you," suggested Mr. Casals. "Try a—"

"I want a cream puff!" Teddy repeated in a loud voice.

Mr. Casals glanced nervously at his grinning fellow passengers, and ordered one.

"Make it four," said Teddy to the attendant.

The attendant made it four. On top of them Teddy ate a whole lobster and a pound of strawberries. He then lay back in his corner, munching a candy bar. Casals lighted a dainty cigarette, and then looked at the boy with unconcealed disgust.

At Dover two blue-jerseyed porters seized their hand baggage and led them through the dungeon-like vestibules under the station and out upon the windy quay. While one of them escorted Casals to his stateroom, the other, who appeared to be nothing more than one of the regular porters, touched his cap to Teddy.

"Hope you have a smooth crossing, Mr. Thwaite," he said. "Stand in the corridor when your train leaves Calais."

The boat churned up the water, and stood out of the harbor for the distant gray hills of France. Teddy joined Casals in his stateroom. He made himself a nuisance by examining all the fittings of the tiny cabin, leaving the port open so that it banged, and losing the soap under Casals' chair.

"Will you please sit down!" ordered the diplomat, who by now was calculating how many more hours he would have to spend in the company of this beastly boy.

Teddy obediently sat down. The boat began to roll in the ceaseless swell of the Channel. The boy's face took on an injured expression. He was so quiet that Casals actually managed to read three pages of his book.

"Mr. Casals!" cried Teddy suddenly. "Oh, Mr. Casals!"

"What is it?"

"Mr. Casals, I think I'm going to be seasick!"

He clutched the unfortunate diplomat, and gave a heart-rending hiccup. Casals led him firmly to the side of the boat, but he was too late. Teddy had had the greatest difficulty in making himself seasick, and having succeeded, he wasn't going to waste his efforts.

Casals, cursing in four languages, mopped his exquisite trousers with an inadequate silk handkerchief and returned to his stateroom. Teddy chuckled to himself. Casals had actually left the bag unguarded while he rushed the boy to the open air. Teddy rightly guessed that by this time he had got so thoroughly on the diplomat's nerves that the man had forgotten everything except his hatred of him.

The desolate-looking town of Calais came racing up from the horizon, and soon the boat nosed alongside the jetty. Casals showed his diplomatic passport, and the two walked serenely through the customs, and on to the station platform. Gold-laced, bearded, and magnificent, the stationmaster led them to their reserved compartment on the Simplon-Orient Express. A narrow corridor ran along one side of the coach, and out of it opened luxurious little rooms. Casals dropped dejectedly into the corner nearest the corridor, with the precious bag on the seat beside him. Teddy sulked in the corner by the window. The famous express slid silently out of the station, and settled down to its seventy miles an hour.

Teddy pushed past Casals' legs and went out into the corridor. Two men, looking like solid English manufacturers, edged past him.

"I hear, Mr. Thwaite," said one, apparently speaking to the other, "that there's a slight obstacle on the line. The train will slow up in five minutes."

Teddy returned to the compartment. "Feeling better now!" he announced. "I guess I could eat another candy bar."

He pulled a half-melted bar from his pocket and started to eat it noisily. The trick worked. Casals got up and stood at the entrance to the compartment, his back to Teddy. The bag remained on the seat. Teddy banged the window down and thrust his head out. Casals glanced around, saw the boy's shoulders heaving, and looked away again, hoping fiercely that the revolting child would fall out. Anything to get rid of him!

As they passed outside the port of Boulogne, the brakes jarred on quietly. Teddy thrust his legs through the open window and balanced on the sill. The speed of the train dropped to ten miles an hour. He leaned back, grabbed the mail sack, and slid, feet foremost, to the track. The bag and his heavy coat broke the fall, and in an instant he was up and skidding down the embankment. At the bottom he shed his coat and sprinted across the open fields toward the gray cottages on the outskirts of Boulogne.

Teddy was no mean runner. He had done the 100 yards in 10 seconds, which was well for the two great countries whose plans depended on his legs. He took a low hedge in his stride, and dropped on one knee behind it to see what was happening. Casals was standing on the embankment, raving. Some of the train crew and passengers were pounding after the fugitive, strung out over the field like a pack of hounds.

"*Au voleur!*" they yelled. "Stop thief!"

Teddy sprang up and skimmed over the ground toward a narrow, cobbled street that seemed to promise dark corners and yards where he might hide. He was nearly in it when out shot a mob of honest citizens, headed by a blue-cloaked French policeman. Teddy swerved like a hare, but he was too late. The *flic* caught him by the collar.

"I arrest you in the name of the law!" he said.

He led Teddy down the street at a rapid walk, surrounded by the excited crowd.

Suddenly he stopped and looked the crowd over, twirling his glorious moustaches with his free hand.

"*Circulez!*" he ordered grandly. "*Circulez donc!*"

The crowd obediently dispersed, but followed at a distance. The policeman turned a corner, and with a catlike spring leaped into a tiny, dark cottage, dragging Teddy after him.

"That was a close shave, Mr. Thwaite!" he said in English.

"Gosh!" exclaimed Teddy. "Are you a Mr. Thwaite, too?"

"Exactly!" replied the policeman.

He hurled his cloak, uniform, and moustaches into a corner, and slipped on a loud tweed suit. In an instant he was transformed into a middle-class English tourist, spending a jolly week-end in Boulogne.

"If anyone catches us," he said, "say that you escaped from the police. I wish I could help you more, old boy. But you've got to play a lone hand. They told you that, I suppose?"

"Sure!" answered Teddy, grinning. "I don't know there are such things as secret agents."

He dressed Teddy in the blue jersey and trousers of a French fishing boy, and tanned his face. The mail sack he dropped into a stout paper bag, and covered it with rolls of bread.

"Off No. 2 pier," he said, "is my motor launch, the *Baby Mine*. She's fast and seaworthy, in spite of her disgusting name. Steal her. Make Folkestone, not Dover, if you can. Your course is due west till the tide starts running down channel, then northwest. I'll have to make an awful row when I find she's gone, but I'll delay pursuit as long as I can."

The two shook hands with a single swift grip. Teddy left the cottage and strolled through the streets toward the port. He saw Casals standing outside the telegraph office, and shot hastily around a corner. Nobody took any interest in him. He might have been a boy from any of the brown-sailed fishing smacks that worked the coast from Ostend to Dieppe.

He got himself rowed out to the *Baby Mine* on the pretense of delivering stores. Standing with his back to the man in the dinghy, so that the movements of his hands were hidden, he started the motor. It roared into life, and before the boatman could recover from his surprise, Teddy had slipped the moorings and was tearing out to sea at a speed absolutely prohibited by the port of Boulogne.

He settled down at the wheel and relaxed. He had the gift of trusting to his luck when there was nothing else to trust to. The *Baby Mine* purred into the sunset at twenty knots an hour. The misty shores of England gradually took on definite shape, and a white cliff gave him a landmark. He found that he was drifting down channel, and altered his course to the northwest. The lights of Folkestone winked in the dusk and he aimed straight for the harbor.

" 'Eave to, and stop yer engines!" came a sharp command.

Teddy, gazing fixedly into the growing darkness, had not noticed the coast-guard cutter that foamed up on his port quarter. He disobeyed the order, trusting to his superior speed. Three times he was challenged; then a fountain of water deluged him as a one-pounder shot plumped into the sea a yard ahead of the *Baby Mine's* bows.

"The next un'll knock yer 'ead off," remarked a grieved voice through a megaphone. "I don't want ter *'ave* ter do it."

Teddy promptly hove to, and the cutter came alongside.

"Aye!" said the captain. "This 'ere's the boat wot was pinched from Boulong 'arbor. Come aboard, young un!"

"But I'm Mr. Thwaite," protested Teddy firmly.

"I don't care if yer the bloomin' prince of Wales," replied the captain. "Come on quietly now!"

Teddy went aboard, and the cutter, taking the *Baby Mine* in tow, ran 'nto Folkestone.

With a seaman on each side of him, he was marched along the jetty to the port offices, still clutching his paper bag, and deposited in a whitewashed and depressing cell. Teddy sat there dejectedly, hoping that his unknown friend in Boulogne had been able to wire Lord Reginald that he was on the way. It was maddening to think that all his work might be undone by the clumsy questioning of the police.

After a short wait he was escorted to the charge room, where a stern inspector looked him up and down disdainfully.

"Name?" asked the inspector.

"Theodore van Ness."

"Nationality?"

"United States citizen."

"Did you steal the launch *Baby Mine* from Boulogne Harbor?"

"I did," answered Teddy calmly.

The inspector snorted, and looked over a telegram lying on his desk. Then he pulled a bell at his side. A stout and helmeted police sergeant answered the ring.

"Sergeant Hawkins," ordered the inspector, "we have instructions from the Foreign Office to send this boy under arrest to No. 6 Clarendon Crescent, where an attaché of the American Embassy will hold him for inquiries. Take him there. Resist any attempt at rescue, and above all, see that his baggage is not disturbed. Where's your baggage?" he asked Teddy.

"Here," said Teddy, indicating the paper bag, and trying hard not to show his delight.

"Balmy!" exclaimed the inspector. "That's what they are, balmy! Still, it's no business of mine. Get a move on, Sergeant Hawkins! You'll just make the boat train if you run."

Sergeant Hawkins trotted leisurely to the station, with the dignified gait of an old cab-horse. He heaved his prisoner and himself into the baggage van just as the train was pulling out. Then he released Teddy, took off his helmet, and mopped his brow.

"Watcher been up to?" he asked sternly. "Been shootin' peas at Mussolini?"

"Yes, sergeant," replied Teddy with the utmost innocence.

The sergeant kept a disapproving silence for a while, but finally slapped his massive knee and winked at Teddy.

"You're a bit of orl right!" he said. "Ever play the game o' 'earts?"

Teddy had. The baggage master pulled out a pack of greasy cards, and the three sat down on the trunks to play.

" 'Alfpenny points?" asked Hawkins.

"Go on!" said the baggage master. "The kid's too young!"

"No, 'e ain't," answered the sergeant. "Not after bein' mixed up with all them dirty furriners, 'e ain't!"

Sergeant Hawkins was right. When the train rattled over the switches into Victoria Station, the pair of them had a profound respect for Teddy's game.

The sergeant led his prisoner to a taxi, and they drove out into the murky London night. A drizzling fog shrouded the great city. The street lamps were pale yellow globes dimly reflected in the soaking pavement. The taxi crawled toward Clarendon Crescent through a maze of wide, elegant squares and terraces, deserted at this hour.

A powerful Rolls Royce pulled up alongside them.

"Hand over your prisoner, sergeant," said a quiet voice with a slight foreign accent.

Sergeant Hawkins jumped. He was looking down the barrel of a revolver. A second was trained on Teddy, while a third man covered the taxi driver. The car stopped with a jerk.

"Nah then!" said Sergeant Hawkins calmly, reaching for his whistle. "Yer can't do this in London, yer know."

"No?" answered Casals' agent. "If you blow that whistle, sergeant, you're a dead man."

"Say, mister!" interrupted Teddy sulkily. "Here's your bag! I only took it for a joke."

He opened the door of the taxi, stepped onto the running board, and offered the bag to the man who had spoken. The secret agent grasped it eagerly. At the same instant Teddy jerked the bottom. The wet paper gave way, leaving the mail-sack in Teddy's hands. He hurled himself sideways under a shower of stale rolls, and ducked behind the back of the car. Two tongues of fire spat at him. A bullet ripped through his sleeve. Another cut a part through his hair. In a fraction of a second he was up and zigzagging through the fog—an impossible target. He heard Sergeant Hawkins blow his whistle, heard it answered at once from the next block. The Rolls Royce whizzed around a corner on two wheels and disappeared.

Teddy jumped the railings of one of the little gardens that line the residential terraces of London, and took cover in some shrubbery. His first impulse was to make a dash for Lund's apartment, but then decided that he should appear to be brought there against his will. The police were scattering through the adjoining street and gardens in search of him. He marked the burly figure of friendly Sergeant Hawkins, to whom he wished to give the honor of his recapture, dashed across the road in front of him, and tripped deliberately over the curb. The sergeant grabbed him in triumph.

"Well," he remarked, "that there was the queerest rescue I ever did see. 'Ang me if them furriners h'acted like yer friends!"

He waited for an explanation, but Teddy offered none, and allowed himself to be led in stony silence to No. 6 Clarendon Crescent, and handed over to Mr. Lund. The attaché looked so sternly at Teddy that Sergeant Hawkins felt positively sorry for the boy.

As soon as the sergeant had left, Lord Reginald, who had kept discreetly out of sight, appeared from the bedroom. Teddy was overwhelmed by his reception. The diplomats, apparently mad with joy, danced around him, cheering incoherently and slapping him on the back.

"Well done! Well done, my Thwaiteling!" yelled Bats. "Lord! I can't and I won't let this boy go without credit! You'll have to wait till the pact is signed, Teddy, but then I'm going to let this tale leak out —and leak where it will do you the most good!"

He ripped open the bag and removed a simple, typewritten document, each paragraph initialed in several hands.

"That's it!" he said, pocketing the document. "They'll miss it, but they can't say anything. Why, our efficient police even recovered the bag for them within eight hours!"

"And now your lordship had better shut up, and take itself down the backstairs," said Lund. "I'll call Casals' chief over, and deliver the bag with many apologies for our spoiled American children. Whatever made you do such a shocking thing, Van Ness?"

Teddy opened his big blue eyes and pretended to be on the verge of tears. "I guess I must have seen too many gangster films!" he whimpered.

Fritz the Master-Fiddler

by John Bennett

A LONG time ago, in fact several years before there was any such thing as time, there lived a sturdy miller and his wife in a cottage at the edge of a great black forest near the village of Weisnichtwo, in the southeast corner of the kingdom of Niemandweis, just this side of the other end of nowhere.

This worthy couple had one son, Fritz, a funny little tow-headed fellow with big blue eyes, rosy cheeks, and baggy little trousers that he could almost turn around in. He was a queer little chap, too; for when the other boys played along the dusty highway and narrow street with whoop and halloo, Fritz crept quietly away to the field or forest, where, among the kaiserblumen or the fern, he would sit alone for hours, singing baby-songs to the brook as it babbled out of the woods, and making quaint little tunes for the lambs to play to—tunes that sounded like the wind in the pines, the birds calling in the tree-tops, or the stream rippling down the rocks to the water-wheel at the mill.

"Father," said he one day, "when I grow up I will be a master-fiddler and make music on the fiddle."

"Stuff and nonsense!" said his father; but he bought him a little yellow fiddle at the next kermess, and let him play it all day long.

It was surprising how soon Fritz could draw melody out of that Swiss-pine box with his stubby bow! He made it fairly laugh and cry and sing and gurgle and whistle and hum, until the birds flew down from the tree-tops and hopped about him; and the lambs came and lay down at his feet; and mother-sheep rubbed their noses against his knees; and the marmots peeped from among the rocks; and the rabbits paused in the thick grass with listening ears; and the brown bees buzzed about his head. None of them were afraid, for Fritz seemed one of themselves.

But he grew up,—as healthy boys will do, who eat good meat, and sweet brown bread, and amber honey with creamy milk as rich as nectar,—and he fiddled better and better every day, until at last he said: "Father, I fiddle too well for Weisnichtwo. These dull villagers care only for the drone of the dudelsack and a bawling song with their muddy beer. I must go out into the world and seek my fortune."

"The little boys followed him down the street"

So he took his cap and his fiddle, was blessed by his father and kissed by his mother, waved a farewell to Weisnichtwo, and went out into the world.

At first he fiddled merrily as he went along, and thought to fiddle himself into a fortune soon. But no one stopped to listen; no one seemed to care whether he fiddled or not; and, no one offering to pay for his music, he might fairly have fiddled himself into the poorhouse if one angry goose-herd had not rated him soundly for scaring the geese with his "nonsensical noise." After that Fritz indignantly tucked his unappreciated fiddle under his arm and trudged on silent and discouraged.

"Oh, dear!" he sighed wearily, "if they won't let me fiddle, how can I ever find my fortune? I wonder where it can be."

So he began to ask the passers-by, "Good sir,"—or "madam," as the case might be,— "have you seen my fortune?"

Some laughed at him. Some told him to mind his business. Others were too busy hunting their own fortunes to pay him any attention whatever. And at last, in one rough village, they called him a silly dunder-head, and pelted him with mud and stones until he took to his heels and ran off. All out of breath as he turned into the cross-road, he tripped over a stone and fell flat upon his fiddle with a dreadful crunch. And when he picked it up out of the dust it was spoiled beyond all hope of repair, with one peg bent up, and one peg down, and one this way, and the other that, while the neck was twisted hopelessly awry.

"Oh, my fiddle, my little fiddle, my dear little fiddle, it is ruined!" he sobbed; and, clasping the spoiled instrument to his breast, he limped ruefully on, hardly caring where he went or what became of him, and only knowing that his beloved fiddle would never make sweet music again.

Just at nightfall he came to the city of the king, and wandered through the gloomy streets heedless of them all.

"Hullo, Master-Fiddler!" called some revelers beside a cozy inn. "Come fiddle for us, and we will pay you well!"

"I do not care to play—pay or no pay," said Fritz bitterly, as he clutched his ruined fiddle to his bosom and passed on.

"What?" cried the amazed revelers, "a fiddler who will not fiddle for pay!" And the little boys took up the shout, and followed him down the street, crying, "Look, here is a fiddler who will not fiddle for pay!" And all the people stopped to see; and many came out of their houses, hearing the cry; and soon the narrow way was so crowded that the king's carriage could not pass, and a footman came to learn the cause of the blockade.

"It is a fiddler who will not fiddle for pay!" yelled the gamins in the gutter.

"Indeed?" exclaimed the king. "Then he must surely be a great fiddler! Tell him he may come to my palace and play."

But Fritz thought only of his poor, twisted fiddle, and replied, "I do not care to play, king or no king!"

"Dear me!" cried his Majesty, surprised; "this must be a very fine fiddler, indeed, who does not fairly jump at the chance to play before a king. I surely must hear him!"

So he sent his coach and a regiment of grenadiers to bring Fritz to the palace, or to take him to prison if he would not play—for he gave him his choice, being a magnanimous king.

Then Fritz was at his wit's end. His clothes were torn, his fiddle was spoiled,—but there was no way to escape; so in sheer despair he faced the music like a man. "If the king *will* hear me play, he shall!" said he grimly, as he climbed into the coach and was whirled to the palace.

"So," said the king, "you are here, are you?"

"Yes," replied Fritz, as he looked about; "I believe I am."

"Then call the court," cried the king; "we will have some first-class A No. 1 music! But where are your notes?"

"This fiddle does not play by note," faltered Fritz; which was very true—it certainly did not!

"Ah," whispered the king to the vice-chancellor, "what did I tell you? This fellow is a genius—he does not fiddle by note."

"Yes," whispered the vice-chancellor, "he must indeed be a genius—just see how very shabby he is!"

But, "Oh, dear!" groaned Fritz to himself, "it is all up with me!" And then, with his heart clear up in his throat, though outwardly smiling, he hastily filled his ears with cotton and began to play.

Such a shrieking, such a squeaking, such a wild, ear-piercing scream as came out of that crooked fiddle! Ugh-h-h-h!

Why, even the sparrows under the palace eaves jumped out of their nests, flew over the fence, and never came back again; the king's pet cat crawled under the cellar door and yowled with fear; while, for a moment, paralyzed with amazement, the courtiers sat motionless and dumb!

They had never heard any such music as that before. It set their teeth on edge, made their flesh creep, and raised goose-flesh in the very marrow of their shivering bones! But there stood Fritz, placidly playing away as if he were producing the sweetest sounds in the world. And had not the king himself said that this fiddler was a genius? Certainly he had! And since the king had said it, it must be so. Consequently, every man Jack of them was afraid to say he did not like it. And no one dared to admit that he saw nothing lovely in it, for fear he would appear more stupid than his neighbor. So they all clasped their hands, and, turning to each other, cried in one ecstatic voice, "Oh, this must be a new school of music—it must be a new school! Isn't it overpowering—isn't it forceful—isn't it thrilling—isn't it just too utterly *ne-plus-ultra* for anything!"

"Ah," said one, "it isn't everybody who can have taste for such music!"

"No, indeed," answered another; "one should know how to listen!"

And then they all listened with rapt attention and clasped hands, while they fairly squirmed, and longed for the roof to fly off, the walls to fall in, the floor to blow up, or something—or anything, oh, anything!—just to stop that horrible noise!

Now it happened that, seven years before, the Crown Princess Hilda's favorite wax doll had fallen head first into the royal soup-tureen one day at dinner; and the soup, being hot, had melted off her nose. Whereat, after one wild burst of childish grief, the princess had been seized with profound grief, and had gone into deep mourning for her disfigured darling, refusing to be comforted, and had never smiled again. The court physician had given her potions and powders until she was pale as a ghost. She had traveled to all of the fashionable watering-places for change of air until she was worn to a shadow. Fabulous rewards had been offered for anything to break her sorrow, but in vain. Her sorrow remained unbroken.

There, attended by a favorite maiden, and with a trusty grenadier within call, upon a raised dais at the end of the great hall, a fragile little waxen princess in gloomy black, brown-haired and hazel-eyed, she sat so deeply wrapped in melancholy that nothing seemed to move her.

But at the first shriek of Fritz's crooked fiddle she jumped with surprise and looked up with a sudden sparkle in her heavy eyes. And as she listened to the squeaking, screaming, shrieking squeal, a gleam lit up her face, she cast one quick look around the vast audience all in its rapt attention, and falling back into her chair broke into a peal of uncontrollable laughter.

"Oh, my!—oh, my!—oh, my!" she cried, holding her sides; "it sounds like—a little pig under—a—gate!" and she laughed until the tears ran down her face.

Oh, the scene of wild excitement that ensued! The king tossed his crown up to the ceiling, the lord high chamberlain fell over two small pages trying to dance a jig, the whole court rolled off their chairs in delighted surprise, and the court physician had three conniption fits in rapid succession behind the Japanese screen—for the melancholy spell was broken, the princess was cured, and his high-salaried situation was at an end!

Then the king fell upon Fritz's neck and kissed him, to his great embarrassment; and the courtiers, delighted that the fiddling had stopped, cheered until they were hoarse, crying, "Long live Fritz, the Master-Fiddler!" And the populace outside, hearing the shout, took up the cry until they were twice as hoarse: "Long live Fritz, the Master-Fiddler!" although they had not the slightest idea what it was all about—which made no difference at all with the populace.

"And now, Sir Master-Fiddler," exclaimed the king, when the hullabaloo had stopped; "since you have cured the princess, of course you will marry her."

"Shall I?" stammered Fritz, blushing like a girl. "Why?"

"Because that is the way I am going to have this story end," said the king, firmly. "And I am not going to have it spoiled by any nonsense!"

"Well," said Fritz, thoughtfully, rubbing his chin; "if I must, I suppose I must —but," he continued uneasily, "I would like to ask the princess one thing before the wedding takes place."

"What is that?" asked the princess, smiling up into his face.

"Will—will—will," he stammered bashfully—"will you marry me?"

"Yes," replied she, shyly dropping her dark eyelashes, and laying her little hand confidingly upon his broad shoulder; "but—"

"But what?" cried Fritz anxiously.

"You must never—"

"What?" gasped Fritz, turning pale with apprehension.

"Play that horrible fiddle around the house!"

"Oh!" ejaculated Fritz, with a smile of relief that spoke volumes, as he removed the cotton from his ears; "I promise you I never will."

And he never did.

"And all went merry as a marriage-bell"

ONAWANDAH

FOURTH SPINNING WHEEL STORY

by Louisa M. Alcott

Long ago, when hostile Indians haunted the great forests, and every settlement had its fort for the protection of the inhabitants, in one of the towns on the Connecticut River lived Parson Bain and his little son and daughter. The wife and mother was dead; but an old servant took care of them, and did her best to make Reuben and Eunice good children. Her direst threat, when they were naughty, was, "The Indians will come and fetch you, if you don't behave." So they grew up in great fear of the red men. Even the friendly Indians, who sometimes came for food or powder, were regarded with suspicion by the people. No man went to work without his gun near by. On Sundays, when they trudged to the rude meeting house, all carried the trusty rifle on the shoulder, and while the pastor preached, a sentinel mounted guard at the door, to give warning if canoes came down the river or a dark face peered from the wood.

One autumn night, when the first heavy rains were falling and a cold wind whistled through the valley, a knock came at the minister's door and, opening it, he found an Indian boy, ragged, hungry, and footsore, who begged for food and shelter. In his broken way, he told how he had fallen ill and been left to die by enemies who had taken him from his own people, months before; how he had wandered for days till almost sinking; and that he had come now to ask for help, led by the hospitable light in the parsonage window.

"Send him away, Master, or harm will come of it. He is a spy, and we shall all be scalped by the murdering Injuns who are waiting in the wood," said old Becky, harshly; while little Eunice hid in the old servant's ample skirts, and twelve-year-old Reuben laid his hand on his cross-bow, ready to defend his sister if need be.

But the good man drew the poor lad in, saying, with his friendly smile: "Shall not a Christian be as hospitable as a godless savage? Come in, child, and be fed; you sorely need rest and shelter."

Leaving his face to express the gratitude he had no words to tell, the boy sat by the comfortable fire and ate like a famished wolf, while Becky muttered her forebodings and the children eyed the dark youth at a safe distance. Something in his pinched face, wounded foot, and eyes full of dumb pain and patience, touched the little girl's tender heart, and, yielding to a pitiful impulse, she brought her own basin of new milk and, setting it beside the stranger, ran to hide behind her father, suddenly remembering that this was one of the dreaded Indians.

"That was well done, little daughter. Thou shalt love thine enemies, and share thy bread with the needy. See, he is smiling; that pleased him, and he wishes us to be his friends."

But Eunice ventured no more that night, and quaked in her little bed at the thought of the strange boy sleeping on a blanket before the fire below. Reuben hid his fears better, and resolved to watch while others slept; but was off as soon as his curly head touched the pillow, and dreamed of tomahawks and war-whoops till morning.

Next day, neighbors came to see the waif, and one and all advised sending him away as soon as possible, since he was doubtless a spy, as Becky said, and would bring trouble of some sort.

"When he is well, he may go whithersoever he will; but while he is too lame to walk, weak with hunger, and worn out with weariness, I will harbor him. He can not feign suffering and starvation like this. I shall do my duty, and leave the consequences to the Lord," answered the parson, with such pious firmness that the neighbors said no more.

But they kept a close watch upon Onawandah, when he went among them, silent and submissive, but with the proud air of a captive prince, and sometimes a fierce flash in his black eyes when the other lads taunted him with his red skin. He was very lame for weeks, and could only sit in the sun, weaving pretty baskets for Eunice, and shaping bows and arrows for Reuben. The children were soon his friends, for with them he was always gentle, trying in his soft language and expressive gestures to show his good will and gratitude; for they defended him against their ruder playmates, and, following their father's example, trusted and cherished the homeless youth.

When he was able to walk, he taught the boy to shoot and trap the wild creatures of the wood, to find fish where others failed, and to guide himself in the wilderness by star and sun, wind and water. To Eunice he brought little offerings of bark and feathers; taught her to make moccasins of skin, belts of shells, or pouches gay with porcupine quills and colored grass. He would not work for old Becky—who plainly showed her distrust—saying: "A brave does not grind corn and bring wood; that is squaw's work. Onawandah will hunt and fish and fight for you, but no more." And even the request of the parson could not win obedience in this, though the boy would have died for the good man.

"We cannot tame an eagle as we can a barn-yard fowl. Let him remember only kindness of us, and so we turn a foe into a friend," said Parson Bain, stroking the sleek, dark head, that always bowed before him, with a docile reverence shown to no other living creature.

Winter came, and the settlers fared hardly through the long months, when the drifts rose to the eaves of their low cabins, and the stores, carefully harvested, failed to supply even their simple wants. But the minister's family never lacked wild meat, for Onawandah proved himself a better hunter than any man in the town, and the boy of sixteen led the way on his snow-shoes when they went to track a bear to its den, chase the deer for miles, or shoot the wolves that howled about their homes in the winter nights.

But he never joined in their games, and sat apart when the young folk made merry, as if he scorned such childish pastimes and longed to be a man in all things. Why he stayed when he was well again, no one could tell, unless he waited for spring to make his way to his own people. But Reuben and Eunice rejoiced to keep him; for while he taught them many things, he was their pupil also, learning English rapidly, and proving himself a very affectionate and devoted friend and servant, in his own quiet way.

"Be of good cheer, little daughter; I shall be gone but three days, and our brave Onawandah will guard you well," said the parson, one April morning, as he mounted his horse to visit a distant settlement, where the bitter winter had brought sickness and death to more than one household.

The boy showed his white teeth in a bright smile as he stood beside the children, while Becky croaked, with a shake of the head:

"I hope you mayn't find you've warmed a viper in your bosom, Master."

Two days later, it seemed as if Becky was a true prophet, and that the confiding minister *had* been terribly deceived; for Onawandah went away to hunt, and, that night, the awful war-whoop woke the sleeping villagers to find their houses burning, while the hidden Indians shot at them by the light of the fires kindled by dusky scouts. In terror and confusion the whites flew to the fort; and, while the men fought bravely, the women held blankets to catch arrows and bullets, or bound up the hurts of their defenders.

It was all over by daylight, and the red men sped away up the river, with several prisoners, and such booty as they could plunder from the deserted houses. Not till all fear of a return of their enemies was over, did the poor people venture to leave the fort and seek their ruined homes. Then it was discovered that Becky and the parson's children were gone, and great was the bewailing, for the good man was much beloved by all his flock.

Suddenly the smothered voice of Becky was heard by a party of visitors, calling dolefully:

"I am here, betwixt the beds. Pull me out, neighbors, for I am half dead with fright and smothering."

The old woman was quickly extricated from her hiding-place, and with much energy declared that she had seen Onawandah, disguised with war-paint, among the Indians, and that he had torn away the children from her arms before she could fly from the house.

"He chose his time well, when they were defenseless, dear lambs! Spite of all my warnings, Master trusted him, and this is the thanks we get. Oh, my poor Master! How can I tell him this heavy news?"

There was no need to tell it; for, as Becky sat moaning and beating her breast on the fireless hearth, and the sympathizing neighbors stood about her, the sound of a horse's hoofs was heard, and the parson came down the hilly road like one riding for his life. He had seen the smoke afar off, guessed the sad truth, and hurried on, to find his home in ruins and to learn by his first glance at the faces around him that his children were gone.

When he had heard all there was to tell, he sat down upon his door-stone with his head in his hands, praying for strength to bear a grief too deep for words. The wounded and weary men tried to comfort him with hope, and the women wept with him as they hugged their own babies closer to the hearts that ached for the lost children. Suddenly a stir went through the mournful group, as Onawandah came from the wood with a young deer upon his shoulders, and amazement in his face as he saw the desolation before him. Dropping his burden, he stood an instant looking with eyes that kindled fiercely; then he came bounding toward them, undaunted by the hatred, suspicion, and surprise plainly written on the countenances before him. He missed his playmates, and asked but one question:

"The boy? the little squaw?—where gone?"

His answer was a rough one, for the men seized him and poured forth the tale, heaping reproaches upon him for such treachery and ingratitude. He bore it all in proud silence till they pointed to the poor father whose dumb sorrow was more eloquent than all their wrath. Onawandah looked at him, and the fire died out of his eyes as if quenched by the tears he would not shed. Shaking off the hands that held him, he went to his good friend, saying with passionate earnestness:

"Onawandah is *not* traitor! Onawandah remembers. Onawandah grateful! You believe?"

The poor parson looked up at him, and could not doubt his truth; for genuine love and sorrow ennobled the dark face, and he had never known the boy to lie.

"I believe and trust you still, but others will not. Go, you are no longer safe here, and I have no home to offer you," said the parson, sadly, feeling that he cared for none, unless his children were restored to him.

"Onawandah has no fear. He goes; but he comes again to bring the boy, the little squaw."

Few words, but they were so solemnly spoken that the most unbelieving were impressed; for the youth laid one hand on the gray head bowed before him, and lifted the other toward heaven, as if calling the Great Spirit to hear his vow.

A relenting murmur went through the crowd, but the boy paid no heed, as he turned away, and with no arms but his hunting knife and bow, no food but such as he could find, no guide but the sun by day, the stars by night, plunged into the pathless forest and was gone.

Then the people drew a long breath, and muttered to one another:

"He will never do it, yet he is a brave lad for his years."

"Only a shift to get off with a whole skin, I warrant you. These varlets are as cunning as foxes," added Becky, sourly.

The parson alone believed and hoped, though weeks and months went by, and his children did not come.

Meantime, Reuben and Eunice were far away in an Indian camp, resting as best they could, after the long journey that followed that dreadful night. Their captors were not cruel to them, for Reuben was a stout fellow and, thanks, to Onawandah, could hold his own with the boys who would have tormented him if he had been feeble or cowardly. Eunice also was a hardy creature for her years, and when her first fright and fatigue were over, made herself useful in many ways among the squaws, who did not let the pretty child suffer greatly; though she was neglected, because they knew no better.

Life in a wigwam was not a life of ease, and fortunately the children were accustomed to simple habits and the hardships that all endured in those early times. But they mourned for home till their young faces were pathetic with the longing, and their pillows of dry leaves were often wet with tears in the night. Their clothes grew ragged, their hair unkempt, their faces tanned by sun and wind. Scanty food and exposure to all weathers tried the strength of their bodies, and uncertainty as to their fate saddened their spirits; yet they bore up bravely, and said their prayers faithfully, feeling sure that God would bring them home to father in His own good time.

One day, when Reuben was snaring birds in the wood,—for the Indians had no fear of such young children venturing to escape,—he heard the cry of a quail, and followed it deeper and deeper into the forest, till it ceased, and, with a sudden rustle, Onawandah rose up from the brakes, his finger on his lips to prevent any exclamation that might betray him to other ears and eyes.

"I come for you and little Laraka,"—
(the name he gave Eunice, meaning "Wild
Rose.") "I take you home. Not know me
yet. Go and wait."

He spoke low and fast; but the joy in his
face told how glad he was to find the boy
after his long search, and Reuben clung
to him, trying not to disgrace himself by
crying like a girl, in his surprise and delight.

Lying hidden in the tall brakes they
talked in whispers, while one told of the
capture, and the other of a plan of escape;
for, though a friendly tribe, these Indians
were not Onawandah's people, and they
must not suspect that he knew the children, else they might be separated at once.
"Little squaw betray me. You watch
her. Tell her not to cry out, not speak me
any time. When I say come, we go,—
fast,—in the night. Not ready yet."

These were the orders Reuben received,
and, when he could compose himself, he
went back to the wigwams, leaving his
friend in the wood, while he told the good
news to Eunice, and prepared her for the
part she must play.

Fear had taught her self-control, and
the poor child stood the test well, working off her relief and rapture by pounding corn in the stone mortar till her little
hands were blistered, and her arms ached
for hours afterward.

Not till the next day did Onawandah
make his appearance, and then he came
limping into the village, weary, lame, and
half starved after his long wandering in
the wilderness. He was kindly welcomed,
and his story believed, for he told only
the first part, and said nothing of his life
among the white men. He hardly glanced
at the children when they were pointed
out to him by their captors, and scowled
at poor Eunice, who forgot her part in
her joy, and smiled as she met the dark
eyes that till now had always looked

kindly at her. A touch from Reuben
warned her, and she was glad to hide her
confusion by shaking her long hair over
her face, as if afraid of the stranger.

Onawandah took no further notice of
them, but seemed to be very lame with
the old wound in his foot, which prevented his being obliged to hunt with the
men. He was resting and slowly gathering
strength for the hard task he had set himself, while he waited for a safe time to
save the children. They understood, but
the suspense proved too much for little
Eunice, and she pined with impatience
to be gone. She lost appetite and color,
and cast such appealing glances at Onawandah that he could not seem quite indifferent, and gave her a soft word now
and then, or did such acts of kindness as he
could perform unsuspected. When she lay
awake at night thinking of home, a cricket
would chirp outside the wigwam, and a
hand slip in a leaf full of berries, or a
bark-cup of fresh water for the feverish
little mouth. Sometimes it was only a
caress or a whisper of encouragement, that
reassured the childish heart, and sent her
to sleep with a comfortable sense of love
and protection, like a sheltering wing over
a motherless bird.

Reuben stood it better, and entered
heartily into the excitement of the plot,
for he had grown tall and strong in
these trying months, and felt that he must
prove himself a man to sustain and defend his sister. Quietly he put away each
day a bit of dried meat, a handful of
parched corn, or a well-sharpened arrow-
head, as provision for the journey; while
Onawandah seemed to be amusing himself with making moccasins and a little
vest of deerskin for an Indian child about
the age of Eunice.

At last, in the early autumn, all the
men went off on the war-path, leaving
only boys and women behind. Then Ona-

wandah's eyes began to kindle, and Reuben's heart to beat fast, for both felt that their time for escape had come.

All was ready, and one moonless night the signal was given. A cricket chirped shrilly outside the tent where the children slept with one old squaw. A strong hand cut the skin beside their bed of fir boughs, and two trembling creatures crept out to follow the tall shadow that flitted noiselessly before them into the darkness of the wood. Not a broken twig, a careless step, or a whispered word betrayed them, and they vanished as swiftly and silently as hunted deer flying for their lives.

Till dawn they hurried on, Onawandah carrying Eunice, whose strength soon failed, and Reuben manfully shouldering the hatchet and the pouch of food. At sunrise they hid in a thicket by a spring and rested, while waiting for the friendly night to come again. Then they pushed on, and fear gave wings to their feet, so that by another morning they were far enough away to venture to travel more slowly and sleep at night.

If the children had learned to love and trust the Indian boy in happier times, they adored him now, and came to regard him as an earthly Providence, so faithful, brave, and tender was he; so forgetful of himself, so bent on saving them. He never seemed to sleep, ate the poorest morsels, or went without any food when provisions failed; let no danger daunt him, no hardship wring complaint from him; but went on through the wild forest, led by guides invisible to them, till they began to hope that home was near.

Twice he saved their lives. Once, when he went in search of food, leaving Reuben to guard his sister, the children, being very hungry, ignorantly ate some poisonous berries which looked like wild cherries, and were deliciously sweet. The boy generously gave most of them to Eunice, and soon was terror-stricken to see her grow pale and cold and deathly ill. Not knowing what to do, he could only rub her hands and call wildly for Onawandah.

The name echoed through the silent wood, and, though far away, the keen ear of the Indian heard it, his fleet feet brought him back in time, and his knowledge of wild roots and herbs made it possible to save the child when no other help was at hand.

"Make fire. Keep warm. I soon come," he said, after hearing the story and examining Eunice, who could only lift her eyes to him, full of childish confidence and patience.

Then he was off again, scouring the woods like a hound on the scent, searching everywhere for the precious little herb that would counteract the poison. Anyone watching him would have thought him crazy as he rushed hither and thither, tearing up the leaves, creeping on his hands and knees that it might not escape him, and when he found it, springing up with a cry that startled the birds, and carried hope to poor Reuben, who was trying to forget his own pain in his anxiety for Eunice, whom he thought dying.

"Eat, eat, while I make drink. All safe now," cried Onawandah, as he came leaping toward them with his hands full of green leaves, and his dark face shining with joy.

The boy was soon relieved, but for hours they hung over the girl, who suffered sadly, till she grew unconscious and lay as if dead. Reuben's courage failed then, and he cried bitterly, thinking how hard it would be to leave the dear little creature under the pines and go home alone to father. Even Onawandah lost hope for a while, and sat like a bronze statue of despair, with his eyes fixed on his Wild Rose, who seemed fading away too soon.

Suddenly he rose, stretched his arms to the west, where the sun was setting splendidly, and in his own musical language prayed to the Great Spirit. The Christian boy fell upon his knees, feeling that the only help was in the Father Who saw and heard them even in the wilderness. Both were comforted, and when they turned to Eunice there was a faint tinge of color on the pale cheeks, as if the evening red kissed her, the look of pain was gone, and she slept quietly without the moans that had made their hearts ache before.

"He hears! He hears!" cried Onawandah, and for the first time Reuben saw tears in his keen eyes, as the Indian boy turned his face to the sky full of a gratitude that no words were sweet enough to tell.

All night, Eunice lay peacefully sleeping, and the moon lighted Onawandah's lonely watch, for the boy Reuben was worn out with suspense, and slept beside his sister.

In the morning she was safe, and great was the rejoicing; but for two days the little invalid was not allowed to continue the journey, much as they longed to hurry on. It was a pretty sight, the bed of hemlock boughs spread under a green tent of woven branches, and on the pillow of moss the pale child watching the flicker of sunshine through the leaves, listening to the babble of a brook close by or sleeping tranquilly, lulled by the murmur of the pines. Patient, loving, and grateful, it was a pleasure to serve her, and both the lads were faithful nurses. Onawandah cooked birds for her to eat, and made a pleasant drink of the wild raspberry leaves to quench her thirst. Reuben snared rabbits, that she might have nourishing food, and longed to shoot a deer for provision, that she might not suffer hunger again on their journey. This boyish desire led him deeper in the wood than it was wise for him to go

alone, for it was near night-fall, and wild creatures haunted the forest in those days. The fire, which Onawandah kept constantly burning, guarded their little camp where Eunice lay; but Reuben, with no weapon but his bow and hunting knife, was beyond this protection when he at last gave up his vain hunt and turned homeward. Suddenly, the sound of stealthy steps startled him, but he could see nothing through the dusk at first, and hurried on, fearing that some treacherous Indian was following him. Then he remembered his sister, and resolved not to betray her resting-place if he could help it, for he had learned courage of Onawandah, and longed to be as brave and generous as his dusky hero.

So he paused to watch and wait, and soon saw the gleam of two fiery eyes, not behind, but above him, in a tree. Then he knew that it was an "Indian devil," as they called a species of fierce wild-cat that lurked in the thickets and sprang on its prey like a small tiger.

"If I could only kill it alone, how proud Onawandah would be of me," thought Reuben, burning for the good opinion of his friend.

It would have been wiser to hurry on and give the beast no time to spring; but the boy was overbold, and, fitting an arrow to the string, aimed at the bright eye-ball and let fly. A sharp snarl showed that some harm was done, and, rather daunted by the savage sound, Reuben raced away, meaning to come back next day for the prize he hoped he had secured.

But soon he heard the creature bounding after him, and he uttered one ringing shout for help, feeling too late that he had been foolhardy. Fortunately he was nearer camp than he thought. Onawandah heard him and was there in time to receive the wild-cat, as, mad with the pain of the wound, it sprang at Reuben. There was no time for words, and the boy could only watch in breathless interest and anxiety the fight which went on between the brute and the Indian.

It was sharp but short, for Onawandah had his knife, and as soon as he could get the snarling, struggling beast down, he killed it with a skillful stroke. But not before it had torn and bitten him more dangerously than he knew; for the dusk hid the wounds, and excitement kept him from feeling them at first. Reuben thanked him heartily, and accepted his few words of warning with grateful docility; then both hurried back to Eunice, who till next day knew nothing of her brother's danger.

Onawandah made light of his scratches, as he called them, got their supper, and sent Reuben early to bed, for tomorrow they were to start again.

Excited by his adventure, the boy slept lightly, and waking in the night saw by the flicker of the fire Onawandah binding up a deep wound in his breast with wet moss and his own belt. A stifled groan betrayed how much he suffered; but when Reuben went to him, he would accept no help, said it was nothing, and sent him back to bed, preferring to endure the pain in stern silence, with true Indian pride and courage.

Next morning, they set out and pushed on as fast as Eunice's strength allowed. But it was evident that Onawandah suffered much, though he would not rest, forbade the children to speak of his wounds, and pressed on with feverish haste, as if he feared that his strength might not hold out. Reuben watched him anxiously, for there was a look in his face that troubled the boy and filled him with alarm, as well as with remorse and love. Eunice would not let him carry her as before, but trudged bravely behind him, though her feet ached and her breath often failed as she tried to keep up; and both children did all they could to comfort and sustain their friend, who seemed glad to give his life for them.

In three days they reached the river, and, as if Heaven helped them in their greatest need, found a canoe, left by some hunter, near the shore. In they sprang, and let the swift current bear them along, Eunice kneeling in the bow like a little figure-head of Hope, Reuben steering with his paddle, and Onawandah sitting with arms tightly folded over his breast, as if to control the sharp anguish of the neglected wound. He knew that it was past help now, and only cared to see the children safe; then, worn out but happy, he was proud to die, having paid his debt to the good parson, and proved that he was not a liar nor a traitor.

Hour after hour they floated down the great river, looking eagerly for signs of home, and when at last they entered the familiar valley, while the little girl cried for joy, and the boy paddled as he had never done before, Onawandah sat erect with his haggard eyes fixed on the dim distance, and sang his death-song in a clear, strong voice—though every breath was pain,—bent on dying like a brave, without complaint or fear.

At last they saw the smoke from the cabins on the hill-side and, hastily mooring the canoe, all sprang out, eager to be at home after their long and perilous wandering. But as his foot touched the land, Onawandah felt that he could do no more, and stretching his arms toward the parsonage, the windows of which glimmered as hospitably as they had done when he first saw them, he said, with a pathetic sort of triumph in his broken voice: "Go. I cannot.—Tell the good father, Onawandah not lie, not forget. He keep his promise."

Then he dropped upon the grass and lay as if dead, while Reuben, bidding Eunice keep watch, ran as fast as his tired legs could carry him to tell the tale and bring help.

The little girl did her part tenderly, carrying water in her hands to wet the white lips, tearing up her ragged skirt to lay fresh bandages on the wound that had been bleeding the brave boy's life away, and, sitting by him, gathered his head into her arms, begging him to wait till father came.

But poor Onawandah had waited too long; now he could only look up into the dear, loving, little face bent over him, and whisper wistfully: "Wild Rose will remember Onawandah?" as the light went out of his eyes, and his last breath was a smile for her.

When the parson and his people came hurrying up full of wonder, joy, and good will, they found Eunice weeping bitterly, and the Indian boy lying like a young warrior smiling at death.

"Ah, my neighbors, the savage has taught us a lesson we never can forget. Let us imitate his virtues, and do honor to his memory," said the pastor, as he held his little daughter close and looked down at the pathetic figure at his feet, whose silence was more eloquent than any words.

All felt it, and even old Becky had a remorseful sigh for the boy who had kept his word so well and given back her darlings safe.

They buried him where he lay; and for years the lonely mound under the great oak was kept green by loving hands. Wild roses bloomed there, and the murmur of the Long River of Pines was a fit lullaby for faithful Onawandah.

THE FLOATING PRINCE

by Frank R. Stockton

THERE was once an orphan prince, named Nassime, who had been carefully educated to take his place upon the throne of his native country. Everything that a king ought to know had been taught him, and he was considered, by the best judges, to be in every way qualified to wear a crown and to wield a scepter.

But when he became of age, and was just about to take his place upon the throne, a relative, of great power and influence in the country, concluded that he would be king himself, and so the young prince was thrown out upon the world. The new king did not want him in his dominions, and it was therefore determined, by his teachers and guardians, that he would have to become a "floating prince." By this, they meant that he must travel about, from place to place, until he found some kingdom which needed a king, and which was willing to accept him to rule over it. If such a situation were vacant, he easily could obtain it.

He was therefore furnished with a new suit of clothes and a good sword; a small crown and a scepter were packed into his bag; and he was started out to seek his fortune, as best he could.

As the prince walked away from the walls of his native city, he felt quite downhearted, although he was by nature gay and hopeful. He did not believe that he could find any country which would want him for a ruler.

"That is all nonsense," he said to himself. "There are always plenty of heirs or usurpers to take a throne when it is empty. If I want a kingdom, I must build up one for myself, and that is just what I will do. I will gather together my subjects as I go along. The first person I meet shall be my chief councilor of state, the second shall be head of the army, the third shall be admiral of the navy, the next shall be chief treasurer, and then I will collect subjects of various classes."

Cheered by this plan, he stepped gayly on, and just as he was entering a wood, through which his pathway led him, he heard some one singing.

Looking about him, he saw a little lady, about five inches high, sitting upon a twig of a flowering bush near by, and singing to herself. Nassime instantly perceived that she was a fairy, and said to himself: "Oho! I did not expect a meeting of this sort." But as he was a bold and frank young fellow, he stepped up to her and said: "Good-morning, lady fairy. How would you like to be chief councilor to a king?"

"It would be splendid!" said the lively little fairy, her eyes sparkling with delight. "But where is the king?"

"I am the king," said Nassime, "or, rather, I am to be, as soon as I get my kingdom together."

And then he told her his story and his plans. The fairy was charmed. The plan suited her exactly.

"You might get a larger councilor than

I am," she said, "but I know a good deal about government. I have been governed ever so much, and I could not help learning how it is done. I'm glad enough to have a chance to help somebody govern other people. I'll be your chief councilor."

"All right," said the prince, who was much pleased with the merry little creature. "Now we'll go and hunt up the rest of the kingdom."

He took the little fairy in his hand and placed her in one of the folds of his silken girdle, where she could rest, as if in a tiny hammock, and then he asked her name.

"My name," she answered, "is Lorilla, chief councilor of the kingdom of—what are you going to call your kingdom?"

"Oh, I haven't thought of a name, yet."

"Let it be Nassimia, after yourself," said Lorilla.

"Very well," answered the prince, "we will call it Nassimia. That will save trouble and disputes, after the kingdom is established."

Nassime now stepped along quite briskly, talking to his little companion as he went, and explaining to her his various ideas regarding his future kingdom. Suddenly he stumbled over what he supposed was the trunk of a fallen tree, and then he was quickly raised into the air, astride of the supposed tree-trunk, which seemed to have a hinge in it.

"What now?" said a great voice, and the prince perceived that he was sitting on the knee of a giant, who had been lying on his back in the wood.

"Don't be afraid," said Lorilla, looking out of her little hammock. "He won't hurt you."

"Excuse me," said the prince, "I did not see you, or I should have been more careful. How would you like to be general of the army of the kingdom of Nassimia?"

"That sounds splendid!" cried little Lorilla.

The giant looked bewildered. He could not understand, at all, what the prince was talking about. But when Nassime explained it all to him, he said he would like very well to be head general of the army, and he accepted the position.

Rising to his feet, the giant offered to carry the prince on his arm, so that they could get along faster, and in this way they traveled, all discussing, with much zest, the scheme of the new kingdom.

About noon, they began to be hungry, and so they sat down in a shady place, the giant having said that he had something to eat in a bag which he carried at his side. He opened this bag, and spread out half a dozen enormous loaves of bread, two joints of roast meat, a boiled ham, and about a bushel of roasted potatoes.

"Is that the food for your whole army?" asked Lorilla.

"Oh, no," answered the giant, who was a young fellow with a good appetite. "I brought this for myself, but there will be enough for you two. I don't believe I should have eaten it quite all, anyway."

"I should hope not," said the prince. "Why, that would last me several weeks."

"And me a thousand years," said Lorilla.

"You will talk differently, if you ever grow to be as big as I am," said the giant, smiling, as he took a bite from a loaf of bread.

When the meal was over, they all felt refreshed, and quite eager to meet the next comer, who was to be the admiral, or commander of the navy, of the new kingdom. For some time, they went on without seeing any one, but, at last, they perceived, in a field at some distance, a man on stilts. He was tending sheep, and wore the stilts so that he could the better see his flock, as it wandered about.

"There's the admiral!" said the giant. "Let me put you down, and run over and catch him."

So saying, he set the prince on the ground, and ran toward the shepherd, who, seeing him coming, at once took to flight. His stilts were so long that he made enormous steps, and he got over the ground very fast. The giant had long legs, and he ran swiftly, but he had a great deal of trouble to get near the man on stilts, who dodged in every direction, and rushed about like an enormous crane. The poor frightened sheep scattered themselves over the fields, and hid in the bushes.

At last, the giant made a vigorous dash, and swooping his long arm around, he caught the shepherd by one stilt, and waving him around his head, shouted in triumph.

The prince and Lorilla, who had been watching this chase with great interest, cheered in return.

"Now we have an admiral," said the fairy, as the giant approached, proudly bearing the shepherd aloft. "Don't you think it would be well for you to get out your crown and scepter? He ought to understand, at once, that you are the king."

So Nassime took his crown and scepter from his bag, and putting the first on his head, held the other in his hand. He looked quite kingly when the giant came up, and set the shepherd down on his knees before him, with his stilts sticking out ever so far behind.

"I am glad to see you," said the prince, "and I herewith make you admiral of my royal navy."

"Admiral?" cried the poor frightened man. "I don't understand."

"Oh, it's all right," exclaimed the merry little Lorilla, as she slipped out of the prince's sash, and ran up to the shepherd. "We're going to have a splendid kingdom, and we're just getting together the head officers. I'm chief councilor, that giant is the general of the army, and we want you to command the navy. There'll be a salary,

after a while, and I know you'll like it."

When she went on to explain the whole matter to the shepherd, his fear left him, and he smiled. "I shall be very glad to be your admiral," he then said, to the prince, whereupon the giant lifted him up on his feet, or rather on to the stilts, which were strapped to his feet and ankles, and the affair was settled. The party now went on, the giant and man on stilts side by side, the prince on the giant's arm, and Lorilla in Nassime's sash.

"What other great officer must we have?" asked she of Nassime.

"The chief officer of the treasury, or chancellor of the exchequer. I see him now."

It was true. Along a road in a valley below them, a man was walking. Instantly all were excited. The giant and the man on stilts wished to run after the newcomer, but the prince forbade it, saying it would be better to approach him quietly.

The man, who halted when he saw them, proved to be a clam-digger, with his clam-rake over one shoulder, and a large basket in his hand. The prince did not waste many words with this person, who was a rather humble-minded man, but briefly explained the situation to him, and told him that he was now the chancellor of the exchequer, in charge of the treasury of the kingdom of Nassimia.

The man, remarking that he saw no objection to such a position, and that it might, in the end, be better than clamdigging, joined the prince's party, which again proceeded on its way.

That night, they all slept in a palmgrove, first making a supper of cocoa-nuts, which the giant and the admiral picked from the tops of the trees.

"Now, then," said Nassime, in the morning, "what we must have next is an aristocracy. Out of this upper class we can then fill the government offices."

"Very true," said the giant, "and we shall want an army. I do not feel altogether like a general, without some soldiers under me."

"And *I* must have a navy," said the admiral.

"And there must be common people," remarked the chancellor of the exchequer. "For we shall need some folks on whom I can levy taxes with which to carry on the government."

"You are all right," said Nassime, "and this is the way we will manage matters. All the people we meet to-day shall be the aristocrats of Nassimia; all we meet to-morrow shall form the army, and all we see the next day shall be taken to make up the navy. After that, we will collect common people, until we have enough."

"I can tell you now," said the admiral, "how to get a lot of aristocrats all together in a bunch. A mile ahead of where we now are is a school-house, and it is full of boys, with a gray-headed master. Those fellows ought to make excellent aristocrats."

"They will do very well," said Nassime, "and we will go quietly forward and capture them all."

When they reached the school-house, Nassime, with his crown on his head and his scepter in his hand, took his position at the front door, the giant crouched down by the back door, the chancellor stood by one window and the admiral tried to stand by the other, but his stilts were so long that he looked over the roof instead of into the window.

"Is not that a well near you?" said the little councilor Lorilla, who was perched on a vine, for safe-keeping. "Step into that, and you will, most likely, be just tall enough."

The admiral stepped into the well, which was close to the house, and found that he stood exactly high enough to command the window. When all were posted, Nassime opened his door, and stepping a short distance into the room, declared his title and position, and called upon them all to consider themselves members of the aristocracy of his kingdom. The moment he said this, the astonished and frightened boys sprang to their feet and made a rush for the back door, but when they threw it open, there squatted the giant, with a broad grin on his face, and his hands spread out before the door-way. They then turned and ran, some for one window and some for the other, but at one stood the treasurer, brandishing his clam-rake, and at the other the admiral, shaking his fists. There was no escape,—one or two, who tried to pass by Nassime, having been stopped by a tap on the head from his scepter,—and so the boys crowded together in the middle of the room, while some of the smaller ones began to cry. The master was too much startled and astonished to say a word.

Then came running into the room little Lorilla, and mounting to the top of the school-master's table, she addressed the school, telling them all about the new kingdom, and explaining what a jolly time they would have. It would be like a long holiday, and although their master would go with them, to teach them what they would have to know in their new positions, it would not be a bit like going to school.

As soon as the boys heard that they would not have to go to school, they agreed to the plan on the spot. Some of them even went out to talk to the giant. As to the master, he said that if his school was to be taken into the new kingdom he would go, too, for he had promised the parents that he would take care of their boys.

So, when all was settled, the whole school, headed by the master, made ready to follow Nassime and his officers. The giant pulled the admiral out of the well, much to the delight of the boys, and all started off in high good humor.

The company went into camp on the edge of a wood, quite early in the evening, because Lorilla said that boys ought not to

The general and the admiral led the procession

be up late. If it had not been for the luncheons which the boys had in their baskets, and which they cheerfully shared with their older companions, many of the party would have gone to sleep hungry that night. As for the giant, it is probable that he did go to sleep hungry, for it would

have taken the contents of all the baskets to have entirely satisfied his appetite.

Early the next morning, he aroused the party.

"Here are a few bushels of coco-nuts," he cried, emptying a great bag on the ground. "I gathered them before any of you were awake. Eat them quickly, for we must be off. To-day is my army day, and I want to get as many soldiers as I can."

As every one was very willing to please the giant, an early start was made, and, before very long, the party reached the edge of a desert. They journeyed over the sand nearly all day, but not a living being did they see. Late in the afternoon, a black man, on an ostrich, was seen coming from behind a hillock of sand, and immediately, with a great shout, the whole party set out in chase.

It is probable that the man on the bird would have soon got away from his pursuers, had not the ostrich persisted in running around in a great circle, while, with whoops and shouts, the giant and the rest succeeded in heading off the ostrich, which tumbled over, throwing his rider on the sand. The bird then ran off as fast as he could go, while the negro was seized by every aristocrat who could get near enough to lay hold of him. The giant now came up, and lifted the man from the midst of his young captors. "You need not be frightened," said he. "You are to belong to my army. That is all. I will treat you well."

"And not kill me?" whimpered the black man.

"Certainly not," said the giant. "I need soldiers too much to want to kill the only one I've got. Fall into line, behind me, and we'll march on and see if we cannot find you some comrades."

But by night-fall the giant's army still consisted of one black man. The party encamped in an oasis, where grew a number of date-palms, the fruit of which afforded a plentiful supper for everybody. The giant had not much appetite, and he looked solemn while gazing at his army, as it sat cross-legged on the ground, eating dates.

The next morning, the admiral earnestly petitioned that they should try to get out of the desert as soon as possible. "For," said he, "I have a dreadful time in this sand with my stilts, and I really need more men in my navy than the giant has in his army. Besides, the best kind of sailors can never be found in a dry desert like this."

As no one could object to this reasoning, they set forth, turning to the east, and, before noon, they saw before them fields and vegetation, and shortly afterward they came to a broad river. Journeying down the bank of this for a mile or two, they perceived, lying at anchor in the stream, a good-sized vessel, with a tall mast, and a great sail hauled down on the deck.

"Hurrah!" shouted the admiral, the moment he set his eyes upon this prize, and away he went for it, as fast as his stilts would carry him. When he reached the water, he waded right in, and was soon standing looking over the vessel's side.

He did not get on board, but, after standing for some time talking to a person inside, he waded back to the shore, where his companions were anxiously waiting to hear what he had discovered.

"There are not many persons on board," he said, rather ruefully. "Only an old woman and a girl. One is the cook and the other washes bottles. There were a good many men on the ship, but the old woman says that they all went away yesterday, carrying with them a vast number of packages. She thinks they were a lot of thieves, and that they have gone off with their booty and have deserted the vessel. She and the girl were simply hired as servants, and knew nothing about the crew. It isn't exactly the kind of navy I wanted, but it

will do, and we may see some men before night."

It was unanimously agreed that the government of Nassimia should take possession of this deserted vessel, and the giant soon managed to pull her to shore, anchor and all. Everybody excepting the giant went on board, Nassime and Lorilla going first, then the government officers, the aristocracy, and the army. The admiral stood on his stilts, with his head up in the rigging, and the ship was formally placed under his command. When all was ready, the

The Kingdom of Nassimia afloat

giant ran the ship out into the stream, wading in up to his middle; and then he very carefully clambered on board. The vessel rocked a good deal as he got in, but it could carry him as long as he kept quiet.

"As my navy is not large enough, just now, to work the ship," said the admiral to Nassime, "and, also, as it doesn't know anything about such work, I shall have to have the help of the aristocracy, and also to ask the general to lend me his army."

"All right," said the giant, "you can have him."

A number of the larger boys, assisted by the negro, now went to work and hoisted the sail. Then the army was sent to the helm, the vessel was put before the wind, and the kingdom of Nassimia began to sail away.

There was a large quantity of provisions on board, enough to last many days, and everybody ate heartily. But not a person was seen that day on either bank of the river.

They anchored at night, and the next morning, setting sail again, they soon entered a broad sea or lake. They sailed on, with the wind behind them, and everybody enjoyed the trip. The admiral sat on the stern, with his stilts dangling behind in the water, as the ship sailed on, and was very happy.

"Now," said the chancellor of the exchequer, as the officers of the government were talking together on deck, "all we want is some common people, and then we can begin the kingdom in real earnest."

"We must have some houses and streets," said Nassime, "and a palace. All those will be necessary before we can settle down as a kingdom."

They sailed all night, and the next day they saw land before them. And, slowly moving near the shore, they perceived a long caravan.

"Hi!" shouted the chancellor of the exchequer, "there are the common people!"

Everybody was now very much excited, and everybody wanted to go ashore, but this Nassime would not permit. Capturing a caravan would be a very different thing from capturing a negro on an ostrich, and the matter must be undertaken with caution and prudence. So, ordering the ship brought near the shore, he made ready to land, accompanied only by the giant and Lorilla.

The giant had found a spare mast on the vessel, and he had trimmed and whittled it into a convenient club. This he took under one arm, and, with Nassime on the other, wearing his crown and carrying Lorilla in his sash, the giant waded ashore, and stopped a short distance in front of the approaching caravan.

Nassime, having been set on the ground, advanced to the leader of the caravan, and, drawing his sword, called upon him to halt. Instantly the procession stopped, and the leader, dismounting from his horse, approached Nassime, and bowed low before him, offering to pay tribute if necessary.

"We will not speak of tribute," said Nassime, "at least, not now. What I wish, is to know who you all are, and where you are going."

"That is easily answered," said the other, giving a glance upward at the giant, who stood leaning on his club, behind Nassime; "we are a company of men of high degree; philosophers and rich merchants, who have joined together to visit foreign lands, to enjoy ourselves and improve our minds. We have brought with us our families, our slaves, and our flocks and other possessions. We wish to offend no one, and if you object to our passing through your dominions——"

"I do not object," said Nassime, "I am very glad you came this way. These are not my dominions. I am king of Nassimia."

"And where is that, your majesty?"

"It is not anywhere in particular, just now," said Nassime, "but we shall soon fix upon a spot where its boundaries will be established. It is a new kingdom, and only needed a body of com—"

"Say populace," whispered Lorilla, from his sash, "the other might offend him."

"And only needed a populace," continued Nassime, "to make it complete. I am the king—of royal blood and education. I have ministers of state and finance; an admiral and a navy; a general of the army, whom you see here," pointing to the giant, "and an aristocracy, which is at present on board of that ship. I have been looking for a populace, and am very glad to have met you. You and your companions are now my people."

"What, your majesty?" cried the astonished leader of the caravan. "I do not comprehend."

Nassime then explained the plan and purpose of his kingdom, and assured the other that he and his countrymen could nowhere be more happy than in the kingdom of Nassimia, where every opportunity of enjoyment and the improvement of the mind would be offered to the people.

The leader, on hearing this, begged permission to consult with his fellow-travelers. Some advised one thing and some another, but the sight of the giant, who every now and then playfully struck the earth with the end of his club in such a way as to make the ground tremble, hastened their decision.

"If we were poor men," said one of the philosophers, "and had no treasures with us, we might scatter in various directions, and many of us might escape. That giant could not kill us all. But we are too rich for that. We cannot run away from our great possessions. We must submit in peace."

So it was settled that they should submit to the king of Nassimia and become his people, and the leader carried the decision to Nassime.

The chancellor of the exchequer now became very anxious to go on shore. He had cast off his clam-digger's clothes, and wore a magnificent suit which he had found in the ship, and which had belonged to the robber captain. He stood on the deck and made signs for the giant to come for him. So the giant was sent for him, and soon returned, bringing also the army, which the chancellor had borrowed of him for a time. This officer, as soon as he had landed, approached Nassime and said:

"These, then, are the common people.

I suppose I might as well go to work and collect taxes."

"You need not hurry about that," said Nassime.

"They will never believe in your government until you do it," urged the chancellor, and so Nassime allowed him to do as he wished, only telling him not to levy his taxes too heavily.

Then the chancellor, with the negro behind him, carrying his old clam-basket, over which a cloth had been thrown, went through the caravan and collected taxes enough in gold and silver to fill his basket. He also collected a horse for himself and one for Nassime. "Now," said he, "we have the foundation of a treasury, and the thing begins to look like a kingdom."

Everything being now satisfactorily arranged, the company began to move on. The giant, with his army at his heels, and his club over his shoulder, marched first. Then rode Nassime with Lorilla, then the chancellor, with his basket of treasure before him on his horse, and after him the caravan. The ship sailed along a short distance from the shore.

In the evening, the land party encamped near the shore, and the vessel came to anchor, the giant shouting to the admiral Nassime's commands. The chancellor wished to make another collection of taxes after supper, but this Nassime forbade.

Lorilla then had a long talk with Nassime, apart from the company, assuring him that what was needed next was the royal city.

"Yes, indeed," said Nassime, "and we are not likely to meet with that as we have met with everything else. We must build a city, I suppose."

"No," said Lorilla, gayly. "We can do much better. Do you see that heavy forest on the hills back of us? Well, in that forest is the great capital city of my people, the fairies. We are scattered in colonies all over the country, but there is our court and our queen. And it is the fairies who can help you to get a royal city. This very evening I will go and see what can be done."

So, that evening, Nassime took Lorilla to the edge of the forest, and while she ran swiftly into its depths, he lay down and slept. Early the next morning, while the stars were still shining, she returned and awoke him, and while they were going to the camp she told him her news.

"Our queen," she said, "will have a city built for you, all complete, with everything that a city needs; but before she will have this done, she commands that someone in your party shall be changed into a fairy, to take my place! This must be a grown person who consents to the exchange, as I have agreed to be your chief councilor of state. And it must be someone whose mind has never been occupied with human affairs."

"I don't believe you will find any such person among us," said Nassime, ruefully.

But Lorilla clapped her hands and cried merrily:

"Ah, yes! The bottle-washer! I believe she is the very person."

Nassime was cheered by this idea, and as soon as they reached the shore, he asked the giant to carry him and Lorilla to the ship. Early as it was, they found the young girl sitting on the deck, quietly washing bottles. She had lost her parents when an infant, and had never had any one to care for. She had passed her life, since she was a very small child, in washing bottles, and as this employment does not require any mental labor, she had never concerned herself about anything.

"She will do," exclaimed Lorilla, when she had found out all this. "I don't believe her mind was ever occupied at all. It is perfectly fresh for her to begin as a fairy."

When the girl was asked if she would be a fairy, she readily consented, for it made no difference to her what she was, and when the admiral was asked if he would give her up, he said: "Oh, yes! To be sure, it will reduce my navy to one person, but, even then, it will be as large as the army. You may take her, and welcome." The bottle-washer therefore was taken to the shore, and Nassime conducted her to the woods with Lorilla. There he left them, promising to return at sunset.

"You must be careful of one thing," said Lorilla to him, before he left, "and that is, not to let those aristocrats come on shore. If they once get among the populace, they will begin to lord it over them in a way that will raise a dreadful commotion."

Nassime promised to attend to this, and when he went back he sent orders to the admiral, on no account to allow any aristocrat to come on shore. This order caused great discontent on the vessel. The boys couldn't see why they alone should be shut up in the ship. They had expected to have lots of fun when the common people were found.

It was, therefore, with great difficulty that they were restrained from jumping overboard and swimming ashore in a body. The master had been made an ancient noble, but his authority was of little avail, and the poor admiral had his hands full. Indeed, he would have been in despair, had it not been for the gallant conduct of his navy. That brave woman seized a broom, and marching around the deck, kept watchful guard. Whenever she saw a boy attempting to climb over the side of the vessel, she brought down the broom with a whack upon him, and tumbled him back on the deck. In the afternoon, however, the giant came to the vessel with a double arm-load of rich fruit, cakes, pastry and confectionery, an offering from the common people, which so delighted the aristocrats that there was peace on board for the rest of the day.

At sunset, Nassime went to the woods and met Lorilla, who was waiting for him.

"It's all right!" she cried; "the bottle-washer is to be magically dwindled down to-night. And when everybody is asleep, the fairies will come here and will see how many people there are and what they are like, and they will build a city just to suit. It will be done to-morrow."

Nassime could scarcely believe all this, but there was nothing to be done but to wait and see. That night, everybody went to sleep quite early. And if the fairies came and measured them for a city, they did not know it.

In the morning, Nassime arose, and walked down toward the shore. As he did so, a lady came out of a tent and approached him. He thought he knew her features, but he could not remember who she was. But when she spoke, he started back and cried out: "Lorilla!"

"Yes," said the lady, laughing, "it is Lorilla. The king of Nassimia ought to have a chief councilor of state who is somewhat longer than his finger, and last night, as the girl who took my place dwindled down to the size of a fairy, I grew larger and larger, until I became as large as she used to be. Do you like the change?"

Lorilla was beautiful. She was richly dressed, and her lovely face was as merry and gay as ever.

Nassime approached her and took her hand.

"The chief councilor of my kingdom shall be its queen," he said, and calling a priest from the populace, the two were married on the spot.

Great were the rejoicings on land and water; but there was no delay in getting ready to march to the royal city, the domes and spires of which Lorilla pointed out to them behind some lovely groves.

Nassime was about to signal for the ship to come to shore, but Lorilla checked him.

"I'm really sorry for those poor aristo-crats, but it will never do to take them to the royal city. They are not needed, and they would make all sorts of trouble. There is nothing to be done but to let the admiral sail away with them, and keep on sailing until they are grown up. Then they will come back, fit to be members of the nobility. They will have their master with them, and you can put three or four philosophers on board, and they can be as well educated, traveling about in this way, as if they were going to school."

Nassime felt sorry for the aristocrats, but he saw that this was good advice, and he took it. A quantity of provisions and four philosophers were sent on board the ship, and the admiral was ordered to sail away until the boys grew up. As he liked nothing better than sailing, this suited the admiral exactly; and after having a few sheep sent on board, with which to amuse himself during calms, he hoisted sail, and was soon far away.

The rest of the kingdom marched on, and in good time reached the royal city. There it stood, with its houses, streets, shops, and everything that a city should have. The royal palace glittered in the center, and upon a hill there stood a splendid castle for the giant!

Everybody hurried forward. The name of the owner was on every house, and every house was fully furnished, so in a few minutes the whole city was at home.

The king, leading his queen up the steps of his royal palace, paused at the door:

"All this," he said, "I owe to you. From the very beginning, you have given me nothing but good advice."

"But that is not the best of it," she said, laughing. "You always took it."

The vessel carrying the aristocrats sailed away and away, with the admiral sitting on the stern, his stilts dangling in the water behind, as the ship moved on.

HOW THE ARISTOCRATS SAILED AWAY

by Frank R. Stockton

For many and many a day, the ship of the admiral of the kingdom of Nassimia, containing the admiral himself, the company of school-boys who had been made aristocrats, the old school-master, the four philosophers, and the old woman, who was cook and navy all in one, sailed and sailed away.

The admiral sat on the stern, his long stilts dangling in the water behind, as the ship sailed on. He was happy, for this was just what he liked; and the four philosophers and the old master and the navy were happy; but the aristocrats gradually became very discontented. They did not want to sail so much; they wanted to go somewhere, and see something. The ship had stopped several times at towns on the coast, and the boys had gone on shore, but, in every case, the leading people of the town had come to the admiral, bearing rich presents, and begging him to sail away in the night. So it happened that the lively young aristocrats had been on land very little since they started on their travels.

Finding, at last, that the admiral had no intention of landing again, the aristocrats determined to rebel, and, under the leadership of the Tail-boy, who was the poorest scholar among them but first in all mischief, they formed a plan to take possession of the ship.

Accordingly, one fine afternoon, as the admiral, the master, and the four philosophers were sitting on the deck of the vessel, enjoying the breeze, six aristocrats, each carrying a bag, slipped quietly up behind them, and, in an instant, a bag was clapped over the head of each man. It was in vain to kick and struggle. The other aristocrats rushed up, the bags were tied securely around the necks of the victims, their hands and feet were bound, and they were seated in a row at the stern of the ship, the admiral's stilts lying along the deck. The Tail-boy then took a pair of scissors and cut a hole in each bag, opposite the mouth of its wearer, so that he could breathe. The six unfortunate men were now informed that if they behaved well they should be treated well, and that, on the next day, a hole should be cut in each of their bags, so that they could see with one eye; on the next day, a hole for one ear; on the next, a hole for the nose; and if they still behaved well, holes should be cut on the two succeeding days for the other ears and eyes. The smartest boy of the school had said, when this arrangement was proposed, that by the time they got this far they might as well take off the bags, but the rest of the aristocrats did not think so; a prisoner whose head was even partly bagged was more secure than one not bagged at all.

The admiral and his companions could think of nothing to do but to agree to these terms, and so they agreed, hoping that, by some happy chance, they would soon be released. It was suggested by a few aristocrats that it would be well to bring up the navy and bag her head also, but the majority decided that she was needed to do the cooking, and so she was shut down below, and ordered to cook away as hard as she could.

The prisoners were plentifully fed, at meal-times, by their captors, who put the food through the mouth-holes of their bags. At first, the aristocrats found this to be such fun that the poor men could scarcely prevent themselves from being overfed. At night, cushions were brought for them to lie upon, and a rope was fastened to the ends of the admiral's stilts, which were hoisted up into the rigging, so as to be out of the way.

The aristocrats now did just as they pleased. They steered in the direction in which they supposed the coast should lie, and, as they were sailing on, they gave themselves up to all manner of amusements. Among other things, they found a number of pots of paints stowed away in the vessel's hold, and with these they set to work to decorate the vessel.

They painted the masts crimson, the sails in stripes of pink and blue, the deck light green, spotted with yellow stars; and nearly everything on board shone in some lively color. The admiral's sheep were adorned with bands of green, yellow, and crimson, and his stilts were painted bright blue, with a corkscrew red line running around them. Indeed, the smell of paint soon became so strong, that three of the philosophers requested that the nose-holes in their bags should be sewed up.

There is no knowing what other strange things these aristocrats would have done, had they not, on the fourth day of their rule on the vessel, perceived they were in sight of land, and of what seemed to be a large city on the coast. Instantly the vessel was steered straight for the city, which

they soon reached. The ship was made fast, and every aristocrat went on shore. The cook was locked below, and the admiral and his companions were told to sit still and be good until the boys should return.

Each of the prisoners now had holes in his bag for his mouth, his nose, one eye, and an ear, but as the eye-holes were all on the side toward the water, the poor men could not see much that was going on. They twisted themselves around, however, as well as they could, and so got an occasional glimpse of the shore.

The aristocrats swarmed up into the city, but although it was nearly midday, not a living soul did they meet. The buildings were large and handsome, and the streets were wide and well laid out; there were temples and palaces and splendid edifices of various kinds, but every door and shutter and gate of every house was closely shut, and not a person could be seen, nor a sound heard.

The silence and loneliness of the place quieted the spirits of the aristocrats, and they now walked slowly and kept together.

"What does it all mean?" said one. "Is the place bewitched, or has everybody gone out of town and taken along the dogs, and the birds, and the flies, and every living thing?"

"We might go back after one of the philosophers," said another. "He could tell us all about it."

"I don't believe he'd know any more than we do," said the Tail-boy, who had now forced his way to the front. "Let us go ahead, and find out for ourselves."

So they walked on until they came to a splendid edifice, which looked like a palace, and, much to their surprise, the great doors stood wide open. After a little hesitation, they went up the steps and peeped in. Seeing no one, they cautiously entered. Everything was grand and gorgeous within, and they gradually penetrated to a large hall, at one end of which they saw a wide stair-way, carpeted with the richest tapestry.

Reaching this, they concluded to go up and see what they could find upstairs. But as no one wished to be the first in such a bold proceeding, they went in a solid body. The stair-way was very wide, so that twelve boys could go up, abreast, and they thus filled three of the stairs, with several little boys on the next stair below.

On they went, up, up, and up, keeping step together. There was a landing above them, but it seemed to be farther up than they had supposed. Some of the little aristocrats complained of being tired; but as they did not wish to be left behind, they kept on.

"Look here," said one of the front row; "do you see that window up there? Well, we're not any nearer to it now than we were when we started."

"That's true," said another, and then the Smart-boy spoke up:

"I'll tell you what it is. We're not going up at all. These stairs are turning around and around, as we step on them. It's a kind of a tread-mill!"

"Let's stop!" cried some of the boys; but others exclaimed, "Oh, no! Don't do that, or we shall be ground up!"

"Oh, please don't stop!" cried the little fellows below, forgetting their tired legs, "or we shall be ground up first."

So on they kept, stepping up and up, but never advancing, while some of them tried to devise some plan by which they all could turn around and jump off at the same instant. But this would be difficult and dangerous, and those little fellows would certainly be crushed by the others if they were not ground up by the stairs.

Around and around went the stairs, each step disappearing under the floor beneath, and appearing again above them; while the boys stepped up and up, wondering if the thing would ever stop. They were silent now, and they could hear a steady click, click, click, as the great stair-way went slowly around.

"Oh, I'll tell you!" suddenly exclaimed the Smart-boy. "We're winding it up!"

"Winding up what?" cried several of the others.

"Everything!" said the Smart-boy; "we're winding up the city!"

This was true. Directly, sounds were heard outside; a dog barked; some cocks crew, and windows and doors were heard to open. The boys trembled, and forgot their weariness, as they stepped up and up. Some voices were heard below, and then, with a sudden jar, the stairs stopped.

"She's wound!" said the Smart-boy, under his breath, and every aristocrat turned around and hurried off the stairs.

What a change had taken place in everything! From without, came the noise and bustle of a great city, and, within, doors were opening, curtains were being pulled aside, and people were running here, there, and everywhere. The boys huddled together in a corner of the hall. Nobody seemed to notice them.

Suddenly, a great gilded door, directly opposite to them, was thrown wide open, and a king and queen came forth. The king glanced around, eagerly.

"Hello!" he cried, as his eyes fell upon the cluster of frightened aristocrats. "I believe it is those boys! Look here," said he, advancing, "did you boys wind us up?"

"Yes, sir," said the Head-boy, "I think we did. But we didn't mean to. If you'd let us off this time, we'd never——"

"Let you off!" cried the king. "Not until we've made you the happiest boys on earth! Do you suppose we're angry? Never such a mistake! What do you think of that?" he said, turning to the queen.

This royal lady, who was very fat, made no answer, but smiled, good-humoredly.

"You're our greatest benefactors," continued the king. "I don't know what we can do for you. You didn't imagine, perhaps, that you were winding us up. Few people, besides ourselves, know how things are with us. This city goes all right for ten years, and then it runs down, and has to be wound up. When we feel we have nearly run down, we go into our houses and apartments, and shut up everything tight and strong. Only this hall is left open, so that somebody can come in, and wind us up. It takes a good many people to do it, and I'm glad there were so many of you. Once we were wound up by a lot of bears, who wandered in and tried to go upstairs. But they didn't half do it, and we only ran four years. The city has been still —like a clock with its works stopped—for as long as a hundred years at once. I don't know how long it was this time. I'm going to get here?"

The boys then told how they had come in a ship, with the admiral, their master, and four philosophers.

"And the ship is here!" cried the king. "Run!" he shouted to his attendants, "and bring hither those worthy men, that they may share in the honor and rewards of their pupils."

While the attendants were gone, the aristocrats waited in the hall, and the king went away to attend to other matters. The queen sat down on a sofa near by.

"It tires me dreadfully to smile," she said, as she wiped her brow; "but I have to take some exercise."

"I hope they won't bring 'em here, bags and all," whispered the Tail-boy. "It would look funny, but I shouldn't like it."

In a short time the king came back in a hurry.

"How's this?" he cried. "My messengers tell me that there's no ship at our piers excepting our own vessels. Have you deceived me?"

The aristocrats gazed at each other in dismay. Had their ship sailed away and left them? If so, they had only been served aright. They looked so downcast and guilty that the king knew something was wrong.

"What have you done?" said he.

The Head-boy saw that there was no help for it, and he told all.

The king looked sad, but the queen smiled two or three times.

"And you put their heads in bags?" said the king.

"Yes, sir," replied the Head-boy.

"Well, well!" said the king; "I am sorry. After all you have done for us, too. I will send out a swift cruiser after that ship, which will be easy to find if it is painted as you say, and, until it is brought back to the city, I must keep you in custody. Look you," said he to his attendants; "take these young people to a luxurious apartment, and see that they are well fed and cared for, and also be very careful that none of them escape."

Thereupon the aristocrats were taken away to an inner chamber of the palace.

When the admiral and his companions had been left on board the vessel, they felt very uneasy, for they did not know what might happen to them next. In a short time, however, when the voices of the aristocrats had died away as they proceeded into the city, the admiral perceived the point of a gimlet coming up through the deck, close to him. Then the gimlet was withdrawn, and these words came up through the hole:

"Have no fear. Your navy will stand by you!"

"It will be all right," said the admiral to the others. "I can depend upon her."

And now was heard a noise of banging and chopping, and soon the cook cut her way from her imprisonment below, and made her appearance on deck. She went to work vigorously, and, taking the bags from the prisoners' heads, unbound them, and set them at liberty. Then she gave them a piece of advice.

"The thing for us to do," said she, "is to get away from here as fast as we can. If those young rascals come back, there's no knowin' what they'll do."

"Do you mean," said the master, "that we should sail away and desert my scholars? Who can tell what might happen to them, left here by themselves?"

"We should not consider what might happen to them if they were left," said one of the philosophers, "but what might happen to us if they were not left. We must away."

"Certainly!" cried the admiral. "While I have the soul of the commander of the navy of Nassimia left within me, I will not stay here to have my head put in a bag! Never! Set sail!"

It was not easy to set sail, for the cook and the philosophers were not very good at that sort of work; but they got the sail up at last, and cast loose from shore, first landing the old master, who positively refused to desert his scholars. The admiral took the helm, and, the wind being fair, the ship sailed away.

The swift cruiser, which was sent in the direction taken by the admiral's vessel, passed her in the night, and as she was a very fast cruiser, and it was therefore impossible for the admiral's ship to catch up with her, the two vessels never met.

"Now, then," said the admiral the next day, as he sat with the helm in his hand,

"we are free again to sail where we please. But I do not like to sail without an object. What shall be our object?"

The philosophers immediately declared that nothing could be more proper than that they should take a voyage to make some great scientific discovery.

"All right," said the admiral. "That suits me. What discovery shall we make?"

The philosophers were not prepared to answer this question at that moment, but they said they would try to think of some good discovery to make.

So the philosophers sat in a row behind the admiral, and thought and thought; and the admiral sat at the helm, with his blue-and-red stilts dangling in the water behind; and the cook prepared the meals, swept the deck, dusted the sail, and put things in order.

After several hours, the admiral turned around to ask the philosophers if they had thought of any discovery yet, when, to his amazement, he saw that each one of them had put his bag upon his head.

"What did you do that for?" cried the admiral, and each of the philosophers gave a little jump; and then they explained that it was much easier to think with one's head in a bag. The outer world was thus shut out, and trains of thought were not so likely to be broken up.

So, for day after day, the philosophers, with their heads in their bags, sat, and thought, and thought; and the admiral sat and steered, and the navy cooked and dusted and kept things clean. Sometimes, when she thought the sail did not catch the wind properly, she would move the admiral toward one side or the other, and thus change the course of the vessel.

"If I knew," said the admiral one day, "the exact age of the youngest of those aristocrats, I should know just how long we should have to sail, before they would all be grown up; when it would be time for us to go back after them, and take them to Nassimia."

The cook remembered that the smallest boy had told her he was ten years old.

"Then," said the admiral, "we must sail for eleven years."

And they sailed for eleven years; the philosophers, with their heads in their bags, trying their best to think of some good thing to discover.

The day after the aristocrats had been shut up in their luxurious apartment, the queen sent a messenger to them, to tell them that she thought the idea of putting people's heads in bags was one of the most amusing things she ever heard of, and that she would be much obliged if they would send her the pattern of the proper kind of bag, so that she could have some made for her slaves.

The messenger brought scissors, and papers, and pins, and the boys cut a pattern of a very comfortable bag, with holes for the eyes, nose, mouth, and ears, which they sent with their respects to the queen. This royal lady had two bags made, which she put upon two of her servants, and their appearance amused her so much that she smiled a great deal, and yet scarcely felt tired at all.

But, in the course of a day or two, the king happened to see these bag-headed slaves sitting in an ante-chamber. He was struck with consternation, and instantly called a council of his chief ministers.

"We are threatened with a terrible danger," he said to them, when all the doors were shut. "We have among us a body of Bagists! Little did we think, in our gratitude, that we were wound up merely that we might go through life with our heads bagged! Better far that we should stay stopped forever! How can we know but that the ship which brought them here may soon return, with a cargo of bag stuffs, needles, thread, and thimbles, and

that every head in our city may be bagged in a few days? Already, signs of this approaching evil have shown themselves. Notwithstanding the fact that these dangerous characters have been closely confined, no less than two of the inmates of my palace have already had their heads bagged!"

At these words, a thrill of horror pervaded the ministers, and they discussed the matter for a long time. It was finally decided that a lookout should be constantly kept on the top of a high tower, to give notice of the approach of the ship, should she return; additional guards were posted at the door of the aristocrats' apartment, and it was ordered that the city be searched every day, to see if any new cases of bagism could be discovered.

The aristocrats now began to be very discontented. Although they had everything they could possibly want to eat and drink, and were even furnished with toys and other sources of amusement, they did not like to be shut up.

"I'll tell you what it is," said the Tail-boy. "I can't stand this any longer. Let's get away."

"But where shall we get away to?" asked several of the others.

"We'll see about that when we're outside," was the answer. "Anything's better than being shut up here."

After some talk, everybody agreed that they ought to try to escape, and they set about to devise some plan for doing so. The windows were not very high from the ground, but they were too high for a jump, and not a thing could be found in the room which was strong enough to make a rope. Every piece of silk or muslin in the curtains or bed-clothes was fine, and delicate, and flimsy. At last, the Smart-boy hit upon a plan. The apartment was a very long one, and was floored with narrow boards, of costly wood, which ran from one end to the other of it. He proposed that they should take up one of these boards, and, putting it out of the window, should rest one end on the ground, and the other on the window-sill. Then they could slide down.

Instantly, every aristocrat set to work, with knife, or piece of tin, or small coin, to take out the silver screws which held down one of the boards.

"It is very narrow," said the Head-boy. "I am afraid we shall slip off."

"Oh, there is no danger of that," replied the Smart-boy. "If we only go fast enough, we cannot slip off. We will grease the board, and then we shall go fast enough."

So the board was taken up, and, after having been well greased with oil from the lamps, was put out of the window.

Then the boys, one at a time, got on the board and slid, with the speed of lightning, to the ground. Most of them came down with such rapidity and force that they shot over the smooth grass to a considerable distance. As soon as they were all down, the Smart-boy took the end of the board, and moved it to one side, so that it rested on the edge of a deep tank.

"Now, then," said he, "if any of the guards slide down after us, they will go into the tank."

It was now nearly dark, and the boys set about finding some place where they could spend the night. They soon came to a large building, the doors of which were shut, but, as they were not locked, they had no trouble in entering. This building was a public library, which was closed very early every afternoon, and opened very late every morning. Here the aristocrats found very comfortable quarters, and having lighted a candle which one of them had in his pockets, they held a meeting, to determine what they should do next.

"Of course the ship will come back, some

day," said the Smart-boy, "for that admiral would be afraid to go home without us. The giant would smash him and his old ship if he did that. So we shall have to wait here until the ship comes."

"But how are we going to live?" asked several of his companions.

"We can sleep here," he answered. "It's a nice, big place, and nobody will ever disturb us, for a notice on the door says it's closed two hours before sunset. And as to victuals, we shall have to work at something."

This was thought good reasoning, and they now began to consider what they should work at. It was agreed that it would be wise for them all to select the same trade, because then they could stand by each other in case of any business disputes, and their trade was to be chosen in this way: Every boy was to write on a piece of paper the business he liked best, and whatever trade or profession was written on the most papers, was to be adopted by the whole company.

When the papers were read by the Head-boy, it was found that nearly every one had selected a different calling; but three of the smaller boys happened to want to be letter-carriers, and so, as there was no business which had so many votes as this, it was determined that they should all be letter-carriers.

The three little boys shouted for joy at this.

"But where shall we get letters to carry?" asked some of the older fellows.

"Oh, we'll see about that in the morning," said the Smart-boy. "There'll be plenty of time before the library opens."

They slept that night on piles of parchments, and in the morning the building was searched to see if any letters could be found for them to carry. In the cellar they discovered a great many huge boxes, filled with manuscripts which had been collecting ever since the city was first wound up and started. These, they concluded, would do just as well as letters, and each boy filled his satchel with them, and started off to deliver them.

Each carrier was assigned by the Head-boy to a different street, and all went to work with a will. The people were glad

"in trying to escape, have all slid into the tank. Let it be walled over, and that will be the end of it. We are fortunate to get rid of them so easily."

But the watch on the high tower was still kept up, for no one knew when the ship might come back with more Bagists.

One day, as the Head-boy was deliver-

The aristocrats winding up the city

to get the manuscripts, for many of them were very instructive and interesting, and they gave the boys a small piece of money for each one. This went on, day after day, and every morning each person in the whole city got a letter.

When the king was informed of the escape of his prisoners, he hurried, in great trouble, to see how they had got away. But when he saw the board which they had left resting on the edge of the tank, he was delighted.

"Those wretched Bagists," he exclaimed,

ing his letters, he met an old man, whom he instantly recognized as his master. At first, he felt like running away; but when the master told him that he was alone, and forgave everything, they embraced in tears. The old man had not been able to find his boys in the town, and had wandered into the surrounding country. In this way, he had never had a letter.

The Head-boy took him to the library that night, and he afterward spent most of his time reading the old manuscripts, and sorting them out for the carriers. Nobody ever came into the cellar to disturb him.

The people of the city were very much benefited by the instructive papers which were brought to them every day, and many of them became quite learned. The aristocrats also learned a great deal by reading the papers to those persons who could not read themselves, and, every evening, the master gave them lessons in the library. So they gradually became more and more educated.

They often looked up to the high tower, because they had heard that a flag was to be hoisted there whenever a ship with a pink and blue sail was seen approaching the city.

Ten years passed, and they saw no flag, but one day they saw, posted up all over the city, a notice from the king, stating that, on the next day, the city would run down, and ordering all the people to retire into their houses, and to shut up their doors and windows. This struck the aristocrats with dismay, for how were they to get a living if they could not deliver their letters?

So they all boldly marched to the palace, and, asking for the king, proposed to him that they should be allowed to wind up his city.

The king gazed upon them in amazement. "What!" he cried. "Do you letter-carriers venture to come to me with such a bold request? Do you think for a moment that you know anything about what you propose doing?"

"We can do it a great deal easier than we did it before," said one of the younger aristocrats, "for some of us were very small then, and didn't weigh much."

"Did it before?" exclaimed the bewildered king, staring at the sturdy group before him.

The Head-boy, who was by this time entirely grown up, now came forward, and,

acknowledging that he and his companions were the boys who had been shut up in the luxurious apartment, told their whole story since their escape.

"And you have lived among us all this time, and have not tried to bag our heads?" said the king.

"Not a bit of it," replied the other.

"I am very glad, indeed, to hear this," said the king, "and now, if you please, I would like you to try if you really can wind us up, for I feel that I am running down very fast."

At this, the whole body of aristocrats ran to the great stair-way, and began quickly to mount the steps. Around and around went the revolving stair-way, twice as fast as it had ever gone before. Click! click! click! went the machinery, and before anybody could really imagine that the thing was true, the stair-way stopped with a bump, and the city was wound up for another ten years!

It would be useless to try to describe the joy and gratitude of the king and the people. The aristocrats were loaded with honors and presents; they and their old master were sumptuously lodged in the palace, and, in their honor, the public library was ordered to be kept open every evening, in order that the people who were busy in the day-time might go there and read the papers, which were no longer carried to them.

At the end of a year, a flag was raised on the top of the high tower, and the admiral's ship came in. The philosophers took off their bags, which were now very old and thin, and the aristocrats, with their master, were warmly welcomed on board. Being all grown up, they were no longer feared. In a few days, the ship sailed for Nassimia, and, as the aristocrats were taking leave of the sorrowing citizens, the Smart-boy stepped up to the king, and said:

"I'll tell you what I should do, if I were you. About a week before the time you expect to run down again, I'd make a lot of men go to work and wind up the city. You can do it yourselves, just as well as to wait for other people to do it for you."

"That's exactly what I'll do!" cried the king. "I never thought of it before!"

He did it, and, so far as is known, the city is running yet.

When the aristocrats reached the city of Nassimia, everybody was glad to see them, for they had become a fine, well-behaved, and well-educated body of nobility, and the admiral, standing high upon his stilts, looked down upon them with honest pride, as he presented them to the king and queen.

Lorilla shook each one of them by the hand. They did not recognize the little fairy in this handsome woman, but when she explained how the change had taken place, they were delighted.

"To think of it!" cried one of the younger aristocrats. "We never missed that bottle-washer!"

"No," said Lorilla; "nobody ever missed her. That is one reason why she was such a good one to be made a fairy. And now you must tell us your whole story."

And so the king and the queen, the giant and his army, the chancellor of the exchequer, and as many of the populace as could get near enough, crowded around to hear the story of the adventures of the aristocrats, which the Head-boy told very well.

"I should like very much to go to that curious city," said Lorilla, "especially at a time when it had run down, and everything had stopped."

"Oh, I don't believe it will ever stop any more," cried the Tail-boy. "We told them how to keep themselves agoing all the time."

THE MAN WHO MADE INSECTS FAMOUS

by Louise Seymour Hasbrouck

Jean Henri Fabre

A LITTLE boy stood in the sunlight in front of a poor farmer's hut on a desolate, wolf-haunted moor in France. His soiled, coarse frock flapped about his bare ankles; his grimy handkerchief, all too frequently lost, had been tied to his waist by a string. One would never have taken him for a scientist. But he was! He was conducting an important experiment.

It had occurred to him to wonder whether he enjoyed the sunlight with his mouth or his eyes! He set about finding out. First, he shut his eyes and opened his mouth. No sunlight! Then he shut his mouth and opened his eyes. The sunlight was there! He repeated each process, with the same result. He had proved, then, by deduction, in the scientific manner, that he saw the sunlight with his eyes. What a discovery! That evening at supper he told the family all about it. Strange to say, they laughed at the "little simpleton," all except the fond grandmother, who was sure her grandchild was a prodigy.

A few days, or perhaps a few months, later, the same little boy heard one evening a faint "jingling" sound from some bushes. What caused it? He must know. But the bushes were very awe-inspiring in the darkness. Wolves had been known to lurk in them before now. All the same, the boy stationed himself behind some tall grass and waited. The evening passed, with no result. The next evening he was there again, and this time he was more fortunate. *Whoosh!* The singer jumped out and was promptly caught in a chubby hand. It was a grasshopper. But this particular child was not nearly so much interested in the fact that the grasshopper was a wonderful jumper, as in the discovery that a grasshopper made that kind of a song. This time, though, he did not tell the family. He did not wish to be laughed at again.

The little boy's name was Jean Henri Fabre, and he was to become one of the greatest entomologists—perhaps *the* greatest—the world has ever known. Some one at this point may say, "Oh, if he was one of those people who collect butterflies and bugs and pin them to cardboard, with long Latin names underneath, I don't want to hear about him." But wait a moment. That is what an entomologist means to most people—but Fabre was one of a different kind. Fabre's entomology meant a study of the live insects; it meant finding out all about their births and deaths, their babies and ways of caring for them, their game-hunting, their building, and their wonderful instincts—those instincts which involve a knowledge, conscious or unconscious on the part of the insect, of laws of higher mathematics, chemistry, and physics which are beyond the comprehension of most humans. It meant finding out about all these things, and then writing about them in such an interesting, vivid, poetic way that even people who are not scientists get as much pleasure out of reading Fabre's works as they do out of reading the most absorbing fiction. If an American were to describe Fabre, he might say he was "the man who made the insect famous." A Frenchman—possibly Victor Hugo—long ago gave him the striking and well-deserved title of the "Homer of the insects."

This scientist, whose works have been widely known only during the last few years, spent all of his long life in poverty, and most of it in obscurity. He was born in 1823 of a poor peasant family. How did he, whose parents and grandparents in most cases could neither read nor write—how did he come by his scientific curiosity and the mind with which to gratify it? Nobody knew—least of all, himself. "Heredity—" he wrote, "the darkness that lies behind that word! There was nothing in heredity to explain my taste for observation."

When a small boy, Fabre attended the village school, a wretched hovel which was not only a school, but a kitchen, bedroom, dining-room, and, at times, chicken-house and piggery as well. The schoolmaster, Fabre's godfather, was also a barber, bell-ringer, farmer, and choir-singer. Naturally, he did not have much time to teach. The youngsters studied their A B C's out of little penny primers at their own sweet will. There were many diversions. Often they slyly opened the door into the barnyard, so that the hens, with their "velvet-coated chicks," and the tiny piggies entered, the latter, in Fabre's words, "troting and grumbling, curling their little tails," poking "their cold pink snouts into our hands in search of a scrap." Little Jean Fabre was much more interested in these animals than in his lessons. He was induced to study his A B C's only by a woodcut of a pigeon that embellished one of the leaves of his primer, and a large print, afterward given him, containing an "animal alphabet."

One of the duties connected with the school was to remove snails from the master's box-hedge. Instead of killing his snails, Jean took them home in his pockets. "They are so pretty!" he wrote long after. "Just think! there are yellow ones and pink, white ones and brown, all with dark spiral streaks." Sometimes the scholars turned out to help the master make hay. Then Jean made the acquaintance of the frog, and the "Hoplia, the splendid scarab who pales the azure of the heavens," the locusts, "spreading their wings, some into a blue fan, others into red," and various other fascinating creatures.

His father, the first of the family to forsake the fields for the town, was a poor innkeeper, always failing in his business. At one of these crises Jean had to leave school and earn his living as best he could, one day selling lemons at a country fair, another working with a gang of laborers on the roads. Once he dined on a few grapes, after exchanging his last sous for a volume of poems. But he never forgot his little winged and creeping friends. In this period of misery, which he felt keenly, he had time to notice the pine-chafer, "that superb beetle whose black or chestnut coat is sprinkled with specks of white velvet; which squeaks when captured, emitting a slight complaining sound, like the vibration of a pane of glass rubbed with the tip of a finger."

After this period of wandering, he managed to attend a secondary and normal school. Natural history at that time was held in utter contempt in educational circles. No one taught it—no one wanted to learn it. The necessity of earning his living made Fabre give up his nature studies, bury his specimens and notes deep in the bottom of his trunk, where they would not tempt him, and apply himself to mathematics and the physical sciences. He made rapid progress, and at the age of nineteen was appointed to a place as primary teacher in the college of Carpentras. His salary here was about $140 a year! It was a melancholy place, looking like a penitentiary rather than a school. The only recreation place was "a yard between four high walls, a sort of bear-pit, where the scholars fought for room for their games." After a few years of discontent, he received a more congenial post at the college at Ajaccio, Corsica, at a salary of about $360 a year. The beauty and interest of the surrounding country was a more considerable gain than the gain in salary. During his scanty spare time, the young schoolteacher applied himself to mathematics, to chemistry, and to collecting geological specimens, shells, and ancient coins, in which the country was rich. He met in some of his walks two traveling scientists, one of whom gave him some sound advice:

"Leave your mathematics," said he. "No one will take the least interest in your formulæ. Get to the beast, the plant; and if, as I believe, the fever burns in your veins, you will find men to listen to you. You interest yourself in shells," he went on. "That is something; but it is not enough. You must look into the animal itself. I will show you how it's done." He took a pair of sharp scissors from a near-by work-basket (this happened at dinner, between the "fruit and the cheese") and then and there showed him the anatomy of the snail in a soup-plate filled with water. It was the first and the only natural-history lesson Fabre ever received. But it was the only one he needed.

From that time on, Fabre took pains to develop his peculiar genius. When he was thirty-two, he finished his first memoir on the insect, a wonderful study of a wasp and its manner of paralyzing its prey. Two years later he published another essay, equally illuminating, on a species of beetle. These papers attracted the attention of scientists and gained him a prize from the French Institute. But, owing to his many school duties and the outside tutoring necessary to support his family, he could devote very little time to his insects, and it was twenty-five long years before the first volume of his "Souvenirs Entomologiques" appeared, a series destined to comprise many volumes.

Printed unattractively and without illustrations, they were read at first by scientists only. Some of these worthy men were displeased because the books were too interesting! They feared, Fabre said, "lest a page that is read without fatigue should not always be the expression of the truth." Fabre defended himself from this extraordinary complaint in a characteristic way:

"Come here, one and all of you," he wrote, addressing his friends the insects, "you, the sting-bearer, and you, the wing-cased armor-clads—take up my defense and bear witness in my favor. Tell of the intimate terms on which I live with you, of the patience with which I observe you, of the care with which I record your actions. Your evidence is unanimous; yes, my pages, though they bristle not with hollow formulas nor learned smatterings, are the exact narrative of facts observed, neither more nor less; and whoso cares to question you in his turn will obtain the same replies.

"And then, my dear insects, if you cannot convince these good people because you do not carry the weight of tedium, I, in my turn, will say to them:

"'You rip up the animal, and I study it alive; you turn it into an object of horror and pity, whereas I cause it to be loved; you labor in a torture-chamber and dissecting-room, I make my observation under the blue sky to the song of the cicadas; you subject cell and protoplasm to chemical tests, I study instinct in its loftiest manifestations; you pry into death, I pry into life. . . . I write, above all, for the young. I want to make them love the natural history which you make them hate; and that is why, while keeping strictly in the domain of truth, I avoid your scientific prose, which, too often, alas, seems borrowed from some Iroquois idiom.'"

The twenty-five years just alluded to formed for Fabre a season of bitter struggle and disappointment. He had married young, his family was large, and though devoted to his wife and children, it was no easy matter to support them and still have time left to develop his specialty. He was a splendid teacher, but had no talent for pushing himself, and consequently did not advance beyond an assistant professorship at a tiny salary. He was not even free from persecution. The other professors at Avignon, where he taught for twenty years, were jealous of him because the free lectures he gave on natural history attracted much favorable attention. In ridicule of his pet study, they nicknamed him "The Fly."

Yet there were a few bright spots in this period. Through his writings and genius, Fabre had gained the friendship of several celebrated men. One of these was Darwin, then at the height of his fame, who called him "the incomparable observer." Another was John Stuart Mill, the celebrated English logician, who lent him three thousand francs without security at a time of special need. The minister of education in France invited him to Paris, had him made a Chevalier of the Legion of Honor, and presented him to the emperor, Napoleon III. This honor did not destroy in the least the poise and simplicity of the country professor. As he stood at court in his shabby-genteel frock-coat (a garb he hated, but was obliged to wear on account of his profession), he thought the emperor a "simple man," and compared the chamberlains in livery who waited on the monarch to "great beetles, clad with café-au-lait wing-cases, moving with a formal gait."

At last, after forty years of drudgery and severest privation, he secured the desire of his heart—a small independent income from his books, releasing him from teaching and enabling him to own his own small cottage and garden, and, more important than either, a piece of waste ground, dedicated to thistles and insects. How he exulted in it!

"This cursed ground," he wrote, "which no one would have had as a gift to sow with a pinch of turnip-seed, is an earthly paradise for bees and wasps. Its mighty growth of thistle and centauries draws them all to me from everywhere around. Never, in my insect-hunting memories, have I seen so large a population at a single spot; all the trades have made it their rallying point. Here are hunters of every kind of game, builders in clay, weavers of cotton goods, collectors of pieces cut from a leaf or the petals of a flower, architects in pasteboard, plasterers mixing mortar, carpenters boring wood, miners digging underground galleries, workers handling goldbeater's skin, and many more.

"It is a little late, O my pretty insects," he writes pathetically,—he was at this time nearly seventy years old,—"I greatly fear the peach is offered to me only when I am beginning to have no teeth wherewith to eat it." But his misgivings were not justified. In his home-made cottage laboratory, in this barren, sun-scorched bit of ground, he was to spend more than twenty happy, laborious years, the devoted wife and young children of his second marriage caring for him and helping him in his work.

Here he completed observations and experiments begun in his young manhood. As an example of his patience, it may be recorded that his observations on the sacred beetle, or "tumble-bug," as we call it, extended over a period of forty years. The remarkable things he found out about it—its bold highway robberies, its stupendous feasts, when it sits over twenty-four hours "at table," the exquisitely shaped little "pear" the mother beetle makes for a couch and for food for her babies—all these discoveries make us regard the tumble-bug with a new and respectful interest as we watch its antics in the fields. His study of the bees and wasps took nearly as long and resulted in even more surprising knowledge. What learned surgeon can surpass in skill the wasp, who, desiring live animal food for her children, who will arrive at the eating stage some months hence, paralyzes without killing a grub by inserting her sting at exactly the spot in the neck which connects with the nerve centers? No battle tale is more exciting and gruesome than the recital of the terrible encounters of the wasp and tarantula; and few stories from human life are more pathetic than that of the shabby Grandmother Bee, who, too old for the labors of the hive, makes herself into a portress to guard its door. But space here is too short to give you more than the barest glimpse of Fabre's true wonder stories—you must read them all for yourself some day. And when you do, you will wonder how one man, with no more elaborate apparatus than you yourself could construct, could discover so many new and wonderful secrets in a domain of science hitherto considered unimportant.

During the last few years of his life, Fabre's fame gradually spread. In 1910, in his eighty-eighth year, some of his devoted disciples arranged a jubilee celebration at his dwelling-place, Serignan. On that day many famous men visited the old man in his cottage; letters and telegrams of congratulation poured in from all parts of the world. There was a banquet, and the presentation of a gold plaque engraved with his portrait. The venerable poet-scientist, so long neglected, so poor, was almost overcome. Tears came into his eyes, and into the eyes of those who watched him. The recognition was indeed belated, but it came in time to brighten the last five years of his life. He died in the fall of 1915; and people in all countries stopped for a time their talk of war and battles to mourn for the man who, loving so much his "pretty insects," interpreted their little lives in a way to illumine the great mystery of the universe itself.

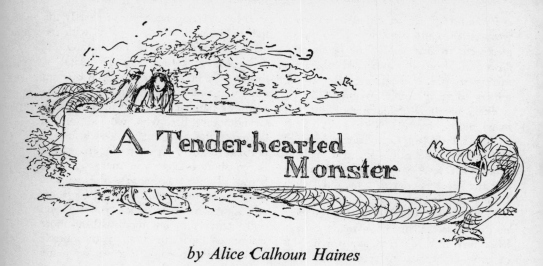

A Tender-hearted Monster

by Alice Calhoun Haines

"Now, see here," said the Dragon, "are you going to betray me?"

"I—I don't know," faltered Molly, clutching her dolly nervously. "I—I don't think mama'd like it if she knew you were here."

"That's just the point," the Dragon answered; "of course she wouldn't. No lady would; and yet, what harm have I done or what harm do I do? It's the only home I've got."

"But it's our garden," Molly said; "and we like to walk in it."

"Well," answered the Dragon, "I don't mind. You may walk in it all you please, and I'll never say a word. I've been here a month already, and nobody's ever guessed it. You wouldn't know it now, but that I told you; and I wouldn't have told you only that I hated to see you crying so hard about your doll when I could give it back to you just as easy as not."

"Yes," said Molly, "it was very good of you." She hugged Arabella, her favorite wax beauty, closer to her heart. "Oh,

Bella," she whispered, "what an adventure you've had! Tumbling into the dried-up well, and spending all this time with a dragon! Goodness, child, I don't see how you ever lived through it! But it *was* good of him to give you back."

"You know," the Dragon continued, "if the Prince should find out my hiding-place it would settle things pretty thoroughly for me. I've almost forgotten how to fight. Anyhow, dragons never *do* beat the princes; you must know that, if you know anything."

"But there isn't any prince," said Molly.

"You don't say!"—the Dragon raised himself high on his hind legs and peered out at her—"you don't say so!" His head was thrust far out of the well now, and Molly drew back in terror. He was a very dreadful-looking beast; but there was also something quite familiar about his appearance. For a moment this puzzled her; but then she saw it was his likeness to a picture in her new fairy-book that caused the feeling.

"Don't be afraid," he said, when he saw

her shrink away; "I won't hurt you. But do you really mean to tell me that there isn't any prince at all?"

"Why, yes," Molly answered faintly; "they all died long ago. At least, there aren't any in this country, I'm quite sure. I thought the dragons were all dead, too."

"I believe they are—all but me. And if it hadn't been for the old fairy Merenthusa I shouldn't be here either. It's a queer story—" he shook his head sadly.

"Oh, tell it," cried Molly—she was a little girl who dearly loved to listen to stories.

"Now, see here," said the Dragon, "I'll tell you the story, if you will promise not to tell your folks about my being here. Come, now—is it a bargain?"

Molly considered for a few moments.

"I'd love to hear the story," she said, "but just think how dreadful it would be if mama or papa were walking alone in the garden, and you should snap off one of their feet."

"I wouldn't," the Dragon answered; "I never eat anybody but just princesses. I say, you aren't a princess, are you?"

"Oh, no!" cried Molly, hastily, "indeed, I'm not. I'm just a little girl—Molly Forster."

"I'm glad of that," he assured her; "I wouldn't like to eat you a bit, but it would be my duty, you know, if you were a princess."

"Would it? How dreadful!" Molly's little face grew quite white with horror.

"You needn't think I'd enjoy it," said the Dragon, "for I never did one bit. I want to whisper to you. It's a terrible thing I have to say, and I'd rather not speak it aloud."

"There's nobody near," Molly objected; "there isn't a soul in the garden but just you and me. I—I'd rather not put my ear down. Can't you say it without that?"

"Well, if I must, I must," grumbled the Dragon. "I did not think you were so suspicious; but nobody trusts me. I'm beginning to get used to it; and yet all the time, you know, *I've got a tender heart.*" He patted his chest with his paw as he spoke. "Yes; I've got a tender heart."

"I'm very glad to hear it," said Molly, cheerfully. "It's a nice thing to have."

"Not for a dragon, my dear," the monster answered; "you're all off there. On the contrary, it's a drawback, a most terrible drawback!"

"Why, I don't see that," Molly cried. "My mama says that there is nothing so bad as a hard heart. You can cure other things, you know, but you can't cure that. If you are really hard-hearted you have just got to stay so. Why, I believe it's the very worst fault there is."

"For a little girl, I'll admit, or for a princess; but not for us. It's what we all aspire after, and most of us have it. I never did." He sighed deeply. "That's one of the particular features of my story. Shall I tell it to you?"

"Yes, indeed," cried Molly.

"Well," said the Dragon, "there were seven of us, and we lived in a cave in the mountains. It was a big cave with lots of cracks and crevices and crannies to play hide-and-seek in, and my! but we had a good time! Our father died when we were babies, and our mother let us do just whatever we chose. She was the most indulgent parent that dragon ever had; and yet *she* didn't have a tender heart. She could eat a princess with all the gusto in the world; and that is the thing I never did manage. Oh! h-m-m! It has embittered my whole life; however, I'm not up to that yet.

"As I said, we had a glorious time up there in our old cave in the mountains. We never went away to school—our mother couldn't part with us—so we had a private tutor, and that was fun, too.

My!—we led him a life! The jokes we played on that poor old fellow would make you split your sides laughing; but I haven't time to tell about them now. I remember one morning in particular—but never mind; I guess I won't tell you that."

"Oh, please do," cried Molly; "I love to hear about naughtinesses."

"No," said the Dragon, "I don't think it would be strictly honorable. You see I'm here in your mother's garden, enjoying

"We had a private tutor, and that was fun, too"

her hospitality,—her guest you might almost say,—so I must be doubly careful, and tell you only those stories that she would care for you to hear—stories that have a moral."

"I don't like that kind," pouted Molly.

"Well, you ought to," said the Dragon; "that's all that concerns me. Shall I go on?"

Molly thought a moment. "What is the moral of this one?" she asked.

"Never be tender-hearted," the Dragon answered. "It's the best one I know."

"Oh," cried Molly, "why, that's not a moral at all!"

"You wait and see if it's not," said the Dragon, with much confidence. "I think I am the best judge of that."

"Go on," Molly whispered. She felt that

she was a very naughty little girl, but she had not time to grieve over the matter just then.

"Well," said the Dragon, "one by one my brothers left the old cave, till at last I alone was left. I had always been delicate, and then, too, I was the baby, so my mother naturally hated to part with me. But when I was about five years old I grew impatient of that quiet life, and determined that it was time for me also to go forth to seek my fortune.

"My mother felt very sad when I told her what was in my mind. 'My dear child,' she said, 'it is what I have been dreading for a long time, but if you feel that you cannot be happy here any longer, why, of course, I can't keep you. Nothing would induce me to make one of my children unhappy for a single moment.' Now wasn't she a good creature?"

"Indeed she was," said Molly.

"Next morning I started upon my travels. I shall never forget how strange everything seemed to me, secluded as I had always been in my happy home among the rocks. I remember well seeing my first man—my heart leaped within me, for I had never see anything like him before, and 'twas only by hearsay that I knew what he was. Of course, the correct thing was to chase him; all my brothers had told me that, so I began at once. I never thought that I should mind. My brothers all enjoyed it, and I expected to also; but when I saw the horror depicted upon the poor fellow's face and heard his breath coming in quick, panting gasps, it gave me such a queer, sick sort of feeling that I stopped running and the man got away.

"At first I could not imagine what was the cause of my weakness, but the meaning flashed upon me all of a sudden. I was tender-hearted! The conviction forced itself upon me and nearly drove me mad."

"Poor Dragon!" said Molly; and then she thought, "Oh, what a bad, bad little girl I am, to be sorry because he did not eat the man! I didn't think I could be so wicked!"

"Yes," said the dragon, "that was how I first knew it, and from that day to this I have never known a happy moment! It's been the same way with everything I've undertaken; I'd go out in the woods and see a lovely princess tied to a tree, a sight that would make most dragons leap for joy, and it would just make me cry! I could not help it, somehow, the tears would come.

"I'd say over and over to myself, 'You're a dragon. You're a dragon. It's your duty to eat her. She won't mind. Princesses never do. It's what they're made for.' But try as I would I could not bring myself to do it. I'd go away and hide in a cave till some one had untied her, and sometimes I'd overhear remarks like this: "They say there is a dragon around here, and, do you know, the Princess Rose, or Belinda, was tied to this tree for three whole days and he never came near her. I wouldn't give much for a beast like that!' Oh, it was most humiliating, and the older I grew the worse it was.

"At last one day things came to a crisis. I was walking in the forest when suddenly I came upon three beautiful maidens, all in a row, tied to sycamore trees. I just turned about and ran! I'm sorry to confess it, but it's true. I scuttled over the ground as fast as I could crawl, slipping under the brushwood and whisking around the tree-trunks, till suddenly I stopped spell-bound, for there—right in front of me—was another of them! I just stood still and looked at her, my eyes almost bulging out of my head!

" 'So this is the way you bear yourself, oh, valiant one!' she cried, her voice full of fury. 'This is the way you devour princesses, oh, ranger of the woods! Very pretty conduct; very pretty, indeed!'

" 'Good gracious!' I gasped, 'do you want me to eat you?' I had never expected this. 'Let others scoff as they will,' I always thought, 'at least I have the sympathy of the princesses.'

" 'Look at me,' she commanded; and then I understood. She was not a woman at all, but a fairy. I knew her at once by her eyes; they were pale green and twinkled like stars. Her name was Merenthusa, and she was both wicked and powerful.

" 'They were my step-daughters,' she said, 'and I tied them to the trees this morning. I knew that there was a dragon near and I wanted to get rid of them. Then I tied myself to this tree, intending to make myself invisible when you passed, and so escape unharmed. When my husband returned he would find me here weeping and wailing over the fate of his three lovely daughters. I would have told him that you were frightened away before you had eaten me. That would have been true, at all events.'

" 'No, it wouldn't,' I cried, and I jumped at her; and, do you know, I really believe I should have eaten her, but she raised her wand, and—that is all I can remember.

"I think she must have put me into a magic sleep, in which I lay for years and years, for about two months ago I woke and found myself in what used to be the forest—it is only a patch of woods now; a great thicket had grown up around me, and I suppose that is how I had escaped detection.

"When I scrambled from it everything seemed changed; nothing was as it used to be, and I felt lost and strange. I traveled a great many miles, always during the night, and hid in the daytime, and after a while I made my way into your garden, found this old well, and here I have been ever since. That's my story. Now remember, you promised not to tell."

"Molly! Molly! Molly!" It was her mother's voice calling.

The little girl started up from the ground, where she had been sitting, and ran toward the house. She felt queer and stiff.

"I don't suppose I can break my word," she whispered, "though mama would love to hear about him. Oh, I wish to-morrow would hurry up and come. I am going to get him to tell me a new story every day."

But, strange to say, next morning when Molly sought her friend the dragon in the garden he was nowhere to be found, and the little girl never saw nor heard of him again.

SOME MAN-EATERS

by Ernest Ingersoll

How the title "man-eaters" is to be understood depends a great deal upon what part of the world you happen to be in. To us North Americans, and to our English cousins, it has a very foreign sound, since there is no animal in our forests, nor hardly any along our coasts, to which the term is commonly applied or would properly belong. If you should say "man-eater" in South America, the native would at once think of the cayman and the jaguar, and similarly, in India, the crocodile would be suggested along the Ganges, and the royal tiger in Bengal. In Africa, it is the lion which would at once be brought to mind. To a West Indian, or to the pearl-fishers of any coast, the shark is the dreaded foe, while the Vancouver Indian looks upon the ugly cuttle-fish as the man-eater of his region, and the Eskimo fears the polar bear.

While all wild carnivorous beasts capable of coping with men may become man-eaters,—since human flesh is no doubt quite as palatable as the flesh of any of the other animals upon which they are accustomed to feed,—yet, properly speaking, only those are called "man-eaters" that, having once tasted human blood, are supposed always afterward to be hankering for it, and never to be quite satisfied with any less noble diet. They are thought to be forever on the watch for men, lying in ambush and seeking every means of destroying them, and never feeding on anything else, excepting to satisfy extreme hunger. Such beasts, being especially dreaded, are credited with extraordinary size, strength and ferocity.

In Africa, every district has a lion of this kind, which is feared by the whole region as much as all the rest of the lions there put together, and the case is equally true of central India. The lion truly deserves the royal name he bears. Although by no means of great size, the strength of his massive shoulders and forelegs, and of the thick muscles of his great neck and firm, square jaws, is so enormous that he can drag down the heaviest buffalo and overthrow the powerful giraffe, whose head towers above the trees, and whose skin is nearly an inch thick. There is no animal, even the elephant, which the lion hesitates to attack; yet notwithstanding the power of the machinery which has been given him for this purpose, it has been packed in such small compass in his lithe body that he can overtake and prey upon quadrupeds as fleet as zebras and antelopes.

Although he has great speed, the lion does not depend so much upon chase in the open field as upon strategy, in securing his prey. He follows about from pasture to pasture, and from spring to spring, the herds of deer and buffaloes as they change their feeding-places at different seasons. Remaining asleep, and concealed in the recesses of the forest or among secluded rocks, during the day, he sallies out at night in company with one or two friends, or perhaps with his mate and two half-grown cubs, or often alone, and repairs to the nearest water-hole. In Africa, water is very scarce. The springs are few and far between, and the animals of the whole region must resort to a particular fountain, sometime during the night, to quench the thirst which there alone can be allayed. The lion knows this, and goes to the vicinity of this spring, choosing the early part of the evening, if the moon is to rise early, or waiting until morning, after the moon has set, if it be on the wane, so as not to show himself. When some convenient prey approaches, he leaps upon it, bears it down with his weight, breaking its neck by the stroke of his heavy paw or the crushing strength of his jaws, and drags the body away into the jungle, to be feasted upon at leisure.

At such times, if you should happen to pass near him, you would hear a low, deep moaning as he eats, repeated five or six times, and ending in faintly audible sighs. At other times, he startles the forest with loud, deep-toned, solemn roars, uttered in quick succession. Often, a troop may be heard roaring in concert, making music inconceivably grand to the hunter's ear. The effect is greatly enhanced when the hearer chances to be all alone in the depths of the forest, at the dead hour of midnight, and within twenty yards of the fountain which the troop of lions is approaching.

In central Africa, many of the native tribes do not bury the bodies of their dead, but simply carry them forth and leave them lying anywhere on the plain. Lions are always prowling about, and, finding many of these corpses, do not hesitate to dine off them, for it is not true that the king of beasts will not eat what he himself has not killed. Afterward, that

lion, particularly if he is an old and cunning fellow, becomes a very dangerous neighbor. I do not believe that the lion has from the first a preference for the flesh of men over fresh venison or beef, but that it is an agreeable discovery to him that men are animals, and good to eat; and, furthermore, that he soon recognizes unarmed men as less able to resist or escape from him than are the four-footed beasts. He therefore keeps an eye out for human prey, since it costs him less trouble.

In the tropical wastes of India, the forest, or jungle, is grown up very densely with cane, stout, tangled grass, creepers, vines, and so on, until the only way to get through it is by following paths kept open by constant traveling. In traversing these dark and narrow passages, the traveler is peculiarly exposed to attack from the lions and tigers which make the jungle their home, and the native Hindoos are often stricken down. Then ensues a grand hunt from the nearest village, assisted by some English officer, who, with his cool courage and precise shooting, usually does more to kill the beast (if he is killed) than all the rest of the villagers combined.

Generally, the animal will try to get away and hide, when he hears the hunters approaching. But if he is a hardened old man-eater, it does not take long to bring him to bay, since he has grown courageous, or reckless, or both. Then those who are on foot look out for their safety as best they can, usually by climbing the nearest tree, and those who are on horseback dismount and get upon the back of an elephant, where, in a sort of basket strapped upon the great animal, two or three will stand together, ready to shoot the moment they get a chance, while the elephant slowly crushes his way toward that spot in the thick jungle where the tiger is heard growling. The books about life in

India, and the letters which sportsmen write home to the English newspapers, are full of accounts of such hunts; but none that I know of is more thrilling, or better shows the terrific danger sometimes encountered in such contests of men-eating lions and tigers with lion-killing men, than an incident related by Charles Waterton, in his charming "Essays on Natural History."

Three English officers and a lot of natives were hunting for two lions, which had made a raid upon a village the night before, and in the course of the day one of the pair was killed, but the other escaped to the jungle. When at last his hiding-place was discovered, the three officers got upon an elephant and proceeded toward the heart of the jungle, to rouse the royal fugitive a second time. They found him standing under a large bush, with his face directly toward them. He allowed them to approach within range of his spring, when he made a sudden leap, and clung upon the elephant's trunk. The men fired, but without avail, and the elephant managed to shake his troublesome visitor off, but was so frightened that he became uncontrollable, and when the lion made another spring at him, rushed in headlong fear out into the clearing. The officers, therefore, had to give up all idea of forcing the elephant to face the lion again, but one of them, Captain Woodhouse, took the desperate resolution to proceed on foot in quest of the game; and finally seeing him, fired though the bushes, the only effect of which was to make the lion retire still deeper into the brake.

Resolved not to let the game escape, his companions, the two lieutenants, now took the elephant, intending to proceed around the jungle, so as to discover the route the lion had taken on the other side. But Captain Woodhouse reloaded his rifle, and alone followed the tracks through the thicket. Finally, Lieutenant Delamain joined him.

Proceeding cautiously, after a few steps the lieutenant saw the lion, and instantly fired, which enraged the beast so that he rushed toward him at full speed. Captain Woodhouse saw the movement, and knew that if he tried to get into a better position for firing, he would put himself directly in the way of the charge, so decided to stand still, trusting that the lion would pass close by him, unaware, when he could perhaps shoot to advantage. But he was deceived. The furious animal saw him, and flew at him with a dreadful roar. In an instant the rifle was broken and thrown out of the captain's hand, his left arm at the same moment being seized by the claws, and his right by the teeth, of his antagonist. At this desperate juncture, Lieutenant Delamain ran up and discharged his piece full at the lion. This caused both beast and man to fall to the ground together, while the lieutenant hastened out of the thicket to reload his gun. The lion now began to crunch the captain's arm; but as the brave man, notwithstanding the pain which this horrid process caused, had the cool, determined resolution to lie still, the lordly savage let the arm drop out of his mouth, and quietly placed himself in a crouching posture, with both his paws upon the thigh of his fallen foe. While things were in this untoward position, the captain unthinkingly raised his hand to support his head, which had got placed ill at ease in his fall. Instantly the lion seized the lacerated arm a second time, and crunched it as before, breaking the bone higher up. This hint was not lost on Captain Woodhouse, who saw at once the imprudence of stirring, and to the motionless attitude which this lesson taught him to keep thereafter he undoubtedly owed his life.

But while death was close upon him, as he lay bleeding and broken in the power of the most mighty enemy which a man can meet in the forest, and was closing his eyes to a world on the point of vanishing forever, he heard the welcome sound of feet approaching. But the lieutenants were in the wrong direction. Aware that, if his friends fired, the balls would hit him after they had passed through the lion's body, Captain Woodhouse quietly spoke, in a low voice, "To the other side! To the other side!" Hearing the voice, they for the first time saw the horrible position of their commander, and having cautiously but quickly made the circuit, Lieutenant Delamain, whose coolness had been conspicuous in many an encounter with wild beasts, fired from a short distance at the lion, over the person of the prostrate warrior. The beast started up a little, quivered, the massive head sank down, and in an instant he lay dead, close beside his intended victim.

The lesson to be learned from this true story of nerve and heroism is that, when a person is in the power of a lion, tiger, leopard or panther, or any other of the great cats, he must feign death and lie absolutely still, if he hopes for life. Let him make a motion, and his foe will pounce upon him as the house-cat does on an escaping mouse; but so long as he keeps still, he has a chance. Yet not every one has the nerve to do so. With dogs, wolves and bears, on the other hand, the only way, when attacked, is to resist sturdily to the last limit of your strength, since, once having a victim in their power, they never cease worrying it until it is utterly dead. Sometimes, nevertheless, resolution and nerve are no protection, since there is no opportunity to exercise them. This was the case in a dreadful tragedy which happened in the lonely camp of that great Nimrod, Gordon Cumming,

during one of his hunting expeditions to the far interior of Africa. Lions had been roaring about all day, but at last their voices ceased, and apparently they all went off. After their supper, three of the men went off to a little fire they had built, near some bushes, at some distance from the main camp-fire, and lay down—two of them under the same blanket.

"Suddenly," says Mr. Cumming, "the appalling voice of an angry lion burst upon our ear, within a few yards of us, followed by the shrieking of the Hottentots. Again and again the deafening roar was repeated. We heard John and Ruyter shriek, 'The lion! the lion!'

"Still, for a few minutes, we thought the lion was no doubt only chasing one of the dogs around the kraal; but, all at once, John Stofolus rushed into the midst of us, almost speechless with fear and terror, his eyes bursting from their sockets, and shrieked out: 'The lion! the lion! the lion! He has got Hendric; he dragged him away from the fire beside me. I struck him with the burning brands upon his head, but he would not let go his hold. Hendric is dead! Oh! Hendric is dead! Let us take fire and seek him!' The rest of my people rushed about, shrieking and yelling as if they were mad. I was at once angry with them for their folly, and told them that if they did not stand still and keep quiet, the lion would have another of us; and that very likely there was a troop of them. I ordered the dogs, which were nearly all fast, to be let loose, and the fire to be increased as far as could be. I then shouted Hendric's name, but all was still. I told my men that Hendric was dead, and that a regiment of soldiers could not help him; and, hunting my dogs forward, I had everything brought within the cattle-kraal, when we lighted our fire, and closed the entrance as well as we could.

"It appeared that, when the unfortunate

Hendric rose to drive in the oxen, the lion had watched him to his fireside; and he had scarcely lain down when the brute sprang upon him and Ruyter (for both lay under one blanket), with his appalling, thunderous roar, and, roaring as he lay, grappled him with his fearful claws, and kept biting him on the breast and shoulder, all the while feeling for his neck, having got hold of which, he at once dragged him away backward around the bush into the dense shade."

The next day, toward evening, knowing the lion would return for a second victim that night, Mr. Cumming decided to seek him out and kill him. So, setting his dogs to work, and following the track along which the mangled body of poor Hendric had been dragged, the hunter soon came up with the savage beast, among some thorn-brush. But let him tell it:

"As I approached, he stood, his horrid head right to me, with open jaws, growling fiercely, his tail waving from side to side. On beholding him, I dashed my steed forward within thirty yards of him, and shouted, 'Your time is up, old fellow!' I halted my horse, and, placing my rifle to my shoulder, waiting for a broadside. This the next moment he exposed, when I sent a bullet through his shoulder, and dropped him on the spot. . . . I ordered John to cut off his head and forepaws and bring them to the wagons, and, mounting my horse, galloped home, having been absent about fifteen minutes. When the Bakalahari women heard that the man-eater was dead, they all commenced dancing about with joy, calling me their father."

Perhaps the next most important class of animal-enemies of men is that of the sharks. Of sharks, there is a large number of species. They are of various sizes and inhabit all seas, from Arctic and Antarctic to tropical latitudes. They are most abundant, of greatest size and of most impor-

tance, in the tropics, however; and it is among the coral rings of the Pacific Islands, and along the shining sands of the Gold Coast, that the shark is the most dreaded.

In the South Sea Islands, everybody swims from infancy, like so many water-dogs. It is asserted that a Mexican is taught to ride before he learns to walk. It is just as near truth—and, indeed, very little removed—to say that a native of the Sandwich or Society Islands can swim before he can creep. Babies a few months old are tossed into the surf, and, before they have cut their teeth, they become as lively and safe in the water as ducks. We have accounts of these people swimming incredible distances. Ten or a dozen miles seem to offer no difficulty whatever to them; and when ships approach the shores of the less civilized islands, they are surrounded by men and women and children, who sport about the bows like dolphins, long before the sailors have thought of taking in sail or preparing to anchor.

But along a tropical coast, where hundreds of people are constantly at play in the surf, and often are far out from shore, it is to be expected that sharks will often get a good meal. Fortunately, all sharks, or nearly all, are surface-swimmers. They do not lurk at the bottom or float in the depths, like the true bony fishes; usually, therefore, their great triangular back-fins appear above the water and give the bathers warning. The sight always produces great consternation, and a rush for the shore takes place, though sometimes the crowd will unite, and, by shouting and splashing, frighten the great fish away. Yet, not infrequently he comes upon them unawares, and, dashing into their midst like a streak of white light, is scarcely observed before the death-scream of some wretched bather is drowned, almost before uttered, as he is dragged down, and the next wave rolls in red with blood, or casts high upon the gleaming beach some torn fragments of what was once their friend. Looking seaward, they see the shark cruising back and forth, eager for another victim, and perhaps they go out to attack him, in revenge. But the surf-riding is over for that day, for the shark will stay there many hours, in hope of more prey.

Perhaps the metropolis of shark life is off the western coast of Africa. They found there always plenty of food, furnished by the slave-ships which used to haunt those waters. There are few good harbors along the whole of that extensive sea-coast. The ships, therefore, were obliged to anchor some distance away, and send back and forth to the shore by the small boats. It was thus that the slaves were taken on board. But the passage through the surf was always dangerous, and often the yawls were capsized. On such occasions, few of the blacks were ever seen again. The sudden activity of the swarms of ever-present sharks, and the blood-stained water, told sufficiently well their fate. Troops of these same sharks would follow a slave-ship clear across the Atlantic, sure of their daily meal of dead and dying captives, which were thrown overboard from those floating dens of the most awful human misery the world has ever seen—misery that we cannot even think of without a sick and shuddering sense of horror.

Some of the Polynesian fishermen before alluded to, nevertheless, do not hesitate to attack and conquer the largest shark in his native element. The fish does not see very well, and is not very quick in any but a straight-ahead movement. The swimmer, armed with a long knife, watches the shark's onslaught coolly, and just as the great fish opens his horrid mouth to seize the brave man in his jaws, the fisherman dives out of reach, and plunges his knife deep into the shark's belly, as the disap-

pointed monster passes over his head. This feat is attempted only by the coolest and ablest divers, you may be sure, but it is done; and it is one of the most splendid examples I know of the success of human pluck against animal force greatly its superior. Should the swimmer fail in his plan by an instant of time, his life must pay the penalty. The pearl-divers in the Gulf of California are said to employ an equally audacious method of fighting the sharks which torment them when at work on the deep-sea beds of the pearl-oyster. They carry with them a stick of hard wood about a foot long, sharp-pointed at both ends. Finding that a shark is meditating an attack, they grasp this stick in the middle, and calmly await him. When he opens wide his mouth, they dexterously shove in the sharp stick, crosswise, and then get out of his way as fast as possible, while the too-eager shark shuts his jaws only to find that he has mortally wounded himself by punching holes in the roof and floor of his mouth. I cannot vouch for this story; the reader must take it for what it is worth.

Not long ago I read, in the New York *Herald,* a diver's narrative of how he escaped from a shark which seemed to have too great curiosity as to his edible qualities. This man was known as "On Deck," and he had an eventful life. A sailor in youth, a diver in manhood, and a "ne'er-do-weel" in old age, he saw more than falls to the lot of most men. In California, in 1851, a ship lost an anchor in the harbor of San Francisco, and "On Deck" was sent for to recover it. While so engaged, he noticed a shark hovering a few feet above him, evidently observing his movements. The fish was at least eighteen feet long, and was known as the "bottle-nose," one of the most voracious of the shark kind. This discovery naturally alarmed the diver. He had found the anchor, made a cable fast to it, and was about ascending, when the appearance of the shark made him pause. He had heard that sharks did not molest men in armor. He doubted this, and did not feel now like risking the experiment. He moved a few paces from the anchor—the shark moved, too. He returned to his former place—the shark followed. He was evidently, to use his own words, "spotted by the bottle-nose for a supper," and, unless signally favored, would fall a victim to its voracity. He hardly knew how to act, when he thought how the cuttle-fish often escapes its enemies by darkening the waters with an inky liquor ejected from its body. He accordingly stirred up the mud at the bottom till the water was darkened around him, cast off weights, and signaled the man to haul him up. The shark snapped at him as he ascended, and three of his toes were taken off. A little more and his foot would have gone, a stout boot only saving it. The happy idea of muddying the water was all that preserved his life.

The shark's mouth is one of the most formidable means of destruction I know of among animals anywhere. It is on the under side of the head, some distance back of the end of the snout, and crescent-shaped. The teeth are in three to seven close, crescentic, parallel rows, the largest and oldest in front, the smaller ones behind—that is, farthest inside the mouth. Some sharks have more than 200 of these teeth. They are three-cornered, exceedingly thin and sharp-pointed, and in some cases have saw-edges. When the mouth is wide open they stand erect, and almost protrude from the lips, but when it is closed they lie down flat, out of the way. When those in the front row wear out or break off, the next row behind is gradually pushed forward to take their places. The shark thus has reserves of teeth which, operated by the tough and exceedingly

muscular mechanism of the jaws, are able to bite through anything, especially since the bite is nearly always accompanied by a rolling or wrenching movement which causes the teeth to act like a saw, and thus cut through the quicker. For some of the larger sharks in the South Seas, it would be only a moderate mouthful to take half a man's body in, and clip him off at the waist. Nevertheless, I believe fewer persons have lost their lives by sharks than we generally suppose, though many narrow escapes are constantly happening.

There are some other fishes which would regard it as very good luck to find a human body in their power,—the old piratical threat, of making "food for the fishes" out of their captives, was not altogether an idle one,—but there are few, if any, besides the sword-fish, that could do a man much harm, or would be likely to. A friend at my elbow suggests the whale; but I object. The whale is not a fish!

There is a sea-beast, nevertheless, which makes a formidable antagonist to man, and does not hesitate to attack him, or anything else that comes in its way. This is the cuttle-fish, which is also known as the devil-fish, in allusion to its frightful appearance and evil disposition. It has a shapeless pouch of a body, spotted, rough and wrinkled, from all sides of which branch stout, elastic arms of a leathery character, some of which are stretched far away, winding in and out among the slimy rocks and stems of sea-weed, and others are shortened up close to the body, as the animal lies concealed in a dark and muddy crevice of a broken rock at the bottom of the sea, patiently waiting for its prey. Two enormous round, bulging eyes are ever staring about, and nothing escapes their attention. Let a living thing come within reach of those arms, and its fate is sealed. Quick as thought, the snaky member clutches the prey, and holds on by a host of little suckers and tiny hooks, in the grasp of which the strongest and slipperiest animal is fast. Other arms whip out to the help of the first, paralysis soon overpowers the unfortunate captive, and slowly the arms are contracted until the prey is brought within reach of the sharp, parrot-like jaws, when it is deliberately eaten up.

Some of these cuttle-fishes are of vast size. They are abundant in the Eastern Mediterranean, on the coast of British Columbia, on the Pacific coast of Asia, on the Banks of Newfoundland and else-where. They lurk near the shore, hiding very quietly among the rocks, where, as they are mud-color, they are not easily seen.

The Indians of Puget Sound eat these cuttle-fishes, baking the flesh in the ground. They go in canoes and hunt for them, spearing them with a long handled harpoon when discovered. It is exceed-ingly dangerous business, and many have lost their lives at it, besides those who now and then are dragged down when bathing over the spot where a cuttle-fish lies in wait.

This frightful tyrant over all the inhabit-ants of the ocean must be allowed a place among our man-eaters; and a great deal more might be said about his peculiar and interesting, though always deadly, habits, were there room.

Turning from salt to fresh waters, no more feared and hated animals stand in the way of human enjoyment than the crocodiles and alligators, which swarm in all tropical rivers from Borneo to Guate-mala. The most famous of these ugly rep-tiles are the long-snouted, hungry gavial of the Ganges, the crocodile of the Nile, the cayman of the Amazonian region, and the alligator of our own Southern States. Their jaws are of great extent and strength, and filled with strong, sharp teeth, while the broad tail is able to deliver so effective a blow as to stun almost any animal which it strikes, and even splinter a stout boat. Nothing can exceed the ugli-ness of their rough, knotted hide, so thick that a rifle bullet glances off without harm, or equal the stony glare of the cold, glassy eyes. The crocodiles haunt the shallows of streams, lurking among the rank vegeta-tion which grows along marshy shores, or lying asleep upon banks and half-sub-merged islands of mud. Sometimes per-sons, finding one thus, have mistaken it for an old water-soaked log of drift-wood, and stepped upon it. It was fortunate if they discovered their mistake in time to get out of the reach of the powerful tail. When swimming, crocodiles move about with only the tip of the snout, where the nostrils are, out of water; and, if they want to escape notice, they will sink altogether beneath the surface so quietly that not a ripple disturbs the water. Thus they stealthily approach any animal swimming in the stream, or drinking upon the mar-gin, and, making a sudden rush when close by, drag it down before it has time to make an effort to escape. The South American and West Indian species, known as caymans, are the most active and dan-gerous of all, and a great many negro slaves and Indians lose their lives through them every year. The same thing happens on the Nile, and, to a less extent, in the bayous of Louisiana and Florida. The peo-ple there get somewhat careless, and forget how quietly the alligator approaches, and how terrible is his attack when within reach. In the United States, however, not many of these disagreeable creatures reach a sufficient size to make them able to drag down and devour a full-grown man.

The history of the natives of India is full of dark and bloody rites, which shock all civilized hearts by their blind superstition and cruelty. Human life seems of very small account to those Eastern nations, and most of their deities are fearful tyrants, to be dreaded and appeased rather than loved and honored. It has always been a pagan idea that, when any misfortune came upon a family or a nation, it was an expression of anger on the part of a god, and that the only way to get rid of present distress, or avert a threatened disaster, was to sacrifice, on an altar consecrated to the particular deity from which the affliction was supposed to come, something of great value. Sometimes it was the first of a farmer's fruit or crops; sometimes the fattest ox or the whitest dove; sometimes quantities of gold and precious stones, which were given for the support of the temples of this god, or made into images of him; and along the Ganges, the Hindoo mothers bid their tender babes a heart-rending farewell, and set them afloat on the tide of that vast stream for the crocodiles to eat.

The subjection of India to England has put a stop to this terrible custom to a great extent, but it is still occasionally followed. The Hindoo mother is suffering under some real trouble, or the village in which she lives is visited by pestilence or some other calamity, or her priest tells her that a catastrophe will follow unless she sacrifices her child. Perhaps there are many mothers who hope similarly to avert the frown of their god and save their neighbors from calamity,—for I do not believe any woman would put her baby to death merely to save herself from suffering; and so these women make little boats of rushes, dress the laughing and crowing infants as though for a festival, heap the little boat up with flowers, and, with the semblance of joy but with hearts almost dead with grief, commit their darlings to the wide, rolling, merciless river, and watch the pigmy craft as the eddies toss it this way

and that, while the current bears it on to where the chubby little hands will be held up in vain, and the delicate voice be hushed forever.

Surely the crocodiles belong in the horrible society of man-eaters.

Returning to four-footed beasts, it is hard to find any, besides the lion and other large cats, that will attack man without any provocation. Some of the bears, when severely pressed by hunger, are very savage, and may perhaps prey upon man at such times, but instances of their doing so are, I think, very rare. The grizzly bear of our Rocky Mountains is the most ferocious of its race, and one authority says of it: "If it is not certain that he will voluntarily attack a human being, it is certain that, if attacked, he will pursue the assailant to the last, nor quit the conflict while life remains." The bears can hardly be classed among man-eaters, I think; yet they are very dangerous enemies of man, and certainly the grizzly and the polar bear should be numbered with the animals that *kill* man. And if such beasts may be mentioned here, we must not forget the "rogue" elephant, as certain old cross leaders of the herd are called, for he is a very dangerous fellow to be in the same grove with; and the black rhinoceros of South Africa, who, when on his native heath, does not wait to do the polite thing, but introduces himself by a fierce snort and a headlong charge as unexpected as it is impetuous. But, of course, the elephant and rhinoceros could not eat any portion of their victims,—their food is wholly vegetable; at the same time, I do not know of beasts more dangerous to meet.

There are no other animals that I know of which could properly be called man-eaters, excepting wolves, and they are timid about attacking, unless they are in packs and starving. So much has been written about them of late, that I refrain from saying a great deal. You cannot do better than to read Mr. Hamerton's talk on this subject in his "Chapters on Animals." It is very rare that a man's life is lost by the attack of wolves, though, like other beasts, they will fight when put in a corner. On our western plains, there is a tradition which seems to have a considerable foundation of truth concerning a mad wolf, which can properly be told here:

Half a century ago, bands of trappers used to wander through the northern Rocky Mountains, shooting and trapping bears, wolves, foxes, beavers, otters, and other animals, for the sake of their fur. When winter came on, it was their custom to settle in a fixed camp at some convenient spot, and make short excursions, while in summer they roamed about the cañons. One winter night, where several companies happened to be close together, the men were all asleep, when suddenly a cry of "Mad wolf! Mad wolf!" rang through the silent camp, and frightened men leaped up from their blankets only in time to see a dark form vanishing swiftly into the darkness, and hear shrill howls die away in the distance. It was not long before the effects began to be seen. Dogs were seized with hydrophobia and shot, till nearly all were gone. Not one alone, but nearly all the camps had been visited, and, one by one, men in each of these little, far-isolated communities were seized with the dreadful disease, and were left to die. How many lives were thus lost I do not know, and no one ever can tell, but there were many; and all through the next summer the skeletons and bodies of wolves were found scattered over that region, and these evidently had been bitten by the rabid animal and died of hydrophobia. It is a horrible story to think of, and a fit conclusion to a talk about "Man-Eaters."

MIDSUMMER PIRATES

by Richard H. Davis

THE boys living at the Atlantic House, and the boys boarding at Chadwick's, held mutual sentiments of something not unlike enmity—feelings of hostility from which even the older boarders were not altogether free. Nor was this unnatural under the circumstances. When Judge Henry S. Carter and his friend Dr. Prescott first discovered Manasquan, such an institution as the Atlantic House seemed an impossibility, and land improvement companies, Queen Anne cottages, and hacks to and from the railroad station, were out of all calculation. At that time "Captain" Chadwick's farmhouse, though not rich in all the modern improvements of a seaside hotel, rejoiced in a table covered three times a day with the good things from the farm. The river, back of the house, was full of fish, and the pine-woods along its banks were intended by Nature expressly for the hanging of hammocks.

The chief amusements were picnics to the head of the river (or as near the head as the boats could get through the lily-pads), crabbing along the shore, and races on the river itself, which, if it was broad, was so absurdly shallow that an upset meant nothing more serious than a wetting and a temporary loss of reputation as a sailor.

But all this had been spoiled by the advance of civilization and the erection of the Atlantic House.

The railroad surveyors, with their high-top boots and transits, were the first signs of the approaching evils. After them came the Ozone Land Company, which bought up all the sand hills bordering on the ocean, and proceeded to stake out a flourishing "city by the sea" and to erect signposts in the marshes to show where they would lay out streets, named after the directors of the Ozone Land Company and the Presidents of the United States.

It was not unnatural, therefore, that the Carters, and the Prescotts, and all the Judge's clients, and the Doctor's patients, who had been coming to Manasquan for many years, and loved it for its simplicity and quiet, should feel aggrieved at these great changes. And though the young Carters and Prescotts endeavored to impede the march of civilization by pulling up the surveyor's stakes and tearing down the Land Company's sign-posts, the inevitable improvements marched steadily on.

I hope all this will show why it was that the boys who lived at the Atlantic House —and dressed as if they were still in the city, and had "hops" every evening—were not pleasing to the boys who boarded at Chadwick's, who never changed their flannel suits for anything more formal than their bathing-dresses, and spent the summer nights on the river.

This spirit of hostility and its past history were explained to the new arrival at Chadwick's by young Teddy Carter, as the two sat under the willow tree watching a game of tennis. The new arrival had just expressed his surprise at the earnest desire manifest on the part of the entire Chadwick establishment to defeat the Atlantic House people in the great race which was to occur on the day following.

"Well, you see, sir," said Teddy, "considerable depends on this race. As it is now, we stand about even. The Atlantic House beat us playing base-ball—though they had to get the waiters to help them —and we beat them at tennis. Our house is great on tennis. Then we had a boat-race, and our boat won. They claimed it wasn't a fair race, because their best boat was stuck on the sand-bar, and so we agreed to sail it over again. The second time the wind gave out, and all the boats had to be poled home. The Atlantic House boat was poled in first, and her crew claimed the race. Wasn't it silly of them? Why, Charley Prescott told them, if they'd only said it was to be a *poling* match, he'd have entered a mud-scow and left his sail-boat at the dock!"

"And so you are going to race again to-morrow?" asked the new arrival.

"Well, it isn't exactly a race," explained Teddy. "It's a game we boys have invented. We call it 'Pirates and Smugglers.' It's something like tag, only we play it on the water, in boats. We divide boats and boys up into two sides; half of them are pirates or smugglers, and half of them are revenue officers or man-o'-war's-men. The 'Pirate's Lair' is at the island, and our dock is 'Cuba.' That's where the smugglers run in for cargoes of cigars and brandy. Mr. Moore gives us his empty cigar boxes, and Miss Sherrill (the lady who's down here for her health) lets us have all the empty Apollinaris bottles. We fill the bottles with water colored with crushed blackberries, and that answers for brandy.

"The revenue officers are stationed at Annapolis (that's the Atlantic House dock), and when they see a pirate start from the island, or from our dock, they sail after him. If they can touch him with the bow of their boat, or if one of their men can board him, that counts one for the revenue officers; and they take down his sail and the pirate captain gives up his tiller as a sign of surrender.

"Then they tow him back to Annapolis, where they keep him a prisoner until he is exchanged. But if the pirate can dodge the Custom House boat, and get to the place he started for, without being caught, that counts one for him."

"Very interesting, indeed," said the new arrival; "but suppose the pirate won't be captured or give up his tiller, what then?"

"Oh, well, in that case," said Teddy, reflectively, "they'd cut his sheet-rope, or splash water on him, or hit him with an oar, or something. But he generally gives right up. Now, to-morrow the Atlantic House boys are to be the revenue officers and we are to be the pirates. They have been watching us as we played the game, all summer, and they think they understand it well enough to capture our boats without any trouble at all."

"And what do you think?" asked the new arrival.

"Well, I can't say, certainly. They have faster boats than ours, but they don't know how to sail them. If we had their boats, or if they knew as much about the river as we do, it would be easy enough to name the winners. But, as it is, it's about even."

Every one who owned a boat was on the river the following afternoon, and those who didn't own a boat hired or borrowed one—with or without the owner's permission.

The shore from Chadwick's to the Atlantic House dock was crowded with people. All Manasquan seemed to be ranged in line along the river's bank. Crab-men and clam-diggers mixed indiscriminately with the summer boarders; and the beach-wagons and stages from Chadwick's grazed the wheels of the dog-carts and drags from the Atlantic's livery-stables.

It does not take much to overthrow the pleasant routine of summer-resort life, and the state of temporary excitement existing at the two houses on the eve of the race was not limited to the youthful contestants.

The proprietor of the Atlantic House had already announced an elaborate supper in honor of the anticipated victory, and every father and mother whose son was to take part in the day's race felt the importance of the occasion even more keenly than the son himself.

"Of course," said Judge Carter, "it's only a game, and for my part, so long as no one is drowned, I don't really care who wins; *but,* if our boys" ("our boys" meaning all three crews) "allow those young whippersnappers from the Atlantic House to win the pennant, they deserve to have their boats taken from them and exchanged for hoops and marbles!"

Which goes to show how serious a matter was the success of the Chadwick crews.

At three o'clock the amateur pirates started from the dock to take up their positions at the island. Each of the three small cat-boats held two boys: one at the helm and one in charge of the center-board and sheet-rope. Each pirate wore a jersey striped with differing colors, and the head of each bore the sanguinary red, knitted cap in which all genuine pirates are wont to appear. From the peaks of the three boats floated black flags, bearing the emblematic skull and bones of Captain Kidd's followers.

As they left the dock the Chadwick's people cheered with delight at their appearance and shouted encouragement, while the remaining youngsters fired salutes with a small cannon, which added to the uproar as well as increased the excitement of the moment by its likelihood to explode.

At the Atlantic House dock, also, the excitement was at fever heat.

Clad in white flannel suits and white duck yachting-caps with gilt buttons, the revenue officers strolled up and down the pier with an air of cool and determined purpose such as Decatur may have worn as he paced the deck of his man-of-war and scanned the horizon for Algerine pirates. The stars-and-stripes floated bravely from the peaks of the three cat-boats, soon to leap in pursuit of the pirate craft which were conspicuously making for the starting-point at the island.

At half-past three the judges' steam-launch, the "Gracie," made for the middle of the river, carrying two representatives from both houses and a dozen undergraduates from different colleges, who had chartered the boat for the purpose of following the race and seeing at close quarters all that was to be seen.

They enlivened the occasion by courteously and impartially giving the special yell of each college of which there was a representative present, whether they knew him or not, or whether he happened to be an undergraduate, a professor, or an alumnus. Lest someone might inadvertently be overlooked, they continued to yell throughout the course of the afternoon, giving, in time, the shibboleth of every known institution of learning.

"Which do I think is going to win?" said the veteran boat-builder of Manasquan to the inquiring group around his boat-house. "Well, I wouldn't like to say. You see, I built every one of those boats that sails to-day, and every time I make a boat I make it better than the last one. Now, the Chadwick boats I built near five years ago, and the Atlantic House boats I built last summer, and I've learned a good deal in five years."

"So you think our side will win?" eagerly interrupted an Atlantic House boarder.

"Well, I didn't say so, did I?" inquired

boats; and if the Chadwick boys win, they'll win because they're the better sailors."

In the fashion of all first-class aquatic contests, it was fully an hour after the time appointed for the race to begin before the first pirate boat left the island.

" 'Which do I think is going to win?' said the veteran boat-builder to the inquiring group around his boat-house"

the veteran, with crushing slowness of speech. "I didn't say so. For though these boats the Chadwick's boys have are five years old, they're good boats still; and those boys know every trick and turn of 'em—and they know every current and sand-bar just as though it was marked with a piece of chalk. So, if the Atlantic folks win, it'll be because they've got the best

The *Ripple,* with Judge Carter's two sons in command, was the leader; and when her sail filled and showed above the shore, a cheer from the Chadwick's dock was carried to the ears of the pirate crew who sat perched on the rail as she started on her first long tack.

In a moment, two of the Atlantic House heroes tumbled into the *Osprey,* a dozen over-hasty hands had cast off her painter, had shoved her head into the stream, and the great race was begun.

The wind was down the river, or toward the island, so that while the *Osprey* was sailing before the wind, the *Ripple* had her sail close-hauled and was tacking.

"They're after us!" said Charley Carter, excitedly. "It's the *Osprey,* but I can't make out who's handling her. From the way they are pointing, I think they expect to reach us on this tack as we go about."

The crew of the *Osprey* evidently thought so too, for her bow was pointed at a spot on the shore, near which the *Ripple* must turn if she continued much longer on the same tack.

"Do you see that?" gasped Charley, who was acting as lookout. "They're letting her drift in the wind so as not to get there before us. I tell you what it is, Gus, they know what they're doing, and I think we'd better go about now."

"Do you?" inquired the younger brother, who had a lofty contempt for the other's judgment as a sailor. "Well, I don't. My plan is simply this: I am going to run as near the shore as I can, then go about sharp, and let them drift by us by a boat's length. A boat's length is as good as a mile, and then, when we are both heading the same way, I would like to see them touch us!"

"What's the use of taking such risks?" demanded the elder brother. "I tell you we can't afford to let them get so near as that."

"At the same time," replied the man at the helm, "that is what we are going to do. I am commanding this boat, please to remember, and if I take the risks I am willing to take the blame."

"You'll be doing well if you get off with nothing but blame," growled the elder brother. "If you let those kids catch us, I'll throw you overboard!"

"I'll put you in irons for threatening a superior officer if you don't keep quiet," answered the younger Carter, with a grin, and the mutiny ended.

It certainly would have been great sport to have run almost into the arms of the revenue officers, and then to have turned and led them a race to the goal, but the humor of young Carter's plan was not so apparent to the anxious throng of sympathizers on Chadwick's dock.

"What's the matter with the boys! Why don't they go about?" asked Captain Chadwick, excitedly. "One would think they were trying to be caught."

As he spoke, the sail of the *Ripple* fluttered in the wind, her head went about sharply, and, as her crew scrambled up on the windward rail, she bent and bowed gracefully on the homeward tack.

But, before the boat was fully under way, the *Osprey* came down upon her with a rush. The Carters hauled in the sail until their sheet lay almost flat with the surface of the river, the water came pouring over the leeward rail, and the boys threw their bodies far over the other side, in an effort to right her. The next instant there was a crash, the despised boat of the Atlantic House struck her fairly in the side, and one of the Atlantic House crew had boarded the *Ripple* with a painter in one hand and his hat in the other.

Whether it was the shock of the collision, or disgust at having been captured, no one could tell; but when the *Osprey's* bow struck the *Ripple,* the younger Carter calmly let himself go over backward and remained in the mud with the water up to his chin and without making any effort to help himself, until the judges' boat picked him up and carried him, an ignominious prisoner-of-war, to the Atlantic House dock.

The disgust over the catastrophe to the pirate crew was manifested on the ,part of the Chadwick sympathizers by gloomy silence or loudly expressed indignation. On the whole, it was perhaps just as well that the two Carters, as prisoners-of-war, were forced to remain at the Atlantic House dock, for their reception at home would not have been a gracious one.

Their captors, on the other hand, were received with all the honor due triumphant heroes, and were trotted off the pier on the shoulders of their cheering admirers; while the girls in the carriages waved their parasols and handkerchiefs and the colored waiters on the banks danced up and down and shouted like so many human calliopes.

The victories of John Paul Jones and the rescue of Lieutenant Greely became aquatic events of little importance in comparison. Everybody was so encouraged at this first success, that Atlantic House stock rose fifty points in as many seconds, and the next crew to sally forth from that favored party felt that the second and decisive victory was already theirs.

Again the black flag appeared around the bank of the island, and on the instant a second picked crew of the Atlantic House was in pursuit. But the boys who commanded the pirate craft had no intention of taking or giving any chances. They put their boat about long before the revenue officers expected them to do so, forcing their adversaries to go so directly before the wind that their boat rocked violently. It was not long before the boats drew nearer and nearer together, again, as if they must certainly meet at a point not more than a hundred yards from the Atlantic House pier, where the excitement had passed the noisy point and had reached that of titillating silence.

"Go about sharp!" snapped out the captain of the pirate boat, pushing his tiller from him and throwing his weight upon it. His first officer pulled the sail close over

the deck, the wind caught it fairly, and, almost before the spectators were aware of it, the pirate boat had gone about and was speeding away on another tack. The revenue officers were not prepared for this. They naturally thought the pirates would run as close to the shore as they possibly could before they tacked, and were aiming for the point at which they calculated their opponents would go about, just as did the officers in the first race.

Seeing this, and not wishing to sail too close to them, the pirates had gone about much farther from the shore than was needful. In order to follow them the revenue officers were now forced to come about and tack, which, going before the wind as they were, they found less easy. The sudden change in their opponents' tactics puzzled them, and one of the two boys bungled. On future occasions each confidentially informed his friends that it was the other who was responsible; but, however that may have been, the boat missed stays, her sail flapped weakly in the breeze, and, while the crew were vigorously trying to set her in the wind by lashing the water with her rudder, the pirate boat was off and away, one hundred yards to the good, and the remainder of the race was a procession of two boats with the pirates easily in the lead.

And now came the final struggle. Now came the momentous "rubber," which was to plunge Chadwick's into gloom, or keep them still the champions of the river. The appetites of both were whetted for victory by the single triumph each had already won, and their representatives felt that, for them, success or a watery grave were the alternatives.

The Atlantic House boat, the *Wave,* and the boat upon which the Chadwicks' hopes were set, the *Rover,* were evenly matched, their crews were composed of equally good sailors, and each was determined to tow the other ignominiously into port.

The two Prescotts watched the *Wave* critically and admiringly, as she came toward them with her crew perched on her side and the water showing white under her bow.

"They're coming entirely too fast to suit *me*," said the elder Prescott. "I want more room and I have a plan to get it. Stand ready to go about." The younger brother stood ready to go about, keeping the *Rover* on her first tack until she was clear of the island's high banks and had the full sweep of the wind; then, to the surprise of her pursuers and the bewilderment of the spectators, she went smartly about, and, turning her bow directly away from the goal, started before the wind back past the island and toward the wide stretch of river on the upper side.

"What's your man doing that for?" excitedly asked one of the Atlantic House people, of the prisoners-of-war.

"I don't know, certainly," one of the Carters answered, "but I suppose he thinks his boat can go faster before the wind than the *Wave* can, and is counting on getting a long lead on her before he turns to come back. There is much more room up there, and the opportunities for dodging are about twice as good."

"Why didn't *we* think of that, Gus?" whispered the other Carter.

"We were too anxious to show what smart sailors we were, to think of anything!" answered his brother, ruefully.

Beyond the island the *Rover* gained rapidly; but, as soon as she turned and began beating homeward, the *Wave* showed that tacking was her strong point and began, in turn, to make up all the advantage the *Rover* had gained.

The *Rover's* pirate-king cast a troubled eye at the distant goal and at the slowly but steadily advancing *Wave*.

His younger brother noticed the look.

"If one could only *do* something," he exclaimed, impatiently. "That's the worst of sailing races. In a rowing race you can pull till you break your back, if you want to; but here you must just sit still and watch the other fellow creep up, inch by inch, without being able to do anything to help yourself. If I could only get out and push, or pole! It's this trying to keep still that drives me crazy."

"I think we'd better go about, now," said the commander quietly, "and instead of going about again when we are off the bar, I intend to try to cross it."

"What!" gasped the younger Prescott, "go across the bar at low water? You can't do it. You'll stick sure. Don't try it. Don't think of it!"

"It is rather a forlorn hope, I know," said his brother; "but you can see yourself they're bound to overhaul us if we keep on—we don't draw as much water as they do, and if they try to follow us we'll leave them high and dry on the bar."

The island stood in the center of the river, separated from the shore on one side by the channel, through which both boats had already passed, and on the other by a narrow stretch of water which barely covered the bar the *Rover* purposed to cross.

When she pointed for it, the *Wave* promptly gave up chasing her, and made for the channel with the intention of heading her off in the event of her crossing the bar.

"She's turned back!" exclaimed the captain of the *Rover*. "Now, if we only can clear it, we'll have a beautiful start on her. Sit perfectly still, and, if you hear her center-board scrape, pull it up, and balance so as to keep her keel level."

Slowly the *Rover* drifted toward the bar; once her center-board touched, and as the boat moved further into the shallow water the waves rose higher in proportion at the stern.

But her keel did not touch, and as soon as the dark water showed again, her crew gave an exultant shout and pointed her bow toward the Chadwick dock, whence a welcoming cheer came faintly over the mile of water.

"I'll bet they didn't cheer much when we were crossing the bar!" said the younger brother, with a grim chuckle. "I'll bet they thought we were mighty foolish."

"We couldn't have done anything else," returned the superior officer. "It was risky, though. If we'd moved an inch she would have grounded, sure."

"I was scared so stiff that I couldn't have moved if I'd tried to," testified the younger sailor with cheerful frankness.

Meanwhile the wind had freshened, and white-caps began to show over the roughened surface of the river, while sharp, ugly flaws struck the sails of the two contesting boats from all directions, making them bow before the sudden gusts of wind until the water poured over the sides.

But the sharpness of the wind made the racing only more exciting, and such a series of maneuvers as followed, and such a naval battle, was never before seen on the Manasquan River.

The boys handled their boats like veterans, and the boats answered every movement of the rudders and shortening of the sails as a thoroughbred horse obeys its bridle. They ducked and dodged, turned and followed in pursuit, now going free before the wind, now racing, close-hauled into the teeth of it. Several times a capture seemed inevitable, but a quick turn of the tiller would send the pirates out of danger. And as many times the pirate crew almost succeeded in crossing the line, but before they could reach it the revenue

cutter would sweep down upon them and frighten them away again.

"We can't keep this up much longer," said the elder Prescott. "There's more water in the boat now than is safe; and every time we go about we ship three or four bucketfuls more."

As he spoke, a heavy flaw keeled the boat over again, and, before her crew could right her, the water came pouring over the side with the steadiness of a small waterfall. "That settles it for us," exclaimed Prescott, grimly; "we *must* pass the line on this tack, or we sink."

"They're as badly off as we are," returned his brother. "See how she's wobbling—but she's gaining on us, just the same," he added.

"Keep her to it, then," said the man at the helm. "Hold on to that sheet, no matter how much water she ships."

"If I don't let it out a little, she'll sink!"

"Let her sink, then," growled the chief officer. "I'd rather upset than be caught."

The people on the shore and on the judges' boat appreciated the situation fully as well as the racers. They had seen, for some time, how slowly the boats responded to their rudders and how deeply they were sunk in the water.

All the maneuvering for the past ten minutes had been off the Chadwick dock, and the Atlantic House people, in order to get a better view of the finish, were racing along the bank on foot and in carriages, cheering their champions as they came.

The *Rover* was pointed to cross an imaginary line between the judges' steam-launch and Chadwick's dock. Behind her, not three boat-lengths in the rear, so close that her wash impeded their headway, came the revenue officers, their white caps off, their hair flying in the wind, and every muscle strained.

Both crews were hanging far over the sides of the boats, while each wave washed the water into the already half-filled cockpits.

"Look out!" shouted the younger Prescott, "here comes another flaw!"

"Don't let that sail out!" shouted back his brother, and as the full force of the flaw struck her, the boat's rail buried itself in the water and her sail swept along the surface of the river.

For an instant it looked as if the boat was swamped, but as the force of the flaw passed over her, she slowly righted again, and with her sail dripping and heavy, and rolling like a log, she plunged forward on her way to the goal.

When the flaw struck the *Wave,* her crew let their sheet go free, saving themselves the inundation of water which had almost swamped the *Rover,* but losing the headway which the *Rover* had kept.

Before the *Wave* regained it, the pirate craft had increased her lead, though it was only for a moment.

"We can't make it," shouted the younger Prescott, turning his face toward his brother so that the wind might not drown his voice. "They're after us again, and we're settling fast."

"So are they," shouted his brother. "We can't be far from the line now, and as soon as we cross that, it doesn't matter what happens to us!"

As he spoke another heavy gust of wind came sweeping toward them, turning the surface of the river dark blue as it passed over, and flattening out the waves.

"Look at that!" groaned the pirate-king, adding, with professional disregard for the Queen's English, "We're done for now, that's certain!" But before the flaw reached them, and almost before the prophetic words were uttered, the cannon on the judges' boat banged forth merrily, and the crowds on the Chadwick dock answered

its signal with an unearthly yell of triumph.

"We're across, we're across!" shouted the younger Prescott, jumping up to his knees in the water in the bottom of the boat and letting the wet sheet-rope run freely through his stiff and blistered fingers.

But the movement was an unfortunate one.

The flaw struck the boat with her heavy sail dragging in the water, and with young Prescott's weight removed from the rail. She reeled under the gust as a tree bows in a storm, bent gracefully before it, and then turned over slowly on her side.

The next instant the *Wave* swept by her, and as the two Prescotts scrambled up on the gunwale of their boat the defeated crew saluted them with cheers, in response to which the victors bowed as gracefully as their uncertain position would permit.

The new arrival, who had come to Manasquan in the hope of finding something to shoot, stood among the people on the bank and discharged his gun until the barrels were so hot that he had to lay the gun down to cool. And every other man and boy who owned a gun or pistol of any sort, fired it off and yelled at the same time, as if the contents of the gun or pistol had entered his own body. Unfortunately, every boat possessed a tin horn with which the helmsman was wont to warn of his approach the keeper of the draw-bridge. One evil-minded captain blew a blast of triumph, and in a minute's time the air was rent with tootings little less vicious than those of the steam whistle of a locomotive.

The last had been so hard-fought a race, and both crews had acquitted themselves so well, that their respective followers joined in cheering them indiscriminately.

The *Wave* just succeeded in reaching the dock before she settled and sank. A dozen of Chadwick's boarders seized the crew by their coat-collars and arms as they leaped from the sinking boat to the pier and assisted them to their feet, forgetful in the excitement of the moment that the sailors were already as wet as sponges on their native rocks.

"I suppose I should have stuck to my ship as Prescott did," said the captain of the *Wave* with a smile, pointing to where the judges' boat was towing in the *Rover* with her crew still clinging to her side; "but I'd already thrown you my rope, you know, and there really isn't anything heroic in sticking to a sinking ship when she goes down in two feet of water."

As soon as the Prescotts reached the pier they pushed their way to their late rivals and shook them heartily by their hands. Then the Atlantic House people carried their crew around on their shoulders, and the two Chadwick's crews were honored in the same embarrassing manner. The proprietor of the Atlantic House invited the entire Chadwick establishment over to a dance and a late supper.

"I prepared it for the victors," he said, "and though these victors don't happen to be the ones I prepared it for, the victors must eat it."

The sun had gone down for over half an hour before the boats and carriages had left the Chadwick dock, and the Chadwick people had an opportunity to rush home to dress. They put on their very best clothes, "just to show the Atlantic people that they *had* something else besides flannels," and danced in the big hall of the Atlantic House until late in the evening.

When the supper was served, the victors were toasted and cheered and presented with a very handsome set of colors, and then Judge Carter made a stirring speech.

He went over the history of the rival houses in a way that pleased everybody, and made all the people at the table feel ashamed of themselves for ever having been rivals at all.

He pointed out in courtly phrases how excellent and varied were the modern features of the Atlantic House, and yet how healthful and satisfying was the old-fashioned simplicity of Chadwick's. He expressed the hope that the two houses would learn to appreciate each other's virtues, and hoped that in the future they would see more of each other.

To which sentiment everybody assented most noisily and enthusiastically, and the proprietor of the Atlantic House said that, in his opinion, Judge Carter's speech was one of the finest he had ever listened to, and he considered that part of it which touched on the excellent attractions of the Atlantic House as simply sublime, and that, with his Honor's permission, he intended to use it in his advertisements and circulars, with Judge Carter's name attached.

THE
LATEST NEWS
ABOUT THE
THREE WISHES

by Rupert Hughes

As every one knows, young folks that never do what they should not do, and never leave undone what they ought to do, run a great risk of meeting some day a good fairy who will say, in a musical voice:

"Thomas" (or "Richard" or "Henry," as the case may be), "since you have been a good boy, the gracious King of the Fairies has decided to reward you bountifully. Any three wishes you may make will be granted, whatever they are. But be very careful what you choose!"

Now, there was once a lad named Albert Crane. He was related to the King of the Fairies by the marriage of a great-uncle, on his mother's side, to the second cousin of an intimate friend of a passing acquaintance of a young man who had once saved the life of a fairy who was caught in a rain-storm about midnight and could not fly home. If she had stayed out till sunrise she would have died, as you all know; and her wings were so wet that she was having a sorry time of it when this young man picked her gently up by the nape of the neck, and hid her under a candle-snuffer till the next night, thus saving her from the fatal glance of the sun. And this is a thing you must all do when you find a fairy in distress; for fairies are like the unfixed proofs of a photograph: they fade into nothing under the glare of the sun.

Well, then, since this young man had befriended the fairy, the fairy King was eager to show his gratitude in any way and every way possible, even to relatives as far removed as the eye could reach. He was very anxious, for this reason, to grant the three wishes to Albert Crane. But Albert was such a mischievous little fellow that it seemed he would never be able to express his gratitude in that direction. The lowest average of good behavior on which the diploma of the three wishes will be granted is three weeks. (No wonder so few young people ever get the wishes!) Albert Crane seemed the most hopeless of all. He was so far from being able to stay good three weeks in succession that nothing could trap him into being good even one day in succession. There is no need of telling you all the mischievous things he did, because, if you have not already done them all yourself before, you might learn something new.

But just as the fairy King was giving up in despair, Albert fell sick, and was kept in bed for a whole month. He was too weak to carry out any mischief, or even to plan it; and the fairy King jumped at the chance to relieve himself of the debt he thought he owed to Albert's mother's uncle's second cousin's intimate friend's passing acquaintance's young man.

So one day,—the first day Albert was strong enough to go out into the woods alone, and before he could rob any birds' nests or do anything else wrongful,—he was surprised beyond expression to see standing before him a beautiful girl with long brown hair and bright blue eyes, and a wand with a star on it. And on her shoulders grew beautiful butterfly wings that must have cost between $3.99 at Browny & Pixie's bargain-counter. Albert recognized her at once from her resemblance to the fairies in the picture-books; and for the first time he saw how true all such pictures are.

Before Albert could make up his mind to do what he usually did when he met pretty girls,—pull their hair till the tears came,—the fairy spoke to him, and said the words quoted above, except that in the printed blank the King had given her was written the name Albert instead of Tom, Dick, or Harry.

When Albert heard the fairy's little speech, which she delivered like a Friday afternoon recitation,—only she forgot the curtsy at the end,—he was too much amazed for a moment to say a word. His memory ran back over all the similar experiences of youngsters who had been accosted by fairies for some good deed. He had never expected any such experience himself, and was not prepared with an immediate answer; but he remembered the fates of several of the children to whom the gift of three wishes had been given.

Some of the boys asked, first, for all the candy they could eat; second, for all the red circus-lemonade they could drink; and third, for all the baseball runs they could score. Albert never forgot the fate of these poor wretches—the terrible stomach-aches the candy gave them, how sick they grew of lemonade, and how their baseball games lasted so long they could never go home to dinner or to bed. Because, of course, the three wishes they wished were fulfilled to the last degree, and they had no extra wish to save them from the penalty of the first three. Albert had read of other boys, who, unlike him, had always enjoyed Sunday-school, and never stole a ride on a wagon or threw a rock through a street-lamp. They always wished, first, for virtue; second, for wisdom; and third, for a chance to do good in the world. But these things did not appeal to Albert at all, for he was a little imp. His father called him a limb, though he never specified whether he was a hickory limb or a limb of "slippery-ellum."

Albert was very much puzzled over his

wishes. He wanted so many things at once that his brain went into a whirl. He felt as if he had been tied in a merry-go-round for weeks. The whole world was one great merry-go-round to him.

The fairy stood and watched the boy till she remembered an appointment she had in China, a few minutes later, to carry the three wishes to a little pigtail, who would probably wish, first, for as much rice as he could eat; second, for as many fire-crackers as he could set off; and last (and least), for good luck with his lessons.

Then the fairy spoke as sharply as a street-car conductor saying "Step lively, there!" and brought Albert to his senses in a moment. Now, Albert was a lawyer's son, and a happy thought struck him. Instead of choosing any three wishes out of the thousands things a boy of his age could wish, he suddenly said, with a bluntness that took the fairy's breath away:

"If I choose one wish only, will you make me three times as sure of getting it?"

The fairy was too much startled to understand what this strange request might mean, and before she thought she accepted:

"Yes, if you wish."

"You promise?" persisted Albert.

"I promise," said the fairy.

"Well, then," said Albert, with the slowness of a judge, "I make this one wish: that every wish I make in all the rest of my life shall be granted."

This was something the fairy had not expected. She had never heard of such a thing, and it almost scared her to death to think what she had done. It would have scared her to death, if there were any death for fairies.

"I shall have to see the King," she cried; and before Albert could grab her by her back hair she had disappeared.

Then Albert stood nonplussed for a moment, and wished he had not been so greedy. It made him sicker than he had been all the month before, and he felt very much like lying down and crying his eyes out. In fact, he had just decided that would be a good thing to do, when there was a buzz and a whizz and a flash, and there stood the King of the Fairies himself.

Albert dropped down on his knees before the bright apparition, and heard the King saying:

"What trick is this you are trying to play on us? You are the worst boy that ever lived! I have been trying for half a year to keep you good long enough to grant you the three wishes, and now you try to play a trick upon me! As a punishment for your presumption, you shall have no wish at all."

But Albert, being a lawyer's son, was not to be put out of countenance, and he said, as if it were the Fourth of July and he were saying, "Give me liberty, or give me death":

"Your Majesty, whatever my past history may be, you have given your sacred promise, and you cannot break it."

The fairy King blustered and stormed and threatened and pleaded; but Albert was obstinate, and finally the King flew away in a great huff, snapping:

"Keep your old wish, then!"

So Albert went home very triumphant. Finding that he had walked a long way and was a little tired and weak from his illness, he wished for a beautiful Shetland pony; and before he knew how it came, there it was. So he got on its back, and just as he wished it would gallop away, even before he could say "Get up," it galloped. But Albert had never learned to ride before, and he was being jolted into a cream-cheese, when he wished that he might be an expert rider. So he was.

Remembering that his home was not a very beautiful one, for his father was a poor lawyer,—in both senses of the word, —he wished that he might find his mother and father and brothers and sisters in a beautiful mansion. So he did.

But when he went into this beautiful home he found that the butcher and the baker and the grocer had got tired of having their bills unpaid, and had refused to give his father any more credit; so, for all the beautiful house, there was nothing to eat; and much as the family was mystified at the change in their dwelling, they were not too much mystified to be hungry. So Albert simply wished all his father's bills receipted, and a beautiful dinner served in the magnificent dining-room. So everything was done as he wished.

It would take all the rest of your life to tell all the beautiful experiences he had, so if you have anything else to do this year, we'll skip most of it. He got his wisher so well trained that he could wish for so many things at one time that the whole fairy court had to quit all other work and attend to him. On beautiful moonlight nights they were too tired to dance in the woods. Besides, Albert was just as likely to wish in his sleep as when he was awake.

The fine thing about Albert's experience was that it was unlike that of the bad boys who had wished for candy and red lemonade. When they made themselves sick, there was nothing to do but suffer. When Albert overate, all he had to do was to wish himself cured. If there was an especially beautiful dinner before him, he wished himself an extra good appetite and digestion till he had finished all there was in sight and was tired of eating.

He wished to have Christmas every day until he got as tired of it as Mr. Howells' little girl grew. Then he wished for Fourth of July every day till that bored

him. Then he wished that he might know all his lessons without going to school, until he found that one of the chief pleasures of knowledge is the pleasure of getting it. He wished that all the trees with birds' nests in them would be easy to climb until he saw how much pain he was causing the mother birds, and how many songs he was hushing in the woods by robbing the nests of the eggs which would some day be songsters.

He wished his baseball nine to win all the games by tremendous scores, till he saw how uninteresting it was to be certain of everything.

In fact, in time he came to believe that, after all, life was very good and full of pleasures and opportunities just as it was, and without fairy power to change it. He saw the use of pain, and, understanding this, came to sympathize with the rest of the world, and to be very merciful and very charitable and very thoughtful.

But even this happiness palled on him. He was ashamed to be so different from the other boys, and he felt that he had no friends at all, because he was no fit companion for boys who had to work hard for all the fun they had, as well as all the serious things they accomplished. He saw that his life was merely one continued story of good luck—a mere fairy story; and he felt that he never deserved pleasures, because he had done nothing to earn them.

Besides, the other boys began to let him severely alone. They wouldn't play with him, they wouldn't go to school with him, and they wouldn't even fight with him. It would have been bad enough to becalled "teacher's pet"; he couldn't endure being called "fairy's pet."

One day, in his loneliness, he cried, "Plague take the wish! I wish I were without it!"

Suddenly he felt something rip, and in a

great fright he gasped, "No; I wish my wish to come back!" But when he wished for a glass of chocolate ice-cream soda to appear on a tree-stump near by, not a thing happened.

The fairy court stood on their heads with joy when Albert's wish came crashing through a window, and they knew their long service was over.

But Albert was happier still, for he was admitted to a ball game when he said he was no longer a professional wisher. And when he put up his hands to catch a "beauty" fly, he muffed it and got a bruised finger to boot. And when he went to bat he missed the ball three times. And he was so happy at being a human boy again that he hugged himself; and that evening he ran home crying: "Hooray! hooray! We lost the game!"

THE SWIFTWATER BUCK

by William Gerard Chapman

ACROSS the sunlit swale came stalking cautiously a whitetail doe with her five-months' fawn stepping daintily at her side, the weanling showing a curious, long, whitish scar on its flank. Before emerging from the dark recesses of the wood, they had stood in the spruce tangle at the forest's edge for several minutes, the doe searching the open with eyes and nose and ears, her fawn as motionless as herself in obedience to an unspoken command.

The mother deer was in mighty fear of humankind, but it is doubtful if the fawn would have evidenced any great terror had one of the tribe appeared, for the same recent experience from which sprang the doe's overpowering dread of man had left the fawn with as great a curiosity concerning him. Early in the spring the doe, driven by wolves, had, in her extremity, leaped among the pasturing herd of a settler, and the cattle, alarmed by her abrupt advent and catching the fever of her fear, had raced to the barn-yard. The doe and her fawn, which had followed at her heels, tolled along by the rush, soon found themselves in a strange, fenced enclosure, and, falling exhausted from their terrific effort, had been captured and imprisoned within a calf-pen by the backwoods farmer. The man had acted on impulse, and, once the pair was safely railed in, wondered what he should do with them, his first thought naturally being of the venison they would provide for his table.

The next day, however, his young son, coming early to the pen to feed and make overtures to the captives, was overjoyed by the sight of the fawn, and thenceforth he devoted himself to cultivating the friendship of the agile and beautiful creature.

One morning, some days later, the boy, peering into the pen, was cut short in his salutations by the sight of a red gash in the flank of the baby deer. The fawn had torn his side deeply, but not dangerously, on a protruding splinter, and the crimson streak in his delicate coat smote the child's heart with horror and sympathy. He lifted the latch of the pen door, which could be fastened only on the outside, and ran to comfort his wounded protégé. The doe backed into the far corner, trembling with terror, then suddenly sprang for the opening, bowling the child over in her rush. At her bleat of command the fawn dashed after her, maternal authority overcoming whatever of reluctance he may have felt in deserting the kind little two-legged animal, and the boy, rising bewildered and with the hot tears springing to his eyes, emerged from the pen just in time to glimpse the two gracefully leaping forms disappearing over the crest of a rise in mid-pasture. With her white flag guiding the youngling, the freed mother deer streaked for the friendly cover that loomed invitingly

156

before her eyes, and quickly doe and fawn were swallowed up in the cool, dim sanctuary of the forest.

SEVERAL years passed, and in the settlements a "scar-sided buck" began to achieve a reputation beyond that of any of his fellows. Known and recognized both by the livid mark on his right flank and the immense size to which he grew, he became famous throughout the Swiftwater country. He was credited either with possessing uncanny craft or the gift of uncommonly good luck, for no magnificently antlered head was more coveted, or more assiduously hunted, than the one that reared itself proudly on his broad, powerful shoulders. And frequently something more than desire to possess the finest head they had known inspired the efforts of the hunters of the region. His depredations on the fields and truck patches of the scattered farmsteads periodically sent irate backwoods farmers on his trail vowing to exterminate this despoiler of their crops. But these usually returned without having seen the big buck, or else, if they caught a glimpse of him, he got himself so swiftly out of sight that no chance offered for a successful shot.

That the buck knew the difference between a man unarmed and a man with a gun was an opinion shrewdly held by one young hunter, who kept this view to himself for reasons of his own. Probably some early experience in being creased by a bullet from one of those fire-spouting, loud-voiced sticks that men sometimes carried had brought an idea into the buck's head. Dogs did not seem to excite any great terror in him, and on numerous occasions he had turned on those that followed his trail and driven them off. But usually he accepted the challenge and gave them an exhilarating run, and, when the game palled, broke his trail craftily and

left the dogs to plod back home foot-sore and chop-fallen.

The history of "Old Scarside," which was the name by which the great buck finally came to be known, was familiar to the settlement folk. Laban Knowles, the farmer who had imprisoned the doe and fawn, and his son Lonny held themselves his sponsors; indeed, Lonny maintained that the buck belonged to him, and always was driven to white anger by the often expressed designs on the deer's life.

Lonny desired above all things that his big buck, who only a few years before, as a captive fawn, had plainly shown his willingness to be friends with him, should live unharmed. Old Scarside, magnificent and storied buck whitetail of the Swiftwater country, had responded to his voice and nuzzled his hand when both were hardly more than babies! The intimate association, unfortunately, had been terminated after all too brief a life, else surely it would have progressed to a thorough understanding; but the friendship so begun still held with one of the parties to it, and the boy's assumption of proprietorship in the biggest deer of the region was known to all the inhabitants of the border country.

Lonny Knowles was by way of becoming a top-notch woodsman, and his skill as a marksman with his twenty-two rifle was a matter of note among his fellows. Whenever his farm duties permitted, he roamed the woods, shooting what small game was needed for the home table, but finding his greatest pleasure in studying the wild life of the great timbered stretches that enclosed the settlement. Of all the wild-wood folk, the scar-sided whitetail deer held first place in his interest. Noiselessly he ranged the feeding-grounds and runways that he had come to know were used by "his buck," and often his careful stalking was rewarded by a sight of the noble animal. His great wish was to overcome the buck's instinctive fear, in the boyish hope that eventually he would succeed in reëstablishing an understanding with his one-time friend. And very patiently and persistently he sought to accustom the buck to his presence. Whenever he came upon his track, easily distinguishable by its size, he trailed him with the silent efficiency of an Indian. When, finally, Old Scarside was sighted, Lonny drew as near to him as cover and wind permitted, and watched him long and admiringly. Then, leaving his rifle on the ground, he would silently rise and show himself, all his movements quiet and restrained and his manner casual. Up would come the buck's head with a snort of surprise at the sudden apparition. Usually he would bound away the instant Lonny showed himself. Sometimes, when Lonny stood forth while the buck's eyes were turned aside, Scarside would suddenly become aware of an alien figure standing astonishingly close where no figure had been an instant before, and, snorting and stamping petulantly, with eyes and nose would seek to penetrate the mystery. Then, suspicion overcoming curiosity, he would wheel and plunge swiftly from the spot.

But gradually, very gradually, the painstaking methods of the young woodsman began to have their effect on the buck. The casual approach, unthreatening manner, and eyes that never fixed themselves disquietingly upon his own, were strangely at variance with what his experience had taught him of the ways of the man tribe, though sometimes the evidence carried on a veering puff of wind would unmistakably proclaim the intruder a member of it. And as time went on, a growing familiarity with this seemingly harmless individual, smaller in stature than his other persecutors and never bearing that abhorrent instrument of noise and flame asso-

ciated with these enemies, slowly wore down the fine edge of his fear. Often he would stand and stamp and snort for minutes, merely backing off slowly as Lonny advanced upon him inch by inch. Then, as a quiver of muscles rippled the sheen of his coat and signaled a break for cover, Lonny would stay him with a bleated *"Mah!"* And for an instant longer the wondering buck would tarry, to puzzle out the meaning of this, before discretion sent him bounding away into the green forest depths. Later, when the buck's departure was still longer delayed, Lonny would utter soothing words to him.

"You ain't afeard o' me, are you, old feller? 'Member when you an' me was babies, you licked my hand. We're friends still, ain't we? Now, don't get skeery an' cut an' run—I ain't a-goin' to harm you!"

Awed and fascinated by the softly spoken words, Scarside would stand a-quiver, then run back a few steps and halt, half hidden, in a near-by thicket, pawing and whistling, his big liquid eyes never leaving this strangely ingratiating one of the enemy kind. In the dim recesses of his brain did some faint memory stir at the voice that, in the first days of his life, spoke to him in the universal language of infant brotherhood? Or perhaps some remnant of that early curiosity of his concerning man creatures remained to weaken the ancestral dread.

The buck's whistling Lonny chose to interpret as a reply to his own remarks.

"Remember, do you? Well, then don't be so bashful. I ain't never a-goin' to hurt you, Old Scarside—it's all along o' that scar that you got away from me when you were jest a little feller. You ain't forgotten, have you? Well, good-by then, if you're a-goin'."

When Lonny described his adventures in friendliness with the deer, Laban scoffed amusedly at his son's firm belief in Scarside's memory of the early incident.

"A deer hain't got no memory—don't you ever believe it. He's jest gittin' used to you an' your quiet ways, like any wild critter will ef you show yourself often enough an' don't pay special attention to 'em at first. He's jest curious about you, an' a deer's as curious a critter as any woman.

"But ef he's your deer, like you claim, you better learn him to keep out o' the clearin's," Laban continued, his whimsical tone changing to half-angry seriousness as he thought of the devastated field of ruta-bagas he had just visited. "The pesky crit-ter's gittin' to be a blame nuisance, eatin' up half the crops. Last night he liked to spile the hull 'baga patch, tromplin' what he didn't eat. I ain't a-goin' to stand him much longer. Ef he don't quit ruinin' the fields, I'll put a bullet inter his big car-cass!"

"Don't you never do it, Pa!" burst out Lonny. "He's only takin' what he thinks is rightly his'n, an' we oughter be able to spare a few 'bagas an' such like. He is my deer, and I won't stand to have him hurted!"

Laban grumbled in his throat and turned away. The generous-hearted farmer was troubled by the knowledge that Old Scarside's continued depredations had reached the unbearable stage. Fences were as nothing to him, and his despoiling of growing crops was now a matter of al-most nightly occurrence. The countryside was becoming inflamed against the big buck, who left his sign manual in each invaded area in the form of tracks that in size resembled those of a calf.

Leaving the boy protesting against the threat, Laban strode off on his way to a neighbor's to assist in raising a new barn-frame. A short cut could be made by pad-dling across the lake that lay between the farmsteads, the trail to this leading over a hard-wood ridge, beyond which stretched the broad sheet of water. On the shelving beach his birch-bark lay among the bushes, and, noting as he shoved it in that a stiff breeze was blowing in his face, he de-cided to weight the bow with a small rock. Otherwise, the light craft would ex-pose so much free-board to the gale that he would have difficulty in keeping its prow in the wind's eye. Bending forward, he was about to deposit the rock carefully in the canoe, when his design was rudely frustrated. His next conscious thought was that the Wendigo—that demon of north-ern Indian legend which seizes men in its talons and bears them off on journeys through space—had savagely snatched at him and sent him whirling dizzily through the air.

Back in the timber of the ridge a big, nobly antlered buck, the pride—and bane —of the Swiftwater country, had watched the striding man with arrogant eyes, eyes that for the moment held no glint of fear. The fever of the sweethearting time was in his blood this crisp November morn-ing, and dread of man was forgotten in the swift anger that blazed within him when his trysting was disturbed. Stiffly he stood for a moment in his screen of bushy hemlock, neck swollen with the madness in his veins, bloodshot eyes glar-ing upon the unsuspecting interloper. Then, intent upon vengeance, he followed after the figure noisily descending the slope. His progress was a series of pranc-ing steps, though his feet fell cunningly without sound, and he shook his mag-nificent head threateningly.

He was only a few paces behind when the man, reaching the shore, suddenly swerved to look about; and the buck froze for a moment before the expected stare of those disconcerting eyes. But the man's gaze did not lift from the ground.

He picked up something and turned his back again and bent over at the water's edge.

The opportunity was too tempting. The buck plunged forward, his lowered head aimed at the crouching figure, and drove at it with all the power of his hard-muscled body. The impact was terrific and the result startling—no less to the object of his attack than to the deer. For the man, with a grunt of astonishment, shot from the shore, turning upside down as he went, and out of the splash that followed emerged not the man, but what appeared to be a smooth brown log, that trembled and rolled crazily among the wavelets and gave forth weird, muffled bellowings!

The backwoodsman, lifted into the air by the amazing assault from the rear, had let go the rock (which at the instant was poised above the canoe) as his hands instinctively reached for the gunwales. As he catapulted into the lake, his grasp on the birch-bark turned it over on him, and he found himself upright in the water, his face above the surface, but in darkness. For a moment utter bewilderment possessed him; then, realizing that he was standing in over five feet of freezing water, his head in the hollow of his capsized canoe, to which he still clung tenaciously, he burst into language and sought to extricate himself.

With a wrench of his arms, he threw the canoe over and turned a wrathful glare toward the bank. Hot indignation choked him momentarily as his eyes fell on the author of his plight pawing the gravel and shaking his antlers in invitation to combat. Then he found his voice.

"Ye confounded, tarnation critter!" sputtered Laban, at a loss for adequate words with which to express his feelings. "So 'twas you butted me into the lake! Ye'll pay fer this—with a bullet through yer hide afore ye're a day older, ye scar-sided imp o' Satan!" He shook his fist at the animal and started to scramble up the steep bottom, continuing his abuse vigorously. But half-way up he came to a stop, perplexed. What should he do when he reached the bank? The buck plainly was in a fighting mood, and no unarmed man was a match for those driving, keen-rimmed hoofs and dagger-like antler-points. Scarside stood his ground, stamping and snorting and lowering his head in challenge.

Laban wondered angrily if he would have to stand there waist-deep in the icy lake until some one came to drive the buck away—and to witness his humiliation! The blood rushed to his bronzed and bearded cheeks at the thought, though he was now shivering to his marrow with the combined cold of water and wind.

In desperation, he suddenly made a great splashing and waved his arms wildly about his head, then gave a piercing yell.

This inexplicable behavior of his victim had its effect on the buck. Irresolutely he fell back a few steps, startled by the wild commotion; and at the terrifying sound that followed, his ardor for battle died. His madness cooling as suddenly as aroused, with a snort of dismay, Scarside whirled in his tracks and dashed off through the trees.

Grim of visage, but with chattering teeth, Laban climbed out of the water, beached his canoe, and hurried homeward, flailing his great arms against his body to restore the circulation of the sluggish blood. Half-way home, he met Lonny coming over the trail.

"Was that you that yelled, Pop? Sounded like some one was terribly hurted, or somethin'. What in time's the matter, anyway? Upset?" Lonny gazed wonderingly at the dripping, angry-faced figure of his father.

"Yes, somethin' happened; but you needn't blat it 'round 'mongst the neighbors. An' somethin' else's goin' to happen, too, mighty soon!"

As his father related his adventure with Old Scarside, Lonny had difficulty in repressing the chuckles that rose to his lips. He covered his mouth with his hand to hide the grin that would persist.

" 'Tain't no laughin' matter," protested Laban, noting the action. "Ef I don't catch pneumony from it, I'll be lucky. Jest as soon as I c'n get some dry duds on, I'm a-goin' to take the rifle an' trail that blame' critter till I git him. 'Tain't enough fer him to be destroyin' the crops; he's started to attack folks, an' he's too dangerous to let live."

He clamped his mouth on his resolution; and Lonny knew that the big buck of the Swiftwater country was doomed.

The scar-sided buck, resting on a mossy knoll in the depths of the spruce wood, raised his head to a suspicious odor that drifted down the wind. He rose to his feet and ran with the breeze for a short distance, then swung around and headed back, paralleling his trail. He halted in a clump of tangled low growth a few rods from it, and waited. Soon a man came swinging along, silent footed, carrying that dreaded black stick, his eyes bent on the ground, but now and again lifting to scan the surrounding bush. Manifestly, as the evidence of nose and eyes indicated, this was the same human so lately visited with his displeasure; and some elemental intuition that reprisal was to be expected warned him that he must be discreet.

When the man had passed, the buck quietly withdrew from his hiding-place and bounded off at right angles to the trail. A mixture of wariness and confidence guided his actions during the succeeding hours. He well knew the danger of giving the man a glimpse of himself in circumstances like these, but his great craft, so often successfully exercised, and his long immunity from harm had bred in him a confidence in his powers that stayed his flight to the barest necessity of keeping out of range. Doggedly the hunter followed, untangling the puzzles of the trail so cunningly woven, his skill the fruit of many a previous stalking of the wily old buck. But whereas on these other occasions he had been content to consider himself the victor in the contest of wits when he finally had come within easy shooting distance of his quarry, bravely withstanding the itch of his trigger-finger, this time there would be a different ending to the hunt.

As the pursuit lengthened, familiar landmarks apprized the backwoodsman that the buck was circling back toward the settlement. This was fortunate, for the afternoon was waning; and furthermore, it afforded him the opportunity of cutting across to the runways along the ridge where, logically, the buck would pass. And then, the finish!

Laban put his plan into operation. If he hurried, he could obtain a vantage-point on a rise of ground commanding the flank of the ridge, and here he would have an ideal chance for a shot as the buck swept across the burning that gashed its forested sides. He neared the spot somewhat winded from his exertions, and paused a moment to regain his breath before carefully threading the thicket of young alder and birch, beyond which the earth fell away into the little valley that lay between. Reaching the fringe of the growth, the opposite slope was revealed to his sight, and he exulted inwardly as he glimpsed the object of his chase just about to cross the burned area. The deer was going steadily, but at no great speed, and though the shot was a long one, he presented an easy chance for a marksman of Laban's skill.

Without hurry, he raised his rifle to his shoulder. At the same instant the buck swerved, stood tense for a second, and began to rear and whirl about in a most astonishing manner. Puzzled by this behavior, which made a killing shot uncertain, Laban lowered his rifle to study the meaning of it. He could discern nothing at first to account for the deer's actions, and when the buck momentarily presented a broadside target, he aimed quickly and pressed the trigger. As he did so, there came to him a flash of understanding— the scene suddenly cleared to his eyes, and his brain fought to restrain the pressure of his finger—but too late! The rifle cracked and the buck went down, and Laban rushed over to the hillside, a numbing fear rising in his heart.

THE scar-sided buck had begun to be annoyed at the pertinacity of the man who followed him. All the cunning that so often in the past had served him seemed of no avail against this creature, who solved each mystery of the trail with such seeming ease. But he was not yet fearful; his bag of tricks was still far from empty. Therefore, without panic, he broke through the trees that bordered the fire-devastated sweep of ground, heading diagonally for the summit, from whence, in the shielding second growth that clothed the spine of the ridge, a view of his adversary's progress might be had. Midway in his flight up the acclivity, a terrifying odor suddenly smote his nostrils. He pivoted sharply as the mingled scent of man and an even worse-hated enemy warned him of danger close by, and he sought warily to locate it.

As his head lifted, his gaze fell on a long, tawny, furtive beast, crawling serpent-wise through the low brush, its tail twitching at the tip, while, at a little distance in front, a small man creature lay twisted on the ground, wriggling frantically, but not moving from the spot. The stricken one's eyes bore on him at the same instant, and a cry came from his lips, cut short as he sagged into an inert heap.

Who shall say what promptings stirred within the whitetail buck, impelling him to leap furiously upon the most dreaded of his animal foes? Whether, at the cry, he recognized the young human who had grown so engagingly familiar to him and sensed the appeal in it, or whether it was that, in the season of his queer flashes of insane courage, his hatred for the slinking beast flamed into uncontrollable rage, no man may say; but the big cat, crouching for the spring and unaware, or unmindful, of the new-comer upon the scene, was assailed from behind by a fury of fierce-driven blows from feet that cut into his flesh like steel knives. His spine was crushed at the first onslaught, and, turning with an agonized snarl, he was flattened to the ground by an irresistible array of stabbing bayonet-points. So sudden and overwhelming was the attack that the panther had never a chance. Almost before he could realize his plight, the deep-cutting feet and battering antlers had reached his vitals, and the spark of his savage life flickered out. But as the victorious buck prodded at the now unresponsive form, a rifle shot shattered the silence, and at the report he gave a convulsive leap forward and fell asprawl, his nose lying against the same hand that he had nuzzled confidingly in a long-past day.

As Laban breathlessly drew near, the full meaning of the strange scene was made plain to him. A sharp pang of regret for the slaying of his son's deliverer came to the backwoodsman as he bent over the huddled, unconscious form, and saw that the child was not seriously hurt. A foot, tightly held in a clump of roots and twisted at the ankle, indicated the nature of Lonny's mishap. Thankful that it was no worse, Laban cut away the detaining tangle and gently chafed the boy back to life. In a few minutes Lonny was sitting up, nursing his sprained ankle, the pain of which was almost forgotten in his wonder at what he beheld.

"Old Scarside saved ye from the painter, Lonny, an' what he got fer it was a bullet! I'd give my rifle if I could have sensed what was up a second sooner. I saw somethin' of what was happenin' all in a flash, but 't was too late. I'm mortal sorry I killed the critter."

Lonny sorrowfully patted the sleek, tawny neck that lay stretched at his feet. Tears were not far from his eyes, but not for the pain of his wrenched foot. "The old feller knew it was me—I allus told you he knew me!—an' he wasn't goin' to let me be chawed up by no painter!" Never thereafter, in the many tellings of the story, was either father or son to permit this altruistic motive for the buck's action to be gainsaid.

"How 'd you git inter such a mess, I want t' know?" asked his father, as the boy thoughtlessly tried to rise to his feet for a closer view of the mangled body of the panther.

Lonny sank back, stifling a yelp of pain. "I come out here to see if I couldn't turn Old Scarside off the ridge, if he happened along with you after him," he admitted; "an' I ketched my foot in this here mess o' creepers an' like to broke my ankle when I fell. I couldn't move, hardly, an' then that ornery painter come lopin' along an' saw me an' started creepin' up——" He shivered at memory of the sinister, stealthy approach of the big cat, its brassy, malevolent eyes fastened with savage purpose on the shrinking lad whom, in its cowardly heart, it knew to be disabled. "I tried to crawl off, but my foot was held tight; an' I jest looked at the varmint an' tried to yell, but was too scairt. An' then I saw Old Scarside amblin' out o' the woods, like he was comin' to help me, an' I called to him—an' that's all I remember.

"You come, didn't you, old feller?" he said, addressing his fallen champion. "It's a blame' shame you got killed fer what you did fer me." The hot tears this time overflowed.

"Wonder where I hit him?" questioned Laban, awkwardly seeking to cover his own very real misery. "Don't see nary mark, an' there ain't no blood far as I kin tell. 'Spose I might as well bleed him," he added, practicalities not to be lost sight of even in the face of tragedy. He drew his knife from its sheath and bent over the body, one hand grasping the antlers.

The moment that followed was the most bewildering in the lives of father and son. For an instant they seemed to be inextricably entangled in a maze of wildly threshing limbs—their own and a deer's—as the "dead" buck rose in the air with a terrified snort, sending Laban spread-eagling over beyond Lonny, and, finding his feet after a few frantic seconds, sped off into the timber.

Astonishment held the two speechless for a space. Then Lonny, ignoring the pain of his foot, throbbing fiercely from the shaking up, gave voice to a yell of joy.

"Go it, Scarside, go it!" he shrieked jubilantly after the vanishing buck. "Couldn't kill you after all, you old rip-snorter, could they?" Full vent for his feelings at the deer's startling resurrection demanded nothing less than the throwing of several handsprings, but Lonny could only toss his hat in the air and wave his arms exultantly. He turned shining eyes on his father, over whose face a delighted grin was breaking as he rubbed his bruises.

"You must've just creased him, Pa, an' only knocked him out fer a spell. Gosh, but I'm glad!"

"You bet I'm glad, too," chuckled Laban, "even ef 't was the second time to-day the critter sent me sprawlin'! Reckon when I pulled the trigger an' then tried not to, all at once, I must've lost my bead an' shot high. Likely the ball nicked him at the base o' the antlers, an' the shock keeled him over, but didn't hurt him none. 'T was a rank miss that I'm proud of—an' 'twill be the last time any one from here-abouts takes a shot at the old buck, I promise ye that! Well, I reckon we better be gittin' home; I'll carry ye pickaback." He swung the lad up to his broad shoulders and started along the back trail for the clearing; and as he strode homeward through the lengthening woodland shad-ows, his chattering, light-hearted burden clinging to his neck, he marveled thank-fully at the outcome of the day's adven-tures, and framed the edict he would send forth upon the morrow—to be violated only at peril of Laban Knowles's ven-geance.

The scar-sided buck, plunging through the twilight aisles of the spruce wood, could not know that from this day he would have nothing to fear from his human neighbors of the wilderness border, nor that, before many hours, the story of his exploit would go ringing through the settlements, colored into a supreme act of devotion to his youthful patron and given an imperishable page in the annals of the Swiftwater country.

THE POOR UNFORTUNATE HOTTENTOT

(NONSENSE VERSE)

by Laura E. Richards

THIS poor unfortunate Hottentot,
    He was not content with his lotten-
        tot;
      Quoth he, "For my dinner,
      As I am a sinner,
There's nothing to put in the pottentot!"

This poor unfortunate Hottentot
Cried: "Yield to starvation I'll nottentot;
      I'll get me a cantaloup,
      Or else a young antelope,
One who'll enjoy being shottentot."

This poor unfortunate Hottentot,
His bow and his arrows he gottentot;
      And being stout-hearted,
      At once he departed,
And struck through the bush at a trotten-
        tot.

This poor unfortunate Hottentot,
When several miles from his cottentot,
      He chanced to set eyes on
      A snake that was p'ison,
A-tying itself in a knottentot.

Then this poor unfortunate Hottentot
Remarked: "This for me is no spottentot!
      I'd better be going;
      There's really no knowing
If he's trying to charm me, or whattentot!"

This poor unfortunate Hottentot
Was turning to flee to his grottentot,
    When a lioness met him,
    And suddenly "et" him,
As a penny's engulfed by the slottentot.

MORAL:

This poor unfortunate Hottentot
Had better have borne with his lottentot,
    And grown even thinner
    For lack of a dinner.
But *I* should have had, then, no plottentot!

UNDER THE HEADLIGHT

by Albert Bigelow Paine

ONE summer morning, nearly twenty years ago, I found myself in New Orleans, Louisiana, with very little money indeed. Being rich in youth and health, this fact did not trouble me. I was rather expert in certain branches of photography, and at once set about obtaining employment at what I was pleased to call my profession.

But it was a poor year and a dull season. I tramped day after day from gallery to gallery, getting always the same reply: "More help than we need now. No chance before cotton time," which was then about three months distant. Finally I went to the photographic supply depot and learned there that a customer at Winona, Mississippi, wanted at once an operator and retoucher, and would pay for his work a fair price, as wages went. I thanked my informant, and said that I would start immediately.

But alas! Winona was more than two hundred and seventy miles from New Orleans, and the fare something over eight dollars. A year or so later I should have stated my case frankly to the supply-dealer and arranged for my ticket. But I did not know of this custom then, and also, being very young, was too proud, or too timid, perhaps, to confess my predicament. Instead, I went back to my cheap room to devise ways and means.

There seemed very few of either. I had precisely twenty-five cents after paying my bill, and the sale of a half-worn heavy coat—not needed in this climate and season—brought me fifty cents more. The remainder of my wardrobe I put into a small valise, and presently set out on foot for the Illinois Central Railroad yards, where freight-trains for the North were made up. I had resolved to beat my way.

I was not altogether unfitted for the undertaking. In still earlier youth I had for one summer been station-agent's assistant, or "cub," at a small Western village, and had learned a good deal about cars, as well as to climb over them while in motion; also the lingo and manner of railroad men, and the kind of talk most likely to obtain a free ride. In fact, during the summer that followed, I had made an extensive trip, in company with a boy-friend, through the great wheat districts of the Central West, earning a good deal of money in the harvest-fields, and paying no railroad fare whatever, though often riding with the trainmen, and in such style as the caboose afforded. I felt confident, therefore, of my ability to get about handily on any part of a running train, and relied as well on a certain railroad freemasonry, though I am bound to say the latter did not count for much in this adventure.

It was a warm day. Even the small valise and my light attire became a burden. Arriving at the yards, the sun beat fiercely down on the cinders and shining steel rails.

Then, the constant switching was confusing, and there seemed to be no train making up that would be ready to start for some hours at least.

I resolved at length to walk to the first small station outside the city, and wait somewhere in the shade until a train came along. Remembering past experience, I counted on making an average of a hundred miles a day, at which rate it would take me about three days to reach Winona.

Beyond the outskirts of the city the road led through a semi-tropical Louisiana swamp, from which the sun drew steam and heavy odors. Here and there I passed gangs of negro railroad laborers, whose shiny blue-black bodies, bare above the waist, and gleaming like polished gun-metal, had a wild look of South African savagery. They chopped and dug at the rank tropical vegetation, and didn't seem to mind the heat, which to me was stifling.

My valise began to drag on me fearfully, and it would bother me still worse later; I resolved to express it, charges collect, from the little station at which, almost overcome by the heat, I at length arrived. Here also I bought a few cents' worth of crackers and, with cold water from a public well, was soon refreshed. Then I went over near the track, and sat down in a shady place to wait.

I had barely rested when a construction train ran in, pausing just long enough for telegraphic orders. When it pulled out, I mounted an empty flat-car at the rear end. By-and-by an employee came back to where I was sitting.

"Where you goin'?" he shouted, above the clatter of the wheels.

"Winona!" I shouted back.

"Can't ride here! Against the rules!"

"Sorry, but I *must go.*"

"Can't allow it. You must get off next stop."

"All right."

The train was for hauling gravel and was very long. I sat on the edge of the flat-car and let my feet swing over the side. The cool wind fanned by, and I enjoyed the scenery. We were making time, too, for a gravel-train, and I thought if I could just keep this up I could increase the daily average. After about a dozen miles, however, we stopped, and I jumped off, as I had agreed to do.

We were at another little village, and I walked for a short distance up a shady street. Then my train whistled to start, and as she got under good headway I resumed my old place on the rear flat-car. Presently my former acquaintance returned and shouted:

"Thought I told you you couldn't ride here!"

"Yes, I believe you did."

"Why didn't you get off back there, then?"

"I did."

He smiled then, too.

"Well," he said, "you can go as far as the lake. We stop there to work. But it's a bad place to lay up in. Mosquitoes will kill you."

"When does the next train come along?"

"About nine o'clock. Passenger-train. Stops at the tank there for water."

That suited me exactly. I could make a station, perhaps two, on the passenger, and some time during the night catch a freight, which, with good luck, I could "hold down" till morning, thus completing my first hundred miles or more.

By and by we came to Lake Pontchartrain bridge, and just beyond it my train ran into a switch and laid up. A gang of painters were employed on the bridge, and with these I soon struck up an acquaintance; for, among the many occupations of a restless youth, I had also painted. The foreman offered me a job, presently, at two dollars a day and board. I thought at first I would take it temporarily, but finally declined, fearing the delay would cause me to lose the other position.

The lake was picturesque. The tall moss-hung cypresses and the placid waters were just as I had seen them in the pictures. The bridge had a draw in the middle of it, and presently this was opened to let a lumber-schooner pass—the *Mary Polly* of New Orleans. As she passed through I looked down on her peaceful decks and wished she were going my way.

At the end of the bridge there was a little store where I ate a light lunch. I did find the mosquitoes rather fierce, but I had nothing to do except to defend myself, and night brought, at last, the rumble of my approaching train. I knew it only stopped here for water, and I could tell just about where the pilot, or cow-catcher, of the engine would be when it stopped. In a line with this and near the track I stood waiting behind some tall weeds and bushes, while the headlight streamed across the bridge, passed me, and the heavy train slowed down and stood panting at the tank. When the big water-pipe was hoisted back to its place and the locomotive began to move slowly, I stepped out and, putting my toe on the lower crosspiece of the cow-catcher, swung myself lightly into place, directly in front of the boiler and beneath the great glaring headlight.

It had grown quite dark by this time, and neither the engineer nor fireman was looking. I felt quite sure I had not been noticed.

Presently we began to go much faster, then still faster. Then we settled down into a steady thirty to thirty-five mile swing, and the rushing wind swept heat, mosquitoes, and weariness far behind.

Faster and still faster! The engine began to rock and hum, and a cloud of small sharp cinders swirled down from above.

They stung my face, but I did not mind them. I was cutting off good miles now. How long I would be allowed to do so, I had no idea; but every two minutes that it lasted meant a mile, at least, nearer my journey's end, and the sensation and excitement of it were glorious. The light from the great eye above me streamed far ahead up the track. On each side was a black wall of night, and between them I was plunging northward at a fearful speed.

On, and still on. Suddenly, with a wild scream from above, we swept through a town without stopping. Country stores were built along the track, after the usual fashion of Southern villages. I saw lights and people. Then woods and blackness again, with the great light streaming ahead.

A new joy now swept over me. My train was the express—the fast mail. It would stop only where railroads crossed, or at large towns, and for water. There are very few railroads or large towns in Mississippi,—fewer then than now,—and an express-locomotive does not take water often. I was good for thirty miles, perhaps, before the first stop. How much better it was than the plodding freights! I looked down the shining steel rails that drew together and vanished in the gloom far ahead, and was exultant, with the careless happiness of youth.

Another village fled by, and another. I was quite settled down to a sense of enjoyment and ownership by this time, and when at last we whistled "down brakes," and I felt our speed slacken for the first stop, it was with a sense of personal injury and ill usage. Perhaps this was to be the end of my glorious ride. It would be more difficult to escape notice in the town than it had been at the lonely water-tank. To add to my dismay, some boys saw me as we swept up to the platform, and ran along by the engine, pointing and calling to the engineer. It was all up, of course. I must get off, and stay off. They had fallen a little behind, however, by the time the engine stopped. I slid off directly in front of the pilot, and walked carelessly away as if I had reached my journey's end. Opposite the platform some ties were piled near the track, and there it was dark. I stepped between them and waited. The boys came up to the pilot, whooping eagerly, and found me gone. I heard them talking loudly and laughing; then their voices grew fainter. The bell clanged to go, and from my place in the shadow I saw the engine move. I stepped out quickly, though with no undue haste, and resumed my place on the pilot. I was, I believe, quite cool. I realized that a scramble might mean a misstep, and a misstep, death. The engineer or fireman may have seen me, but, if so, they gave no sign. The town became scattering houses, with only here and there a light; then came woods again, and the rushing black walls.

I rejoiced greatly that I was good for at least one more stage of my journey. I believed that I had already covered no less than thirty miles on the pilot, and that the next stop would mean as many more. Every village that we dashed through added to my satisfaction; and when the engine screamed, I shouted with it. Then I sang hymns and jubilee songs to the roar and rhythm and rock of the locomotive.

No boys troubled me at the next stop. Perhaps it was too late for them. Nevertheless, I got off instantly, on the side opposite the platform, and walked back to the mail-car. I knew that it had a step on the front, and that the door leading out to this step was rarely opened. It was dark there, and I sat on the end of a tie just below until the train moved; then I climbed aboard, and away we went once more.

This was a harder place to ride, for the cinders and smoke were terrible; but I was determined to make at least one more run, and I felt that the engineer and fireman, who must have seen me, would be on the watch and prevent my boarding the pilot again.

Either the run was unusually long this time, or it seemed so because of the discomforts of my position. Then, too, for some reason, a postal employee came out there and found me. He shouted to me to get off, and stay off, at the next stop. I did not waste words with him. It was no place for argument. I had resolved to "get off and stay off" his old car, anyway. I did so, and went quietly forward to the friendly engine.

My engineer and fireman were off their guard now, it seemed, and I lay in the shadow of some freight-cars on the siding until the pilot moved. Then I mounted as before, and with renewed joy and confidence. This was something like. On the mail-car was no proper place for a gentleman to ride. Perhaps the wildness and excitement of it all had made me desperate by this time, for I was seized with a determination to ride till daybreak.

"I won't get off till morning!
I won't get off till morning!
I won't get off till morning,
    Till daylight doth appear!"

I shouted.

But there are some things easier to sing than to do. I went along without difficulty and with increasing confidence for several stations. Then, all at once,—at Canton, I think,—we changed engines. There was broad light everywhere, and a number of employees were about the cab. The conductor, too, came up presently to chat with the engineer, and from my concealment in the shadow of a small tool-house I could hear what they said. I heard the conductor speak of the hot night and a black cloud, and say that it was going to rain. I wished that it would pour instantly, so that everybody would go away.

This it did not do, and the engineer oiled and wiped while the conductor and yard employees lingered and talked. There would be no chance whatever to get back on the pilot,—none, so far as I could see, to get anywhere,—unless these fellows went away. The employees did so presently, but the conductor lingered and talked on. Then, for some unknown reason, he turned and walked directly to where I was sitting. It would have been foolish to run. I closed my eyes and pretended to be asleep. He came up and held his lantern to my face. Then he called to the engineer: "Here's a fellow going to get wet, Bill!"

The engineer laughed, but did not seem interested enough to look. The conductor left me, and I heard him talking to the engineer again—something about tramps and getting killed. He talked on, and I concluded that he meant to stay there until the train started and get on the first coach as it passed. The situation was becoming desperate. After all, perhaps it would be as well to stop over one train at Canton.

But when the bell began to ring it brought me to my feet. The conductor had walked back a few yards to the end of the platform. If he got on the step of the mail-car there was no hope. The train was moving now, and gaining speed with every foot. He was a heavy man, and would hardly take chances on waiting for the coach. The baggage-car passed him, and the mail-car came on at good speed.

He looked at the step as it came abreast of him, made a slight movement with his body, and—let it pass.

I hesitated no longer. He would not look around again. I stepped quickly over to the track, and as the mail-car step swept by, almost on a level with my head, I caught the handles and made a quick, swinging leap. An instant later I was seated on the upper step, my heart thumping and my breath coming quick and hard. The step had been very high and was going very fast. It was the greatest feat of my life.

The postal employee did not come out this time, perhaps because it was sprinkling and very discouraging out there. At the next stop I went back to my old post on the pilot.

Now it began to rain in earnest—great splashing drops at first, with quick lightning and thunder. I was drenched through at once, of course. Then followed one of the fiercest thunder-storms of that semitropical country: a continuous blue flare, crashing thunder, a torrent of water that bore upon me as if from a broken dam. The conductor's prophecy had come true: I *was* wet. It was cool, though, and a relief after the mail-step. I bent my head to it, and laughed aloud at the wildness of the situation. I thought, if we should only strike a cow now, there would be nothing left to happen, and the fact that we were rushing on to the North through it all exhilarated me till I shouted and sang and laughed wth the rain beating and blinding me. The storm slackened at last, then ceased. The air was much cooler, and I began to feel chilly with the rushing wind in my wet clothes. But the boiler behind me was warm, and I pressed back against it. As my clothes dried I grew very sleepy.

For a time I could scarcely hold my

eyes open, and it was only the occasional stop, and the interest and exercise of regaining my position, that kept me awake.

And so on through the night. I do not know how many stops we made in all—how many times I concealed myself behind the ties, weeds, cars, sheds, or whatever came handiest; but it could not have been less than a dozen in all. Of these places I caught a few of the names as we passed the station placards. I remember dimly Crystal Spring, Jackson, the State capital, and, more clearly, Canton (I think), where we changed engines. I had counted on the night seeming very long, and I could scarcely believe that it was more than two o'clock when all at once I realized that daylight was coming. The sky was clear now, and the stars were fading back into the white light of morning. Bushes and trees on either side began to show in dim outline as we whirled past. At the next stop the fireman came around and met me as I left my seat. He carried a lantern and an oil-can, and did not seem surprised.

"Don't you ever get tired?" he asked.

I knew then that he must have been aware of me for some time. I said that I *was* rather tired—that travel was not all pleasure. He laughed, and throwing his light in my face, looked at me intently. Then he laughed again. I suppose the soot and cinders that had gathered on my features and mixed with the rain had something to do with his mirth. He was goodhearted, though, and went back to his cab with a pleasant word. If he sees this, and remembers, I want him to know that if I wasn't clean, I was grateful for his kindness.

The next stop was a water-tank in the woods. The sun was on the horizon, and the wet green trees were loud with birds. The conductor came forward and saw me.

"This is your place to get off," he said.

"Well," I replied, "I guess I *will* stop over here."

I sat down on a green bank, and the train went on. Then I went to a barrel of fresh rain-water that stood near the tank, and plunged in my arms and head. When I had finished I believed I had the soot and cinders pretty well off. I learned my mistake when, later, I came face to face with a mirror. But, at least, I was refreshed, and sat down to think and congratulate myself on the night's run. I believed that it was about four o'clock, and that I had been seven hours on the train. I could not have made less than two hundred miles, which, with the distance beyond Lake Pontchartrain, would make a total not far from two hundred and twenty-five, leaving perhaps fifty still to go. I could take a good rest, and, with any luck at all, still complete my journey a day sooner than I had calculated.

I realized suddenly that I was thinking all this aloud, and repeating some of it over and over. My head felt light, and I knew that I was slightly delirious from loss of sleep and excitement. I was tempted to lie down at once, but decided to walk on to the first village and get something to eat. There were open fields just ahead, where meadow-larks sang and the grass sparkled with dew. The morning air was fresh and sweet—much better, I thought, than the heavy Louisiana atmosphere. I felt perfectly well in body, but found it hard not to think aloud. The mind is very easily unsettled.

All at once I came to a little road that led across the track and connected two fields. A small negro boy was driving a cow across, and just beyond him was a white post with black figures on it. I looked closer and saw that they formed the number "271." I stared at them steadily

—272 would be my destination. I was not quite sure of my brain. Then I asked of the little darky:

"How far is it to the next town?"

He looked at me, grinning, before he spoke.

"'Bout a mile," he said. "You can see it f'm right up yon'er a li'l' piece."

"What's the name of it?"

"Winona."

I made him repeat it to be sure.

"Yes, sah; Winona. Mighty nice town, sah."

I gave him five of the sixty cents still left in my pocket. Then I hurried on, and going to a cheap railroad restaurant, ate whatever I could get the most of for the least money. They had a wash-room there, and a mirror. In the latter I saw what I most needed, and took it, for towel and basin were there and soap that was strong and plentiful. After breakfast I went to a barber shop, and came out penniless but respectable. I reached my employer's gallery just as he was opening his morning mail. It contained a letter from New Orleans, stating that a man such as he needed would start at once. It referred to me, and had come on the same train. He was glad to see me, and I remained with him a year. We became the best of friends in time, and one day I told him about my trip.

"Well," he laughed, "you were here on time, anyway."

And so I was. But I would not willingly go through such a night again, and many a poor fellow since then has lost his life in just that sort of an undertaking.

THE BROWNIES MEND THE DAM

by Palmer Cox

As Brownies talked in spirits good,
  Beside a broken dam they stood,
  To watch the water as it flew
From many holes the timbers through.
Said one: "The noise that strikes the ear
Would tell that something's lacking here,
If one had not an eye to see
The water spouting out so free;
It surely finds no lack of room
To make escape without the flume,
Where it's supposed to lie and wait
With patience till they raise the gate."

Another said: "This dam supplied
The needs of all the country wide;
It drove the millstone round about,
And ground the grain that kept folk stout,
From grandsires, with their gruel bowl,
To babes just learning how to roll.
It made the saw play up and down,
And furnished lumber for the town
To build its homes so snug and warm,
And give protection from the storm."
A third exclaimed: "Now here's a task
That will have all that one could ask,
In way of struggle and of strain,
Who seeks distinction to attain!
And I, for one, don't want to miss
Or put aside a chance like this.

The work begun was work indeed,
Of all their strength they felt the need,
And skill to plan, and power to stick,
Or make a leap both sure and quick.
For water, if there be enough
And running fast, is dangerous stuff,
And those who went above the flow
Were not more safe than those below.

We all can see there's danger here,
Even for us, who never fear,
And, if a river talks at all,
Quite plainly says this waterfall,
'Begin, begin, to stop the leaks,
You'll need no other bath for weeks.'
But where the human kind would dread
To make a move, we push ahead,
And in this way the honor win
That only comes from wading in.
If men with chisel, saw, and bore,
Could patch this break, we can do more,
Because their skill is ours too,
Besides some gifts they never knew."
What need we with our knowledge great
Of Brownie band do more than state
The task, as you've already guessed,
Was soon commenced with all their zest?

'T was hard above to check the rush,
And hard below to meet the gush;
The logs, that down the stream they ran
To aid in working out their plan,
Were seldom checked at boom or bar,
And, to their sorrow, went too far,
While Brownies with the sticks were
    tossed,
And for a time were counted lost.
For logs rolled over as they ran,
And changed at once the Brownies' plan,
By keeping heads a foot below
Where it was thought the feet would go.
Some might have laughed who saw the
    sight,
But there's no fun in such a plight.
Some bravely faced the danger great,
While more went backward to their fate,
And on the timbers round or square

That they had shaped with art and care,
There was no moment, do their best,
When one could let his prudence rest.
'T would have been painful to behold
If one knew not traditions old,
That these wee people can win through
The trials that would us undo.

To carry out their plans entire,
That failure may not mock desire.
Like bees in hive, or ants in hill,
They show a common stir and will,
And though at times they crowded seem,
They're only working out their scheme,
Each calculation made aright

PALMER COX.

There is no mourning at the home
When they lose breath beneath the foam,
Or grieving at the fireplace,
If they are missing for a space.
They're up and active as a clock
Nor ever suffer from the shock,
Or they would not for years have run
From page to page as they have done.
A mortal scarce can comprehend
The energy they all expend

To reach success and honor bright.
If one would judge them ere they're
        through,
While all's confusion and to-do,
You'd think success would never crown
Such crazy acts, or bring renown.
At such a time advice is lost,
As all have plans and won't be bossed,
But carry out as firm as stone
The part each thinks to be his own.

Strange things were into service press'd
That in their hurry promised best,
And few the objects that escaped
Their eyes, if they were rightly shaped,
Or could with labor small be made
To stop a leak if rightly laid.
They used some gates that long had swung
A welcome wide to old and young,
But now were sagging in their place
With faithless hinge and broken brace.
The task was hard, and tried the best,
And all were anxious for a rest.

But that was not the place to stay
And face the coming glare of day.
So those who still had strength to spare
To weaker comrades gave their care,
For some were heated, some were chilled,
And some with aches and pains were filled,
While more had bruises, or were sore
With work they never tried before.
They hastened to a safe retreat
Where no surprises they would meet,
However bright the day might be,
Or mortals hope to find the key.

PALMER COX.

THE DEAF MUSICIAN

I T was over a hundred and thirty years ago. The opposite neighbor of the Beethovens, who was standing in front of his comfortable home, saw Ludwig, Carl, and Johann Beethoven turn in at their gate and bravely help their staggering father up the steps. He watched them solemnly. "Herr van Beethoven has been drinking again," he thought. Many times after that he saw the same sight—the three Beethoven boys almost lifting that sagging burden into the house.

But what wonderful music came through the open door of the house across the way! At his best, Herr van Beethoven sang beautifully. Ludwig, when he was only four, had sat in his father's lap at the harpsichord, rapt not in the fascination of flying fingers, but in satisfied love of the music. Then Herr van Beethoven had stopped, and, letting the baby hands take their turn on the cold, white keys, had felt with a thrilling, bounding confidence that no ordinary child touched the instrument. Out of it stole the same melody that he had played. And so, when Ludwig was only four or five, his father began his musical training; when he was nine years old,

a big man named Pfeiffer, who lived with the Beethovens, gave him regular lessons. As the oldest son and a possible genius, Ludwig was to have his chance. While the Beethoven boys were playing, Herr Pfeiffer would come to the door and thunder, *"Ludwig, komm' ins Haus";* and the child, sometimes crying, would stop his fun and stamp into the house to that dull practising. At times, they say, his teacher had to use something harsher than his big, harsh voice.

But once indoors, Ludwig was not miserable; he handled the keys with love. Sometimes Herr Pfeiffer would pick up a sweet-voiced flute, and, standing there beside the boy, he too would play. And the people going by would stand still to listen, and perhaps even Carl and Johann would stop their games to listen, too, for they were German boys, and music made them happy.

One day, the neighbors learned that the Beethovens had sold their linen and their silver service; another day, that much of the furniture and tableware had been sold. Frau van Beethoven grew paler and paler, and the father kept on drinking. Sometimes Ludwig would go away to play at public concerts. At that time, no one knew that Herr van Beethoven, in order to gain a large audience, reported the child a year younger than he really was. He was such a little fellow for his age that this was easily believed. When, "aged six," he was advertised to give a series of concerts in Cologne, he was really seven. But he was only ten when he made a concert tour through Holland with his mother, and he was only fourteen when he was appointed assistant to the court organist.

People used to love to have him "describe the character of some well-known person" on the piano. He could do with the piano what a painter does with his brush.

Before Beethoven was out of his teens, his brave, good mother died. "There was once some one to hear me when I said, 'Mutter,'" thought the lonely boy. Soon after, his father, who was less than a cipher, lost his position through drink, and so Ludwig was made head of the family, with the weight of his brothers' education and all his father's debts.

Hoping to have his genius recognized and perhaps to take a few lessons, he went from Bonn to Vienna to play before the great Mozart. But Mozart was absorbed in composing an opera; he did not want to be bothered. He looked at the short young man with the "snub nose," and thought little of him; heard him play, and still thought him commonplace. In fact, he believed that Beethoven had learned his pieces by heart just to show off. Then, on fire with disappointment, Beethoven asked Mozart to give him a subject, and, just as an author might make up a story on a given subject, he sat down and played a wonderful piece of music. The older genius was astounded. "This youth will some day make a noise in the world!" he exclaimed.

Before Beethoven was thirty, he began to grow deaf. Think of it! Think of a painter losing his sight; never again to see the changing beauty of cloud and river, the chasing light on a field of waving grain, or the sparkle in a baby's eyes. It was as heart-breaking for a musician to grow deaf as for a painter to be struck blind. "The noblest part of me, my sense of hearing, has become very weak," Beethoven wrote in sorrowing confidence. "Please keep as a great secret what I have told you about my hearing." Then followed years of torment mingled with terrible sensitiveness, even to the point of running away for fear people would learn that he was deaf, and show pity in their faces. It was not possible for him to say, "Speak louder, shout, for I am deaf." "A feeling of hot anxiety" overwhelmed him, and at the same time a pathetic wistfulness, when he thought that perhaps his companions could hear "a distant flute" or a "shepherd singing." When he went to concerts, he had to lean forward close to the orchestra to get the sound. This sealing of his dearest sense must have made him feel like "a house half ruined ere the lease be out."

With time, in spite of all his doctors, the humming in his ears grew worse. At last, deafness drove him to ear-trumpets and written conversations; saddest of all, he could no longer hear the sounds made by his own fingers on the piano.

It would be both impossible and misleading to systematize a life of Beethoven. Eccentric genius that he was, his life had next to no system. Though many of his days were much alike, domestic explosions of one kind or another broke into them and kept him harried and confused. We must think of him as seldom at peace. His youth was spent in the city of Bonn, his manhood in or near Vienna, with some of his summers at Baden. He never married, and he never had a home, in any real sense, though his great, affectionate heart would have dearly loved one.

Now fretted by small suspicions and petty wants, now upborne by the power of great emotion, he was a wonderful combination of pygmy and giant. Judged by his letters, the veriest trifles made up life; judged by his music, life was too vast for our poor human groping. And so one person called him "a growling old bear"; another, "the cloud-compeller of the world of music." Almost as helpless as a child, in some respects, he expected his friends to look after all sorts of things: wrote to Ries for half a dozen sewing-needles, and to the ever patient Zmeskall for quills for his pens, a watch, the cost of re-vamping his servant's boots, and, at last, "Please send me for a few hours the looking-glass which hangs next to your window; mine is broken"; and even, "Send me at once your servant."

If ever a man needed a guardian, it was Beethoven. Wholesome Frau Streicher, the wife of one of his friends, did all she could to help him in his many domestic difficulties. "Yes, indeed," he wrote her, "all this housekeeping is still without keeping, and much resembles an *allegro di confusione.*" To her the poor man turned for dusters, blankets, linen, scissors, knives, and servants; and to her he complained of having to "carry in his head so many pairs of trousers, stockings, shoes, etc."

"Man stands but little above other animals, if his chief enjoyments are limited to the table," Beethoven would often say. Under inspiration, for days together he "forgot all about time and rest and food." On the other hand, when he did eat, he was particular. He generally made his own coffee for breakfast, allowing sixty beans to a cup, and counting them as precisely as if coffee were all-important. Not only

was he as fond of soup as are most other Germans, but he thought himself the highest authority on that great subject, and would argue hotly on the best way to make it. "If Schindler had declared a bad soup good, after some time he would get a note to this effect: 'I do not value your judgment about the soup in the least, *it is bad,*'" or perhaps a savory sample to prove Beethoven's knowledge. Indeed, Germany's mighty composer made very superior soup!

"There is music in running water," says Van Dyke. To Beethoven there surely was; but his landladies must have regretted it. If, for any reason, Beethoven could not go out-of-doors, he had a way of creating inspiration in his room. He would go to the wash-bowl, "pour several jugs" of water over his wrists, and dabble there till his clothes were drenched. If this had been all, no one else would have cared; but often, in his absent-minded rapture, he poured out a great deal more water than the bowl would hold, and, before long, buxom old Frau von R——, who roomed below him, would find her ceiling dripping. To her there was no "music in running water," and she took pains to explain as much to the landlady. And then there would be one more change of lodging for Beethoven. Often, when he moved, he would leave part of his things behind, and sometimes he was paying for "two, three, and at one time four, dwelling-places at once."

One day, a ten-year-old boy was taken to see Beethoven, and this is his memory of the visit:

"We mounted five or six stories high . . . and were announced by a rather dirty-looking servant. In a very desolate room, with papers and articles of dress strewn in all directions, bare walls, a few chests, hardly a chair except the rickety one standing by the piano, there was a party of six or eight people. Beethoven was dressed in a jacket and trousers of long, dark goat's-hair, which at once reminded me of 'Robinson Crusoe,' which I had just been reading. He had a shock of jet-black hair, standing straight upright."

When Frau Streicher was in Baden, Beethoven wrote to her: "If you wander through the mysterious fir-forests, think it was there Beethoven often poetized, or, as it is called, composed." "Strolling among the mountain clefts and valleys," with a sheet of music-paper in his hand, he would "scribble a lot for the sake of bread and money—daub work for the sake of money," so that he might "stand the strain of a great work."

Never understood, that great, mysterious soul with its tremendous inner struggles must have suffered incurable loneliness. Indeed, Beethoven was twice solitary— through deafness and through greatness. In all seasons and in all weathers, beneath the open heavens, he sought society in winds and lightning, as well as gurgling brooks and restful moonlight. Away into the woods he would go. The hurry of business, the clatter of wagons and of many feet—these things suffocated his inspiration. Solitude gave it life. Tempests filled him with power; clouds, with their far-away peace; but not even in his greatest music could he utter it all. And so he had the pain, not only of loneliness, but of being forever unsatisfied. After his deafness came on, he could not hear the wind in the pine-trees, or the singing-bird that soared up, up into the blue; but he could see the green boughs bend, and watch the joyous flight, and he could *remember*. In his little notebook he would feverishly jot down his ideas, waiting a while to let the melody and its variations settle. Then at dusk, half afraid that it might all slip away, his hat gone and his bushy head bowed, he would stride home through the city streets, seeing and hearing no one, not even his best friends.

"Just Beethoven!" they would laugh, getting out of his mad way; "only his body is in the world!"—or some such thing. Though he had lost nothing in the woods but his hat, very likely strangers thought he had lost his wits. On the contrary, he had found a wonderful something that made his heart swell. In that heart a great symphony struggled for creation and release, and all the elements of earth and sky cried out to be immortalized in music.

God has a few of us whom He whispers
  in the ear;
The rest may reason and welcome; 't is
  we musicians know.

When Beethoven reached home, he dashed in, and, keeping his hat still on (if he *happened* not to have lost it) and throwing his coat anywhere, he rushed to the piano. There, leaning low over the keys, to catch all the beauty his deafness would allow, he played rapturously, not knowing who or where he was, not knowing, above all, that a crowd had gathered outside the forgotten open door to hear the great, free concert.

"He has three sets of apartments in which he alternately secretes himself," said a friend—"one in the country, one in the town, and a third on the ramparts."

Just as his eccentricity scattered his servants and enraged his landladies, so it broke out to his friends, his orchestra, his pupils, in a hundred hot-headed actions.

His friends had to be very patient and believing. Von Breuning, Ries, and Schindler were repeatedly tested by his shifting trust and suspicion. There would be a terrible word-explosion or a letter of the never-speak-again kind, and then, "warm out of the heart," but in abominably illegible handwriting, would gush a little note begging for forgiveness and the same old place in their affections. It was a fragment of the child left in him. "I fly to you, . . . Your contrite, faithful, and loving friend, Beethoven." "I know I have rent thy heart." Then, after pages of penitent pleading, "Now perhaps thou wilt fly back into my arms." Notes of two successive days read: "Do not come any more to me. You are a false fellow," and "You are an honorable fellow . . . so come this afternoon to me." One day he calls Schindler "arch-scoundrel," later, "best of friends" or "trusty one, I kiss the hem of your coat." This is one unique invitation: "You can come to midday meal, bring your provisions with you—be ready—we are ready."

Once, in the middle of a public concert, when his orchestra had not pleased him, he stopped, quite as if he were giving a lesson, and shouted, "Begin again! From the beginning!" The orchestra obeyed. He never treated a lord with a whit more respect than a peasant. When Duke Raimer came late to his music-lesson, Beethoven revenged himself on the young man's fingers.

"Why are you so impatient?" asked the duke.

"You make me lose my time in the anteroom, and now I cannot get patient again," answered Beethoven. After that, Duke Raimer never kept him waiting. As we can imagine, the tediousness of counting his pupils' time wore terribly on the great composer. He did it for bread. But rather often he excused himself, on the ground of illness, from lessons to the Archduke Rudolph. "Your Imperial Highness," he called him, or oftener, "Y. I. H." The same old reason crept again and again into his profoundly respectful letters. We must remember, however, that Beethoven suffered for years from rheumatism, indigestion, and finally from dropsy. He seems never to have been really well.

Just as eccentric in public as in private, when he led an orchestra he would make himself smaller and smaller to compel softened sounds. Then, as he wanted the sounds louder, his head would "gradually rise up as if out of an abyss; and when the full force of the united instruments broke upon the ear, raising himself on tiptoe, he looked of gigantic stature, and, with both his arms floating about in undulating motion, seemed as if he would soar to the clouds. He was all motion, no part of him remained inactive."

Few things are more irritating to musical people than drifting attention. It is as if, sensitive to every thought and feeling, the power to play leaves the musician's hands if his listeners are not with him. A frivolous audience scattered the great Beethoven's inspiration like wind-blown leaves. And he could not recall it. As a rule, though, he did not care to; he gave way to justified impatience. One day, during a duet by Beethoven and Ries, some young people began to talk and laugh in the next room. Suddenly Beethoven stopped, grabbed Ries's hands from the piano, and sprang to his feet with an angry exclamation. And no one could persuade him to finish the piece.

"You prelude a great while; when are you going to begin?" was his tart comment when Himmer competed with him in improvising. It sounds bitter and conceited, but Beethoven was equally hearty in his appreciation, and in offers of assistance. "Truly in Schubert dwells a divine fire," he said. He admired the "scene-painting" of Rossini; but particularly the work of Mozart, Bach, and Handel. And he was unstinted in his praise of "The Messiah." "Handel is the greatest composer who ever lived," he sweepingly declared. One letter, practical, loving, tender, he wrote to help raise money for Bach's daughter, who was "aged and in want." He asked earnestly for help—"before this daughter of Bach dies, before this *brook* dies up, and we can no longer supply it with water." (Bach is German for brook.) Beethoven was apt to make puns in his letters, just as he was to begin them with a bar of music.

With his hands too full of his own work, he wrote, nobly and freely, "With pleasure, my dear Drieberg, will I look through your compositions, and if you think me able to say anything to you about them, I am heartily ready to do it." And he wrote to a little girl of eight or ten who "raved over him": "If, my dear Emilie, you at any time wish to know something, write without hesitation to me. The true artist is not proud; he unfortunately sees that art has no limits; he feels darkly how far he is from the goal. . . . I would, perhaps, rather come to you and your people than to many rich folks who display inward poverty."

Just such a democratic spirit as this ruled his life. Passion and pride moved him to all sorts of unexpected acts. He refused to take off his hat to royalty. When his brother Johann wrote him a letter signed "Landowner," Beethoven signed his answer "Brain-owner." When he was asked in court to prove his right to his title of nobility, he said, raising his rough head grandly and flashing his brilliant little eyes, "My nobility is here and here," and he pointed to his head and heart. In his warm hero-worship he had dreamed that Napoleon meant to make France a republic, and he intended to dedicate his "Heroic Symphony" to him. But, just as he was completing it, he heard that the emperor had been crowned. With mingled passion and disappointment, he tore off

the title page bearing the word "Bonaparte," and flung the whole thing to the floor. "After all, he's nothing but an ordinary mortal!" he exclaimed bitterly. And so, though the original manuscript still bears faint traces of the fallen hero's name, it was published merely: "To the Memory of a Great Man."

As Louis Nohl says, the march in this symphony gathers into one picture "the glad tramp of warlike hosts, the rhythm of trampling steeds, the waving of standards, and the sound of trumpets."

To Beethoven the greatest element in music was spiritual. Not only did he long to lift the audience heavenward, but every one of the orchestra. His own feeling was so immense that he judged the best musical performance as nothing if it had no soul. "Read Shakspere," he said to some one who wanted to play. Those who would interpret Beethoven must be full of poetry. For that reason, those who are mere piano gymnasts, no matter how good, had better try shallower compositions.

There is the music of imitation and the music of feeling. One of Beethoven's early teachers had complained, in despair, "He will never do anything according to rule; he has learned nothing." But even then the young genius was *feeling* something no follower of rules could teach. Before him lay a conquest of sound so glorious that strong men would bow their heads and sob aloud at its power.

Like a mighty heart the music seemed,
That yearns with melodies it cannot speak.

Sir George Grove said of Beethoven's "Funeral March," "If ever horns talked like flesh and blood, they do it here." That solemn march stirs us to the depths. But hard labor had gone hand in hand with feeling. Though Beethoven could neither play nor write formally, he often worked for years on a piece of music, changing, cutting, and improving. They say that of his opera "Fidelio" he made as many as eighteen different versions.

He had the power of imitation, too, though that was not his greatest strength. As we can see the sunlight flash on the leaping fish in Schubert's "Trout," so we can see a heavenly shimmer in Beethoven's "Moonlight Sonata." His "Pastoral Symphony" carries us from the scene by the brook, through the gathering of the peasants, a thunder-storm, a shepherd's song, and a final rejoicing. We hear the murmur of the brook and the mutter of thunder; the violins make flashes of lightning; the flute, oboe, and clarinet mimic the nightingale, quail, and cuckoo. One part of the symphony pictures "a rustic merrymaking, the awkward, good-natured gambols of peasants," and one old fellow who sits on a barrel and is able to play only three tones.

The great, lonely composer gave and craved much love. But no friend, no *one* ever held a place in his heart equal to his nephew Carl's. At eight, the boy had been left by his father's will to his Uncle Ludwig, and immediately that uncle assumed all a father's responsibility and love. His one great thought, aside from music, was Carl. Much of his music, even, was written to get money for the boy's education. We follow the uncle through all his early hopes. Believing he saw scientific genius "in the dear pledge intrusted" to him, he sent the boy to a fine school and gave him, besides, lessons in drawing, French, and music. For years he chose him the best tutors, watched over him like a mother, and called him all kinds of pet names: "lovely lad," "my Carl," "dear little rascal," "best ragamuffin," "dear jewel," but, oftenest of all, "my son." How willingly he adjusted his own program to suit the boy's convenience! He believed he found

in the handsome little fellow all the things he longed for: honor, tenderness, affection; and he vowed to do his "best for him to the end of his life," and leave him everything after death.

To those who read Beethoven's letters, even the awful, increasing deafness seems less cruel than Carl's ingratitude. The empty-hearted fellow had no loyalty. As he grew older, he grew calculating and defiant. It is not too hard to say that he loved his uncle's money, not his uncle. At twenty, he was publicly expelled from the university, and later sent to prison, his uncle getting him out and securing him a commission in the army. With all this, the selfish nephew even begrudged Beethoven his society. The uncle, in his wistful loneliness, wrote him the most pathetic letters. "I should be so glad to have a human heart about me in my solitude," he said, touchingly.

How often the great composer must have looked from his sick-room window! The long days lagged by, and many suns set gloriously behind the trees; but Carl, beloved and longed for, did not come. Meanwhile, "in his remote house on the hill," the "Solitary of the Mountain" fought out his final conquest. On his writing-table stood his framed motto: "I am all that is, all that was, and all that shall be; no mortal man hath my veil uplifted." "He had learned in suffering what he taught in song." His life had been one battle after another, all the way: the child Ludwig had begun by caring for a drunken father and shouldering big debts; the man had driven himself through humdrum lessons. Then came the approach of closing deafness, and, in the darkness of desperation, Beethoven had looked up and said, "Art, when persecuted, finds everywhere a place of refuge; Dædalus, though inclosed in the labyrinth, invented wings which carried him into the air; oh! I also will find those wings." Lonely for Carl and hungry for his own music, he said to himself, "Poor Beethoven, there is no external happiness for you! You must create your own happiness." "O God, grant me strength to conquer myself," he prayed. And so he determined to give to others what he, himself, could not get— a wonderful rapture of sound; he would not leave this earth till he had revealed what lay within him. For this, he had been sent of God.

His tempestuous fight ended March 26, 1827, after a long illness. He died in the midst of a great thunder-storm. None of his dearest friends were with him. Carl was not there; Schindler and von Breun-ing had gone out on errands. Beethoven's clock stopped, as it had often done when it lightened. But the warring elements had been the composer's lifelong friends, and often before had carried his soul above this little world. In the midst of the flashes and the rumbling, he thought, "I shall hear, in heaven."

He might have thought that he would be immortalized on earth. Twenty great composers bore Beethoven to his last sleeping-place, and twenty others carried torches in the grand, somber procession.

"No mourning wife, no son, no daughter wept at his grave; but a world wept at it."

TAKEN AT HIS WORD

by Elizabeth Stuart Phelps

HEROD'S STORY

"THERE, go!" said I; "and I don't care if I never see you again!"

I am almost an old man now, with gray hairs and rheumatism, and an objection to draughts; so old that I wear my rubbers in dry, cold weather, and don't take off a comforter before May, and don't go out after dewfall in the summer, and don't keep track of the last engagement, and don't think much about the church sociables and whom I shall take to a lecture.

You can think how old that must be! But old as I am, I remember just how I said those words; where the accent fell; how they sounded; how the wind caught them and blew them around the corners of the house; and how they seemed to come around and knock on the windows, to be let in again, after I had shut the door. Nothing has happened to me in all my life since they were spoken that has helped in the least to make me forget them.

It may be only an old man's notion, but sometimes I am forced to wonder if anything will happen in the next life that can make me forget them.

There is this about a next world's life, girls and boys: It is no fun, to my mind, to carry a thing on into it that you want to forget and *can't* forget. And we all know how dreary anything is when there's "no fun" in it.

There was fun enough in what I have to tell, at the first of it. At least Trollo thought so, I suppose. Trollo was my brother. He was a little chap, eight years old. I was fourteen. They all had gone off and left us alone in the house, and Trollo had plagued me half out of my senses. That's the way, you know, it seemed to *me*. It seemed to *him* quite different, I've no doubt.

This is how it happened.

My sister Mary lived in New Haven. That was fifteen miles away. Mary's husband had got into some trouble about money, and father thought he would go on and see about it; and Mary's baby was sick with something or other, and mother thought she would go on and see about that.

Mary's husband was always getting into trouble about money, and Mary's baby was always getting sick; but they didn't often come on poor Mary together. At any rate, father and mother thought they would go on; and as they would be gone only over the second night, and because I was fourteen years old, and because Trollo said he would be good, and because Keziah Phipps said she would come over and "do" for us, and stay nights, unless "the old man got his back up,"—and because, on the whole, we didn't very much

186

care, but thought it would be rather nice, and that if Keziah Phipps' old man *should,* by any providential accident, "get his back up," we would make molasses corn-balls, with vanilla in them,—we were left alone.

It was dark and cloudy, the day they went away. Mother said she was afraid it was blowing up for a storm; but father said he thought not. And he told me to be sure and not let the fire go out, nor the pigs go hungry, nor the horse go un-blanketed; and mother kissed us both—but she kissed Trollo twice—and told me to take good care of Trollo, and let the cat sit by the fire; and then the stage rattled away with them, and Trollo and I stood looking after it.

"I wish they'd come back to-morrow; don't you, Herod?" said Trollo.

My name was Hurdley. But Trollo used to call me Herod, just to see what I would say; and when he found I didn't say any-thing, he called me so because he had got into the way of calling me so; and by the time he'd got into the way of calling me so, I didn't much mind, but rather liked it. Only when the boys laughed at it, or I felt cross, it used to seem an ugly name. But Trollo had a gentle, little, pleasant voice, and generally I liked the sound he gave it.

I said no, I didn't wish they were com-ing *right* back; for I was thinking about the vanilla corn-balls. And Trollo said he didn't know as he did either.

"But you're to be good, you know," said I.

I felt very old and superior to Trollo, and I rather liked it to feel that I could order him around for two days.

"I hadn't said I wasn't, had I?" said Trollo, firing up to begin with.

Then I fired up a little, and told him he was to behave himself, at all events; and that was the beginning of it. I thought

afterwards it would have been nicer in me not to have preached at him before he'd had a chance to behave one way or another. But I didn't think of it at the time. Boys don't, you know.

So we both sulked a little, and Trollo went to school; but when he came home to dinner we'd got over it, or very nearly. We only quarreled about his piece of pie. I said it was bigger than mother let him have. And we got the foot-rule and a tape-measure, and measured it off. Then he ate it down in three mouthfuls, to pay me for that.

I didn't go to school myself. I was to stay and watch the house, and look after the horse, and so forth; for it was only two days, and I could study at home, and such a thing might never happen again. And Keziah Phipps came over and got dinner and went away again, and came again to supper, and stayed all night. Keziah Phipps was our nearest neighbor; she lived a quarter of a mile away. Ours was rather a lonesome house, with pine trees in the front yard and a long stretch of fields behind, where the snow drifted; it always drifted in the road by our house, too. We lived on a very windy road.

It was a cold day, and the wind blew pretty high. Trollo came in from school the last time that afternoon with red cheeks, and as full of mischief as he could hold. He stamped off the snow in the entry and flung his mittens at me when I told him not to. One of them hit me in the eye.

Trollo was a good aim—a lithe, little, quick-eyed chap, always up to something.

"Oh! I didn't mean to!" he said, when the mitten hit.

But I was mad. It didn't hurt me much; but I'd been having a cold time with the horse and had spilled the pigs' supper, and, I suppose, didn't feel like myself exactly, from not going to school as usual, but loafing around and sitting by the fire so much. At any rate, I was mad. So I shook him.

He didn't say much, and I don't think he cared much. He'd come home as wild as a witch, and there wasn't anything he wasn't ready to do to make mischief that night. And because I was mad, he wouldn't mind me.

He tied his rubber boots to the door-bell. He stuffed his wet mittens down my neck. He set the cat in the platter with the turkey bones, and then set platter, cat, bones and all upon the table, when Keziah Phipps had begun to eat. He ran out with a new squash pie to give to the horse, and dropped it and fell on it before he got there. He put salt in my tea, and sugar on my pickles, and green wood on the fire; and when I scolded him, he whistled.

Then, after tea, we sat down to study. Somehow, everything that Trollo did seemed to me to be wrong that night. He banged his boots against the table-leg. He wouldn't put on his slippers. His nails were dirty; he wouldn't clean them. He asked Keziah for another piece of cake, and, after all he had done, he got it. He sang "Hail, Columbia!" on a very flat squeak for twenty minutes. He sat down on the cat. He wouldn't brush his hair. He got Keziah to show him his sums. He flung sofa-pillows at the ceiling, and they came down on the custard batter. He seemed to me the most disagreeable boy I ever knew. When he went to bed, I told him so.

I remember just how he looked, standing—with our little brass bed-lamp in his hand—in the entry, to say good-night. It was one of those old-fashioned, one-wicked lamps, that gave almost no light. His face looked dim and odd behind it in the dark entry.

He started to say something, but gave it up and didn't speak,—only laughed,—and trotted off up stairs, kicking his boots off and letting them drop down through the balusters. He was a merry, happy-go-lucky little chap. If he minded anything, he wouldn't say so. If you were cross to him, he might plague you; but he wouldn't scold a great deal himself.

The next morning it was much the same. It was a very dark morning, and snowing in a slow, hard way. We woke late, and I had to hurry Trollo up. I don't suppose I was very gentle. And he threw pillows at me, and when I ordered him down to see if Keziah had got breakfast, he hid my tooth-brush. I needn't have ordered him around so much, but I thought that was part of the fun of having father and mother gone. I rather liked it to be able to say "you must" and "you mustn't" to Trollo. It didn't occur to me to wonder how Trollo liked it.

Well, it was one thing and another between Trollo and me till school-time. Such little things they seem now! But they did not seem little to me then. I was cross and cold. And I was afraid Keziah Phipps' old man wouldn't get his back up, after all, and we shouldn't get our corn-balls. And everything hit me, somehow, just the crooked way. You know how it is on a cold morning. Not that I want to excuse myself. I wouldn't excuse myself for the wide, wide world, for what I said to Rollo at the last.

He'd plagued me about his luncheon,—for it was so snowy Keziah thought he'd better stay over till afternoon,—or I thought he plagued me. He nibbled at the pie, and took a squash cooky Keziah made for me. And when I told him how much trouble he was, he said:

"Hee-he-hee-e-e-ee!"

He had a funny way of laughing out, like a waterfall or a little bell, or a little shower. When I felt pleasant, I liked to hear him laugh. When I didn't, it didn't make me any pleasanter.

"It's nothing to laugh at," said I.

"Hee-hee-he-ee-ee!" said Trollo.

I didn't say anything to that, but hurried him along a little to the door. I didn't push him *exactly*.

"Come, Herod!" said Trollo; "le' me alone, and say good-by!"

"My name is *not* Herod!" said I, with an awful air.

"Oh, well," said Trollo, "don't let's be so cross. I wished you were coming, too. Just see it snow!"

He stood a minute on the steps, turning his face towards the road—the pretty, mischievous little round, red face! It looked graver, somehow, that minute, as he stood looking at the storm. And he spoke back in his gentlest, prettiest little way, as he went down the steps and waded into the snow that had already begun to drift in shallow, grayish piles against the fence.

"Good-by, Herod!" said Trollo.

But still I felt a little cross; and he called me Herod. And I didn't want to give in to him that way, I suppose. However it came about, I called after him down the walk:

"There, go! And I don't care if I never see you again!"

Trollo did not answer. The wind blew in between us. He trudged off stoutly into the storm, his little red tippet flying in the wind across his shoulder. The snow whirled up, and in a minute or less I lost sight of the little tippet, and came in and shut the door.

I shut the door, but I did not shut away the words I had spoken to Trollo. As I told you, they seemed to me to come back and knock on the window to be let in again. If I could, I would have unsaid them, I think, even then. I wished I had said something a little different, somehow.

I passed rather a lonesome morning. The storm grew worse. Keziah Phipps warmed over the hash and a piece of squash pie for me, and went home early. She said maybe she shouldn't come over again. "The old man was riley about it to-day, anyhow—his potatoes burned yesterday—and then it did set in and snow at such a rate!" But she'd come if she could, for she'd promised my ma, and I could heat up the coffee myself, for she'd cut the bread and butter.

So I said, "Very well," and I didn't urge her to come, for I was thinking about the corn-balls. I hoped Trollo would get home in good season, and we'd have some fun. I opened Keziah's old umbrella for her, and kicked her a little path to the gate, and then came back and stood in the door till she had got out of sight, and then I came into the house alone.

It did seem lonesome, do the best I would. My footsteps echoed up and down the stairs. The doors slammed after me and made me start. The fire winked at me, as if it were going to sleep. I built it up, and put things in order a little, picking up some slippers and an old mitten of Trollo's, that he had left kicking around. I wished that Trollo would come. It gave me an unhappy feeling to see the little slippers, as if I had been homesick.

I went to the barn for company before long, and fed the pigs and shook down hay for Hautboy—that was the horse— for the night, although it was early, and locked everything up, and came back again, wondering what I should do next. I wished that Trollo would come.

I had been in the barn some time, and when I crossed the little side-yard to come from the barn to the house, I was surprised to see how the storm had gained. It was blowing, by that time, a furious gale; the wind came up in long waves like an incoming tide. It took my breath as I stood in the barn door. The air was gray and dense with snow and sleet. There was a deep drift in the yard at the corner where I crossed. I waded through to get to the house. It came almost to my waist. I could hardly get the door together. I wished that Trollo were at home.

I wished so again when I had got into the house by the fire. It looked so deadly cold out of doors, I wondered how anyone could see his way to walk in that great whirl of snow and wind. And such a little fellow—only eight years old!

I looked at the clock. It was almost four. Just about that time he would be starting to come home. The school-house was a mile and a quarter away, beyond the church and beyond the town. Trollo had rather a lonely road to come, and a very windy one, as I said. There were two ways, where the road branched off. He might take one or he might take another; but both were bad enough.

I began to think that I should feel better to go and meet him. But I remembered that he would have started long before I could get there, and that I could not tell which way he would come. If he came alone, he would come by the church. When he came with Jenny Fairweather, he came the other way. Jenny Fairweather and Trollo were rivals in the spelling class, but the best of friends outside of it.

So I gave up the idea of going to meet him, for if I missed him, and he came home cold and found me gone, I should be sorry, I thought. I ran up into the attic once, to see if I could see anything of him. It had begun to grow a little dark. I thought I could see as far as the church clock, for I often got the time by the attic window. But I could not even see the church. I could not see the road. I could see nothing but wind and snow. It seemed to me as if I could *see* the wind. From the

attic window, the whole world seemed to have become a whirlpool of wind and snow. Oh, for a sight of the little red tippet! a glimpse of the round, red, mischievous little face!

It seemed to me still as if those ugly words were blowing about in the storm, and had come up to the attic window, and were knocking and knocking to be let in.

"I don't care if I never see you again!"

"I—don't—care if I—never—see you—again!" I actually tried to open the window and let them in,—I felt so uncomfortable in the attic. But the window was frozen and stuck.

I went downstairs and tried to amuse myself by putting the molasses candy on to boil. Keziah Phipps had not appeared, and I thought it as good as settled that the old man's back would be up to-night. She would not come. We would have the candy. Trollo would be so pleased! He would come in wet and cold. I would have a good, hot fire. I would get him some dry stockings. Perhaps we would roast some apples in the ashes. Trollo always liked to roast apples. We should have a nice time that night. He should see that I *was* glad to see him again, after all! He should know that I *didn't* think him the most disagreeable boy I ever knew. I shouldn't say much about it, for it was not our way. But he should know.

So I put the molasses on, and then I went to the window to look for Trollo. Then I got out the bread and butter and coffee, that they might be ready for his supper; and I went down into the cellar and picked out the biggest Baldwin I could find, to roast for him. Then I went to the window again. I was very restless. I could not keep away from the window. The storm was beating against the house in an awful way.

Half-past four. Trollo had not come. Five. No Trollo. Quarter past five. Where *was* Trollo?

It came upon me very suddenly that it was dark, and that Trollo ought to have been at home half an hour ago,—three-quarters, perhaps. It came *into* me, like the thrust of a sharp knife, that something had happened to keep the child away. Had he gone home with Jenny Fairweather? Had he not started at all? Had he got angry with me because of what I said, and gone on to Keziah's to frighten me? Or had he started, and *not* got anywhere? Where *could* he be?

I was too restless, wretched and anxious by that time to sit any longer, asking myself questions to which I got no answer. I determined to harness up the horse, and start out to find my brother.

It took me some time to do this, for Hautboy was of the opinion that the barn was the warmest place for a horse of any sense that night. He would not take the bits, and made me trouble. I had to hunt up a barrel and stand on it to reach his head—for I was not tall for my age. It was quite dark by the time I got harnessed and drove out into the yard.

I drove as fast as I could, but that was scarcely over a walk. The long, dim, bleak road stretched, a solid drift, before me. Hautboy broke it angrily, tossing the snow back into my face, and blinding me again and again. I took the road to Jenny Fairweather's, as nearly as I could make out where the road might be. I thought I would inquire there first.

"Surely Trollo must be there!" I said to myself, as I drove along. "Trollo will be there!"

I looked out into the drifts as I rode along. An awful fear had crept into my heart. I would not own it to myself. I said, "He will be at Jenny Fairweather's." But I looked at all the drifts. Sometimes I poked them with the butt end of my whip. Sometimes I called out. I did not call Trollo,—for, of course, Trollo *must* be at Jenny Fairweather's. But I thought I would shout a little,—it did no harm.

I knew the Fairweathers' by the light in the sitting-room behind the red curtains. I drove up close to the back door, and went in without knocking. I carried the reins in with me, so that Hautboy should not overturn the sleigh in the drifts, from being restless. I knocked with my whip on the sitting-room door.

Mrs. Fairweather came to the door. She held a light, and had her hand up before her eyes to shield them. I could see into the sitting-room. Jenny Fairweather sat there alone, studying her atlas at the table. My heart gave a sickening bound; but I spoke up—or I tried to—manfully:

"Is Trollo here, Mrs. Fairweather?"

"Trollo? No! Where is he?"

"That's what I don't know. He hasn't come home from school at all. I thought he must have come with Jenny. I thought you had kept him on account of the storm."

"Why, he started when I did!" said Jenny. She, too, came to the door and looked at me. "He started, but he went the other way. I came with Tommy Larkins. Trollo didn't come with us at all. He went the other way, alone."

"Where can he be?" exclaimed Mrs. Fairweather.

I did not answer. I could not speak. Mrs. Fairweather and Jenny followed me to the door. They said things that I did not hear. I only remember telling Mrs. Fairweather that he must have gone to some of the neighbors, and that I should drive up the other way; and I remember her saying that I must have help,—the child must be found! And that she wished she and Jenny were men, to go with me.

I got into the sleigh, and started out again into the storm.

I was now very cold; but I did not think much about it. I whipped and whipped poor Hautboy, and we blundered along,—freezing, frightened, stumbling,—into the other road. I could just see the church. I thought if I could get as far as the church, I would go to the first house I came to and get help. I shouted as I went along, and called out Trollo's name. But I could scarcely hear my own voice. I could not see. I could not breathe. My hands were stiff. I dropped the reins two or three times. The wind blew savagely up the other road. It blew in our faces. Hautboy did not like it. He puffed and backed and bothered me.

The first thing I knew, the horse stood still. I whipped him, but it did no good. I shouted, but he would not stir. I got out to see what was the matter. We had stuck in a mighty drift, which came to the creature's haunches.

So fast and so frightfully our old-fashioned Connecticut storms come down!

I turned around as well as I could, and Hautboy put for home. I sat still, in a stupid way, in the sleigh. I let the reins hang, for I could not hold them. I felt very numb and sleepy. I wondered if I were freezing to death. I thought how I should look, when Trollo found me in the morning; how Hautboy would get as far as the barn-door, and stick, with the sleigh; how I should be sitting up there, straight under the buffalo, half in, half out the door.

Then I thought that, perhaps, Trollo would never find me at all. Stupidly, I seemed to think that Trollo was frozen too. In a dreamy, meaningless way, I remembered telling Trollo that I hoped I should never see him again; and I won-

dered if, when *he* was freezing, *he* remembered it too.

All at once I felt myself aroused. Something had happened. Hautboy stood stock still beside a fence. He whinnied, and turned his neck to look at me.

"What is it, Hautboy?" said I, sleepily. I managed to get out. Had we got home? Had we gone on to Keziah's? What had happened?

We had got home—or nearly. We were just outside the gate, in an enormous drift. I could see the light in the kitchen and the cat sitting in the uncurtained window.

That brought me to my senses. Perhaps Trollo had got home. I called out as loud as I could: "Trollo! Trollo! Oh, *Trol*-lo!" Did something answer me? Did Hautboy whinny? Was it the cat mewing in the window? Or was it—? Oh, what was that?

Whoa, Hautboy! Whoa! Whoa, sir! Whoa! You'll tread on it! You'll crush him! Back, sir! Back!

Is it under your feet—across the drift! I have my hand beneath it! I can lift it up—the still, cold thing! The awful precious thing!

I have it in my arms. Oh, Hautboy, I'm so weak! Don't tread on me! We shall drop back beneath the drift! Back, sir! back! Good pony. Good old fellow. There!

Oh, Trollo, here we are! Here's the door-latch! We are getting up the steps. It's warm inside; and I set the candy on, and I went to meet you, Trollo. Oh, Trollo, can you hear?

Can he hear? Can he ever hear again? Does he know that I hold him; that I love him; that my heart is breaking, while we crouch by the stove that he may feel the red-hot glow? Does he stir? Do his eyelids move? Has Heaven taken me at my word?—that dreadful word! Shall I never see him move again?

Oh, what shall I do? What shall I do? All alone in the house this awful night with this awful little burden in my lap! If any grown-up soul were here, they would know how to save the child!

I do the best I can. I rub him and rub him with my numb, cold hands; I get hot water—for the fire has kept like a furnace, thank God! I fetch water and mother's blankets, and I get him upon the old lounge, and I rub and rub and wrap him and breathe on him. Now and then I speak to him, but I get no answer. Once or twice I think I will say my prayers, but I only say, "Our Father," for I can think of nothing else.

There! While I am rubbing and sobbing, curled on my knees in a little helpless heap beside the lounge,—oh, there! he *did* draw a little, little breath. He chokes and stirs; his eyelids flutter.

I remember then that there is brandy on the lower cupboard shelf. I spring to get it, calling, "Trollo! Trollo!" lest he drop away and lie still again before I can get back. I get it, somehow, down his throat. I keep on calling, "Trollo! Trollo! Trollo!" How long before it happens I cannot say; how it happens I do not know; but while I am kneeling and sobbing, calling and spilling brandy wildly down his neck, and doing everything wrong, and nothing right, except to love him and to hate myself, as if my heart would break with love and hate, a little feeble, pleasant voice speaks up:

"Her-od?"

"Oh, Trollo, I *did* want to see you all the afternoon! I did! I did!"

"Yes, Herod; I *hoped* you'd come to meet me, Herod."

"Oh, Trollo, just look here! You *know* you're not the most disagreeable boy I ever——"

"Oh, yes, I know. It isn't any matter, Herod. I'm warm as toast, I guess, only a little queer, somehow. But the pains ain't *very* bad. Did Keziah's old man get his back up? Did you put the candy on?"

Our poor candy has bubbled and boiled away to a burn on the stove. But little want have we of candy this long, strange night. Trollo is very weak and suffers much. I cannot leave him to get help. I do the best I can. Towards morning he feels better, and I crawl out to look at Hautboy, who has broken his harness and got safely under cover. In the gray, cold dawn in the breaking storm I crawl into mother's bed beside my brother, and we drop asleep heavily, holding hands.

We sleep long and late,—I don't know how late it is. I am wakened by Keziah Phipps; she has fires going and hot coffee, and she throws up her hands and says: "Laws mercy on me! What is the matter? What has ever happened to you?"

And when she knew what it was that happened, she says we are to lie in bed till our ma comes home, and she makes beefsoup for Trollo, and cries into it, so that he makes faces when he drinks it.

Trollo is very weak, but pretty well. So when the broth is gone, we both lie still. By-and-by Jenny Fairweather comes over to see if Trollo has been found, but we feel too weak to see her. Then, by-and-by, we hear the whistle of the early train, —well-belated this morning,—by which father and mother will be hurrying home to see how we have stood the storm.

We do not talk much. We lie very still, holding each other's hands in bed.

Only once, I say, "Trollo?" and Trollo says, "Well, Herod?" and I say, "If I live to be an old, old man I shall never forget this night. Shall you?"

Trollo says, no, he doesn't think he ever shall. Then I say again, "Trollo?" But when he says, "What, Herod?" I only hold his hand a little closer, for I cannot speak.

AN ALPHABET FROM ENGLAND

by Christina G. Rossetti

A is the Alphabet, A at its head;
A is an Antelope, agile to run.

B is the Baker Boy bringing the bread,
Or black Bear and brown Bear, both
    begging for bun.

C is a Cornflower, come with the corn;
C is a Cat with a comical look.

D is a dinner which Dahlias adorn;
D is a Duchess who dines with a Duke.

The comical cat

194

E is an elegant, eloquent Earl;
E is an Egg whence an Eaglet emerges.

F is a Falcon, with feathers to furl;
F is a Fountain of full foaming surges.

The eloquent earl

G is the Gander, the Gosling, the Goose;
G is a Garnet in girdle of gold.

The gander, the gosling, the goose

H is a Heartsease, harmonious of hues;
H is a huge Hammer, heavy to hold.

I is an Idler who idles on ice;
I am I—who will say I am not I?

A hammer heavy to hold

J is a Jacinth, a jewel of price;
J is a Jay full of joy in July.

K is a King, or a Kaiser still higher;
K is a Kitten, or quaint Kangaroo.

L is a Lute or a lovely-toned Lyre;
L is a Lily all laden with dew.

A jay full of joy in July

M is a Meadow where Meadow-sweet
blows;
M is a Mountain made dim by a mist.

N is a nut—in a nutshell it grows;
Or a Nest full of Nightingales singing—
oh, list!

O is an Opal, with only one spark;
O is an Olive, with oil on its skin.

A pony, a pet in a park

P is a Pony, a pet in a park;
P is the Point of a Pen or a Pin.

Q is a Quail, quick chirping at morn;
Q is a Quince quite ripe and near dropping.

A red-breasted robin

R is a Rose, rosy red on a thorn;
R is a red-breasted Robin come hopping.

S is a Snowstorm that sweeps o'er the Sea;
S is the Song that the swift Swallows sing.

T is the Tea-table set out for tea;
T is a Tiger with terrible spring.

U, the Umbrella, went up in a shower;
Or Unit is useful with ten to unite.

The umbrella

Policeman X exercised

V is a Violet veined in the flower;
V is a Viper of venomous bite.

W stands for the water-bred Whale;
Stands for the wonderful Wax-work so
gay.

X, or X X, or X X X is ale,
Or Policeman X, exercised day after day.

Y is a yellow Yacht, yellow its boat;
Y is the Yucca, the Yam, or the Yew.

Z is a Zebra, zigzagged his coat,
Or Zebu, or Zoöphyte, seen at the Zoo.

"Seen at the Zoo"

PARLOR MAGIC

by Leo H. Grindon

EXPERIMENTS REQUIRING CHEMICAL SOLUTIONS

To prepare these solutions, purchase of a druggist a small quantity of the solid crystals of the substance needed for the experiment you wish to try. Dissolve the crystals in clear pure water, and keep the solution in a little bottle, labeled with the name. It is seldom that the solutions need be strong. When the crystal is a colored one, enough should be used to give the water a light tint, blue, yellow, or what it may be. None of these solutions will do any harm to the hands, unless there is a cut or a wound of any kind upon the skin. It is well also, not to let a drop of any of them fall upon the clothes, or upon furniture, for some of them will stain. And none of them should ever be tasted, or touched by the lips or tongue, many of them being acrid and even poisonous.

With the acids still greater care is needed, the stronger acids being corrosive and poisonous. The greater portion of these substances must likewise not be smelled, as the fumes or vapors would affect the nostrils painfully.

For the proper performance of these experiments with solutions, etc.,—at all events for the neatest and most elegant performance of them,—there should be obtained from the chemist's shop about a dozen test-tubes. These are little glass vessels, manufactured on purpose, and very cheap. Do not take glasses that may afterward be used for drinking or household purposes. Be careful to have every one of your experiment glasses perfectly clean.

To Produce a Beautiful Violet-Purple Color

Take a nearly colorless solution of any salt of copper. The sulphate is the cheapest and handiest. Fill the test-tube or other experimenting-glass about two-thirds full. Then drop in, slowly, a little liquid ammonia. It will cause a beautiful blue to appear, and presently a most lovely violet-purple, which, by stirring with a glass rod, extends all through the fluid.

If now you drop into this a very little nitric acid, the fluid will again become as clear as pure water.

To Make a Splendid Scarlet

Again take some solution of sulphate of copper. Add to it a little solution of bichromate of potash. Then add a little solution of nitrate of silver, and there is produced a splendid scarlet color.

To Make a Deep Blue

Now, take a nearly colorless solution of sulphate of iron, and drop into it, slowly, a small quantity of solution of yellow prussiate of potash. This will induce a beautiful deep blue, quite different from the blues that are produced from copper salts.

To Make a Yellow Color

Take a solution of acetate of lead, and add a few drops of solution of iodide of potassium, and a most lovely canary-yellow color is produced.

Invisible Inks

Nearly all those experiments which result in the production of color may be performed in another way, and be then applied to the purposes of secret writing. Thus:

Write with dilute solution of sulphate of copper. The writing will be quite invisible, but become blue when held over the vapor of liquid ammonia.

Write with the same solution, and wash the paper with solution of yellow prussiate of potash, and the writing, previously invisible, will become brown. If you choose you may reverse this method, writing with solution of the prussiate of potash, and, washing the paper with solution of the copper salt.

Write with solution of sulphate of iron, and the writing will again be invisible. Wash it over with tincture of galls, and it becomes black.

Write with sulphate of iron, and use a wash of yellow prussiate of potash, and the writing will come out blue. This experiment may likewise be reversed, and with similar result.

How to Copper a Knife-Blade

Make a rather strong solution of sulphate of copper. Let a clean and polished piece of steel or iron, such as the blade of a knife, stand in it for a few minutes, and the iron will become covered or encrusted with a deposit of pure copper.

To Make Beautiful Crystals

Dissolve, in different vessels, half an ounce each of the sulphates of iron, zinc, copper, soda, alumina, magnesia, and potash. The solutions can be made more rapidly by using warm water. When the salts are all completely dissolved, pour the whole seven solutions into a large dish, stir the mixture with a glass rod, then place it in a warm place, where it will not be disturbed. By degrees, the water will evaporate, and then the salts will recrystallize, each kind preserving its own proper form and color. Some occur in groups, some as single crystals. If carefully protected from dust, these form extremely pretty ornaments for the parlor.

Alum Baskets

These may be prepared by dissolving alum in water in such quantity that at last the water can take up no more, and the undissolved alum lies at the bottom of the vessel. The solution thus obtained is called a saturated one. Then procure a common ornamental wire basket, and suspend it in the solution, so as to be well covered in every part. There should be twice as much solution as will cover the basket. The wires of the basket should be wound with worsted, so that the surface may be rough. Leave it undisturbed in the solution, and gradually the crystals will form all over the surface. Before putting in the basket, it is best to further strengthen the solution by boiling it down to one half, after which it should be strained.

The Lead-Tree

Dissolve half an ounce of acetate of lead in six ounces of water. The solution will be turbid, so clarify it with a few drops of acetic acid. Now put the solution into a clean phial, nearly filling the phial. Suspend in the solution, by means of a thread attached to the cork, a piece of clean zinc wire. By degrees the wire will become covered with beautiful metallic spangles, like the foliage of a tree.

UN ALPHABET FRANÇAIS

par Laura Caxton

A—ANNETTE A UN TRÈS JOLI PETIT AGNEAU.

B—BAPTISTE A UNE PAIRE DE GRANDES BOTTES.

C—CÉCILE EST CHARMÉE DE FAIRE ROULER SON CERCEAU.

D—DENIS PLEURE PARCEQU'IL A MAL AUX DENTS.

E—ÉDOUARD VA GAIEMENT À L'ÉCOLE,
    AVEC SES LIVRES.

F—FANCHON FAIT UNE CRAVATE POUR
    SON FRÈRE.

G—GABRIELLE A ÉTÉ GRONDÉE PAR
    SON GRAND-PÈRE.

H—HENRI VA PATINER SUR LA GLACE
    PENDANT L'HIVER.

I—ISABELLE EST UNE PAUVRE PETITE INVALIDE

J—JACQUES S'AMUSE TOUTE LA JOURNÉE AVEC SES JOUJOUX.

K—K EST LA LETTRE QUE JEAN TIENT SOUS LA MAIN.

L—LOUISE DONNE DES LÉGUMES À SES PETITS LAPINS.

M—MARIE A DES MARGUERITES POUR SA CHÈRE MAMAN.

N—NARCISSE A TROUVÉ DES OISEAUX DANS UN NID.

O—OLIVIER, AVEC SON PARAPLUIE, N'A PAS PEUR DE L'ORAGE.

P—PAULINE A BEAUCOUP DE PLAISIR AVEC SA PETITE POUPÉE.

Q—QUENTIN AIME À JOUER AUX
QUILLES DE BOIS.

R—ROLAND REMPLIT UN POT POUR Y
PLANTER SON ROSIER.

S—SUSETTE A UN MORCEAU DE SUCRE
POUR SON SERIN.

T—THÉRÈSE EST TRISTE PARCEQUE SON
TABLIER EST SALE.

U—URBAIN A LE DRAPEAU DES ÉTATS-UNIS.

V—VIRGINIE ARROSE SES VIOLETTES CHAQUE MATIN ET CHAQUE SOIR.

W—WINIFRED EST AMÉRICAINE, ELLE N'EST PAS UNE PETITE FRANÇAISE.

X—XÉNOPHON EST LE GÉNÉRAL RENOMMÉ À QUI PAUL CROIT RESSEMBLER.

Y—Y A-T-IL UNE AUTRE PETITE FILLE
DE SI JOLIS YEUX?

Z—ZÉNOBIE SAIT COMPTER D'UN JUSQU'À
ZÉRO.

THE CREATURE WITH NO CLAWS

by Joel Chandler Harris

"WEN you git a leetle bit older dan w'at you is, honey," said Uncle Remus to the little boy, "you'll know lots mo' dan you does now."

The old man had a pile of white oak splits by his side and these he was weaving into a chair-bottom. He was an expert in the art of "bottoming chairs," and he earned many a silver quarter in this way. The little boy seemed to be much interested in the process.

"Hit's des like I tell you," the old man went on; "I done had de speunce un it. I done got so now dat I don't b'lieve w'at I see, much less w'at I year. It got ter be whar I kin put my han' on it en fumble wid it. Folks kin fool deyse'f lots wuss dan yuther folks kin fool um, en ef you don't b'lieve w'at I'm a-tellin' un you, you kin des ax Brer Wolf de nex' time you meet 'im in de big road."

"What about Brother Wolf, Uncle Remus?" the little boy asked, as the old man paused to refill his pipe.

"Well, honey, 't ain't no great long rigamarole; hit's des one er deze yer tales w'at goes in a gallop twel it gits ter de jumpin'-off place.

"One time Brer Wolf wuz gwine 'long de big road feelin' mighty proud en high-strung. He wuz a mighty high-up man in dem days, Brer Wolf wuz, en 'mos' all de yuther creeturs wuz feard un 'im. Well, he wuz gwine 'long lickin' his chops en walkin' sorter stiff-kneed, w'en he happen ter look down 'pon de groun' en dar he seed a track in de san'. Brer Wolf stop, he did, en look at it, en den he 'low:

"'Heyo! w'at kind er creetur dish yer? Brer Dog ain't make dat track, en needer is Brer Fox. Hit's one er deze yer kind er creeturs w'at ain't got no claws. I'll des 'bout foller 'im up, en ef I ketch 'im he'll sholy be my meat.'

"Dat de way Brer Wolf talk. He followed 'long atter de track, he did, en he look at it close, but he ain't see no print er no claw. Bimeby de track tuck 'n tu'n out de road en go up a dreen whar de rain done wash out. De track wuz plain dar in de wet san', but Brer Wolf ain't see no sign er no claws.

"He foller en foller, Brer Wolf did, en de track git fresher en fresher, but still he ain't see no print er no claw. Bimeby he come in sight er de creetur, en Brer Wolf stop, he did, en look at 'im. He stop stock-still and look. De creetur wuz mighty quare-lookin', en he wuz cuttin' up some mighty quare capers. He had big head, sharp nose, en bob tail; en he wuz walkin' roun' en roun' a big dog-wood tree, rubbin' his sides ag'in it. Brer Wolf watch 'im a right smart while, he acts so quare, en den he 'low:

"'Shoo! dat creetur done bin in a fight en los' de bes' part er he tail; en w'at make he scratch hisse'f dat away? I lay I'll let 'im know who he foolin' 'long wid.'

"Atter 'while, Brer Wolf went up a leetle nigher de creetur, en holler out:

"'Heyo, dar! w'at you doin' scratchin'

yo' scaly hide on my tree, en tryin' fer ter break hit down?'

"De creetur ain't make no answer. He des walk 'roun' en 'roun' de tree scratchin' he sides en back. Brer Wolf holler out:

"'I lay I'll make you year me ef I hatter come dar whar you is!'

"De creetur des walk 'roun' en 'roun' de tree, en ain't make no answer. Den Brer Wolf hail 'im ag'in, en talk like he mighty mad:

I fus' holler atter you, but I ain't gwine ter let you off now. I'm a-gwine ter l'arn you a lesson dat 'll stick by you.'

"Den de creetur sorter wrinkle up he face en mouf, en Brer Wolf 'low:

"'Oh, you nee'n'ter swell up en cry, you 'ceitful vilyun. I'm a-gwine ter gi' you a frailin' dat I boun' you won't forgit.'

"Brer Wolf make like he gwine ter hit de creetur, en den——"

Here Uncle Remus paused and looked

"Well, suh, dat creetur des fotch one swipe dis away, en 'n'er swipe dat away"

"'Ain't you gwine ter min' me, you imperdent scoundul? Ain't you gwine ter mozey outer my woods en let my tree 'lone?'

"Wid dat, Brer Wolf march todes de creetur des like he gwine ter squ'sh 'im in de groun'. De creetur rub hisse'f ag'in de tree en look like he feel mighty good. Brer Wolf keep on gwine todes 'im, en bimeby w'en he git sorter close de creetur tuck'n sot up on his behime legs des like you see squir'ls do. Den Brer Wolf, he 'low, he did:

"'Ah-yi! you beggin', is you? But 'tain't gwine ter do you no good. I mout er let you off ef you'd a-minded me w'en

all around the room and up at the rafters. When he began again his voice was very solemn.

—"Well, suh, dat creetur des fotch one swipe dis away, en 'n'er swipe dat away, en mos' 'fo' you can wink yo' eye-balls, Brer Wolf hide wuz mighty nigh teetotally tor'd off 'n 'im. Atter dat de creetur s'antered off in de woods, en 'gun ter rub hisse'f on 'n'er tree."

"What kind of a creature was it, Uncle Remus?" asked the little boy.

"Well, honey," replied the old man in a confidential whisper, "hit want nobody on de top-side er de yeth but old Brer Wild-cat."

EDITHA'S BURGLAR

by Frances Hodgson Burnett

I WILL begin by saying that Editha was always rather a queer little girl, and not much like other children. She was not a strong, healthy little girl, and had never been able to run about and play; and, as she had no sisters or brothers, or companions of her own size, she was rather old-fashioned, as her aunts used to call it. She had always been very fond of books, and had learned to read when she was such a tiny child, that I should almost be afraid to say how tiny she was when she read her first volume through. Her papa wrote books himself, and was also the editor of a newspaper; and, as he had a large library, Editha perhaps read more than was quite good for her. She lived in London; and, as her mamma was very young and pretty, and went out a great deal, and her papa was so busy, and her governess only came in the morning, she was left to herself a good many hours in the day, and when she was left to herself, she spent the greater part of her time in the library reading her papa's big books, and even his newspapers.

She was very fond of the newspapers, because she found so many curious things in them,—stories, for instance, of strange events which happened every day in the great city of London, and yet never seemed to happen anywhere near where she lived. Through the newspapers, she found that there were actually men who lived by breaking into people's houses and stealing all the nice things they could carry away, and she read that such men were called burglars. When she first began to read about burglars, she was very much troubled. In the first place, she felt rather timid about going to bed at night, and, in the second place, she felt rather sorry for the burglars.

"I suppose no one ever taught them any better," she thought.

In fact, she thought so much about the matter, that she could not help asking her papa some questions one morning when he was at breakfast. He was reading his paper and eating his chops both at once when she spoke to him.

"Papa," she said, in a solemn little voice, and looking at him in a very solemn manner, "papa dear, what do you think of burglars—as a class?" (She said "as a class," because she had heard one of her papa's friends say it, and as he was a gentleman she admired very much, she liked to talk as he did.) Her papa gave a little jump in his chair, as if she had startled him, and then he pushed his hair off his forehead and stared at her.

"Burglars! As a class!" he said, and then he stared at her a minute again in rather a puzzled way. "Bless my soul!" he said. "As a class, Nixie!" (that was his queer pet name for her.) "Nixie, where is your mother?"

"She is in bed, papa dear, and we mustn't disturb her," said Editha. "The party last night tired her out. I peeped into her room softly as I came down. She looks so pretty, when she is asleep. What *do* you think of burglars, papa?"

"I think they're a bad lot, Nixie," said her papa, "a bad lot."

"Are there no good burglars, papa?"

"Well, Nixie," answered papa, "I should say not. As a rule, you know,—" and here he began to smile, as people often smiled at Editha when she asked questions, —"as a rule, burglars are not distinguished for moral perspicuity and blameless character."

But Editha did not understand what moral perspicuity meant, and besides she was thinking again.

"Miss Lane was talking to me the other day, about some poor children who had never been taught anything; they had never had any French or music lessons, and scarcely knew how to read, and she said they had never had any advantages. Perhaps that is the way with the burglars, papa,—perhaps they have never had any advantages,—perhaps if they had had advantages they might n't have been burglars."

"Lessons in French and music are very elevating to the mind, my dear Nixie," papa began in his laughing way, which was always a trial to Editha, but suddenly he stopped, and looked at her rather sadly.

"How old are you, Nixie?" he asked.

"I am seven," answered Editha, "seven years, going on eight."

Papa sighed.

"Come here, little one," he said, holding out his strong white hand to her.

She left her chair and went to him, and he put his arms around her, and kissed her, and stroked her long brown hair.

"Don't puzzle your little brain too much," he said, "never mind about the burglars, Nixie."

"Well," said Editha, "I can't help think-ing about them a little, and it seems to me that there must be, perhaps, one good burglar among all the bad ones, and I can't help being rather sorry, even for the bad ones. You see, they must have to be up all night, and out in the rain some-times, and they can't help not having had advantages."

It was strange that the first thing she heard, when she went up to her mamma's room, was something about burglars.

She was very, very fond of her mamma, and very proud of her. She even tried to take care of her in her small way; she never disturbed her when she was asleep, and she always helped her to dress, bring-ing her things to her, buttoning her little shoes and gloves, putting the perfume on her handkerchiefs, and holding her wraps until she wanted them.

This morning, when she went into the dressing-room, she found the chamber-maid there before her, and her dear little mamma looking very pale.

"Ah, mem! if you please, mem!" the chamber-maid was saying, "what a bless-ing it was they didn't come here!"

"Who, Janet?" Editha asked.

"The burglars, Miss, that broke into Number Eighteen last night, and carried off all the silver, and the missus's jewelry."

"If burglars ever do break in here," said mamma, "I hope none of us will hear them, though it would almost break my heart to have my things taken. If I should waken in the night, and find a burglar in my room, I think it would kill me, and I know I should scream, and then there is no knowing what they might do. If ever you think there is a burglar in the house, Nixie, whatever you do, don't scream or make any noise. It would be better to have one's things stolen, than to be killed by burglars for screaming."

She was not a very wise little mamma, and often said rather thoughtless things;

but she was very gentle and loving, and Editha was so fond of her that she put her arms round her waist and said to her:

"Mamma, dearest, I will never let any burglars hurt you or frighten you if I can help it. I do believe I could persuade them not to. I should think even a burglar would listen to reason."

That made her mamma laugh, so that she forgot all about the burglars and began to get her color again, and it was not long before she was quite gay, and was singing a song she had heard at the opera, while Editha was helping her to dress.

But that very night Editha met a burglar.

Just before dinner, her papa came up from the city in a great hurry. He dashed up to the front door in a cab, and, jumping out, ran upstairs to mamma, who was sitting in the drawing-room, while Editha read aloud to her.

"Kitty, my dear," he said, "I am obliged to go to Glasgow by the 'five' train. I must throw a few things into a pormanteau and go at once."

"Oh, Francis!" said mamma. "And just after that burglary at the Norris's! I don't like to be left alone."

"The servants are here," said papa, "and Nixie will take care of you; won't you, Nixie? Nixie is interested in burglars."

"I am sure Nixie could do more than the servants," said mamma. "All three of them sleep in one room at the top of the house when you are away, and even if they awakened they would only scream."

"Nixie wouldn't scream," said papa, laughing; "Nixie would do something heroic. I will leave you in her hands."

He was only joking, but Editha did not think of what he said as a joke; she felt that her mamma was really left in her care, and that it was a very serious matter. She thought about it so seriously that

she hardly talked at all at dinner, and was so quiet afterward that her mamma said, "Dear me, Nixie, what *are* you thinking of? You look as solemn as a little owl."

"I am thinking of you, mamma," the child answered.

And then her mamma laughed and kissed her, and said: "Well, I must say I don't see why you should look so grave about me. I didn't think I was such a solemn subject."

At last bedtime came, and the little girl went to her mother's room, because she was to sleep there.

"I am glad I have you with me, Nixie," said mamma, with a rather nervous little laugh. "I am sure I shouldn't like to sleep in this big room alone."

But, after she was in bed, she soon fell asleep, and lay looking so happy and sweet and comfortable that Editha thought it was lovely to see her.

Editha did not go to sleep for a long time. She thought of her papa trying to sleep on the train, rushing through the dark night on its way to Scotland; she thought of a new book she had just begun to read; she thought of a child she had once heard singing in the street; and when her eyes closed at length, her mind had just gone back to the burglars at Number Eighteen. She slept until midnight, and then something wakened her. At first she did not know what it was, but in a few minutes she found that it was a queer little sound coming from down-stairs,—a sound like a stealthy filing of iron.

She understood in a moment then, because she had heard the chamber-maid say that the burglars broke into Number Eighteen by filing through the bars of the shutters.

"It is a burglar," she thought, "and he will awaken mamma."

If she had been older, and had known more of the habits of burglars, she might have been more frightened than she was. She did not think of herself at all, however, but of her mother.

She began to reason the matter over as quickly as possible, and she made up her mind that the burglar must not be allowed to make a noise.

"I'll go down and ask him to please be as quiet as he can," she said to herself, "and I'll tell him why."

Certainly, this was a queer thing to think of doing, but I told you when I began my story that she was a queer little girl.

She slipped out of bed so quietly that she scarcely stirred the clothes, and then slipped just as quietly out of the room and down the stairs.

The filing had ceased, but she heard a sound of stealthy feet in the kitchen; and, though it must be confessed her heart beat rather faster than usual, she made her way to the kitchen and opened the door.

Imagine the astonishment of that burglar when, on hearing the door open, he turned round and found himself looking at a slender little girl, in a white frilled night-gown, and with bare feet,—a little girl whose large brown eyes rested on him in a by no means unfriendly way.

"I'll be polite to him," Editha had said, as she was coming down-stairs. "I am sure he'll be more obliging if I am very polite. Miss Lane says politeness always wins its way."

So the first words she spoke were as polite as she could make them.

"Don't be frightened," she said, in a soft voice. "I don't want to hurt you; I came to ask a favor of you."

The burglar was so amazed that he actually forgot he was a burglar, and staggered back against the wall. I think he thought at first that Editha was a little ghost. "You see I couldn't hurt you if I wanted to," she went on, wishing to encourage him. "I'm too little. I'm only seven,—and a little over,—and I'm not going to scream, because that would waken mamma, and that's just what I don't want to do."

That did encourage the burglar, but still he was so astonished that he did not know what to do.

"Well, I'm blowed," he said in a whisper, "if this aint a rummy go!" which was extremely vulgar language; but, unfortunately, he was one of those burglars who, as Miss Lane said, "had not had any advantages," which is indeed the case with the majority of the burglars of my acquaintance.

Then he began to laugh,—in a whisper also, if one can be said to laugh in a whisper. He put his hand over his mouth, and made no noise, but he laughed so hard that he doubled up and rocked himself to and fro.

"The rummiest go!" he said, in his uneducated way. "An' she haint agoin' to 'urt me. Oh, my heye!"

He was evidently very badly educated, indeed, for he not only used singular words, but sounded his h's all in the wrong places. Editha noticed this, even in the midst of her surprise at his laughter. She could not understand what he was laughing at. Then it occurred to her that she might have made a mistake.

"If you please," she said, with great delicacy, "are you really a burglar?"

He stopped laughing just long enough to answer her.

"Lor' no, miss," he said, "by no manner o' means. I'm a dear friend o' yer Par's, come to make a evenin' call, an' not a wishin' to trouble the servants, I stepped in through the winder."

"Ah!" said Editha, looking very gravely at him; "I see you are joking with me, as papa does sometimes. But what I wanted to say to you was this: Papa has gone to

Scotland, and all our servants are women, and mamma would be so frightened if you were to waken her, that I am sure it would make her ill. And if you are going to burgle, would you please burgle as quietly as you can, so that you wont disturb her?"

The burglar stopped laughing, and, staring at her, once more uttered his vulgar exclamation:

"Well, I'll be blowed!"

"Why don't you say, 'I'll be blown?'" asked Editha. "I'm sure it isn't correct to say you'll be blowed."

She thought he was going off into one of his unaccountable fits of laughter again, but he did not; he seemed to check himself with an effort.

"There haint no time to waste," she heard him mutter.

"No, I suppose there isn't," she answered. "Mamma might wake and miss me. What are you going to burgle first?"

"You'd better go upstairs to yer mar," he said, rather sulkily.

Editha thought deeply for a few seconds.

"You oughtn't to burgle anything," she said. "Of course you know that, but if you have really made up your mind to do it, I would like to show you the things you'd better take."

"What, fer instance?" said the burglar, with interest.

"You mustn't take any of mamma's things," said Editha, "because they are all in her room, and you would waken her, and besides, she said it would break her heart; and don't take any of the things papa is fond of. I'll tell you what," turning rather pale, "you can take my things."

"What kind o' things?" asked the burglar.

"My locket, and the little watch papa gave me, and the necklace and bracelets my grandmamma left me,—they are worth a great deal of money, and they are very pretty, and I was to wear them when I grew to be a young lady, but—but you can take them. And—then—" very slowly, and with a deep sigh, "there are—my books. I'm very fond of them, but——"

"I don't want no books," said the burglar.

"Don't you?" exclaimed she. "Ah, thank you."

"Well," said the burglar, as if to himself, and staring hard at her brightening face, "I never see no sich a start afore."

"Shall I go upstairs and get the other things?" said Editha.

"No," he said. "You stay where you are —or stay, come along o' me inter the pantry, an' sit down while I'm occypied."

He led the way into the pantry, and pushed her down on a step, and then began to open the drawers where the silver was kept.

"It's curious that you should know just where to look for things, and that your key should fit, isn't it?" said Editha.

"Yes," he answered, "it's werry sing'lar, indeed. There's a good deal in bein' eddicated."

"Are you educated?" asked Editha, with a look of surprise.

"Did yer think I wasn't?" said the burglar.

"Well," said Editha, not wishing to offend him, "you see, you pronounce your words so very strangely."

"It's all a matter o' taste," interrupted the burglar. "Oxford an' Cambridge 'as different vocabillaries."

"Did you go to Oxford?" asked Editha, politely.

"No," said he, "nor yet to Cambridge."

Then he laughed again, and seemed to be quite enjoying himself as he made some forks and spoons up into a bundle. "I 'ope there haint no plated stuff 'ere," he said. "Plate's wulgar, an' I 'ope yer parents haint wulgar, cos that 'd be settin' yer a werry bad example an' sp'ilin' yer morals."

"I am sure papa and mamma are not vulgar," said Editha.

The burglar opened another drawer, and chuckled again, and this suggested to Editha's mind another question.

"Is your business a good one?" she suddenly inquired of him.

"'Taint as good as it ought to be, by no manner o' means," said the burglar. "Every one haint as hobligin' as you, my little dear."

"Oh!" said Editha. "You know you obliged me by not making a noise."

"Well," said the burglar, "as a rule, we don't make a practice o' makin' no more noise than we can help. It haint considered 'ealthy in the perfession."

"Would you mind leaving us a few forks and spoons to eat with, if you please? I beg pardon for interrupting you, but I'm afraid we shall not have any to use at breakfast."

"Haint yer got no steel uns?" inquired the burglar.

"Mamma wouldn't like to use steel ones, I'm sure," Editha answered. "I'll tell you what you can do: please leave out enough for mamma, and I can use steel. I don't care about myself, much."

The man seemed to think a moment, and then he was really so accommodating as to do as she asked, and even went to the length of leaving out her own little fork and knife and spoon.

"Oh! you are very kind," said Editha, when she saw him do this.

"That's a reward o' merit, cos yer didn't squeal," said the burglar.

He was so busy for the next few minutes that he did not speak, though now and then he broke into a low laugh, as if he was thinking of something very funny indeed. During the silence, Editha sat holding her little feet in her nightgown, and watching him very curiously. A great many new thoughts came into her active brain, and at last she could not help asking some more questions.

"Would you really rather be a burglar than anything else?" she inquired, respectfully.

"Well," said the man, "p'r'aps I'd prefer to be Lord Mayor, or a member o' the 'Ouse o' Lords, or heven the Prince o' Wales, honly for there bein' hobstacles in the way of it."

"Oh!" said Editha; "you couldn't be the Prince of Wales, you know. I meant wouldn't you rather be in some other profession? My papa is an editor," she added. "How would you like to be an editor?"

"Well," said the burglar, "hif yer par ud change with me, or hif he chanced to know hany heditor with a roarin' trade as ud be so hobligin' as to 'and it hover, hit's wot I've allers 'ad a leanin' to."

"I am sure papa would not like to be a burglar," said Editha, thoughtfully; "but perhaps he might speak to his friends about you, if you would give me your name and address, and if I were to tell him how obliging you were, and if I told him you really didn't like being a burglar."

The burglar put his hand to his pocket and gave a start of great surprise.

"To think o' me a forgettin' my cardcase," he said, "an' a leavin' it on the pianner when I come hout. I'm sich a bloomin' forgetful cove. I might hev knowed I'd hev wanted it."

"It is a pity," said Editha; "but if you told me your name and your number, I think I could remember it."

"I'm afeared yer couldn't," said the burglar, regretfully, "but I'll try yer. Lord Halgernon Hedward Halbert de Pentonwille, Yde Park. Can you think o' that?"

"Are you a lord?" exclaimed Editha. "Dear me, how strange!"

"It is sing'lar," said the burglar, shaking his head. "I've hoften thought so myself. But not wishin' to detain a lady no longer than can be 'elped, s'pose we take a turn in the lib'ery among yer respected par's things."

"Don't make a noise," said Editha, as she led the way.

But when they reached the library her loving little heart failed her. All the things her father valued most were there, and he would be sure to be so sorry if one thing was missing when he returned. She stood on the threshold a moment and looked about her.

"Oh," she whispered, "please do me another favor, wont you? Please let me slip quietly upstairs and bring down my own things instead. They will be so easy to carry away, and they are very valuable, and—and I will make you a present of them if you will not touch anything that belongs to papa. He is so fond of his things and, besides that, he is so good."

The burglar gave a rather strange and disturbed look at her.

"Go an' get yer gimcracks," he said in a somewhat grumbling voice.

Her treasures were in her own room, and her bare feet made no sound as she crept slowly up the staircase and then down again. But when she handed the little box to the burglar her eyes were wet.

"Pape gave me the watch, and mamma gave me the locket," she whispered, tremulously; "and the pearls were grandmamma's and grandmamma is in heaven."

It would not be easy to know what the burglar thought; he looked queerer than ever. Perhaps he was not quite so bad as some burglars, and felt rather ashamed of taking her treasures from a little girl who loved other people so much better than she loved herself. But he did not touch any of papa's belongings, and, indeed, did not remain much longer. He grumbled a little when he looked into the drawing-room, saying something to himself about "folks never 'avin' no consideration for a cove, an' leavin' nothin' portable 'andy, a-expectin' of him to carry off seventy-five pound bronze clocks an' marble stattoos;" but though Editha was sorry to see that he appeared annoyed, she did not understand him.

After that, he returned to the pantry and helped himself to some cold game pie, and seemed to enjoy it, and then poured out a tumbler of wine, which Editha thought a great deal to drink at once.

"Yer 'e'lth, my dear," he said, "an' 'appy returns, an' many on 'em. May yer grow up a hornyment to yer sect, an' a comfort to yer respected mar an' par."

And he threw his head very far back, and drank the very last drop in the glass, which was vulgar, to say the least of it.

Then he took up his bundles of silver and the other articles he had appropriated, and seeing that he was going away, Editha rose from the pantry step.

"Are you going out through the window?" she asked.

"Yes, my dear," he answered, with a chuckle, "it's a little 'abit I've got into. I prefers 'em to doors."

"Well, good-bye," she said, holding out her hand politely. "And thank you, my lord."

She felt it only respectful to say that, even if he had fallen into bad habits and become a burglar.

He shook hands with her in quite a friendly manner, and even made a bow.

"Yer welcome, my dear," he said. "An' I must hadd that if I ever see a queerer or better behaved little kid, may I be blowed —or, as yer told me it would be more correcter to say, I'll be blown."

Editha did not know he was joking; she thought he was improving, and that if he had had advantages he might have been a very nice man.

It was astonishing how neatly he slipped through the window; he was gone in a second, and Editha found herself standing alone in the dark, as he had taken his lantern with him.

She groped her way out and up the stairs, and then, for the first time, she began to feel cold and rather weak and strange; it was more like being frightened than any feeling she had had while the burglar was in the house.

"Perhaps, if he had been a very bad burglar, he might have killed me," she said to herself, trembling a little. "I am very glad he did not kill me, for—for it would have hurt mamma so, and papa too, when he came back, and they told him."

Her mamma wakened in the morning with a bright smile.

"Nobody hurt us, Nixie," she said. "We are all right, aren't we?"

"Yes, mamma dear," said Editha.

She did not want to startle her just then, so she said nothing more, and she even said nothing all through the excitement that followed the discovery of the robbery, and indeed, said nothing until her papa came home, and then he wondered so at her pale face, and petted her so tenderly, and thought it so strange that nothing but her treasures had been taken from upstairs, that she could keep her secret no longer.

"Papa," she cried out all at once in a trembling voice, "I gave them to him myself."

"You, Nixie! You!" exclaimed her papa, looking alarmed. "Kitty, the fright has made the poor little thing ill."

"No, papa," said Editha, her hands shaking, and the tears rushing into her eyes, she did not know why. "I heard him, and —I knew mamma would be so frightened,—and it came into my mind to ask

him—not to waken her,—and I crept down-stairs—and asked him;—and he was not at all unkind though he laughed. And I stayed with him, and—and told him I would give him all my things if he would not touch yours nor mamma's. He—he wasn't such a bad burglar, papa,—and he told me he would rather be something more respectable."

And she hid her face on her papa's shoulder.

"Kitty!" papa cried out. "Oh, Kitty!"

Then her mamma flew to her and knelt down by her, kissing her, and crying aloud:

"Oh, Nixie! if he had hurt you,—if he had hurt you."

"He knew I was not going to scream, mamma," said Editha. "And he knew I was too little to hurt him. I told him so."

She scarcely understood why mamma cried so much more at this, and why even papa's eyes were wet as he held her close up to his breast.

"It is my fault, Francis," wept the poor little mamma. "I have left her too much to herself, and I have not been a wise mother. Oh, to think of her risking her dear little life just to save me from being frightened, and to think of her giving up the things she loves for our sakes. I will be a better mother to her, after this, and take care of her more."

But I am happy to say that the watch and locket and pearls were not altogether lost, and came back to their gentle little owner in time. About six months after, the burglar was caught, as burglars are apt to be, and, after being tried and sentenced to transportation to the penal settlements (which means that he was to be sent away to be a prisoner in a far country), a police officer came one day to see Editha's papa, and he actually came from that burglar, who was in jail and wanted to see Editha for a special reason. Editha's papa took her to see him, and the moment she entered his cell she knew him.

"How do you do, my lord?" she said, in a gentle tone.

"Not as lively as common, miss," he answered, "in consekence o' the confinement not bein' good fer my 'e'lth."

"None of your chaff," said the police officer. "Say what you have to say."

And then, strange to say, the burglar brought forth from under his mattress a box, which he handed to the little girl.

"One o' my wisitors brought 'em in to me this mornin'," he said. "I thought yer might as well hev 'em. I kep' 'em partly 'cos it was more convenienter, an' partly 'cos I took a fancy to yer. I've seed a many curi's things, sir," he said to Editha's papa, "but never nothin' as bloomin' queer as that little kid a-comin' in an' tellin' me she wont 'urt me, nor yet wont scream, and please wont I burgle quietly so as to not disturb her mar. It brought my 'art in my mouth when first I see her, an' then, Lor', how I larft. I almost made up my mind to give her things back to her afore I left, but I didn't quite do that—it was agin human natur'."

But they were in the box now, and Editha was so glad to see them that she could scarcely speak for a few seconds. Then she thanked the burglar politely.

"I am much obliged to you," she said, "and I'm really very sorry you are to be sent so far away. I am sure papa would have tried to help you if he could, though he says he is afraid you would not do for an editor."

The burglar closed one eye and made a very singular grimace at the police officer, who turned away suddenly and did not look round until Editha had bidden her acquaintance good-bye.

And even this was not quite all. A few weeks later, a box was left for Editha by a very shabby, queer-looking man, who quickly disappeared as soon as he had given it to the servant at the door; and in this box was a very large old-fashioned silver watch, almost as big as a turnip, and inside the lid were scratched these words:

To the little Kid,
From 'er fr'end and wel wisher,
Lord halgernon hedward halbert
de pentonwill, ide park.

MAULED BY AN ELEPHANT

by J. Alden Loring

"BUTIABA, Uganda, Africa; Jan. 5, 1910. On the shore of Albert Nyanza." So begins one of the entries in my journal during the Roosevelt African Expedition, of which I had the good fortune to be a member.

We were due at Butiaba the day before, but were detained a day by waiting at the last camp to secure the tusks and feet of an ugly old rogue elephant that the Colonel had killed at the earnest solicitation of the natives.

The great brute was a sort of outcast among his fellows, and for some time had been wandering about terrorizing the people by visiting the "shambas" (gardens) at night and feeding on the crops. He had wrecked several grass huts and killed one native; and, as our coming was heralded through the country several months in advance, the childish people, who were apparently at the brute's mercy, anxiously awaited our arrival.

We were not in camp fifteen minutes before the chief of the district appeared and asked the Colonel to relieve his people of their tormentor. For several days, the cunning old native had stationed men to watch the rogue, and he said that the two men who accompanied him were guides that had just left the brute taking his midday siesta under a tree less than a mile from camp.

The Colonel heard the story in silence, and then said: "But, Cuninghame, tell him

that I have secured all the elephants I want, and that we lack the men to carry the skin and skeleton even though we *did* want it."

"Yes, Colonel, that's true," said Cuninghame; "but this animal is really a pest to the country, and, if he is not killed, his depredations may compel the people to desert their village and move from the locality. Such an occurrence is not unusual. Besides, it is one of the customs of the country, a thing that these natives expect of a white man—that he should deliver them from a rogue elephant—and if you do not acquiesce, they will look upon it as a lack of courtesy, so to speak."

"Oh, well, if that's the case, certainly I will try my best."

So saying, he called to Kermit, and in a few minutes the two, accompanied by their gun-bearers, left with the guides, after being warned by the chief that the rogue was dangerous, and would probably charge as soon as it saw or scented them.

As they disappeared, I thought how typical of the Colonel this dialogue was, for, during the eleven months that we were in Africa, he rarely shot an animal that was not used for a specimen or for food,—the only exception being crocodiles, which every year kill hundreds of women and children as they wade out to fill their water-jars.

Seizing a bag of traps, I called to my boys and started out to collect some small mammals. I had set only a few traps when I heard a shot, then another, and finally several in rapid succession. The roar of the heavy 405 Winchester and the double report of the Colonel's Holland rifle were unmistakable. A few minutes later I heard the exultant shouts of the gun-bearers and the guides, and I knew that the rogue elephant was an animal of the past.

The hunters had come upon the brute in the tall grass, and, true to the chief's warning, it charged the instant that it saw them, and before a shot had been fired.

After seeing the brute, I did not wonder that the natives hesitated about attacking it, for it measured ten feet nine inches from the soles of its front feet to the top of the back, and its tusks weighed one hundred and ten pounds.

As we marched into Butiaba, we were met by Captain Hutchison, then head of the Uganda Marine, which was at the time a fleet of several miniature naphtha launches. He congratulated the Colonel on his recent feat, adding that escape from a charging elephant of any kind, and particularly a "rogue," deserved congratulations, as he could testify from a certain "close call" he once had in elephant-hunting.

"Now, Captain," spoke up the Colonel, "I feel sure that you have an interesting story to relate, so please give it to us at once."

"Well, it was a bit awkward, I must admit," began the captain, "and so upset me that I have never 'taken on' an elephant since.

"It happened just north of the Lado country. I had been out ivory hunting for some time without having much luck, when one of my boys brought in word that he had struck a herd in which, judging from the enormous track, there was an immense tusker. He guided me to the spot, and, sure enough, there was a huge track that was well worth following.

"The trail was made several hours before, and evidently there were about twenty elephants in the bunch. They were traveling at a good rate, and we knew that they probably would not stop before feeding time, late in the afternoon.

"Elephants may look slow and clumsy in captivity, but when they are walking at an ordinary gait, a person must step along at almost a dog-trot in order to overhaul them. It was about ten o'clock when we took the 'spoor' (a sign of any kind), and we knew that it meant a hard twenty-mile journey at least, before we should overtake them. Frequently ivory hunters will follow a herd of elephants for days before catching up with their game. The trail was not hard to keep, for a herd of twenty elephants, following single file through the ten-foot elephant-grass, makes more than a well-worn path.

"As they marched along, they had amused themselves by snatching a bunch of grass and tossing it aside; then, as they had passed through a grove of thorntrees, they had broken off limbs and dragged them a hundred yards or more before dropping them. Several times one had halted long enough to dig a hole in the ground three or four feet in diameter with his tusks, and then we saw where he had galloped on to overtake his comrades. Once they gave us an advantage by stopping for some time to wallow in a water-hole, and, as they emerged, they rubbed their bodies against the first trees they passed, leaving the mud plastered ten feet high on the bark. These and other signs, growing fresher and fresher all the time, told us that we were slowly overtaking our game.

"About five o'clock, we surmised that, if the elephants were still traveling, we must be within five miles of them; but, as it was feeding time, I thought it practical to send my best tracker ahead to reconnoiter, while we followed more slowly. In an hour he returned, and reported that he had overhauled the herd feeding in a grove of thorn-trees, of which they are particularly fond.

"By the time we had arrived, they had passed out of the grove and were again in the elephant-grass, which, owing to its height and density, made it impossible for us to see them. Even when we mounted an ant-hill, the growth was so tall that we got only an occasional glimpse of a back or of a few snakelike trunks waving about in the air. The wind was scarcely in our favor, so we circled them to a large tree, and I sent one of the boys up to see if he could locate the big tusker.

"Our prize was on the far side of the herd, and in such a position that, should we attempt to stalk him, there would be risk of some of the elephants catching the scent and giving the alarm. Nothing could be done, therefore, but to keep watch until he had worked around to a more favorable position.

"At last, the long-looked-for time arrived, for the tusker was on the outskirts of the herd, and the wind was favorable. We circled to his side, and stealthily drew near—my gun-bearer, tracker, and myself—while the other boys remained in the rear.

"The tall grass prevented us from even catching a glimpse of the beasts, but it was easy to locate them by the noise they made while feeding.

"We held to the elephant trails, as no one could penetrate that jungle of grass and travel silently. Next to silence we had to watch the wind, for, once the animals caught our scent, they would either dash away or charge.

"So far, our plans had worked out admirably; the elephants, unconscious of our presence, were still tearing up the grass directly in our front, while my boys and myself proceeded inch by inch and strained our eyes to catch sight of the brutes. These boys had been my companions on many an elephant-hunt, and I had the utmost confidence in them, knowing well that, if it were necessary, they would not hesitate to give up their lives to save mine.

"I don't care how many elephants a man may have encountered, while he is sneaking up on his game, a feeling of uneasiness steals over him until the critical moment arrives; then things happen so quickly and his brain works so rapidly, that all sense of fear is for the moment lost.

"With both hammers of my rifle raised, I cautiously sneaked nearer and nearer, my faithful boys following at my very heels. At last, we were within fifty feet of the elephant, and, as he moved toward me, I could see the top of the grass swaying violently from side to side. Suddenly, fate turned against us, for a shifting current of air must have warned the brute of danger. I saw a huge trunk rise above the grass, heard a shrill, deafening trumpet, and knew that the fight was on. The grass parted as though a snow-plow were being driven through it, and the next instant there loomed up, not twenty feet away, a monster head with wing-like ears protruding on either side like the sails on a dhow. Two shiny tusks of ivory, fully six feet long, were pointed at my chest, and the towering trunk between them gave the head a fiendish look not often found outside of Hades. The other elephants took up the trumpeting, and the uproar was appalling.

"My rifle was at my shoulder from the second the brute began his charge, and the instant that he hove in sight, I fired both barrels point-blank into his face. Without a second's hesitation, I reached back to my gun-bearer for the '450,' and brought it to position. Immense though the brute was, he looked three times his normal size as I cast my eyes along the barrels leveled at his head not five feet away. I pressed one trigger, then the other, but there was no report, and, with a sickening feeling of horror, I realized that my gun-bearer, in the excitement of the moment, had failed to raise the hammers.

"Before I could lower the rifle from my shoulder, the brute was upon me! With a scream of rage he twined his trunk about my body, and, lifting me high above his head, brandished me about in the air as though I were a feather. Every instant I expected to be hurled fifty feet or more through space, which I welcomed as the only possible likelihood of escape. But no, at that moment I struck the ground with a thud. Three times I was lifted high and brought crashing through the grass to earth. The last time the elephant uncoiled his trunk and left me lying there, stunned and dazed, and staring blankly into his wicked little eyes, now hot with rage.

"Then dropping to his knees before me, he knelt there hesitating, as though to give me time to deliberate before the end should come. But he did not keep me waiting long, for slowly the two great tusks began descending. With all my waning strength I threw my body snug up against his bending knees, and the tusks passed harmlessly over me, just grazing my back, and tore great holes in the earth beyond. Again the ponderous head was raised, and again his tusks bore down upon me and probed deeply into the earth behind me.

"Evidently the animal had been somewhat blinded by my shots, for, assuming that he had done his work, he started to rise, and as he did so, the sudden thought came over me that he would probably attempt to trample me to death, the usual method that an elephant employs to obliterate an enemy. So, as he slowly rose, in some unaccountable manner I managed to scramble between his fore feet, and grabbed him by the leg, then loosed my grip, and, working back, seized hold of his hind foot.

"Once more I felt the snakelike trunk being wound around me, next I was being waved about over the grass-top—then the ground seemed suddenly to rise and meet me, and I lost consciousness. How many times I was hammered on the ground I do not know.

"Three hours later, I came to myself and found my boys dashing water into my face. When I opened my eyes, I saw the gun-bearer holding a smoking rifle in his hands. He had just returned from the scene of my mauling, and brought in my rifles, one of which he had attempted to unload, and, in some manner, had accidentally discharged. The explosion had no doubt assisted to revive me.

"My men told me that my life was saved by the quick action of my tracker, who appeared on the scene with a spear at about the time that I lost consciousness, and, rushing in, plunged the spear into the elephant's side. Leaving me, the animal took after its new tormentor, and the agile native, twisting and doubling in the thick grass, managed finally to escape. The elephant had devastated the grass, bushes, and small trees in his search for the man, and, fortunately, had not returned to me.

"While it is undoubtedly true that the native's action had much to do with saving me, one reason why I was not dashed to death lies in the fact that an elephant's trunk is the tenderest part of his body, and being twined about me, it received the brunt of the blow each time that I struck the ground, and evidently the pain kept the animal from using the force needed to kill me.

"As a result of this mauling, I was laid up for six weeks before I was well enough to hobble about again.

"That elephant may be alive at this present moment, for all I know. My native attendants were too terror-stricken over the outcome of the hunt to give the brute any further attention after I was mauled, so no one followed him up to discover what damage my shots had done. But, judging from the amount of vigor that was left in his great hulk at the time he put me to sleep, he could not have been seriously wounded.

"Well, as I have said, Colonel," concluded Captain Hutchison, "that hunt used up my stock of courage, and I doubt if I shall ever 'take on' another elephant, unless in self-defense."

The Gossips

Painted by Arthur Rackham

Marjorie and Margaret

Painted by Arthur Rackham

Mother Goose

Painted by Arthur Rackham

A BARREL OF TACKS

by Foster Rhea Dulles

JOHN COLLINGS gripped his oar and pulled as he never had before in his life. He dared not look around—that was the first rule of the whaleboat—but from the excited and frantic pleas of the first mate, clinging grimly to his long steering oar as they shot through the crested waves which broke in a fine spray over the boat's crew, he knew that they must be getting close to the whale. But that was not his business. He had only to row; and with the sweat pouring down his face and his heart thumping noisily, he put every ounce of energy into it. No one would be able to say that he was not worth his weight when it came to chasing whales.

They had lowered from the whaleship *Angus Parker* so quickly that the lookout's long-drawn-out call of "There she blows!" was still reverberating in their ears when they pushed off and headed toward that distant spot where the whale's filmy jet had broken the surface. It was the first whale they had sighted in three weeks. Captain Hooker had become so gloomy that not even the mates dared approach him, and the crew were so sick of loafing about the decks that they grumbled all day and half the night. If they didn't get this whale there was bound to be trouble. Nerves had been stretched to the breaking point.

But if this was the way the *Angus Parker's* crew in general felt about things,

the lowering was even more important to John Collings. It was his first chance in the boats. Ten months before, he had shipped as a cabin boy. Throughout the long voyage about Cape Horn, throughout those endless weeks of cruising in the South Pacific, he was always afraid that Captain Hooker would never give him his opportunity. He was afraid that he would be helping the cook and the steward, running errands, until the *Angus Parker* at last tied up again at her berth in New Bedford. And that was not what he had come to sea for. He had come to hunt whales. But now here he was in the first mate's boat, actually going after a whale. John pulled with all the strength of his eighteen years.

"Give it to her, boys," the mate was shouting. "Oh, he's a beaut, a beaut. Just a hundred yards ahead of us now. Pull, you scoundrels, pull! What are you loafing for? Do you think this is some blamed regatta? We're after whales and we're going to get this one. Come on now, all together. Pull, pull. What are you holding back for? Do you think we're out here for fun? It's oil we're after and this thumping crittur is just oozy with it. We can get him if you'll only wake up. Pull, will you, pull, pull!"

The boat was now shooting through the water, each man almost breaking his back as he dragged on his heavy oar. The waves cascaded over the bow and drenched them to the skin. The water shot by. Any minute now should see them close enough for the harpooner to let his iron fly. He was ready there in the bow, the long weapon in his hands, his knee braced against the gunwale. The line still lay loose along the thwarts and there was not a hitch in the neat coils in the after tub, but it was not hard to imagine it running out when the harpoon had been hurled. Any minute now and they might be fast, off for a "Nantucket sleigh ride" as the whale made its dash for freedom.

John was so excited he could hardly breathe. His hands seemed stuck to the oar, his heart had stopped. He thought he could hear the whale wallowing in the deep swells; he thought he could smell it. The spray which broke over him seemed hot and scalding. He was sure it was from the whale's spout. He'd have given any-thing for a quick glance over his shoulder to see what was happening. But he clung to his oar and pulled as if his life depended on it.

Suddenly the mate whispered a com-mand to the harpooner to stand ready. The time had come. John leaned forward for a final long stroke, caught his oar on the top of a wave, and was tumbled off the thwart as he swung back. The whaleboat seemed to hesitate a fraction of a second and just at that moment the harpooner let go his iron. But he was thrown off his balance and the harpoon fell short. Before a second could be hurled, the whale had sounded. As the whaleboat rocked in the rolling swells, a cloud of bubbles rose to the surface as sole evidence that there had ever been a whale.

No one in the boat said a word except the mate, who was cursing steadily under his breath. John struggled up and grabbed the oar which had been knocked out of his hand.

"I . . ." but he could get no further. Never did a boy wear a more rueful ex-pression, a more beaten, hang-dog look. He had had his chance. He had failed. He would have given anything in the world to be back home on his father's farm. He couldn't face the men in the boat.

For a little while the whaleboat re-mained at the spot where the whale had sounded, its weary and discouraged crew resting on their oars. They kept their thoughts to themselves but John could feel the unspoken bitterness of their re-sentment. If the whale should break water again not too far off, the chase might be renewed, but as minute after minute passed without a sign of it, this hope slowly faded. Finally far in the distance a faint spout was sighted by the harpooner, but he merely pointed at it with a listless ges-ture. It was much too far away to make any renewal of the hunt at all practical. As the whale disappeared in the distance the whaleboat's bow was swung around toward the waiting *Angus Parker* and the boat crew started on the long row back to the ship.

As they drew near Captain Hooker could be seen on the quarterdeck and from his angry expression it was clear he had some idea of what had happened.

"Well, what do you think you were doing?" he shouted as soon as the boat was within hailing distance. "Did you trip over yourselves or did you get scared? Of all the stupid, clumsy, dodgasted ways of going on a whale . . ."

"What do you expect when you give us a farmer who still thinks he's handling a hoe instead of an oar?" shot back the mate angrily. "Your smart young cabin boy is about as much use in a boat as a blind organ grinder furling sails in a Cape Horn blow."

As John clambered up the ropes and

stood on deck he steeled himself for a terrible dressing-down. But Captain Hooker took one look at him and turned abruptly.

"Go back to the galley," he ordered in a gloomy tone, "and tell the cook you're to do whatever he wants from now on. If I ever let you in a boat again, may the barnacles on the ship's bottom turn into pansies!"

For five weeks after this incident John was kept hopping about by the cook and by anyone else who could think of a disagreeable task which would keep him busy. He could hardly face a potato, he had peeled so many of them; the sight of food made him ill, he had spent so many hours in the stifling galley. Never was a boy's life more completely miserable. If more whales had been sighted and there had been a chance to lower and make a kill, it would not have been so bad. But not once in those five weeks did the glad cry of "There she blows!" ring out. Even though John knew he would not be allowed in the boat, he would have given anything for a little excitement to break the deadly monotony of working in the galley.

For the officers and men it was almost as bad. Every day they became more morose and quarrelsome. They blamed John not only for missing that one whale, but for all their bad luck. No one would speak to him. He felt himself to be a Jonah and hardly dared to go down in the forecastle.

Finally, with supplies running low, the *Angus Parker* was headed toward the Pelew Islands, where Captain Hooker thought he could get some fresh vegetables and fruit by bartering with the natives. The ship's stores were broken out to see what they had for trade. Among the miscellaneous assortment of cloth goods, trinkets, iron nails, and other such stuff, was a barrel of tacks.

"By the flukes of the great white whale," Captain Hooker exploded, "what do they expect me to do with tacks? Do they think we came out here to lay a carpet or to catch whales?" Suddenly he had an idea. "Here you, Collings," he called. "No shore leave for you while we're layin' off the Pelews and here's something you can do. Count these tacks so I can make a report to the owners showing how careful I am of the ship's supplies. And count 'em right."

A few days later they anchored in a little harbor on a palm-fringed island with a long sandy beach. In spite of himself John could not help getting excited. What fun it would be to go ashore! What fun to swim off that beach! The other members of the crew gathered at the rail and began to talk of what they were going to do. Forgetting the captain's orders, John started to join them. At that moment the mate spied him.

"What about those tacks?" he shouted.

With a start John remembered, and sadly went over to where the barrel had been put in the ship's waist with another empty barrel beside it. One by one he began taking the tacks out of the first barrel and putting them into the second. "So this is what a whaling voyage is," he thought bitterly. "So this is why I've sailed around Cape Horn and across the Pacific. To be made sport of by Captain Hooker! To count a barrel of tacks!"

When a number of canoes put out from the shore filled with natives—fierce-looking beings with wild, unkempt hair and roving eyes—it was all he could do to keep from rushing over to the ship's side to get a better look at them. They were the first South Sea Islanders he had ever seen and it made him more than ever bitter to be kept at such a stupid task when he might be trying to barter with these fascinating natives for the yams, coconuts, oranges, and pineapples they were bringing out to the *Angus Parker*.

Among the other members of the crew little attention was paid to the natives. It was often necessary to be pretty much on guard when such savages came aboard ship. One could not tell what they might do if their cupidity was aroused by sight of a vessel's stores. But these islanders seemed peaceful enough, for all the savagery of their appearance, and they had no weapons of any kind with them. Captain Hooker carelessly motioned to them to stay forward and leisurely prepared to look over their fruits and vegetables before trying to barter with them. The crew were ordered not to trade until he had arranged for what the ship needed.

Suddenly there was a startling yell from one of the natives and at that abrupt signal the savages rushed amidships with hair-raising shouts. There on the racks the whalemen kept the weapons of their trade: long harpoons with their heads sharpened to a razor-like edge, keen-pointed lances, cutting-in spades and heavy axes. Before the startled crew of the *Angus Parker* realized what was happening the savages had seized these weapons, and, brandishing them aloft with bloodcurdling yells, started to advance upon the quarterdeck.

Captain Hooker and the mates had instinctively retreated to their own deck at the savage chief's first signal. Some of the crew were with them but most of the foremast hands had by now either dived down the open hatchways or sprung into the rigging. The natives appeared to have won control of the deck by their unexpected rush for the ship's whaling weapons, and the fate of the men on the quarterdeck

and eventually of every man on the ship hung in precarious balance.

It had all happened too quickly for the crew to take any effective measures to defend themselves and in their wild panic their only thought was of immediate escape. Even Captain Hooker was staggered by the sudden attack. Another minute and he knew the savages would be upon him, and against the harpoons, lances, and spades with which they had armed themselves, there was no protection.

At this moment, when every man's life was at stake, an idea flashed into the mind of John Collings. He had jumped up at the first bloodcurdling yell and sprung into the rigging. But now he dropped lightly to the deck and dashed back to where he had been counting the tacks. Plunging his hands into the open barrel he scooped out great handfuls of them and began to strew them over the deck. Again and again he plunged in his hands and, with the sweeping motion he had learned in planting seed, scattered the tacks full across the ship. The deck was soon covered with them.

The savages paid no attention to him. They had their eyes on the quarterdeck. They knew that if they could cut down the little group of officers and men still holding their ground, the ship was theirs. They could pick off the rest of the crew at will and plunder to their hearts' content. As their chief sprang forward they followed him in a rush aft. But their charge was halted as quickly as it had started. Some enchantment had converted the wooden deck into a torturous field of knives and spears which cut cruelly into their bare feet and burned like fire.

A chorus of frightful shrieks rose from the pain-maddened savages. They jumped and danced about the deck in agony and with every jump more tacks were embedded in their bare soles. The attack had become a rout. The natives howled and yelled. First one man and then another dove over the ship's side to escape this stabbing deck. Soon the whole savage band had dropped their weapons and plunged headlong into the sea. They did not stop to climb into their canoes; they swam for shore without a backward glance. The ship was enchanted!

John himself scarcely realized what had happened. He was wildly excited. The frantic din made by the pain-maddened savages still rang in his ears as he looked at his bleeding hands and at the half-emptied barrel of tacks.

Captain Hooker strode from the quarterdeck and looked at the boy a moment without saying anything. Then he stretched out his hand, caught sight of the boy's bleeding fingers, and withdrew it. He hesitated, cleared his throat gruffly.

"Well, John, never mind about counting the tacks. Get your hands in shape so you'll be able to pull the bow oar in my boat next time we lower."

OLD MORDECAI'S COCKEREL

by Sargent Flint

"GRAND old trees," said Mamma, "a fine view from the piazza, and pleasant inside."

"I see no fault," said Papa.

"Except that hideous little house at the foot of the garden," said Aunt Amy.

"And that horrible old man, sitting all day close up to our fence," said Bob.

"Both his legs is shorter than the other," said little Lucy.

"He sits on his own land," said Papa.

"And he minds his own business," said Mamma.

"Nevertheless, he is a very Mordecai at our back gate," said Aunt Amy.

But the summer went, and, despite the hideous little house at the foot of the garden, and the old man smoking his pipe so near the fence, everybody had seemed quite merry. The grand old trees were bare now, and a great, melancholy pile of leaves in the garden was all that was left of their glory. Aunt Amy wished the pile had been a little higher, that it might have hidden old Mordecai's house.

"I like Old Mortify," said Lucy; "he hands me my kitten when she runs away." She had grown used to seeing the old man walking from side to side, on his poor old rheumatic legs, and felt kindly toward him. She had smiled first at his little grand-daughter, and then asked her if she were Mortify's little girl.

"What you mean?" said the child.

"Are you his little girl?" asked Lucy. "He is my grandpa; I am Sadie."

Lucy handed some white roses through the fence, and Sadie handed back a plum. To be sure, the plum was very hard, and Lucy could not eat it; but she believed it was the best her little neighbor had, and always spoke to her afterward.

Now the weather had become so cold that Mordecai no longer sat by the fence, or walked in his little garden; and Lucy had not seen Sadie for a long time.

In a week it would be Thanksgiving. The sky was gray and cold, and the tall trees waved their bare branches to keep warm until the snow should come to cover them.

"Everything looks awfully homesick," said Bob, standing at the window. "This is the meanest place I ever saw."

At that moment a loud, defiant crow fell upon his ears.

"That's Old Mordecai's cockerel," he said angrily.

"Yes," said Lucy. "I can see him down at the pile of leaves."

"I told him never to crow on our side of the fence," said Bob.

Lucy laughed.

"You may laugh, but you just see if he crows on our side again, Lucy Jackson."

Once again the cockerel crowed, loudly and triumphantly. Once more Lucy laughed. Bob went out, and Lucy saw the cockerel scratching the leaves. Then she saw Bob creeping toward him with a bow and arrow. She laughed again, for she considered Bob a very poor shot. Aunt Amy had often said that, if no one but Bob cared for archery, a target would last forever.

Mordecai's cockerel seemed to be of the same opinion, for he stopped a moment to turn his eye toward the young archer, then began to scratch again more diligently than before.

Lucy did not see the arrow fly from the bow, but she saw Bob flying to the stable with the cockerel in his arms. She was so much excited that she ran out at once, bare-headed, to find Bob just drawing out the arrow from the poor fowl's breast.

"Oh, Bob!" she whispered, "that will hurt him dreadfully."

"Do you 'spose he likes it that way?" said Bob, sarcastically.

"Oh, Bob!" she continued, "I didn't believe you could ever hit anything."

"Nor I, either."

She turned away her head while he drew out the arrow. The cockerel flapped his wings a little, then closed his eyes and lay quite still.

"He's going to die," whispered Lucy.

"That's just like a girl! Why don't you help a fellow out?"

"I will do anything you want me to, Bob."

"A girl ought to know more about such things than a boy."

"I know it," sighed Lucy. "I'm trying to think, but all I can remember is arsenicum and Jamaica ginger. He hasn't sneezed, so I don't believe it's arsenicum he needs. Shall I go for some ginger?"

"Do you think it would do any good?"

"He opened one eye; maybe, if he had some ginger, he could open both."

"Well, go get it; we can try it." And Lucy went for the ginger.

"Hope you stayed long enough," said Bob, when she appeared at the stable-door with a cup in her hand.

"That mean cook wouldn't give me the sugar, and I hurried so I spilled the ginger in the closet. How is he?"

"He keeps on breathing, but he doesn't notice much."

Bob took the cup, and gave the cockerel a spoonful of the ginger. The bird staggered to his feet and flapped his wings. Lucy thought surely he meant to crow again on their side of the fence, but the next instant he lay motionless before them.

"He's gone!" said Bob, solemnly.

"I wish we had tried the arsenicum," said Lucy, sadly. "What will Old Mortify say?"

"I guess I shall be Old Mortify, if Papa finds it out. How strong this ginger smells! —how much did you put in?"

"Five spoonfuls. I thought he was so awful sick he ought to have a lot."

"Five spoonfuls! Then *you* killed him."

"Oh, Bob, don't say that!" she cried. "What would Sadie say to me?" and she lifted the bird's head tenderly, but it fell back again upon the stable-floor. Old Mordecai's cockerel would never crow again on either side of the fence. Little Lucy stood shivering, with tears in her eyes.

"Run in the house," said Bob.

"What shall you do?"

"I am going to hide him under the leaves. And mind you, it's my place to tell of it, and not yours."

"But you are going to tell, Bob?"

"You run in, and wait and see."

She went in and stood by the window, and saw him come carelessly out of the stable and walk about the garden, then return with the dead cock and cover him hastily with leaves.

When he came in, he said: "Don't stand

staring at that pile of leaves. It's done, and can't be helped. Nothing but an old rooster, anyway! No business crowing on our side of the fence. I gave him fair warning."

"But he didn't understand, Bob."

"Well, he does now," said Bob.

That night, after the children had gone to bed, the old man came up to inquire if any one had seen his cockerel.

Aunt Amy went up to ask Bob.

"Yes," said that young gentleman; "tell him I saw him on the wrong side of the fence about four o'clock."

As the days went by, little Lucy felt more and more uneasy, as she thought of what lay under the leaves. She had seen Sadie out, and had heard her call and call for the poor cockerel that never came. Still she had kept quiet, waiting for Bob to speak.

The day before Thanksgiving she sat alone in the library. Her mother and Aunt Amy had gone to the city to meet her grandmother, and Lucy felt a little lonely. Bob saw her as he passed the door, and stepped in, saying:

"What is the matter with you, Lucy? Why can't you brighten up? You've had the doleful dumps for a week."

"Oh, Bob!" she answered, "why don't you tell about that cockerel? It worries me awfully."

He glanced around at all the doors, then came savagely up to his sister and took her roughly by the arm. "I suppose," he whispered almost fiercely, "you mean that old rooster under the leaves. Now, never say another word to me about it. You have twitted me enough."

She looked very much astonished, as she had never referred to it in any way before. A mightier voice than little Lucy's had been calling to him ever since he hid the bird under the leaves.

She saw that his conscience troubled him, and gained courage. "If you would only tell Mamma, she would tell you what to do. Oh, Bob! I can't walk on that side of the garden for fear I shall see Sadie. She came out yesterday, and looked over our fence, and I heard her call the cockerel several times."

Bob looked down into Lucy's face and wished he had not taken hold of her quite so roughly. He went back to the kitchen and got a large bunch of raisins and gave them to her, with a pat on the head, which she understood very well. "Too bad," he declared, "that you can't go out to-day."

After he had gone, she took up the raisins, when, happening to look out of the window, she saw Sadie looking over the fence. "I will give her my raisins," thought Lucy.

The cook rapped sharply as she passed the kitchen window, for she knew Lucy ought not to go out.

"Don't give me all," said Sadie, as Lucy passed the great bunch through the fence.

"Tomorrow we shall have a whole box-ful," said Lucy.

"We can't find our rooster," said Sadie. "Grandpa sold all but him; we kept him for Thanksgiving. I don't see how he got out of the coop. We can't have any Thanksgiving now."

"Too bad!" said little Lucy, very faintly.

"Grandpa's looked everywhere for him, till he tired himself out, and got rheumatism dreadfully. He thinks some of the neighbors have killed him."

Lucy turned a little pale, and said she had a very bad cold and must go in.

Sadie would have been surprised had she looked out a few minutes later, for she would have seen Lucy running toward the provision store.

"Anything wrong, Miss Lucy?" said the red-cheeked boy who drove the wagon.

She went in timidly, and when she stood

close by his side, she whispered, "How much do you ask for roosters?"

"A hen wouldn't do?" he asked, laughing.

"No," she said, with a sigh, as she compared in her mind the proud strut of Mordecai's cockerel with the walk of any hen she had ever met. "No, I want a rooster."

"What's it for?" he said, confidentially.

"For Thanksgiving."

"I just took two fine gobblers up."

"It's for—for somebody else's Thanksgiving."

"Oho! Why not get a small turkey? Just the thing."

Why had she not thought of it before! Perhaps that would help Mordecai to forgive them. (She had begun to blame herself with Bob, for had she not prepared the fatal ginger?)

The red-cheeked boy held up a plump little turkey.

"Is that a dollar?" she asked.

"That's heavier than I thought," he said, after he had thrown it into the scales. "That will cost, all told,—let me see,—one dollar thirty-eight."

She began feeling about her neck, as if she kept her money concealed somewhere about her jugular veins, and the tears came to her eyes.

The red-cheeked boy became again confidential. "Come, now," he said, in a low tone, "how much do we want to pay? What is just the little sum we were thinking of, when we came in?"

"I have only one dollar," answered Lucy, with her hand still guarding a jugular.

"A dollar is quite enough to pay for a small, nice, plump little turkey, if the right person comes for it."

Lucy hoped she was the right person. "If you please," she said, as he showed her another turkey, the smallest one she had ever seen, "are you sure it's a turkey? I don't want a rooster, now."

"My word for it, Miss Lucy, yesterday afternoon that fowl said 'Gobble.' Shall I send it to your house?"

"If you would do him up so he would look like a dress, I would be very much obliged to you."

While he was gone, she again put her hand to her neck and took off a small gold chain; attached to this was a gold dollar. She had worn it since she was a baby; her fingers seemed unwilling to take it off. Her little head said, "Take it off!" and her little heart said, "Oh, no!"

When the boy came back with the turkey, looking as much like a dress as a provision man could make it, the small coin still remained firmly attached to the chain.

"If you please, will you undo this?" said Lucy.

He looked at it a moment, without taking it in his hands, and said, "Why don't you charge it, Miss Lucy?"

"Oh, no, no," she said, hastily; "Papa is not to pay for this. I must pay for it myself."

"I understand; you don't want your good works talked about either, Miss Lucy. But I don't want to take this."

"Come, come," said his employer from the other side of the store; "fly around there!"

The boy hurriedly unfastened the dollar, and said: "You may have it back any time, Miss Lucy."

She took the turkey in her arms and went out. When she had walked a few steps she stopped suddenly and turned and went back. The boy was just getting into the wagon. She pulled his coat, and, as he turned, said timidly: "You are so kind, will you tell me how to spell 'Mordecai?' Not Mortify, but Mordecai."

"It's a joke," he said, grinning.

"Oh, no!" groaned poor Lucy.

"Mordecai," he said, pausing, with one foot on the wheel: "M-o-r—Mor—d-y—Mordy—k-i—Mordyki."

She thanked him and hurried home.

When Bob came in, she pulled him into a corner and whispered: "I have bought a little turkey, the littlest one you ever saw, but a sure turkey, for Mordecai! Run out, before you take off your coat, for it's in the stable, in the oat-box; and will you take it to Mordecai's house? Go quick, before it gets dark."

He turned toward her with an angry gesture.

"Oh, Bob! Sadie can't have any Thanksgiving, because we killed the rooster, and I knew you would be so sorry."

He made no reply, but ran with great haste to the stable. He soon found the bundle and brought it to the little window, when he saw there was a little letter, pinned with several pins, on the outside. The afternoon light was fast fading, and it was with some difficulty he read the note, of which this is a copy:

> "DEAR MISTER MORDYKI BOB AND ME KILLED YOUR RUSTER PLEAS TAKE THIS
> LUCY"

"The good, generous little thing!" muttered Bob, gazing solemnly at the brown bundle, which was supposed to resemble dry goods. "I wonder where in time she got the money! And to say *she* killed it, or had anything to do with killing it! Oh, I hope she wont grow up and be one of those good kind of folks that never have any fun and give all their money away. Where in the world *did* she get the money?" He folded the note carefully and put it in his pocket. "I never felt meaner," he thought, as he seized the turkey, with no gentle hand, and ran to Mordecai's house.

The old man sat at the front window, and Bob thought he looked a little sour as the gate opened; but he came to the door as fast as he could hobble, for fear Mrs. Mordecai might get there first. Bob held out the turkey and said: "I shot your rooster, sir. My little sister thought you were saving him for Thanksgiving, and she sent you this turkey."

"So *you* killed my cockerel, did ye?" said the old man; "a mighty fine cockerel he was!" He punched with his thumb the turkey that he could not see, as if he wondered if it could possibly be as fine as the cockerel.

"I had no idea I should hit him," said Bob. "I am a most awful shot, sir. Would you rather have a live rooster?"

"N-no," said old Mordecai. "Though my wife misses his crowing in the morning—overslept every morning since he went."

"We should have killed him for Thanksgiving," said Mrs. Mordecai, a tired-looking little woman, who looked as if she could oversleep, in spite of all the warnings that might be sounded. "A turkey, Father, is better than a cockerel; and so we have lost nothing."

"You don't like to feel that yer neighbors is standin' round armed, ready to destroy yer property,—do you, eh?"

"No, but I like to know that, if they do happen to destroy it, they stand ready to pay more than it's worth."

"Yer allays did like young folks," said Mordecai, dryly, and hobbled back to the front window.

"You are a good boy," said his wife. "Don't mind him; he'll speak better of you behind your back."

"'T was Lucy sent it; I only killed the cockerel," said Bob, turning away.

"I have carried the turkey down," he said to Lucy on his return. "Now, tell me where you got the money."

"I had to take my gold dollar." Lucy

could not keep the tears from filling her eyes.

"Whew!" he said, "the one on your chain?"

She nodded.

"Born with it on, weren't you?"

"I don't 'member when I got it," said she, a little more cheerfully. "Don't go out again, Bob," as he started suddenly toward the door, and she saw him run across the garden with his skate-bag under his arm.

"Hang the old rooster!" he said, as he passed the little house and saw old Mordecai sitting at the window. "It's going to cost me a pretty sum. I won't do it!— It's good enough for her, to go spend that dollar—just like a girl—I hope he won't take them. Hang Mordecai!" Still he walked on rapidly until he came to Johnny Bang's house. "Hope he's gone away," he said, as he pulled the bell, which was answered by young John himself, whose eyes brightened as he saw the skate-bag; but he waited for Bob to speak.

"You said last night you would give me two and a half; say three and they're yours," said Bob.

"Do you suppose I made a half a dollar in my sleep?" said Johnny, with a grin.

"Can you give me three?"

"No, I can't."

"Jerry will; I came to you first, because you made the first offer. I must have three or nothing."

"You come in and sit down, and I'll see if I can work Mother up to it."

Johnny's mother proved a person easily "worked up," for in a few minutes he returned with three crisp bills in his hand.

"I told her they cost five dollars, and you had had them only two weeks; was that straight?"

"Yes," said Bob, "that's straight."

"She asked me if you had a right to sell them without asking your father, and I told her you bought them yourself with your own money that you had saved; was that straight?"

"Yes," said Bob, his mouth twitching a little, "that's straight."

He took the skates from the bag and handed them to his friend.

"Won't throw in the bag?" said Johnny.

"Oh, I'll throw in the whole family," said Bob, sarcastically, as he left the house.

The first call he made was on the red-cheeked boy at the provision store; then he went to the city.

After supper, when little Lucy was sitting with her father, talking about Thanksgiving, he came in, looking rather tired, and gave her a tiny box. She opened it and found first a note, which said to her:

"DEAR LUCY: You did the square thing by me and I won't forget it. Hang these on your chain in remembrance of Old Mordecai's rooster.   "BOB."

And under some pink cotton lay her own little dollar, and beside it a small gold cockerel, as proud-looking as Old Mordecai's before Bob's unlucky shot.

A WONDERFUL PAIR OF SLIPPERS

*(WITH LETTERS CONCERNING THEM FROM
MARK TWAIN AND ELSIE LESLIE LYDE)*

MARK TWAIN'S LETTER

Hartford, Oct. 5, '89.

Dear Elsie: The way of it was this. Away last spring, Gillette and I pooled intellects on this proposition: to get up a pleasant surprise of some kind for you against your next visit—the surprise to take the form of a tasteful and beautiful testimonial of some sort or other, which should express somewhat of the love we felt for you. Together we hit upon just the right thing—a pair of slippers. Either one of us could have thought of a single slipper, but it took both of us to think of two slippers. In fact, one of us did think of one slipper, and then, quick as a flash, the other thought of the other one. It shows how wonderful the human mind is. It is really paleontological; you give one mind a bone, and the other one instantly divines the rest of the animal.

Gillette embroidered his slipper with astonishing facility and splendor, but I have been a long time pulling through with mine. You see, it was my very first attempt at art, and I couldn't rightly get the hang of it along at first. And then I was so busy that I couldn't get a chance to work at it at home, and they wouldn't let me embroider on the cars; they said it made the other passengers afraid. They didn't like the light that flared into my eye when I had an inspiration. And even the most fair-minded people doubted me when I explained what it was I was making—especially brakemen. Brakemen always swore at it, and carried on, the way ignorant people do, about art. They wouldn't take my word that it was a slipper; they said they believed it was a snow-shoe that had some kind of a disease.

But I have pulled through, and within twenty-four hours of the time I told you I would—day before yesterday. There ought to be a key to the designs, but I haven't had time to get one up. However, if you will lay the work before you with the forecastle pointing north, I will begin at that end and explain the whole thing, layer by layer, so that you can understand it.

I began with that first red bar, and without ulterior design, or plan of any sort— just as I would begin a Prince and Pauper, or any other tale. And mind you it is the easiest and surest way; because if you invent two or three people and turn them loose in your manuscript, something is bound to happen to them,—you can't help it; and then it will take you the rest of the book to get them out of the natural consequences of that occurrence, and so, first thing you know, there's your book all finished up and never cost you an idea. Well, the red stripe, with a bias stitch, naturally suggested a blue one with a perpendicular stitch, and I slammed it in, though when it came daylight I saw it was green—which didn't make any difference, because green and blue are much the same anyway, and in fact from a purely moral point of view are regarded by the best authorities as identical. Well, if you will notice, a blue perpendicular stitch always suggests a ropy red involved stitch, like a family of angle-worms trying to climb in under each other to keep warm—it would suggest that, every time, without the author of the slipper ever having to think about it at all.

Now at that point, young Dr. Root came in, and of course he was interested in the slipper right away, because he has always had a passion for art himself, but has never had a chance to try, because his folks are opposed to it and superstitious about it, and have done all they could to keep him back; and so he was eager to take a hand and see what he could do. And it was beautiful to see him sit there and tell Mrs. Clemens what had been happening while we were off on summer vacation, and hold the slipper up toward the end of his nose, and forget the sordid world, and imagine the canvas was a "subject" with a scalp wound, and nimbly whirl in that lovely surgical stitch which you see there—and never hesitating a moment in his talk except to say "Ouch" when he stuck himself, and then going right on again as smooth and easy as nothing. Yes, it was a charming spectacle. And it was real art, too,—realistic; just native untaught genius; you can see the very scalp itself, showing through between the stitches.

Well, next I threw in that sheaf of green rods which the lictors used to carry before the Roman Consuls to lick them with when they didn't behave,—they turned blue in the morning, but that is the way green always acts.

The next week, after a good rest, I snowed in that sea of frothy waves, and set that yellow thing afloat in it and those two things that are skewered through it. It isn't a home-plate, and it isn't a papal tiara with the keys of St. Peter; no, it is a heart—my heart—with two arrows stuck through it—arrows that go in blue and come out crimson—crimson with the best drops in that heart, and gladly shed for love of you, dear.

Now, then, as you strike to the south'ard and drift along down the starboard side, abaft the main-to'-gallant scuppers you come to that blue quarter-deck which runs the rest of the way aft to the jumping-off place. In the midst of that blue you will see some big red letters—M. T.; and west'ard, over on the port side, you will see some more red letters—to E. L. Aggregated, these several groups of letters signify, Mark Twain to Elsie Leslie. And you will notice that you have a gift for art yourself, for the southern half of the L, embroidered by yourself, is as good as anything I can do, after all my experience.

There, now you understand the whole work. From a professional point of view I consider the Heart and Arrows by all odds the greatest triumph of the whole thing; in fact, one of the ablest examples of civil engineering in a beginner I ever saw—for it was all inspiration, just the lightning-like inspiration of the moment. I couldn't do it again in a hundred years,—even if I recover this time and get just as well and strong as I was before. You notice what fire there is in it—what rapture, enthusiasm, frenzy—what blinding explosions of color. It is just a "Turner"—that is what it is. It is just like his "Slave Ship," that immortal work. What you see in the "Slave Ship" is a terrific explosion of radiating rags and fragments of flaming crimson flying from a common center of intense yellow which is in violent commotion—insomuch that a Boston reporter said it reminded him of a yellow cat dying in a platter of tomatoes.

Take the slippers and wear them next your heart, Elsie dear; for every stitch in them is a testimony of the affection which two of your loyalest friends bear you. Every single stitch cost us blood. I've got twice as many pores in me now as I used to have; and you would never believe how many places you can stick a needle into yourself until you go into the embroidery line and devote yourself to art.

Do not wear these slippers in public, dear; it would only excite envy; and, as like as not, somebody would try to shoot you.

Merely use them to assist you in remembering that among the many, many people who think all the world of you is your friend,

Mark Twain.

ELSIE'S REPLY

New York, October 9, 1889.

My dear Mr. Clemens: The slipper the long letter and all the rest came this afternoon, I think they are splendid and shall have them framed and keep them among my very most prechus things. I have had a great many nice things given to me and people often say very pleasant things but I am not quite shure they always mean it or that they are as trustable as you and "Leo," and I am very shure they would not spend their prechus time and shed their blood for me so you see that is one reason why I will think so much of it and then it was all so funny to think of two great big men like you and "little Willie" (that is what "Leo" calls himself to me) imbroidering a pair of slippers for a little girl like me of corse you have a great many large words in your letter that I do not quite understand. One word comencing with P. has fifteen letters in it and I do not know what you mean by pooled unless you mean you and Leo put your two minds together to make the slippers which was very nice of you both I think you are just right about the angle worms thay did look like that this summer when I used to dig them for bate to fish with please tell Dr. Root I will think of him when I look at the part he did the Surgicle Stich I mean I hope you will be quite well and strong by the time you get this letter as you were before you made my slipper it would make me very sad if you were to be ill. Give my love to Mrs. Clemens Susie Clara Gene I-know and you-know and Vix and all of my Hartford friends tell Gene I wish I was with her and we would have a nice jump in the hay loft. When you come to New York you must call and see me then we will see about those big words my address is up in the top left corner of this letter.

To my loyal friend
     Mark Twain
     From his little friend
          Elsie Leslie Lyde.

THE FAIRPORT NINE

by Noah Brooks

CHARACTERS IN THE STORY

THE FAIRPORT NINE	THE WHITE BEARS
Pitcher—Ned Martin	*Pitcher*—Jake Coombs
Catcher—John Hale, otherwise "The Lob"	*Catcher*—Eph Weeks
1st Base—Jo Murch	*1st Base*—Joe Patchen
2d Base—Hi Hatch	*2d Base*—George Bridges
3d Base—James Pat Adams	*3d Base*—Sam Booden, Captain
Short Stop—Sam Perkins, Captain	*Short Stop*—Eph Mullett, otherwise "Nosey"
Left Field—Sam Black, otherwise "Blackie"	*Left Field*—Dan Morey
Center Field—Billy Hetherington	*Center Field*—Joe Fitts
Right Field—Bill Watson, otherwise "Chunky"	*Right Field*—Peletiah Snelgro

The whole assisted by a large number of young ladies and gentlemen, who do not belong to any base-ball nine, but who hope to, if they live long enough.

CHAPTER I

RINGING THE BELL

IN Fairport, every boy slept with some other boy on the night before the Fourth of July. If any boy did sleep in his own bed, it was because he had a playmate with him. But, for the most part, the boys of that period thought it poor fun to sleep at home on that eventful night. They all preferred to sleep in barns, haymows, or some other out-of-the-way and unusual place. It was a sign that a fellow was a milk-sop if he slept in a real bed on that night, except under such circumstances as have just been referred to. For there was a great deal to be done on the night before the Fourth. In the first place, there was a bonfire to be built on the common. There was a large, bare spot in the middle of the common where the grass refused to grow from one year's end to another, because the bonfire was built there on the night before the Fourth. And to feed that fire, it was necessary to gather much fuel from various and distant places. Spare barrels, store-boxes, and occasionally a loose board from off some careless person's fence, were to be brought in. The boys did not take gates off their hinges to kindle the fire, as tradition said that their older brothers did, when they were boys. The time of which I write was a great improvement on that elder period. No boy fed the bonfire with anything more valuable than the few loose things that could be picked up without alarming the neighbors. The neighbors were easily alarmed, anyhow. There was a class of old ladies in Fairport who never remembered from one Fourth of July to another that, on the night before it, the boys, ever since there were any boys, built a bonfire on the common. So, when the bright flames began to rise up in the darkness, one or more of these timid women would be sure to come out on her door-step and cry: "Boys! Boys! What are you doing? You'll set the town a-fire, you pesky boys!"

Jo Murch (his whole name was Jotham Augustus Murch) used to be very much mortified when his mother came out like that, and he would say: "Now, Ma, don't be so foolish. There isn't any danger of our setting anything a-fire!" Once, one of the Selectmen of the town, a very dignified and truly awful person, came upon the common to see what the boys were at. It was nearly midnight, and it seemed as if something alarming was about to happen when the great man came out at that time of night. But he only looked the party of boys all over, as if to be sure that he would know them again, if anything happened, and then he went away, telling them to be careful of the sparks.

"My! Wasn't I afraid he would see old Snelgro's wheelbarrow!" said Ned Martin, when the Selectman was gone.

At midnight, as near as they could guess, it was necessary that the meeting-house bell should be rung. At least, every Fairport boy thought it was necessary; and it was rung. There was a bell on the school-house at the right of the common, only, as nobody but the nearest neighbors objected to the ringing of this bell, the boys did not much enjoy ringing it. They took a pull at it, once in a while, for fear that the folks around would not know that the glorious Fourth had arrived. The folks usually found it out before day-break. The town bell was on the Unitarian meeting-house, below the school-house, and facing the street which skirted the bottom of the common. To ring this bell was not only necessary, but it was also a great feat. The Selectmen had forbidden that the bell should be rung by anybody but the town sexton, except in case of fire. From time immemorial, Old Fitts had been the town sexton, and if any man really hated boys, Old Fitts did. Probably he never was a boy. It seemed absurd to think that he ever could have been a boy. Boys were his natural enemies. They used to shin up the lightning-rod of the church and catch the pigeons which he reared in the belfry; and they used to ring the bell on the night before the Fourth of July. Generation after generation of boys had done this; but, somehow, Old Fitts could never become reconciled to it. On the particular night about which I am going to write, Old Fitts had not only nailed up one of the two church doors and put an extra padlock on the other, but he had carried away the bell-rope. The Fairport boys were a curious set. They laughed among themselves when they saw him going home, after he had rung the nine o'clock bell, with the long bell-rope coiled up on his back. But when they flew to the doors, after he was well out of sight, and beheld the defenses which he had put on them, they began to think that, for the first time in the history of the world, the bell would not be rung on the night before the Fourth of July.

As the boys scattered to the barns and hay-mows where they had chosen to sleep, Ned Martin said to his crony, Sam Perkins:

"I'll ring that bell before daylight, you see."

"But how, Ned?"

Now, Sam was the leader of the boys in almost all of the mischief that was afoot, and he was, besides all that, the captain of the Fairport Nine. For Fairport had a baseball nine, and it was the terror of the surrounding villages. Of course, Sam did not want any other boy to lead off in a feat of this kind unless he had a hand in it himself. But Ned Martin knew a thing or two, and Sam was sure that he would ring the bell, if he said so. And when the boys, three of them, for Hi Hatch bunked in with them that night, were safely hidden in the hay, Ned unfolded to them his plan. It was a good scheme, and all agreed to it.

In all the world, probably, there is no stillness like that which comes between nine o'clock and the time when the Fairport boys get up to ring the bell and build their bonfire, on the night before the Fourth of July. At least, Hiram Hatch thought so that night, as he lay awake in the hay in his father's barn, listening to the heavy breathing of his mates. The spears of hay tickled his ear so that he could not get to sleep; and the stillness was awful. He almost wished that he was snug in his own bed, and he wondered why Ned and Sam should go to sleep so soon, and he should be so broad awake. There was a sound of something on the barn floor below. It was a tread! Then he heard a ghostly whisper, and he felt the hair rising on his head. Desperately poking Sam in the back he whispered:

"There is something climbing up the ladder!"

Sam bounced up and cried: "What's—what's that!"

There was a scrambling and a rush of feet below, and all was still again. But Hiram was too badly scared to go to sleep at once, and when, tired out by his long vigil, he did drop off into slumber, he slept so soundly that Sam had hard work to wake him, as he shook him and shouted in his ear:

"Remember you have got to play second base, to-day."

"What do you s'pose that was in the barn, just now?" shivered Hiram, for the midnights in Fairport are cool, seeing that the town is on Penobscot Bay, on the cold coast of Maine.

"Oh bother!" said Sam. "Let's get out of this as still as we can. If your father should hear us, as likely as not he'd fire that double-barreled shotgun at us."

Hiram held his peace, for the double-barreled shotgun was a sore subject with him, since he had promised to carry it off on the sly and have it for firing the usual midnight salute. He was comforted now by the reflection that he had not the responsibility of that gun on his mind; and Ned assured him that the noise in the night was probably only made by some of the other boys who had intended to steal a place to sleep, without waking up the rightful tenants.

Silently, and as if bent on some dreadful deed, dark forms now stole in from all around, and clustered in the middle of the common. A crockery crate, filled with straw, and stuck all around with pickets from some slothful man's dilapidated fence, was set on fire. The cheerful blaze, ascending, lighted up the fronts of the houses on the edge of the common, and shed a lurid glare on the tall elms which stood tremulously in the midnight air. The flames warmed the boys, and revived their spirits, somewhat damped by cold and lack of sleep.

"Hurrah for the Fourth of July!" shouted Bill Watson, a burly little chap, the right fielder, and better known as "Chunky." Then every other fellow cried "Hurrah for the Fourth of July!" And it was felt that the fun had begun.

Amidst great enthusiasm, Pat Adams now fired off his gun. It was only a single-barreled one, to be sure, but it spoke well for itself. Pat's name was James Patterson Adams, but he was known, for short, as Pat Adams, and, when the boys were not in much of a hurry, he was called Jim Pat Adams, to distinguish him from another Jim whose name was not Adams. When the bang of Pat's gun rent the air, there was a sound of opening windows, and the boys knew that angry looks were directed toward them from some of the houses roundabout. There was a wild hurrah when Sam Black, assisted by Billy Hetherington, staggered up to the fire with the better part of a tar-barrel, which they had hidden away some days before. There is no aristocracy among real boys, and it was an evidence of this truth that Sam Black, who was the only Negro boy in Fairport, was a crony of Billy Hetherington, whose father was the county judge, and had been to Congress. If any boy had a right to be "stuck up," it was Billy, whose family held themselves very high in Fairport. But Billy never once thought of such a thing. If he had, his mates would have cut him at once, and he would have found himself alone in the village of boys. It was curious that the only black boy in the town should be Black by name. So Sam, who was a great favorite with his comrades, was usually called "Blackie," a term which carried with it no idea of contempt. Blackie was the best fellow of the boys of that generation, and, moreover, he knew more of the habits of the birds, beasts, fish, and all manner of living wild things, than most of the naturalists who write thick books about the animal kingdom. The times and seasons when birds come and go, and when they mate, and where they build their nests, as well as the secret lairs of the small game of the woods and fields, were all as familiar to Blackie as if he had been born in the wilderness, and not in a house on stilts at the harbor's edge.

"Three cheers for the left fielder!" cried Jo Murch, as Blackie, his face shining with satisfaction and pride, helped Billy Hetherington heave the tar-barrel on the blazing pile. "And now, boys, for the bell," he added, for it was already past twelve, one of the boys having reconnoitered, through the kitchen window of a neighboring house, to ascertain the time of night.

Ned Martin looked around on the little group of lads in his superior way, and said:

"Which of you fellows is the best on shinning a lightning-rod?" There was a great laugh when John Hale stoutly answered: "I am!" for John was so big and lubberly that he was never called anything

but the "lob." In Fairport, the 'longshoremen call any craft which is clumsy and unwieldy "lob-sided," meaning, perhaps, that it is lop-sided, a phrase which may be found in the dictionaries. If one but stuck out a fist at Johnny Hale he fell over. And when the schoolmaster tried to get him up on the tall stool where it was the custom for boys to be hoisted for punishment, the master and Johnny invariably came down in a heap together on the floor, the "lob" was so very clumsy and so very heavy. Nevertheless, the "lob," for all his awkwardness, was the champion catcher in Fairport, and the envy of the White Bears, the rival club from the south end of town.

The "lob" was rejected as the champion climber, however, and little Sam Murch, Jo's brother, was selected for the feat of shinning up the lightning-rod of the church.

As an aid, in case of need, the volunteered services of Blackie were also promptly accepted, for the Fairport Nine never did anything that was not "shipshape and Bristol fashion," or, otherwise, according to rule and discipline.

Old Major Boffin's house stood so near the meeting-house that one could toss a biscuit from the roof of one to the other; and the Major's grandson, Ike, was a member of the party, though not of the famous "Nine." This was lucky; and it was also lucky that the roof of the Major's house was nearly flat, and that it had at each of the angles of said roof a big, square chimney, so big that two or three boys might hide behind one of them without fear of detection. And when it was remembered that the roof of the Major's house could be reached by a lightning-rod, much easier of ascent than that on the meeting-house, it was evident that fortune favored the brave when it was necessary for the brave to ring the bell on the night before the Fourth of July. The testy old Major, calmly sleeping in his bed, could not have dreamed how much his property was contributing to the celebration of the glorious Fourth, when, in addition to all this, Ned Martin, carefully stripping the sheets, shirts and pillow-cases from the clothes-line in the Major's garden, took the line and making one end fast to the ankle of little Murch, gave him a hoist, and told him to "go it" up the lightning-rod of the meeting-house.

The projection of the eaves of the building set the rod out from the side of it a great way, and, as the rod was jointed in two or three places, it swayed fearfully while Sam laboriously shinned up it. Now and again he would be flung round and round by the swinging rod, as he passed over the clanking joints, the clatter of which threatened to bring the choleric Major down upon them at any moment.

"Hold fast, little one," hoarsely whispered Captain Sam from below, for Sam, with his usual facility for taking command, had now assumed the direction of things. "Hold fast, or Blackie will be on your heels." And Blackie, dancing up and down with impatience, was ready to make a spring at the rod when little Murch should be out of his way.

"Bully for Sam," half shouted Ned Martin, for the little fellow had reached the edge of the far-projecting eaves, and was now struggling to get over the most difficult part. The boys below held their breath, for it was a perilous place. The lightning-rod, after turning up the edge of the shingles, was fastened to the roof by strong staples which held it firmly down and afforded almost no hold to which even a boy's small and hook-like fingers could cling. But little Sam was "clear grit," as his brother proudly remarked in a suppressed whisper, and while the silent spectators below all looked up, with their hearts in their mouths, he turned the edge

of the eaves and went picking his way up the roof, hand over hand. It was now Blackie's turn to go up, but Captain Sam interfered, and declared that if both of the best climbers went up into the meeting-house belfry, there would be nobody to shin up to the roof of the Major's house and carry the rope from the bell, when it was made fast. Half-a-dozen boys volunteered to go up the Major's lightning-rod, but Ike Boffin agreed to "hook in" by the back door, steal up the stairs to the roof, and take care of the rope when there.

"So, then, you are to have all the fun of ringing the bell, are you?" demanded Captain Sam, sarcastically.

"Well," said Ike, "you pick out four other fellows, and I will undertake to get them up on our roof, if they will promise to be mighty still about it."

Accordingly, Captain Sam, Ned Martin, Hi Hatch and Chunky were chosen to go up on the Major's roof, guided by Ike, who, with a quaking heart, opened the back door and let in these midnight conspirators. No cat could have climbed the stairs more softly than the five boys, Ike at the head. Barefoot and breathless, they stole by the door of the sacred chamber where the old Major, snoring manfully, was sleeping in happy unconsciousness of what was going on around him. Drawing a long breath, the five boys found themselves out on the roof at last. To their great delight and relief, they saw little Murch just shinning up the part of the rod which led from the roof to the belfry, not a very difficult job, in comparison with that which he had just finished. In a moment more he was in the belfry, and pausing on the balustrade which decorated the rim, he gave a noiseless cheer, dropped over to the inner side, and made fast to the clapper of the bell the end of the line which he had brought up with him. Ned Martin now dropped down from the roof of the Major's house one end of a mackerel line which he had with him. To this the boys below fastened the end of the line from the bell-clapper, and it was drawn up to Captain Sam, who took it up behind his chimney with great joy. The boys on the ground now scattered to all parts of the common, at a whispered command from Captain Sam, and then the big bell struck a peal of mighty strokes, pulled by the sinewy hand of Sam. The night air quivered with the blows on the bell. Old Fitts' pigeons, affrighted by the midnight booming of the bell, flew out in crowds, scaring Sam Murch as they dashed in his face. The brave little lad swung himself over the balustrade, and sliding down the roof in a hurry, was soon on the long and swaying rod below, and on firm ground once more, and then safe among his comrades.

"Those pesky boys," sighed Grandmother Boffin, as she turned uneasily in her sleep, but awake enough to know what was the cause of the horrible din which rent the air. The Major got out of bed, and, putting his head out of the window, addressed the darkness, commanding all in sound of his voice to disperse and go home, or take the consequences. But the old Major never forgot that he had been a boy once himself, although that was a great many years ago; and when he went back to bed, smiling grimly to himself as the bell answered his warning with a yet louder peal, he said: "Well, mother, boys will be boys, you know. There's no law ag'in ringing the meeting-house bell on the night before the Fourth." The Major, although a hot-tempered man, remembered that he had fought in "the last war" —that of 1812—and something was due, he thought, to the day we celebrate.

A sudden idea struck the good grandmother. She crept out of bed, stole to the bedroom of her grandson, passed her hand over the vacant bed, and then going back to her chamber-window, cried into the air, as the Major had done, "You, Ike, wherever you are, don't you dare to come into the house for your breakfast!" Ike, who was now taking his turn at the clothesline, laughed to himself. He remembered that he had a share in a boiled ham, a basket of apples and a paper of crackers, stowed away in Hatch's barn, under the hay.

Suddenly there was an alarm of "Fitts! Fitts!" from the boys stationed on the court-house steps, from which post they could see all the way down Howe's lane, up which the old sexton must come to the defense of his precious bell. Fortunately for the boys, Fitts never stirred out of doors, no matter how light the night, without his lantern. And the rays from that familiar lantern, "like a lightning-bug," as Billy Hetherington declared, now bobbed along the ground as Fitts climbed the hilly lane.

Warned in time, not a boy was in sight when the old sexton, grumbling to himself, reached the top of the hill and went across the bottom of the common toward the meeting-house. The bell continued to ring, much to the delight of the boys hidden behind the chimneys and stowed away in various nooks and corners below. With infinite trouble, Old Fitts got the door open, and with many a hard word for the boys, toiled up the long stairs which led to the belfry. "Now, then, Ned, give her a good one," whispered Captain Sam, as the old Sexton's lantern, shining through the belfry windows, showed that he was almost up to the bell, and, sure enough, as Fitts put his head out of the scuttle which opened to the deck of the belfry, a tremendous and audacious peal boomed directly over his head.

The old man walked all around the big bell. Not a boy was to be seen. The rope, he knew, was safe in his own house, and there was no sign of anything by which the bell could be rung. The light line leading to the roof of the Boffin house was too small to be noticed as it lay on the slanting deck of the belfry. The boys chuckled to themselves as they watched the puzzled old man walking around the bell, again and again peering over the balustrade, as if to see if some small boy were circling around in the air with the scared pigeons which silently flew about their master's head. It was very queer, so it was.

Just then, the "lob," who was never known to stand up when he could fall down, slipped on the roof behind the Boffin chimney that hid him. He might have slid off to the ground below if he had not put out his hand to save himself by grabbing at the boy next to him, which happened to be Sam, who tried to shake the "lob" from him. It was in vain, and the two boys came down in a heap behind the chimney, Sam pulling the rope with him. As he fell, the bell, of course, was given another peal, and the rope in the belfry flew up before the astonished eyes of the old sexton. Fitts stopped, cut the line, and, shaking his fist in the direction of the Major's house, cried, "I've stopped your fun this time, you young varmints;" and so he had. When he had carefully locked the scuttle of the belfry, descended the stairs and gone home, his light disappearing in the distance, the four boys on the roof, somewhat crestfallen, silently slid down the Major's lightning-rod, and made their way up to the bonfire. The "lob" was overwhelmed with ridicule for his share in the failure of the bell-ringing feat. "And he wanted to shin up the meeting-house lightning-rod!" said Captain Sam, derisively.

Blackie, however, soon found a way to remedy the mischief. He went up the lightning-rod again with the agility of a cat, spliced the line, then, disdaining to go up through the Major's house, he shinned up its lightning-rod and speedily had the bell a-ringing merrily. Meantime, the boys about the bonfire were doing their best to celebrate the night by firing the few pieces of small-arms which they had; and their fire-crackers were exploded—sparingly, however, as it was borne in mind that the Fourth was yet to come, and more noise would be needed for the day.

Hiram Hatch, returning from a visit to the back of Major Boffin's house to encourage Blackie, who was pulling away lustily at the bell-rope, cast his eyes on the fire, and, to his horror, spied the remains of the leaching-tub which he knew ought to be standing on his father's barn floor. "Where did that come from?" he demanded. Nobody knew, but Chunky guessed that Jo Murch and George Bridges had thrown it on the fire.

"That came out of my father's barn," said Hi, stoutly, "and the fellow that took it is a mean sneak, and I don't care who he is."

"I don't see that it is any meaner to take that leaching-tub out of Deacon Hatch's barn than it is to steal old Boffin's clothes-line, or Judge Nelson's chicken-coop, so there," said Jo Murch.

As the Judge's coop had been ravished by Hiram, he felt condemned; but he replied, hotly, that there was a big difference between taking an old chicken-coop, only fit for kindlings, anyhow, and stealing a leaching-tub out of a man's barn. Then, suddenly remembering the mysterious noises which he had heard while he was trying to go to sleep, he exclaimed, with his small fist before Jo Murch's nose, "And you came in there and stole that tub while we were in the hay-loft. I heard you."

"Yes, and mighty scared you were, too," Jo replied, with an unpleasant sneer.

There were symptoms of a fight, when one of the sentries on the court-house steps shouted "Fitts! Fitts!" Then all the boys, in their anxiety for the bell, scattered to points about the meeting-house from which they could see the fate of Blackie, who, perceiving the lantern of the old sexton coming, improved the time by giving the bell as many and as vigorous strokes as possible.

Grumbling and groaning to himself, the sexton slowly climbed the belfry stairs once more, and was soon on the upper deck. "Why, oh why, didn't I nail down that scuttle?" groaned little Blackie, as, from behind his chimney, he saw the old man emerge upon the belfry deck. Blackie consoled himself with the reflection that he would do this the next time the coast was clear. But he was doomed to disappointment. Fitts, as soon as he had cut the line, for the second time, gave it a strong pull, and a sudden pull, and poor Blackie, not for a moment dreaming what was going to happen, was jerked out from behind the chimney, and, still holding on, across the scuttle, which had been left open.

"Aha! It's you, is it? you, you black limb, is it?" cried Old Fitts, exultingly, as the boy came dimly into sight from behind the chimney. "Major Boffin! There's a burglar on your roof!" shouted the old man, as he tugged at the line which Blackie sturdily refused to let go.

"Shame! Shame! Old Fitts!" shrieked several of the boys below, in their concealment. "He's no burglar, and you know it."

In the midst of the racket, Major Boffin, with a grim smile on his face, put his head out of the window, and, after shouting "Thieves! Thieves!" at the top of his voice, fired into the sky a horse-pistol which he kept loaded for the entertainment of the midnight cats that sometimes disturbed his slumbers. A profound silence followed this volley. Even Old Fitts was quiet in his belfry; and Blackie, taking advantage of the lull, dropped the line which he had held, and softly crept down the roof, clutched the lightning-rod, slid to the ground, and made off in the darkness.

"If I catch those pesky boys around here again to-night," said the angry sexton, "I'll put a load of buckshot into some of 'em."

"Never you fear," answered the Major, "you will never catch them. Sooner catch a lot of weasels." And the old man shut down his window with a bang.

Fitts descended into the little loft below the belfry, and, though the boys waited for his appearance beneath, his lantern did not shed its beams again on the outside of the meeting-house.

"He's camping in the steeple!" cried the boys, in alarm. And so he was. Determined to stop the ringing of the bell, and afraid to leave his post of duty, the old man lay down on the floor of the loft, secure in the knowledge that no enemy could scale the roof without awakening him. The boys gathered in a knot below, examined the ground and confessed that, for once, they were circumvented.

It was growing toward morning. The east was pale with the first streaks of dawn. It had been a tiresome night. The great baseball match was coming off on that day. The bell had been rung. The Nine went to bed, and Fairport was quiet at last.

HOW PINKEY DELIVERED AN ADDRESS

by Captain Harold Hammond, U.S.A.

CHILDREN'S DAY at the church was drawing near, and each day Pinkey Perkins was becoming more and more impressed with a sense of his personal importance. He had been selected to deliver the "Welcome Address to the Fathers and Mothers" on that occasion. When he had been informed of the fact in the beginning, he had not looked on it with favor. Heretofore his oratorical efforts had been confined to the school-room, and he lacked the necessary confidence to attempt such a courageous feat. But his mother had been assured by the lady who consulted her on the subject, that the committee had carefully considered all the boys available for the honor, and had decided that of all these Pinkey was the one to make the address.

When the task had been turned over to him and he had set about practising, it was with a pardonable air of superiority that Pinkey, on occasions, when invited to join in some after-school game of "scrub" or take part in an attack on some newly discovered bumble-bees' nest, would reply, with a sort of bored air: "I wish I could, but I've got to go and rehearse."

True, there were others who had "to go and rehearse," but not in the way that Pinkey did. While they devoted their time to singing and went to practise collectively, he went alone to Miss Lyon, his Sunday-school teacher. That lady, being a teacher of elocution, had taken the task of drilling Pinkey in the most effective delivery for his first public oration.

"Humph! You needn't feel so smart," retorted Bunny Morris one day when Pinkey had referred rather loftily to "my address"; "you're not the only one who has to practise."

It happened that Bunny was one of eight who were to sing in chorus on Children's Day, and, although he would not admit it, the fact that Pinkey had been selected to make the "Welcome Address" rankled in Bunny's bosom.

When Bunny had made this stinging remark, Pinkey merely replied in his condescending way: "I don't 'practise.' I rehearse."

Pinkey had really entered on his work with a will, and a week before the eventful Sunday he had committed the whole of his address to memory and could recite it perfectly.

This statement, however, must be slightly modified. Sometimes, in rehearsing, he would have difficulty with certain portions of it, and that difficulty came about in this way:

Once in two weeks Miss Vance, Pinkey's school-teacher, required one half of her pupils to "recite a piece," either prose or poetry. For Pinkey's part in one of these bi-weekly punishments, as they were looked upon by the pupils, she had assigned him "The Supposed Speech of John Adams." Pinkey had surprised her by acquitting himself with credit on the occasion, for he had spent hours and days of careful preparation on it—"just to make her think it was easy," as he expressed it.

For some time, Red Feather, as she was known among her pupils, had not made Pinkey's school-life a bed or roses. Since one memorable Monday morning, when she had found four able-bodied mice secreted in her desk, she had always felt certain that he was responsible for their presence. From that day, the examples hardest to work, the States hardest to bound, and the words hardest to parse, according to Pinkey's standard, had fallen to his lot. It was to this "partiality" that Pinkey attributed his assignment of the "Supposed Speech."

Now, the author of the "Welcome Address," when in search of suitable material for that literary effort, had evidently used as a reference work "Great Speeches of Great Men," wherein was printed "The Supposed Speech of John Adams." Owing to this fact, several portions of the "Supposed Speech," either word for word or slightly modified, had found their way into the "Address." Oratorical flights were scattered all through it, such as: "Let not those beneath these vaulted roofs, within these hallowed walls, upon this memorable occasion, forget the incontestable vital truth that it is the young blood, the young mind, that we look to for our support," and so forth—sentiments more appropriate to John Adams's speech than to a Children's Day address.

In rehearsing, Pinkey found it hard not to confuse the two orations. In fact, neither was to him much more than a series of high-sounding phrases, intended more to impress the ear than to enlighten the mind. This is why it is necessary to modify the statement that Pinkey knew his address perfectly a week before the date appointed for its delivery.

As a reward for his diligence, Pinkey's mother promised him what had long been his heart's desire—a pair of patent-leather shoes that laced up the front and had sharp-pointed toes incased in fancy-edged tips.

Besides, since his unfortunate experience on the way home from Red Feather's party, he felt that he had been continually losing ground with his Affinity, and he hoped that the possession of a pair of patent-leather shoes might turn her in his favor.

Eddie Lewis, his arch-rival for her affections, had been paying her marked attention of late, and to Pinkey it seemed that she regarded these attentions as more or less acceptable.

Pinkey felt that the important moment when his Affinity must choose once and for all between him and Eddie would be when he should appear on the rostrum and, by his manly bearing and glowing oratory, win everlasting approval or disapproval. Consequently, he set great store by the promised shoes, which he felt would be not a small factor in making his appearance all that could be desired and thereby serve as an aid in fanning back to life the waning affections of his Affinity.

Saturday evening came at last, and, to Pinkey's delight, he was allowed to go down-town with his father and try on the coveted shoes, and to carry them home. He insisted on putting them on again when he got home, just to show his mother how well they fitted him and how far superior they were to anything he or any of the boys had ever had before, and how high the heels were and how bright and shiny the toes. And Pinkey was doubly proud of them on account of the squeak that accompanied each step. Before he went to bed, he carefully wrapped them up again and replaced them in their box, in order that no speck of dust might get on them and mar the luster that he depended on to melt the heart of his Affinity.

As he lay in bed that night, reciting his address over and over, and making his gestures in the darkness, he pictured the envy of the others as they saw him in his new shoes mount the platform to declaim his welcome. He had said nothing to any-one about the shoes his mother had prom-ised him,—not even to Bunny,—and he looked forward to the envy they would arouse among his less fortunate compan-ions.

When Pinkey awoke next morning, it was raining; but no rain could dampen his

spirits on such an occasion as this. He wore his ordinary "Sunday shoes" to Sun-day-school that morning, desiring not to show his patent-leathers until the time came for his address.

On account of the rain and mud, Mrs. Perkins suggested that it might be better not to wear the new shoes to the exercises; but Pinkey could not think of such a blow to his plans, and his mother had not the heart to wound his pride by insisting on her suggestion, and, besides, she feared he might not do so well with his speech if he were plunged into disappointment after all his anticipations.

"Pinkey," said his mother, after putting the last finishing touches to his toilet, "since you *must* wear your new shoes in all this rain and mud, I want you to put on these high overshoes of mine, to keep your shoes clean."

To this compromise Pinkey reluctantly assented, but later found his action to be a wise one, as he encountered the muddy crossings on the way to church, against which his own rubbers would have been but little protection.

Pinkey's heart swelled with pride as he strutted along between his father and mother on the way to the church. But as he saw the people entering the building, several of whom spoke encouraging words to him about his forthcoming address, he began to feel a little shaky and noticed his heart beating faster than he liked. He kept trying to swallow a lump of suppressed ex-citement that would go neither up nor down.

If Pinkey gave these symptoms more than a passing thought, he attributed them to his inward exultation and not to any manifestation of stage-fright—a malady of which, up to that time, he had never known the existence.

Pinkey left his parents at their pew and marched on up the carpeted aisle, looking neither to right nor left. He mounted the rostrum and took his seat on one of the uncomfortable, high-backed, hair-cloth chairs which, since time immemorial, had occupied space at either end of the equally uncomfortable, though not so high-backed, hair-cloth sofa on the platform. The top of the seat was rounded in form, and Pinkey found it hard to retain his position and his composure at the same time.

As the time drew near for the exercises to begin, Pinkey became more and more nervous. The church became full to over-flowing, despite the bad weather, and, look where he would, Pinkey found hundreds of eyes gazing at him. He envied those in the chorus, because they each had seven others to assist in the singing, but he must get up and do his part all alone.

Presently the minister appeared and attempted to put the children at their ease by shaking hands with each one and uttering a few words of encouragement.

The members of the chorus were seated on a long bench on one side of the rostrum, and were partly hidden by the banks of flowers, while Pinkey sat alone on the other side, out in full view of the congregation, where he could get only an occasional, uncertain view of the others. His Affinity was there, but he could not muster up the courage to look at her.

He tried to look unconcerned, but he knew the utter failure he was making. Once he saw Putty Black grin and whisper something behind his hand to the girl next to him, and then they both looked at Pinkey and tittered.

By and by the last bell stopped ringing and the exercises began. By the time the chorus had sung the "Welcome Carol," and the minister had made the opening prayer, Pinkey had partly regained his composure. But the minister's reference to the "bright young faces" around him, and the pleasure he felt and that he was sure every member of the congregation must feel "on such an occasion," made the pitapat of Pinkey's heart seem to him loud enough to drown all other sounds.

After a few other appropriate remarks, during which Pinkey's discomfort became more and more marked, the minister announced his "pleasure in presenting to the congregation the orator of the day," who would welcome the fathers and mothers on this joyous occasion—"Master Pinkerton Perkins."

Pinkey slid from his perch on the haircloth chair as the minister seated himself on the mate to it at the other end of the sofa.

With shaking knees, he walked to the front. When he stopped, his legs trembled so violently that he felt sure every one in the congregation must notice his quaking knees.

He could distinguish nothing. All before him was an indistinct blur. Beyond, at the rear of the auditorium, he could make out a hazy, arched opening. That, he knew, was the door. He looked for his mother, but his eyes would focus on nothing, and the intense stillness that pervaded the whole room only added to the suffering he was undergoing.

Then he began. Automatically the words came, but his voice sounded hollow and strange. His throat was parched, and it was with difficulty that he could get his breath. The roaring in his ears made his voice sound as though it came from far in the distance. The perspiration stood in beads on his forehead, and he felt hot and cold by turns. Still on he went, though it seemed that each word must be his last.

About midway of his speech, in order to allow the full import of his words to awe his hearers, Pinkey had been taught to strike an attitude and pause for effect. Reaching that point, he paused, right hand uplifted, left foot advanced. As he put his foot forward, a nauseating wave of sudden mortification swept over him. *Now* he knew why Putty Black had whispered to the girl next to him. *Now* he knew why they had both tittered as they looked at him. Gradually he bent his head and looked down until his gaze met his feet. The sight that greeted his eyes sickened him.

He had forgotten to take off his mother's overshoes!

The shock of this realization, combined with his stage-fright, rendered Pinkey utterly helpless. He stood as one petrified, speechless, before the assembled throng. He stared glassily at his overshoes; they seemed fascinating in their hideousness. A stir in the congregation awakened him to the fact that he had been standing mute, he knew not how long.

He tried to continue his address, but the words had taken wings. Miss Lyon attempted to prompt him, but all her efforts proved futile. He could not take up the broken thread.

Yet he dare not quit the platform with his speech unfinished and go down to ignominious failure before the eyes of the congregation, of his father, his mother, and, above all, his Affinity.

Then came a brilliant thought. "The Supposed Speech of John Adams"! Since the two speeches were so similar, why would not that do instead of the one he could not remember?

Without further delay, he began: "Sink or swim! live or die! survive or perish! I give *my* hand and *my* heart to this vote! It is true that, in the beginning, we aimed not at Independence; but there's a Divinity that shapes our ends—" and so on, without hesitation, clear to the end.

Delivering his school-room speech, he regained his school-room composure, and as he spoke he gathered courage. His voice became natural and his lost faculties, one by one, returned. His knees became firm again, and his heart became normal. What had been but a hazy blur became a sea of faces, and all within the church began to take definite form.

As Pinkey concluded, he made a sweeping bow, once more possessed of all his customary assurance.

Spontaneously the congregation burst into applause, such as the old walls had never heard on any occasion. Every one had seen his overshoes, and had been moved to sympathy when they saw his embarrassment on discovering them. That he had left out part of his address, which he had plainly forgotten, and delivered another entirely out of keeping with his subject and the occasion, only increased their admiration for his determination and grit.

With his head erect, Pinkey faced about and returned to his chair. As he did so he gave a look of triumph at his Affinity, and received in return a look that told him, plainer than words, that, overshoes or no overshoes, he had won her unqualified approval.

When he reached his place, he knelt down, calmly removed the overshoes, and, with his heart swelling with pride at the ringing applause, resumed his seat on the hair-cloth chair.

ANN MARY—HER TWO THANKSGIVINGS

by Mary E. Wilkins

"GRANDMA."

"What is it, child?"

"You goin' to put that cup cake into the pan to bake it now, Grandma?"

"Yes; I guess so. It's beat 'bout enough."

"You ain't put in a mite of nutmeg, Grandma."

The grandmother turned around to Ann Mary. "Don't you be quite so anxious," said she with sarcastic emphasis. "I allers put the nutmeg in cup-cake the very last thing. I ruther guess I shouldn't have put this cake into the oven without nutmeg!"

The old woman beat fiercely on the cake. She used her hand instead of a spoon, and she held the yellow mixing-bowl poised on her hip under her arm. She was stout and rosy-faced. She had crinkly white hair, and she always wore a string of gold beads around her creasy neck. She never took off the gold beads except to put them under her pillow at night, she was so afraid of their being stolen. Old Mrs. Little had always been nervous about thieves, although none had ever troubled her.

"You may go into the pantry, an' bring out the nutmeg now, Ann Mary," said she presently, with dignity.

Ann Mary soberly slipped down from her chair and went. She realized that she had made a mistake. It was quite an understood thing for Ann Mary to have an eye upon her grandmother while she was cooking, to be sure that she put in everything that she should, and nothing that she should not, for the old woman was absent-minded. But it had to be managed with great delicacy, and the corrections had to be quite irrefutable, or Ann Mary was reprimanded for her pains.

When Ann Mary had deposited the nutmeg-box and the grater at her grandmother's elbow, she took up her station again. She sat at a corner of the table in one of the high kitchen-chairs. Her feet could not touch the floor, and they dangled uneasily in their stout leather shoes, but she never rested them on the chair round, nor even swung them by way of solace. Ann Mary's grandmother did not like to have her chair rounds all marked up by shoes, and swinging feet disturbed her while she was cooking. Ann Mary sat up, grave and straight. She was a delicate, slender little girl, but she never stooped. She had an odd resemblance to her grandmother; a resemblance more of manner than of feature. She held back her narrow shoulders in the same determined way in which the old woman held her broad ones; she walked as she did, and spoke as she did.

Mrs. Little was very proud of Ann Mary Evans; Ann Mary was her only daughter's child, and had lived with her grandmother ever since she was a baby. The child could not remember either her father or mother, she was so little when they died.

Ann Mary was delicate, so she did not go to the village to the public school. Miss Loretta Adams, a young lady who lived in the neighborhood, gave her lessons. Loretta had graduated in a beautiful white muslin dress at the high-school over in the village, and Ann Mary had a great respect and admiration for her. Loretta had a parlor-organ and could play on it, and she was going to give Ann Mary lessons after Thanksgiving. Just now there was a vacation. Loretta had gone to Boston to spend two weeks with her cousin.

Ann Mary was all in brown, a brown calico dress and a brown calico, long-sleeved apron; and her brown hair was braided in two tight little tails that were tied with some old brown bonnet-strings of Mrs. Little's, and flared out stiffly behind the ears. Once, when Ann Mary was at her house, Loretta Adams had taken it upon herself to comb out the tight braids and set the hair flowing in a fluffy mass over the shoulders; but when Ann Mary came home her grandmother was properly indignant. She seized her and re-braided the tails with stout and painful jerks. "I ain't goin' to have Loretty Adams meddlin' with your hair," said she, "an' she can jest understand it. If she wants to have her own hair all in a frowzle, an' look like a wild Injun, she can; you sha'n't!"

And Ann Mary, standing before her grandmother with head meekly bent and watery eyes, decided that she would have to tell Loretta that she mustn't touch the braids, if she proposed it again.

That morning, while Mrs. Little was making the pies and the cake and the pudding, Ann Mary was sitting idle, for her part of the Thanksgiving cooking was done. She had worked so fast, the day before and early that morning, that she had the raisins all picked over and seeded, and the apples pared and sliced; and that was about all that her grandmother thought she could do. Ann Mary herself was of a different opinion; she was twelve years old, if she *was* small for her age, and she considered herself quite capable of making pies and cup-cake.

However, it was something to sit there at the table and have that covert sense of superintending her grandmother; and to be reasonably sure that some of the food would have a strange flavor were it not for her vigilance.

Mrs. Little's mince-pies had all been baked the Saturday before; to-day, as she said, she was "making apple and squash." While the apple-pies were in progress, Ann Mary watched her narrowly. Her small folded hands twitched and her little neck seemed to elongate above her apron; but she waited until her grandmother took up an upper crust, and was just about to lay it over a pie. Then she spoke up suddenly. Her voice had a timid yet assertive chirp like a bird's.

"Grandma!"

"Well, what is it, child?"

"You goin' to put that crust on that pie now, Grandma?"

Mrs. Little stood uneasily reflective. She eyed the pie sharply. "Yes, I be. Why?" she returned in a doubtful yet defiant manner.

"You haven't put one bit of sugar in."

"For the land sakes!" Mrs. Little did not take correction of this kind happily, but when she was made to fairly acknowledge the need of it, she showed no resentment. She laid the upper crust back on the board and sweetened the pie. Ann Mary watched her gravely, but she was inwardly complacent. After she had rescued the pudding from being baked without the plums, and it was nearly dinner-time, her grandfather came home. He had been over to the village to buy the Thanksgiving turkey. Ann Mary looked out with delight when he drove past the windows on his way to the barn.

"Grandpa's got home," said she.

It was snowing quite hard, and she saw the old man and the steadily tramping white horse and the tilting wagon through a thick mist of falling snowflakes.

Before Mr. Little came into the kitchen, his wife warned him to be sure to wipe all the snow from his feet, and not to track in any, so he stamped vigorously out in the shed. Then he entered with an air of pride. "There!" said he, "what do ye think of that for a turkey?" Mr. Little was generally slow and gentle in his ways, but to-day he was quite excited over the turkey. He held it up with considerable difficulty. He was a small old man, and the cords on his lean hands knotted. "It weighs a good fifteen pound'," said he, "an' there wasn't a better one in the store. Adkins didn't have a very big lot on hand."

"I should think that was queer, the day before Thanksgivin'," said Mrs. Little. She was examining the turkey critically. "I guess it'll do," she declared finally. That was her highest expression of approbation. "Well, I rayther thought you'd think so," rejoined the old man, beaming. "I guess it's about as good a one as can be got,— they said 'twas, down there. Sam White he was in there, and he said 'twas; he said I was goin' to get it in pretty good season for Thanksgivin', he thought."

"I don't think it's such very extra season, the day before Thanksgivin'," said Mrs. Little.

"Well, I don't think 'twas, nuther. I didn't see jest what Sam meant by it."

Ann Mary was dumb with admiration. When the turkey was laid on the broad shelf in the pantry, she went and gazed upon it. In the afternoon there was great enjoyment seeing it stuffed and made ready for the oven. Indeed, this day was throughout one of great enjoyment, being full of the very aroma of festivity and good cheer and gala times, and even sweeter than the occasion which it preceded. Ann Mary had only one damper all day, and that was the non-arrival of a letter. Mrs. Little had invited her son and his family to spend Thanksgiving, but now they probably were not coming, since not a word in reply had been received. When Mr. Little said there was no letter in the post-office, Ann Mary's face fell. "Oh, dear," said she, "don't you suppose Lucy will come, Grandma?"

"No," replied her grandmother, "I don't. Edward never did such a thing as not to send me word when he was comin', in his life, nor Maria neither. I ain't no idee they'll come."

"Oh, dear!" said Ann Mary again.

"Well, you'll have to make up your mind to it," returned her grandmother; she was sore over her own disappointment, and so was irascible toward Ann Mary's. "It's no worse for you than for the rest of us. I guess you can keep one Thanksgivin' without Lucy."

For a while it almost seemed to Ann Mary that she could not. Lucy was her only cousin. She loved Lucy dearly, and she was lonesome for another little girl; nobody knew how she had counted upon seeing her cousin. Ann Mary herself had a forlorn hope that Lucy still might come, even if Uncle Edward *was* always so particular about sending word and no word had been received. On Thanksgiving morning she kept running to the window, and looking down the road. But when the stage from the village came, it passed right by the house without slackening its speed.

Then there was no hope left at all.

"You might jest as well be easy," said her grandmother. "I guess you can have a good Thanksgivin' if Lucy *ain't* here. This evenin' you can ask Loretty to come over a little while, if you want to, an' you can make some nut-candy."

"Loretta ain't at home."

"She'll come home for Thanksgivin', I guess. It ain't very likely she's stayed away over that. When I get the dinner ready to take up, you can carry a plateful down to Sarah Bean's, an' that'll be somethin' for you to do, too. I guess you can manage."

Thanksgiving day was a very pleasant day, although there was considerable snow on the ground, for it had snowed all the day before. Mr. Little and Ann Mary did not go to church as usual, on that account.

The old man did not like to drive to the village before the roads were beaten out. Mrs. Little lamented not a little over it. It was the custom for her husband and granddaughter to attend church Thanksgiving morning, while she stayed at home and cooked the dinner. "It does seem dreadful heathenish for nobody to go to meetin' Thanksgivin' day," said she; "an' we ain't even heard the proclamation read, neither. It rained so hard last Sabbath that we couldn't go."

The season was unusually wintry and severe, and lately the family had been prevented from church-going. It was two Sundays since any of the family had gone. The village was three miles away, and the road was rough. Mr. Little was too old to drive over it in very bad weather.

When Ann Mary went to carry the plate of Thanksgiving dinner to Sarah Bean, she wore a pair of her grandfather's blue woolen socks drawn over her shoes to keep out the snow. The snow was rather deep for easy walking, but she did not mind that. She carried the dinner with great care; there was a large plate well filled, and a tin dish was turned over it to keep it warm. Sarah Bean was an old woman who lived alone. Her house was about a quarter of a mile from the Littles'.

When Ann Mary reached the house, she found the old woman making a cup of tea. There did not seem to be much of anything but tea and bread and butter for her dinner. She was very deaf and infirm, all her joints shook when she tried to use them, and her voice quavered when she talked. She took the plate, and her hands trembled so that the tin dish played on the plate like a clapper. "Why," said she, overjoyed, "this looks just like Thanksgiving day, tell your Grandma!"

"Why it *is* Thanksgiving day," declared Ann Mary, with some wonder.

"What?" asked Sarah Bean.

"It is Thanksgiving day, you know." But it was of no use, the old woman could not hear a word. Ann Mary's voice was too low.

Ann Mary could not walk very fast on account of the snow. She was absent some three-quarters of an hour; her grandmother had told her that dinner would be all on the table when she returned. She was enjoying the nice things in anticipation all the way; when she came near the house, she could smell roasted turkey, and there was also a sweet spicy odor in the air.

She noticed with surprise that a sleigh had been in the yard. "I wonder who's come," she said to herself. She thought of Lucy, and whether they *could* have driven over from the village. She ran in. "Why, who's come?" she cried out.

Her voice sounded like a shout in her own ears; it seemed to awaken echoes. She fairly startled herself, for there was no one in the room. There was absolute quiet through all the house. There was even no sizzling from the kettles on the stove, for everything had been dished up. The vegetables, all salted and peppered and buttered, were on the table—but the turkey was not there. In the great vacant place where the turkey should have been was a piece of white paper. Ann Mary spied it in a moment. She caught it up and looked at it. It was a note from her grandmother:

We have had word that Aunt Betsey has had a bad turn. Lizz wants us to come. The dinner is all ready for you. If we ain't home to-night, you can get Loretty to stay with you. Be a good girl.
GRANDMA

Derby, and Derby was fourteeen miles away. It seemed a long distance to Ann Mary, and she felt sure that her grandparents could not come home that night. She looked around the empty room, and sighed. After a while she sat down and pulled off the snowy socks; she thought she might as well eat her dinner, although she did not feel so hungry as she had expected. Everything was on the table but the turkey and plum-pudding. Ann Mary

"When Ann Mary reached the house, she found the old woman making a cup of tea"

Ann Mary read the note and stood reflecting, her mouth drooping at the corners. Aunt Betsey was Mrs. Little's sister; Lizz was her daughter who lived with her and took care of her. They lived in

supposed these were in the oven keeping warm; the door was ajar. But, when she looked, they were not there. She went into the pantry; they were not there either. It was very strange; there was the dripping-pan in which the turkey had been baked, on the back of the stove, with some gravy in it; and there was the empty pudding-dish on the hearth.

"What has Grandma done with the turkey and the plum-pudding?" said Ann Mary aloud.

She looked again in the pantry; then she went down cellar—there seemed to be so few places in the house in which it was reasonable to search for a turkey and a plum-pudding!

Finally she gave it up, and sat down to dinner. There was plenty of squash, and potatoes, and turnips, and onions, and beets, and cranberry-sauce, and pies; but it was no Thanksgiving dinner without turkey and plum-pudding. It was like a great flourish of accompaniment without any song.

Ann Mary did as well as she could; she put some turkey-gravy on her potato and filled up her plate with vegetables; but she did not enjoy the dinner. She felt more and more lonely, too. She resolved that after she had washed up the dinner dishes, and changed her dress, she would go over to Loretta Adams's. It was quite a piece of work, washing the dinner dishes, there were so many pans and kettles; it was the middle of the afternoon when she finished. Then Ann Mary put on her best plaid dress, and tied her best red ribbons on her braids, and it was four o'clock before she started for Loretta's.

Loretta lived in a white cottage about half a mile away toward the village. The front yard had many bushes in it, and the front path was bordered with box; the bushes were now mounds of snow, and the box was indicated by two snowy ridges.

The house had a shut-up look; the sitting-room curtains were down. Ann Mary went around to the side door; but it was locked. Then she went up the front walk between the snowy ridges of box, and tried the front door; that also was locked. The Adamses had gone away. Ann Mary did not know what to do. The tears stood in her eyes, and she choked a little. She went back and forth between the two doors, and shook and pounded; she peeked around the corner of the curtain into the sitting-room. She could see Loretta's organ, with the music book, and all the familiar furniture, but the room wore an utterly deserted air.

Finally, Ann Mary sat down on the front doorstep, after she had brushed off the snow a little. She had made up her mind to wait a little while, and see if the folks would not come home. She had on her red hood, and her grandmother's old plaid shawl. She pulled the shawl tightly around her, and muffled her face in it; it was extremely cold weather for sitting on a doorstep. Just across the road was a low clump of birches; through and above the birches the sky showed red and clear where the sun was setting. Everything looked cold and bare and desolate to the little girl who was trying to keep Thanksgiving. Suddenly she heard a little cry, and Loretta's white cat came around the corner of the house.

"Kitty, Kitty, Kitty," called Ann Mary. She was very fond of Loretta's cat; she had none of her own.

The cat came close and brushed around Ann Mary. So she took it up in her lap, and wrapped the shawl around it, and felt a little comforted.

She sat there on the doorstep and held the cat, until it was quite dusky, and she was very stiff with the cold. Then she put down the cat, and prepared to go home. But she had not gone far along the road when she found out that the cat was following her. The little white creature floundered through the snow at her heels, and mewed constantly. Sometimes it darted ahead and waited until she came up, but it did not seem willing to be carried in her arms.

When Ann Mary reached her own house the lonesome look of it sent a chill all over her; she was afraid to go in. She made up her mind to go down to Sarah Bean's and ask whether she could not stay all night there.

So she kept on, and Loretta's white cat still followed her. There was no light in Sarah Bean's house. Ann Mary knocked and pounded, but it was of no use; the old woman had gone to bed, and she could not make her hear.

Ann Mary turned about and went home; the tears were running down her cold red cheeks. The cat mewed louder than ever. When she got home she took the cat up and carried it into the house. She determined to keep it for company, anyway. She was sure, now, that she would have to stay alone all night; the Adamses and Sarah Bean were the only neighbors, and it was so late now that she had no hope of her grandparents' return. Ann Mary was timid and nervous, but she had a vein of philosophy, and she generally grasped the situation with all the strength she had, when she became convinced that she must. She had laid her plans while walking home through the keen winter air, even as the tears were streaming over her cheeks, and she proceeded to carry them into execution. She gave Loretta's cat its supper, and she ate a piece of mince-pie herself; then she fixed the kitchen and the sitting-room fires, and locked up the house very thoroughly. Next, she took the cat and the lamp and went into the dark-bed-room, and locked the door; then she and the cat were as safe as she knew how to make them. The dark-bedroom was in the very middle of the house, the center of a nest of rooms. It was small and square, had no windows, and only one

door. It was a sort of fastness. Ann Mary made up her mind that she would not un-dress herself, and that she would keep the lamp burning all night. She climbed into the big yellow-posted bedstead, and the cat cuddled up to her and purred.

Ann Mary lay in bed and stared at the white satin scrolls on the wall-paper, and listened for noises. She heard a great many, but they were all mysterious and inde-finable, till about ten o'clock. Then she sat straight up in bed and her heart beat fast. She certainly heard sleigh-bells; the sound penetrated even to the dark-bed-room. Then came a jarring pounding on the side door. Ann Mary got up, unfast-ened the bedroom door, took the lamp, and stepped out into the sitting-room. The pounding came again. "Ann Mary, Ann Mary!" cried a voice. It was her grand-mother's.

"I'm comin', I'm comin', Grandma!" shouted Ann Mary. She had never felt so happy in her life. She pushed back the bolt of the side door with trembling haste. There stood her grandmother all muffled up, with a shawl over her head; and out in the yard were her grandfather and another man, and a horse and sleigh. The men were turning the sleigh around.

"Put the lamp in the window, Ann Mary," called Mr. Little, and Ann Mary obeyed. Her grandmother sank into a chair. "I'm jest about tuckered out," she groaned. "If I don't ketch my death with this day's work, I'm lucky. There ain't any more feelin' in my feet than as if they was lumps of stone."

Ann Mary stood at her grandmother's elbow, and her face was all beaming. "I thought you weren't coming," said she.

"Well, I shouldn't have come a step to-night, if it hadn't been for you—and the cow," said her grandmother in an indig-nant voice. "I was kind of uneasy about you, an' we knew the cow wouldn't be milked unless you got Mr. Adams to come over."

"Was Aunt Betsey very sick?" inquired Ann Mary.

Her grandmother gave her head a toss. "Sick! No, there wa'n't a thing the matter with her, except she ate some sassage-meat, an' had a little faint turn. Lizz was scairt to death, the way she always is. She didn't act as if she knew whether her head was on, all the time we were there. She didn't act as if she knew 'twas Thanksgivin' day; an' she didn't have no turkey that I could see. Aunt Betsey bein' took sick seemed to put everythin' out of her head. I never saw such a nervous thing as she is. I was all out of patience when I got there. Betsey didn't seem to be very bad off, an' there we'd hurried enough to break our necks. We didn't dare to drive around to Sarah Bean's to let you know about it, for we was afraid we'd miss the train. We jest got in with the man that brought the word, an' he driv as fast as he could over to the village, an' then we lost the train, an' had to sit there in the depot two mortal hours. An' now we've come fourteen mile' in an open sleigh. The man that lives next door to Betsey said he'd bring us home, an' I thought we'd better come. He's goin' over to the village to-night; he's got folks there. I told him he'd a good deal better stay here, but he won't. He's as deaf as an adder, an' you can't make him hear anythin', anyway. We ain't spoke a word all the way home. Where's Loretty? She came over to stay with you, didn't she?"

Ann Mary explained that Loretta was not at home.

"That's queer, seems to me. Thanksgivin' day," said her grandmother. "Massy sakes, what cat's that? She came out of the settin'-room!"

Ann Mary explained about Loretta's cat. Then she burst forth with the question that had been uppermost in her mind ever since her grandmother came in. "Grandma," said she, "what did you do with the turkey and the plum-pudding?"

"What?"

"What did you do with the turkey and the plum-pudding?"

"The turkey an' the plum-puddin'?"

"Yes; I couldn't find 'em anywhere."

Mrs. Little, who had removed her wraps, and was crouching over the kitchen-stove, with her feet in the oven, looked at Ann Mary with a dazed expression.

"I dunno what you mean, child," said she.

Mr. Little had helped the man with the sleigh to start, and had now come in. He was pulling off his boots.

"Don't you remember, Mother," said he, "how you run back in the house, an' said you was goin' to set that turkey an' plum-pudding away, for you was afraid to leave 'em settin' right out in plain sight on the table, for fear that somebody might come in?"

"Yes; I do remember," said Mrs. Little. "I thought they looked 'most too temptin'. I set 'em in the pantry. I thought Ann Mary could get 'em when she came in."

"They ain't in the pantry," said Ann Mary.

Her grandmother arose and went into the pantry with a masterful air. "Ain't in the pantry?" she repeated. "I don't s'pose you more 'n gave one look."

Ann Mary followed her grandmother. She fairly expected to see the turkey and the pudding before her eyes on the shelf and to admit that she had been mistaken. Mr. Little also followed, and they all stood in the pantry and looked about.

"I guess they ain't here, Mother," said Mr. Little. "Can't you think where you set 'em?"

The old woman took up the lamp and

stepped out of the pantry with dignity. "I've set 'em somewhere," said she in a curt voice, "an' I'll find 'em in the mornin'. You don't want any turkey or plum-puddin' to-night, neither of you!"

But Mrs. Little did not find the turkey and the plum-pudding in the morning. Some days went by, and their whereabouts as much a mystery as ever. Mrs. Little could not remember where she had put them; but it had been in some secure hiding-place, since her own wit which had placed them there could not find it out. She was so mortified and worried over it, that she was nearly ill. She tried to propound the theory, and believe in it herself, that she had really set the turkey and the pudding in the pantry, and that they had been stolen; but she was too honest. "I've heerd of folks puttin' things in such safe places that they couldn't find 'em, before now," said she; "but I never heerd of losin' a turkey an' a plum-puddin' that way. I dunno but I'm losin' what little wits I ever did have." She went about with a humble and resentful air. She promised Ann Mary that she would cook another turkey and pudding the first of the week, if the missing ones were not found.

Sunday came and they were not discovered. It was a pleasant day, and the Littles went to the village to church. Ann Mary looked over across the church after they were seated and saw Loretta, with the pretty brown frizzes over her forehead, sitting between her father and mother, and she wondered when Loretta had come home.

The choir sang and the minister prayed. Suddenly Ann Mary saw him, standing there in the pulpit, unfold a paper. Then *the minister began to read the Thanksgiving Proclamation*. Ann Mary cast one scared glance at her grandmother, who returned it with one of inexpressible dignity and severity.

As soon as meeting was done, her grandmother clutched her by the arm. "Don't you say a word about it to anybody," she whispered. "You mind!"

When they were in the sleigh going home, she charged her husband. "You mind, you keep still, Father," said she. "It'll be town-talk if you don't."

The old man chuckled. "Don't you know, I said once that I hed kind of an idee that Thanksgivin' weren't quite so early, and you shut me up, Mother," he remarked. He looked good-naturedly malicious.

"Well, I dunno as it's anything so very queer," said Mrs. Little. "It comes a whole week later than it did last year, and I s'posed we'd missed hearin' the proclamation."

The next day a letter arrived saying that Lucy and her father and mother were coming to spend Thanksgiving. "I feel jest about beat," Mrs. Little said when she read the letter.

Really, she did feel about at her wit's end. The turkey and pudding were not yet found, and she had made up her mind that she would not dare wait much longer before providing more. She knew that another turkey must be procured, at all events. However, she waited until the last minute Wednesday afternoon, then she went to work mixing a pudding. Mr. Little had gone to the store for the turkey. "Sam White was over there, an' he said he thought we was goin' right into turkeys this year," he reported when he got home.

That night the guests arrived. Thanksgiving morning, Lucy, and Ann Mary, and their grandfather, and Lucy's father and mother, were all going to meeting. Mrs. Little was to stay at home and cook the dinner.

Thanksgiving morning, Mr. Little made a fire in the best-parlor air-tight stove, and just before they started for meeting, Lucy and Ann Mary were in the room. Lucy, in the big rocking-chair that was opposite the sofa, was rocking to and fro and talking. Ann Mary sat near the window. Each of the little girls had on her coat and hat.

Suddenly Lucy stopped rocking and looked intently over toward the sofa.

"What you lookin' at, Lucy?" asked Ann Mary, curiously.

Lucy still looked. "Why—I was wondering what was under that sofa," said she slowly. Then she turned to Ann Mary, and her face was quite pale and startled—she had heard the turkey and pudding story. "Oh, Ann Mary, it does look like —oh——"

Both little girls rushed to the sofa, and threw themselves on the floor. "Oh, oh, oh!" they shrieked. "Grandma—Mother! Come quick, come quick!"

When the others came in, there sat Ann Mary and Lucy on the floor, and between them were the turkey and the plum-pudding, each carefully covered with a snow-white napkin.

Mrs. Little was quite pale and trembling. "I remember now," said she faintly, "I run in here with 'em."

She was so overcome that the others tried to take it quietly and not to laugh much. But every little while, after Lucy and Ann Mary were seated in church, they would look at each other and have to put their handkerchiefs to their faces. However, Ann Mary tried hard to listen to the sermon, and to behave well. In the depths of her childish heart she felt grateful and happy. There, by her side, sat her dear Lucy, whose sweet little face peeped out from a furry winter hat. Just across the aisle was Loretta, who was coming in the evening, and then they would pop corn and make nut-candy. At home there was the beautiful new turkey and unlimited pudding and good cheer, and all disappointment and mystery were done away with.

Ann Mary felt as if all her troubles would be followed by thanksgivings.

THE BILGED MIDSHIPMAN

by Thomas A. Janvier

I USED to know a Bilged Midshipman. He was rather a nice sort of fellow, and we got along together very well. But we should have liked him much better, at first, I think, if he had not been so dismal a character. I never did know any boy (except a boy whom we named the "Sea-Calf," because he was all the time blubbering) who seemed to be so thoroughly miserable. Why, I've known that Bilged Midshipman to refuse to join a swimming party of five as good fellows as ever walked—I was one of them, myself—and to spend all the afternoon of a half-holiday in moping.

None of us knew much about him except that he had been a midshipman and had been bilged. This much he said himself, when Clarence Detwiler, by virtue of seniority, asked him about himself on the first day that he came to the school. He didn't begin regularly, but in the middle of the term, and so he was something of a curiosity.

"Yes," he said sadly, "I was a midshipman at Annapolis, but I was bilged!" Then he turned away and looked as if he might take to crying—blinky about the eyes, you know.

Now, not one of us had the least idea of what "bilged" was, or how it felt to be in that condition. But as he seemed to take it hard we concluded that it must be an uncommonly bad thing to have, and we came to an understanding among ourselves not to bother him by talking about it. I think that he understood our good intentions and was grateful to us for trying to do the handsome thing by him. Anyhow, he certainly tried to make himself agreeable, in a cheerfully dismal sort of fashion; and sometimes he succeeded.

His first success was won by splicing the clothes-line. In the interest of Science, a lot of us had borrowed the clothes-line from the laundry and had begun a series of very interesting experiments on the Levitation of Solids. For want of better solids to work with, we were using ourselves—each one of us knew about how much he weighed—and we were levitating ourselves up into some remarkably fine chestnut-trees. In the midst of an interesting experiment—we had Pud Douglass up in the air—the clothes-line broke. It was a new line, but Pud was too much for it. Luckily, he was only about ten feet up, and the tumble didn't hurt him. But the clothes-line separated into two pieces; and what made it worse was that the break was just about in the middle.

We were in something of a dilemma. We knew that a knot in the middle of the new line would excite critical comment, and probably would lead to very unpleasant consequences. For, apart from the fact that we had obtained the line rather informally, the chestnut-trees were quite out-of-bounds. We felt low in our minds. Then we all went back to the school and were as dismal as possible. However, we comforted ourselves a little by abusing Pud for being so inordinately fat.

Close by the wood-shed we fell in with the Bilged Midshipman. He was in his usual mournful mood; but we were mournful too, so we stopped to tell him of our tribulations.

"Pooh!" said the Bilged Midshipman, when we had told our tale of woe. "Is that all?"

We said that it was, and that we rather thought it was more than enough.

"Pooh!" said he again (he was a great fellow to say "Pooh!"). "Just you let me have the line and I'll splice it so its own mother won't know it's been broken!"

We were too much pleased to stop for argument with him over a clothes-line's having a mother, and we all sat down in a row behind the wood-shed, and little Billy Jenks pulled the line out from under his jacket. What Billy wished to do, was to go straight to the Doctor and tell him all about it and offer to pay for the clothes-line—but that always was Billy's way.

The Bilged Midshipman really seemed almost cheerful for once; and he went to work with a will. He made what he called a "long splice." It was a wonderful piece of work. He untwisted two strands of the rope for three or four feet, and then he "crutched them together," as he called it. Then he untwisted some more from one of the ends, and into the space where the strand had been he twisted a strand from the other. He did this both ways from the "crutch," and ended up by tucking all the ends snugly away. When he had cut the ends off smoothly and had rolled the rope under his foot, it would have taken a pretty good pair of eyes to see that it ever had been broken! It seemed almost a miracle to us, and only prudential reasons kept us from giving the Bilged Midshipman three cheers on the spot. But

we all shook hands with him and told him solemnly that we thought that he was "a brick." For a minute or two he seemed really pleased. Then he subsided suddenly and his countenance grew as dismal as Clarence Detwiler's on the day when he ate more green apples than were good for him.

"What's the use of it all?" he said, half to himself. "I'm bilged,—bilged!" Then he went sorrowfully away.

After that he often did bits of knotting and splicing for us, and seemed to find it rather comforting. But he always ended by going moping off, muttering to himself something about bilging. It was very mysterious.

We looked up "bilged" in the dictionary, and found that it was "nautical" and meant "having a fracture in the bilge." As applied to a midshipman, the "nautical" was good; but the rest wasn't. To cut things short, I may say that we all were completely puzzled. Finally, we concluded to have the matter settled definitely. It was growing too rasping to be borne. So we called a meeting of the school and elected Clarence Detwiler Chairman, and little Billy Jenks Secretary—not because there was anything in particular for a secretary to do, but because we wanted to make things pleasant for Billy. You see, Billy's father had just failed and he was naturally a little cut up about it.

When the meeting was fairly under way, the chairman appointed Pud Douglass and me a Committee of Two to bring in the Bilged Midshipman. As he was just around the corner of the wood-shed, waiting to be brought, this did not take long— and he could have been brought even sooner if "Clumsy" Skimples hadn't tumbled down from above among the rafters just as the procession was entering, and so spoiled the effect. But "Clumsy" was always tumbling down from somewhere or other,—he generally kept himself bumped black and blue,—so nobody minded it much.

Detwiler made a speech, in which he explained that we all were curious to know how a fellow who seemed to be all right could be bilged, if the dictionary gave the true meaning of the word; that we did not wish to press him too hard upon a delicate subject; but that, as we now cherished a very high esteem for him as a companion and as a—a boy, we should be very much obliged to him if he would explain this mysterious matter once and for all. Detwiler was a capital hand at speech-making, and this speech was even better than usual. When he concluded, we all clapped our hands, and then we looked at the Bilged Midshipman and waited for him to begin.

He blinked his eyes for a minute or two, in his queer, sorrowful way, and then he braced up and said he supposed he might as well tell about it, and have done with it;—we'd all been kind to him and we had a right to know.

"You see," said the Bilged Midshipman, "down at Annapolis 'bilged' is what they call it when a cadet fails to pass his examinations, or is sent adrift for misconduct. It's a sea term, and means that a barrel, or cask, is stove in and done for; a cadet is done for when the Academy throws him overboard, and so the sailors say that he is bilged. That's all;—*I* was bilged—terribly!" Then he hitched up his trousers in sailor fashion—he was as fond of this action as Dick Deadeye—and looked dismaler than ever.

"If you don't mind telling," said Clarence Detwiler, "the meeting would like very much to know what bilged you. Everybody in favor of his telling what bilged him, will please say 'aye.'" (Of course we all said "aye.") "The ayes have it, gentlemen."

"Well," said the Bilged Midshipman, in a most forlorn and solemn way, "it was a cat; a big, black tom-cat! Yes, I know it sounds queer, but it's true, all the same; that cat finished my naval career—*bilged* me! You see, it happened in this way: It was the beginning of my second year at the Academy, and my prospects were bright. I had passed the examinations and stood well up in my class, and the professors seemed to like me. But I couldn't get along comfortably with the Commandant of Cadets. He was a peppery sort of a man, a Commander in the service; and he had a way of snapping a fellow up short and setting him down hard, that made it uncomfortable to get along with him. And then he never would listen to what a fellow had to say. He was always talking about discipline. His pet speech was: 'The discipline of the service demands, my boy, that when I give an order you are to obey it, instantly and implicitly. Discipline and argument are utterly incompatible.' He'd say this over a dozen times a day: and so we always called him 'Old Discipline.'

"Well, I had a way of sliding into scrapes and Old Discipline had a way of catching me. At last things began to look squally. The Admiral—who was a trump—sent for me and gave me a good talking-to, just such a talking-to as my father gives me sometimes; and he made me see that it really wouldn't do for me to be careless, if I 'ever hoped to be an officer and a credit to the service,' as he put it. He was just as kind as he could be, but he wound up by telling me that I must steer a straight course or take the consequences; and, to give me a clear idea of what the consequences would be, he said that if I was reported to him again for misconduct during the term I certainly would be sent adrift from the Academy. I promised him with all my heart that I would turn over a new leaf then and there. And then the old gentleman, in his kind way, shook hands with me and said that he was sure I really meant to be steady, and would live to be as good an officer as ever trod a deck."

The Bilged Midshipman stopped for a minute or two and seemed very low in his mind. "It makes me feel dismal," he said presently, "when I think what the Admiral must think of me now. But it wasn't my fault that I was bilged—at least, not entirely.

"For a week or two after I was 'warned,' I was the best-behaved cadet in the Academy. 'Old Discipline' was on the lookout to catch me tripping, but I was on the lookout not to trip, and he couldn't. Two or three times he thought he had me, for the cadets were always playing tricks on him, but every time it turned out to be somebody else, and I was not in the wrong.

"But he did catch me at last, and that wretch of a black tom-cat was at the bottom of it. The cat was a good-for-nothing sort of a cat that used to drift about the Academy grounds by the kitchen. It was forever getting picked up by the cadets and put into places where a cat didn't belong—such as the professors' desks and the officers' hat-boxes.

"Well, one day it happened that the Commandant had to go down to the Norfolk Navy Yard for some stores, and a detail of cadets was told off to go with him. On the strength of my recent good conduct I was put in the detail; and I was glad enough to have the little cruise. Just as the tug was pushing off from the Academy wharf, 'Old Discipline' found that he had forgotten his valise—and as he was going to stay all night at Norfolk and go to a ball, and as the valise contained his dress-uniform, leaving it behind was not to be thought of. So he ordered the tug back to the wharf and, as I had the bad luck to be standing close by him, he directed me to jump ashore and run up to the Academy and get it. It was in his room, he said, all ready. Now this was orderly-service, and he had no business to send me on it. But I did not dare to hesitate; and I feared, too, that if I made the least objection, he would order me ashore and go off without me. I didn't like to give in when I knew I was right, but neither did I like to lose the cruise; so away I went as fast as my legs would carry me.

"I found the valise all right, seized it and bolted back to the tug—but I hadn't taken a dozen steps before I thought I felt something alive, squirming around inside the valise. Then it flashed upon me, all in a minute, that one of the fellows had stowed the old black Tom there, in a coil with the Commandant's dress-uniform. When I found that the Commandant, in his hurry, had left his keys hanging in the lock of the valise, the whole business was clear to me, and I just chuckled with delight. I put the keys into my pocket and hurried toward the wharf. But before I reached the tug I had stopped chuckling, and was thinking over the matter seriously. Of course I hadn't much sympathy with the Commandant, but I could not help worrying over my promise to the Admiral that I would keep out of scrapes. I stopped and attempted to open the valise; but either I mistook the key or failed to understand the lock, for I really could not open it. I tried faithfully until I dared delay no longer, and then feeling I had done my best, I ran for the tug. Still, I was very uneasy, and afraid of blame or something worse. To be sure, I hadn't put the cat in the valise, and I didn't even know, positively, that there was a cat in it at all. It wasn't my valise and it wasn't my cat; and, finally, the Commandant had no right to send me on orderly-duty. This was one side of the case. On the other was my promise to the Admiral that I would do my best to behave like an officer and a gentleman while I remained at the Academy—and I couldn't help admitting to myself that a cadet reasonably suspected of having anything to do with stowing a cat in the same valise with a dress-uniform might well be thought neither officer-like nor gentlemanly.

"Well, the long and short of it was that by the time I got down to the tug, I had made up my mind to tell the Commandant about the cat, and thus to clear my conscience of breaking my promise to the Admiral; and I must confess that I thought it would be rather good fun to see the Commandant open his valise and let black 'Tommy' come bouncing out of it on the deck, while all the sailors and cadets would be grinning at the jolly lark and at the way 'Old Discipline' would rage over it. But, as things turned out, I didn't have a chance to tell, after all,—more's the pity!" Here the Bilged Midshipman stopped for a minute or two to be miserable.

"When I got down to the tug," he went on, "the Commandant was hurried and flurried—for the Admiral had come down to the dock in the interval, and had asked why the tug had not started—and so, as I tumbled on board and handed him his keys, he blazed away:

" 'Now, sir, I should like to know where you have been spending the morning. Are you so utterly incapable of all useful duty that you cannot run an errand without dawdling over it all day? Take the valise below, at once, and remain below until we reach Norfolk! Boatswain, see that the lines are cast off. Mr. Pivot, you will oblige me by getting under way immediately.'

"I was all in a rage at this unfair attack. It wasn't my fault that the Commandant

had come off without his valise, that he had ordered the tug to wait while he sent back for it, and that the Admiral had come down and caught him at the dock when he ought to have been well downstream; and I knew that I hadn't dawdled a bit. Then, to crown it all, he had ordered me below for the cruise, and so spoiled every bit of my fun. A big lump came up in my throat, and I felt rather wicked.

"But somehow, right in the thick of it I remembered my promise to the Admiral. So I gulped down the lump, by a great effort, and began:

" 'If you please, sir, I——'

" 'But I don't please,' he said angrily. 'Go below, sir!'

" 'If you please,' I began again, for I was determined to do my duty, 'in the valise there's——'

"I don't think he heard what I was saying, he was in such a passion. He burst out: 'How *dare* you reply! The discipline of the service demands that when I give an order you are to obey it instantly and implicitly. Discipline and argument are utterly incompatible. Go below, this instant! You are under arrest. I shall report you to the Admiral for gross misconduct!'

"That settled the whole thing. There was nothing more to be said. I went down into the cabin and—I hope you fellows won't think it was mawkish—I just burst out crying. The whole business was so wretchedly full of injustice. Here I was trying my best to do my duty as an officer and a gentleman, and, for no fault of mine, I was under arrest and was to be reported for misconduct."

A sort of sympathetic thrill ran around the wood-shed. Clarence Detwiler formulated the sense of the meeting by observing that the Commandant was "a terror"; and little Billy Jenks crossed over from the secretary's seat—on the saw-horse—and put his arm over the Bilged Midshipman's shoulder. Billy always was a good-hearted little beggar.

After a while the Bilged Midshipman went on with his story: "After all," he said, "I don't believe that the Commandant would have reported me, when he came to think the matter over quietly, if it hadn't been for the cat—and he certainly had a right to raise a row over that part of the performance. You see, there was a stiff east-wind blowing that kicked up a heavy swell in the bay, and the tug rolled and tumbled about so that you fairly had to 'hang on with your teeth to keep your footing,' as one of the cadets said. Down in the cabin, things went bumping around in a very reckless sort of way, and I had to stow myself between a locker and the after-bulkhead to keep from bumping about, too. The valise was down in the cabin; and as it was not clewed fast it had the range of the whole place—sailing away first to starboard and next to port, and then taking a long roll up and down amidships, as the tug pitched in the short seas. Of course no cat was going to stand such nonsense as that without remonstrance; especially such a determined old scoundrel as Tommy. At first he sent up a lot of plantive 'me-ows!' but presently, when he found that 'me-owing' didn't do any good, he took to howling at the very top of his voice, and trying to scratch his way out. I could hear the sound of tearing cloth as he rattled his claws through and through the Commandant's dress-uniform, and—as I was in a rather wicked frame of mind by that time—I didn't object. If ever poetical justice got hold of a fellow it was then and there—and the fellow was 'Old Discipline' and the poetical justice was that ripping and raging cat who was tearing those ball-room clothes to scraps and tatters. I felt in my

bones that there was a tremendous storm ahead for me; but I was so angry that I hadn't much sympathy with the Commandant."

The wood-shed responded promptly to this sentiment, Clarence Detwiler leading a roar of laughter at the Commandant's expense. Only little Billy Jenks looked solemn. When we had got through laughing he said that he thought it was all right so far as the Commandant was concerned, but he couldn't help feeling that it was rather rough on the old cat. (You see, Billy was a very soft-hearted little chap about animals. Why, that little fellow once wanted to fight Clarence Detwiler, who was three years older and a whole head taller and who had taken boxing lessons, because Detwiler was going to drown a stray puppy so as to see whether or not he could bring it to life again by a plan that he had been reading about in some scientific paper. Detwiler was angry at first, but Billy was so much in earnest about it that he wound up by shaking hands with Billy and letting the puppy go—"sacrificing Science to Friendship," as he explained in his clever way. But that has nothing to do with the story.)

When we were all through laughing, the Bilged Midshipman continued:

"Well, the Commandant did not go to the ball! He came back to the Academy the next day, raging, and the storm which I knew to be brewing burst out at once. I have never heard what he said to the Admiral, but the case against me was black enough. The upshot of the matter was that I was dismissed from the Academy right out-of-hand—just 'bilged' without being summoned or having a chance to say a word in my own defense. This seemed to me the crowning injustice of all. I did not think that the Admiral would have treated me in that way, and I had expected to make it all right when I was summoned; for, you see, I really had tried to do my duty, and could have explained the whole matter so that the Admiral and all other officers would have seen that I was not to blame. But I had been in mischief several times since I entered the Academy and so everybody believed I had been larking again: and so I came to grief. Instead of believing me innocent until I was proved guilty, I was believed guilty from the start,—for there certainly seemed to be plenty of evidence against me,—and I wasn't given even an opportunity to prove my innocence.

"But I didn't see all this as plainly then as I do now, and I was angry at the clear injustice which had been done me, and concluded that the sooner I got away from the Academy the better. If the Admiral did not believe in me after my promise, it was he who was not behaving like an officer and a gentleman, this time. I hated him, and I hated everybody, myself included; and I was eager to get away, and so I didn't even try to explain matters and have my dismissal canceled. The Admiral had lost faith in me, and that settled the whole matter.

"And so, the short and long of it was, that I was 'bilged'—kicked out of the service in disgrace—all because some other fellow had put that miserable black cat in with 'Old Discipline's' dress-uniform! That's all there is to tell. And the reason I'm so miserable is that I can't help thinking all the time that if I'd kept reasonably steady from the start I should not have been dismissed at all. It was the cat that finished me, but the root of the whole wretched business was my bad name.

"I did love the service with all my heart, and I'd give almost anything to get back into it again; but I'm out of it forever— and I've nobody but myself to thank for my bad luck!"

The Bilged Midshipman sat down on the pile of kindling-wood just behind him and blinked his eyes quickly. I'm not sure that he wouldn't have broken down altogether, but just then Clumsy Skimples managed to tumble from the top of the wood-pile, bringing a whole load of wood down with him, and this raised a general laugh, and gave the Bilged Midshipman time to recover. When Clumsy had finished piling up the wood, and things were quiet again, Clarence Detwiler made a very handsome speech, in which he told the Bilged Midshipman how sorry we all felt for him and how badly we thought that he had been treated "while in the service of our common country" (Detwiler said that over twice, and we all applauded); and how, in short, we all hoped that it wouldn't happen again. Others of us made sympathetic speeches, and the meeting wound up by adopting a preamble and resolutions in which we just gave it to the United States Government in general and to the Commandant at the Naval Academy in particular.

But what seemed to please the Bilged Midshipman more than anything else, was the way in which little Billy Jenks got up from the saw-horse, walked across the wood-shed and said that he thought the Bilged Midshipman was a "gentleman, all the way through!" and he would like to have the honor of shaking hands with him. So Billy and the Bilged Midshipman solemnly shook hands, and then the small chap, in his dignified way, walked back across the wood-shed and sat down on the saw-horse again. Billy was such a queer little dick! He was always doing odd, old-fashioned things in the most natural sort of a way;—and yet, when you came to think about them, you always saw that they were just the right things to do, and you couldn't help respecting Billy for doing them. It is a solemn fact that there was more real, downright dignity about that little fellow than there was about Clarence Detwiler himself—though, of course, nobody at the school would have dared say so. And so the Bilged Midshipman seemed better pleased with Billy's shaking hands with him that way, than he was with our vote of censure upon the National Government.

Then the meeting broke up.

Now perhaps you think that this is the whole story of the Bilged Midshipman. But it isn't. At least, it has a very short sequel that is a great deal pleasanter than the story itself.

When the Bilged Midshipman was sent home, it seems, he told his father just how the whole thing happened, and his father, without saying anything to his son, wrote it all out and forwarded it to the Admiral. The Admiral immediately began an investigation of the case, and the result of it all was that the cadet who put the cat in the valise was found out, and was "bilged" in no time. Then the Admiral wrote back that he thought it would be a good plan to let our Bilged Midshipman stay at school quietly until the next term at the Academy began, without telling him that he was all right, so as to give him a good opportunity to think over what had happened and see what his failure to maintain a good record at the Academy had cost him,—it was to give him a sort of moral lesson, you see. And that was just what his father had concluded to do. Next year he was reinstated at the Academy, and two years later he was graduated, almost at the head of his class. He is an Ensign now, cruising around out on the East India Station. I had a letter from him the other day, telling how he had been in a rumpus with a Malay pirate, and had ridden on an elephant, and had eaten mangoes.

And so, the short and long of it was, you see, that the Bilged Midshipman was not really bilged, after all!

DEBORAH'S CHANGE OF HEART

by Helen Ward Banks

"OF course I can't have what the others have. I'm too homely," murmured Deborah. "But I hate her when she talks like that."

The corners of her mouth drooped, and her eyes filled with tears. There were so many things Deborah hated: the bare, angular house perched on the hillside, the plainness of her daily living, the vision she saw reflected in the mirror,—a small figure clothed in checked-brown gingham, and a pale face with drooping mouth and hair drawn tightly back into two braids. She could have seen eyes blue as gentians if she had looked long enough, but she always turned away after the first glance.

"I don't love a thing but my garden," thought Deborah. "It's the only beautiful thing I have. Maybe I love Aunty Jones a little scrap, and I used to love Josie, because she's so pretty. I hate ugly things. I'm going to hate people now, too. I hate Josie when she talks like that."

Pretty Josie Fenton walked on down the hill with Fred Dillon, unconscious that her words had been overheard. "It's too bad Debby is so homely," she had said carelessly.

Deborah watched them out of sight. She would have given all she owned to walk unconcernedly down the street with Fred. He was so merry and good-looking; any girl would be glad to have him for a friend. She picked up her trowel from the door-sill, and went slowly down the walk, her back to the ugly little house. She knelt among her flowers, and laid a caressing hand on the nearest. The garden was gay now with foxglove and sweet-William and columbine. Later it would run riot with tiger-lilies and larkspur and hollyhocks.

"I love you! I love you!" she whispered passionately. "You're the only thing I have to love. Why do I have to be so ugly when I hate ugly things with all my soul!"

She dug vigorously among her pansies for some time. Presently she left the trowel sticking in the earth, and settled back, her hands clasped around her brown gingham knees. She was too shy to have friends to talk to; she was used to thinking things out for herself.

"I am ugly," she thought, "and Aunty Jones is ugly, and the house is ugly. It must hurt everybody to look at us all, for ugliness is hateful. Why can't the world just be full of beauty?"

For a long time she sat thinking about it, and then she slowly went back to her pansies.

"I suppose really to make all the world beautiful, everyone ought to put a little beauty into it. All I have is my garden, but that's the prettiest in town, and I can make it prettier even than it is. It's the only point I have to start from, but I'll

272

do it. I sha'n't pay any more attention to people, whether they're pretty or not. I'm going to hate people, and hate ugly things all my life, and just give myself up to putting beauty into the world."

She rose to her feet and surveyed her garden with a dreamy look. Her eyes showed the blue in this direct glance, and the corners of her mouth did not droop quite so pitifully. She had at least an object in life.

"Yes," she said. "The larkspur is in just the right place, and the hollyhocks will be lovely against the fence. The phlox needs thinning,—but it's time to go and help Aunty Jones get dinner now."

As she walked back toward the house, her eyes traveled farther up the hill. A new house was rising on the hilltop, and the newly graded earth made more raw ugliness in the landscape.

"It's a beautiful house," thought Deborah. "It makes ours worse than ever by contrast. But it will take forever to get the new look off the place. How lovely rock-pinks would be on that slope!"

A sudden thought struck her, so daring that it sent the unaccustomed color over her face. Was this a broader chance in her mission of bringing beauty into the world? Could she take it out of the confines of her own little garden and spread it abroad?

"Oh, I couldn't! I'd never dare!" she exclaimed. "I've plenty of pinks, and they spread like lightning, but I'd never dare offer Mr. Danvers any."

She could not get the thought out of her mind, however. Every morning for a week, with a quick-beating heart, she watched Mr. Danvers walk by on his visit of inspection to his new house. Then one day, before she knew she had done it, she had opened the gate and was speaking to him.

"Rock-pinks would be lovely on that slope," she gasped, her cheeks aflame. "I have lots of them. Could I plant some out there?"

Mr. Danvers looked at her quizzically.

"You're the girl with the pretty garden, aren't you?" he said, "and we are neighbors. I've tried to speak to you before, but you always looked the other way. And you want to share with me? That's very kind of you."

"Don't you mind?" stammered Deborah.

"I shall be very grateful. I'm not much at flowers, and Mrs. Danvers won't be coming till later, for I want things settled before she arrives."

"And could I put a little bunch of pink phlox by the barn?" asked Deborah, eagerly. "The color will be so pretty against the gray."

"It will be extremely pretty. Do whatever you want to. How do you like my house?"

"I love to look at it," said Deborah, fervently.

The glow stayed on Deborah's face all through dinner-time. She had never before spoken to a stranger of her own accord, and it was exciting. So was the permission to pour some of the beauty of her own little garden-plot into her neighbor's wide domain.

"I'm really doing it!" she thought. "I'm really putting beauty into the world out of my own garden!"

Then she stopped, struck by a sudden thought. Was she going to be able to carry out perfectly her plan of hating people as she spread beauty? How could she hate Mr. Danvers while she was giving him flowers out of her garden?

She did not have time to find an answer to her question just then, for transplanting kept her very busy. Josie Fenton's father was building the house, and he watched Deborah with interest as, day by day, she came over with a new perennial clump to tuck into its fitting nook. Deborah did not know he was watching her until he spoke to her.

"Are you sharing up that white piny? It's the handsomest one in town."

"Do you think so?" Deborah asked shyly. "I didn't know any one ever noticed it."

"When it's in bloom, I come down this way just to look at it," Mr. Fenton said.

"Oh, do you?" Deborah asked, with a little smile. She did not often smile. Then she added, shyly, "Would you like a root, too?"

"Indeed I would, if it won't be robbing you."

"I'd like to give it to you," Deborah answered, and went home wondering if she could leave out from her hating the people who loved flowers.

She dug so hard at her peony roots that before she knew it she had kneed a hole straight through her brown gingham frock. She showed it in dismay to Aunty Jones.

"Never mind," said the kind old lady. "It's an old one. You go up to the store this afternoon and get you some new gingham, and I'll make you some new dresses. I'm slack of work just now; and I don't read as easy as I did once."

To the second brown gingham, clean and starched, Deborah added a brown sailor hat over hair tied tightly with a brown ribbon, and went to the store. She had to wait a long time for attention, for an automobile stood outside, and the two ladies who owned it were inside buying many things. Deborah sat patiently on a high stool and waited. She looked a good deal at the young lady who was matching embroidery silk, for she was very pretty. Presently the young lady looked up and met the gaze. She smiled at Deborah,

and Deborah had shyly smiled back before she knew what she was doing.

"I'm afraid we're keeping you waiting," said the older girl.

"I don't mind," answered Deborah. "I only want some brown gingham, and I have lots of time."

"If you're going to buy yourself a dress," the automobile girl said impulsively, "don't buy another brown; buy blue, to match your eyes. See, there's a lovely piece up there."

"Why," faltered Deborah, "I've always had brown."

"But that's no reason you always should. The blue costs the same, and pretty things are much nicer to look at than ugly ones, aren't they?" said her new friend, with a smile.

"Oh, yes!" exclaimed Deborah.

The young lady had the blue-and-white check pulled down, and held it against Deborah's face. Her cheeks flushed, and her eyes were bright as she looked up.

"It's very becoming," said the older lady, with a satisfied nod. "I am going to make you a present of a blue hair-ribbon to match, so that when you look in the glass and find how nice you look, you will remember what I tell you. Outside beauty doesn't always strike in, but inside beauty always strikes out in time, though young folk aren't apt to think so. Will you remember that? Every girl wants to be pretty, and no girl can carry a brave, honest, merry heart without having it shine through, finally, to make people call her beautiful."

"My mother is preaching you quite a sermon," laughed the young lady. "Now remember, too, what *I* tell you. Just wear blue always, and never touch another inch of brown. Wait a minute! I have a hat out in the car that would just suit you, I know, and it isn't my style at all. Will you take it to remember *my* little sermon? My mother's ribbon will make you remember to be good, and my hat will make you remember to wear becoming clothes. They're both very important."

The young lady dashed out to find the hat, and dashed back to leave it on Deborah's lap. Then she smiled once more, and she and her mother buzzed off in the automobile, leaving Deborah's head buzzing as fast as the car. She went home, scarcely knowing who she was, the blue gingham and the blue hair-ribbon done up in one parcel, and the hat—such a pretty one!—in another.

"I'm getting all mixed up on my hating plan," she thought as she went. "I've given Mr. Danvers and Mr. Fenton flowers; that's all right. But I like them both. And I like the pretty young lady and the hair-ribbon lady, too."

Aunty Jones chuckled comfortably when she saw the gingham. "I declare, Debby! I don't know as my needle'll take to anything but brown. We might have thought of blue long ago, for it's a sight prettier. I'll enjoy sewing on it."

"I could read to you while you sew, if you like," ventured Deborah, quite thrilling with the soft, clear shade of her new dress. Aunty Jones's face brightened. "It would be a great treat. Maybe you'd read me my Bible piece first."

Deborah found the Bible marker at the account of Jehoshaphat going to meet the Moabites. She liked the swing of the old Jewish story. "He appointed singers unto the Lord and that they should praise the beauty of holiness," she read finally, and stopped to think what the words meant. The beauty of holiness was a thing she had not thought about, but in a flash she saw it was the only true beauty in the world; one must cultivate beautiful thoughts and deeds as well as beautiful

flowers. That was what her hair-ribbon lady had meant, and that was why she found it hard really to hate people. Hating must always be ugly. To bring beauty into the world, one must bring love into it. Oh, but it would be much harder than transplanting flowers and wearing blue ribbons!

She finished the story, and shyly kissed Aunty Jones when she went to bed. The old lady looked up lovingly.

"She isn't so awfully ugly," thought Deborah, wonderingly, as she went upstairs. "I guess she's beautiful inside, and it's shining through. I never noticed. I wonder if I couldn't make her something soft and white to wear at her neck. Then she would look like the hair-ribbon lady."

Even transplanting the beauty of love wasn't so hard when Deborah really tried it. Maybe the blue frock helped along, for it was much more friendly than the old brown ones. Deborah, before she knew it, was having long flower discussions with Mr. Fenton, and a good many of her roots made their way into his garden. She found, too, that Mr. Danvers's head painter was very fond of milk, and she carried him a pitcherful for his lunch every day. When she proposed white muslin curtains for the sitting-room, Aunty Jones was quite ready to agree, and she brought out bags of carpet-rag pieces to start a new rug. Deborah chose all the blue, and while the old lady peacefully cut and sewed and rolled, her niece read aloud all sorts of books that they both enjoyed. For the first time, the house had a gleam of home in it, because somebody had begun to love it.

All her spare time Deborah spent in Mr. Danvers's place. He had been away for a fortnight, and came back to find new little bunches of growing things in all sorts of odd places, and Deborah busy with her seedling zinnias.

"You're a born gardener," said Mr. Danvers, "but you need more material for this big place. Suppose you had everything you wanted, what would you put in over here?"

"Oh," said Deborah, "I've shut my eyes and seen that place over and over; it's full of dahlias—yellow ones!"

Mr. Danvers nodded approvingly. "Yes, that's good. I'll get some. Now how about over here?"

Before the morning was over, Deborah and Mr. Danvers had planned the entire garden. Deborah forgot to be dumb or bashful. She chattered and laughed and glowed like any other happy, human creature.

Presently Mr. Danvers looked at his watch. "My! how the time runs away. I don't know when I've enjoyed a morning more. I have a train to catch now, and I shan't be back till next month. Are you going to oversee all this planting for me? If you will, I'll give you a percentage for yourself out of the dahlias and all the other things. And now I tell you what I want to do, Miss Deborah. If you have to look up at my place, I have to look down at yours. You have beautified my slopes; now I want to add a little beauty to your house. I have lumber here I'm not going to use, and I want Fenton to put a porch along the south side of your house. Will you let him? It will take down the height and will make a pretty little house of it. I want to do it for my own sake, if you'll let me."

Then he ran for his train, and Deborah did not really know whether she had said "No, thank you," or "Yes, thank you." But it must have been yes, for the very next morning Mr. Fenton's men began to saw and fit and hammer by the little, dingy house.

Those were exciting days. Boxes of plants and seeds arrived, and there was an experienced gardener at Mr. Danvers's who lived for nothing but to plant beauty as Deborah ordered it. The porch took on its outline and filled out to completeness. One day the painter whom Deborah had fed with milk handed back the jug with a very grave face.

"That there milk seems to have some magic in it," he said solemnly. "I declare if it ain't turned into white paint; enough to cover your whole house. If you'll say the word, I'll smear it over odd times after hours; it'll be a good-looking little place when it gets whitened up."

"Haven't you got some green cheese around, too?" laughed Mr. Fenton. "I was just thinking I've got some blinds piled under a lot of rubbish over at the shop that would just fit these little windows. I took 'em off an old house ten years ago. I'll hang 'em if you'll daub 'em over with green cheese."

"Oh!" cried Deborah. "Everybody is so good. Could I really have blinds? Not having them has always made the house look like a person without any eyebrows."

"It's nothing to put those on," Mr. Fenton said; "and it's all the house needs to make it match the garden. My new flowers are doing finely. Why don't you come over and see 'em? Don't you ever come to see my girl?"

"She wouldn't want to me to," stammered Deborah. She could not forget how homely Josie thought her.

"Of course she'd want you," answered Mr. Fenton. "I'll send her down here to prove it."

"Oh, don't," Deborah wanted to protest, but she didn't. Would she even have to love Josie Fenton?

The paint and the blinds were on before Josie came. Debby tried to be cordial and entertaining, but it was Josie who did most of the talking. They discussed the weather and the garden, and all the time Josie was casting little flying glances at Deborah.

"Oh, Debby!" she exclaimed abruptly at last. "Will you be mad? I'm just crazy to fix your hair. I never noticed before how thick and soft it is. You could be stunning if you did it right. Come on upstairs and let me try."

Most unwillingly Deborah led the way to her room and sat down before her dressing-table.

"Why, it's gorgeous!" cried Josie, as Debby's loosened hair flowed over her shoulders. "But you mustn't drag it back tight as if you were stuffing a pincushion. It's got lots of wave in it. There, you must always roll it like that and keep it soft—so. Now where's your blue ribbon? Why, Debby, you're *lovely!* Just look!"

Confused, yet pleased, Deborah looked in the mirror which had so often reflected her plain face. But what did she see now? A warm flush in the pale cheeks; a happy smile on the discontented lips; a friendly look in the downcast eyes; softly waving hair instead of the scalp-tight locks—and all this set off by a blue ribbon and a blue dress that made her eyes look like forget-me-nots. It wasn't herself; it couldn't be! She was so ugly, and this girl was a joy to look at! It was too good to be true.

"Don't you ever dare do it any other way!" said Josie. "There's Father going home. I'll catch a ride. Come and see me, Debby."

Debby felt almost too conscious to go down to supper. She stole another glance at herself in the mirror, and smiled at what she saw. "I'm not ugly," she thought with a throb of joy. "People won't have to hate looking at me. Something has shined through, but I don't know what it is."

She went out to water her flowers after supper, with the smile still in the corners of her lips, the flush on her cheeks, and the brightness in her eyes. When Fred Dillon walked by, instead of turning her back, Deborah looked up and smiled. It was a friendly smile, born of her new sense of self-assurance.

"Hello, Debby!" the boy said. "If you'll invite me in, I'll carry that water-pot for you. My, what a dandy porch you've got! You'll have to have a house-warming for that, for sure!"

"So I can!" cried Deborah. "I'll do it just as soon as the moon is full."

"Then I'm invited, am I?"

"Yes," said Debby, "only I can't let you pass lemonade if you spill as much as you're spilling out of that watering-pot."

"They're wet enough anyhow," said the boy. "Let's go sit on the porch and look at how much good we've done them."

Debby led the way to the porch, her heart beating with a new glad glow of life. It was all so wonderful. Above her, Mr. Danvers's beautiful house stood against the evening sky, and his lawns sloped to her own pretty little home, painted and porched and shuttered, worthy of the garden in which it stood. Fred had come to see her, as he called to see other girls, and she was talking and laughing, and she wasn't homely. Life was full of joy, where a few months ago there had been only heaviness and hopeless loneliness. And she loved everything and everybody.

"Loving is the biggest beauty in the world," Deborah thought. "The really ugly things are just hating and hatefulness. I guess we can put beauty anywhere if we have loving enough."

WHEN I WAS A BOY ON THE RANCH

by J. Frank Dobie

THERE were six of us children and our ranch was down in the brush country of Texas between the Nueces River and the Rio Grande. The automobiles have outrun the horses since then; radios have drowned out many a cricket's voice and many a coyote's wailing cry; in many a ranch yard the lights of Delco plants have dimmed the glowing points of the fireflies—"lightning bugs," we called them. But the ranch of our childhood is still a ranch. And south of it clear to the Mexican border, and northwest of it into the Rocky Mountains and on up beyond the line where Montana joins Canada, there are millions and millions of acres of other ranches on which boys and girls live.

Despite automobiles these boys and girls still ride horses. Despite radios they still listen in the evening to crickets and frogs, and sometimes in the night to the wailing cries of coyotes. As for electric lights on the ranches, they light such small spaces that the fireflies in the grass and the stars in the sky never notice them. The country is still country. For all the changes brought by invention, ranches are still ranches.

So if I tell how we children lived on our ranch, I'll also be telling how children still live on other ranches scattered all over the western half of the United States.

We liked ranching so much that our best game used to be "playing ranch." There were fine live oak trees between the yard fence and the pens about the stables and barns, and it was in the shade of these trees, especially during the summer, that we built our "ranches."

To build a pasture we drove little stakes close together in the ground until a plot about as big as a kitchenette was inclosed; sometimes the pasture was made by setting up "posts" of stakes in the ground and then stretching cords, in imitation of barbed wire, from one corner of the "pasture" to the other. Each ranch had several pastures, and of course each ranch had headquarters, where houses and corrals were built. The houses were generally of boards; the corrals were of pickets laid between pairs of upright posts.

Fencing in the pastures was never so much fun as getting them stocked. It took work to fence in land and improve it with dirt tanks, which never would hold water very long. It took patience to construct corral gates that would open and shut and to make a house that would not fall down when a turkey stepped on it or a pup ran against it. But stocking this land with cattle and horses and goats was nothing but fun.

We had two kinds of cattle—high-grade cattle and common "stuff." The horn tips of real cattle—which were clipped off at branding time—became our pure-bred animals. Sometimes we had hundreds of them. Our "common Mexican cattle" were represented by oak balls.

But we prized our horses far more than

our cattle. Horses consisted of sewing-thread spools; most of our clothes were made on the ranch, and those clothes took an astonishing amount of thread. Moreover, when we went visiting we had our eyes open for discarded spools, but visits of any kind were rare and those that brought spools were rarer. A spool has a long "side" that can be branded and it has a long "back" that can be saddled. I can't think of any better kind of play-horse than a spool.

The ranches in our part of the country had herds of white Mexican goats. White-shelled snails were abundant in our neighborhood, and these shells became our goats. A live snail would not stay in a pasture, for he can climb straight up and carry his shell with him, so our goats were always empty shells. There were no sheep in the country; we had never heard anything particularly good connected with sheep men; and so we had no sheep—just cattle, horses, and goats.

Each of us had a brand. Mine was NEv , which an uncle of mine named Neville used. Fannie's was , Elrich's was an *E;* Lee's brand was *L.* The two younger children were too small to build ranches and brand herds by themselves; consequently if Henry and Martha got into the game, they got in as "hired help." Our branding irons were short pieces of bailing wire, with a crook at one end. This kind of branding iron is called a "running iron." When we had occasion to brand, we built a fire close to ranch headquarters, heated the "running irons," and burned our brands on the spool-horses, the common oak-ball cattle, and the fine horn cattle.

Like real ranchmen, we bought and sold stock. When a trade was made, the cattle or horses—we seldom traded goats—had to be gathered up, driven to the shipping pens, loaded on the railroad cars, trans-ported, and delivered. Then after they were delivered they had to be branded with the brand of the new owner. (A great many of the "common cattle" were decayed on the inside and when they were branded collapsed into nothing!) We had to sell cheap for the very simple reason that dollars were scarce and cattle were plentiful.

The dollars we had, however, were extraordinarily good dollars of sound coinage and pure metal. The ranch kitchen used a considerable amount of canned goods, particularly canned tomatoes, salmon, and sardines, along with some peaches and corn. We held the empty can in a fire with tongs until the solder started to run, and then caught the solder in an old spoon, pouring it into a round wooden box that had once held bluing. The diameter of this round bluing box was—and still is—about that of a silver dollar. The dollars we coined were sometimes thicker than a silver dollar and they were always heavier, but in buying cattle they were worth just as much.

We had another source of metal for our dollars. In the fall of the year hunters would be on the ranch, either camped out or staying with us at the house. They usually shot up a good many boxes of shells practicing on trees. After the shooting was over, we children gouged out the lead bullets lodged in the trees and melted them into dollars.

I spoke of shipping cattle. The train was a string of empty sardine cans coupled to each other with wire hooks. Motive power was the chief problem. We tried hitching horned frogs and green lizards to it, but neither pulled with any strength. A horned frog would sometimes pull an empty wagon made of a cardboard match box. Old Joe, the best dog we ever had, would pull the train pretty well if he went in a straight line, but when he didn't, he caused several bad wrecks that overturned cars and spilled cattle out. If a delivery of cattle had to be made promptly, the simplest and surest way to make the engine pull the train was to tie a string to it and pull it yourself.

Of course there were *real* horses and *real* cattle to interest us. Children brought up on a ranch usually learn to ride only a little later than they learn to walk. Old Stray, Dandy, and Baldy were the horses on our ranch that could be trusted with the youngest children. Old Stray was a common Mexican pony that some Mexican had ridden down and turned loose on our ranch. When we first saw him he was as thin as a stick-horse. Nobody claimed him, so after a while we used him. He seemed to appreciate having plenty of grass to eat but he had no intention of ever·exerting himself again. In short, he was not only gentle but "pokey." If a child fell off him, he would stop and graze until the child got up again. Baldy was an enormous horse, and by the time a boy was big enough to scramble upon his back without help from a man or a friendly fence, that boy was nearly ready for "long pants."

Dandy was a black horse of thoroughbred trotting stock. He alone of all the horses was entitled to corn the year around. The other horses lived mostly on grass. We rode Dandy sometimes as well as drove him, but he had too much life in him for mere beginners. He was as kind and intelligent as he was lively. One time when my brother Elrich was very small he toddled into Dandy's stall while Dandy was eating. The flies were bothering Dandy and he was switching his tail and stamping his feet. He knew that the little boy was in danger. He put a hind foot against the child and shoved him out of the stall. He did not kick him—just shoved him.

By the time I was eight years old I had several horses to ride. There was Maudie, a little Spanish mare, that would kick up when I punched her in the shoulder with my finger or pointed my hand down toward her flank or tail. Later there was Buck, a horse raised on the ranch. He was a bay with a white face and stocking feet. I kept him as long as he lived and he died on the ranch where he was born. He could be turned loose in camp and would not stray off. Once when I was running to head some wild steers and Buck gave a quick dodge, the saddle, which was loosely girted, turned, throwing me to the ground and nearly breaking my hip. Buck could "turn on a dime" and stop as quickly as one can snap a finger. On this occasion he stopped so suddenly that he did not drag me a foot, though I was still in the saddle when my hip struck the ground. He was the best cowhorse I ever rode. Often when we were alone I talked to him. By the time I was twelve years old and a regular ranch hand, I was sometimes on him from daylight until long after dark. More than once I went to sleep riding him. I loved him and he loved me. I think of Buck oftener now than I think of many people who have been my friends.

As range cows do not give as much milk as dairy cows, we usually had a pen full of them to milk, especially in the summertime. Each cow had her calf, and the calves were allowed part of the milk. A Mexican man usually did the milking, but it was the privilege of us boys to bring in the calves from the calf pasture each evening and then to ride them.

Now, riding calves is about as much fun as a ranch boy can possibly have. The calf is roped around the neck, and a half hitch, called a "bosal," is put around its nose. Then, using the rope as a bridle, the boy mounts. Until the calf is gentled, it will "pitch like a bay steer." One calf that I remember particularly was a black heifer with a white face. She became very gentle and we named her Pet. I trained Pet so well that I could mount her and guide her all over the calf pasture. Usually, no matter how well "broke" to riding, a calf won't go where you want it to go. It won't go anywhere. Saddles don't fit calves or grown cattle and, although it was sometimes fun to saddle yearlings, what actual riding we did was bareback. As we grew older we caught range cattle coming into the big pen to water and rode the calves and yearlings.

Each of us children had a few head of cattle to call our own. They were for the most part dogies or of dogie origin. A "dogie" is a motherless calf. When one was found on the range, it would be brought in and some cow with a calf of like age would be tied at night and morning and forced to let the motherless calf share her milk. We had one old muley cow that was so kind to dogies that the dogie always fared better than her own offspring. She would moo to it and lick its hair and otherwise mother it.

Pet was originally a dogie. When she grew up and had calves of her own, we milked her. If she was a good "saddle horse," a red-roan calf that she had was a better one. Pet had so many calves and those calves grew up and had so many calves of their own that the little stock of cattle coming from her helped materially to put me through college one year.

We went to a country school, which was on our own ranch, where the children of five or six other ranch families attended. Most of them rode to school horseback. One of our games was "cats and dogs." This we boys—for girls did not join in it—played at noon recess. The "cats" would set out in the brush afoot. About three minutes later the "dogs," mounted on horses and yelling like Apache Indians, would take after them. The brush had thorns and

the idea of the "cat" was to get into brush so thick that the "dog" could not follow him, or to crawl into a thicket where he could not be seen. Sometimes the chase would last until long after the bell had sounded. I remember one great chase that kept us out until three o'clock. An hour later eight or nine boys were alone with the teacher and a pile of *huajilla* switches.

Another game on horseback that the older boys played was "tournament." Three posts are erected in a line a hundred yards apart. Each post has an arm of wood about a yard long. Hanging from this arm is a metal ring about two inches in diameter. It is held by a spring clasp so that it can be easily disengaged. The runner takes a sharpened pole—the "tournament pole"—in his right hand and, holding it level, with the point out in front of him, runs lickety-split down the line of rings trying to spear them. The game requires skill. Buck was a wonderfully smooth-running horse, and he and I together hooked plenty of rings.

My sisters and girl cousins joined us in playing Indian and in making houses. Our ranch was built on a dry arroyo, or creek, named Long Hollow. Just below the house this creek had bluffs about forty feet high. For years we children worked periodically at digging caves back into the bluffs. Here we played Indian. If the soil had not been so gravelly and consequently inclined to cave in, we might have made dwelling places as ample as some of the ancient cliff dwellings. As it was, we got the caves big enough for us to hide in. When Long Hollow ran water after a rain, we made water wheels of sticks and cornstalks and watched them turn.

The house of our own construction that we enjoyed most was in a tree. It was a live oak called "the Coon Tree," from the fact that a coon hungry for chickens had once been found in it. Climbing up into this tree was an enormous mustang grape-vine. This grapevine afforded us a kind of ladder to the limbs of the Coon Tree. We took planks up to these limbs and nailed them so that we had a solid floor.

In our country we did not have many fruits, but around the ranch house were prolific pomegranate bushes. No matter how dry the season, these pomegranates always bore fruit. In the summertime we would pick pomegranates, borrow some sugar, spoons, and glasses from the kitchen, and, with a jug of water, gather on the platform in the Coon Tree for a picnic. We had a rope with which to pull up the jug and a bucket containing the other articles. The point of the picnic was to make "pomegranateade" out of sugar, the fruit seeds, and water.

Sometimes we took books and read in the Coon Tree. *Beautiful Joe* and *Black Beauty* were favorites. Our real house had matting on the floor, and when this mat-ting was discarded and we covered the platform in the Coon Tree with it, we felt that we had reached the height of luxury. I don't understand why none of us ever fell out of the Coon Tree.

I have spoken of our life with horses and calves. There were other animals to interest us, as there always are in the country. The trees about the ranch were inhabited each spring and summer by hun-dreds of jackdaws, a kind of blackbird. They built their nests in the trees so flimsily that disaster to the newly hatched birds was inevitable. Before they could fly or even walk, young birds would fall out of the trees and sprawl helpless on the ground, a ready prey for cats, turkeys, and other enemies. The distressed cries of the parent jackdaws were at times almost deafening, but these parents could do noth-ing toward getting their young back into the nests. We used to pick up the young birds and put them in straw-filled wooden nail-kegs, which we placed on the roofs of a shed and smokehouse under the Coon Tree. I have seen three or four par-ent jackdaws feeding their young at the same time in one of these kegs. Some-times each keg held as many as eight young birds.

Scissortails built their hanging nests in the very tops of the higher trees, but their young never fell out. We never tired of watching the scissortails fly, especially if they were chasing a hawk, darting at his head and driving him away. The wrens nested in tool boxes in the stable, in coils of rope, even in the leather toe-fenders—called *tapaderos*—covering the stirrups of saddles. When we found these nests, we made it our duty to warn our father and the Mexican laborers not to disturb them. One time a saddle had to go unused for weeks until a wren that had built in the *tapadero* of one stirrup had brought off her brood.

Under Mother's direction we raised chickens, turkeys, and guineas. The guineas were good "watchdogs," alarm-ing, with their wild cries, everything and everybody within hearing distance when a hawk was approaching. Hawks, chicken snakes, and coyotes were constant enemies of the barnyard. We boys sometimes set traps for the coyotes. I remember seeing my mother, before I was old enough to handle a gun, shoot one with a rifle very near the house.

The evening call of the bob-white brought—as it yet brings—a wonderful peace. In the early mornings of certain times of the year we could hear wild tur-keys "yelping" out in the brush back of the field. Once a large flock of them grazed up to the schoolhouse, but the teacher would not let us out to chase them. Al-though deer were plentiful, and some other children in the country had a pet fawn, we never had one. Once while riding in the pasture I halted a long time to watch a doe kill a rattlesnake.

I can honestly say that we did not enjoy "tormenting" animals and that we did not rob birds' nests. But when we snared lizards with a horse hair looped on the end of a pole; when we poured buckets of water down the holes of ground squirrels to make them come out; and when we hitched horned toads to match boxes, we no doubt did torment those animals, though we seldom injured them. I have since killed noble buck deer, mountain lions, wild boars, and other game, but no memory of hunting is so pleasant as that of rescuing little jackdaws, of restoring a tiny dove fallen from its nest, and of watching, without molesting them, baby jack-rabbits in their cotton-lined nest against the cow pen fence—memories all of a ranch boy.

Ranch girls and boys always find so many ways to play and so many creatures of nature to interest them that the days are never long enough. And no life can be long enough for a ranch-bred boy or girl to forget the full times of childhood.

PERCY RAY'S TRICK BOAT

Nathan Haskell Dole

"FATHER, I'm going to build a boat."
"Build a boat! You couldn't
build a boat!"

There was no conviction in the father's
tone. Alexander Ray, who was satisfied
with himself, with all his possessions, and,
above all, with his only son, in his heart
believed that his son could do anything,
just as he believed that he himself could
do anything. Percy looked like his father.
He had the same bright blue eyes, the same
aquiline nose, the same determined mouth.
His hair stood up on his head with the
same aggressive fierceness. They both had
a quick, eager way of speaking.

"What is your plan?" asked Percy's
father.

"Well, I'm going to build it in the barn.
I'll get some wood over at the sawmill. I
saw some over there which looked just
right."

"What kind of a boat?"

"No flat-bottomed punt, I tell you! I
want one that will sail. I'll build her with
a keel and a rudder."

"Have you made a sketch of it?"

"No; only in my own mind."

"You want a carefully drawn sketch of
it. I'll help you."

Mr. Ray got some large sheets of brown
paper, and he and Percy were soon deeply
engrossed in making measurements to
scale. Both had considerable skill in drawing, and the boat as it took shape gave
promise of being a joy forever. They
reckoned about how much lumber would
be necessary, and Percy borrowed a team
of a neighbor and went to the mill to
make his purchase.

The old harness-room in the barn had
been converted into a carpenter's shop; it
contained a solid bench, and a fairly complete assortment of tools. The main body
of the barn afforded ample room for the
boat-building. The big folding doors could
be flung wide open, and the view, as one
looked out, comprised a small grove of
maple-trees with one big oak and one tall
pine, and, far beyond, the main village and
the slope of a high hill covered with old
apple-trees. Out of sight lay the wide river
into which the boat would be launched.
The barn stood lower than the house,
which was of brick, with huge chimneys.
One could stand on the front door-step and
fling a stone into the water.

Percy went to school in the morning; he
had, therefore, only three or four afternoon hours and his Saturdays in which to
work on the boat. If he had not been eager
to have it finished by the beginning of the
summer vacation, he would have been
rather jealous, and have objected to his
father's pushing it forward while he himself was engaged in reading how Cæsar
constructed the bridge or Odysseus made
his raft. Mr. Ray puttered more or less, but
Percy did the larger part of the work. It
was wonderful to see the boat grow. The
keel was laid with great care, and the ribs,

skilfully shaped, took their proper places. One thing Percy's father could do, and that was to make shavings. He handled the plane like a master, and he did yeoman's work in smoothing the boards. It was to be a lapstreak.

The pounding and general clatter could not fail to attract attention, and there was always a little crowd of critics who watched the operations with the keenest interest. When the work began, the ice was still in the river. It went out as usual on Sunday, and there was even a first-class freshet. Another barn, standing a little lower, was inundated, and Caleb Loring had to take a flat-bottomed punt and rescue the Widow Jones's cow. Percy was sorry that his craft was not in readiness to engage in such a deed of mercy.

At last, the school examinations were finished, and the boat was ready to be launched. All the boys of the village, and not a few men, gathered to watch and assist. In the olden days, before the bridge was built, long before the war, there had been a ferry, and the road leading diagonally down the rather steep bank still existed. Indeed, it was always used in winter when there was teaming on the ice. Percy arranged two pairs of wheels taken from a hay-cart, and, with the assistance of willing hands, got the boat safely and steadily established between solid crutches. Strong ropes were attached to the forward axle. Ropes were also fastened to the rear axle, so as to hold back when going down the incline. A team of shouting boys were waiting the word of command to march forward with the glittering equipage. Glittering? It was painted white, with two parallel green lines. The name, *Speranza,* was delicately lettered on the stern. Two parts of brass rowlocks were in place. Four small boys disputed the honor of carrying the four oars.

The procession started. An excited crowd was on hand to witness the launching. Percy had in some way procured a small yacht-cannon. It was all ready to fire a salute to the young queen of the river. Everything went like clockwork. The lads at the ropes walked in step. A couple of the taller ones moved at each side to give a steadying hand if it were necessary. Under the tall hackmatack trees that lined the street, the sunlight pouring down from a cloudless sky, went the boat. It soon reached the old ferry road. The team changed places, taking hold of the rear ropes. It was all admirably managed. Percy's heart swelled with pride. He realized that he occupied a commanding position among his fellows. Every one in town had been praising his enterprise and ingenuity. This was his day of triumph.

The river flowed by in a calm and sedate manner. There was not a breeze. Every bush and tree was reflected in its soft brown water. Occasionally, a little fountain of bubbles would mount to the surface— gas from some decaying log buried in the muddy bottom. Now and then a fish would leap and cause a spreading circle to mar the images depicted on the mirror. There was a beach of clean white sand; the bottom sloped gradually for perhaps ten feet, and then went down suddenly. It was an ideal place to launch the bonny craft. It did not take much imagination to see that the *Speranza* was quivering with anticipation. It seemed to be actually alive. Very carefully she was pushed out into the stream until she floated. Then Percy, taking the end of the painter, towed her round to his float. This was constructed of large logs fastened together with parallel planks and securely anchored. All the boys would have piled in at once, but he kept them off. "No," said he, "I'll try it myself first. You shall have your show afterward." He took one pair of the oars, and carefully, so as not to scratch the paint, stepped in. He was just inserting one oar into the rowlock, having drifted away a few feet from the float, when suddenly, without the least warning, the boat rolled over, tipping the proud owner into the river. A shout went up from the crowd on the bank; but they all knew Percy could swim like a duck. He came up sputtering, but a few strokes brought him and the boat to shallow water.

Here Mr. Ray asserted himself.

"You were careless," he said; "there's no sense in managing a boat like that! I thought you knew how to handle oars. Here, give it to me. I will show you how!"

It was hot in the sun, so there was no danger of Percy's getting cold, though the water was streaming from his clothes and from his thick hair.

Mr. Ray, assisted by several of the boys, brought the boat to the float again.

He took the oars, and crept cautiously over the bow and seated himself on the middle thwart. He then tried to insert both oars simultaneously, saying rather boastfully, "I was brought up in a boat. I know all about them—" The next instant he was floundering in the water. When the crowd saw the expression of his face, a mighty howl of unholy joy went up which might have been heard a mile. It was too bad, but Mr. Ray, in spite of many admirable qualities, enjoyed among his fellow-townsmen the reputation of being a little too boastful. He was so often justified in his pretensions that, to see him for once humiliated, relieved the disappointment which all felt at the failure of the *Speranza* as a passenger-carrying craft. Both oars and Mr. Ray's new hat went sailing down the current together. Percy had to swim after them and bring them back.

As poor Mr. Ray waded ruefully ashore, he was overwhelmed with suggestions as to what should be done. One thought that the keel should have a lead shoe; another proposed to get some bricks for ballast.

"She sets just like a swan," said Harry Manning. "She doesn't look as if she'd be so cranky. Here comes Caleb Loring; perhaps he'll try her."

Caleb Loring was a half-witted fellow who got his living from the river. He had a flat-bottomed punt which he navigated backward or forward with a paddle. With it he collected cords of driftwood; from it he fished near the sunken piers of the old bridge that had been carried away during a January thaw, many years before. Caleb Loring was always the first to cross the river on the ice after it had closed over.

"What's the trouble?" he asked as he came lumbering down over the bank. He wore a ragged straw hat, a blue flannel shirt, and trousers hitched to his shoulders by pieces of hemp rope. He was barefooted. "Oh, I see," he continued, "boat too high-studded. Wait, I'll get a stun'." He went a few rods up the bank, and soon returned, bringing a water-worn boulder which he had used for an anchor. "There!" he exclaimed, "this'll make her set deeper. Now she'll be all right."

"You try her, Caleb," shouted several.

"I'd ruther paddle her," said Caleb; "I'll use the oar f'r a paddle."

With perfect confidence he stepped into the *Speranza,* but he had not taken two strokes before the mischievous craft, with all the agility of a bucking bronco at a circus, flopped on her side, spilling Caleb Loring, just as she had spilled Percy and his father, into the smiling river.

Loring came up puffing like a grampus —a most ludicrous object. His straw hat and one oar went sailing down the current. The boat righted herself and floated gracefully, looking as innocent as she was beautiful.

"There's something wrong with her," said Mr. Ray, with the water still dripping from all his garments; "I can't imagine what it is. She was built on measurements. We've got to take her up to the barn again."

This time it was more like a funeral than like a wedding procession. The boys hauled her out of the stream and lifted her on the wheels. Then they all took hold and rushed her up the bank, and back to the place of her nativity. Nothing was talked about in the village during the next few days except Percy Ray's "bucking boat," and those who missed the great spectacle of Alexander Ray following Percy over her side, had no difficulty in imagining the scene, so vividly was it narrated by the various eye-witnesses.

Percy and his father were sitting, a few days later,—in dry clothes, of course, and with a somewhat chastened spirit—talking about the still unsolved problem of the bucking boat, as it was universally called. The door-bell rang. The visitor was the proprietor of a little hotel at "the Pond." This was a resort about six miles from the village. Picnic parties frequently went there for sailing, swimming, rowing, and fishing. Ebenezer Junkins had originally been a farmer, and his acres skirted the Pond. He had found it more profitable to rent his grove, to take boarders, and gradually to enlarge his fleet of boats, than to practise farming. He was a character. He had very blue eyes, sandy hair, and a straggly beard under his chin. His clothes consisted of a pair of very baggy pantaloons, a rusty black coat, and cowhide boots. He was regarded as extremely shrewd. He took a seat, and, twisting his broad-brimmed rusty black hat in his big, hairy hands, which carried around with them a goodly share of the rich soil of his farm, he hemmed and hawed for a while, and then burst out suddenly:

"I hearn tell about that there boat o' yourn. That was plum funny—the way she upsot ye. I'd 'a' giv' a dime to 'a' seen that circus-show. What I come f'r is to find out if ye'd sell her."

"I don't think it would be fair to palm her off on any one," said Mr. Ray; "do you, Percy?"

"Why, no; it wouldn't be safe for any one to try to go out in her," said the boy.

"Well, I'd take the resk o' that," eagerly urged Mr. Junkins. "I've got quite a stack o' boats, and I'm mighty keerful how I let 'em. What will ye take f'r her?"

"Let me see," mused Mr. Ray. "It cost us about twenty dollars, didn't it, Percy?"

"I kept the accounts very carefully," replied Percy. "Not reckoning our time, the bare materials stood us about twelve dollars. That doesn't include the oars. One of them went down the river."

"I'll give ye six dollars f'r her. She ain't no good to you nohow."

"I don't think I want to sell her," decided Percy. "I'm bound to discover what was the trouble with her, and if I can't make her carry me, I'll take the material and build another. What do you want of her, anyway?"

Ebenezer Junkins's desire to get the boat was so evident that the boy's bright mind was filled with all sorts of conjectures.

"Ef ye don't want to sell her, will ye rent her to me?"

"Tell us what you want to do with her," insisted Mr. Ray.

"If ye'll either sell her or rent her, I'll tell ye what my scheme is," replied Ebenezer, after a little consideration, during which he scratched his sandy hair vigorously.

"I'd just as lief rent it," said Percy. "Now tell us what you propose to do."

"Wall, I went to the circus onc't, and I see a bucking mule named Maud. Ther' was a standin' offer of five dollars to any one who'd stay three minutes on her back, an' I never see no one git it. When I heerd about your 'buckin' *boat,*' 't occurred to me that I might try the same scheme with *her.* I'll offer a dollar to the boy or man who will row or paddle her acrost fr'm the float over to the p'int 'thout gittin' tipped over—'t 's about as fur 's fr'm here up to the corner yonder. I'll charge ten cents a try at it. There's hundreds o' boys an' men come every season an' go in swimmin'. 'T'will be a grand card."

"What would you be willing to pay for it for the summer?"

At first he offered a lump sum, but, after some bargaining, it was decided that Percy should have twenty-five per cent. of all the profits.

"I come down in my hay-cart," said Ebenezer, "an' I s'pose I may 's well take her now 's any time. That's all right, ain't it?"

A little later, the village was astonished to see Ebenezer Junkins, whom every one knew, deliberately driving through the streets and across the bridge with the *Speranza,* apparently enjoying the sensation she was creating.

A week later, the Sunday-school which Percy was regularly attending held its annual picnic at the Pond. Every one was going. It was known that Percy's trick boat would be going through her paces. All the boys and a good many of the girls carried their bathing-suits, and an extra dime and the resolution to conquer the mischievous little craft. It was a perfect summer day, not even the prospect or threat of a shower to mar its festivity. There was the usual motley array of equipages—wagons which looked as if they had been made before the flood, old-fashioned chaises, barges, and carts piled high with sweet-scented new hay. Baskets filled with home-made goodies were not lacking, and the train started off promptly, with shouts and songs.

Percy, though he was going to play on the side of the Academy boys against the outsiders in a game of base-ball, managed, first of all, to steal away and get a look at his masterpiece—the bonny *Speranza.* Yes, there she floated, demure and graceful! He could not help feeling proud of her nice lines—a pride tempered, indeed, by the consciousness that she had played him false. Ebenezer saw him as he stood contemplating her.

"She's a swan!" exclaimed Percy, with a burst of enthusiasm he could not repress.

"I sh'd call her a duck!" chuckled Ebenezer. "Nobody ain't tamed her yit. More 'n forty's tried her so fur. That gives ye a dollar. Guess we'll make ye another to-day."

There was a hurry call for Percy, whose heart, it must be confessed, was not in the game. At least he did not play so well as usual. Nevertheless, the Academy boys came out ahead: the score stood five to four. When the nine innings were finished, there was a rush for the water. Three or four boys piled into each of the bath-houses, and, in an incredibly short time, the pond was alive with heads of every color—black, yellow, brown, red. Some dived from the float; others jumped; many raced in, leaving a foamy wake and making a prodigious splash. Several tried to see how far they could swim under water. But after the first general cooling off, there was a simultaneous convention gathered to tame Percy's trick boat. Ebenezer supervised the trials. A painted sign announced the terms: each competitor was to pay ten cents; any number might try at once. Whoever succeeded in propelling the *Speranza* from the float to the point without overturning should receive a dollar.

Percy himself was the first to try the game. He had an inward lurking hope that his first experience with his beautiful boat might have been only a dream—a dreadful nightmare. But the trick boat was true to her principles. She seemed to be actually alive. She took a mischievous delight in deceiving, for a moment, the careful venturer, and then, with a little shake, flinging him into the shining waters of the pond, the next moment riding calm and serene, as if no such impulse had ever entered her perverse feminine heart.

Half a dozen of the larger boys in succession tried to tame her; they all floundered, one after the other. Then companies of twos, threes, and fours, and, finally, half a dozen at once, experimented. The *Speranza* stood nobly to her reputation. She was no Atalanta: she would not be bribed by a golden apple; she was as tameless as Pegasus. She and her antics made the event of the picnic. Even the girls—a few of them, at least—with no little self-confidence, thought they might have better success; but the *Speranza* was proof against even this appeal to the sex pride— she refused to be wheedled.

Ebenezer pocketed the dimes.

It chanced that a sailor on shore leave arrived at the Pond. He heard of the unruly lady of the waters. He knew he could conquer her. He scorned to take off his watch. "I never saw a boat yet that I couldn't manage," he boasted. The *Speranza* heard him; she played with him after the manner of her kind. She let him row away ten or a dozen strokes from the dock. "This is an easy one!" he was saying to himself; but—the thought was finished in the cooling, gurgling waters. From the shore it could be seen how the tameless one exulted in her pride. The sailor knew not how to swim, but half a dozen of the boys bore down to his aid, and got him ashore, where he stood for a rueful moment, his wide trousers clinging limply to his legs, and streams of water like tears running

from his head; then he disappeared, all his boastfulness melted within him.

All that summer, Percy Ray's trick boat was the drawing attraction of Ebenezer Junkins's picnic grounds. Her fame traveled far and wide; men came from distant places to discover the cause of such a freak. As the *Speranza* sat on the water, she looked as innocent and harmless as a dove. Yet ever there lurked that tricksy spirit of mischief, ready to spill the would-be conqueror.

Percy's receipts for the season amounted to about fifty dollars. When the autumn came, it was the time for fairs; in such places as had streams or ponds easily accessible, there Ebenezer exhibited the *Speranza,* offering a prize of ten dollars for the successful mastery of the boat, and charging a quarter for the privilege. As the price went up, the boat's pride increased. She bridled with the witchery of her unconquerable nature. One would have thought that a more docile spirit might have come to her in time—that she would have tired of exhibiting what has been called "the total depravity of inanimate things." Inanimate? If ever a boat was animate, she was! She exerted an irresistible fascination. Men could not seem to help making the futile attempt to manage the fickle creature. But never once did the ten-dollar gold piece change hands.

When the weather became too cold, the *Speranza* was stored in a shed on Ebenezer Junkins's farm. One October morning, the shed was burned to the ground. It was supposed that some tramp who had slept in it had smoked his pipe and thrown a match into rubbish. The *Speranza* perished in the conflagration, with several more innocent boats. Ebenezer was inconsolable. She was the only boat of her class. Percy, with a part of the money which he received as his share of the sea-

son's proceeds, bought a second-hand mo-
tor-boat at a great bargain. It was an in-
novation on the river, and he soon covered the cost of it in taking excursion
parties to the Glen and the Old Indian
village, and other points of interest on
the river.

But he will wonder to his dying day
what caused the *Speranza* to deceive the
promise of its beautiful lines.

THE BOY WHO BORROWED TROUBLE

By Frederick B. Opper

Though extremely fond of coasting, this most peculiar lad,
  While flying swiftly down the hill, would wear a look of pain;—
For already he was thinking—and it really made him sad—
  That very soon he'd have to climb the whole way up again.

THE MAN WHO DID N'T BELIEVE IN CHRISTMAS
BY MARY AUSTIN

Albertine Randall Wheelan

PERSONS OF THE DRAMA

THE REAL PEOPLE
Alan, a lonely boy   Mr. Hardmann, his father
Mammy Delia, the housekeeper

THE PASSERS-BY
Grocer's Boy   Shopping Girl
Old Woman   Newsboy

THE STORY PEOPLE
Red Riding Hood   The Three Bears
Captain Kidd   Fairy Princess
Toby, the Clown   The Wizard of Oz
Dare-Devil Dick, the Indian Fighter
Clarice, the World's Empress
Bareback Rider
TIME: The Present, Christmas Eve.

ACT FIRST

SCENE.—The living-room of a comfortably furnished house in any American city. At the back is a deep window-seat looking on the street; at the left, a fireplace, with a dull glow of coals; in front of it, a table with a reading-lamp, unlighted; near that a Morris chair. One or two other chairs are arranged about the room, and over the mantel is the portrait of a lady. A strong light comes in from the window, but the corners of the room are in darkness.

A boy of seven or eight is seated among the cushions of the window-seat, turning over a pile of books. From time to time he glances out of the window.

A grocer's boy goes by with a basket from which the top of a bunch of celery and a chicken's legs may be seen sticking out. The boy inside opens a small book and begins to read. Little Red Riding Hood comes out of the dusk on the right of the room and goes briskly across with her basket. As she disappears on the left you can just see the Wolf, joining her. The boy turns the pages, and from somewhere in the dusk the Three Bears materialize,

*each with his appropriate spoon. ("Who's
been eating out of my spoon?") The boy
keeps his eyes on the book and wriggles
with appreciation.*

*A pretty girl, with her arms full of parcels,
passes outside and calls, "Hello, Alan!"
Turning to look at her and wave his hand,
the boy lets his book fall, and the Three
Bears disappear. He watches the girl out
of sight. An old woman with wreaths of
holly on her arm holds up one, inviting
him to buy, but he shakes his head, and
with a sigh turns to his books again. This
time he selects a larger one; and as he
reads, the Fairy Princess, who looks very
like the young lady who just smiled at
him, steps daintily across the room, and
then other figures appear indistinctly. A
newsboy outside, passing, cries, "Merry
Christmas," and a man with a small fir-
tree in his arms goes by. Alan answers,
"Merry Christmas," but it ends in a sigh
and a choke, and he turns to his books.*

*Now the shadowy figures grow plainer.
Captain Kidd, with a cutlass in his mouth,
buries a chest of Spanish Treasure behind
the Morris chair, and Dare-Devil Dick,
the Indian Fighter, comes scouting along
the trail. Dick catches sight of the largest
of the Three Bears, draws a bead on him,
misses fire, and, drawing his bowie-knife
as the bear rears on his hind legs, they
clinch.*

*Just at the most dramatic moment the
sound of a door opening causes them all
to vanish; and Alan, who has been showing the most intense appreciation of what
he reads, puts down his book to talk to
the housekeeper, who enters from the
right.*

*All this time the room has been growing
dark, lit only by the glow of the street
lamp outside. Now delicate flakes of snow
begin to fall. Mammy Delia brings in a
tray with Alan's supper, which she places
on the table, turning on the reading-lamp,
diffusing a warm glow over the room.*

DELIA. Law sakes, honey, ef you ain't
a-strainin' of you' eyes ag'in over them old
story-bookses! Ef you' daddy was to catch
you at it, you gonna hear somepin go
smack, I reckon.

ALAN (*still absorbed in what he has
been reading*). Mammy Delia, were you
ever scalped? Or had to walk a plank?

DELIA. Who, me? (*Alan nods.*) Law
bless you, chile, ain't no plank gonna hold
me; I take the whole sidewalk.

ALAN. Oh, no, Delia, I mean as a pirate
makes you. Captain Kidd, you know
(*Pantomime*). But I guess they didn't do
that to ladies. Pirates were always awfully
kind to ladies; and the ladies sometimes
got so fond of them that the pirates just
couldn't drive them away.

DELIA (*moving about the room, drawing the curtains and setting the furniture
to rights*). Oh, couldn't they!

ALAN. No. Don't you think that shows
they have kind hearts, Delia?

DELIA (*placing a chair at the table*).
Well, I reckon pirates is a whole lot like
other people. They got as kind hearts as
they can affo'd to have 'ithout spilin' their
business.

ALAN. I'm glad you think so, because
I really wouldn't *care* to be a pirate if they
weren't kind. Sometimes I think I'd rather
be an Indian fighter, because pirates have
to fight perfectly good people sometimes;
but Indian fighters only kill bears and red-
skins and things of that kind. (*While
Delia has her back turned he creeps upon
her from behind with pantomime of scalping.*) Scalped! (*War-whoop*).

DELIA (*in mock terror*). Fo' de laws' sake, you ain't skelped me ag'in, is you? I reckon you' daddy'll do that, though, ef he comes home and catches you settin' up. (*She draws a chair invitingly.*) Come, now!

ALAN. It's very perplexing, don't you think, Delia, trying to decide what you'll be when you grow up?

DELIA (*tying his napkin*). Well, I guess havin' you' supper will help some with the growin'. (*Pushes him up.*)

ALAN (*catching sight of the bread and jam*). Oh—e! Strawberry jam! (*He reaches for it, but Delia catches his hand*).

DELIA. Porridge first! (*She brings a cushion to make him high enough, giving his napkin a final tuck*). Mind now, don't spot! You know you' daddy says you got to be a gen'man jes' the same when you's alone as when you got company.

ALAN. Uh—huh (*eating carefully*). Delia, why don't we have some Christmas in this house?

DELIA. Well, you know, you' pa, he don't believe in Chris'mus.

ALAN. Yes, but isn't it *there?* In the street and everywhere, just like Thanksgiving and—Sunday? I don't see how you can help believing in it if it is *there*.

DELIA. Well, leastways, he don't believe in makin' a fuss about it.

ALAN. Every window in this street has got some Christmas in it but ours.

DELIA (*with a quick glance up at the portrait on the wall*). You poor lamb!

ALAN (*following her glance*). If we had a mother in our house, *we'd* have a Christmas, too, wouldn't we, Delia?

DELIA. Yes, honey, you' mother, she was one for all kinds of doin's and fixin's. Seemed like we wasn't hardly done with Thanksgivin' till we was fixin' for Chris-mus. An' them ole story-books what you been readin', she was fond of 'em up to the

last. 'Pears like this ole house ought to be plumb full of pirates an' b'ars an' fairy princesses an' sich, they was that alive to her.

ALAN (*kindling*). Oh, it is. Every time I open a book they just come right out. (*Mysteriously*) There's a chest of Spanish Treasure right over there behind that chair, Delia, and back there in that corner there's the most awful, horrible—grizzly bear!

DELIA. Awk! (*She gives a squeal of fright, and then recovers herself*). If you ain't the beatenest chile!

ALAN. I should think they wouldn't like it not to have any Christmas in the window.

DELIA (*to herself*). Poor lamb! (*Aloud*) But we don't have to have Chris'mus in the window, honey. We can have it right here in ou' hearts.

ALAN (*taking it seriously*). I don't know just what that means, Delia.

DELIA. Why, jus' lovin' and givin'. That's what Chris'mus is, honey lamb. We can love people in ou' hearts and give them things in ou' hearts. We can have that kind of Chris'mus.

ALAN (*soberly*). Can we? (*Absorbed in the subject, he absently lets the porridge fall from his spoon, and then puts the spoon in his mouth without noticing*).

DELIA. Mind you' napkin! You know what you' pa is always sayin'.

ALAN (*regarding the drip of his spoon thoughtfully, and then suddenly taken with an idea*). Why—of course we can have that kind of a Christmas. (*He finishes his porridge carefully, with great attention to keeping his napkin spotless, takes a careful drink of milk, and begins on his bread and jam.*)

DELIA. Besides, you jes' wait an' see what I got for dinner to-morrow.

ALAN (*interested*). Turkey?

DELIA. You jes' wait an' see!

ALAN. I know. Turkey and stuffing and celery—and mashed potato—and cranberry —and mince pie—ouch! (*In his excitement he has almost dripped the jam, but remedies that by licking the crust once around.*)

DELIA. (*Who has been piling up the books with her back to him.*) Ain't you 'most finished? You' pa is likely to be along home any minute now.

ALAN (*bolting the last mouthful*). Almost—Thank you. (*He licks his fingers, and, taking off his napkin, surveys its spotlessness with satisfaction.*) Not a one!

DELIA (*taking it from him*). Quite the little gen'man you're gettin' to be. Wait a minute! (*She attempts to wipe on the napkin the jam which he has not quite succeeded in removing from his countenance with his tongue.*)

ALAN (*drawing back*). No, no. No, sir-ee! (*He takes out his handkerchief and polishes his cheeks with it.*) Now it's all right.

DELIA. And now you better run along to bed before you' pa—

ALAN. Please, Delia—I just have to stay up tonight until Daddy comes. There's something I have to ask him.

DELIA. You know what he said—

ALAN. He said I could stay up when it was necessary, and this is, Delia. It's *most* important.

DELIA (*reluctantly, as the boy strokes her cheek coaxingly*). Oh, well— But don't you try no 'maginary pufformances on you' pa, honey; he ain't built for 'em. (*Goes out with the tray.*)

(*Alan brings his book to the table, kneels in the chair to bring himself in the right relation to the lamp, and begins to turn the pages slowly. As he turns, Captain Kidd and Dare-Devil Dick come out of the shadow; they are joined by the Fairy Princess, and as the three talk the Three Bears lumber up and stand listening*).

CAPTAIN KIDD (*motioning to Dare-Devil Dick to draw near and regarding Alan with pride*). What a pirate he'd have made if they'd just let him have his chance in life!

DICK. Well, now, *I* think he rather favors trailin' an' scalpin'. But ain't it a plumb shame the poor kid don't have no Christmas? Ain't there nothing we can do about it?

CAPTAIN KIDD. Well, maybe if we made that father of his walk the plank—

PRINCESS. Oh, no, *she* wouldn't like that (*indicates picture*). You know, if it hadn't been for her, we wouldn't be here.

DICK. No, we can't go against the feelings of a lady.

PRINCESS. Don't you remember how all the time the boy was a tiny baby she kept calling us around her? She was afraid she would have to leave him, and she said if he could have *us* for friends—

CAPTAIN KIDD (*much moved*). Well, the *Jolly Roger* isn't exactly the school for Christmas angels, ma'am, but if you think of anything—

PRINCESS. We must *all* think—

DICK. The first thing is to lay for the father—

PRINCESS. Hush! I think he's coming! (*They slip back into the shadow and as the outer door is heard to close, Alan closes his book and they completely disappear. Mr. Hardmann is heard stamping in the entry, and immediately enters with his coat still on and hat in hand.*)

ALAN (*getting down from chair*). Hello, Daddy!

HARDMANN. Well, son! Been a good boy to-day?

ALAN. Yes, Daddy. (*They kiss formally.*)

HARDMANN. (*To Delia, who has en-*

tered and who takes his coat.) Just hang it where it will dry; there's quite a bit of snow falling. (*Exit Delia. Hardmann takes newspaper from pocket and draws up the Morris chair.*) A bit late, isn't it, for you, young man?

ALAN (*who stands touching him with timid affection.*) I wanted to ask you something.

HARDMANN. Well, out with it. (*He takes the boy's hand, not unkindly, but with stiffness.*)

ALAN. I wanted—to ask—if you would mind our having a little Christmas in the window to-morrow—

HARDMANN (*stiffening*). Who's been talking to you about Christmas? I thought I had made Delia understand—

ALAN (*alarmed*). No, Father, truly. I just thought of it by myself. You see, every house but ours—

HARDMANN. *Of* course! It's a conspiracy of tradespeople. The more fools they can get to buy their gimcracks—Christmas giving! Christmas getting would be more like it. I'll have nothing to do with it.

ALAN (*desperately*). I thought you wouldn't mind. I could take the money out of my bank—and we needn't put it up until after you had gone to the office— Daddy!

HARDMANN (*rising and taking an attitude before the fireplace*). Now, Alan, you have really hurt my feelings! You are talking as though I were a cruel and neglectful parent. I thought I had made you understand that, in doing my best to bring you up useful and successful, I had tried to avoid everything that is not eminently practical.

ALAN (*forlornly*). Yes, Daddy.

HARDMANN. Now what is there practical about Christmas? And Santa Claus? What's Santa Claus? Driving reindeer through the air! Sliding down chimneys! Stuff and nonsense! Do you understand?

ALAN (*choking back his disappointment and glancing back toward his storybook for support*). I—I think so, Daddy.

HARDMANN. Well, then, you mustn't disappoint me by indulging in such nonsense. It stimulates the imagination unduly. Your poor dear mother had too much imagination. It was her one failing, and I shouldn't be doing right by her son if I didn't try to correct it. Come now, kiss me good night, and let us hear no more of Christmas.

ALAN (*kissing him*). Good night, Daddy. (*He looks at his book and then back at his father, and, when he thinks the latter isn't looking, tries to slip the book away unobtrusively.*)

HARDMANN. Here, what's this? Reading in bed?

ALAN. I wasn't going to read. I was just —taking it. For company.

HARDMANN. Well, let me see what company you keep. I suppose it is time I began to supervise your reading. Come.

ALAN (*reluctantly yielding it*). It's a very nice book, Father. It—it isn't at all— imaginative.

HARDMANN (*reading the title*). Boy's Story-book. We'll see (*turning the pages*). Captain Kidd—h'm—Aladdin—Sindbad—

ALAN. Good night, Father.

HARDMANN (*abstracted*). Good night, son.

(*He adjusts the light and the Morris chair and begins to turn over the pages of the book, showing strong disapproval. He says "Pish!" and "Tut-tut!" and "This is worse than I thought!" But in spite of himself he grows interested, tries to pretend he is not, finally surrenders and settles down to enjoyment. As he reads, the story people gather in the dark corners of the room. They whisper and make signs to one another. Captain Kidd takes off his sash and offers it to Dare-Devil Dick, making signs what he shall do with it. Dick and Captain Kidd steal up on either side of Hardmann.*)

DICK. "Hands up!" (*They bind his hands behind him with the sash, and Dick takes off his own handkerchief to make a gag. Hardmann sputters.*)

CAPTAIN KIDD. There now, don't you make any more noise than you have to!

DICK (*with the gag*). He won't have any more chance to than the coon had with Davy Crockett. Now then! (*Slumping him back in the chair*). You look more the way a man ought to look who's been putting it all over a poor kid. Just because he's your'n! I've a notion to skelp you. Eh, Cap?

CAPTAIN KIDD. Walking the plank is too good for *him*. Shiver my timbers! Don't believe in Christmas!

RED RIDING HOOD. Why doesn't he?

ALL. *Yes, why don't you?* (*Hardmann makes inarticulate protest.*)

CAPTAIN KIDD. There wasn't a pirate ship on the Spanish Main that didn't have an extra grog and a plum pudding for Christmas.

RED RIDING HOOD. Why, you're worse than a pirate!

THE OTHERS. Yes, you are worse than a pirate!

PRINCESS. A great deal worse. You've had a chance to learn better.

RED RIDING HOOD. I think he ought to be magicked away to some place *where nothing ever happens.*

DICK. That's no good. That kind don't know when anything happens, anyway.

PRINCESS. Oh, I've thought of something! Listen! (*They all gather around her to whisper.*)

DICK. Hist! You, Pete! (*He motions to the Father Bear to take his place while he joins the others.*)

CAPTAIN KIDD. You, mate! (*He panto-*

mimes to the Mother Bear to take her place beside the prisoner). Fo'castle council!

(*Hardmann, who has not seen the bears, as soon as the others turn their backs tries to get out of his chair on one side, and is terrified back by the open jaws of Father Bear; he tries to sneak out on the other side, and confronts Mother Bear. He sinks back in the chair, and Baby Bear comes sniffing about his toes. He begins to kick out frantically and makes sputtering noises. This attracts the others.*)

DICK. Hold on there, hold on! (*Separating him from Baby Bear.*) Ain't you got no feelings for the young? He was just having fun with you. Why, I knew a man had his whole arm et off and didn't make so much fuss about it. Take his gag off and let him talk some. It'll relieve his feelings.

(*While this is being done there is music and a whoop-halloo outside, and Toby the Clown comes tumbling into the room, holding a hoop through which the Bareback Empress suddenly bounces and pirouettes about the circle.*)

PRINCESS. Oh! I never saw you before. Did *you* come out of a book?

CLARICE. Out of a circus, and that's pretty near the same thing. I heard you were having a party, and this gentleman (*kissing her hand to Hardmann*) is a friend of mine.

HARDMANN. I—really, there's some mistake, I—really!

CLARICE. And what's more, he once admired me very much. (*Sensation.*)

HARDMANN. I?—preposterous!

CLARICE. You did. You were eleven and a half when your father took you to a circus, and you saw me there.

CLOWN. What's more, you admired *me*. You were going to be *me* when you grew up. You used to practise this out in the barn (*tumbles*).

CLARICE. Yes, and when your own boy wanted to go to the circus this summer you—said—it was—enervating!

THE OTHERS. Oh! You never! How could you!

HARDMANN. I didn't! That is—I mean I don't know this lady. I won't be responsible for what people like that say about me.

DICK. Why, it's the best thing I ever heard about you. If you was to *be* one of them things, you'd have to be doing something every minute.

CLOWN. You betcha! (*Business of clowning*) Like that!

CAPTAIN KIDD. That's why boys like to read us, real healthy boys. We're always doing something.

PRINCESS. It's very stimulating to the imagination.

THE OTHERS. Yes. Of course it is. Didn't you know *that?*

PRINCESS. And that's what gave me my idea.

CLARICE. What's that?

PRINCESS. Why, that he should have to be each one of us in turn until he finds out what we are for.

THE OTHERS. Yes! That's the idea. Make him find out!

CLARICE. Well, you're rather old to begin my business. They generally break a leg or an arm when they begin at your age. Still, that's nothing, and if you fall, the horses hardly ever step on you.

HARDMANN (*alarmed*). Really, I—

CAPTAIN KIDD. There's nothing like pirating to keep you limber. Why, I've seen the time when the scuppers were running full and the rigging half over, and the sea swarming with sharks—And there was Old Flint. Remember Flint? (*Sings*).

Fifteen men on the dead man's chest,
(*The others join*)

Yoho, and a bottle of rum!

HARDMANN. I'm a respectable citizen—

DICK. That won't do you no good when you get into the redskin's country. (*Fixes his gag again.*) Now, don't you try no funny business. We're going to learn you something. Let's begin. (*Hardmann shows extreme terror as Dick begins pantomime of Indian war-dance and scalping.*)

CLARICE. Well, I think we ought to do something for the poor kid first.

RED RIDING HOOD. He ought to have some kind of Christmas.

THE OTHERS. Yes, of course he ought. (*They consider.*)

PRINCESS. I know! Let's ask the Wizard of Oz.

CLARICE. Well, he doesn't seem to be among those present—

PRINCESS. Oh, *that's* easy. I only have to make a figure like this with my wand, and wave it like this—and this—and turn around three times—and stamp my foot—

(*There is a flash of light, a flash of darkness, then the lights are at normal again and the Wizard of Oz is seen.*)

And there he is!

WIZARD (*proceeding at once to do tricks of magic and legerdemain*). What can I do for you?

PRINCESS. We want you to make a Christmas.

RED RIDING HOOD. For a little boy who never had any.

CLARICE. Christmas-trees and toys and candy.

WIZARD. Produce your boy.

PRINCESS. Why, we can't, you know. He's upstairs, asleep.

WIZARD. I see. You want a dream Christmas. Nothing easier. Make the magic circle there.

(*They make a circle, pushing back the furniture, the Wizard producing whatever he needs by magic, describes circles in the air with his wand, and begins to pace a magic figure, chanting*)

> Cabala, quabala,
> Abracadabra,
> Zamiel, Amiel, Abaron, Tymayel,
> Shemeshiel, Malkahiel,
> Tetragram, Pentagon,
> Fee! Foo! Fum!

(*As he paces, the others circle in back, moving from right to left as he moves from left to right, each one using movements appropriate to his character.*)

STORY PEOPLE (*dancing and chanting*).

> Intry, Mintry, Cutery corn,
> Apple seed and briar thorn,
> Onery, oery, ichory Ann,
> Phillison, phollison,
> Nicholas, John—

WIZARD OF OZ (*his voice rising above the others as smoke begins to arise within the circle and a strange light shines about him*).

> Shemeshiel, Malkahiel,
> Macaroni, piebald pony,
> Samiel and Grimalkin,
> Cabala, quabala,
> Abracadabra,
> Ding, Dong, Dell—

(*As the last word thunders out, the smoke clears and shows a small Christmas-tree in the middle of the circle.*)

ALL. Oh, lovely!

WIZARD. Now for the gifts. (*He goes about extracting small toys from each of them—a ball, a top, etc.*)

PRINCESS. But I want to give him something my own self. Christmas-trees have stars, don't they? (*She takes the star from her wand and fixes it to the top of the tree. The Wizard waves his wand, and suddenly the star glows, amid exclamations of delight.*)

CLARICE. I want to be in on this. (*She takes the spangles from her dress; the clown hangs up his whistle.*)

CAPTAIN KIDD (*lugging his treasure-chest*). Just let him get his hands into this! (*He opens it at the foot of the tree and holds up a handful of gold*). Spanish Treasure!

DICK (*showing a bowie-knife*). These long marks are for the Injuns I've killed, and these notches are for grizzly bears, and the crosses are for life-and-death struggles.

PRINCESS. Dear me, there seem to be a great many of them!

DICK. Yes, ma'am; and if he finds he needs any more, I can easy put 'em on for him. (*He hangs it on the tree and at the same time Red Riding Hood produces a cake from her basket and puts it on the treasure-chest.*)

WIZARD. Now, produce your boy! (*They all look blank.*)

PRINCESS. Well, of course, it's only a dream Christmas—(*she looks troubled*).

CLARENCE. Well, he could walk in his sleep, couldn't he?

PRINCESS. The very thing. I know a fairy spell! You must all help me. Somebody open the door.

(*Red Riding Hood sets the door open. The Princess begins to dance and to sing softly. A fairy light plays over the whole scene. The others stand back and accompany her dance with a low crooning*).

PRINCESS (*singing*)

> All you sleeping in this house,
> Man and child and creeping mouse,
> Hearken to my fairy spell!

> (*Chorus*)
> Hearken to her fairy spell!

Hark, but do not wake to hear,
Be your slumber without fear,
While the dream is hovering near,
Slumber deep and well!
(*Chorus*)
Slumber deep and well!

You, dear child, for whom we wait,
Come you through the Dreamland Gate,
Listening to my fairy spell!
(*Chorus*)
Listening to her fairy spell!

Come you softly down the stair,
Of the darkness unaware,
Come to those who speak you fair
And who love you well!
(*Chorus*)
All who love you well!

(*She pauses to listen at the doorway, turns to the others and nods reassuringly, and sings softly*)

Now the dream is at its best,
Day is neither East nor West,
Come but do not break your rest,
Come, oh come!
(*Chorus*)
Come, dear dreamer, come!

(*The Princess backs away from the door, dancing still with beckoning movements as she draws Alan, who appears at the door in his night things, with his shoes and stockings in one hand and his little coat in the other.*)

ALAN (*vaguely*). I thought somebody called me. Oh—ee! (*catching sight of the tree*). Christmas-tree! (*He drops his clothes and advances, entranced, discovering the others*). Why, you are all here! (*Timid for a moment, he suddenly remembers*) Merry Christmas! Everybody!

ALL. Merry Christmas! Merry Christmas!

ALAN. Captain Kidd, and Dare-Devil Dick the Indian Fighter, and the Fairy Princess, and—and everybody. (*Wistfully*) Is that your tree?

PRINCESS. No, it's yours. See, this is what I gave you. (*Alan is overcome*).

DICK. And look-a-here, Pard. This is from me.

CAPTAIN KIDD (*thrusting his hands in the chest*). Pieces of Eight!

RED RIDING HOOD (*giving him cake*). Now sit right down and eat every bit. It's got pink icing.

ALAN (*sitting down, cake in hand, on the treasure-chest*). And who is this? I don't believe I know your story?

CLARICE. Oh, I'm Mademoiselle Clarice, the World's Bareback Empress!

ALAN (*looking at her back interestedly*). Oh! (*Wishing to be polite*) Don't you ever catch cold?

CLARICE. Well, what do you think of that? That's what comes of keepin' kids away from the circus.

ALAN. Oh—ee, circus! Oh, won't you please do a little of it now?

CLARICE. Why, sure. That's what I'm here for. Hoop-la, Toby!

(*The clown and Clarice begin their act, and one by one the others join in, doing things for Alan's entertainment, the Wizard pulling rabbits out of people's collars, etc., Captain Kidd dancing a hornpipe with Father Bear, until the boy is quite beside himself with laughter and sounds of delight. In the meantime Alan's father, who has been sitting in the background, gagged and tied, has worked the handkerchief from his mouth, and calls attention to himself with various spluttering noises. When the fun is at its height he breaks out.*)

HARDMANN. Stop, stop! I object. That's not the sort of thing I want my son to see. It's foolish, it's impractical—

ALAN. Father! (*Goes up to him.*) Why, your hands are tied!

HARDMANN. I tell you, I'll not sit here and have my son hear such things—

DICK. Easy, old scout.

ALAN. What are you doing to my father? Untie his hands!

PRINCESS. You see, my dear, we don't regard him as a suitable kind of father for a nice, imaginative boy like you—

ALAN (*almost crying*). What are you going to do with him?

CAPTAIN KIDD. Walking the plank's too good for—

DICK (*stopping him*). Why, you see, he was going to take your book away. And then where would you be without us?

RED RIDING HOOD. And he doesn't believe in Christmas!

PRINCESS. And the fairy folk don't care much about staying around a house where there isn't any Christmas, not a teenty little smidge of it.

ALAN (*laying his hand on his father's arm*). You—you mean that you won't stay if my father stays—

PRINCESS. You see, it isn't only the fairy folk who leave! There are lots of other nice things go out of a house where there isn't any Christmas—you'll find when you grow up—and lots of ugly things come in — You'll have to choose.

ALAN (*stoutly struggling with tears*). It isn't true that there isn't any Christmas in this house. There is some right here in my heart. Christmas is loving—Mammy Delia said it was. And—I love you, and I love my father—

PRINCESS. Christmas is giving, too, little boy.

ALAN (*dashing away the tears triumphantly*). Well, I was giving something, too. I was giving my father a Christmas gift. I—I'm a nawful careless little boy —an' I spot my napkin and sometimes the tablecloth—and disappoint my father. And I didn't spot them to-night. And I wasn't going to, *ever*—and I was giving it to him for a Christmas gift. (*He bursts into tears and throws himself upon his father's breast*). And I don't want him to go away, I want him to sta—ay!

(*At the boy's first sob, the story people look at one another in consternation, and at the next, all the lights but the reading-lamp go out, and they all vanish. The lights go up a little and show Alan sobbing in his father's arms in the Morris chair.*)

HARDMANN. There, there, son (*petting him*).

ALAN. Father, Father! I don't want you to go away!

HARDMANN. Why, I'm not going. I'm here, son. You've been dreaming. Hush—hush.

DELIA (*entering, in dressing-gown*). 'Scuse me, Mr. Hardmann, I thought I heard Master Alan cryin'.

HARDMANN. He's been walking in his sleep, and he's had a dream or two.

ALAN (*now fully awake and puzzled*). I thought Daddy was going away.

HARDMANN. Why, I couldn't leave you, son. I—why, I would get to be quite an old fogy without my boy—I— Isn't that so, Delia?

DELIA. Well, you suttenly was aidgin' in that direction, Mr. Hardmann.

HARDMANN. Yes, I—(*embarrassed*)—I think you'd better take him right up to bed. There are—several things I want to do (*gives her the boy*). I—suppose you couldn't tell me if the shops on this street are open, Delia?

DELIA (*as she takes Alan, now drowsing*

off again). Yes, sir, they's right smart sto's, keeps open till midnight, along of tomorrow bein' Chris'mus.

ALAN (*rousing sleepily*). Merry Christmas, Daddy.

HARDMANN. Aw—er—Merry Christmas! (*Delia bursts into a laugh which she tries discreetly, but unsuccessfully, to check as she goes out with Alan in her arms or drowsily stumbling along beside her*).

(*Left alone, Hardmann goes to the window, drawing the curtain to look up and down the street. The old woman with holly wreaths holds up one. Hardmann makes signs that he wishes to buy, opens the sash, hands out the money, and is heard to say emphatically, "Two, please." Receives the two wreaths, hangs them up in the window and hurries to the door. He stumbles over Alan's shoes and stockings, picks them up, is struck with an idea, and, timidly looking up at his wife's picture for approval, hangs up one stocking at the mantelpiece, and then hurries out at the door like a man bent on a pleasant errand. Christmas chimes are heard.*)

CURTAIN.

THE COOPER AND THE WOLVES

by Hjalmar H. Boyesen

TOLLEF KOLSTAD was a cooper, and a very skillful cooper he was said to be. He had a little son named Thor, who was as fond of his father as his father was of him. Whatever Tollef did or said, Thor was sure to imitate; if Tollef was angry and flung a piece of wood at the dog who used to come into the shop and bother him, Thor, thinking it was a manly thing to do, flung another piece at poor Hector, who ran out whimpering through the door.

Thor, of course, was not very old before he had a corner in his father's shop, where, with a small set of tools which had been especially made for him, he used to make little pails and buckets and barrels, which he sold for five or ten cents apiece, to the boys of the neighborhood. All the money earned in this way he put into a bank of tin, made like a drum, of which his mother kept the key. When he grew up, he thought, he would be a rich man.

The last weeks before Christmas are, in Norway, always the briskest season in all trades; then the farmer wants his horses shod, so that he may take his wife and children to church in his fine, swan-shaped sleigh; he wants bread and cakes made to last through the holidays, so that his servants may be able to amuse themselves and his guests may be well entertained when they call; and, above all, he wants large tubs and barrels, stoutly made of beech staves, for his beer and mead, with which he pledges every stranger who, during the festival, happens to pass his door. You may imagine, then, that at Christmas time coopers are much in demand, and that it is not to be wondered at if sometimes they are behindhand with their orders. This was unfortunately the case with Tollef Kolstad at the time when the strange thing happened which I am about to tell you. He had been at work since the early dawn, upon a huge tub or barrel, which had been ordered by Grim Berglund, the richest peasant in the parish. Grim was to give a large party on the following day (which was Christmas eve), and he had made Tollef promise to bring the barrel that same night, so that he might pour the beer into it, and have all in readiness for the holidays, when it would be wrong to do any work. It was about ten o'clock at night when Tollef made the last stroke with his hatchet on the large hollow thing, upon which every blow resounded as on a drum. He went to a neighbor and hired from him his horse and flat sleigh, and was about to start on his errand, when he heard a tiny voice calling behind him:

"Father, do take me along, too!"

"I can't, my boy. There may be wolves on the lake to-night, and they might like to eat up little boys who stay out of bed so late."

"But I am not afraid of them, Father. I have my whip and my hatchet, and I'll whip them and cut them."

Thor here made some threatening flourishes with his weapons in the air, indicating how he would give it to the wolves in case they should venture to approach him.

"Well, come along, you little rascal," said his father, laughing, and feeling rather proud of his boy's dauntless spirit. "You and I are not to be trifled with when we are angered, are we, Thor?"

"No, indeed, Father," said Thor, and clenched his little mittened fist.

Tollef then lifted him up, wrapped him warmly in his sheep-skin jacket, and put him between his knees, while he himself seized the reins and urged the horse on.

It was a glorious winter night. The snow sparkled and shone as if sprinkled with starry diamonds, the aurora borealis flashed in pale, shifting colors along the horizon, and the moon sailed calmly through a vast, dark-blue sea of air. Little Thor shouted with delight as he saw the broad expanse of glittering ice, which they were about to cross, stretching out before them like a polished shield of steel.

"Oh, Father, I wish we had taken our skates along, and pulled your barrel across on a sled," cried the boy, ecstatically.

"That I might have done, if I had had a sled large enough for the barrel," replied the father. "But then we should have been obliged to pull it up the hills on the other side."

The sleigh now struck the ice and shot forward, swinging from side to side, as the horse pulled a little unevenly. Whew! how the cold air cut in their faces. How it whizzed and howled in the tree-tops! Hark! What was that? Tollef instinctively pressed his boy more closely to him. Hush!—his heart stood still, while that of the boy, who merely felt the reflex shock of his father's agitation, hammered away the more rapidly. A terrible, long-drawn howl, as from a chorus of wild, far-away voices, came floating away over the crowns of the pine-trees.

"What was that, Father?" asked Thor, a little tremulously.

"It was wolves, my child," said Tollef, calmly.

"Are you afraid, Father?" asked the boy again.

"No, child, I am not afraid of one wolf, nor of ten wolves; but if they are in a flock of twenty or thirty, they are dangerous. And if they scent our track, as probably they will, they will be on us in five minutes."

"How will they scent our track, Father?"

"They smell us in the wind; and the wind is from us and to them, and then they howl to notify their comrades, so that they may attack us in sufficient force."

"Why don't we return home, then?" inquired the boy, still with a tolerably steady voice, but with sinking courage.

"They are behind us. Our only chance is to reach the shore before they overtake us."

The horse, sniffing the presence of wild beasts, snorted wildly as it ran, but, electrified, as it were, with the sense of danger, strained every nerve in its efforts to reach the farther shore. The howls now came nearer and nearer, and they rose with a frightful distinctness in the clear, wintry air, and resounded again from the border of the forest.

"Why don't you throw away the barrel, Father?" said Thor, who, for his father's sake, strove hard to keep brave. "Then the sleigh will run so much the faster."

"If we are overtaken, our safety is in the barrel. Fortunately, it is large enough for two, and it has no ears and will fit close to the ice."

Tollef was still calm; but, with his one disengaged arm, hugged his little son convulsively.

"Now, keep brave, my boy," he whispered in his ear. "They will soon be upon us. Give me your whip."

It just occurred to Tollef that he had heard that wolves were very suspicious, and that men had often escaped them by dragging some small object on the ground behind them. He, therefore, broke a chip from one of the hoops of the barrel, and tied it to the lash of the whip; just then he heard a short, hungry bark behind him, and turning his head, saw a pack of wolves, numbering more than a dozen, the foremost of which was within a few yards of the sleigh. He saw the red, frothy tongue hanging out of its mouth, and he smelt that penetrating, wild smell with which every one is familiar who has met a wild beast in its native haunts. While encouraging the reeking, foam-flecked horse, Tollef, who had only half faith in the experiment with the whip, watched anxiously the leader of the wolves, and observed to his astonishment that it seemed to be getting no nearer. One moment it seemed to be gaining upon them, but invariably, as soon as it reached the little chip which was dragging along the ice, this suddenly arrested its attention and immediately its speed slackened. The cooper's hope began to revive, and he thought that perhaps there was yet a possibility that they might see the morrow's sun. But his courage again began to ebb when he discovered in the distance a second pack of wolves, larger than the first, and which, with terrific speed, came running, leaping, and whirling toward them from another direction. And while this terrible discovery was breaking through his almost callous sense, he forgot, for an in-

stant, the whip, the lash of which swung under the runners of the sleigh and snapped. The horse, too, was showing signs of exhaustion, and Tollef, seeing that only one chance was left, rose up with his boy in his arms, and upsetting the barrel on a great ledge of ice, concealed himself and the child under it. Hardly had he had time to brace himself against its sides, pressing his feet against one side and his back against the other, when he heard the horse giving a wild scream, while the short, whining bark of the wolves told him that the poor beast was selling its life dearly. Then there was a desperate scratching and scraping of horseshoes, and all of a sudden the sound of galloping hoof-beats on the ice, growing fainter and fainter. The horse had evidently succeeded in breaking away from the sleigh, and was testing his speed in a race for life. Some of the wolves were apparently pursuing him, while the greater number remained to investigate the contents of the barrel. The howling and barking of these furious creatures without was now incessant. Within the barrel was pitch darkness.

"Now, keep steady!" said Tollef, feeling a sudden shock, as if a wolf had leaped against their improvised house with a view to upsetting it. He felt himself and the boy gliding a foot or two over the smooth ice, but there was no further result from the attack. A minute passed; again there came a shock, and a stronger one than the first. A long, terrible howl followed this second failure. The little boy, clutching his small cooper's hatchet in one hand, sat pale but determined in the dark, while with the other he clung to his father's arm.

"Oh, Father!" he cried, in terror, "I feel something on my back."

The father quickly struck a light, for he fortunately had a supply of matches in his pocket, and saw a wolf's paw wedged in between the ice and the rim of the barrel; and in the same instant he tore the hatchet from his son's hand and buried its edge in the ice. Then he handed the amputated paw to Thor, and said:

"Put that into your wallet, and the sheriff will pay you a reward for it. For a wolf without paws couldn't do much harm."

While he was yet speaking, a third assault upon the barrel lifted one side of it from the ice, and almost upset it. Instead of pushing against the part nearest the ice, a wolf more cunning than the rest had leaped against the upturned bottom.

You can imagine what a terrible night father and son spent together in this constant struggle with the voracious beasts, that never grew weary of attacking their hiding-place. The father was less warmly clad than the son, and, moreover, was obliged to sit on the ice, while Thor could stand erect without knocking against the bottom of the barrel; and if it had not been for the excitement of the situation, which made Tollef's blood course with unwonted rapidity, it is more than probable that the intense cold would have made him drowsy, and thus lessened his power of resistance. The warmth of his body had made a slight cavity where he was sitting, and whenever he remained a moment still, his trousers froze fast to the ice. It was only the presence of his boy that inspired him with fresh courage whenever hope seemed about to desert him.

About an hour after the flight of the horse, when five or six wolves' paws had been cut off in the same manner as the first, there was a lull in the attack, but a sudden increase of the howling, whining, yelping, and barking noise without. Tollef concluded that the wolves, maddened by the smell of blood, were attacking their wounded fellows; and as their howls

seemed to come from a short distance, he cautiously lifted one side of the barrel and peered forth; but in the same instant a snarling bark rang right in his ear, and two paws were thrust into the opening. Then came a howl of pain, and another paw was put into Thor's wallet.

But hark! What is that? It sounds like a song, or more like a hymn. The strain comes nearer and nearer, resounding from mountain to mountain, floating peacefully through the pure and still air:

"Who knows how near I am mine ending;
So quickly time doth pass away."

Tollef, in whose breast hope again was reviving, put his ear to the ice, and heard distinctly the tread of a horse and of many human feet. He listened for a minute or more, but could not discover whether the sound was coming any nearer. It occurred to him that in all probability the people, being unarmed, would have no desire to cope with a large pack of wolves, especially as to them there could be no object in it. If they saw the barrel, how could they know that there was anybody under it? He comprehended instantly that his only chance of life was in joining those people, before they were too far away. And, quickly resolved, he lifted the boy on his left arm, and grasped the hatchet in his disengaged hand. Then, with a violent thrust, he flung the barrel from over him, and ran in the direction of the sound. The wolves, as he had inferred, were lacerating their bleeding comrades; but the moment they saw him, a pack of about a dozen immediately started in pursuit. They leaped up against him on all sides, while he struck furiously about him with his small weapon. Fortunately, he had sharp steel pegs on his boots, and kept his footing well; otherwise the combat would have been a short one.

His voice, too, was powerful, and his shouts rose high above the howling of the beasts. He soon perceived that he had been observed, and he saw in the bright moonlight six or eight men running toward him. Just then, as perhaps in his joy his vigilance was for a fraction of a second relaxed, he felt a pull in the fleshy part of his right arm. He was not conscious of any sharp pain, and was astonished to see the blood flowing from an ugly wound. But he only held his boy the more tightly, while he fought and ran with the strength of despair.

Now, the men were near. He could hear their voices. But his brain was dizzy, and he saw but dimly.

"Hello, friend; don't crack my skull for my pains!" some one was shouting close to his ear, and he let his hatchet fall, and fell himself, too, prostrate on the ice.

The wolves, at the sight of the men, had retired to a safe distance, from which they watched the proceedings, as if uncertain whether to return.

As soon as Tollef had recovered some-what from his exhaustion and his loss of blood, he and his boy were placed upon a sleigh, and his wound was carefully bandaged. He now learned that his rescuers were on their way to a funeral, which was to take place on the next day, but, on account of the distance to the church, they had been obliged to start during the night. Hence their solemn mood, and their singing of funeral hymns.

After an hour's ride they reached the cooper's cottage, and were invited to rest and to share such hospitality as the house could offer. But when they were gone, Tollef clasped his sleeping boy in his arms and said to his wife: "If it had not been for him, you would have had no husband to-day. It was his little whip and toy hatchet that saved our lives."

Eleven wolves'-paws were found in Thor's wallet, and, on Christmas eve, he went to the sheriff with them and received a reward which nearly burst his old savings-bank, and compelled his mother to buy a new one.

"CHRISTMAS GIF'"

by Ralph Henry Barbour

JIMMY STROUD slammed the door behind him and joyfully assaulted his room-mate. "I got you in!" he announced triumphantly. "I worked it!"

"Hey, hold on!" protested Tom Wayne. "Got me in what?"

"Hal's Christmas party, of course. I told you about it yesterday, stupid!"

"Yes, but you didn't say anything about me!"

"Course not." Jimmy slid into a chair and beamed. "Wasn't certain I could swing it for you and didn't want you disappointed. But it's all right, old chap. Trust little James! Hal was about decided for Ted Winslow, but I fixed that. Why, shucks, Ted wouldn't fit in at all! Not in this bunch."

"Well, but—"

"Hal will be around to invite you pretty soon. Say, it's going to be some party, Tom! He was telling about this house where he lives, and I'll bet it's a corker. It's in the country, sort of, only you can get into New York in almost no time, he says. And it's got just about everything; billiard-room and skating-pond—"

"In the house?" ejaculated Tom.

"And cars and horses and—and—"

"But look here, Jimmy," the listener interrupted, "I didn't suppose you were going to—to get Hal to ask me! Do you think he really wants me?" Tom's incredulity was natural, for Hal Townsend was the acknowledged and admired leader of a considerable coterie at Embury School, of which Tom was at the best no more than a quasi-member—and that by virtue of his acquaintance with Jimmy. He couldn't help feeling flattered.

"Of course he wants you," answered Jimmy impatiently. "I had to talk you up a bit, but he came around. Besides, I showed him what a dim bulb Ted would be at a house-party. Why, gosh, I don't suppose he even owns a dress-suit!"

"I kind of wish you hadn't knocked him, though. Ted's an awfully decent sort."

"Sure, but listen, Tom. You don't get it. This is a bang-up affair. Dinners and dances and theaters. 'Evening clothes obligatory.' Where'd Ted be? He wouldn't enjoy it a bit!"

"Still," Tom murmured, "I don't see why Hal asks me."

"You don't, eh?" Jimmy chuckled. "Well, for one thing, you had a mighty good press-agent. Besides, Hal likes you anyhow. He says you know how to wear your clothes and aren't dumb. And you dance pretty well, too, and there'll be girls there. Say, what are you looking so sunk for? Gee, I thought you'd be tickled!"

"I am, Jimmy, and it was awfully decent of you to take so much trouble," answered Tom earnestly. There were occasions when he wasn't particularly enthusiastic about his room-mate, but present gratitude obliterated the memory of them. "I'd like awfully to go, too, but—oh, gosh, Jimmy, I don't see how I can!"

"Why not, for Pete's sake?" asked the other amazedly.

"Well, I—I've always been home for Christmas. I don't believe Mother would like me to be away. You see, there's just the three of us, and—no, I guess it wouldn't do, Jimmy." Tom shook his head regretfully. "Maybe if I'd known sooner I could have kind of prepared them, but it's all settled now."

"Sooner! Why, gee, it's eleven days to Christmas, Tom! What's eating you? Write home and say you've had a bid to a corking house-party and that you simply can't afford to turn it down. And you really can't, Tom. It means a lot to a fellow to be invited home by Hal Townsend. In a way it's your duty to accept. Hal's a fine chap, but if he's down on you—and don't forget that you haven't got your place on the team cinched by any means, Tom. Of course Hal isn't one of the baseball crowd, but he's a senior and he can pull a lot of strings. I don't mean that he'd do anything nasty—"

"I wouldn't be afraid of what he'd do to me," replied Tom a trifle coldly. "I'd really like to go, of course. But if I can't—well, I just can't. If he asks me I'll simply tell him how it is, and—"

"No, wait! Don't be a goof, Tom! Tell him you'll go. Then if anything happens you can get out of it later. But I don't see why your mother shouldn't let you; honest, I don't!"

"Oh, I guess she'd let me," murmured Tom, "it isn't that."

"What is it, then?"

"I'm afraid they'd be awfully disappointed, Jimmy; Mother and Ellen. They sort of look forward to having me home at Christmas, and there's been no question of

my not going, and so—well, I sort of hate to—spoil it."

"Shucks, what's one Christmas in so many? Besides, Hal's only asking us from Wednesday to Monday. That'll give you a whole week at home. Be your age, Tom!"

"That's so," replied Tom, brightening a little. "Well, I—I guess it won't do any harm to write and see how Mother feels about it."

"Course it won't! And, listen, Tom, put it strong, eh?"

The invitation came a few hours later, and Tom, although forewarned, accepted it with such evidences of embarrassment and gratitude that Hal's vanity was pleased and he concluded that perhaps, after all, he hadn't erred in allowing Jimmy Stroud to persuade him against Ted Winslow. Tom tried hard to approach that difficult letter to his mother, but it wasn't until the following afternoon that he finally got it off. And all the rest of the day, after he had dropped it in the letter-box he wished it back again.

Jimmy professed to hold it certain that Tom was to be one of the fortunate five destined to enjoy the hospitality of the Townsends, and brought frequent tidings regarding the magnificence of the Townsend home, the number of servants employed there, the plans for entertainment, and so on. "Hal says there'll be something doing every night. His father has already bought theater tickets for two shows in New York, and we're to dine in town beforehand. Then there's a dinner-dance at the Country Club on Christmas Eve, and a luncheon somewhere on Christmas Day—"

"But don't we eat at home ever?" asked Tom perplexedly.

Jimmy shrugged. "Oh, I guess so, but Hal says they dine out a lot. More fun, I dare say."

"Y-yes, but what's the good of all those servants you told about? Gee, that's a funny way to live!"

The letter from his mother didn't come until Saturday, and when it did Tom hesitated for a long minute before he opened it. But having read it he sighed with vast relief. Everything was quite all right! "Of course, dear," Mrs. Wayne wrote, "we're a little disappointed, for Ellen and I have been looking forward to seeing you for so long, but I quite understand your wish to accept such a nice invitation, and since we're to have you from Tuesday on it won't seem quite so bad. I suspect that Ellen means to write, too, dear, but you mustn't mind what she says. She is young and thoughtless, and a little upset just now. When she is older she will learn that she can't always have things her own way. I do hope you'll have a splendid time in New York, but don't let your friends keep you too long. We shall be thinking of you often on Christmas Day, my dear boy."

There was much more: news of Aunt Emmie and Uncle Marsh; of the horses and dogs and cousins and neighbors; also the announcement that Tom's presents would be awaiting him at home. But this portion Tom only skimmed over on first reading, the fact that he was free to attend Hal's party overshadowing everything else. It was only when he reread the letter that doubts assailed him. Mother had made light of her disappointment, he mused, but she wasn't fooling him. For some moments he wavered. It still wasn't too late to change his mind. But in the end he placed the letter back in its envelope and frowningly locked it away.

His sister's letter arrived the next morning. It wasn't a pleasant letter, for Ellen called him a selfish pig and several other things no more flattering; said that Mother had cried when his news had arrived; declared that for her part she didn't care a picayune if he didn't come home at all, that she hoped he'd have a perfectly beastly time in New York and that she hated him. Tom scowled considerably during the perusal and then crumpled up the agitated epistle and hurled it in the wastebasket. "She's crazy," he muttered angrily. "Wish I hadn't sent her a thing!" But it was too late now, for he had despatched his mother's present and hers the day before. They weren't as nice as he had intended, for, although this visit to the Townsends was, theoretically at least, to entail no expenditure on his part, Jimmy had reminded him that it would cost a lot in tips. "It's a quarter every time you turn around in New York," he said complacently. "And then you're expected to tip the servants when you leave. Better take plenty, Tom."

Not so easy, though, for Tom had had to buy a pair of new patent leathers, not to mention four dress collars and a tie, and these expenditures left him woefully short; moreover, there was still the price of a ticket to Carver's Run, Virginia, to be reckoned with. However, financial worries were soon forgotten in the joys of anticipation as the term neared its end and Christmas holidays drew closer. The only incident to mar that period of pleasant suspense was a near quarrel with Jimmy. They were discussing the social merits of the other three fellows whom Hal had selected for his party, comparing them with several who had been considered and passed over, when Jimmy inadvertently revealed a secret.

"He asked Bruce Ellery first of all, but Ellery turned him down," said Jimmy thoughtlessly. And then, observing Tom's expression, he tried to cover up his indiscretion, but too late.

"Bruce Ellery!" exclaimed Tom. "Jimmy, he never! You mean he actually invited *him?*"

"Sure! Why not?"

"Why—why—but Bruce Ellery! I don't see how Hal had the nerve, Jimmy!"

Jimmy bristled. "Where's the nerve?" he demanded. "I guess Ellery would have been glad to go if—if he hadn't had another date or something. He said so!"

But Tom smiled gently and shook his head. "Hal ought to have known he couldn't get *him,* Jimmy."

"Oh, you make me tired! Listen, Bruce Ellery isn't any better than Hal Townsend, even if he is so high-and-mighty!"

"Bruce Ellery," said Tom firmly, "is about everything a fellow can get to be. He's President of the Student Government, Senior Class President, President of S. D. S., Chairman—"

"Well, what of it? That doesn't—"

"And he's the only fellow in the history of the school," continued Tom inspiredly, "who ever refused a football captaincy! He won the Norton game for us—"

"Aw, rats! Now listen here—"

"And he can have his pick of Graduation Day offices—"

"He's a swell-head, if you want my opinion!"

"And I don't believe there's another fellow in school cheeky enough to do what Hal did! It's a wonder to me he didn't ask Prexy to his party!"

"That's all right," declared Jimmy irately. "Ellery was asked, and he'd have accepted too, if he could have. You're perfectly daffy about him. He makes fellows think he's the grandest thing around, but he's no better than lots of others. Hal says his folks aren't even known in New York!"

"Never mind," answered Tom loyally. "He's known here!"

It continued for another ten minutes,

at the end of which period Jimmy went out and slammed the door very hard behind him. But the disagreement was forgotten by morning.

Christmas recess began on Wednesday, the twenty-second, to last twelve days. The exodus started almost the moment that breakfast was over, and in something less than two hours nearly three hundred joyous youths took their departure. Most of them left by train, but many sped away in motor-cars, and of the latter were Hal Townsend and his five guests. There was a big limousine for the boys and a smaller car for the baggage, and no automobile that rolled away from the school that morning was so well-appointed, so immaculately shining, so impressively chauffeured as those. Tom's vacation began on a high note of luxury and never faltered from it during his stay at Valley View.

The house was enormous, and even more wonderful than Jimmy had pictured it. There were acres of grounds surrounding it. There were servants galore, indoors and out, anticipating one's every intention. And there were Mr. and Mrs. Townsend. The former was stout, jovial of manner, rather loud of voice; a man of well on toward fifty trying to look thirty-five, and almost succeeding. Tom liked Mrs. Townsend better; a tall, pretty woman, much younger than her husband, who wore beautiful clothes and much jewelry and was never still. For that matter, remaining quiet for more than a half-hour was evidently an impossibility for any one at Valley View. The boys reached the house in time for a late luncheon and then were whisked off immediately to a round of neighboring houses. Tom recalled the afternoon as a confusion of things to eat and drink, of dozens of girls, youths, and older folks, of music and impromptu dances. He returned dazed, tumbled into a bath, dressed, and went down to dinner. It had been explained by Mrs. Townsend that this first evening was to be spent quietly at home, and so subsequent proceedings rather surprised him. Fourteen persons, many of whose names he never learned, sat down at table. Later as many more arrived, appearing and disappearing bewilderingly. The music-room rug was rolled away and dancing began. Tom liked to dance, but the steps indulged in by his partners were often most disconcerting. There was a light supper at midnight, and after experimenting with two kinds of salad and a lot of strange delicacies, he stole off to bed in the big yellow-toned room which he had all to himself. He didn't fall asleep readily, but the music and voices from downstairs were still in his ears when he did.

Thursday was a day of rain, but that made little difference to the restless spirits of the house-party. Their motto was, evidently, "Never a dull moment"! Breakfast almost merged into luncheon, luncheon into tea, and tea into dinner in town. Between times Tom was sped here and there, trotted after Hal and the others, tried his hand at billiards, danced a few times, changed his clothes twice, longed for a moment's respite and failed to find it save in the big amber-hued bathtub. The party, fifteen strong, dined at a hotel, hurried to a theater to occupy three boxes, took supper at a second hostelry and finally, long after midnight, sped back over wet, glistening roads to Chesterville. Tom enjoyed the play, although he thought some of it rather silly, ate his first broiled lobster, nodded most of the way back and had horrible dreams when he got to bed.

Perhaps the lobster was to blame, not only for his dreams, but for the state of mind in which he awoke. The rain had changed in the night to snow, and the view from his window was lovely, but somehow the Christmas landscape increased rather than dissipated his depression. He sat down on the edge of his bed and looked facts in the face.

He wasn't having a good time, after all. On the contrary, he was bored and tired and rebellious and—yes, he might as well say it—homesick. Hal, in his own home, was irritatingly bossy and patronizing. Two of the other fellows, distantly admired by Tom at school, were distinctly ill-mannered. Even Jimmy was changed. He dogged Hal about and truckled to him disgustingly. The place was oppressively comfortable. Everything was soft and pillowed, and Tom longed for a hard angle once more. Besides, although he had locked his mother's letter away from sight days ago, he couldn't get it out of his mind. Nor Ellen's, either, although he discounted that; Ellen was just a crazy kid. And tomorrow was Christmas Day and no one seemed to think a thing about it here. Why, they probably wouldn't even stay at home long enough to find out! This afternoon there was a shindig somewhere and to-night they were to dine at the Country Club; and if they made him sit next to that doll-faced girl they called Pam just once more he'd—he'd—

He got up and turned the water on in the tub, taking satisfaction in the thought that he had beaten the lantern-faced valet to it. He was Spartan this morning, only tempering the icy flood with a brief flow from the hot faucet. He plunged in, shivering, dried himself on a towel so large that he became all tangled up in it, and finally emerged from the bathroom with his mind made up. He was going home.

It required courage. He hid himself in the big drawing-room with a morning paper, deaf to the summons of Jimmy and the others, and awaited the appearance of his hostess, who was seldom visible until just before luncheon. Mrs. Townsend was very nice about it, although it was plain that she considered him slightly deficient. That any one could deliberately renounce the hospitality of Valley View was strong evidence of mental failing. But she helped him break the news to Hal after luncheon, and kindly invited him to come again. Hal, after the first shock of the announcement, was pitying and ironical. Oh, of course, if Tom was bored with them he was quite right to go. Probably they couldn't hope to provide the entertainment awaiting him in—what was the place? Oh, yes—Carver's Run! Tom felt so guilty that he fairly groveled in apologies, without, however, winning forgiveness from Hal. Jimmy was, in a way, even worse, for he charged Tom with a total lack of appreciation of his efforts in his behalf, accused him of being "small-town," and finally intimated that Tom had disappointed him most terribly. He ended his tirade on a note of warning. Tom was making an enemy of Hal, and that, he declared, was dangerous.

The others apparently cared little whether Tom went or stayed. Mr. Townsend was in the city, and the deserter was spared one leave-taking. At the last Jimmy relented somewhat and offered to accompany Tom to the station—the latter had declined Mrs. Townsend's offer to have him driven to New York—but Tom refused the sacrifice and departed alone, trying to look at ease but feeling exceedingly otherwise. To increase his discomfort, he remembered that he had come away without giving a single tip, and the two dollars he slipped into the willing palm of the chauffeur at the little station failed to restore his self-respect.

It was almost four o'clock when he finally reached the Pennsylvania Station, and he had most of an hour to wait. He bought his ticket and a parlor-car seat and repaired to a bench. The station was crowded and grew more so from minute to minute. The snow had turned back to rain at noon, and the hurrying throng trailed moisture from coats and umbrellas, giving off odors of rubber and damp garments. Almost everyone was burdened with parcels, evidences of last-minute Christmas buying, and it seemed to Tom that a holiday spirit somewhat softened their irritable excitement. Suddenly he began to feel excited, too; excited and very happy. He could forget his social failure and realize that in the morning—Christmas morning—he would be at home with his mother and Ellen, good old Aunt Emmie and Uncle Marsh, and Stuart and Tug. The last two were just dogs, but they seemed most important factors of the reunion. Gee, it was great! Christmas at home!

Presently he had an idea, and, finding that the hands of his watch had hardly moved since his last inspection, surreptitiously counted his money. He mentally laid aside a dollar for his supper, twenty-five cents for the porter, a half-dollar for unforeseen incidentals, and found that he had nearly four dollars left. Afraid to leave his two bags behind, he tugged them to a distant counter and there bought two boxes of candy; very beautiful boxes bearing winter scenes and much red ribbon. It was while he was retracing his steps to his bench that the stupendous happened. Dodging through the stream of traffic he brought a suitcase into violent collision with a pair of long legs and a patiently remonstrant voice exclaimed: "Hey, feller! Look out where—" And then the tone changed and the assaulted pedestrian said, "Why, hello, Wayne!"

As Tom told himself later, you could have knocked him down with a baseball bat! For there was Bruce Ellery smiling down at him! Tom stared gasping out something made up of surprise, embarrassment and apology, and Bruce shoved him into a back-water of the stream. "Where are you off to?" he inquired. "Thought you were at Townsend's house-party."

"I am," answered Tom. "I mean I was! But—but I thought I'd go home."

"H'm, that sounds like a wise thought. When does your train go? Oh, well, you've gobs of time. Come over and sit down a minute." Tom followed, incredulous of his fortune. Why, at school if Bruce Ellery even recognized him with a smile and a nod he had been proud for hours! And here he was invited to sit and talk with him! Well, this was turning out to be a wonderful Christmas; Bruce had left his bag on a bench, something Tom wouldn't have dared, and when he had removed it there was room for them both. "So you decided to tear yourself away from the fleshpots, eh?" he asked, smiling encouragingly. "What was it like there?"

Tom started circumspectly, but was presently opening his heart. "I shouldn't have gone in the first place, you see," he ended.

"Oh, well, I can't say I blame you," replied Bruce, taking a quizzical look at the other. "Sounded pretty attractive, I guess. Where do you live, Wayne?"

Tom told him, and Bruce said, nodding, "Virginia, eh? I was in Richmond once with my father. I was only about seven or eight, I think, but I can remember it pretty clearly. It was in winter, late winter, I guess; but there was always sunlight, as I remember it. Do you suppose the sun will be shining when you get home?"

"Oh, yes," answered Tom confidently. "And not a bit like this. Maybe there'll be ice on the ponds—just a skin, you know; but it'll be right warm by ten or eleven. Gee, Virginia winters are great, Ellery!"

"Are, eh?" He looked at his watch. "Hello!" he muttered, made as though to

seize his suitcase and then relaxed again. "My train's just about pulling out," he said.

"Oh, I'm sorry! Can't you make it?"

Bruce shrugged. "Shan't try. There'll be another one after a while. This is the second I've missed since I got here. Fact is, Wayne, I'm not awfully keen on my visit. You see, I haven't any folks now. Father was killed in France. My guardian's a foggy old chap and we don't enjoy each other much. I've just spent a couple of days with him and now I'm off to my aunt's, my mother's sister. She's an estimable lady, but I can't bear the kids. There are three of them, from nine to fourteen, and they make things."

"Make things?" repeated Tom vaguely.

Bruce nodded gloomily. "Yes. Last year it was model airplanes. The Christmas before it was ships. They all do it. There's a workshop off the living-room and the house smells of glue and paint and shavings. They never do anything else, it seems. Not when I'm there. Pestiferous kids, I call 'em. Christmas at Aunt Justine's is about as merry as the Burial of Sir John Moore!"

Tom tried to think who Sir John Moore was, but didn't, because words sprang to his lips and got past before he could stop them. "Gee, I wish you could come home with me!" he exclaimed. The enormity of his offense brought the blood to his cheeks, and Bruce's startled *"What?"* added to his discomfort. Embarrassment held him, and Bruce was making the situation more painful by staring hard. Then, while Tom still struggled for speech, Bruce spoke again.

"What did you say, Wayne?" he insisted.

"I said—" Tom gulped nervously, tried a placating smile that faded almost before it was under way, and tried again. "I didn't mean to be cheeky, Ellery! I didn't think when—"

"Cheeky be hanged!" replied the big

fellow surprisingly. "Do you mean you'd really like me to go with you?"

Tom nodded silently but vehemently.

"Well, but—but what would your folks say?" Bruce sounded and looked almost excited.

"They'd love it," said Tom earnestly. "I —they've heard about you. You don't mean that—that you could, Ellery!"

"No, I don't suppose I do." Bruce sighed and settled back. "Only, you oughtn't to tempt a fellow, Wayne. Virginia sounds —well, it sounds pretty wonderful to me. If you knew Hopewell-in-the-Hills and Aunt Justine—bless her heart—and those three plaguy kids as I do, you'd understand. And—" Bruce turned a threatening scowl on his companion—"it would serve you right if I held you to it. Only," he muttered, "I shan't."

Tom never knew afterwards how he got the courage for what he did next. He actually grabbed Bruce Ellery by the arm and cried, "Quick! Let's get your parlor-car seat before they're all gone! And you can send a wire to Aunt Whose-this. We've got thirteen minutes! Oh, do hurry, *please!*"

Wonderful, miraculous things still happen in this delightful world, and perhaps, if the facts could be known, most of them happen around Christmas-time. That, at least, was Tom's conclusion as he and Bruce sped through the rain-swept darkness toward Washington. Having crossed his Rubicon, Bruce was the most delightful of companions. He still pretended to view pessimistically the effect on Tom's mother of his appearance at "Far Fields," but that didn't keep him from being very care-free and jolly. Tom found himself wondering why he had held Bruce Ellery in such awe, because when you knew him he wasn't awe-inspiring at all. He was just —well, he was just corking!

They had supper in the dining-car and made it a very merry meal. At Washington they alighted, whiled away almost two hours, and then embarked on a leisurely train for Carver's Run. Fortunately they obtained berths, even if they were uppers, and long after midnight Tom, too blissfully excited to sleep, lay and tried to realize that farther along the swaying, darkened car was Bruce Ellery! He was still trying when slumber at last claimed him.

They were awakened at dawn, dressed, and presently stepped out into a frosty world. At the end of the tiny station a weather-beaten sign proclaimed "Carver's Run." They left their bags and started off along the red clay road that rose and fell before them between broad fields. There was a good two-mile walk ahead, but they swung out briskly and merrily, Bruce proclaiming to the wide and empty world in a fine tenor that

"The old team fights till it can't fight no more,
Pilin' up, pilin' up a great big score!"

The sun came up, the stubble of the fields turned to gold, birds twittered, and a covey of quail took flight across a rail fence. The frosty clay began to yield to the warmth, and their feet skidded at times and got themselves laughed at. The sound of distant bells reached them and Bruce stopped to listen and wonder. "Christmas chimes," laughed Tom. But it sounded like fairy music until at last the big wagon came into sight and Bruce saw that the bells were on the three great black horses that drew it. "That's one of Cousin Harrison's," explained Tom, and when the wagon drew abreast, the negro driver, astride a wheel-horse, stilled the jangling bells and he and Tom exchanged news while Bruce marveled at and admired the gay caparisons.

The bells took up their pleasant song again and the big, wide-tired wheels rolled on. Trees marched across a sunny field to meet the travelers, drenched them with cool shadow for a while, and retreated. A low white house appeared on a distant rise and a column of blue smoke arose straightly against the sky. A dog barked and another answered. Tom tried to keep his voice steady. "Yonder it is," he said. "That's 'Far Fields'."

"It's lovely," answered Bruce softly.

Tom only nodded, keeping his face averted. It was so silly to have your eyes get moist at the sight of sunlit fields, a kind of tumble-down old white house, a grove of leafless trees, and the barking of a dog! But it all spelled home, and, wonder of wonders, he was coming back to it! And—why, he had almost forgotten! This was Christmas Day! He turned suddenly to cry, "Christmas gif', Bruce!"

"Say, that's right! Same to you, old man. But what's 'Christmas gift' mean?"

"Means you must give me a present, of course," Tom explained, laughing. "I said it first, you see."

"Oh, that's it, eh? The idea being to pop out on folks and yell 'Christmas gift!' before they beat you to it?"

"Yes. 'Chrismas gif' the darkies say it. You'll hear it plenty of times to-day when they begin to come around."

They turned in at a gate and followed a lane. A red-and-white setter came bounding toward them, followed no less eagerly but, of necessity, less speedily, by a basset-hound. There were joyous barks and bays, whines and yelps, and Tom's voice trying to hush the clamor. It was still no more than breakfast-time, if so late, and he wanted to walk in unannounced. Bruce had suggested sending a warning telegram from Washington, but Tom had laughingly assured him that unless they delivered it themselves it probably wouldn't reach its destination before noon. After a prolonged frenzy of welcome the dogs con-

sented to "hush up," and Tom and Bruce went on silently to the house, Bruce lagging as they reached it.

Tom tried the front door, found it unlocked as usual, and entered stealthily. A wonderful aroma of coffee almost made him gasp! He tiptoed along the hall, tried to peek in the dining-room where, as he knew from the sounds, fat old Aunt Emmie was lumbering around the table, and would have done so undetected if Stuart, the setter, hadn't gone bounding past him. Aunt Emmie gave a shout and a dish clattered to the floor.

"Miss Lizzie! Miss Lizzie! He's done come home!"

There was a startled exclamation beyond the door and then Tom was holding his mother very tightly, and an amazed but happy voice was crying: "Why, Tom! Oh, I can't believe it! My dear, dear boy, is it really you?"

"Yes'm," said Tom sort of chokily. "You see, Mother, I—I changed my mind."

Then Ellen was there, trying to kiss him, too, and Uncle Marsh, attracted by the hubbub, was scraping and bobbing at the back door and grinning all over his old black face. And Stuart and Tug barked as loud as they could.

"Oh, gee!" gasped Tom. "Bruce! Bruce, where are you?"

"Here," answered a voice from the hall, and the momentarily forgotten guest appeared. If Mrs. Wayne was surprised she kept it quite to herself, and Bruce could have no doubt of his welcome.

"And this," went on Tom, with an almost approving glance at his pretty sister, "is Ellen, Bruce."

"How do you do, Miss Wayne?" said Bruce gravely as he shook hands. "Christmas gif'!"

"Of course," said Jimmy weightily a week later, "it was a pretty rotten thing to do, Tom, and Hal was mighty sore about it, but I guess he's most over it now. If I were you, though, I'd see him and sort of—well, you know; sort of smooth him down."

"What for?" asked Tom, looking up from the bag he was unpacking.

"What for?" gasped Jimmy. "Gee whiz, you aren't crazy, are you? Why, you can't afford to have as—as influential a fellow as Hal Townsend down on you! Not if you're going to get anywhere next spring! Don't be a goof, Tom. Just drop over there and tell him—"

He was interrupted by a knock on the door, and when it opened, there, to Jimmy's amazement, stood Bruce Ellery.

"Say, Tom," announced Bruce, "I called up Wiggins on the 'phone and he says he's got a couple of pretty decent saddle nags. I told him to feed 'em some oats and we'd try 'em about four o'clock. How's that? Suit you?"

"Sure, Bruce," replied Tom. "I'd like a ride mighty well."

"Good," said the visitor, and nodded. "Meet you downstairs at quarter to four."

The door closed. Tom stole a glance at Jimmy. Jimmy's mouth was wide open and his eyes looked glazed.

A STORY OF A VERY NAUGHTY GIRL; OR, MY VISIT TO MARY JANE

from the pen of 'Lizbeth Hall

WHEN Mary Jane Hunt left Tuckertown last summer, she invited me to come to the city and make her a visit.

"If I were sure Mrs. Hunt wanted you, 'Lizbeth, I would like to have you go," said Mother, "for it's good for young folks to widen their horizon now and then, and you would enjoy seeing the sights."

I didn't care anything about my horizon, but I did want most awfully to see the sights; but, although I teased and teased, Mother wouldn't let me go.

There was a great church bother in Tuckertown that year, but our folks weren't in it. The trouble began in the choir, who couldn't agree about the tunes. On some Sundays the organist wouldn't play, and on others the singers wouldn't sing. Once, they all stopped short in the middle of "Greenland's Icy Mountains," and it was real exciting at church, for you never knew what might happen before you came out; but folks said it was disgraceful, and I suppose it was. They complained of the minister because he didn't put a stop to it; so at last he took sides with the organist, and dismissed the choir, and declared we would have congregational singing in the future. 'Most everybody thought that would be the end of the trouble; but, mercy! it was hardly the beginning! Things grew worse and worse. To begin with, the congregation wouldn't sing. You see, they had had a choir so long, people were sort of afraid to let out their voices; and besides, there was Elvira Tucker, who had studied music in Boston, just ready to make fun of them if they did. For she was one of the choir, and they were all as mad as hornets.

In fact, the whole Tucker family were offended. They said folks didn't appreciate Elvira, nor what she had done, since she returned from Boston, to raise the standard in Tuckertown. I don't know, I am sure, what they meant by that, for I never saw Elvira raise any standard; but I do know that they were real mad with the minister, and lots of people took their side and called 'emselves "Tuckerites."

You see, the Tuckers stand very high in Tuckertown, and other people try to be just as like them as they can. They were first settlers, for one thing, and have the most money, for another; and they lay down the law generally. The post-office and the station are at *their* end of the village. *They* decide when the sewing-societies shall meet, and the fairs take place, and the strawberry festivals come off. If there is to be a picnic, *they* decide when we shall go, and where we shall go, and just who shall sit in each wagon. If anybody is sick, Mrs. Tucker visits 'em just as regularly as the doctor, and she brings

317

grapes and jelly, and is very kind, though she always scolds the sick person for not dieting, or for going without her rubbers, or something of that sort. If Mother had a hand in this story, not a word of all this would go down. She says they are very public-spirited people, and that they do a great deal for Tuckertown. I suppose they do; but I've heard other people say that they domineer much more than is agreeable.

The people on the minister's side were called "Anti-Tuckerites"; but, as I said, our folks weren't in the quarrel at all. The consequence of being on the fence was, that I could not join in the fun on either side, and I think it was real mean. Every now and then, the Tuckerites would plan some lovely picnic or party, just so as not to invite the Anti-Tuckerites. Then, in turn, *they* would get up an excursion, and not invite any of the Tuckerites. Of course, *I* wasn't invited to either, and it was just as provoking as it could be.

One day, when I went to school, I found that Elvira Tucker was going to train a choir of children to take the place of the old choir.

"I went over to call on Elvira last evening," I heard Miss Green tell our schoolteacher, "and I found her at the piano playing for little Nell to sing. It was just at dusk, and they did not see me; so I stood and listened, and wondered why we couldn't have a choir of children instead of the congregational singing. Elvira said she thought it would be lovely."

Now, I had been to singing-school for two winters, and the singing-master said I had a good voice; so I thought I ought to belong to the choir.

"You can't, 'cause only Tuckerites are going to belong," said 'Melia Stone. "And your folks are just on the fence. They aren't one thing or another."

I couldn't stand being left out of all the fun any longer, so I said: "I'm as much a Tuckerite as anybody, only our folks don't approve of making so much trouble about a small affair."

"I want to know!" said Abby Ann Curtiss. "Well, I'll ask Miss Elvira if you can belong there."

Mercy me! I had jumped from the fence and found myself a Tuckerite! I was sure Mother would be real mad if she knew what I had said, for I suspected in my heart of hearts that, if *she* had jumped from the fence, she would have landed on the minister's side. I made up my mind that I would not tell her what had passed, for maybe, after all, Miss Elvira would decide that I was no real Tuckerite. But the very next day she sent word to me by Abby Ann that she would like to have me join the choir.

I told Mother that I was wanted in the children's choir because I had a good voice, and I never said a word about being a Tuckerite.

"A children's choir," said she. "That's a real good idea—a beautiful idea."

She never suspected how I was deceiving her.

Well, we had real fun practicing. That week we learned a chant and two hymns. One day Miss Green came in.

"How does *she* happen to be here?" I heard her ask Miss Elvira, with a significant look at me.

"Oh, she has a real good voice," answered Miss Elvira, laughing. "Most of the children who can sing are on the Tuckerite side. Besides, from something she said to Abby Ann, I think at heart the Halls sympathize with us."

What would my folks have said to that? I felt half sick of the whole affair, and went home and teased Mother to let me go to the city and visit Mary Jane.

I never shall forget the Sunday I sang in the choir. Miss Elvira played for us on the organ, for when the real organist heard that only the Tuckerite children were to belong to it she refused to play. Everybody seemed surprised to see me in it, and even Dr. Scott looked at me in a mournful sort of way, as if he thought the Halls had gone over to the enemy. What troubled me most, though, was the look Mother gave me when she first realized that the choir was formed only of the

But I never sang but just that once in the choir, for next Sunday I spent with Mary Jane, in Boston.

The way it happened was this. That night Mother sent me to bed right after supper, as a punishment for not telling her all about the choir before I joined it; and, as I undressed, she had a great deal to say about the defects in my character. She talked to me a long time about my faults,

"Mercy! how we did sing!"

Tuckerite children, and that she had not found it out before.

But, in spite of all this, I enjoyed the singing. We sat, a long row of us, in the singers' seats up in the gallery. After the hymn was given out and we stood up, Miss Elvira nodded to me and whispered: "Now, don't be afraid, girls. Sing as loud as you can."

Mercy! how we *did* sing! Twice as loud as the grown-up choir. Luella Howe said, afterward, that we looked as if we were trying to swallow the meeting-house.

and she went down-stairs without kissing me goodnight. I was thinking what a miserable sinner I must be, and was trying to cry about it, when I heard her go into the sitting-room and say to Father, who was reading his paper there:

"I just put 'Lizbeth to bed; but she isn't half so much to blame as some other folks. If grown people act in such a way, you can't expect much of the children. I declare, I wish I could send her away from Tuckertown till this choir-matter is settled."

"Well," says Father, "why don't you let her go and see Hunt's girl? You know she invited her, and 'Lizbeth wants to go."

"Oh, no," says Mother. "They have so much sickness there. I'm afraid she would be in the way," and she ended her sentence by shutting the door with a slam.

I got right up and sat on the stairs for a long time, to see if they would say anything more about my visiting Mary Jane, but they didn't. Father began to talk of the black heifer he had just bought, and then about the Presidential campaign, and several other unimportant things like that. Not a word about me.

But I began early the next morning and teased steadily to go and visit Mary Jane. Finally, Tuesday morning Mother said I might write Mary Jane that, if it were perfectly agreeable to her mother, I would now make them the promised visit, and, if I heard nothing to the contrary from them, would start on Friday in the early train for Boston.

Well, Tuesday passed and Wednesday came, and Thursday came, and at last— at last Friday came, and no letter from Mary Jane. My trunk was all packed. I took my best dress and my second-best dress, and most of the every-day ones, and Mother lent me her hair jewelry. I had my shade hat, and my common one, and my too-good hat. That last is one I've had for years—ever so many years,—fully two years, I guess,— and it's always too good to wear anywhere, and that's why it lasts so long. At the last, Mother declared she was sorry she had ever consented to let me go, for she was afraid Mrs. Hunt didn't like to write that my coming would be inconvenient. She declared that I ought to have written I would go if I heard that it would be agreeable.

I had fifty frights that morning before I was finally put in Deacon Hobart's care in the cars, for he, too, was going to Boston that day.

He promised my mother that, if no one was at the depot for me, he would put me in a carriage, so that I should get safely to Mrs. Hunt's house.

I was real mad to have him tag along— it would have been such fun to travel alone, and I did hope, when he stood so long on the platform talking to Father, the cars would go off without him; but he jumped on just as they were starting. However, when we finally got to Boston, and I found that nobody was waiting for me there, I was glad enough to have him with me.

I must say that, as I rode along in the carriage, I thought it was real queer and rude for no one to come to meet me; but the city was so interesting, I had forgotten about it by the time we had stopped at the Hunts' door. The house had a kind of shut-up look, and I felt queer for a moment, as I thought perhaps they were all away from home; but, just then, Mary Jane flew down the steps, and Dot came squealing behind her.

"Now, you just hush!" said Mary Jane to her, after she had kissed me. "You wake Lucy up, and see what you'll get." (She is always awful domineering to Dot, Mary Jane is.)

"Why, what's the matter with Lucy?" I asked. "Why is she asleep in the day-time?"

"Why, she is sick," said Mary Jane.

"Oh, awful sick!" cried Dot.

"'T isn't catching, though; so come right in, Beth," added Mary Jane, and in we went.

She had the hackman carry my trunk up into her room, and she went up behind him all the way, ordering him to be quiet, and slapping Dot and holding up her finger at me, and making more noise herself than all the rest of us put together.

"You see, I have to take care of everything," she said, when we were up at last. "Mother has to stay with Lucy all the time, and Dot is so thoughtless. But, what have you got in your trunk?"

"Yes, why don't you unpack?" asked Dot.

It took me some time to get to the bottom of my trunk, but I showed them everything that was in it. After that, Mary Jane said she must go and see about tea. When we got down-stairs we found the table set.

"Why! there's no preserves on it," said Mary Jane to Bridget, who tossed her head, and answered:

"Your ma didn't order any, and I won't open 'em without her telling me."

"Oh, my!" cried Mary Jane; "you are very particular just now, aren't you? You don't mind so much when your aunt's step-mother's cousin comes."

Bridget turned as red as a beet. "Now, just you take yourselves out of my kitchen!" she said, and, as true as you live, she shut the door right in my face!

"Hateful old thing!" cried Mary Jane. "Well, never mind, I'm going to the china-closet to get some. But, which do you like best, peach preserves or raspberry jam?"

"Peach preserves, o' course," answered Dot. "Everybody does."

I don't see why Dot had to say that. It was just enough, and I knew it would be, to make Mary Jane take the jam. When we went back to the dining-room, we found Susan (that's the nurse) had come in with the baby.

"Here, Mary Jane," said she, "your ma said you were to take care of Baby while I'm upstairs."

Mary Jane looked as cross as two sticks. "Oh, bother! I can't! I have Dot to take care of, and Beth and the house, and everything. Bridget ought to do that."

But just then Mr. Hunt came down. He looked real worried, but he spoke to me just as kind, and asked after the Tucker-town folks. I tried to tell him about the singing affair, but he didn't seem to take much interest, and soon went upstairs again.

"He hasn't eaten any of his supper," said Dot. "I'm going to give his jam to Baby."

The baby had been sitting in a high chair up to the table, and hadn't had a thing but a piece of graham cracker to eat. I thought he was real good.

"He can't have any jam. Here! give it to me," said Mary Jane. "I'll eat it."

Of course, at that he banged his cracker on the floor, and began to cry for the jam. But Mary Jane didn't take the slightest notice of him. She went on eating the jam as calmly as if he was asleep in his cradle. Dot had been sent out on an errand, so I tried to amuse him; but he was afraid of me, and screamed louder than before.

"Don't pay any attention to him," said Mary Jane. "I'm going to break him of screaming so much. I always longed to break him of it, and at last I've got a chance. When he finds no one takes any notice of him, he'll stop it, I guess."

While he was still screaming, Mrs. Hunt came down. She had on her wrapper, and her hair was just bobbed up, and she looked as if she hadn't slept for a month.

"Mary Jane, why don't you amuse him?" she said, after she had shaken hands with me, and had taken Baby in her arms. "You know that the noise disturbs Lucy, and yet you'll let him cry."

"It's too bad," said I. "I would amuse him, only he is afraid of me."

"Why, I'll amuse him, of course," said Mary Jane.

So her mother went upstairs again, and we had that child on our hands till seven o'clock, when Susan came and took him to bed.

The next morning I told Mary Jane that I thought I ought to go home.

"Oh no!" she begged. "You are here, and you might as well stay, and Lucy will be better soon."

"Oh," said Dot, "don't go! You can help us take care of Baby, you know."

"I don't see how I can be in your mother's way, when I hardly ever see her," said I. "Besides, it would be real mean to leave you while you are in trouble." So I decided to stay.

I should have had a splendid time of it, had it not been for the baby; but we never began any interesting play but Susan would come and leave him with us, and then he always had to be amused. I never saw such a child—never quiet a moment. They said it was because he was so bright. If I ever have a child, I hope it will be one of the stupid kind, that will sit on the floor and suck its thumb all day.

He was particularly in the way when we went to see the sights. We went to the State-house and the Art Museum, and one day Mary Jane showed me a place where they were having a baby show.

"Mercy!" said Mary Jane, "*who* would ever want to go to that?"

"Lots o' people are going in, anyhow," said Dot.

We had started on, but all at once Mary Jane stopped short. "Lizbeth," said she, "I'll tell you what. Let's take Baby to the baby show. I mean to exhibit him, and p'raps he'll take a prize, and we will have the money."

Wasn't it a splendid idea? The trouble was, we didn't know how to get in. At last, Mary Jane told the ticket-master what we wanted, and he sent for the manager.

"And so you want to put this little chap in the show," said he. "How old is he?" Mary Jane told him.

"Well, he *is* a whopper," said the man.

"Is it too late for him to get the prize?" we asked.

"Oh, he won't stand so good a chance as if he had come at first. You see, the babies are all numbered, and each person, when he goes out of the show, gives the number of the baby he thinks is the finest, and the one that has the most votes, so to speak, gets the prize. Those folks that came yesterday, you see, haven't voted for *your* baby, but then you'll have part of to-day and to-morrow."

"Why, will we have to stay all the time?" asked Mary Jane.

"No, you can take him out when you choose; but the more he is here the more votes he'll get."

"Well, if there's a prize for the baby that can cry loudest, he'll get it," said Dot.

But they didn't give any prize for that.

We gave Baby's name and address to the manager, who then took us in to the show. His number was three hundred and twelve, and a paper telling his age, and number of teeth, and so on, was tacked over the little booth where we sat.

There were lots of people in the room, but when any one came near *our* baby he cried.

"I do believe he won't get a single vote," said Mary Jane, in despair. But somebody gave him some candy, and that pacified him for a while, and ever so many persons said he was the finest child in the show. We were so encouraged, we planned just how we would spend the money, and we stayed till dinner-time, when Mary Jane thought we ought to go home.

Mrs. Hunt was real pleased that we had kept him out so long. It was a pleasant day, she said, and the air would do him good.

"We will take him out again this afternoon," said Mary Jane.

When we went back, Baby was so tired he went to sleep in Dot's lap. They looked awful cunning, and everybody raved over them; but we had to promise Dot everything under the sun to keep her quiet.

Lucy was worse that night, and the next morning Mrs. Hunt sent us right out after breakfast. We stayed at the show all day, but the baby wasn't good a bit. He screamed and kicked, and looked, oh, so red and ugly! We had to send Dot for some candy for him, and we felt worried and uncomfortable.

The doctor's carriage was at the door when we went home at last, and Mr. Hunt was walking up and down in the parlor. He called Mary Jane and Dot in, and I went upstairs, for Susan said the postman had left a letter for me. I thought it was from Mother; but it was a printed thing from the Dead-letter Office, saying that a letter for me was detained there for want of postage. It had been sent to Tuckertown, and the postmaster had forwarded it to Boston. I had spent all my money, except just enough to buy my ticket home; but I thought I would take out enough for the stamps, and borrow six cents from Mrs. Hunt. I went out right off and mailed my letter with the stamps, so as to get the other letter that was in the Dead-letter Office. When I came back I found Mary Jane crying in the hall.

Lucy was worse and the doctor had given her up.

"And I have always been so cross to her," sobbed Mary Jane.

"Yes, so you have!" put in Susan, who was coming down stairs with a tray. "I hope you'll remember now to be kinder to Dot and the baby."

"But they are so healthy," she sniffed. but she seemed to feel real bad, and it's no wonder, for Lucy is a darling! I couldn't help crying myself.

That night, poor little Three Hundred and Twelve was taken sick. Mr. Hunt and the doctor came to our room to ask what we had given him to eat, and when we told them about the candy (we didn't dare say a word about the show) they were angry enough.

I sha'n't forget that night in a hurry. I didn't think it would ever come to an end, and we both lay and cried till the sun shone into our window in the morning, when Susan came to tell us that Lucy was sleeping beautifully, and was going to get well, after all. After breakfast, we went into Mrs. Hunt's room, which was next to the nursery, where Lucy lay, and she took us all in her arms—there was room for me too—and we just cried with joy together.

The baby had got all over his colic, and Mary Jane and I had just concluded we had better tell Mrs. Hunt where we had taken him, when a letter came for Mrs. Hunt.

It was a notice that number three hundred and twelve had taken the third prize at the baby show.

It could not have come at a better time for us, for how could she scold, with Lucy coming back to life, as it were, after those dreadful hours of suspense and suffering? But I know she did scold Mary Jane afterward, for it wasn't right to keep the baby in that stuffy place when she thought he was in the fresh air; but that was after I went home, which happened a few days later.

And what do you think!—Just as the carriage came to take me to the depot, the postman left a sealed envelope from the Dead-letter Office. I opened it as the cars started, and while I was traveling home, I read the very letter Mrs. Hunt had written in answer to the one I wrote her to tell her I was about to visit them in Boston. And in that letter she had asked me to postpone my visit till some later date, on account of the illness of little Lucy!

RALPH CHANTS A DITTY

by Franklin M. Reck

WHEN Ralph Pickens gets inspired, he's pretty sure to carry the day. I think he could argue a marble statue into doing setting-up exercises.

Anyhow, he got me to go to Prince Edward Island with him. Not only that, but he talked me into passing all my final exams two weeks ahead of time so that we could leave State College the last week in May. And that's talking.

"Prince Edward Island is a paradise," he told me up in my room, where I had become slightly unconscious from organic chemistry. "It's a sparkling emerald set in the Atlantic Ocean. It's a land of beautiful trout-streams, cultivated farms, pine forests, and red cliffs dipping down into the sea."

"Swell," I murmured. "What are we going to do in paradise?"

"Catch codfish."

I woke up in alarm. But Ralph was in earnest.

"You can catch a thousand pounds a day," he asserted. "You get a cent and a half a pound. We'll earn a lot of money, have a great vacation, and fill ourselves with sea-food."

I wasn't particularly interested in sea-food, but the thought of riding the gray Atlantic every day, seeing new sights, swimming in the surf, and making money attracted me aplenty. So the last week in May, with our exams safely behind us and a slim fund of cash in our pockets, we took the train to Chicago and got on a Grand Trunk for Montreal.

It wasn't until we arrived at Charlottetown, the capital of Prince Edward Island, that I began to suspect Ralph of having some other purpose besides codfishing in planning this far-off trip. Riding in a day-coach up the St. Lawrence through Quebec, down the wild and beautiful Matapoedia valley, and through New Brunswick to Cape Tormentine, we planned and chatted until in our minds we became codfish millionaires. But the minute the train-ferry had taken us across twelve miles of rough and rolling Atlantic to the island, Ralph grew abstracted.

And when we registered at the hotel in Charlottetown for the night, I detected an excited glow in his eyes. He was humming a tune in his snappiest tenor when we signed our names:

"Casey Jones, mounted to the cabin,
  Casey Jones, with his orders in his
    hand—"

He put down the pen and looked at the room-clerk affably. "My favorite tune," he grinned. "Ever hear it before?"

"Can't say I have," replied the clerk, and I'll be blamed if Ralph's face didn't fall noticeably!

The next morning, on the train for Couris, the fishing town at the eastern end of the island, Ralph was humming it again when the conductor came through for our tickets:

"—mounted to the cabin,
And he took his farewell trip to the
    Promised Land."

The conductor smiled at us.
"That song has about a thousand verses," Ralph said casually.
"I've heard at least nine hundred," ad-

Souris," I told the official. I was getting nervous over Ralph's behavior. "How are they running this year?"
"Dunno," he said. "The fishermen are just getting their lines out."
"Hm," Ralph murmured. "I thought they started earlier than that!"
"It's a late season. There's been ice on the shore up to last week."
"Holy Smoses!" breathed Ralph. "Holy Smoses!"

" 'Just what does "Casey Jones" have to do with codfishing?' I asked."

mitted the conductor, punching our tickets.
"Where?" Ralph asked eagerly.
"I used to work in the States."
"Oh," muttered Ralph, disappointed. "Thought maybe you'd heard it up here."
"We're going to do some codfishing at

Startled, I looked at Ralph and caught him gazing at the conductor with what seemed to be pleading hope in his eyes. But the conductor merely said:
"Codfishing's always good at Souris."
Again it seemed to me that Ralph's face fell, as though he had hoped for some

kind of response to his fool expression. When the conductor had passed on, I turned to Ralph half-peeved.

"Just what does 'Casey Jones' have to do with codfishing?" I asked him. "Do you use him for bait? And is 'Holy Smoses' the patron saint of fishermen, or what?"

But Ralph didn't answer.

DURING our first two days at Souris, we were a pair of excited and busy land-lubbers. We got a room for next to nothing per week and arranged to use a small oil-burner so that we could cook our own meals. We figured it wouldn't cost us more than five dollars a week, apiece, to live, providing we ate lobster and fish most of the time.

Ralph had studied up on the art of catching cod, but we learned a lot from William Poole, who runs the general store. We learned that we'd have to set out about a mile of trawl-line, with at least 1,400 hooks on it. We learned that we'd need a buoy at each end of the line and one in the middle, and three anchors to hold the line in place. The best fishing-ground was about five miles out, where the water was twenty fathoms deep.

Mr. Poole solved the boat problem for us by renting us his for two dollars a trip. But we'd have to go out for our cod at eleven in the morning—not at six, as the rest of the fishermen did, because Mr. Poole used the boat himself at the earlier hour.

That afternoon, loaded with gear, we marched down the straggling street to the water's edge. We were in high spirits and chattering like parrots. Suddenly Ralph burst into song:

"Casey Jones, mounted to the cabin,
  Casey Jones, with his orders in his
    hand—"

Then he turned to Mr. Poole, who was going with us to show us the boat.

"Ever hear that song?" he asked.

"I don't recollect it."

Ralph seemed to bear up under the sad news better this time, and he was still talking gaily when we walked out on the long wharf.

"Here's the boat," Mr. Poole said, cutting in on Ralph's babbling. "Know how to start it?"

"Sure," Ralph replied. "I've run lots of engines."

So after a few final instructions, the storekeeper left us and we started loading things into the boat. It was a stout one, with a heavy-duty one-cylinder engine. As we worked, I began to get all excited over the prospect of chugging through those Atlantic rollers and wresting a living from the green depths.

"What you going to do with all that gear?" asked a voice.

I looked up and saw several men standing on the dock, gazing down at us. They were all dressed in oilskins, and their lined faces were the color of tanned leather. The speaker, a broad, stumpy guy with a square jaw, looked distinctly hostile.

"See if we can't catch a little cod this summer," I explained.

"Plannin' on living here?" he asked.

"Until fall," I replied. "We go back to school then."

"Going to catch all the fish you can and then leave?" he queried coldly.

"Any objections?" I asked, getting a little hot under the collar. I wondered why Ralph wasn't taking any part, and I looked around half expecting to see him preparing to jump out of the boat and swim to a more friendly spot. But instead he was gazing at the stumpy guy with a curious interest.

"The banks are crowded now," grunted the fisherman, walking away. He was followed by one of the others. The man who was left had a friendly wrinkle around his eyes. He was square-shouldered and well set up. I looked at him doubtfully.

"Don't mind Follabee," he said. "He's all right."

"Do the rest of 'em feel the way he does?" I asked, worried.

"I don't think so. Follabee's lived by himself too long. But at heart he's a good enough man."

"Has he always lived here?" asked Ralph in a tone of suppressed excitement, breaking into the conversation for the first time.

" 'Bout fifteen years, I think."

"Where'd he come from?" Ralph asked quickly.

"Don't think he's ever told anybody."

"I wonder—" Ralph began, but instead of finishing what he was wondering he started to stow buoys in the stern. I got busy myself, because we had a lot to do in the next few hours. In a couple of more minutes, after the fisherman had told us how to cut the herring into diagonal chunks for bait, we were plowing toward the end of the breakwater at a snappy five miles an hour. Beyond the breakwater, the gentle swells hit us, and before we knew it the shore began to look far away.

I acquired a funny feeling inside of me —not seasickness—but a sort of excitement like what you feel when you step to the platform for your first public speech.

I steered and Ralph stood in the front of the boat.

"I feel like a viking," he said happily. Then he swept his arm toward the horizon and I knew he was about to be seized with an attack of poetry. "Think of it! The boundless ocean, stretching out before our eyes! Away off there is England and Europe. What if we kept on going east— away from the setting sun?"

"We'd go about thirty miles and then run out of gas," I told him. "Let's catch cod instead."

All the while, I was looking back at shore. Mr. Poole had told me to set a course by two points on shore, and I had selected a little white farm-house overhanging the red cliffs and a clump of high trees on a hill, farther inland.

For about thirty minutes we steered straight out to sea on this course, and then we began to look for buoys. We passed one about fifty yards to port—a bobbing calked keg just like the ones we had in the boat. For about five minutes more we chugged along, and then we took soundings. The water was about a hundred feet deep and, after shaking hands solemnly, we let out our first anchor and moored our first buoy. Then we began paying out the long trawl, I steering my course and Ralph baiting each hook with a chunk of herring.

Before we were finished, I was feeling a lot funnier inside. I got so I couldn't bear to see Ralph bait a hook—it wasn't seasickness, but just an unwillingness to see even a dead herring cut up in that remorseless fashion. It pained me to think of his tail on one hook and his head on another, may be twenty feet away.

Ralph chattered unceasingly on the way back. He sat on the engine-housing, his eyes dancing and his round, firm body all tense. Ralph looks fat, but if you try to poke your finger in him any place, you're likely to break it. He's hard. Three years of high-school football did it.

"To-morrow at eleven," he chortled, "we go out and haul in our first cod. A thousand pounds! Enough for fifteen hundred meals of flaky, creamed—" He broke off and looked at me. "You look pale," he accused me. "You're seasick. Why don't you use a little will-power?"

I didn't bother to reply to his insult. I was steering straight for the edge of the breakwater, three miles away, and I was in one of those moods where you don't want to think about more than one thing at a time.

I felt more talkative after we'd been on shore a while, and that night, in our rooms, we visioned ourselves reaching the very pinnacle of the codfish aristocracy.

To learn, first-hand, the way to haul in a trawl, we went out at six in the morning with Mr. Poole. He's a big, knotty, large-boned man, just about as kindly as they make 'em, and he taught us a lot. The way you do is to haul up your line from the bottom and run it over the bow of the boat. The line is guided sternward by sticks set upright in the bow. Then you just haul, pulling the boat forward and unhooking each cod as you come to it. Some of 'em weigh more than eighty pounds!

Cod isn't all you get, either. Now and then you bring up a haddock, a less freckled fish than the cod, and flatfish— queer things about a foot from top to bottom and about an inch thick. On the menu they're called sole. Then again you get skates, scrapping fish shaped like a flatfish, but all gristle. Skates are a total loss, and so are starfish, with their six tentacles wrapped around the bait.

We felt like old-timers when we set out alone at eleven. I'd like to tell you how elated we were when we started hauling our own line—when the tug got heavy, and looking down into the green depths we caught the flash of a white belly! The first one must have weighed about thirty pounds, but it looked like a whale to us!

A cod is a submissive creature. He hardly struggles at all when you take him up, and when you toss him back into the boat he just heaves a big sigh, gazes at you reproachfully, and passes out without a wiggle. He seems to know, somehow, that he's destined to be creamed and eaten on potatoes.

At the dock, in the middle of the afternoon, our friendly fisherman—Mr. Poole had told us his name was John Roach— showed us how to clean the fish. Weighed in, our catch totaled 900 pounds. That was $13.50 and, deducting our costs, we figured we'd netted a profit of at least $8.00! We slept sweetly that night.

The next afternoon we came in with our boat loaded half-way to the gunwales, and when we started tossing them out on the dock, we caught the stumpy, hostile fisherman, Follabee, looking at us in a manner that made us feel uncomfortable. But the catch weighed in at 1200 pounds—$18.00—and we didn't care what Follabee thought.

The third day's catch was 1100, and we began to compare ourselves favorably with the wealthy oil and automobile magnates. Only one thing marred my joy in our good fortune. One night we called on Cliff Cox, the resort owner, and Ralph sang him about six verses of "Casey Jones."

"Aside from the fact that your voice is even less your fortune than your face," I told him later, in our room, "most people have heard 'Casey Jones' and they get practically no kick at all from hearing you repeat it. Why do you do it? You used to be a good guy."

But Ralph just rolled over and shut his eyes. I went on:

"You've sung it both to Mr. Poole and Mr. Cox. What have those two men done to you?"

No reply from Ralph, so I continued:

"Furthermore, you pretend to get excited about something, and then you bark 'Holy Smoses!' Explain yourself."

But Ralph was snoring. When a guy acts like that there's nothing much you can say, so I went to sleep myself.

THE next day we were due for a shock. Ralph steered the boat out to our line and I took a turn at hauling the trawl. Before we had pulled the boat a hundred yards I knew something was wrong. In that distance I took in only one twenty-pound cod. I pulled a couple of hundred yards more and got one skate and a haddock.

"What are you doing to 'em?" Ralph asked. "Throwin' 'em back into the water?"

"No, eating 'em," I grunted. "Didn't have enough breakfast."

It ceased to be funny before we got half through our line. In that time we had just four fish, and at the last buoy our catch wasn't more than two hundred pounds. We just sat there and looked at each other with a gone feeling in the pit of our stomachs.

"Did you bait the hooks yesterday?" I asked, knowing blamed well that he did.

I wondered if some fisherman—maybe Mr. Follabee—had taken our cod. But the more I thought about it, the more incredible it seemed that anybody would deliberately rob us.

"Probably just an off day," Ralph suggested, and I agreed with him because there was nothing else to do.

Just the same, when we chugged out past the breakwater the next day, I had a gnawing fear that our disappointment was going to be repeated. The waves were crested just a bit with white, this morning, and Ralph had a hard time steering.

I hauled the trawl again, and when we had gone a short distance, my worst fears were justified. Not a fish!

In desperation I pulled feverishly until my arms were sore, and the reward was one small cod. I quit and faced Ralph.

"Somebody's stealing our fish!" I announced emphatically. "And I'll bet it's old man Follabee. He doesn't like us and he doesn't care if we know it."

"Somebody's taking 'em, that's a cinch," Ralph agreed. "But I don't think it's Follabee."

"Why not?"

But Ralph just looked at me queerly. "I —" he started—and then shut his lips tightly.

Exasperated, I turned and started hauling. I kept it up for fifteen minutes and then stopped in disgust.

"There's no use in going on," I told Ralph, "because we won't find any fish. If we don't want our summer to be a total flop, we've got to find out who's robbing our line!"

Down in my heart, I felt sure that if anybody would do it, Follabee was our man. But how could we catch him at it? He was probably robbing us early in the morning, but we couldn't get a boat at that time because they were all in use. I suggested going to Mr. Poole, or the friendly Mr. Roach, but Ralph shook his head. I could see that he was doing some deep and painful thinking, so I waited quietly. Suddenly his face brightened.

"I know what we can do," he muttered. "Pull along until we come to the first good fish and then mark him! To-morrow, when the fishermen come in, we'll watch as they throw 'em out on the dock. See which one has the marked cod!"

"Good old Sherlock," I murmured delightedly. "That's brain-work."

I turned to and started hauling again.

The waves were choppy and the pulling was twice as hard as ordinarily, but I made the boat fairly sing through the crests. After about twenty empty hooks, I came to a good-sized fish—a forty-pounder.

"Cut a diagonal piece off his tail," Ralph suggested. "Not too big."

I did it without taking him off the hook.

THAT night we strolled over to Cox's hotel. A few tourists were beginning to arrive and we anticipated talking to somebody from the United States. About half-way there, we passed a small shack close to the road. The door was partly open and the sound of whistling floated out. Ralph stopped and grabbed my arm.

"Do you hear that?" he hissed.

"Sure," I said. "What of it?"

"He's whistling 'Casey Jones'!"

There it was again! Ralph getting mysterious about that old bromide! But before I could remonstrate, he had pushed through the little gate and entered the house. I followed.

Ralph stood near the door, facing Follabee, who was sitting in a rocker with a newspaper in his hand, looking blankly at the intruder.

"Where did you live before you came here?" Ralph asked, right out of a clear sky.

Follabee recovered from his surprise. "What business is it of yours?" he asked quietly.

But a knowing look stole into Ralph's eyes. "Did you ever sing 'Casey Jones' at a high-school concert?" he asked.

I don't know what kind of a response Ralph expected, but all he got was a blank look—just the kind of look such a question deserved. Ralph seemed to realize he was on the wrong track. For a moment he stood there, while a red flush crept up his neck, and then he stammered an awkward apology and backed out.

When we were on the street once more, I took him by the arm.

"We're not going to the hotel," I told him. "We're going back to the room and we're going to stay there until you tell me what all this tommyrot is about."

We didn't exchange a word as we walked back, and when I lit the lamp in our room I could see that Ralph looked weary.

"We're about as close to each other as two fellows can get," I told him. "Why did you come to Prince Edward Island?"

"To catch codfish," he said firmly.

"That doesn't go," I declared flatly, "and you know it. I don't like to be left out in the cold this way. Why did you come here?"

"Partly to catch cod," Ralph insisted defiantly, "and partly"—he hesitated—"to find my uncle."

"Your uncle!"

Ralph nodded. After a moment's silence he cleared his throat.

"My uncle disappeared twenty years ago."

The statement surprised me, but Ralph's queer conduct had led me to expect anything, and I waited quietly for him to go on.

"After Dad died, Uncle Walter took care of money matters for Mom. He was a bug for aviation—even in those days—and he urged Mom, against our lawyer's advice, to buy stock in an airplane company. She put nearly all her money into it."

"And the company went broke?" I asked, trying to be helpful.

"Went out of business," he said. "But that wasn't the worst of it. Our lawyer told Mom that the deal looked funny. A sort of a stock swindle, with Uncle Walter getting his share out of it.

"Mom didn't believe it, but she let the

lawyer call a little conference with just the three of them present. The old fellow sort of hemmed and hawed and talked a lot about family honor and all that. When Uncle finally got what the lawyer was driving at, he just looked at Mom, and back at the lawyer. Then, without a word, he got up and left the room. That's the last time she ever saw him. She can't forget how hurt he looked."

"But—" I started.

"During the war," Ralph went on, "the airplane company reorganized under a new name. And since then it's made a lot of money. But there wasn't anything in the papers about the reorganization and I don't suppose Uncle Walter knows anything about it. Mother's been hoping for years he'd come back."

"But why did you come *here* to look for him?" I began to feel like a detective grilling a victim, but I had to get the whole story.

"Once or twice a year we get an unsigned letter. It usually has two or three hundred-dollar bills in it—Canadian bills, wrapped in plain paper. And they're mailed from Nova Scotia."

"That's not Prince Edward Island."

"But it's not far away—just across the Northumberland Straits. Uncle Walt served two years on a coastwise boat and he used to talk about Prince Edward Island a lot—called it a paradise, a land of red cliffs dipping down into the sea, and all that."

"Same line you fed me," I murmured. "Then this vacation—"

"A shot in the dark."

"But why did you pick on Souris? Prince Edward Island is more than a hundred miles long and has a score of towns."

"Souris is on the eastern end of the island, and I had a notion Uncle Walt would pick some little town as far away as possible—where we wouldn't be likely

to look for him. Mom says he was mighty sensitive, prob'ly wouldn't ever show up until he thought the account was squared."

"But where does 'Casey Jones' come in?"

"Well," Ralph cleared his throat and half grinned. "Mom told me the story. It seems that Uncle Walt was on the program to sing 'Casey Jones' at a country-school concert. You know how it goes: 'Casey Jones, mounted to the cabin, Casey Jones with his orders in his hand, Casey Jones, mounted to the cabin and took his farewell trip to the Promised Land—'"

"Never mind!" I groaned, "I've heard it before. Go on."

"Uncle Walt got up, sang the verse and chorus through once, and couldn't remember the second verse. But his accompanist started right out and began to get ahead of him, so he couldn't do anything but sing the first verse and chorus through again. Well, he sang it through four times before the audience broke down and drowned him out. Uncle Walt used to say that experience was the making of him. And ever since, whenever he had a big job to do, he used to sing the whole song through to prove he had his wits about him. He was always humming it, Mom says.

"I figured that wherever he went he probably took a new name, and I'd have to trace him down through his favorite song or his favorite expression—'Holy Smoses!' I didn't have anything else to go by."

"Don't you even have a picture of him?"

"The only picture we have shows him at sixteen."

"What made you think Follabee was your uncle?"

"Well, he lives by himself, he doesn't talk much to anybody, he's been here about the right number of years, and when I heard him whistling that tune I thought maybe he might be. Uncle was a square-set guy. Besides, Mr. Poole told me that Follabee goes to Nova Scotia pretty often."

I whistled. Talk about slim clues! Right then I decided that there wasn't one chance in a thousand of locating the lost uncle, and that the best thing to do was to get Ralph to forget it.

"Better get some sleep," I suggested. "Our job, now, is to catch the codfish thief. If we earn enough money at this business, I'll travel all over Canada with you, singing 'Casey Jones' and shouting 'Holy Smoses!'"

And we shook hands on it.

THE next morning, at nine thirty, we were down on the dock waiting for the first fisherman to return with his catch. Two fellows we didn't know came in at ten, and we eagerly watched them toss out their fish. But we didn't see the marked cod. Then Mr. Poole came in. We knew he didn't have it. A half-dozen more and no bob-tailed fish. We weren't discouraged, because we figured that the man who hauled two lines—his own and ours— would be late.

The last two were Roach and Follabee. With a significant glance at Ralph I went over and helped Follabee tie up his boat, while Ralph went to the friendly Mr. Roach. I kept my eyes glued on each fish as it skidded on the wet boards. Right down to the last fish—and no bob-tail.

Half disappointed, I strolled over to Ralph, sure that he had discovered nothing—sure that our luckless cod was still moored to a hook five miles off-shore. But the minute I looked at his face, I knew differently. His eyes, big as saucers, were fixed on a mess of fish. I followed his gaze. And there it was—a forty-pounder with a diagonal piece cut off his tail. No mistaking it.

He looked at each other blankly, dismayed. The friendly Mr. Roach who'd showed us how to clean fish! Slowly we walked off the dock—neither of us felt like accusing him.

"He's the one," Ralph muttered when we were on shore.

"What'll we do?" I asked.

Ralph's lips were set in a firm line and I could see he was getting red-headed.

"The old hypocrite," he grated. "He said hello to me like an old friend and tossed those fish of ours out on the dock without a quiver. Let's—let's get a boat and catch him at it to-morrow morning."

"All the boats are in use," I pointed out.

We were strolling along aimlessly and found ourselves opposite the Cox Hotel. An idea struck both of us at the same time.

"Maybe Mr. Cox has a boat," Ralph ventured, and I nodded.

Mr. Cox had one, a four-cylinder, fairly speedy launch, for the convenience of his guests. In jig time we arranged to use it the next morning.

"He can't get away from us—not with us in this baby," Ralph whispered to me.

We didn't go out for our cod that afternoon—we knew it'd be no use. Instead we took a long walk east of town, along the cliffs overhanging the sea. For a long time we watched the gulls swooping down to the water and mewing at each other. Neither of us had any taste for our job— to catch, red-handed, the man who had been so thoroughly friendly in two short contacts. But it was either that or leave Souris—and we intended to stay. We loved it. Ralph's Uncle Walt had named it correctly—Paradise.

The next morning at seven, gray-eyed from lack of sleep, we purred out into the harbor from Mr. Cox's wharf. There was no sun—the sky was overcast, and the crests of the waves beyond the breakwater were curling. By this time, we figured, the fishermen would be at their buoys, commencing to haul.

The going was hard, farther out, and I found myself hanging to the gunwale. Ralph steered. As he set the course by our two points on shore, he slowed down the engine. Mr. Roach might haul his own line first. We didn't want to interrupt him until he started on ours.

The shore receded. After a while I made out, far to the east, a tiny spot. Away south, another. Neither of them near our line. Gradually, as we bucked the waves seaward, I saw another speck—squarely ahead of us. My heart began to pound furiously.

In another ten minutes, we felt certain that we had our man. A half-mile more and I knew that the boat contained Mr. Roach. Ralph's eyes were glowing with battle-light.

It seemed strange to me that as we drew close to Mr. Roach he made no move to escape, or showed any concern whatsoever.

"Hallo, boys!" he hailed. "You're out early."

There he was, calmly hauling *our* line —tossing *our* cod into his boat. Cast-iron nerve! I lost all patience with him, and so did Ralph. We drew alongside.

"What's the idea!" burst out Ralph, his voice trembling slightly.

"Which idea?" Mr. Roach asked pleasantly.

Ralph had let go the helm and the launch had turned broadside to the waves. The crest of a roller splashed against the side and drenched us both. But Ralph didn't notice it.

"The idea," sputtered Ralph, almost lurching out of the launch, "of standing there like an oily hypocrite, smiling at us, and swiping our fish—"

Mr. Roach quit hauling and watched in amazement while another wave drenched my indignant pal. Ralph was so hot I almost expected the water to sizzle when it hit him.

"You've been pulling this off for two days—coming out here and cleaning our line—and you're going to cut it out!"

I could see that Mr. Roach didn't know whether to laugh or reach over and gaff Ralph with that mean-looking hook he had in his hand. But if he did, he'd find Ralph harder to handle than a meek, fat cod. Ralph can scrap.

"You're just a common thief!" Ralph concluded.

And then Mr. Roach exploded.

"Are you trying to say that I'm taking your cod?" he boomed, and his eyes burned at Ralph so fiercely that I thought they'd singe the blond hair off his head. "Why, you fresh skate, you! Why—" For a moment he stopped, utterly dumfounded, and then he bellowed, "Why, HOLY SMOSES! You two youngsters—"

Ralph's jaw dropped. His eyes popped out. He sank back into the stern of the boat with one arm over the side. Awe crept into his eyes.

"Uncle—Uncle Walt," he said weakly. "Uncle Walt!"

At those words it was Mr. Roach's turn to stop and stare. The gaff he was holding dropped from his limp hand.

"Who—who are you?" he asked, huskily.

"Ralph Pickens," Ralph almost whispered.

"Nan Pickens's boy—my nephew?"

Mr. Roach's Adam's apple was doing its daily dozen and his hand was trembling slightly. I felt something choking my own throat, and just to be doing things I stumbled back to the helm and tried to turn the boat into the wind.

Of the two limp relatives, Mr. Roach came to life first. He quickly cast off the trawl-line, tied his boat to the stern of ours, and climbed over.

Things were explained in no time at all. Mr. Roach—Uncle Walt—hadn't been hauling our line at all. We'd been hauling his. On the two days when the catch had been so poor, Ralph had been steering the boat and he'd unerringly guided us to the wrong buoy. They all look alike. The ocean is a wide place, without traffic signs or route marks, and it's the easiest thing in the world to get a point or two off the course. Even the old-timers sometimes have trouble locating the right buoys. We had been the robbers—only we hadn't stolen much. Our own line—untouched for two days—was probably loaded with cod.

But that wasn't important anyhow. The important thing was that Ralph had found his uncle and was able to tell him that the investment he'd made for Ralph's mother had kept her in bread and butter for ten years. And all the money Uncle Walt had sent home was in a bank, waiting for him.

Gosh, it was one of the sweetest fairytales in which I ever acted. In fact we almost had a lovely ride home. Almost.

"We'll celebrate to-night," smiled Uncle Walt.

"You bet," Ralph said dreamily, sitting close to the big, stalwart fisherman.

The launch was diving up and down like an indignant bronco, only less jerky. A sudden rising—then a falling away that left your stomach suspended.

"Sure—sure will," Ralph repeated faintly.

"We'll start out with cod tongue. Did you ever eat it?" Uncle Walt said contentedly.

Ralph shook his head and looked a little pale.

"Then creamed haddock for entrée—" Ralph shut his eyes.

"Oysters, maybe. And lobsters—two or three fat ones—broiled—"

Ralph's nerveless hand fell to his lap.

"—a slice of bacon on top. And then pie. Your mother used to bake big, juicy mince-pies—"

The pies finished Ralph. Finished him with a completeness that left very little to the imagination. He felt much better when we reached shore. Good, solid ground. And eventually we had our feast. Mr. Follabee was invited because he was the man who'd mailed all those anonymous letters for Uncle Walt from Nova Scotia.

Boy, we had a wonderful summer! Uncle Walt staked us to another complete outfit and we hauled two trawls instead of one—doubled our income. We went home with $600 net profit apiece.

And before we got to Chicago, Uncle Walt had taught us thirty-nine verses of "Casey Jones."

THE INDIA-RUBBER TREE

bp William B. MacHarg

THIS yarn was told to a pea-jacket boy,
  On a wide breakwater walk,
By a short old salt with auburn hair,
And a most engaging, experienced air,
  And a tendency to talk:

———

Now, a-settin' right here on this empty
    cask,
  A-talkin' this way with you,
It'd sound kind o' queer, it seems to me,
If you was to say, "Your Majestee,"
  An' give me a bow or two.

Yet I oncet was a king (said the sailor-
    man);
  I don't look it now (said he);
But I oncet was king of a savage race
In a sort of exceedin' bewilderin' place
  In the middle of Afrikee.

I had hunderds of servants a-standin'
    around,
  Withouten a thing to do
But just keep fandin' of me with fands,
An' just continual obey the commands
  I continual told 'em to.

But I give 'em a too benif'cent rule,
  Peace bein' my only port,
An' a enemy come when the night was
    dark,
A-sailin' along in their boats of bark,
  An' a-cuttin' my kingdom short.

335

They walloped them peaceful soldiers of
    mine
  Like they didn't amount to a thing;
An' when there weren't any more to be
    found,
Why, then they started a-lookin' around,
  A-seekin' the peaceful king.

An' that peaceful king he was me, you
    know,
  An' as scared as scared could be;
An' a single soldier of dusky 'ue,
As painted his features white an' blue.
  Was all that was left with me.

An' together we flees through the forest
    thick,
  An' we flees 'crost the burnin' sand;
But a-gaining be'ind us all the w'ile,
An' a-comin' closer with every mile,
  Is a blood-stained African band.

I couldn't see no way out o' that mess,
  Not *one* way out could I see;
But that peaceful soldier of dusky 'ue,
Though there weren't much else he was
    fit to do,
  Knowed the country better 'n me,

An' after a time we come to a place
  Where trees was a-growin' round,
With their tops a-pointin' up to the sky
Maybe several feet, maybe not so high,
  An' their roots stuck into the ground.

An' in one of them trees is a little hole,
  It might be as big as a pea;
An' the soldier puts his finger inside,
An' he stretches it out till it's two foot
    wide—
  It's an injia-rubber tree!

An' in we climbs, an' the tree snaps shut,
  An' the heathens they rage an' shout;
But there we're as safe as a bug in a rug,
An' just as contented, an' just as snug,
  With a little hole to look out.

An' so I escapes them savage troops
  In a way as I'm proud to boast,
An' comes back home in the "Adam
    M'Cue";
But that peaceful soldier of dusky 'ue
  Keeps store on the Guinea Coast.

The Prince's Councilors

by Tudor Jenks

As the Prince and a Page were coming from a game of tennis, a newsboy ran along crying: "Extra—extra-a! Here y' are; extra-a! Ter'ble los' life!"

"Boy!" called the Prince.

"Extra?" asked the boy.

"Yes, please," answered the Prince, drawing a gold coin from his purse.

"I can't change that," said the boy.

"Never mind the change," said the Prince. The boy's eyes sparkled. He hastily handed over two papers, and ran off with the coin, shouting as before, while heads popped from windows and people tried to find out the news without paying for it.

Meanwhile the Prince and the Page read their papers.

EXTRA

THE PRINCESS PARAGON!
POSSIBLY PERISHING!!
ALONE AND ADRIFT!!
ROYALTY TO THE RESCUE!!!

By this time both had dropped the rackets and were reading rapidly down the big print so as to get at the facts. The finer print told the story in simple words.

The position of the Princess Paragon—at present entirely unknown—is for that very reason most alarming. With her Royal Father she this morning went sailing in their private yacht. In spite of His Majesty's well-known skill with tiller and tackle, he lost control for an instant of the stanch little vessel, and, fearing the worst, courageously jumped overboard and waded ashore, intending to bring assistance to her Royal Highness, the unfortunate Princess. Having lost one of his shoes in the wet sand, His Majesty was delayed by his efforts to find it that the yacht had drifted beyond reach of those on shore before the fishermen sent by the intrepid King could reach the beach.

Distracted by his loss, the King now most generously offers his daughter's hand and a princely dowry, also half his Kingdom (subject to a first and second mortgage), to the noble youth who shall restore to him his daughter and the valuable necklace of diamonds she wears.

We commend the quest to the young Prince and the brave youths of his court. Further particulars in the regular edition this afternoon. The boat, we learn, was fully insured.

"There!" said the page, throwing aside the paper. "That's just what I'm looking for!"

"What is that?" asked the Prince, as he folded his paper and put it in his pocket.

"An opportunity to distinguish myself—to become renowned!" said the Page, proudly.

"You shall have it," answered the Prince, graciously. "You have always served me well, and you play tennis nearly as well as I do." (The score that afternoon was six sets love in favor of the Page.)

"Then you are willing I should try this adventure?" asked the Page, in surprise.

"Certainly," replied the Prince. "I shall take you with me, of course."

"Oh!" said the Page, in quite a different tone. He had been surprised at the Prince's generosity, but now he understood it better. Then he turned to the Prince and said, "When shall you start?"

"In a few days, I think," said the Prince, as he stooped to pick up his racket. "It depends on how long it will take to decide upon the best plan, to get things ready, and to pack up my robes, and put my fleet in order."

"Indeed!" said the Page. Then he added, "As I'm quite willing to go alone, because I'm in a hurry, I think I won't wait. In fact, I'll start now."

Then, coolly turning on his heel, he walked off down the street, leaving his racket where it had fallen, and the Prince where he stood.

"His last week's wages aren't paid, either," said the Prince to himself; "and I don't believe he'll ever come back for that racket of his. Reckless boy!"

The Prince picked up the racket and went leisurely home to the palace, where he was received by two long lines of footmen, who bowed low as he entered.

There were quail on toast for supper, and the Prince was so fond of these little birds that he ate seven of them, and was so busied over it that he could not find time to say a word until he was quite done. The Queen was telling the King all about a new gown; and the King was thinking how he could persuade the treasurer that there was a little too much money instead of much too little; and the Jester was wondering what chance he might have to make a living as a farmer; and the nobles were trying to attract the King's attention; so there was hardly a word spoken at the table until the Prince was quite through with his seven small birds. Then said the Prince:

"Oh, by the way, Papa, I almost forgot to ask you something. Will you please tell the treasurer to give me three or four bags of gold to-morrow? I'm going to take a little journey."

But the King at first paid no attention.

"What did you say?" he asked, at length.

"You tell him," suggested the Prince to the Jester.

So the Jester gave the King a hasty outline of the news in the paper, and told him that the Prince thought of going in search of the Princess. The King took little interest in the story until there was mention of the three or four bags of gold. Then he awoke to animation.

"To be sure," he cried. "It is an excellent plan. I will give you an order on the treasurer for six bags of gold, and I will keep the rest so as to send out a search expedition for you when you get lost."

The King knew the treasurer would not dare refuse the money for so worthy an object as the rescue of a princess adrift. Even if the treasurer did not want to give up the money, the people would never support an economy that would keep the Prince from so worthy an expedition. Indeed, the King's order was at once obeyed, and the Prince began his preparations.

First the Prince called a council of the wisest of the court.

"I suppose you have all read the news about the Princess?" he asked, when his councilors had assembled.

"Yes," they answered.

"I am desirous of not making a blunder at the outset, and so have resolved to secure the assistance of the wisest men of the kingdom. What, then, would you advise?"

"It seems to me," said the Chief Secretary, who was so venerable that his hair and beard seemed turned to cotton-batting, "that we ought first to ascertain whether the report is confirmed."

A low murmur of assent arose from them all; and the Prince, accepting the suggestion, said: "Let us then appoint a committee of investigation. Who knows how to go about the appointing of a committee?"

After a brief pause for consideration, another old courtier arose and said that he had a neighbor who was skilled in such matters, and if they would take an adjournment for a day or two he would ascertain just how to go about it.

The Prince thought the request was very reasonable, and announced that the council would meet again in two days. So they separated, and the Prince betook himself to the tennis-courts again, this time, however, with another page. The Prince found during the games that the former page's racket was a very good one; and this reminded him that the owner of it had started to seek the lost Princess.

Suddenly stopping the game, he said to one of his attendants:

"On second thought, I think I ought not to have sent after the man who knows how to appoint a committee. Suppose you go after the man who went after him, and tell him to come back."

Away went the attendant, and the Prince returned to the palace, resolved to prosecute the search with vigor. The council was again called together, and the Prince told them that without waiting to verify the report of the loss of the Princess, he meant to seek her at once.

"But in which direction will you go?" asked the Court Geographer.

"Oh, in any direction!" said the Prince, indifferently. "There is no telling where a boat may drift to."

"In that case," said the Court Mathematician, smiling, "the chances are about one in three hundred and sixty that you will hit upon the right way. Let me show you."

So the Court Mathematician sent a page to the kitchen for some beans. Away ran the boy; only to return in a few moments with the report that the cook wished to know whether he wanted "a pint, or a quart, or how many?"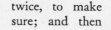

"I want three hundred and sixty white ones, and one black one," said the Mathematician.

This time the page was gone a long while. When he returned, he explained that it took the cook longer to count the beans than one would think. That they had disagreed, and had counted them twice, to make sure; and then

Some of the Councilors

had to send to the grocer's for a black bean, since there was none in the palace.

"There was no need of that," said the Mathematician, impatiently. "I can mark one of the white ones, and it will do quite as well."

So the page ran to overtake the messenger who had started for the grocer's, and meanwhile the Mathematician made an ink mark on one of the white beans, put them all into a hat, and shook them well. "Now, draw one," he said, offering the hat to the Prince.

The Prince drew one. It was the marked bean.

"Well," he said, "what does that prove?"

"It really doesn't prove anything," said the Mathematician, a little out of temper. "Try again." So the Prince returned the marked white bean to the hat, and after they were well shaken, drew again. This time he drew a plain bean.

"You see," said the Mathematician, triumphantly.

"What do I see?" asked the Prince.

"You didn't get the right one."

"But I did the first time," argued the Prince. "All your experiment proves is that I may hit it right the first time, and miss it the second, if I should try again. But if I hit it right the first time, I sha'n't have to try over again; so your rule doesn't apply. Isn't that so?"

"It does sound reasonable," answered the Mathematician, who was honest though clever.

"Perhaps you'd like to go home and try the experiment for yourself," said the Prince, kindly.

The Mathematician borrowed the beans, and went home, promising to send a written report of his trials after a few days.

"Now that we have settled the mathematical side of the question," said the Court Meteorologist, "we can go at the problem scientifically. Here is the way it appears to me, your Royal Highness."

Then the Meteorologist unrolled a map and pinned it on the wall.

"The present position of the lost Princess," said he, "depends upon the joint action of the winds and tides. The Gulf Stream has little or nothing to do with the problem, as the boat was abandoned beyond the sphere of its influence. The trade-winds for a similar reason may perhaps be disregarded. There is no question here of simoon or sirocco, and—"

"Maybe it would be as well to leave out the things that have nothing to do with it," suggested the Prince, a little impatiently.

"But how shall we know what to leave out unless we go over them to see?" asked the lecturer.

"True," said the Prince; "but as that will take some time, you might run over the list at home and report to me, say, the day after to-morrow."

"I will do so," replied the Meteorologist, rolling up his map and departing with an air of great importance.

"I don't see," remarked the Prince, uneasily, "that we are making real progress."

"There has been nothing but nonsense, so far," said a bluff old Admiral. "What I say is to take a boat and go after the young lady in shipshape style!"

The Prince was so much encouraged by this direct way of putting the matter that he let the undignified mention of the Princess pass without reproof.

"And what would you advise?" he asked the Admiral.

"Take the fastest brigantine you can find —" begun the officer; but he was interrupted.

"In a case of less importance," broke in the voice of a portly Commodore, "I should not venture to interrupt my superior officer. But here the matter admits of no false hesitation because of etiquette."

"What suggestion have you to make?" inquired the Prince.

"A brigantine," the Commodore said impressively, "is an unreliable craft at best. I say, take a frigate, at once."

"Pshaw!" broke in the Admiral explosively.

"Gentlemen," said the perplexed Prince, "I cannot presume to decide between you. I am a novice in these matters. Suppose you discuss the question fully, and report in writing?"

When the naval officers had departed, there were left only a few small fry who asked that they might have a day or two to think the whole matter over before committing themselves to a decided opinion. Upon their withdrawal, the Prince found only the Jester.

"Perhaps," said the Prince, a little sarcastically, "you have some advice to give?"

"Perhaps," replied the Jester; "but first I have a plan to suggest."

"What is that?"

"You might take a small army and go after the page who started out to seek the Princess. By the time you have come up with him, he will perhaps have found her. Then you can sail in and take her away from him, and bring her home yourself. That's the way kings and princes often do."

"But that seems hardly fair," said the Prince, after a few moments' reflection.

"Of course it isn't fair," said the Jester; "but it's your only chance. I have no doubt he has found the Princess long ago."

"Do you think so?" asked the Prince.

"No doubt of it," said the Jester. "You see, he didn't wait for any advice, but started off at once."

"Isn't advice a good thing?"

"Yes," said the Jester, "for lawyers and councilors. They make their living by it. Advice is good, when it's good; but the best qualities are hard to find, and the time it takes to find them is sometimes worth more than the advice when found."

"Then you wouldn't advise me to take advice?" said the Prince, thoughtfully.

"My advice is," said the Jester, "don't take mine, or anybody's."

"Isn't that rather a difficult course to follow?" asked the Prince, after a momen's reflection.

"Very," the Jester agreed.

"I think," the Prince went on, "that I shall start now, and take my chances."

"I'll go with you," replied his companion.

So they started toward the palace gate; but just as they reached it and had called for the gate-keeper, there came a summons from without. When the gate was opened there was the Page. He seemed weary, and his shoes showed that he had traveled a long way on foot.

"Did you find the Princess?" asked the Prince, eagerly.

"Yes," said the Page, very calmly. "I found her."

"Fortunate boy!" said the Prince, a little enviously.

"I don't know about that," said the Page. "She was as cross as two sticks about having been left to go adrift. It rained, you know; and when I rowed out to the yacht, I found that everything on board was soaking wet, and she hadn't had anything to eat for two days, and—my goodness!—she was hopping mad!"

"What did she say?" asked the Jester.

"She said she'd like to box my ears," said the Page, earnestly. "Then I told her if she wasn't more polite I wouldn't rescue her. That quieted her, quick! So then she didn't say anything, but she looked about as pleasant as cold gravy. As soon as I towed the boat ashore, she gave me some money and told me to get along home. So I did, and I was glad to get away. I didn't tell her who I was, and I don't think she will ever find me. You won't tell, will you?" pleaded the Page, as he finished.

"No," said the Prince, laughing. "I won't tell. But perhaps you didn't treat the Princess with proper courtesy. No wonder she was out of humor, after being adrift so long."

"I'll tell you," said the Page, suddenly, "what we'll do. I found the Princess, and I suppose I'm entitled to the reward. Now, can't you arrange it that you'll marry the Princess? I think she'll just suit you. She is a fine-looking Princess, and I don't believe she meant to be cross. Do you think you can arrange it? It would be a splendid thing for the kingdom, you know. It would unite the two kingdoms, and there'd be all sorts of advantages. You can say that I went with your permission, you know, and that I'm engaged to be married, and wouldn't presume to aspire to a princess's hand."

"It's a good suggestion," said the Jester; "for otherwise there'll be war, of course. The other king will be bound to know why this young man won't accept his daughter's hand, and then there'll be a lot of diplomatic correspondence, ultimatums, protocols, and all sorts of goings-on. If you don't mind, I think you would do well to marry this Princess."

"I don't mind at all," answered the Prince; "and I think I'll write a letter to her this very day. But how," he went on, turning to the Page, "did you come to be engaged? I didn't know anything about it."

"The fact is," said the Page, "I'm not quite engaged; but there's one of the maids of honor who will have me, I'm sure. She told me the other day that she wished it was leap-year every day; and I think that's a distinct encouragement, don't you?"

His friend agreed that it was a marked observation.

"You'll be safe for a day or two," remarked the Jester to the Page; "and meanwhile you can be getting your clothes brushed and your shoes mended. The Prince will write to-day."

Early on the following morning, as the Prince came down to breakfast, he was told that a deputation was awaiting him in the Council-Room. "Who are they?" he asked.

"The Councilors with their reports," answered the messenger.

"But," said the Prince, "they are—"

"Hush!" said the Jester; "let us not lose their words of wisdom."

"Very well," the Prince agreed, smiling. So the Prince, the Jester, and the Page entered the room where the Council were assembled. All bowed profoundly.

"Your Royal Highness," began the Secretary, "in order to verify the report of the loss of the Princess, I sent an inquiry to a friend of mine who stands very high in favor at her father's court. It was thus worded: 'Is the Royal Princess absent from the Court?' And I have his sealed reply: 'She is not.' That I consider conclusive. Is it not?"

"Yes," said the Jester; "it is not."

"I have no doubt," said the Prince, "that your information is correct; and I thank you for your diligence."

The Secretary bowed and was seated.

"I," began the Meteorologist, "have prepared a list of the things that may be disregarded in the search. It contains 872 items, with two appendices and voluminous notes. I will read it."

"Never mind," said the Prince, very graciously. "I will order it filed in the Royal Archives. We will now listen to the Mathematician."

"I have tried the bean-experiment several hundreds of times," said the Mathematician, "and have not yet succeeded in drawing the marked bean. The formula of chances I have worked out. I find that 'If

"I am not prepared to dispute you," said the Prince, "and I will ask leave therefore to express my indebtedness to you."

The Councilors return to the palace with their reports

Henry puts 360 white beans into a hat, and John draws a good many times, no one can tell whether he will draw the marked bean the first time, or not at all.' I consider that an exact statement of the matter."

"We," said the Admiral, speaking for himself and the Commodore, "I regret to say, have as yet arrived at nothing more advanced than a compromise. We have agreed to recommend a squadron composed of equal numbers of brigantines and frigates. Thus you will secure the advantages of both forms of craft."

"A wise conclusion," said the Prince; "and I gladly offer to you both my fervent gratitude."

A few of the smaller fry of Councilors yet remained to be heard, but the Prince announced that he had bestowed upon each councilor The Order of the Brazen Owl. But, as he was about to leave the room, the Councilors, after a moment's consultation, begged permission to ask a question. It was granted.

"We should like to know what use Your Highness wished to make of the information we have furnished?"

"To find the Princess who was lost," answered the Prince.

"Oh, yes," said the Councilors' spokesman. "We had forgotten what it was all about. But it's of no consequence now."

"No," said the Prince; "she is rescued."

"Indeed?" said the Councilors, with polite interest. Then they put on their cloaks, and went their several ways, all reading their reports to one another, and none listening.

The Prince and Princess were married soon after, and the Page and the Maid of Honor were best man and bridesmaid.

The Prince pensioned the Councilors and sent them to America. They all sailed in one ship. The vessel is several days overdue, but undoubtedly will arrive in safety after the Admiral and the Commodore have settled a little difference of opinion as to where they had better land.

The Page and the Maid of Honor are married, and keep a candy-store where they sell a dollar's worth of candy for five cents. They sent me the address, but you'll be sorry to learn that I have mislaid it.

IN THE KNOB MOUNTAIN TOWER

by Merritt P. Allen

As far back as he could remember, Ray Rand had loved the woods; and about the time he was ten years old he had decided to spend his life in them. This determination did not waver as time advanced; but from his early dreams of being a hermit or a trapper, he turned to an earnest, whole-hearted desire to enter the forestry service, not as a second-rate man, but as a college graduate with an M.F. (Master of Forestry) after his name.

It takes money to go to college, especially to a high-class forestry college, and there was very, very little money in the Rand family. Ray was seventeen when he graduated from high school, a time when a boy's life must necessarily take a turn, for he either goes to college then or he never goes, as a rule. Sometimes circumstances force the decision, but more often it depends on the boy himself.

When Ray graduated he had less than ten dollars of his own, but he had an abundance of clean, solid grit. Searching the papers for a summer's job, he found an announcement by the chief forester of the Adirondack Mountain region that a man was wanted to watch for forest fires from the Knob Mountain lookout-station. The salary was one hundred dollars a month and camp. It sounded good, and eventually Ray appeared in the chief forester's office.

"What can I do for you?" the broad-shouldered, keen-eyed official asked.

"I am applying for the Knob Mountain job."

"Know what it is like?"

"No, sir; but I think I can watch for fires."

"It is a man-sized job, son. The work isn't much, but it is the solitude that gets you, unless you like it. I seldom get a man to stay the season through. It is seven miles straight back in the woods. There are no camps near, and you are not allowed to leave your post night or day. There is a telephone, but you don't use it for pleasure, since it only runs to this office. Twice a month we send a man up with supplies, and I drop in occasionally; you will probably see no other persons until you come out in the fall."

"I like the woods," Ray said. "I shouldn't be lonesome."

The chief looked doubtful. "Why not get a pal to go with you?" he suggested. "You could make a camping-trip out of it and have considerable fun, alternate the work and divide the wages."

Ray shook his head. "I need all the money," he said.

The chief's face became thoughtful, for he had once been a boy in need of money. "What's the idea?" he asked kindly.

Ray told him.

The chief smiled. "Want to enter the service, eh? Well, that puts a different face on the matter. I guess, after all, there is no reason why you shouldn't have the job."

Within a week, Ray was established on Knob Mountain with two weeks' provisions, a few books, a clock, a camera, and a light rifle of his own, besides the professional equipment provided by the service. His camp was the watch-tower itself. It was of steel, round, and rose twenty feet above the rocks of the mountain peak. The ground floor was a tiny kitchen, the next a sleeping-room, and the third and top, the observation-post. Such a view! On clear days Ray could see through the binoculars hundreds and thousands of acres of land and water, deep forest for the most part, except for occasional small valley clearings and lakes, and on the east, the long, glistening expanse of Lake Champlain. When the sun was just right, the spires of Montreal glistened a hundred and more miles to the north; and at night, lights, none nearer than seven miles, twinkled here and there below.

Over this mighty tract it was Ray's duty to watch and, should smoke appear, to locate it as best he could on his maps and telephone the news to the chief's office. There was plenty of rain that season, and he had but two small fires to report.

The chief called up frequently, partly to keep in touch with the boy to whom he had taken a fancy, and partly in an attempt to catch him away from his post. But he never did; for though Ray longed to steal away for a ramble in the woods, he always kept within sound of the telephone-bell as he had promised to do. A man came up with fresh supplies once a fortnight, and the chief dropped in unannounced three or four times; but aside from them, Ray saw no one except at a distance through the glasses.

On a sleepy afternoon in August, the chief was on the wire. "I am going to be away for a few days," he said, among other things. "If anything happens, ask for Mr. Adams, who will be in charge here."

"Yes, sir," Ray answered. And after more talk, he asked as usual, "Any news?"

"No. Oh, yes! the Lake Placid bank was robbed last night of a hundred thousand in cash. The police think the thieves got away through Malone. That's all. Goodby."

Lake Placid, the famous summer resort, was not so very far away, about fifteen miles through the woods to the southwest, but hidden from the Knob tower by an interposing mountain. The robbery was of no consequence to Ray, but for some reason it was so much in his thoughts after that, that at first he believed it to be a dream when he was awakened in the night by a light and opened his eyes to see three men in his room, one with a drawn revolver.

"Get up," the man commanded, "and find us some grub."

"Who are you?" Ray asked, knowing it was no dream.

"Never mind that."

Ray looked about quickly.

"We've got your rifle," the man said. "No use making a fuss. Get up!"

Ray got up, dressed, and went downstairs between two of the men. Without a word, he set out some provisions, and the men ate hungrily, one of them standing guard at the door and all of them casting frequent glances at three canvas packs on the floor. When they finished, dawn was breaking, and he could see their faces better—cruel, hard faces.

"Climb!" the leader said suddenly, pointing up the stairs with his revolver. "Go clean to the top and stay there, or I'll shoot you down like a hedgehog." And there was no doubt but that he meant it.

Ray went up the stairs obediently, for there was nothing else to do; he stood no show against three armed men.

"He can't signal from there, can he?" one asked anxiously.

"No," another answered. "Nothing there but the 'phone. I know these places."

Ray went up through his bedroom to the observation-post, and, looking through the window, saw, as he expected to, the severed telephone-wires dangling from their rock-propped pole a hundred feet away. He went back to the head of the stairs. The two flights were in line, so that from where he stood, he could look directly down on the table on the ground floor. The men were dumping the three canvas packs upon the table—and those packs were full of money. Gold, silver, but mostly bank-notes, lay in a great pile. The leader glanced up suddenly, saw Ray, and, quick as lightning, snatched his gun and fired. The bullet missed the boy by a few inches, glanced from the steel roof over his head, and crashed through a window. Not a word was said, and none was necessary. Ray tumbled back out of range and sat down.

He had seen enough, though, to tell him that those men were the bank-robbers who, instead of going through Malone, had fled straight into the woods. While the police were searching every car on the highways and railways, the bandits were counting their loot on the mountain-top. Only one person besides themselves knew this, and that one was cooped up in the top of a steel tower, helpless.

There was no possible way of getting down, for the outside of the tower was smooth, and to jump the twenty feet to the rocks below would mean a broken leg if nothing more. There was nothing to do but wait; so he waited. If only some one would happen along! He took up his post by the window, and about noon could scarcely believe his eyes when up the trail came the man who brought his supplies.

Regardless of the circumstances, Ray leaned as far out as he dared and shouted wildly: "The men who robbed the Lake Placid bank are downstairs. They will shoot. Run!"

The man stopped in his tracks, then came on again; and out of the tower door calmly walked the leader to meet him. They were in league!

Ray sank back in dismay. His last hope was gone. There was not one chance in a thousand that another person would come that way. How long would the bandits stay in the tower? What would they do with him? They dare not let him go. Would they kill him? They looked capable of it. Whatever they did, it would not be pleasant.

Ray could hear them talking, and, dropping flat on the floor, put his ear as near the head of the stairs as he dared and listened. The supply man was relating how the search was progressing, which was the very reason for which he had been planted in the village below. The fact that they were supposed to have gone west or north pleased the men immensely, and in louder and more confident tones they began outlining their plans. At dark they would go down into separate valleys, and the next day, passing as trampers, would go to the nearest railroad points and get away by train. The supply man would go back as usual, but would soon receive a telegram saying that his brother was dead in New York, after which, of course, he might be expected to depart hurriedly. "And the boy?" some one asked. They would tie him up and leave him, they decided. It might mean his death by starvation, but they couldn't help it. Ray shivered.

After a while the supply man left the others and came up the two flights of stairs.

"Make out a list of the things you want brought up next time," he said. "I'm going down about three o'clock."

He made no attempt to explain his friendship with the bandits. Ray wondered if the man thought him fool enough to be unable to put two and two together. At any rate, he decided to be as taciturn as the next one and merely agreed to have the list ready.

The man went downstairs again, and shortly after, Ray heard the tower door shut and the key turn on the outside. Looking down from his window he saw the supply man and two others spreading blankets and coats on the rocks in the shade of the tower. They were tired after their night's work and lay down heavily. Evidently the leader preferred a softer couch, for Ray heard him coming up the first flight of stairs; then the cot in the tiny bedroom creaked, and soon all was still below.

The boy sat down to think, and decided that rather than be tied in the tower to die by inches, perhaps, he would jump to the rocks, when the time came, and take his chances, slim as they were. As he laid his plans the only sound was the ticking of his alarm-clock on a shelf beside him. It was a very small clock, which he had bought because it could be easily packed up the mountain, thicker, but not much more in diameter, than a watch. It had a modest tick, for a clock, but when it was aroused, it *would* ring!

Ray's thoughts turned idly to this clock; and of a sudden he had an idea. He pondered it for a full two minutes, then, looking down again and making sure that the men outside the tower were sound asleep, he stole to the stairs and peered into his bedroom. The bandit leader was sleeping furiously. The boy went back for the clock and holding it carefully in his hands, began descending the stairs very, very cautiously. His heart was in his throat, for he knew that if he awoke the man, he might be shot. He reached the floor, and, not daring to pause, so precious was every fraction of a second, crept past the cot on his tiptoes and so on down to the ground floor.

The three packs full of money were on the table and he had a great desire to open them, but he knew that time was more precious than money, and went about his work. Moving silently as a ghost, he took down a good-sized tin can partly full of dried hulled corn, emptied two thirds of the corn out on the table, leveled off the remainder inside the can, and on this corn placed an empty cocoa can. Taking a pencil and a leaf from his note-book, he wrote:

The three men who robbed the Lake Placid bank are in the Knob tower with the money. They will leave at dark, separately, for railroad stations. The man who brings me supplies is in with them and will get away to-night if you don't nab him. Telephone wires are cut and I am a prisoner in the tower.   RAY RAND.

This note he placed in the small can inside the larger one, then, taking up the little clock, he wound it and set the alarm at half-past five. Smiling a little, he placed the clock upon the note, put the cover on the cocoa can, then proceeded to bury it completely with the corn from the table. He felt the weight of the large can in his hands, held it close to his ear in an attempt to detect the clock's ticking, then set it back on the shelf, confident that no one could guess that it contained anything but the article advertised on its outside. Three minutes later he was safely back upstairs.

"Got that list ready?" the supply man called up from the kitchen an hour later.

Ray dropped it down to the man, who eyed it sharply to see that it contained no hidden message, then put it in his pocket.

"I wish that you would take back that package of hulled corn and tell the merchant you got it of that I ordered popcorn," Ray said to him.

"I ain't going to fuss with that," the man growled.

"Take it along," the leader commanded. "It will make things look more natural."

"Well, where is it?"

Ray directed him to the shelf and held his breath while he took down the can and thrust it into his pack-basket. But the man suspected nothing and soon started away.

It was already dark in the valleys when the bandit chief ordered Ray to come down. As the boy stepped into the kitchen he was seized, and in two minutes was bound hand and foot and laid on the floor.

"You're a gritty chap," the leader said, standing over him in the darkness. "I hate to leave you this way, but we must get away and don't want you telling what you know too soon. If things go right, I may be able to send you help in two or three days. I will leave a dish of water and some food on the floor and perhaps you can get enough of it to keep you going."

Two or three days or a week to remain bound, with only a little food and water picked off the floor, dog fashion! He might never be found until it was too late. He wished then that he had jumped to the rocks as he had planned.

"We'll be moving," the bandit said to the others. "You know where to go from here."

Silently they picked up their precious packs and stepped out into the darkness. Then came the sound of many feet, blows, a couple of shots, and presently a big voice boomed:

"Got 'em tied up, boys? Anybody hurt? Good! Now where's Rand?"

"Here!" Ray shouted, "inside!"

Two electric torches flashed through the doorway. A man wearing a sheriff's badge entered and cut Ray's bonds.

"There's your friends," he said, pointing outside, where the robbers were nicely handcuffed and guarded by a dozen men. "We got the other one down in the village. Found your note, you see. And say! that was a mighty bright idea fixing the alarm-clock as you did. I happened to be in the store when the fellow brought in that hulled corn. The clerk set it back on the shelf, and a few minutes later—*rippity bang!* We couldn't think what was up till we dug into the corn and found the little clock going like a cyclone. And there was the note under it! Best thing I ever heard of. Say, I guess you'll come in for a fat slice of the reward."

Ray did come in for his share of it, and later, after the chief had heard the story, he received a scholarship to a forestry school that is second to none. He is there now.

TOM SAWYER ABROAD

by Huck Finn. Edited by Mark Twain

CHAPTER X

Tom said it happened like this.

A dervish was stumping it along through the desert, on foot, one blazing hot day, and he had come a thousand miles and was pretty poor, and hungry, and ornery and tired, and along about where we are now, he run across a camel-driver with a hundred camels, and asked him for some alms. But the camel-driver he asked to be excused. The dervish says—

"Don't you own these camels?"

"Yes, they're mine."

"Are you in debt?"

"Who—me? No."

"Well, a man that owns a hundred camels and ain't in debt, is rich—and not only rich, but very rich. Ain't it so?"

The camel-driver owned up that it was so. Then the dervish says—

"Allah has made you rich, and He has made me poor. He has His reasons, and they are wise, blessed be His name. But He has willed that His rich shall help His poor, and you have turned away from me, your brother, in my need, and He will remember this, and you will lose by it."

That made the camel-driver feel shaky, but all the same he was born hungry after money and didn't like to let go a cent, so he begun to whine and explain, and said times was hard, and although he had took a full freight down to Balsora and got a fat rate for it, he couldn't git no return freight, and so he warn't making no great things out of his trip. So the dervish starts along again, and says—

"All right, if you want to take the risk, but I reckon you've made a mistake this time, and missed a chance."

Of course the camel-driver wanted to know what kind of a chance he had missed, because maybe there was money in it; so he run after the dervish and begged him so hard and earnest to take pity on him and tell him, that at last the dervish give in, and says—

"Do you see that hill yonder? Well, in that hill is all the treasures of the earth, and I was looking around for a man with a particular good kind heart and a noble generous disposition, because if I could find just that man, I've got a kind of salve I could put on his eyes and he could see the treasures and get them out."

So then the camel-driver was in a state; and he cried, and begged, and took on, and went down on his knees, and said he was just that kind of a man, and said he could fetch a thousand people that would say he wasn't ever described so exact before.

"Well, then," says the dervish, "all right. If we load the hundred camels, can I have half of them?"

The driver was so glad he couldn't hardly hold in, and says—

"Now you're shouting."

So they shook hands on the bargain, and the dervish got out his box and rubbed the salve on the driver's right eye, and the hill opened and he went in, and there, sure enough, was piles and piles of gold and jewels sparkling like all the stars in heaven had fell down.

So him and the dervish laid into it and they loaded every camel till he couldn't carry no more, then they said good-by, and each of them started off with his fifty. But pretty soon the camel-driver came a-running and overtook the dervish and says—

"You ain't in society, you know, and you don't really need all you've got. Won't you be good, and let me have ten of your camels?"

"Well," the dervish says, "I don't know but what you say is reasonable enough."

So he done it, and they separated and the dervish started off again with his forty. But pretty soon here comes the camel-driver bawling after him again, and whines and whimpers around and begs another ten off of him, saying thirty camel-loads of treasures was enough to see a dervish through, because they live very simple, you know, and don't keep house but board around and give their note.

But that warn't the end, yet. That camel-driver kept coming and coming till he had begged back all the camels and had the whole hundred. Then he was satisfied, and ever so grateful, and said he wouldn't ever forgit the dervish as long as he lived, and nobody hadn't ever been so good to him before, and liberal. So they shook hands good-by, and separated and started off again.

But do you know, it warn't ten minutes till the camel-driver was unsatisfied again —he was the lowdownest reptyle in seven counties—and he come a-running again. And this time the thing he wanted was to get the dervish to rub some of the salve on his other eye.

"Why?" said the dervish.

"Oh, you know," says the driver.

"Know what?" says the dervish.

Says the driver—

"Well, you can't fool me. You're trying to keep back something from me, you know it mighty well. You know, I reckon, that if I had the salve on the other eye I could see a lot more things that's valuable. Come—please put it on."

The dervish says—

"I wasn't keeping anything back from you. I don't mind telling you what would happen if I put it on. You'd never see again. You'd be stone blind the rest of your days."

But do you know, that beat wouldn't believe him. No, he begged and begged, and whined and cried, till at last the dervish opened his box and told him to put it on, if he wanted to. So the man done it, and sure enough he was as blind as a bat, in a minute.

Then the dervish laughed at him and mocked at him and made fun of him; and says—

"Good-by—a man that's blind hain't got no use for jewelry."

And he cleared out with the hundred camels, and left that man to wander around poor and miserable and friendless the rest of his days in the desert.

Jim said he'd bet it was a lesson to him.

"Yes," Tom says, "and like a considerable many lessons a body gets. They ain't no account, because the thing don't ever happen the same way again—and can't. The time Hen Scovil fell down the chimbly and crippled his back for life, everybody said it would be a lesson to him. What kind of a lesson? How was he going to use it? He couldn't climb chimblies no more, and he hadn't no more backs to break."

"All de same, Mars Tom," Jim said, "dey *is* sich a thing as learnin' by expe'ence. De Good Book say de burnt chile shun de fire."

"Well, I ain't denying that a thing's a lesson if it's a thing that can happen twice just the same way. There's lots of such things, and *they* educate a person, that's what Uncle Abner always said; but there's forty *million* lots of the other kind—the kind that don't happen the same way twice —and they ain't no real use, they ain't no more instructive than the smallpox. When you've got it, it ain't no good to find out you ought to been vaccinated, and it ain't no good to get vaccinated afterwards, because the smallpox don't come but once. But on the other hand Uncle Abner said that a person that had took a bull by the tail once had learnt sixty or seventy times as much as a person that hadn't, and said a person that started in to carry a cat home by the tail was gitting knowledge that was always going to be useful to him, and warn't ever going to grow dim or doubtful. But I can just tell you, Jim, Uncle Abner was down on them people that's all the time trying to dig a lesson out of everything that happens, no matter whether—"

But Jim was asleep. Tom looked kind of ashamed, because you know a person always feels bad when he is talking uncommon fine and thinks the other person is admiring, and that other person goes to sleep that way. Of course he oughtn't to go to sleep, because it's shabby; but the finer a person talks the certainer it is to make you sleep, and so when you come to look at it it ain't nobody's fault in particlar, both of them's to blame.

Jim begun to snore—soft and easy-like, at first, then a long rasp, then a stronger one, then a half a dozen horrible ones like the last water sucking down the plug-hole of a bathtub, then the same with more power to it. And when the person has got to that point he is at his level best, and can wake up a man in the next block, but can't wake himself up although all that awful noise of his'n ain't but three inches from his own ears. And that is the curiosest thing in the world, seems to me. But you rake a match to light the candle, and that little bit of a noise will fetch him. I wish I knowed what was the reason of that, but there don't seem to be no way to find out. Now there was Jim alarming the whole Desert, and yanking the animals out for miles and miles around, to see what in the nation was going on up there; there warn't nobody nor nothing that was as close to the noise as *he* was, and yet he was the only cretur that wasn't anyways disturbed by it.

We yelled at him and whooped at him, it never done no good, but the first time there come a little wee noise that wasn't of a usual kind it woke him up. No, sir, I've thought it all over, and so has Tom, and there ain't no way to find out why a snorer can't hear himself snore.

Jim said he hadn't been asleep, he just shut his eyes so he could listen better.

Tom said nobody warn't accusing him.

That made him look like he wished he hadn't said anything. And he wanted to git away from the subject, I reckon, because he begun to abuse the camel-driver, just the way a person does when he has got catched in something and wants to take it out of somebody else. He lit into the camel-driver the hardest he knowed how, and I had to agree with him; and he praised up the dervish the highest he could, and I had to agree with him there, too. But Tom says—

"I ain't so sure. You call that dervish so dreadful liberal and good and unselfish, but I don't quite see it. He didn't hunt up another poor dervish, did he? No, he didn't. If he was so unselfish, why didn't he go in there himself and take a pocket-full of jewels and go along and be satisfied? No, sir, the person he was hunting for was a man with a hundred camels. He wanted to get away with all the treasure he could."

"Why, Mars Tom, the dervish was willin' to divide, fair and square; he only struck for fifty camels."

"Because he knowed how he was going to get all of them by and by."

"Mars Tom, he *tole* de man de truck would make him blind."

"Yes, because he knowed the man's character. It was just the kind of a man he was hunting for—a man that never believes in anybody's word or anybody's honorableness, because he ain't got none of his own. I reckon there's lots of people like that dervish. They swindle right and left, but they always make the other person *seem* to swindle himself. They keep inside of the letter of the law all the time, and there ain't no way to git hold of them. *They* don't put the salve on—oh, no, that would be sin; but they know how to fool *you* into putting it on, then it's you that blinds yourself. I reckon the dervish and the camel-driver was just a pair—a fine, smart, brainy rascal, and a dull, coarse, ignorant one, but both of them rascals, just the same."

"Mars Tom, does you reckon dey's any o' dat kind o' salve in de worl' now?"

"Yes, Uncle Abner says there is. He says they've got it in New York, and they put it on country people's eyes and show them all the railroads in the world, and they go in and get them, and then when they rub the salve on the other eye the other man bids them good-by and goes off with their railroads. Here's the treasure-hill, now. Lower away!"

We landed, but it warn't as interesting as I thought it was going to be, because we couldn't find the place where they went in to git the treasure. Still, it was plenty interesting enough, just to see the mere hill itself where such a wonderful thing happened. Jim said he wouldn't a-missed it for

three dollars, and I felt the same way.

And to me and Jim, as wonderful a thing as any was the way Tom could come into a strange big country like this and go straight and find a little hump like that and tell it in a minute from a million other humps that was almost just like it, and nothing to help him but only his own learning and his own natural smartness. We talked and talked it over together, but couldn't make out how he done it. He had the best head on him I ever see; and all he lacked was age, to make a name for himself equal to Captain Kidd or George Washington. I bet you it would a-crowded either of *them* to find that hill, with all their gifts, but it warn't nothing to Tom Sawyer; he went clear across the Sahara and put his finger right on it.

We found a pond of salt water close by and scraped up a raft of salt around the edges and loaded up the lion's skin and the tiger's so as they would keep till Jim could tan them.

CHAPTER XI

WE went a-fooling along for a day or two, and then just as the full moon was touching the ground on the other side of the Desert, we see a string of little black figgers moving across its big silver face. You could see them as plain as if they was painted on the moon with ink. It was another caravan. We cooled down our speed and tagged along after it, just to have company, though it warn't going our way. It was a rattler, that caravan, and a mighty fine sight to look at, next morning when the sun come a-streaming across the Desert and flung the long shadders of the camels on the gold sand like a thousand grand-daddy-longlegses marching in procession. We never went very near it, because we knowed better, now, than to act like that and scare people's camels and break up their caravans. It was the gayest outfit you ever see, for rich clothes and nobby style. Some of the chiefs rode on dromedaries, the first we ever see, and very tall, and they go plunging along like they was on stilts, and they rock the man that is on them pretty violent and stir him up considerable, I bet you; but they make noble good time and a camel ain't nowheres with them for speed.

The caravan camped, during the middle part of the day, and then started again about the middle of the afternoon. Before long the sun begun to look very curious. First it kind of turned to brass, and then to copper, and after that it begun to look like a blood red ball, and the air got hot and close, and pretty soon all the sky in the west darkened up and looked thick and foggy, but fiery and dreadful like it looks through a piece of red glass, you know. We looked down and see a big confusion going on in the caravan and a rushing every which way like they was scared, and then they all flopped down flat in the sand and laid there perfectly still.

Pretty soon we see something coming that stood up like an amazing wide wall, and reached from the Desert up into the sky and hid the sun, and it was coming like the nation, too. Then a little faint breeze struck us, and then it come harder, and grains of sand begun to sift against our faces and sting like fire, and Tom sung out—

"It's a sand-storm—turn your backs to it!"

We done it, and in another minute it was blowing a gale and the sand beat against us by the shovel-full, and the air was so thick with it we couldn't see a thing. In five minutes the boat was level full and we was setting on the lockers, all

of us buried up to the chin in sand and only our heads out and we could hardly breathe.

Then the storm thinned, and we see that monstrous wall go a-sailing off across the Desert, awful to look at, I tell you. We dug ourselves out and looked down, and where the caravan was before, there wasn't anything but just the sand ocean, now, and all still and quiet. All them people and camels was smothered and dead and buried—buried under ten foot of sand, we reckoned, and Tom allowed it might be years before the wind uncovered them, and all that time their friends wouldn't ever know what become of that caravan.

Tom said—

"*Now* we know what it was that happened to the people we got the swords and pistols from."

Yes, sir, that was just it. It was as plain as day, now. They got buried in a sand-storm, and the wild animals couldn't get at them, and the wind never uncovered them again till they was dried to leather. It seemed to me we had felt as sorry for them poor people as a person could for anybody, and as mournful, too, but we was mistaken; this last caravan's death went harder with us, a good deal harder. You see, the others was total strangers, and we never got really acquainted with them at all. But it was different with this last caravan. We was huvvering around them a whole night and most a whole day, and had got to feeling real friendly with them, and acquainted. I have found out that there ain't no surer way to find out whether you like people or hate them, than to travel with them. Just so with these. We kind of liked them from the start, and traveling with them put on the finisher. The longer we traveled with them, and the more we got used to their ways, the better and better we liked them and the gladder and gladder we was that we run across them. We had come to know some of them so well that we called them by name when we was talking about them, and soon got so familiar and sociable that we even dropped the Miss and the Mister and just used their plain names without any handle, and it did not seem unpolite, but just the right thing. Of course it wasn't their own names, but names we give them. There was Mr. Elexander Robinson and Miss Adaline Robinson, and Colonel Jacob McDougal, and Miss Harryet McDougal, and Judge Jeremiah Butler, and young Bushrod Butler, and these was big chiefs, mostly, that wore splendid great turbans and simmeters, and dressed like the Grand Mogul, and their families. But as soon as we come to know them good, and like them very much, it warn't Mister, nor Judge, nor nothing, any more, but only Elleck, and Addy, and Jake, and Hattie, and Jerry, and Buck, and so on.

And you know, the more you join in with people in their joys and their sorrows, the more nearer and dearer they come to be to you. Now we warn't cold and indifferent, the way most travelers is, we was right down friendly and sociable, and took a chance in everything that was going, and the caravan could depend on us to be on hand every time, it didn't make no difference what it was.

When they camped, we camped right over them, ten or twelve hundred foot up in the air. When they et a meal, we et ourn, and it made it ever so much homeliker to have their company. When they had a wedding, that night, and Buck and Addy got married, we got ourselves up in the very starchiest of the Professor's duds for the blow-out, and when they danced we jined in and shook a foot up there.

But it is sorrow and trouble that brings you the nearest, and it was a funeral that done it with us. It was next morning, just in the still dawn. We didn't know the diseased, but that never made no difference, he belonged to the caravan, and that was enough.

Yes, parting with this caravan was much more bitterer than it was to part with them others, which was comparative strangers, and been dead so long, anyway. We had knowed these in their lives, and was fond of them, too, and now to have 'em snatched from right before our faces whilst we was looking, and leave us so lonesome and friendless in the middle of that big Desert, it did hurt us.

We couldn't keep from talking about them, and they was all the time coming up in our memory, and looking just the way they looked when we was all alive and happy together. We could see the line marching, and the shiny spear-heads a-winking in the sun, we could see the dromedaries lumbering along, we could see the wedding and the funeral, and more oftener than anything else we could see them praying, because they don't allow nothing to prevent that; whenever the call come, several times a day, they would stop right there, and stand up and face to the east, and lift back their heads, and spread out their arms and begin, and four or five times they would go down on their knees, and then fall forwards and touch their forehead to the ground.

Well, it warn't good to go on talking about them, because it didn't do no good, and made us too downhearted.

When we woke up next morning we was feeling a little cheerfuller, and had had a most powerful good sleep, because sand is the comfortablest bed there is, and I don't see why people that can afford it don't have it more. And it's terrible good ballast, too; I never see the balloon so steady before.

Tom allowed we had twenty tons of it, and wondered what we better do with it;

it was good sand, and it didn't seem good sense to throw it away. Jim says—

"Mars Tom, can't we tote it back home en sell it? How long'll it take?"

"Depends on the way we go."

"Well, sah, she's wuth a quarter of a dollar a load, at home, en I reckon we's got as much as twenty loads, hain't we? How much would dat be?"

"Five dollars."

"By jings, Mars Tom, le's shove for home right on de spot! Hit's more'n a dollar en a half apiece, hain't it?"

"Yes."

"Well, ef dat ain't makin' money de easiest ever I struck! She jes' rained in—never cos' us a lick o' work. Le's mosey right along, Mars Tom."

But Tom was thinking and ciphering away so busy and excited he never heard him. Pretty soon he says—

"Five dollars—sho! Look here, this sand's worth—worth—why, it's worth no end of money."

"How is dat, Mars Tom? Go on, honey, go on!"

"Well, the minute people knows its genuwyne sand from the genuwyne Desert of Sahara, they'll just be in a perfect state of mind to git hold of some of it to keep on the whatnot in a vial with a label on it for a curiosity. All we got to do is, to put it up in vials and float around all over the United States and peddle them out at ten cents apiece. We've got all of ten thousand dollars' worth of sand in this boat."

Me and Jim went all to pieces with joy, and began to shout whoopjamboreehoo, and Tom says—

"And we can keep on coming back and fetching sand, and coming back and fetching more sand, and just keep it agoing till we've carted this whole Desert over there and sold it out; and there ain't ever going to be any opposition, either, because we'll take out a patent."

"My goodness," I says, "we'll be as rich as Creosote, won't we, Tom?"

"Yes,—Creesus, you mean. Why, that dervish was hunting in that little hill for the treasures of the earth, and didn't know he was walking over the real ones for a thousand miles. He was blinder than he made the driver."

"Mars Tom, how much is we gwyne to be worth?"

"Well, I don't know, yet. It's got to be ciphered, and it ain't the easiest job to do, either, because it's over four million square miles of sand at ten cents a vial."

Jim was awful excited, but this faded it out considerable, and he shook his head and says—

"Mars Tom, we can't 'ford all dem vials—a king couldn't. We better not try to take de whole Desert, Mars Tom, de vials gwyne to bust us, sho'."

Tom's excitement died out, too, now, and I reckoned it was on account of the vials, but it wasn't. He set there thinking, and got bluer and bluer, and at last he says—

"Boys, it won't work; we got to give it up."

"Why, Tom?"

"On account of the duties."

I couldn't make nothing out of that, neither could Jim. I says—

"What is our duty, Tom? Because, if we can't git around it, why can't we just do it? People often has to."

But he says—

"Oh, it ain't that kind of duty. The kind I mean is a tax. Whenever you strike a frontier—that's the border of a country, you know—you find a custom-house there, and the gov'ment officers comes and rummages amongst your things and charges a big tax, which they call a duty because it's their duty to bust you if they can, and if you don't pay the duty they'll take your sand. They call it confiscating. Now if we try to carry this sand home the way we're pointed now, we got to climb fences till we git tired—just frontier after frontier—Egypt, Arabia, Hindostan, and so on, and they'll all whack on a duty, and so you see, easy enough, we *can't* go *that* road."

"Why, Tom," I says, "we can sail right over their old frontiers; how are *they* going to stop us?"

He looked sorrowful at me, and says, very grave—

"Huck Finn, do you think that would be honest?"

I hate them kind of interruptions. But I said nothin'. I didn't feel no more interest in such things, as long as we couldn't git our sand through, and it made me low-spirited, and Jim the same. Tom he tried to cheer us up by saying he would think up another speculation for us that would be just as good as this one and better, but it didn't do no good, we didn't believe there was any as big as this. It was mighty hard; such a little while ago we was so rich, and could 'a' bought a country and started a kingdom and been celebrated and happy, and now we was so poor and ornery again, and had our sand left on our hands. The sand was looking so lovely, before, just like gold and diamonds, and the feel of it was so soft and so silky and nice, but now I couldn't bear the sight of it, it made me sick to look at it, and I knowed I wouldn't ever feel comfortable again till we got shut of it, and I didn't have it there no more to remind us of what we had been and what we had got degraded down to. The others was feeling the same way about it that I was. I knowed it, because they cheered up so the minute I says, "Le's throw this truck overboard."

Well, it was going to be work, you know, and pretty solid work, too; so Tom he divided it up according to fairness and strength. He said me and him would clear out a fifth apiece, of the sand, and Jim three fifths. Jim he didn't quite like that arrangement. He says—

" 'Course I's de stronges', en I's willin' to do a share accordin', but by jings you's kinder pilin' it onto ole Jim this time, Mars Tom, hain't you?"

"Well, I didn't think so, Jim, but you try your hand at fixing it, and let's see."

So Jim he reckoned it wouldn't be no more than fair if me and Tom done a *tenth* apiece. Tom he turned his back to git room and be private, and then he smole a smile that spread around and covered the whole Sahara to the westward, back to the Atlantic edge of it where we come from. Then he turned around again and said it was a good enough arrangement, and we was satisfied if Jim was. Jim said he was.

So then Tom measured off our two tenths in the bow and left the rest for Jim, and it surprised Jim a good deal to see how much difference there was and what a raging lot of sand his share come to, an' he said he was powerful glad, now, that he had spoke up in time and got the first arrangement altered, for he said that even the way it was now, there was more sand than enjoyment in his end of the contract, he believed.

Then we laid into it. It was mighty hot work, and tough; so hot we had to move up into cooler weather or we couldn't 'a' stood it. Me and Tom took turn about, and one worked while t' other rested, but there warn't nobody to spell poor old Jim. We couldn't work good, we was so full of laugh, and Jim he kept fretting and fuming and wanting to know what tickled us so, and we had to keep making up things to account for it, and they was pretty poor inventions, but they done well enough, Jim didn't see through them. At last when we got done we was most dead, but not with work but with laughing. By and by Jim was most dead too, but it was with work; then we took turns and spelled him, and he was as thankful as he could be, and would set on the gunnel and heave and pant, and say how good we was to him, and he wouldn't ever forgit us. He was always the gratefulest feller I ever see, for any little thing you done for him. He was only black outside; inside he was as white as you be.

MARCH

By Lucy Larcom

March! March! March! They are coming
   In troops, to the tune of the wind
Red-headed woodpeckers drumming,
   Gold-crested thrushes behind;
Sparrows in brown jackets hopping
   Past every gateway and door;
Finches with crimson caps stopping
   Just where they stopped years before.

March! March! March! They are slipping
   Into their places at last,—
Little white lily-buds, dripping
   Under the showers that fall fast;

Buttercups, violets, roses;
   Snowdrop and bluebell and pink;
Throng upon throng of sweet posies,
   Bending the dewdrops to drink.

March! March! March! They will hurry
   Forth at the wild bugle-sound,
Blossoms and birds in a flurry,
   Fluttering all over the ground.
Hang out your flags, birch and willow!
   Shake out your red tassels, larch!
Grass-blades, up from your earth-pillow
   Hear who is calling you—March!

THE BLACK HERO OF THE RANGES

by Enoch J. Mills

THE pungent odor of the camp-fire drifted down the swale, and carried with it the savory smell of the cooking supper. All afternoon, the Diamond H riders had been arriving; word had been passed that a feast would be spread at sundown, in honor of the owner of the "Diamond H" ranch, who had arrived for his first visit to the ranch in three years.

The riders had all arrived but young "Hank"—he of the shiny spurs and new "chaps." No rider in the outfit possessed such complete trappings. Though Hank was not a regular "puncher," it pleased him mightily to be called one. He was a kind of messenger-boy for the outfit, and rode far and wide carrying orders from the foreman, or going down to the post for the mail. When in camp, he assisted the cook, a task he detested as being beneath his dignity. But Hank was proud of the Diamond H, and boasted that no ranch in Nevada had such riders and ropers.

The feast was nearing the end in the soft dusk of evening, when Hank charged down upon the scene at a reckless gallop, and stopped abruptly within the circle of the firelight.

The foreman straightened up with observing eye upon the foaming horse. "Didn't I tell you not to run Old Baldy any more?"

Every cow-puncher eyed Hank, and several tried to divert the foreman by witty remarks and laughter.

But Hank did not wither under the accusation.

"I had a try at the Black Stallion," he observed, as he fixed his eyes on the owner.

"Where?" came a half-dozen demands at once. "Where?" rapped out the owner. It was like an explosion in their midst. The feast was scattered, and instantly there was a stampede of talk. Each rider was possessed of the same thought—to capture that wonderful steed that had so long led his herd whither he would, defying capture, daring to go where no horse ever had gone before, and upon whose head was set a price.

"I thought you said the Black Stallion never came down from the rough country?" The owner waited eagerly for the foreman's answer.

"It's the first time he's shown up, down here, since we had the chase after him two years ago."

"Jess, I'd like to have that horse, and I'm willing to go to any amount of trouble to get him. But the question is, 'can we?'"

The foreman looked into the fire and ran his hands thoughtfully through his hair. At length he turned to the owner. "I believe we've got the best chance at him, now that he's left the rough country, that we've ever had. He's an old fox, though, and there's nothing he doesn't know about

359

being chased. It's about as easy to round up a bird as to try to corner him. Still, the water's all gone, higher up, and he's got to range down here. If we only had more men and a mustang outfit, I believe we could—" The owner's heavy hand reached the foreman's shoulder and stopped him midway of the prediction.

"Get the men and the outfit. I'll foot the bills. If you get him, I'll hand you a year's salary. You can promise the men whatever reward you like, but the thing is, *get that horse!*"

Hank moved opposite the two men, and leaned forward across the embers of the fire.

"Where did you see him, Hank?"

"About three miles up the valley by the spring. There were twenty in the herd he was leading."

"All right, Hank; get a fresh horse and ride down to the post and pick up every rider you can. Find old Sam Higler, and tell him he's to be here with his canvas corral outfit by to-morrow night. Tell every one you see that the black's come down, and there's a reward of a thousand dollars for the man who drops his rope on him and brings him in." Hank vanished in the direction of the rope corral, and five minutes later was riding rapidly toward the post. After he had gone, the owner turned to the foreman. "Jess," said he, "did I ever tell you where the stallion came from?" The foreman's interested face invited him to proceed.

"It was five years ago that a Syrian peddler was killed by a couple of half-breeds because he had this wonderful black stallion. The Indians took the horse clear across the desert to make their escape, but just when they were about to sell him, the stallion killed one, and lamed the other with his heels, and got away. It was not long before he appeared with a wild-horse herd, and since then he's been the terror

of the range, and there's not a man in Nevada who can boast of ever getting near enough to drop his rope on him. I doubt if he's ever taken alive. Before I quit the ranch three years ago, I'd ridden in a couple of chases after him, and I tell you he's got sense, and legs that can put him over a hundred miles any day."

They sat in silence, each looking into the embers of the fire.

TWENTY Diamond H riders surrounded the valley early in the morning, and from the passes looked down at the wild-horse band led by the big black stallion. It was a long, narrow valley, and the eastern wall had but a single pass where anything but winged creatures could escape. At the upper end the valley narrowed, and leading down into it was an old, time-worn pass; here were posted three men with as many extra horses. West of the valley, the ridge rose abruptly. In ten miles it had only five breaks, where steep cañons penetrated its rocky top and broke the barrier. At each break, two men posted themselves and waited. They gained these passes by circuitous routes. The lower end of the valley was guarded by three men, who lounged about, allowing their horses to graze.

At noon, Hank arrived upon a jaded horse, and singly, or by twos and threes, the other "punchers" came in during the afternoon, each mounted on his best horse, and with carefully coiled ropes. At dark, Sam Higler put in appearance with his mustang trap, which was set up over night across the lower end of the valley. This trap consisted of a brown canvas twelve feet high, which represented an impassable wall. Near the center the wall curved sharply, making a natural corner with an inviting opening leading into a canvas corral beyond. It was a cunning contrivance, and in it scores of wild mustangs had been captured. It was here that they hoped to capture the famous stallion.

Extra men were sent to reinforce the guards at all the passes. Fifteen of the best ropers were kept at camp, and these were to take part at the finish of the chase.

From the main ranch there had been sent up a dozen thoroughbred, long-legged, racing horses, which were to be used in case the stallion broke through the barrier and escaped from the valley, or were to be held in reserve until the chase had tired out the crafty leader. Then they were to appear suddenly from behind the canvas wall, and go after the herd like the wind.

Orders were to shoot the stallion if he broke through the lines. The rest of the herd was worth four thousand dollars, and their addition to the ranch stock would be valuable.

The only ones at breakfast at the chuck wagon that morning were the owner, the foreman, and Hank. While the men settled the final details of the chase, Hank tidied up the camp things and saddled his horse.

"Hank, one of the boys rode back yesterday to report that there's still a little water at the muddy spring water-hole." Hank was silent; sudden fear had chilled him. The foreman continued: "If the foxy old stallion gets away from us in the valley, that's the only place in a hundred miles he can get water; and I guess after we've run him a hundred miles or so, he'll be wanting water, too. You'd better ride up to the muddy spring, Hank, and stick it out there until dark. There's no telling what may happen to-day, but whatever comes, the chase will end at dark."

Hank turned away, blinking fast and swallowing hard. His hopes of riding with the foreman and the owner were thus suddenly blasted, leaving behind a sense of revolt that fairly hurt. After discovering the horse, he would lose all the excitement of the chase.

Soon after daylight, the foreman and the owner rode into the valley above the canvas wall. They galloped easily toward the spring where Hank had seen the horses two days before. When they rounded a knoll a half-mile below the water-hole, they sighted the wonderful stallion on guard on a slight elevation, with the herd feeding quietly below. Instantly the band was off up the valley, and the foreman was riding rapidly in pursuit. The owner stopped at the spring, where he would wait until the time came for the concerted dash and capture of the big black. It was a waiting game, and patience was to play an important part.

Ten miles up the valley, straight for the steep trail at the upper end, swept the black leader at the head of his herd. But a quarter of a mile from the pass he stopped, wheeled, and doubled back. The foreman was riding near the western wall, and the band passed him on its return trip without being forced into too close quarters.

One of the men on guard at the pass dashed down with a fresh horse, and five minutes later the foreman was after the herd again with the second horse. He galloped along a half-mile behind the stallion, and not once did he press the chase or excite the band unduly.

At the sight of the brown canvas wall barring his way, the stallion spun around and fled wildly up the valley again. But three of the others went straight on through the narrow opening at the center, and were easy victims in the canvas corral. On another fresh horse, the foreman continued the chase. Not once did he come nearer than the half-mile, and never did he permit the band to stop for more than a minute or two at a time.

When within a quarter of a mile of

the pass, the stallion again scented danger, and again wheeled back down the valley. Once more a man dashed out from hiding with a fresh horse, and the chase continued. It was settling down now to one of dogged endurance, with the odds against the stallion. Fresh horses were in plenty for the foreman, but the wonderful black kept on, hour after hour, leading his dwindling band with what seemed tireless energy. Ceaselessly they kept him moving. Three round trips of the valley, sixty miles, and ten of his mates were out of the chase, and before the fourth round of the valley was finished, they were dropping out rapidly, being roped and dragged in submission to the canvas corral.

Frequently now the stallion would stop and watch until his relentless pursuer was within a hundred yards; then he would be off again. His black coat was covered with foam; he was becoming uncertain on his feet, and stumbled often. He approached the water-hole, but it was guarded. Wearily he turned back down the valley because it was easier going.

The foreman fired three quick signal shots, and from behind the brown canvas wall rode the best ropers of the region, mounted on the fleetest horses. The stallion sloped his flight and went on down the valley along the western side. The riders waited across the valley until he had passed, then they spread out across the level floor.

Ten abreast, and absolutely certain of success, they galloped easily along behind the stallion as he went on straight toward the canvas barrier. They did not hurry; there was no need; an easy gallop kept pace with the stallion's now unsteady gait. A hundred yards from the barrier, he wheeled defiantly. Facing them, he waited. The foreman shouted an order, and they dashed wildly forward, each eager to be first to drop his rope over the wary head

and win eternal fame in the region as the subduer of the most wonderful horse in Nevada.

The stallion waited their coming with heaving sides and flaming eyes. When the nearest riders were fifty feet away, he charged directly toward them, getting into his full stride in spite of his weariness, and by the time he reached them, he was going at top speed. His unexpected charge threw the riders into confusion. Their racing horses were not trained to the roping game like their cow-horses; besides, each rider was racing wildly, and each had his full length of rope ready for a long cast in order to be first.

Straight between two riders went the stallion. The men were alert and active in spite of their mounts. They made casts at the same instant, and their ropes met in mid air above his head. One loop dropped short, and the other was so large that he leaped half through before the man could snake the slack with a quick backward jerk of his hand and tighten up. Even then, his horse was broadside when the plunging stallion reached the end of the rope with a tremendous charge that lifted the racer clear of his feet and flung him violently to the ground.

To save himself, the man instinctively let go the rope, which he had snubbed around the saddle horn, and at the stallion's first lunge it slipped from the saddle and went trailing off behind the black. Three leaps more, and it dropped harmlessly to the ground. The stallion was free again.

The very number of his pursuers was his advantage. A hundred feet away the side of the valley rose at half pitch, and rough rocks and dense scrub were scattered thickly up the slope. Up he went over ragged rock slabs, forcing his way through the scrub where no ridden horse could follow.

Straight up the mountain the great horse fought his way, though it was strewn with huge blocks of bare rock piled in a forbidding mass of debris. The route looked impossible to any animal except a man.

"Don't shoot! He's all in," ordered the foreman. From above came the shouts of the men guarding the pass: "Let him come! We'll get him."

Desperately the men below tried to follow, and impatiently the men at the top waited and watched his slow upward progress. They straightened their ropes, tightened their cinches, and made sure that every detail was ready. Behind them, back of the ridge top, lay a narrow plateau, and beyond rose a second ridge. Upon this level bench they would capture the famous stallion, and the reward.

A hundred feet from the top, the stallion doubled back, leaped boldly over a narrow chasm, and followed along a narrow ledge of bare rock that ran along the face of the cliff. It was barely wide enough for him to edge along, and there was every chance that it might pinch out.

But the ledge did not pinch out, and the stallion came to the end of it fifty yards farther, where a section of the barrier had gone out with the rock slide. Up over the rock slabs the horse fought his mad way, always toward the top. His progress was slow and painful. Often he was minutes gaining a few feet. Still, nothing daunted nor defeated him. The men watching from above laughed, exulted at the sight.

A narrow rock-filled gully ran back across the plateau toward the ridge beyond. Scrub growth filled in between the rocks. It was to the mouth of this gully that the horse finally forced his way.

The men were waiting for him on foot. Each dropped his rope over the coveted head with a yell of triumph.

No sooner did the ropes tighten upon the stallion's neck than he became an explosion of action. Up the slope toward the level ground he charged, and the men, confident of success, let him go.

Once in the open, they stopped him by throwing their weight against their ropes. With flaming eyes, mouth open, and ears laid flat, the stallion came down at them, a terrible monster of rage.

The horse was within ten feet of the men, when one of them let go his rope and dived aside as the black bulk lurched by. The other threw his weight against his rope, and the stallion turned upon him with bared teeth, and awful, flashing eyes. He saved himself only by leaping blindly into the scrub in the gully.

When the men recovered their feet, they rushed to their horses, and were after the runaway pell-mell. But the stallion continued along the broken top of the ridge, where it seemed as if he would surely tumble headlong back into the valley. He dared every obstacle for liberty, leaped treacherous gaps in the rock barrier where his enemies dared not follow, and made his way across fields of huge, broken rocks where no other horse had ever dared.

On the level, the fresh horses of the men could easily have overtaken him; but among the rocks and chasms of the ridge top, they had difficulty in keeping him in sight. Their horses were not fighting a life-and-death battle, and could not follow the way the stallion went. They had to make detours where the black forged straight up the slope.

Seeing that he was about to gain the second ridge top, the men opened on him with their six-shooters, but he plunged desperately into the growth of scrub just back of the second ridge top, and went crashing headlong out of sight, and safe from the spiteful guns.

Ten minutes after the stallion disappeared in the scrub, the men reached the top of the ridge and saw the plain trail where he had entered the thicket. They separated and started circling around the copse in opposite directions, chagrined at their failure to either capture or kill the wonderful black horse. They rode desperately to intercept him when he should emerge from the far side of the sheltering growth. But, as soon as they were out of hearing, the crafty animal came out at the spot where he had entered the thicket, and started westward along the rough ridge top. Sometimes he stopped for a moment to rest, and always he watched the back trail. When he went on again, he followed the roughest way he could find.

An hour later, the men from the valley came up and found his tracks, which told once more how the big black stallion had won his freedom. In the second valley, they found where he had joined another wild-horse band. But they knew he would soon leave the band and seek shelter; so they scattered and began careful search for tracks near every thicket. They hoped to find him before he had sufficiently rested to run away from them.

It was a game for life and freedom by the stallion, and he never gave up. Leaving the wild herd abruptly, he rested a few minutes, then pushed on to a hiding-place. But he allowed little time for rest; always he went on and on, putting as much distance between himself and his enemies as his strength would permit. Thus it was, he worked his way to the lonely water-hole.

Through all the long hours, Hank waited at the muddy spring beside it. While he kept lonely vigil, his heart welled up against the foreman and the others. He almost hoped that the stallion would get away. Surely the chase was over, long since, for the sun was dropping low. However, his orders were to wait until dark, and he would stick it out. Not because he cared what any of them thought, or said, or did, but because he was a boy—and almost a man. They had not given him a fair chance, and he knew that they would give the stallion even less.

At four in the afternoon, Hank unsaddled Old Baldy, hobbled him, and allowed him to graze away from the spring. Behind a scrub where the sand had drifted, he scooped out a hole with his hands, and snuggled in the bottom with his six-shooter within touch. Long rides, loss of sleep, and constant vigil had wearied him more than he knew. In five minutes he was asleep. The sun touched the distant mountains and sank slowly behind them.

A wild snort awakened him, and he started up stupidly, half awake, gun in hand. He arose cautiously. Thirty feet away stood the stallion, legs braced wide apart to keep from falling, muscles all a-quiver. He was reeking with foam and dirt. But his eyes were blazing with that terrible fear and hate of man. The breeze carried the man-smell away from the stallion, and undersized Hank, standing knee-deep in the sand-pit, did not look formidable.

For a moment they faced each other across the water-hole, each immovable with surprise. Instinctively, Hank's gun hand crept out and rose slowly in front, sliding out toward the stallion. He covered a foam fleck between the blazing eyes, held the gun steady there for a second, then he lowered it. "He can't get away anyhow," he said aloud.

At the sound of his voice, the stallion pulled himself together with a jerk. Plainly though, he was at the end of his race. He must have water or perish. Slowly he advanced. A few steps from the spring he halted, his instinct warning him against nearer approach to his hated enemy. But he was too weak to run away, and, after hesitating, he staggered forward and dropped to his knees at the water-hole.

"All right, old fellow, you win!" and Hank replaced his gun in its holster and stood watching as the horse buried his nose in the muddy water and drank in great, sobbing gulps, until the water-hole was empty. Hank was glad he had dug it out in the morning. The little hole held perhaps two buckets of dark water, but it made only a taste for the stallion.

"Looks like they'd given you a run for your life, old fellow," and Hank moved forward slowly, continued talking, and edging nearer. Soothingly he talked his way forward while the horse held his hot muzzle pressed against the wet sand, eagerly sucking up the water as it flowed slowly forth. Its slowness made him impatient, and he began pawing wildly.

"Now don't do that!" Hank chided; "don't you see you've filled up the hole?"

Far back in his mind, the stallion must have remembered that men *had* been kind to him, for he was not afraid now of this first man-being who had been kind to him since he escaped the Indians. There was something in the gentle touch of the boy that thrilled him with vague memories. He waited patiently while with bare hands Hank scooped out the water-hole.

Tears were streaming down Hank's boyish face as he loosened the two ropes and tossed them aside. Patting the foam-flecked neck, he talked on and on. The horse waited impatiently for the water that came so maddeningly slow. After his second draft, he nosed Hank and whinnied eagerly.

Darkness settled unnoticed. Suddenly the stallion lifted his head alert and looked intently toward the east, ears pricked sharply forward, and alarm in his manner. Hank could see or hear nothing, but he watched the revived horse keenly. A moment later came distant hoof-beats, and the stallion galloped stiffly away into the darkness.

Soon the rough voice of a man greeted Hank as he stood motionless by the water-hole.

"Hello, fellows! Did you get him?" his question saved him from having to answer that question himself, and conveyed to the men exactly what he wished it to. He had scooped out a hole in the sand, tossed the ropes into it, and smoothed the sand over them.

Hank was silent on the homeward ride. His heart was filled with conflicting emotions, and he heard only part of the talk about the dare-devil horse that had climbed rock walls and fought for his freedom. It seemed to be the general opinion that the stallion had joined another band.

FIFTEEN miles across the rough country Hank rode every Saturday afternoon. He had asked, then demanded, of the foreman this half-holiday, and had at last secured it through strategy. In his pockets were lumps of sugar, offerings of salt, bread, and other treats for the stallion. Twice during the first month he had sighted the wonderful black, and had coaxed him to approach and accept the offerings he had brought to cement their friendship. If the stallion failed to keep the tryst, Hank would return to the ranch dejected and morose.

It was near round-up time, and some extra work had delayed Hank past his usual starting time. He did not take the precaution of starting off and circling back to throw the others off his trail, but took a short cut up the valley, climbed the steep trail at its upper end, and emerged through the pass that overlooked the muddy spring. He went down the opposite slope at a rapid pace. Baldy had once been a famous cow-horse, but had grown too old for active service. They were going down the smooth slope like the wind, when Baldy stepped into a hole and plunged downward, turning completely over in his fall. Hank was flung from the saddle, but one foot stuck in its stirrup. Then he lost consciousness.

Pain in his leg roused him after a few minutes, and he sat up, dazed.

Noticing that his right toe was twisted in, he tried to reach out to it, but his hand refused to obey the summons—his collarbone was injured, too. His head cleared, and he realized what had happened. Baldy lay with his head doubled under his body; his neck was broken.

Hank crawled painfully to his saddle and cut the thongs that bound his slicker. Out of it, with his left hand, he cut strips and slowly bound the throbbing ankle, and made a sling for his useless arm. When he had finished his bandaging, he started crawling slowly toward the spring. On one hand and both knees he dragged himself along, stopping often to rest.

The stallion snorted at the strange crawling object and circled until he got the wind; the smell convinced him, and he decided to venture nearer. Sitting quiet, Hank coaxed, gave sugar sparingly, and a little salt too. When the stallion was used to his new appearance, he pressed firmly with his left hand behind the horse's knees. "Lie down, lie down, lie down," he begged, but the black horse did not understand, and edged away.

Water at the hole revived Hank, but at times during the night he was half delirious, calling out for the stallion to come to him; and all night the stallion kept vigil about the spring. Frequently at the call, he would approach and nose the boy, whinny eagerly, and walk round and round him.

At daylight, the great black horse was still waiting beside the boy. Sometimes Hank would rouse himself with an effort and try to get the horse to lie down. Toward noon, Hank's head cleared, and he crawled slowly to an upthrust of rock and coaxed the stallion to him. With a painful effort he dragged himself upon the mighty back, and turned the stallion's head toward the ranch. They traveled slowly. Many times the rider reeled recklessly, and came near tumbling off. At such times, the horse would stop and wait until Hank gave the word to go on again.

FIFTEEN cow-punchers were lolling away Sunday afternoon in the shade of the bunk house. Hank's absence was being discussed. Around a point two hundred yards away came the stallion. At the sight of the men he stopped quickly, and Hank narrowly saved himself from pitching headlong to the ground.

The stallion turned his head and looked at Hank. "It's all right, old fellow; I'll see you through. Go on!" And the horse went forward at an easy pace, with Hank clinging with his left hand tightly to the flowing mane.

Fifteen punchers held the attitude they were in when the horse appeared—they were frozen with astonishment. Not one of them broke the silence nor moved a hand.

At the gate the stallion stopped, and Hank crumpled into the arms of one of the punchers, and then to the ground. He lay quiet so long that the horse gently pawed at him and whinnied anxiously. "I'm all right, old pal." Hank said aloud, through clenched teeth. "You hit the trail; I'll see you again, when I'm able to travel."

With head and tail high, mane flowing in the breeze, the stallion galloped away, swinging his magnificent head from side to side as he went, and looking backward continually.

But not a man stirred.

PLANTATION STORIES

by Grace MacGowan Cooke

I.—MRS. PRAIRIE-DOG'S BOARDERS

Texas is a near-by land to the dwellers in the Southern States. Many of the poorer white people go there to mend their fortunes, and not a few of them come back from its plains, homesick for the mountains, and with these fortunes unmended. Daddy Laban, the half-breed, son of an Indian father and a Negro mother, who sometimes visited Broadlands plantation, had been a wanderer; and his travels had carried him as far afield as the plains of southwestern Texas. The Randolph children liked, almost better than any others, the stories he brought home from these extensive travels.

"De prairie-dog a mighty cur'ous somebody," he began one day, when they asked him for a tale. "Hit lives in de ground, more samer dan a ground-hog. But dey ain't come out for wood nor water; an' some folks thinks dey goes plumb down to de springs what feeds wells. I has knowed dem what say dey go fur enough down to find a place to warm dey hands— but dat ain't de tale I'm tellin'.

"A long time ago, dey was a prairie-dog what was left a widder, an' she had a big fambly to keep up. 'Oh, landy!' she say to dem dat come to visit her in her 'fliction, 'what I gwine do to feed my chillen?'

"De most o' de varmints tell Miz. Prairie-Dog dat de onliest way for her to git along was to keep boarders. 'You got a good home, an' you is a good manager,' dey say; 'you bound to do well wid a boardin'-house.'

"Well, Miz. Prairie-Dog done sent out de runners to run, de fliers to fly, de crawlers to crawl, an' tell each an' every dat she sot up a boardin'-house. She say she got room for one crawler, and one flier, an' dat she could take in a whole passel o' runners.

"Well, now you knows a flier's a bird— or hit mought be a bat. Ef you was lookin' for little folks, hit mought be a butterfly. Miz. Prairie-Dog ain't find no fliers what wants to live un'neath de ground. But crawlers—bugs an' worms an' sich-like— dey mostly does live un'neath de ground, anyhow, an' de fust pusson what come seekin' house-room with Miz. Prairie-Dog was Brother Rattlesnake.

"'I dest been flooded out o' my own house,' Mr. Rattlesnake say; 'an' I like to look at your rooms an' see ef dey suits me.'

"'I show you de rooms,' Miz. Prairie-Dog tell 'im. 'I bound you gwine like 'em. I got room for one crawler, an' you could be him; but—'

"Miz. Prairie-Dog look at her chillen. She ain't say no more—dest look at dem prairie-dog gals an' boys, an' say no more.

"Mr. Rattlesnake ain't like bein' called a crawler so very well; but he looks at dem rooms, an' low he'll take 'em. Miz. Prairie-Dog got somethin' on her mind, an' 'fore de snake git away dat somethin' come out.

367

'I's shore an' certain dat you an' me can git along,' she say, 'ef—ef—ef you vow an' promish not to bite my chillen. I'll have yo' meals reg'lar, so dat you won't be tempted.'

"Old Mr. Rattlesnake' powerful high-tempered—yas, law, he sho' a mighty quick somebody on de trigger. Zip! he go off, dest like dat—zip! Br-r-r! 'Tempted!' he hiss at de prairie-dog woman. He look at dem prairie-dog boys an' gals what been makin' mud cakes all mornin' (an' dest about as dirty as you-all is after you do de same). 'Tempted,' he say, 'I should hope not.'

"For, mind you, Brother Rattlesnake is a genterman, an' belongs to de quality. He feels hisself a heap too biggity to bite prairie-dogs. So *dat* turned out all right.

"De next what come to Miz. Prairie-Dog was a flier."

"A bird?" asked Patricia Randolph.

"Yes, little mistis," returned the old Indian. "One dese-hyer little, round, brown squinch-owls, what allers quakes an' quivers in dey speech an' walk. 'I gits so dizzy —izzy—wizzy! up in de top o' de trees,' de little brown owl say, as she swivel an' shake. 'An' I wanted to git me a home down on de ground, so dat I could be sure, an' double sure, dat I wouldn't fall. But dey is dem dat says ef I was down on de ground I might fall down a hole. Dat make me want to live in you' house. Hit's down in de ground, ain't hit? Ef I git down in you' house dey hain't no place for me to fall off of, an' fall down to, is dey?' she ax.

"Miz. Prairie-Dog been in de way o' fallin' down-stairs all her life; dat de onliest way she ever go inter her house—she fling up her hands an' laugh as you pass her by, and she drap back in de hole. But she tell de little brown owl dat dey ain't no place you could fall ef you go to de bottom eend o' her house. So, what wid a flier an' a crawler, an' de oldest prairie-dog boy workin' out, she manage to make tongue

and buckle meet. I is went by a many a prairie-dog hole an' seen de owl an' de rattlesnake what boards wid Miz. Prairie-Dog. Ef you was to go to Texas you'd see de same. But nobody in dat neck o' woods ever knowed how dese folks come to live in one house."

"Who told *you*, Daddy Laban?" asked Pate Randolph.

"My Injun gran'mammy," returned the old man. "She told me a many a tale, when I lived wid my daddy's people on de Cherokee Res'vation. Sometime I gwine tell you 'bout de little fawn what her daddy ketched for her when she's a little gal. But run home now, honey chillens, or yo' mammy done think Daddy Laban stole you an' carried you plumb away."

II.—SONNY BUNNY RABBIT'S GRANNY

OF all the animal stories which America, the nurse-girl, told to the children of Broadlands plantation, they liked best those about Sonny Bunny Rabbit.

"You listen now, Marse Pate an' Miss Patty an' my baby child, an' I gwine tell you de best tale yit, 'bout de rabbit," she said, one lazy summer afternoon when they were tired of playing marbles with chinaberries.

"You see, de fox he mighty hongry all de time for rabbit meat; yit, at de same time, he 'fraid to buck up 'gainst a old rabbit, an' he always pesterin' after de young ones.

"Sonny Bunny Rabbit' granny was sick, an' Sonny Bunny Rabbit' mammy want to send her a mess o' sallet. She put it in a poke, an' hang de poke round de little rabbit boy's neck.

"'Now, my son,' she says, 'you tote dis sallet to yo' granny, an' don't stop to play wid none o' dey critters in de big Woods.'

"'Yassum, mammy,' say Sonny Bunny Rabbit.

"'Don't you pass de time o' day wid no foxes,' say Mammy Rabbit.

"'Yassum, mammy,' say Sonny Bunny Rabbit.

"Dest as he was passin' some thick chinkapin bushes, up hop a big red fox an' told him howdy.

nothin'—an' ain't know dat right good. 'Stead o' sayin', 'I'se gwine whar I's gwine —an' dat's whar I's gwine,' he answer right back: 'Dest 'cross de hill, suh. Won't you walk wid me, suh? Proud to have yo' company, suh.'

"'An' who-all is you gwine see on t'other side de hill?' ax Mr. Fox.

"'My granny,' answer Sonny Bunny Rabbit. 'I totin' dis sallet to her.'

"'Is yo' granny big?' ax de fox. 'Is yo' granny old?' he say. 'Is yo' granny mighty

"'Come back Hyer, you rabbit trash, an' he'p me out o' dis trouble!'" he holler

"'Howdy,' say Sonny Bunny Rabbit. He ain't study 'bout what his mammy tell him now. He 'bleege to stop an' make a miration at bein' noticed by sech a fine pusson as Mr. Fox. 'Hit's a fine day—an' mighty growin' weather, Mr. Fox.'

"'Hit am dat,' say de fox. 'Yass, suh, hit sho'ly am dat. An' what you puttin' out for, ef I mought ax?' he say, mighty slick an' easy.

"Now, right dar," said America, impressively, "am whar dat little rabbit boy fergit his teachin'. He act like he ain't know

pore? Is yo' granny tough?' An' he ain't been nigh so slick an' sof' an' easy any mo' by dis time—he gittin' mighty hongry an' greedy.

"Right den an dere Sonny Bunny Rabbit wake up. Yaas, law! He come to he senses. He know mighty well an' good dat a pusson de size o' Mr. Fox ain't got no reason to ax ef he granny rough, less'n he want to git he teef in her. By dat he recomember what his mammy done told him. He look all 'bout. He ain't see no he'p nowhars. Den hit com in Sonny Bunny Rabbit' mind dat de boys on de farm done sot a trap down by de pastur' fence. Ef he kin git Mr. Fox to jump inter dat trap, his life done save.

"'Oh, my granny mighty big,' he say; 'but dat's 'ca'se she so fat she cain't run. She hain't so mighty old, but she sleep all de time; an' I ain't know is she tough or not—you dest better come on an' find out,' he holler. Den he start off on er long, keen jump.

"Sonny Bunny Rabbit run as hard as he could. De fox run after, most nippin' his heels. Sonny Bunny Rabbit run by de place whar de fox-trap done sot, an' all kivered wid leaves an' trash, an' dar he le'p high in the air—an' over it. Mr. Fox ain't know dey ary trap in de grass; an', blam! he stuck he foot squar' in it!

"'Oh-ow-ow! Hi-hi-hi! Hi-yi! Yi-yi-yi!' bark de fox. 'Come back hyer, you rabbit trash, an' he'p me out o' dis trouble!' he holler.

"'Dat ain't no trouble,' say Sonny Bunny Rabbit, jumping high in de grass. 'Dat my granny, what I done told you 'bout. Ain't I say she so fat she cain't run? She dest love company so powerful well, dat I 'spect she holdin' on to you to hear you talk.'

"An' de fox talk," America giggled, as she looked about on her small audience.

THE TIME SHOP
by
John Kendrick Bangs

OF course it was an extraordinary thing for a clock to do, especially a parlor clock, which one would expect to be particularly dignified and well-behaved, but there was no denying the fact that the Clock did it. With his own eyes, Bobby saw it wink, and beckon to him with its hands. To be sure, he had never noticed before that the Clock had eyes, or that it had any fingers on its hands to beckon with, but the thing happened in spite of all that, and as a result Bobby became curious. He was stretched along the rug in front of the great open fireplace, where he had been drowsily gazing at the blazing log for a half hour or more, and looking curiously up at the Clock's now smiling face, he whispered to it.

"Are you beckoning to me?" he asked, rising up on his hands and knees.

"Of course I am," replied the Clock in a soft, silvery tone, just like a bell, in fact. "You didn't think I was beckoning to the piano, did you?"

"I didn't know," said Bobby.

"Not that I wouldn't like to have the piano come over and call upon me some day," the Clock went on, "which I most certainly would, considering him, as I do, the most polished four-footed creature I have ever seen, and all of his family have been either grand, square, or upright, and if properly handled, full of sweet music. Fact is, Bobby, I'd rather have a piano playing about me than a kitten or a puppy dog, as long as it didn't jump into my lap. It would be awkward to have a piano get frisky and jump into your lap, now, wouldn't it?"

Bobby had to confess that it would; "But what did you want with me?" he asked, now that the piano was disposed of.

"Well," replied the Clock, "I am beginning to feel a trifle run down, Bobby, and I thought I'd go over to the shop, and get in a little more time to keep me going. Christmas is coming along, and everybody is so impatient for its arrival that I don't want to slow down at this season of the year, and have all the children blame me because it is so long on the way."

"What shop are you going to?" asked Bobby, interested at once, for he was very fond of shops and shopping.

"Why, the Time Shop, of course," said the Clock. "It's a shop that my father keeps, and we clocks have to get our supply of time from him, you know, or we couldn't keep on going. If he didn't give it to us, why, we couldn't give it to you. It isn't right to give away what you haven't got."

"I don't think I understand," said Bobby, with a puzzled look on his face. "What is a Time Shop, and what do they sell there?"

"Oh, anything from a bunch of bananas

371

or a barrel of sawdust up to an automobile," returned the Clock. "Really, I couldn't tell you what they don't sell there if you were to ask me. I know of a fellow who went in there once to buy a great name for himself, and the floor-walker sent him up to the third floor, where they had fame, and prosperity, and greatness for sale, and ready to give anybody who was willing and able to pay for them, and he chose happiness instead, not because it was less expensive than the others, but because it was more worth having. What they've got in the Time Shop depends entirely upon what you want. If they haven't got it in stock, they will take your order for it, and will send it to you, but always C.O.D., which means you must pay when you receive the goods. Sometimes you can buy fame on the instalment plan, but that is only in special cases. As a rule, there is no charging things in the Time Shop. You've got to pay for what you get, and it is up to you to see that the quality is good. Did you ever hear of a man named George Washington?"

"Hoh!" cried Bobby, with a scornful grin. "Did I ever hear of George Washington! What a question! Was there anybody ever who hasn't heard of George Washington?"

"Well, yes," said the Clock. "There was Julius Cæsar. He was a pretty brainy sort of a chap, and he never heard of him. And old Father Adam never heard of him, and Mr. Methusaleh never heard of him, and I rather guess that Christopher Columbus, who was very much interested in American history, never heard of him."

"All right, Clocky," said Bobby, with a smile. "Go on. What about George Washington?"

"He got all that he ever won at the Time Shop; a regular customer, he was," said the Clock; "and he paid for what he got with the best years of his life, man or boy.

He rarely wasted a minute. Now I thought that having nothing to do for a little while but look at those flames trying to learn to dance, you might like to go over with me and visit the old shop. They'll all be glad to see you and maybe you can spend a little time there whilst I am laying in a fresh supply to keep me on the move."

"I'd love to go," said Bobby, starting up eagerly.

"Very well, then," returned the Clock. "Close your eyes, count seventeen backward, then open your eyes again, and you'll see what you will see."

Bobby's eyes shut; I was almost going to say with a snap. He counted from seventeen back to one with a rapidity that would have surprised even his school-teacher, opened his eyes again and looked around, and what he saw—well, that was more extraordinary than ever! Instead of standing on the parlor rug before the fireplace, he found himself in the broad aisle of the ground floor of a huge department store, infinitely larger than any store he had ever seen in his life before, and oh, dear me, how dreadfully crowded it was! The crowd of Christmas shoppers that Bobby remembered to have seen last year when he had gone out to buy a lead-pencil to put into his father's stocking was as nothing to that which thronged this wonderful place. Ah me, how dreadfully hurried some of the poor shoppers appeared to be, and how wistfully some of them gazed at the fine bargains to be seen on the counters and shelves, which either because they had not saved it, or had wasted it, they had not time to buy!

"Well, young gentleman," said a kindly floor-walker, pausing in his majestic march up and down the aisle, as the Clock, bidding Bobby to use his time well, made off to the supply shop, "what can we do for you to-day?"

"Nothing that I know of, thank you,

sir," said Bobby. "I have just come in to look around."

"Ah!" said the floor-walker with a look of disappointment on his face. "I'm afraid I shall have to take you to the Waste-Time Bureau, where they will find out what you want without undue loss of precious moments. I should think, however, that a nice-looking boy like you would be able to decide what he really wanted and go directly to the proper department and get it."

"Got any bicycles?" asked Bobby, seizing upon the first thing that entered his mind.

"Fine ones—best there are," smiled the pleasant floor-walker, very much relieved to find that Bobby did not need to be taken to the bureau. "Step this way, please. Mr. Promptness, will you be so good as to show this young gentleman our line of bicycles?"

Then turning to Bobby, he added: "You look like a rather nice young gentleman, my boy. Perhaps never having been here before, you do not know our ways, and have not provided yourself with anything to spend. To encourage business we see that new comers have a chance to avail themselves of the opportunities of the shop, so here are a few time-checks with which you can buy what you want."

The kindly floor-walker handed Bobby twenty round golden checks, twenty silver checks, and twenty copper ones. Each check was about the size of a five-cent piece, and all were as bright and fresh as if they had just been minted.

"What are these?" asked Bobby, as he jingled the coins in his hand.

"The golden checks, my boy, are days," said the floor-walker. "The silver ones are hours, and the coppers are minutes. I hope you will use them wisely, and find your visit to our shop so profitable that you will become a regular customer."

With this and with a pleasant bow the floor-walker moved along to direct a gray-haired old gentleman with a great store of years in his possession to the place where he could make his last payment on a stock of wisdom which he had been buying, and Bobby was left with Mr. Wiggins, the salesman, who immediately showed him all the bicycles they had in stock.

"This is a pretty good wheel for a boy of your age," said Mr. Promptness, pulling out a bright-looking little machine that was so splendidly under control that when he gave it a push it ran smoothly along the top of the mahogany counter, pirouetted a couple of times on its hind wheel, and then gracefully turning rolled back to Mr. Promptness again.

"How much is that?" asked Bobby, without much hope, however, of ever being able to buy it.

"Sixteen hours and forty-five minutes," said Mr. Promptness, looking at the price-tag, and reading off the figures. "It used to be a twenty-five-hour wheel, but we have marked everything down this season. Everybody is so rushed these days that very few people have any spare time to spend, and we want to get rid of our stock."

"What do you mean by sixteen hours and forty-five minutes?" asked Bobby. "How much is that in dollars?"

Mr. Promptness smiled more broadly than ever at the boy's question.

"We don't do business in dollars here, my lad," said he. "This is a Time Shop, and what you buy you buy with time: days, hours, minutes, and seconds."

"Got anything that costs as much as a year?" asked Bobby.

"We have things that cost a lifetime, my boy," said the salesman; "but those things, our rarest and richest treasures, we keep up-stairs."

"I should think that you would rather do business for money," said Bobby.

"Nay, nay, my son," said Mr. Promptness. "Time is a far better possession than money, and it often happens that it will buy things that money couldn't possibly purchase."

"Then I must be rich," said Bobby.

The salesman looked at the little fellow gravely.

"Rich?" he said.

"Yes," said Bobby, delightedly. "I've got no end of time. Seems to me sometimes that I've got all the time there is."

"Well," said Mr. Promptness, "you must remember that its value depends entirely upon how you use it. Time thrown away or wasted is of no value at all. Past time or future time are of little value compared to present time, so when you say that you are rich you may be misleading yourself. What do you do with yours?"

"Why—anything I happen to want to do," said Bobby.

"And where do you get your clothes, your bread and butter, your playthings?" asked the salesman.

"Oh, my father gets all those things for me," returned Bobby.

"Well, he has to pay for them," said Mr. Promptness, "and he has to pay for them in time, too, while you use yours for what?"

Bobby hung his head.

"Do you spend it well?" asked the salesman.

"Sometimes," said Bobby, "and sometimes I just waste it," he went on. "You see, Mr. Promptness, I didn't know there was a Time Shop where you could buy such beautiful things with it, but now that I do know you will find me here oftener spending what I have on things worth having."

"I hope so," said Mr. Promptness, patting Bobby affectionately on the shoulder. "How much have you got with you now?"

"Only these," said Bobby, jingling his time-checks in his pocket. "Of course next week when my Christmas holiday begins I shall have a lot—three whole weeks—that's twenty-one days, you know."

"Well, you can only count on what you have in hand, but from the sounds in your pocket I fancy you can have the bicycle if you want it," said Mr. Promptness.

"At the price I think I can," said Bobby, "and several other things besides."

"How would you like this set of books about wild animals?" asked Mr. Promptness.

"How much?" said Bobby.

"Two days and a half, or sixty hours," said Mr. Promptness, inspecting the price-tag.

"Send them along with the rest," said Bobby. "How much is that electric railroad over there?"

"That's rather expensive," Mr. Promptness replied. "It will cost you two weeks, three days, ten minutes, and thirty seconds."

"Humph," said Bobby. "I guess that's a little too much for me. Got any marbles?"

"Yes," laughed Mr. Promptness. "We have china alleys, two for a minute, or plain miggles at ten for a second."

"Put me down for two hours' worth of china alleys, and about a half an hour's worth of miggles," said Bobby.

"Very good, sir," said Mr. Promptness, with a twinkling eye. "Now can you think of anything else?"

"Well, yes," said Bobby, a sudden idea flashing across his mind. "There is one thing I want very much, Mr. Promptness, and I guess maybe perhaps you can help me out. I'd like to buy a Christmas present for my mother, if I can get a nice one with the time I've got. I was afraid I couldn't get her much of anything with what little money I had saved. But if I can pay for it in time, Mr. Promptness—why, what couldn't I buy for her with those three whole weeks coming to me!"

"About how much would you like to spend on it?" asked Mr. Promptness, with a soft light in his eye.

"Oh, I'd *like* to spend four or five years on it," said Bobby, "but, of course—"

"That's very nice of you," said the salesman, putting his hand gently on Bobby's head, and stroking his hair. "But I wouldn't be extravagant, and once in a while we have special bargains here for kiddies like you. Why, I have known boys to give their mothers presents bought at this shop that were worth years, and years, and years, but which haven't cost them more than two or three hours because they have made up the difference in love. With love you can buy the best treasures of this shop with a very little expenditure in time. Now what do you think of this for your mother?"

Mr. Promptness reached up to a long shelf back of the counter and brought down a little card, framed in gold, and printed in beautiful colored letters, and illustrated with a lovely picture that seemed to Bobby to be the prettiest thing he had ever seen.

"This is a little thing that was written long ago," said Mr. Promptness, "by a man who spent much time in this shop buying things that were worth while, and in the end getting from our frame department a wonderful name which was not only a splendid possession for himself, but for the people among whom he lived. Thousands and thousands of people have been made happier, and wiser, by the way he spent his hours, and he is still mentioned among the great men of time. He was a fine, great-hearted fellow, and he put a tremendous lot of love into all that he did. His name was Thackeray. Can you read, Bobby?"

"A little," said Bobby.

"Then read this and tell me what you think of it," said Mr. Promptness.

He handed Bobby the beautiful card, and the little fellow, taking it in his hand, read the sentence: MOTHER IS THE NAME OF GOD IN THE LIPS AND HEARTS OF LITTLE CHILDREN.

"You see, my dear little boy," said the kindly salesman, "that is worth—oh, I don't know how many years, and your mother, I am sure, would rather know that that is what you think, and how you feel about her, than have you give her the finest jewels that we have to sell. And how much do you think we charge you for it?"

"Forty years!" gasped Bobby.

"No," replied Mr. Promptness. "Five minutes. Shall we put it aside for you?"

"Yes, indeed," cried Bobby, delighted to have so beautiful a Christmas gift for his mother.

So Mr. Promptness put the little card aside with the bicycle, and the wild animal books, and the marbles, putting down the price of each of the things Bobby had purchased on his sales slip.

They walked down the aisles of the great shop together, looking at the many things that time well expended would buy, and Bobby paused for a moment and spent two minutes on a glass of soda water, and purchased a quarter of an hour's worth of peanuts to give to Mr. Promptness. They came soon to a number of large rooms at one end of the shop, and in one of these Bobby saw quite a gathering of youngsters somewhat older than himself, who seemed to be very busy poring over huge books, and studying maps, and writing things down in little note-books, not one of them wasting even an instant.

"These boys are buying an education with their time," said Mr. Promptness, as they looked in at the door. "For the most part they haven't any fathers and mothers to help them, so they come here and spend what they have on the things that we have in our library. It is an interesting fact that what is bought in this room can never be stolen from you, and it happens more often than not that when they have spent hundreds of hours in here they win more time to spend on the other things that we have on sale. But there are others, I am sorry to say, who stop on their way here in the morning and fritter their loose change away in the Shop of Idleness across the way—a minute here, and a half hour there, sometimes perhaps a whole hour will be squandered over there, and when they arrive here they haven't got enough left to buy anything."

"What can you buy at the Shop of Idleness?" asked Bobby, going to the street door, and looking across the way at the shop in question, which seemed, indeed, to be doing a considerable business, if one could judge from the crowds within.

"Oh, a little fun," said Mr. Promptness. "But not the real, genuine kind, my boy. It is a sort of imitation fun that looks like the real thing, but it rings hollow when you test it, and on close inspection turns out to be nothing but frivolity."

"And what is that great gilded affair further up the street?" asked Bobby, pointing to a place with an arched entrance gilded all over and shining in the sunlight like a huge house of brass.

"That is a cake shop," said Mr. Promptness, "and it is run by an old witch named Folly. When you first look at her you think she is young and beautiful, but when you come to know her better you realize that she is old, and wrinkled, and selfish. She gives you things and tells you that you needn't pay until to-morrow and this goes on until some day to-morrow comes, and you find she has not only used up all the good time you had, but that you owe her even more, and when you can't pay she pursues you with all sorts of trouble. That's all anybody ever got at Folly's shop, Bobby —just trouble, trouble, trouble."

"There seem to be a good many people there now," said Bobby, looking up the highway at Folly's gorgeous place.

"Oh, yes," sighed Mr. Promptness. "A great many—poor things! They don't know any better, and what is worse they won't listen to those who do."

"Who is that pleasant-looking gentleman outside the Shop of Idleness?" asked Bobby, as a man appeared there and began distributing his card amongst the throng.

"He is the general manager of the Shop of Idleness," said the salesman. "As you say, he is a pleasant-looking fellow, but you must beware of him, Bobby. He is not a good person to have around. He is a very active business man, and actually follows people to their homes, and forces his way in, and describes his stock to them as being the best in the world. And all the time he is doing so he is peering around in their closets, in their chests, everywhere, with the intention of robbing them. The fact that he is so pleasant to look at makes him very popular, and I only tell you the truth when I say to you that he is the only rival we have in business that we are really afraid of. We can compete with Folly but—"

Mr. Promptness's words were interrupted by his rival across the way, who, observing Bobby standing in the doorway, cleverly tossed one of his cards across the street so that it fell at the little boy's feet. Bobby stooped down and picked it up and read it. It went this way:

THE SHOP OF IDLENESS
PROCRASTINATION,
General Manager.
Put Off Everything And Visit Our Shop.

"So he's Procrastination, is he?" said Bobby, looking at the man with much interest, for he had heard his father speak of him many a time, only his father called him "old Putoff."

"Yes, and he is truly what they say he is," said Mr. Promptness; "the thief of time."

"He doesn't look like a thief," said Bobby.

Now it is a peculiarity of Procrastination that he has a very sharp pair of ears, and he can hear a great many things that you wouldn't think could travel so far, and, as Bobby spoke, he turned suddenly and looked at him, waved his hand, and came running across the street, calling out to Bobby to wait. Mr. Promptness seized Bobby by the arm, and pulled him into the Time Shop, but not quickly enough, for he was unable to close the door before his rival was at their side.

"Glad to see you, my boy," said Procrastination, handing him another card. "Come on over to my place. It's much easier to find what you want there than it is here, and we've got a lot of comfortable chairs to sit down and think things over in. You needn't buy anything to-day, but just look over the stock."

"Don't mind him, Bobby," said Mr. Promptness, anxiously whispering in the boy's ear. "Come along with me and see the things we keep on the upper floors— I am sure they will please you."

"Wait just a minute, Mr. Promptness," replied Bobby. "I want to see what Mr. Procrastination looks like close to."

"But, my dear child, you don't seem to realize that he will pick your pocket if you let him come close—" pleaded Mr. Promptness.

But it was of no use, for the unwelcome visitor from across the way by this time had got his arm through Bobby's and was endeavoring to force the boy out through the door, although the elevator on which Bobby and Mr. Promptness were to go up-stairs was awaiting them.

"When did you come over?" said Procrastination, with his pleasantest smile, which made Bobby feel that perhaps Mr. Promptness, and his father, too, for that matter, had been very unjust to him.

"*Going up,*" cried the elevator boy.

"Come, Bobby," said Mr. Promptness, in a beseeching tone. "The car is just starting."

"Nonsense. What's your hurry?" said Procrastination. "You can take the next car just as well."

"*All aboard!*" cried the elevator boy.

"I'll be there in two seconds," returned Bobby.

"Can't wait," cried the elevator boy, and he banged the iron door to, and the car shot up to the upper regions where the keepers of the Time Shop kept their most beautiful things.

"Too bad!" said Mr. Promptness, shaking his head, sadly. "Too bad! Now, Mr. Procrastination," he added fiercely, "I must ask you to leave this shop, or I shall summon the police. You can't deceive us. Your record is known here, and—"

"Tutt-tutt-tutt, my dear Mr. Promptness!" retorted Procrastination, still looking dangerously pleasant, and smiling as if it must all be a joke. "This shop of yours is a public place, sir, and I have just as much right to spend my time here as anybody else."

"Very well, sir," said Mr. Promptness, shortly. "Have your own way if you prefer, but you will please remember that I warned you to go."

Mr. Promptness turned as he spoke and touched an electric button at the back of the counter, and immediately from all sides there came a terrific and deafening clanging of bells; and from up-stairs and down came rushing all the forces of time to the rescue of Bobby, and to put Procrastination out. They fell upon him like an army, and shouting, and struggling, but still smiling as if he thought it the greatest joke in the world, the unwelcome visitor was at last thrust into the street, and the doors were barred and bolted against his return.

"Mercy me!" cried Bobby's friend the Clock, rushing up just as the door was slammed to. "What's the meaning of all this uproar?"

"Nothing," said Mr. Promptness. "Only that wicked old Procrastination again. He caught sight of Bobby here—"

"He hasn't hurt him?" cried the Clock.

"Not much, if any," said Mr. Promptness.

"You didn't have anything to do with him, did you, Bobby?" asked the Clock, a trifle severely.

"Why, I only stopped a minute to say how do you do to him," began Bobby, sheepishly.

"Well, I'm sorry that you should have made his acquaintance," said the Clock; "but come along. It's getting late and we're due back home. Paid your bill?"

"No," said Mr. Promptness, sadly. "He hasn't had it yet, but there it is, Bobby. I think you will find it correct."

He handed the little visitor a memorandum of all the charges against him. Bobby ran over the items and saw that the total called for a payment of eight days, and fifteen hours, and twenty-three minutes, and nine seconds, well within the value of the time-checks the good floorwalker had given him, but alas! when he put his hand in his pocket to get them they were gone. Not even a minute was left!

Procrastination had succeeded only too well!

"Very sorry, Bobby," said Mr. Promptness, "but we cannot let the goods go out of the shop until they are paid for. However," he added, "although I warned you against that fellow, I feel sorry enough for you to feel inclined to help you a little, particularly when I realize how much you have missed in not seeing our treasures on the higher floors. I'll give you five minutes, my boy, to pay for the little card for your mother's Christmas present."

He placed the card in the little boy's hand, and turned away with a tear in his eye, and Bobby started to express his sorrow at the way things had turned out, and his thanks for Mr. Promptness's generosity, but there was no chance for this. There was a whirr as of many wheels, and a flapping as of many wings. Bobby felt himself being whirled around, and around, and around, and then there came a bump. Somewhat terrified he closed his eyes for an instant, and when he opened them again he found himself back on the parlor rug, lying in front of the fire, while his daddy was rolling him over and over. The lad glanced up at the mantel-piece to see what had become of the Clock, but the grouchy old ticker stared solemnly ahead of him, with his hands pointed sternly at eight o'clock, which meant that Bobby had to go to bed at once.

"Oh, let me stay up ten minutes longer," pleaded Bobby.

"No, sir," replied his father. "No more Procrastination, my son—trot along."

And it seemed to Bobby as he walked out of the room, after kissing his father and mother good-night, that that saucy old Clock grinned.

INCIDENTALLY let me say that in the whirl of his return Bobby lost the card that the good Mr. Promptness had given him for his mother, but the little fellow remembered the words that were printed on it, and when Christmas morning came his mother found them painted in watercolors on a piece of cardboard by the boy's own hand; and when she read them a tear of happiness came into her eyes, and she hugged the little chap and thanked him, and said it was the most beautiful Christmas present she had received.

"I'm glad you like it," said Bobby. "It isn't so very valuable though, Mother. It only cost me two hours and a half, and I know where you can get better looking ones for five minutes."

Which extraordinary remark led Bobby's mother to ask him if he were not feeling well!

AN AZTEC FRAGMENT

It is not alone the dreadful morning bath
That fills this hieroglyphic Babe with wrath.
His complacent Brother's jeers
Start those two resentful tears,—
But behold! the Father cometh with a lath.

The King's Pie

by Abbie Farwell Brown

THERE was great excitement in Blessington, for the king was coming with his young bride, and the town was preparing to give them a famous welcome.

Hugh, the lord mayor, was at his wit's end with all that must be done. As he sat in the town hall holding his aching head, while a mob of decorators and artists and musicians, costumers, jewelers, and florists clamored about him, there came to him a messenger from Cedric, his son. Cedric was one of the king's own courtiers, and he knew his Majesty's taste well. So he had sent to the lord mayor a hint as to how the king might best be pleased. Being a man of few words, this is how his message ran:

"His Majesty is exceedingly fond of pie."

Long pondered the lord mayor over this mysterious message, reading it backward and forward, upside down and crisscross, and mixed up like an anagram. But he could make nothing of it except what it straightforwardly said: that the king was exceedingly fond of pie.

Now in those days pie meant but one thing—a pasty, that is, meat of some sort baked in a dish covered with dough. At that time there was no such thing known as a pie made of fruit or mincemeat. Pie was not even a dainty. Pie was vulgar, ordinary victuals, and the lord mayor was shocked at his son's even mentioning pie in connection with the king.

"Pie indeed!" he shuddered. "A pretty dish to set before a king on his wedding journey! How can pie be introduced into my grand pageant? The king can get pie anywhere, in any hut or hovel along his way. What has Blessington to do with pie?"

The lord mayor snorted scornfully, and was about to dismiss his son's hint from his mind, when he had an idea! A pie! A great, glorified, poetic, symbolic pie such as could be carried in procession decorated with flowers! That was a happy thought. The lord mayor dismissed every one else and sent for all the master cooks of the city.

It was decided to accept Cedric's hint for what it was worth, and make pie the feature of the day. There should be a grand pageant of soldiers and maskers and music. And, following the other guilds, last of all should come the cooks, with their ideas of pie presented as attractively as might be, for the edification of the king. Moreover, the lord mayor said, in dismissing the white-capped company:

"To whichever of you best pleases his Majesty with the pie, I will give this reward: a team of white oxen, a hundred sacks of white flour, and a hundred pieces of white silver."

"Hurrah!" shouted the cooks, waving their white caps. Then away they hurried to put on their *thinking*-caps instead and plan for the building of the king's pie.

Now, among the cooks of Blessington there were two brothers, Roger and Rafe. Roger, the elder, had one of the hugest kitchens and shops in Blessington. But Rafe, the younger, had only a little old house on an acre of land under a little red-apple tree, with a little red cow who gave a little rich cream every day. Rafe was very poor, and no richer for having a brother well-to-do like Roger. For the thrifty cook had little to do with Rafe, whose ways were not his ways.

Rafe cooked in his little kitchen for the poor folk of the town, charging small prices such as they could pay. Indeed, often as not he gave away what he had cooked for himself to some one who seemed hungrier. This is a poor way to make profit of gold, but an excellent way to make profit of affection. And Rafe was rich in the love of the whole town.

Roger was among the cooks whom the lord mayor summoned to consult about the king's pie. But Rafe knew nothing at all of it, until one afternoon he was surprised by a visit from his brother, who had not darkened his door for many a day.

"Well, Brother," said Roger, briefly, "I suppose you are not busy, as I am. Will you work for me for a day or two? In fact, I need you."

"Need me!" said Rafe, in surprise. "How can that be, Brother?"

"I have a great task at hand," said the master cook; "a task that needs extra help. You must come. Your own work can wait well enough, I judge."

Rafe hesitated. "I must cook for my poor people first," he said.

Roger sneered. "Your poor people, indeed! I am cooking for the king! Will you hesitate now?"

"Cooking for the king!" cried Rafe. "Ah, but he is not so hungry as my neighbors will be to-morrow without their rabbit-pies."

"Rabbit-pies! It is a pie for the king that I am making!" shouted Roger, in high dudgeon,—"such a pie as you and your louts never dreamed of. Now what say you? Will you come?"

"I must do my own small cooking first," said Rafe, firmly.

"Very well then," growled Roger. "Cook for your beggars first, but come to me to-morrow. Every cook in town but you is engaged. I must have your help."

"I will come," said Rafe, simply, and Roger bade him a surly good-by without thanks or promises.

The next morning, when his own simple tasks were done, Rafe hied him to his brother's kitchen, and there he found great doings. Roger was superintending the preparations for baking an enormous pie. A group of masons had just finished building the huge oven out of doors, and about a score of smiths were struggling with the pie-dish, which they had forged of iron. It was a circular dish ten feet across and four feet deep; and it looked more like a swimming-tank than anything else.

Rafe stared in amazement. "Is that to hold your pie, Brother?" he asked.

"Yes," growled Roger. "Now get to work with the other men, for the crust must be baked this morning."

Three assistant cooks in caps and aprons were busy sifting buckets of flour, measuring out handfuls of salt and butter. Others were practising with long rolling-pins made for the occasion, so big that a man had to be at each end. On the ground lay a great round piece of tin, ten feet across, pierced full of holes.

"What is that?" whispered Rafe to one of his fellow-cooks.

"That is to be the lid of the pie," answered the cook. "See, they are lifting it onto the dish now. It will have a strong hinge, and it will be covered with crust."

"And what is to fill this marvelous pie?" asked Rafe, wondering still more. "Tender capon? Rabbits? Venison? Peacocks? What is suitable for a king? I do not know."

"Ah, there you show your lack of imagination!" cried the cook. "Master is a great man. This is a poetic pie. It is to be filled with flowers, and on the flowers will be sitting ten beautiful little children, pink and sweet as cherubs, dressed all in wreaths of flowers. And when the pie reaches the king, the top will be opened, and they will all begin to sing a song in honor of their Majesties. Is it not a pretty thought?"

"Well, if the king be not too hungry," said the practical Rafe, doubtfully.

"Nonsense!" cried the cook, testily. "Would you make out our king to be a cannibal, indeed?"

"Nay," said Rafe; "that is why I doubt. However, I am here but to assist in this colossal plan. Hand me yon bag of salt."

All day long at Roger's kitchen the cooks worked over the king's pie. At noon came a band of ten mothers, each with a rosy, smiling baby. They placed the children in the great shell to see how they would look. Every one cried: "Charming! Superb! But ah! we must not tell any one, for Roger has paid us well, and the other cooks must not know how he is to win the prize to-morrow!"

Weary and unthanked, with his meager day's wage,—a little bag of flour and a pat of butter, sugar and a handful of salt,—Rafe went home, musing sadly. "A team of white oxen; a hundred sacks of white flour; a hundred pieces of white silver,—what a prize! If only I could earn these I should be rich indeed and able to help my poor neighbors. But Roger will win the prize," he thought.

He spread on the table his frugal supper. He had emptied his larder that morning for a sick woman. He had but a few apples and a bowl of cream. It was the first food that he had eaten that day, for his brother had forgotten to bid him to his table.

As he was taking a bite from one of the rosy-cheeked apples, there came a tap at the door.

"Enter!" cried Rafe, hospitably. The door creaked, and there tottered in a little, bent, old woman in a long black cloak, leaning on a staff.

"Good evening, Son," she said, in a cracked voice. "Are you a man of charity, or will you turn away a poor old soul who has had nothing to eat for many hours?"

Rafe rose and led her to the table. "Sit down, Mother," he said kindly. "Sit and share my poor supper: a few apples from my little tree, a sup of the cream which my good little red cow gives me,—that is all; but you are welcome."

"Thanks, Son," said the old woman, and without further words she began to eat. But when she had finished she sat for a few moments looking into the empty bowl. Then she said:

"Son, why do you not bake a pie for the king?"

"I!" cried Rafe, astonished. "How can I make a pie? You see all I have in my cupboard. There is nothing but a little bag of flour, a pat of butter, a handful of sugar and salt."

"It is enough," said the stranger. "Son, I will show you a secret. You have been kind to me. Now I will tell you that which until this day no man has known. You shall make the king a pie indeed!"

"But, Mother," interrupted Rafe, smiling, "you do not know what manner of pies are being made. I have seen but one— a giant pie, a glorious pie, all golden crust and flowers and pink little babies who sing!"

"Humph!" grunted the old woman. "A pie for a pasteboard king. Why not cook a pie to tempt a hungry man?"

"The king is indeed a man," mused Rafe.

have tasted them." She leaned forward, whispering earnestly: "Make your pie of them, my son!"

"Apples! A pie of apples!" cried Rafe. "Who ever heard of such a thing!" (And at this time, indeed, no one had.)

" 'Son, why do you not bake a pie for the king?' "

"But how shall I make a pie without viands of any sort?" (As I have said, to speak of a pie in those days meant always a dish of meat or game or poultry.)

"I will tell you," said the old woman. "Have you not a tree of red apples? Yes, luscious apples of a goodly flavor, for I

"Nay, you need not laugh so scornfully," said the old crone. "You shall see! I will help you."

At her command Rafe fetched out the bag of flour and the butter, salt and sugar. Then he went to gather a basket of apples, while the old woman mended the fire and mixed the dough. Wonderingly he watched her pare the apples, core and slice them, and cover all with a blanket of crust laid softly over, but not tucked in at the edges as for an ordinary pasty. Soon the pie was baked, all flaky and brown. When it came smoking hot from the oven, the old woman slipped a knife under the blanket of crust and lifted it aside.

"See," she said, "the apples are steamed and soft. Now I will mash them with a knife and mix the butter and sugar generously therein. This one must ever do, Son, last of all. This is the crown of my secret, the only recipe for a perfect pie."

Rafe watched her curiously, by no means convinced. Then, from a pouch somewhere concealed in her robe, she drew out a strange round nut, such as Rafe had never seen before.

"This is the final blessing," she said. "See, I will grate a little of this magic nut into the pie." Forthwith it was done, and a whiff of spicy fragrance reached Rafe's nose, and, more than anything, gave him confidence in this strange new pie.

"It smells worthy," said Rafe, hungrily.

Without a word the stranger drew from under a cover a little pie baked in a tiny tin, an exact copy of the other. "Eat," she said. "Eat and judge if my secret be worth keeping."

Rafe sunk his teeth into the warm, crisp crust and ate eagerly. His eyes sparkled, but he spoke no word till the last crumb was gone.

"Oh!" he said. "It is a magic pie! Never such have I met before! Never, in all my life!"

The old woman nodded. "A magic pie," she said. "And still better when you serve it with the yellow cream of your little red cow."

"It is a pie for a king," said Rafe. "But shall I be allowed in the procession, Mother?"

"All the cooks in Blessington who choose may march with that guild," said the old woman. "Bear your pie proudly in your own hands, wearing your cap and apron. I will send some one to walk beside you and carry the jug of cream. She shall be here to-morrow when you milk the little red cow. Treat her kindly for my sake."

"Mother, how can I ever thank you—" began Rafe. But, with a quickness which seemed impossible to her years, the old woman had slipped out of the door and was gone.

The next morning bright and early Rafe went out to milk his cow. And there in the stall stood a young maid, the fairest he had ever seen.

"Good morning, Rafe," said the maid, dropping a curtsy. "I am Meg, and I have come to help you carry the king's pie." She smiled so sweetly that Rafe's heart danced a jig. She was dressed in a neat little gown of blue, with a white apron and a dainty cook's cap on her flaxen curls. And she wore red stockings and shoes, with silver buckles. From under her apron she drew a little blue jug. "See, I have brought this to hold the cream," she said, "and it is full of red strawberries for your breakfast. Milk the little red cow, Rafe, and then we can eat and be gone as soon as the cream has risen."

In a happy daze Rafe did as she bade. Merrily they breakfasted together on milk and berries and a wheaten loaf which the maid had brought, as if she knew how hungry Rafe would be. Then Meg skimmed the cream for the blue jug, and they were ready to start. Rafe, in his white cap and apron, bore the precious pie, while Meg walked along at his side. A merry, handsome couple they were.

When they came to the market-place they found a great crowd assembled. "Ho, Rafe! Rafe!" people shouted to him, for every one knew and loved him. "Come here! Come with us!"

But Rafe answered: "Nay, I am going to walk in the procession with the other cooks. I have a pie for the king."

"A pie! A pie!" they cried good-naturedly. "Look at Rafe's pasty! Of what is it made, Rafe? Grasshoppers or mice?" For they knew how poor he was.

But Rafe only smiled and pushed his way to where the cooks were gathered. They, too, greeted him with jests. But he insisted that he must march with them. So they gave him place at the very end of the line, with the little maid at his side. But when he saw the wonderful pies all around him, he sighed and shook his head, looking ruefully at his own simple offering. The little maid, seeing him so look, said:

"Never mind, Rafe. You are giving your best to the king. No one can do more than that."

The people waited. The hands of the great clock in the market-place crept slowly around until they marked noon. Every one began to feel uneasy, for it was close upon the dinner-hour, and the long procession had not moved. The king and queen were late.

At last there sounded the blast of a trumpet, which told that the king and his bride had arrived, and that the lord mayor had led them to their seats on the balcony in front of the town hall. Every one gave a sigh of relief. But then there was another long wait, while the hands of the clock crept on—on, and the people watched and craned their necks eagerly. The lord mayor was making his speech, and it was very long. Finally arose more shouts and huzzas, not because the speech was good, but because it was ended. And presently another trumpet gave signal for the procession to start.

Off they went, through the streets full of cheering, hungry people. Soldiers and bands of music led the way; then came the maskers and the flower-maidens, the city guilds and all the arts and crafts. Finally passed along the yoke of snowy oxen, with ribbons in their ears, drawing a white wain in which were the bags of flour and silver, the prize for the best pie-maker of Blessington. When the company of white-capped cooks came within sight of the king, he laughed merrily and said:

"Cooks! Now we shall have something worth while, for I am growing hungry indeed!" And the young queen whispered: "So am I!"

Then came the pies. And such pies! Carried on the shoulders of sturdy boys, drawn by teams of ponies, wreathed in flowers and stuck over with mottos, the pies passed along before the hungry king. And not one of the pies was real! The king's smile gradually faded.

There was a wonderful big pie fashioned like a ship,—rigged with masts and sails and manned by sailor-dolls. There was a fine brown pasty like a bird's nest, and when it passed the king, off came the cover, and out flew four-and-twenty blackbirds croaking lustily.

"Good-by, dinner!" sighed the king, looking after them wistfully. The queen nudged him and said: "Sh! Behave, your Majesty!" But she also began to look hungrier and hungrier.

There passed a pie in a carriage drawn by six mules. It seemed piping hot, for steam came out of it. But when it reached the king it blew up with a *bang!* scattering showers of blossoms over the royal party.

"My faith!" cried the king, "methought this was the end of all things. But it seems not. Here come more and more empty pies!" The queen smelled of her salts and grew paler every moment.

One pie had a musical box inside and played a sweet tune as it passed the king.

In one was hidden a tiny dwarf, who popped out like a jack-in-the-box when the queen pulled a golden cord.

Still the procession moved on, and so did the hands of the clock, and the king's hands moved to his ample girdle, which he tightened sharply. But both he and the pale young queen were too polite to ask the lord mayor for buns or something to sustain them.

The pie which caused the greatest excitement as it passed along, drawn by four white horses, was that of Roger, the master cook, who walked proudly beside it. When he came opposite the king the carriage stopped, the cover was lifted, and ten beautiful babies on a bed of roses waved their little hands and began to sing. The queen leaned forward eagerly, forgetting to be hungry. "How sweet! The darlings!" she murmured. "Oh, this is the best of all!" Roger the cook heard her and flushed with triumph.

But the king grumbled: "Humph! They look good enough to eat, but—my faith, I hope that this is the end, for soon I must eat something, or I shall become a cannibal!"

"Your Majesty!" protested the queen, faintly. But the king interrupted her.

"What comes here?" he cried. "This looks sensible!" It was Rafe and the pretty maid bringing up the rear of the procession. Side by side they walked in cap and apron, he bearing the small, delicately browned pie, she with a jug of yellow cream. No one paid any attention to them, but closed in around them, following Roger's chariot.

When Rafe and Meg came opposite the king and queen, they turned and Rafe bowed low, holding up the pie as high as he could. The pretty maid curtsied gracefully, and offered the cream-jug with a winsome smile. The crowd was fain to hustle them on; but the king struck the floor with his staff and pointed eagerly at the pie.

"Hold!" he cried, "What have you there?"

Everyone stopped and began to stare. Rafe bowed again.

"'Tis a pie, your Majesty," said Rafe, simply, "an apple pie."

"With cream for the top," lisped the little maid, curtsying again.

"Apple pie!" cried the king. "Who ever heard of an apple pie! A pie should be of savory meat. But of *apples!*" Words failed to express his astonishment.

"Butter and sugar, Sire, go to the making of it, and the dust of a wondrous nut. Will you taste it, Sire?" Rafe held out the pie temptingly.

"With thick cream to pour on the top,— yellow, sweet, rich, thick cream!" said Meg, lingering over each word as if it melted on her lips.

"Give hither that pie!" almost shouted the hungry king. "I will look into this matter." And, drawing a dagger from his girdle, he seized and stabbed the pie to the heart. Sniffing at it eagerly, his eyes grew round, and he smacked his lips. "It is good, I wager my scepter!" he cried. "Hand me the cream, fair maid."

The little maid stepped up and daintily poured cream upon the shattered pie, and without more ado the king began to eat with his dagger. (This was not considered bad manners in those days.) After the first mouthful he stopped only to say: "Food of the fairies! Pie of the pixies! Cook, you are a magician!" He went on at a rate which threatened not to leave a mouthful. But the queen pulled at his sleeve. "A bite for me, your Majesty," she begged. And, with an apology, the king handed her what was left, watching her wistfully till she ate the last crumb.

"Delicious! I never tasted anything finer," she cried. "I must have the recipe."

"*I* must have the cook!" cried the king, turning to Rafe, with a broad grin on his merry, fat face. "You must come with me and cook such pies for every meal. Yes, I will have them for breakfast, too," he insisted, in response to a protest from the queen.

Then up stepped Hugh, the lord mayor.

"Sire," said he, bowing low, "will your Majesty deign to point out to me the pie which has best pleased you, that I may have it set in the place of honor, and give the prize to the maker?"

"That I cannot do," said the king, "for the pie no longer exists. It is *here*," and he slapped his generous waistband. "But give whatever prize there may be to this worthy fellow, whom I now dub Baron Applepy. Baron, wear this ring in token of my pleasure in your pie." He drew a fine ruby from his finger and gave it to Rafe.

"And this is for the little maid," said the queen, taking a beautiful pearl necklace and tossing it over Meg's curls.

But Roger, the master cook, stood by and tore his hair when he saw what was happening.

Then up came the yoke of white oxen drawing the cart bearing the prize. And the lord mayor gave a goad into Rafe's hands, with words of congratulation.

"Now mount and come with me," said the king. But Rafe hesitated.

"Your Majesty," he replied, "I see no way to make another pie like this which has pleased you. For I have no more of the magic nuts wherewith to flavor a second."

The king frowned. "What! No more pie! Is this to be the first and the last? Sirrah, I am not pleased!"

Then little Meg stepped forth. "The magic nut is the nutmeg," said she. "My name is Meg, and Granny called the magic nuts after me. I know where is hidden a store of them. These are my dower." She emptied her pockets of the nuts which

they held, and they were a precious handful.

"Ha!" cried the king, eagerly, "you must marry Baron Applepy, that he may use your dower in our behalf."

Rafe and the maid looked sidewise at one another.

"You are willing, my dear?" said the queen, smiling upon Meg.

"Yes," whispered she, with red-apple cheeks.

"Yes, indeed!" cried Rafe when the queen looked at him. But again he seemed troubled.

"Your Majesty," he said, "I cannot leave my poor neighbors. There will be no one to cook for them at my prices."

"You shall have your own price from me," said the king.

Rafe bowed low. "You do me great honor," he said humbly. "But I cannot leave my poor people, my house and my cow and my apple-tree; indeed I cannot."

The king looked very angry and raised his staff with a gesture of wrath. But the queen laid her hand upon his arm.

"Why may he not live where he will and yet cook the pies for us?" she said. "A messenger on a fleet horse can bring them to us every day. We shall then have pies like that first delicious one, made from apples from that very same red-apple tree of his. They would be best of all."

"True," said the king, reflecting for a moment.

"Please, your Majesty," said Meg, in her most winsome tones, "I do so long to help Rafe pick the red apples for your pies and skim the yellow cream of the little red cow. And please, I do so long to help him cook for his poor neighbors, who will miss him so. Now that we have the prize, we can do much for them. Please, your Majesty!"

"Please, your Majesty!" begged the queen. So the king hemmed and hawed and yielded. "But see, Baron Applepy," he said, "that you make me three fine pies every day, for which my swiftest messenger shall call. Now farewell to thee—and to all. We must be off."

"Heaven bless your Majesties," said Rafe and Meg, bowing and curtsying low. Then Rafe lifted the little maid into the white cart beside the hundred sacks of flour and the bag of silver, and amid shouts and cheers away they drove the white oxen toward the little house on the acre of land under the red-apple tree, where the little red cow was waiting for them. And there they lived happily ever after, making three pies a day for the king at an enormous price, and feeding the beloved poor people, his neighbors, for no price at all.

THE HIDDEN RILL

(Translated from the Spanish)

By WILLIAM CULLEN BRYANT

Across a pleasant field, a rill unseen
   Steals from a fountain, nor does aught betray
Its presence, save a tint of livelier green,
   And flowers that scent the air along its way.
Thus secretly should charity attend
   Those who in want's dim chambers pine and grieve;
And nought should e'er reveal the aid we lend,
   Save the glad looks our kindly visits leave.

THE RIP VAN WINKLE MAN-O'-WAR

(AN "AS-IT-*MIGHT*-HAVE-HAPPENED" STORY)

by H. Irving Hancock

"**S**AIL two points off sta'bu'd bow, sir!" came up to the bridge from the bow watch of the second class battle-ship *Tecumseh,* of the United States Navy.

Lieutenant Rowland, officer of the watch, nodded slightly, spy-glass at his eyes, for he had made out the stranger at the same moment.

It was morning, just after daylight, on Monday, April 20, 1908. The *Tecumseh,* southbound, and going at slow cruising speed, was in latitude about 30° S. and longitude 35° W., that is to say, about six hundred and fifty miles southeast of Rio Janeiro.

Patches of light-brown, smoky, thick haze that is peculiar to the South Atlantic at this season of the year hung about the trim, bristling, white watercraft. Here and there were open streaks showing deep blue water and unclouded skies overhead.

Out of one of these patches of haze, less than a quarter of a mile away, poked a black bowsprit, topped by a spread of old yellow canvas. This was followed by the looming up of a rusty black hull, high out of water; and then a foremast came into view. But what caused officer and bow watch to start in intense astonishment was the muzzle of a long, old-style, 32-pounder bow-gun that, peering out of its canvas jacket, appeared at the stranger's starboard bow.

"The *Flying Dutchman?*" wondered the bow watch.

The men in the wheel-house and the few other members of the crew on duty forward rubbed their eyes. Whatever he felt within, the calm young officer on the bridge kept his outward composure admirably. The vessel that now came wholly out of the haze proved to be a wooden ship of nearly four thousand tons. Her three masts bore a full spread of much-patched, time-seared canvas, while from a single funnel wood smoke floated indolently. Steam was plainly only auxiliary on this craft. Despite the revolutions of the side paddle-wheels the stranger was making barely six knots an hour northward. A few deck-guns were visible, while white-painted, closed ports along the side perhaps concealed others.

It came as a shock to all beholders aboard the *Tecumseh* that this rather ghostly old craft displayed, aft, an old United States flag of many years ago.

"We'll soon know something about this marine ghost, or whatever it is!" said Lieutenant Rowland to himself, as, with a hand on the lever of the mechanical signaling apparatus, he gave the order for the stopping of the battle-ship's propeller-shafts. His verbal command to a marine brought Ensign Waite and Cadet Midshipman Ellis hastily forward.

"Give 'em a blank shot, Mr. Waite!" directed Rowland. "Mr. Ellis, my compliments to the captain and the executive officer, and tell 'em—"

As a puff of white smoke and a sharp report left one of the *Tecumseh's* lighter forward guns, the stranger's colors dipped, while a clump of signal-flags was hauled to the old craft's maintop and there broken out.

"I can't make out that bunting gibberish!" muttered Rowland, impatiently, as he studied the flags through his glass. "Any orders, sir?" he asked, from force of habit, as the executive officer reached the bridge just ahead of the captain.

"No," said both. "Wait."

As the old black craft, in slowly stopping headway, turned and came somewhat nearer, the *Tecumseh's* signal-flags shook out the challenge, "Who are you?" But the stranger replied only with a single deep-throated blast from her whistle.

"Mr. Thornton," said Captain Loring, turning to an ensign in the group of officers that had hastened close to the bridge, "you're our authority on everything ancient in the navy. Can you place the craft yonder?"

"She carries about an 1856 flag, sir, and looks like one of our old line-of-battle ships before the war. But there's no such craft in commission to-day, sir."

From the davits at the starboard waist of the stranger a cumbersome black rowing cutter was lowered in rather seamanlike manner, though the sailors going stiffly down a side gangway to the cutter appeared to be all old, white-haired men. A feeling somewhat of awe crept over the hundreds of watchers now on the white battle-ship's decks.

Though with a stiffness of movement suggestive of something between old age and rheumatism, the men in the cutter got away from their own vessel in good old naval style. Officers and blue-jackets on the *Tecumseh* watched the approaching cutter until Captain Loring roared through a megaphone: "What ship are you from?"

From a white-haired, venerable-faced man of at least seventy years, who sat in the stern-sheets of the cutter, and who wore a curious, dingy, old-style blue uniform, even to the ancient "cheese-box" cap of the old navy, came the response.

"We couldn't read your signals, sir, any better than you could make out ours. Our craft is the line-of-battle ship *Neponset,* United States Navy. Sailed from New York November 18, 1858, and frozen in below the Antarctic Circle almost ever since—now free, thank heaven, to return to the United States! Your flag, sir, and your strange, wonderful craft, show us that our country still lives! We—"

The ancient officer's speech ended in a huskiness that he could not choke down. Yet his words would not have been heard, for one blue-jacket on the *Tecumseh,* gazing hard, forgot discipline and roared hoarsely:

"Mates, we're gazing on wot's left of the Old Navy, that saved this country of our'n and kept it for the New Navy!"

What a mighty tempest of a cheer went up from six hundred throats as the meaning of that speech broke on these gallant sailors of to-day! Even their officers forgot their dignity and joined in the hearty salute. As the cutter came in closer, a side gangway was quickly lowered, while captain and executive officer hurried to receive the wonderful guests.

Only the aged officer who had answered the hail came up the narrow steps. He paused long enough to say to a white-haired brother officer in the cutter:

"Keep all hands in the boat, Midshipman."

"Aye, aye, sir!" came cheerily from that "boy" of past threescore. Then, as this ranking officer, looking as though he had stepped from an old-time print, started to ascend, Ensign Thornton, at a nod from his captain, ran down to give the old man a reverentially supporting arm.

"I am Captain Loring, and I welcome you most heartily, sir, on my own behalf and that of my brother officers," said the *Tecumseh's* commander in husky tones, as the pair reached the head of the gangway.

"I tender you my most respectful thanks, sir," came simply, in a now strong, clear voice from the old man. "I am Second Lieutenant Raymond, ranking surviving officer of the old *Neponset*. I have brought our crumbly old ship's papers, sir, for your inspection."

"Come down to my cabin," begged Captain Loring, and led the way.

While the two commanders were below, recovered discipline prevented any curious hails or conversation between the men on the battle-ship and those in the cutter that rode on the ground-swell at a little distance from the ship's side. It was not long ere the *Tecumseh's* executive officer, Mr. Stayton, was sent for. He soon returned to the deck, saying:

"Mr. Rowland, hail the cutter, and ask the men, with Captain Loring's compliments, to come aboard. Mr. Waite, clear away cutters number three and four, placing Mr. Ellis in charge of one. Go aboard the *Neponset* and hand this invitation to Lieutenant Clover. Gentlemen," to the other officers gathered about, "the captain presents his compliments and invites all not on duty to join our guest and guests-to-come in the ward-room."

As the officers filed below they found the mess-servants flying about in the greatest bustle.

"Gentlemen," began Captain Loring, "this strange tale of the *Neponset* seems proven by the papers that Mr. Raymond brought. You will not be surprised at learning that I have invited the other officers of the *Neponset*—only seven survive, I regret to say—to come aboard and breakfast with us. Until that meal has been met and vanquished I feel that we shall do well to postpone asking for the story that I know every one is waiting in the utmost suspense to hear."

In a few moments more Midshipman John Dalton, sixty-five years old, and the youngest survivor of the *Neponset*, came below, while his venerable-looking boat's crew were being received with tremendous cheers by the *Tecumseh's* enlisted men overhead. Nor were the two steam-launches long in reaching the old black craft and in returning with the remaining officers and some thirty members of the *Neponset's* crew. Undoubtedly the most disappointed man on the old-time fighting ship was Boatswain Peterson, who was obliged to remain in temporary command.

Only greetings and pleasantries of the day followed the introductions between the officers of the Old Navy and the New. They seated themselves at the ward-room tables, old Mr. Raymond at the post of honor.

For nearly an hour, on account of the tension of waiting for the story to come, the meal proceeded rather solemnly. Only once did Lieutenant Raymond touch upon the past, when, looking down at his plate, he sighed: "It seems good to eat such food again, after half a century."

His words were echoed by a murmur from the other aged officers of the *Neponset*, yet, being "youngsters" in point of service rank, they left the remarks mainly to their commanding officer.

When the meal was being cleared away the first surprise came to the nattier officers of the *Tecumseh*. The waiters brought the choicest cigars of the mess. Looking down into a box held before him, Lieutenant Raymond, with an odd, far-away expression in his eyes, said slowly:

"It is good to see the weed, thank you. We've been nearly fifty years away from tobacco, and so we've lost the habit. But we'd like to try these!"

Then Captain Loring asked:

"Will it be agreeable to you, now, sir, to begin some account of your fifty years in the navy but out of the world?"

"I fear you will be disappointed, there is so little to tell," smiled the old man. "We have about the same story to tell as Rip Van Winkle told when he came back from his long sleep. In fact, sir, of late years I've often thought of the good old *Neponset* as the Rip Van Winkle of the United States Navy.

"I have told you the date when we left New York. Our commanding officer, Captain Howard, was ordered by the Navy Department to go as far south of the Antarctic Circle as possible, for the double purpose of making magnetic observations and geographical discoveries. We were expected to be away for two years, and were provisioned for three. Our only stop was at Rio Janeiro, for more fuel.

"Then we plunged boldly southward. On that side of the equator, of course, the summer season is the reverse of that at the north. So we neared the extreme southern seas in what was the height of summer. It was an unusually warm year in the Antarctic, I remember. The sea was so open that we made for the South Orkney Islands without trouble. After stopping there for two days we went somewhat out of our direct course, passing several large tracts of land, but not stopping until we reached Graham Land, which, as you know, is just on the Antarctic Circle. At Graham Land we remained for a week. While some of our officers made volumes of magnetic observations and calculations, Captain Howard kept his eye on the sea conditions.

"Though icebergs dotted the sea in all directions, the water yet remained won-derfully open for the South Polar region. Captain Howard, therefore, decided upon a swift dash southward, even though we ran the risk of becoming ice-bound until the following year.

"It seemed well worth the trying. I may add, sir and gentlemen, that we made the dash with bold and cheery hearts. Though we had to be content with slow progress past the increasing number of icebergs, yet for days we kept on to the southward. One daybreak found us close to a great wall of ice. That wall, sir, was at least two hundred feet high. Captain Howard decided to skirt that great barrier of ice. Going westward at only about four knots an hour, we followed that wall for over four hundred miles.

"Then, one morning, our eyes were amazed by the sight of great, snow-clad mountain peaks on the further side of the ice wall. Our mathematicians quickly figured that the three visible peaks were from eleven to twelve thousand feet high.

"Within two hours of that time, sir and gentlemen, we found an open passage through the ice wall. We followed that passage through, discovering the ice wall, at that point, to be some two thousand feet thick. But beyond, sir, at the bases of those great mountains, we found the bare black rocks jutting out. The water, too, near this land, was much warmer than any we had encountered in days. By noon we sighted a fourth mountain, a live volcano with smoke issuing from its top.

"As we neared the base of this fourth mountain Captain Howard determined to send several officers and two boats' crews ashore. Almost their first discovery was a rock-lined entrance to a cove beyond. Skirting the cove, hemmed in by the mountains, was a valley of warm, fertile land, comprising some three square miles. Throughout this tract of land geysers of warm water spouted and the creeks formed by their waters kept the land warm and genial in that Antarctic summer. Vegetation grew freely, and at least half of the valley was covered by trees that could not be called stunted in latitude 82° S."

"Eighty-two?" cried Captain Loring, astonished.

"Eighty-two, sir," replied Lieutenant Raymond, gravely.

"Pardon me, sir. I did not mean to interrupt you. But your expedition went further south than any before or since!"

"And *stayed there longer!*" sighed Mr. Raymond. "For we were fascinated, and reveled in explorations ashore until one morning, a fortnight later, we made the awful discovery that our gap in the ice wall had closed. It has remained closed, ever since, until about a fortnight ago."

A gasp of astonishment—almost of horror—went round the *Tecumseh's* officers.

"Well, sir," continued Lieutenant Raymond, "there is not much more to be told. We were unable to get out, but we kedged our stanch old *Neponset* into that cove, and later built an especial basin in which we kept her all these years, diverting enough of the flow of the geysers into that basin so that the water about our ship's hull never froze.

"The climate was, of course, cold in winter, but our little three-mile kingdom had as comfortable a climate, winter or summer, as New York can boast. We had plenty of timber for houses and fuel, while the great mountains kept off the iciest Antarctic blasts. Our apothecary had, in a chest, several kinds of vegetable seeds and wheat, from which we harvested a good crop the first summer. There were fish in the waters, a species of seal and several varieties of birds, so that we fared well enough. We were well stocked with cloth, and made much use also of sealskins and the skins of the larger birds.

"Through it all, sir and gentlemen, we tried never to forget that we belonged to the United States Navy, and that we had one of the nation's vessels and a proud old flag to be returned to the American people. As the years went on I will admit that we often despaired of ever seeing our beloved country again. Our officers fell from eighteen to seven, and our crew from two hundred and eighty-nine to seventy-one. Still we felt that we had enough stout hearts to take the old *Neponset* home. Never once did we grow slack in our duty of fitting in new ship's timbers wherever an old one showed signs of giving out. We actually hoarded our uniform cloths, sir, that we might return home with some of the dignity befitting our country's service.

"Even our paint supply we hoarded, that the good old ship herself might go home shipshape and clean. Our ammunition we could not keep, for, with our best care, it gradually became worthless.

"It was twenty-six years ago that Captain Howard, full of hope and the love of duty to the last, died. His last words were: 'Do not despair, gentlemen. We have all made a brave fight of it. You will yet get back home.'

"Sir and gentlemen, a fortnight ago we discovered an opening in the wall of ice; and we were ready, as we had been for fifty years. An hour we spent, in reverent homage, at the graves of our beloved comrades in that ice-bound little valley. Then, with the boldest hearts possible, we left the place of our ship's long sleep, came safely through the great ice barrier, and—well, the rest of our tale you see before you."

Lieutenant Raymond's fine old eyes gleamed wet as he slipped from his seat at the table for a look through one of the port-holes at the not far distant *Neponset*.

"Now," said Captain Loring, speaking very softly, though heard by all, "we younger men understand more of the spirit of the Old Navy. Your ship's company waited a full half-century for your one chance of escape, and then, with true American pluck, took it the first instant that the chance came. Mr. Raymond, may we again shake the hand of each of the *Neponset's* officers? It will make better American sailors of us."

Before the hand-shaking was finished it rounded off into hearty cheering by these younger men of the New Navy. During the tumult the *Neponset's* aged officers looked actually abashed.

"At the time we—left the world," said Lieutenant Raymond, "war with England was feared in our country. I would like to ask if that war ever came about?"

"No, sir; and England and the United States to-day, sir, are two of the firmest friends in the world. But," added Captain Loring, very gravely, "within three years after your enforced exile, the Northern and Southern States clashed in the most gigantic war of modern times. Ten years ago we fought Spain. To-day, a portion of the United States Navy has just completed a cruise around the world—the most formidable naval fleet that ever made so long a cruise."

"A cruise around the world by a whole fleet!" cried Lieutenant Raymond and some of his brother officers in concert. "And the North and South at war! Tell us about that, I beg you!" pleaded the *Neponset's* commander.

"Mr. Thornton, as our historian aboard, I think you are best qualified for that performance," suggested Captain Loring. "While you are getting ready I will pass the word for such of the *Neponset's* crew as are aboard to come and listen with their officers."

A score and a half of the visiting white-haired enlisted men, all scrupulously neat in their darned and mended, faded blue uniforms, came down, gathering at the far end of the ward-room. They would have

stood, but Captain Loring insisted that chairs be placed for these old heroes.

For nearly two hours Thornton described the deeds of the American navy in the Civil War. At first there was deep awe over the story of the great national quarrel. Later the speaker was often interrupted by hoarse cheers from his enthused listeners. Porter, Farragut, Van Brunt, Mercer, Tatnall, Rodgers, Parker, Morris —these and scores of other names were those of living comrades to the *Neponset's* officers and men, who cheered the valor of their old-time friends to the echo. There were few dry eyes.

Ensign Thornton passed at last to the few but bright glories of the war with Spain. Dewey was a youngster, known to Lieutenant Raymond and two of his brother officers, but Admirals Sampson, Schley, and Evans were names over which they shook their heads even while their eyes brightened.

"You will want books to read on the rest of your homeward cruise, that you may 'pick up' and get into the world again," wound up Mr. Thornton. "I will bring you all that I think will be of use to you."

As he went in search of the books, brother officers excused themselves on the same errand. In a few minutes the old-timers had been supplied with more reading matter than could be digested in a year.

"We shall be as poor in purse as in comprehension of to-day's world, I imagine," said Mr. Raymond, musingly. "Of course our pay will have been stopped long ago."

"Poor in purse!" Captain Loring exclaimed, bringing a hand down heavily on the table. "I wish I had your prospects of a rich old age. Why, sir, every officer and man of you will be entitled to fifty years of back pay, for you've never been mustered out. And the country will certainly compel Congress to add compound interest at at least four per cent."

"Can that be so?" murmured Mr. Raymond, looking rather uncomfortable.

"Why, it will mount up into millions, altogether!" cried old Midshipman Dalton, after doing some frantic figuring on paper.

"Can that be so?" repeated Mr. Raymond, glancing at his astonished-looking brother officers. "Can the United States stand such a drain?"

"Yes! yes! Of course it can! We are a very rich country, now!" laughed Captain Loring. "But, gentlemen of the *Tecumseh,* as our guests must all be mentally tired, I ask you to take them above for a turn in the deck air."

"We can't seem to pick up any craft between here and Rio that has a wireless installation, sir," reported Ensign Waite, approaching his commander. The guests stared so curiously at that that they had to listen, with heads that must have throbbed, to the wonderful story of the wireless telegraph.

Captain Loring arranged with Lieutenant Raymond to have both vessels now shape their course toward Rio Janeiro.

"From there we will cable the Navy Department at Washington," Captain Loring explained, and then remembered that even the submarine cable was new to these men of the Rip Van Winkle man-o'-war.

The guests were now taken to the turrets to inspect the great rifled guns, the wonderful aiming mechanisms, the range-finders, and electric firing apparatus. These men of the Old Navy gazed with awe even at the hoisting of massive ammunition from the depths of this steel monster. The torpedo-tubes and the great Whitehead messengers of destruction almost made them shudder. The twentieth-century engine-room fascinated them. They saw a thousand wonders and new inventions in quick succession, and tried to comprehend each new marvel, yet cried out that they could not.

"We shall suffer collapse if you show us more to-day," urged Lieutenant Raymond, with a wavering smile. "We have been asleep for fifty years! Now, by the great Paul Jones, it will take us another fifty to wake!"

"We will lunch, then," suggested Captain Loring, and led the way once more to the ward-room. Through the meal the seven guests sat in an almost stunned silence. They were doing their best to recollect what they had heard and seen of naval progress in fifty wonder-filled years.

"With your approval, sir, we shall return to our ship, to think over what has come to us to-day," proposed Lieutenant Raymond, when luncheon was over. "And to rest," he added truthfully. "You will understand, sir, when we say that our heads never seemed so near to bursting. But we shall be glad, sir, if as many of you as possible will board us, at dark, and dine with us on the simple fare of which we have an abundance."

That invitation was gladly accepted. Most of the officers and crew of the *Tecumseh* spent a good deal of the afternoon gazing across at the drowsy black hull of the *Neponset* lumbering along over the ground-swell.

Never had any officer of the big white battle-ship sat at a simpler meal than the guests of the evening partook of aboard the old Rip Van Winkle man-o'-war. The meats were unfamiliar flesh that had been hunted far below the Antarctic Circle, though most of the vegetables were ordinary. There was wheat bread, though of a peculiar flavor.

After dinner it needed but a bare hour for the guests to see the little that was to be seen aboard the old *Neponset*. To modern eyes it was a primitive wooden ship. The furnaces under the boilers would burn either wood or coal. Mr. Raymond explained that they were now burning the former but had coal in reserve. The cannon were of the old smooth-bore type; the few shells in the magazine were worthless from age.

Just as the *Tecumseh's* officers stepped out upon deck, accompanied by their hosts, the great electric search-light of the white battle-ship turned its glaring eye on them, flooding the old man-o'-war's decks with an intense glow. A cry of amazement and even fear went up from the white-haired old sailors forward. They turned their faces from this brilliant glare, strangest of all equipment wonders of a modern seafighter.

The leave-taking between visiting officers and their hosts was simple but affecting. Then, in a reverent silence, the younger, nattier men went over the side into the steam-launch.

For some time there was complete silence among the *Tecumseh* group. Finally Mr. Stayton, the executive officer, said: "It was the *men,* not the *machines,* that made the Old Navy great!"

THE course for the night had been arranged between the respective commanding officers. The vessels were to keep as close together as wisdom in ship-handling permitted. But, as it happened, by six bells, long before midnight, the sky had darkened so as to blot out of sight the stars. A half-hour later a gale suddenly arose that quickly gave the officers of both ships all they wanted to think about. It was like a veritable West Indian hurricane, with a roaring wind and blinding sheets of rain, so that in a jiffy, as it seemed, each vessel lost sight of the other's lights. At first, the old ship's whistle could be heard in answer to the *Tecumseh's* deep-throated notes. Then even the husky old whistle ceased as a sound of near-by presence. No officer

on the *Tecumseh* slept that night. The raging winds and waters gave even the modern cruiser a struggle for life, and every man had to be at his post. And the dawn brought no relief, for nothing could be seen even a few ship-lengths away through the solid wall of fiercely driven rain. But, about three hours after daylight, the storm abated, and then the *Tecumseh's* officers swept the sea in vain with their glasses. The *Neponset* had vanished.

Captain Loring searched unceasingly for three days. His officers, well-nigh sleepless, shared the stern vigil with him. The *Neponset* was not seen again, nor was a single piece of wreckage found.

"I cannot bear to think of those grand old fellows going to the bottom!" said Captain Loring, that night, when he dined in the ward-room.

"Do you know, sir," smiled Mr. Thornton, wistfully, "I've just a notion that neither the *Neponset* nor the crew went under the waves?"

'Why, what else can have befallen them, sir?" demanded the captain of his young subordinate.

"Well, sir," went on the ship's historian, slowly, "you remember how awed those fine old men felt over the way the world has gone ahead since their day. Then, too, they didn't have any comprehension of how our country has grown. Why, sir, officers and men alike seemed absolutely scared at thought of coming back into a world and life that were utterly strange to them!"

"So you think—"

"Think?" cried Mr. Thornton, while his brother officers gazed at him with varying emotions. "Why, sir, it looks to me like a nine-to-one chance that the *Neponset* did weather that gale. She was old, but had been admirably kept up. So, sir, what more likely than that the gale gave those splendid old fellows the impulse to put about and make off back to their cove at 82° South? They knew that their naval hulk and their report were almost worthless to the country; they felt awed, exiled, and behind the times; they were certain that none of their old comrades still lived nor the relatives they had once known. I overheard one of them say as much to a comrade."

As Thornton ceased, there was a very long pause.

Who *knew?* It seemed sacrilege merely to *guess.* The captain rose slowly.

"Any orders, sir?" asked the lieutenant.

"Keep to the course, Mr. Wildman. We will put in at Rio Janeiro and cable the Navy Department. I fear we are going to have a hard time finding people to believe us when the whole story is told. But—for ourselves—we shall always treasure loving thoughts of those fine men of the Old Navy!"

BETTY'S BEST CHRISTMAS

by *Alice Hegan Rice*

IT was a long, long time ago, in the early days of the Civil War, when two little cousins lay under the shade of a broad beech-tree in Kentucky, and asked each other, for all the world like little girls of the present day, "What can we do next?"

They had swung on the willow-boughs that hung above the creek where it ambled sleepily between its banks of fern and mint; they had climbed the hay-loft and jumped off until they were tired. Now, in the heat of the afternoon, they lay on the grass, eating large slices of bread and jam and trying to think of something to do next.

"I know what I'd say if you weren't a goody-goody!" said Betty, a fair-haired, blue-eyed person of nine, with red lips that pouted when they weren't smiling, and eyes that could dance while the tears still stood in them.

"I'm *not* a goody-goody!" said the older girl, indignantly, "only with Daddy sick in the hospital and Aunty and Grandmother both away, I think we ought to mind Mammy."

"There's always some reason!" said Betty, with a rebellious toss of her curls. "They've been telling us that the Yankees would get us if we did this or that, until I 'most wish they would!"

"They wouldn't hurt me," said Jane, proudly, "because my father is a Union man."

"Well, your grandfather ain't, or Mother, or me, or Mammy. We wouldn't be Yankees for anything!"

A troubled expression crossed Jane's delicate, serious face. She was only eleven, but the tragedy of the terrible war had already thrown its sinister shadows across her life. Her little home in the North had been broken up, her mother was off in a distant hospital nursing the dear father who had given his right arm for his country, and she was here at Hollycrest, her mother's old home in Kentucky, where she hardly dared mention her father's name. "Rebels" and "Yankees"! How she hated the words! It made her just as angry to hear her grandfather called the one, as it did to hear her father called the other.

"I know what I am going to do," announced Betty, whose thoughts had gone back to that forbidden something that started the argument. "I'm going over to the office."

The office was a one-room log-building across the road, where Grandfather kept his books and papers and fled for refuge when the big house became too noisy with the coming and going of kith and kin. It was the one place on the estate forbidden to the children, and, by a strange law of nature, also the most fascinating.

Betty was a person who always suited the action to the word, and before Jane could remonstrate she was leading the way across the yard. As they passed the milk-cellar they encountered an obstacle. In fact, they encountered two of them. Two woolly little colored girls, who had been sliding down the slanting door, disentangled themselves from the bunch in which they had landed, and demanded in one breath: "Whar you-all gwine at?"

"Not any place you can go," said Betty, with a superior air.

"Kin too! Can't I, Miss Jane?" asked the blackest of the little girls, whose name was Lily White. Then as she saw them about to slip off, she added: "I bet I knows whar you-all's gwine. You gwine slip in Marse Jim's office! Ef you don't take me 'long, I'm gwine tell Mammy on you!"

Mammy's voice could be heard from the depths of the milk-cellar singing "Swing Low, Sweet Chariot." A word from her would put an end to the expedition.

"Well, we can't take Rose," said Betty, impatiently; "what you going to do with her?"

They all looked at the fat little darkey, who stood stolidly awaiting the verdict. If it was favorable, all would be well; if unfavorable, she was prepared to make trouble.

Rose was only four, but she had found a way of getting everything she wanted in the world. When things did not go exactly to suit her, she drew in her breath in one long piercing shriek, and held it. Held it until her eyes rolled back in her head, and her short kinky hair stood on end, and Mammy had to be summoned to shake her and dash water in her face. Even Betty, who was in the habit of having her way about most things, had to give in to Rose.

"Oh, well," she said, "bring her along. But if we play Indian, she's got to be the white child that's scalped."

The little procession made its way round the big white house, with its pillared porticoes, down the oleander-bordered avenue, and across the road. The door of the office was always locked, but the windows were often left open, and it was easy for the nimble Betty to scramble over the low sill and lend a hand to the others. It took all three of the older girls to get the fat little Rose up and over, especially as she helped herself not at all, but hung like a bag of meal, half in and half out.

"Marse Jim'll be comin' back heah an' ketchin' us, fus' thing you know!" panted Lily.

"He won't either!" said Betty; "he's gone to town for the day, and he won't come back till he brings Grandmother and Mother from the quilting-bee. Come on; let's see what's in the secretary!"

Of all the forbidden things in the office the most alluring was the secretary. The top part was a bookcase, filled with queer, musty old volumes, and the lower part looked like a chest of drawers. But if two of you pulled very hard on the top knobs and pressed up as you pulled, a shelf opened out into a writing-desk and revealed all sorts of mysteries. There were dark little pigeonholes, and a secret drawer lined with velvet that none of the children could open except Betty, and she wouldn't do it unless you hid your eyes and crossed your heart and body. There was a queer, two-walled inkstand, and one side held red ink that wouldn't come off your fingers no matter how hard you rubbed.

"Let's paint Rosie's face with it," cried Betty, "and stick rooster-feathers in her hair, and play she's a Indian chief!"

The experiment was tried, but the red ink made no show on Rosie's chubby black cheeks, and the project was abandoned in favor of a more daring scheme.

"I wish we could reach those big books on the top shelf," said Betty, jumping up and down in the leather chair; "they're bound volumes of the old magazines, and they've pictures in them."

"Miss Jane, she could reach 'em ef we wuz to put de hassock on toppen de writin' desk," suggested Lily.

Jane did not want to do it, but she didn't want to be left out of the play, either; so she climbed up on the secretary while four black hands and two white ones steadied the hassock. By hooking one finger over the edge of one of the uniform volumes she was able to bring it crashing down in their midst.

They knelt on the floor around it while Betty turned the pages. The first five minutes proved disappointing; then suddenly the pictures took on a personal interest. There were fashion-plates of quaint ladies in frilled petticoats over wide hoop-skirts, with lace mantillas and small dress bonnets; there were adorable little girls in low-necked, short-sleeved frocks, with wide pantalettes and pointed black slippers with ankle-straps.

"Paper dolls!" cried Betty, and even Jane's pulse quickened at the thought.

"Grandfather will never miss them," went on Betty, "besides, he wouldn't want to read the fashions. Let's each choose a family and cut them out."

Excitement ran high, for each mother wanted a good old-fashioned family of not less than twelve children, and the volume had to be ransacked to supply the demand. Moreover, there was but one pair of scissors to be found, and argument over them waxed furious until Rose settled things by demanding, with a threatening wheeze, that her order be executed first.

At the end of an hour four large families of paper dolls had set up light housekeeping in the four corners of Squire Todd's private office, the floor was littered with cut paper, and a large mutilated volume lay face downward on the leather chair.

Suddenly two fair heads and two kinky black ones were raised with a jerk.

"Hush!" cried Jane. "What's that?"

The furious barking of dogs came up the avenue. "Somebody's comin'!" whispered Lily, the whites of her eyes gleaming in terror. "Let's climb outen de winder quick as we kin. I'll go fust, an' you-all han' me Rosie."

Betty dropped everything and did as she was bidden, following the fat Rosie over the window-sill as fast as her legs would carry her. But the conscientious Jane stopped to pick up some of the litter, and had just succeeded in getting her apron full when the key turned in the lock and the door was flung open.

Grandfather, bareheaded and panting, stood on the threshold. He didn't seem to see Jane at all, but strode to the desk and began dragging papers out of the pigeon-holes and drawers.

"Grandfather," began Jane timidly, "I am so sorry—"

But he cut her short. "Child," he said more sternly than he had ever spoken to her before, "stand there at the window and tell me the moment you hear horses' hoofs."

Jane took her position by the window, and her heart began to thump uncomfortably as she saw him tie up package after package of papers and fling them into an old valise.

"Grandfather," she asked fearfully, "is it —is it—the Yankees?"

But he did not seem to hear her; his whole mind was bent on the task before him. After a few moments he stopped, as if he suddenly remembered something.

"Jane," he said, "run up to the house as fast as you can and tell the servants to hide—"

A warning finger stopped him.

"I hear horses, Grandfather!" whispered Jane; "they are coming up the Smithfield pike!"

"Watch if they turn this way or go toward town!"

Jane could feel her heart thump, thumping against the window-sill as she leaned out. "They are coming this way," she said, "two—four—no, six of them!"

Grandfather flattened himself against the wall, and signaled for Jane to do likewise. The clatter of horses' hoofs was growing louder. They passed under the window, passed the open door, then turned into the avenue across the road that led up to the house.

"Jane," said Grandfather, and his words came quick and tense, "those men are after me! They mustn't know I have been here. Hide the rest of those papers and this money before they come back. Don't tell anybody where you put them. Don't tell that you have seen me!"

He seized the valise, and with three strides to the back window was over the sill and gone.

Meanwhile Betty, scrambling through the lilac-bushes with Lily and Rose, made the exciting discovery that it wasn't the family returning from town after all, but a troop of soldiers on horseback, who had reined up at the front porch.

"Whose place is this?" asked the officer.

"Grandfather's," said Betty.

"What is his name?"

"Squire Todd."

The officer nodded to the man behind him. "I thought so," he said. "We'll have a look around."

It was at this point that Mammy, attracted by the voices, opened the front door. At sight of the blue-coated soldiers she gathered the children close, like an old hen protecting her chicks.

"Naw, sir, dey ain't nobody at home," she said; "dey ain't nobody 't all at home." Then with growing alarm as she saw the soldiers dismounting she added: "I ain't gwine 'low you-all to come traipsin' through our house when ole Miss ain't here. She won't like it, I tell you! She—"

But the soldiers brushed right past Mammy and went marching through the wide front door without even stopping to wipe their muddy boots on the mat. When they came out, they carried Grandfather's old flint-lock musket and the two dueling-pistols that used to hang in the dining-room but of late had stood behind the hall door, where nobody was allowed to so much as peep at them.

"Any papers?" asked the officer.

"None of consequence," said a soldier.

Then the officer turned to Mammy. "When do you look for your master to return?"

"Not 'fore sunset, Boss. He gwine bring ole Miss an' Miss Sue home f'um de quiltin'-bee."

"You are sure he hasn't been here in the last hour?"

"Naw, sir, he ain't been here sence breakfus'. Is he, Betty?"

Betty shook a positive head.

The officer looked at them suspiciously. "Two of you men guard the house," he said; "the rest of us will search the premises."

They circled the grounds several times, looking in the milk-cellar and the smoke-house and the negro cabins and all about; then they came back and got on their horses and rode down the avenue.

"Is that a house over there in the bushes?" asked the officer, with a sharp glance at the small log-building across the road. "Better take a look inside."

One of the soldiers strode through the high grass and flung open the door.

Sitting on the floor was a sweet-faced, demure little girl, apparently absorbed in her paper dolls.

"Are you Squire Todd's daughter?" asked the soldier.

"No, sir," said the little girl, looking up. "I am Captain Mitchell's daughter, of the Fourteenth Massachusetts."

"A good little Yankee, eh?" said the soldier, smiling.

"Yes, sir," said Jane, "my father lost his arm at Chickamauga."

The soldier returned to his chief, and after a brief parley they rode away, two to the north and two to the south.

An hour later, Jane and Betty, hanging anxiously over the big gate at the end of the avenue waiting for Grandmother and Mother to come home, saw two of the horsemen returning, with somebody riding between them.

"Why, it's Grandfather!" cried Betty, joyfully, and she waved her hand.

But Grandfather looked neither to right nor left. His white hair blew back from his stern white face and his brows met in a heavy scowl.

"He's awful mad!" said Betty; "he's mad at us for cutting his book."

But Jane knew better. In a terrible flash of understanding she knew that he had been captured, that he was being marched away to prison. She wanted to scream out in fear and protest, but because she was the daughter of a soldier, and because she wanted very much to let him know that she had been true to her trust, she scrambled up on the gate-post and shouted out as loud as she could:

"Good-by, dear Grandfather! I'll take care of everything for you till you come back!"

"TILL he came back!" How little either of them dreamed that he was never to come back, and that even if he had, no little Jane would have met him at the gate. For at the end of the dreadful war Jane and her grandfather lay side by side in the old graveyard on the hill-top, and only Betty and her mother and poor crippled grandmother were left in the old homestead at the cross-roads.

And what a change had come to Holly-crest! The once beautiful garden, with its dancing daffodils and spicy old-fashioned pinks, was trampled under foot; fences were down, outhouses burned. In the house itself every window was broken, and quilts were tacked up to keep out the rain. Mammy no longer sang "Swing Low, Sweet Chariot" as she made fat butter-pats in the cool milk-cellar; Lily and Rose no longer tumbled in the sun. They were all gone, gone with the happy, care-free days that the war had banished forever.

For soon after that fatal day when Grandfather was captured and his old valise found to contain incriminating papers, General Banks's army had marched down from the north, sweeping everything before it. The big house at the cross-roads had been sacked and plundered; every paper of value, every piece of silver, every object of worth had been confiscated. At the end of the war all that Mother had left was the ruined homestead and a bag full of Confederate money that would purchase nothing.

The only bit of happiness left to the family was Betty, now a tall girl of fourteen. But even Betty's dancing blue eyes grew wistful, and the laugh died on her lips when she saw the shadow that never lifted from Grandmother's face and the worn look of her dear mother, who was fighting day by day to keep poverty from the door.

"If I could only help!" was Betty's constant cry.

"You do help, dear," said Mother, wearily. "You help in a hundred ways. If it weren't for you, Grandmother and I wouldn't have the courage to go on."

"But I want to be earning some money!" said Betty. "If I could only go to the art school and learn designing, then I could take care of us all!"

Mother sighed. The art school had been the goal of all their hopes, for Betty had inherited from her artist father a gift for drawing, and had taken all the prizes that her school had to offer. But ambitions and dreams had to give way to the immediate need for food and clothes. And now that winter had come, the problem of keeping warm was looming up biggest of all. All the front part of the house was closed, and only Grandmother's room and the kitchen were lived in.

Day after day Betty tried to think of some way she could make some money; but everybody in the neighborhood was poor like themselves, and there seemed nothing for a girl of fourteen to do. And then one day a happy thought came to her. She had seen at school a set of hand-painted paper dolls that had come from New York, and the idea occurred to her that perhaps, if she made some very pretty ones, she could sell them, too.

Without saying anything to anybody about her plan, she took her paint-box after lunch and went down to the little log-house across the road, the only spot about the place that had been left untouched since the old days. For an hour she worked, only at the end of it to tear up all that she had done. She could paint the little figures with real daintiness and skill, but it took a more experienced hand than hers to make the drawing sufficiently accurate. Very much discouraged, she was about to give up, when another happy thought popped into her head, this time a veritable inspiration!

Jumping up, she ran over to the old secretary, and, reaching up to the top shelf, took down one of the dusty volumes of the bound magazines that had never been disturbed since the day five years ago when Grandfather was marched away to prison.

There they were! The quaint old-fashioned ladies in frilled petticoats over wide hoop-skirts, with their lace mantillas and dress bonnets; and smiling little girls, low-necked and short-sleeved, with wide pantalettes showing below their knees.

All the afternoon Betty worked furiously, cutting the figures out and mounting them with great care on cardboard. Then came the fun of coloring them, and the result was even more charming than she had dreamed. When a set of six was finished, she sat looking at them for a long time, then she went over to the secretary and rummaged until she found a long envelope. This she addressed to the aunt in Massachusetts whose picture Grandmother kept on her bureau, but whose name was never mentioned. Betty wrote:

Dear Aunt Fan: Will you please see if you can sell these paper dolls for me, and get some orders for more? They are just like the ones Jane and I used to play with, and I thought maybe the little Boston girls might like them as much as we did. Mother wouldn't like it if she knew I was writing this, so please don't tell her.
Your loving niece,
BETTY TODD.

Every day after that for a week Betty watched for the mail-carrier, and got to the letter-box before he did; but he always shook his head and passed on. Just when she was giving up hope a letter came. It ran:

Dear Betty: Your letter was the first word I have had from Hollycrest for over two years, and it warmed my heart! It brought back the happy days before the war when my darling Jane was living and my family held me dear. Indeed I can sell your dolls for you. A friend wants twenty sets for her kindergarten, provided you can get that number finished in time for Christmas.
Your loving aunt,
FANNIE TODD MITCHELL.

Betty was so excited over the order that she scarcely thought of the rest of the letter. One hundred and twenty paper dolls to be made, and Christmas only a month off!

That afternoon, as soon as school was over, she rushed home to begin her task, but Mother met her at the door.

"Betty," she said, "I hate to ask you, dear, but you will have to help me with the ironing to-day."

A quick protest sprang to her lips, but one look at her mother's tired face made her get out the ironing-board and fall to work with what patience she could muster. Every afternoon it was the same way; sometimes the dishes had to be washed, sometimes an errand had to be run, and sometimes, hardest of all, she had to sit by the hour playing checkers with Grandmother, trying to help her forget the terrible sorrows that had come to her in her old age.

But whenever a spare moment came, she fled to the office and worked like mad, cutting and pasting and tinting until her fingers grew numb with the cold.

Now and then a crowd of boys and girls, with their skates hung over their shoulders, would pass on the road below, and Betty would lift her head long enough to send a wistful glance after them. But there was no time these days for play: all she asked was time for work. If she could only make some money to help Mother pay those terrible bills over which she cried until her pillow was wet every night!

When all the volumes but one had been ransacked, Betty met with a disappointment that brought her air-castle tumbling about her in ruins. On opening the musty book she found the fashion-plates already cut out! It was the very volume she and Jane had been playing with on the day the soldiers had taken Grandfather away.

Aunt Fan's condition had been that she should send the full number, and here at the last minute she found herself one set short.

Her head went down on the table and she sobbed as if her heart would break. How could she have forgotten to make allowance for that volume? There had been more than enough plates to start with, but she had destroyed all but the prettiest ones, thinking she had more than enough to choose from. And now all her hard work would go for nothing. Mother would find no gold-piece under her plate on Christmas morning, the bills would come in, and then—

She flung back her curls with resolution, and something of Grandfather Todd's rebel spirit flashed in her eyes. She wouldn't give up! She would search every book in that old secretary until she found something she could use! Snatching up the volume before her to put it back on the shelf, she saw something flutter out from its pages and fall on the floor at her feet. Betty had thought so much about money lately that she was almost afraid she was dreaming now; but when she stooped and put out her hand, her fingers actually touched a twenty-dollar bill very old and soft.

For a moment she stood looking at it in bewilderment, then her eyes flew back to the book in her hand. With a quick drawn breath she began feverishly turning its pages. Wherever the fashion-plates had been cut out lay row after row of neatly piled bills, and at the very back, as if it had been thrust there hurriedly, a sheaf of loose papers.

Betty tumbled the treasure, book and all, into her apron, and sped to the house as if she had wings on her feet.

"Mother! Mother!" she kept shouting every step of the way.

Mrs. Todd straightened her tired back above the ironing-board as the impetuous figure burst into the kitchen.

"Look what I've found, Mother!" cried Betty, breathlessly. "In one of Grandfather's old books. It's money! Heaps and heaps of money!"

Mrs. Todd touched the bills with trembling fingers. "In a book?" she kept repeating, like one dazed.

"Grandfather must have hid it there when he thought the soldiers were coming," said Betty. "Count it, Mother, quick! Will there be enough to pay what we owe?"

But Mrs. Todd was not thinking about the money; she was examining the papers with growing excitement.

"Why, these are bonds!" she cried, "for thousands and thousands of dollars! And they've been there all this time and we never knew! Oh, my little girl, my little girl!"

And Mother, who had been so brave during all the years of poverty, broke down completely, now that relief was in sight, and buried her head on Betty's shoulder. Then the story of the paper dolls came out, and Grandmother had to be told, and Aunt Fan's letter was produced and cried over and laughed over in the same breath.

And in the midst of the excitement, with Mother preparing to take the money and papers to the bank, and Grandmother actually writing to Aunt Fan for the first time since Lee's surrender, Betty suddenly remembered her unfinished task!

The sudden good fortune that had dropped from the skies would have made many a girl forget all about those six paper dolls. But Betty was not one to be easily turned aside from an undertaking. Rushing back to the office, she searched in the scrap-basket until she found enough pieces to get together one more little family. The last pink rose was painted on the last bonnet by the flickering light of a candle, and the twenty sets, neatly packed, were addressed and slipped into the mail-box before Betty, tired but happy, trudged up the snowy avenue in time for supper.

On Christmas morning, for the first time in years, a huge log crackled merrily on the stone hearth in the dining-room; Grandmother occupied her old place at the head of the table and poured the coffee; while Lily White, a tall girl now, flew back and forth from the kitchen, bearing plates of crisp brown batter-cakes and piles of hot beaten biscuit. And on the table in the corner were presents, beautiful presents that had come from Boston for everybody down to Mammy and fat little Rose, who had come back to live in the cabin under the hill.

"And the best of all is this!" cried Mother, with eyes as bright as Betty's own. And she held up a shining gold-piece and a card on which was written:

For dearest Mother. The first money I ever earned.

THE ORIGIN OF A PROVERB

by Ralph Henry Barbour

WHAT I am going to tell you about happened many years ago, so many that you couldn't count them on your toes and fingers if you were twins. It happened in the Kingdom of Faraway, which, as you doubtless remember, lies between Hereabouts and Just-beyond. The capital of Faraway is the royal city of Tingalingo, a very wonderful city indeed, filled with beautiful houses and crowned by a golden palace, wherein, at the time of my story, good King Acorn the First lived and ruled. He was a very kind and just and wise monarch, and was greatly loved by all his subjects, as was also his lovely Queen Goldenheart.

And so when one day the bells in the palace towers rang merrily, and the royal heralds rode forth to announce the birth of an heir to the throne, all Tingalingo rejoiced. King Acorn was so pleased that he decreed a period of celebration to last seven days, during which all loyal subjects were to dance and sing and be merry. Moreover, declared the edict, any one found with a long face would be instantly banished. So every one took special pains to be happy and gay, and never before was there such dancing and singing and merry-making, since of course nobody wanted to be banished. At the end of the time you couldn't have heard a sound from one end of the kingdom to the other, for all the people were so tired from being happy that they fell right to sleep and didn't wake up for three days!

But up at the palace there was noise a-plenty. It seemed that the royal baby had just made up his royal mind to be bad right from the start. He cried and he cried and he *cried,* and the seven royal nurses and their seven assistants shook golden rattles in front of him, made all the funny faces they knew how to make,—and some of them were extremely funny indeed!—sang all the lullabies they had ever heard of, and did everything they could to make him stop crying; but all to no purpose. The louder the seven royal nurses and the seven assistant nurses shook the golden rattles, the louder Prince Nimblenod cried, and the lullabies and the funny faces had no effect at all.

I can assure you things got to a truly awful state at the palace! Nobody was able to sleep a wink, and everybody went about looking terribly worried.

At last the King issued a proclamation: any one who would make Prince Nimblenod stop crying was to receive thirty bags of gold, which, since the King, besides being a just king was also a wise one and knew the value of money, was considered very generous. So almost in a twinkling the palace courtyard was filled with persons who believed they could earn the reward. One by one they were conducted to the royal nursery where the prince lay in a beautiful gold cradle, surrounded by the seven royal nurses and their seven assistants, and kicked his royal heels in the air and cried just as hard as he knew how.

They tried all sorts of ways. Some sang, some danced, some stood on their heads, some walked on their hands, and some turned somersaults.

It was a very funny scene, and every one, including the King and the Queen, laughed until their sides shook. Every one, that is, except the royal baby. He just lay in his golden crib and howled and howled and *howled*. It seemed that nothing could stop him, and finally the King and the Queen and the Prime Minister and the Lord High Chamberlain and the First, Second, and Third Lords of the Treasury, and the Exalted Keeper of the King's Bees, and the thirty-three ladies in waiting, and —oh, the whole court of Faraway stopped laughing, and grew very much disturbed, and wrung their hands, and cried, "Oh dear! what shall we do?"

When, at last, all the persons who had come to seek the reward had each one sung or danced or turned somersaults without success, the King smote his hand with a royal thump on the arm of the throne (much to the distress of the Queen, who was very careful of the royal furniture), and said crossly:

"We never heard such nonsense! Do you mean to tell us that not one among you is able to stop a baby from crying? Eh? What? Why doesn't somebody say something? Why doesn't somebody *do* something? We are very much displeased— very much displeased indeed!"

Whereupon the Court Jester, whose name was Addlepate, arose from the step of the throne and bowed low before the King with "May it please Your Majesty!" He was a very sad-faced fellow, owing possibly to the fact that his parents, intending him for the position of court jester, had made him sleep each night in a bureau-drawer so that he would grow up a dwarf.

"Your Majesty," said the Jester, making a very comical face, "it may be that a pin is sticking into Prince Nimblenod."

"Ha!" said the King. "We feel certain that that is it! Why didn't some one think of it before? Examine the Prince at once!"

So the seven royal nurses, aided by their seven assistants, hurried to the cradle and made the examination; and sure enough, there was a pin sticking right into the royal baby's princely tumtum! Did you ever!

When they informed the King, he instantly shouted in a ter-r-rible voice, *"Behead it!"* So the pin was promptly beheaded by the royal executioner. And while the beheading was going on the Jester twitched the King's sleeve.

"Your Majesty," said Addlepate, making a perfectly ridiculous grimace which almost sent the thirty-three ladies in waiting into hysterics, "referring to the thirty bags of gold—"

"To be sure!" replied the King. And he summoned the First Lord of the Treasury and instructed him to deliver the reward forthwith to the Jester.

When he was surrounded by the thirty bags of gold and had signed a receipt for them, Addlepate was very much pleased, and everyone shook hands with him, and told him he was a fine fellow, and invited him to dinner or luncheon. Every one, that is, except the good King Acorn. Times were hard just then, and thirty bags of gold were not to be sneezed at. But, being a just king, he stood by his bargain. Subsequently, however, being also a wise king, he called the royal executioner to him.

"Tie those thirty bags of gold to this varlet and drop him into the moat," he said. "Afterward restore the gold to the royal treasury and advertise for a new jester."

"Your gracious Majesty," said Addlepate with rare presence of mind, "I have long been convinced that the possession of wealth does not make for happiness, and that poverty is the natural heritage of genius. Consequently, Your Majesty, I had determined to devote to charity the treasure which your bounty so generously bestowed upon me, and would request Your Majesty to take charge of it and dispose of it at your pleasure."

"H-m," said the good King Acorn, "h-m! A very wise resolve. We will attend to the matter. Remove the gold."

Whereupon, Addlepate, watching the disappearance of his wealth, sighed with relief. Then he sighed again, this time with regret, and observed sadly, "A fool and his money are soon parted!"

A saying which has survived to this day.

THE MONEY-JUG

(*A Rhyme of the Doll-House*)

By KATHARINE PYLE

THE earthen money-jug sat on the shelf,
 Fat with pennies, and round and red;
"You shall marry the little china doll
 When you are full," the old rag-mother
 said.
"Only a few more pennics," said he,
"Will fill me as full as I can be."

The poor little china doll below
 Sat in the doll-house, very sad,
For she did not want to marry the jug,

In spite of the pennies and dimes he
 had;
And she would not look at the nursery
 shelf,
Where he sat in his pride and puffed himself.

"Two more days and it's Christmas Day;
 I shall be quite full by then, I know,"
Said the money-jug; but sadder still
 Was the little doll in the house below.

A MATCH FOR HIS CAPTORS

by C. H. Claudy

Cutey stood on her ear. Then she slithered sidewise down a mud-bank, waddled over its top, and stuck her nose down a ditch-side, into which, after pausing inquiringly, she dropped with a squashy, squelching sound of oozy mud and slime.

Cutey—Little Cutey, to give her full name—apparently liked her mud-bath and her acrobatics. But those who found refuge from mud, now, and would from shells and bullets, later, in the cavernous, clanking complication which was at once One-Sixty-Seven's interior department, engine-room, and fighting-top, had no appreciation of the beauties of *Little Cutey's* performance.

"The main—dif-ference," grunted Sandy McTodd, "between *Cutey* and—a bucking broncho—oh! is that—you can—get off a broncho—when you—want to—ugh!"

Punctuated with lurches, words shaken from him with vibration, interrupted with the inferno of noise which is inseparable from the operation of the best-brought-up tanks, Sandy voiced the feelings of all her crew. As Sergeant Dill said,—of course he was "Pickles" when off duty!—"It isn't as if we didn't know how to run the old girl! Here we've been training and trailing around in the mud for *years,* posilutely, and no action! Aren't they *ever* going to let us get in the scrap?"

They wanted to get "in the scrap," very badly. All the "tankers" did. But the military powers-that-be had a pale idea that those tanks which stayed longest in the mud-wallows and had the greatest amount of instruction from competent tank officers would probably do the most damage when, indeed, it did finally come their turn to go "over the top." And so the tanks—which had numbers officially, but were affectionately known to their crews as *Little Cutey,* and her sister *Mischievous Maud,* and their near relatives *Go Get 'em* and *Huncatcher* and *The Peacemaker* and *Skiddoo Bill*—wallowed around in the great mud-fields of the training-camp and learned to crawl uphill and down ditches, and tumble into deep trenches, and fall into shell-craters and claw their way up again, and to face about with the quickness of a scared cat (no automobile can turn around so quickly), and to retreat with the speed of chilly molasses flowing uphill. Meanwhile, the human occupants of these most curious of war's new weapons learned to use their cumbersome vehicle and shoot machine-guns, take care of the mechanism and keep their feet and not get seasick, no matter what didos the state of the terrain and the orders of the day caused their movable forts to perform, and not to fall into the machinery, and keep their faces away from gun-slits when duty didn't call them there, and understand signals which couldn't be heard, and not mind living all day in a noise like a boiler-factory.

Except for the impatience of waiting for

that day when their training should bear fruit in action, the tank corps as a whole and the crew of *Little Cutey* in particular were a happy lot. They believed in a great many things with a belief which simply couldn't be shaken. Starting with the Stars and Stripes, and Wilson and Pershing, and the Allies, and the undoubtedness of that sight-seeing trip to Berlin they had promised themselves, they kept right on believing that of all armies there was none as good as the U. S. Army, of all tank corps there was none like theirs, and of all tanks there was none quite so good and obedient and mudworthy and handleable and impregnable as *Little Cutey*. Even Sandy McTodd believed these things, although he was stubborn when it came to saying that a Scottish regiment wasn't just as good as any in the world. Sandy was a good American, but he had a weakness for the kilties of his ancestors. Not that he had very much trouble with his mates on that score—the war record of the kilted soldiers from Bonny Scotland needed no defense from any one!

What Sergeant Dill did want to quarrel with Sandy about rather often was Sandy's pipe. Not that Pickles had any objection to the pipe as a pipe, or to Sandy as a smoker thereof—something must be conceded to the best tank engineer in the outfit.

"But inside *Cutey* is no place for it, Sandy, and you know it. It wouldn't be so bad if she was filled from outside. But you know as well as I do that it's dangerous to have matches around gas-tanks. Suppose some one left the cap off? Now you mark my words—you keep on getting caught smoking in here, and I'll have you sent to the rear!"

And Sandy would smile gently and put out his pipe, only to light it again the next time Pickles was absent.

"What makes you so stubborn, Sandy?"

asked Reddy Baldwin, the youngest and most enthusiastic member of One-Sixty-Seven's enthusiastic crew, late one afternoon. "Pickles'll blow up some day, and then we'll go into action without you!"

"Well, wouldn't you like that?" countered Sandy. "You'd be chief engineer then!"

"Like fun I would! Me, with only three months tanking behind me? No, I'd rather have you boss the job until I learn more. Why wasn't *Cutey* built to fill outside, like *Maud?*"

"Ask the man who made her! Experimental, all these—"

"Hi—inside! Tumble out! Captain's inspecting!"

It was a voice through a slit, and *Little Cutey's* crew crawled out to stand at attention by the little iron door while Captain Hammond looked them over. Then he motioned and they made way for him to go inside. He went in alone, presumably looked the complicated interior arrangements over at his leisure, and then crawled out.

"Very clean and orderly. But I found this!" Captain Hammond held up a half-filled, somewhat dirty, box of ordinary safety-matches. "I don't know whom it belongs to. I don't want ever to find its mate. It's against orders in any tank—particularly in this one. If I find this again, One-Sixty-Seven will lack a member of her crew."

No one said anything. There was nothing to say. And Captain Hammond passed on to look into *The Peacemaker,* standing at attention a score of yards away, and left *Little Cutey's* crew to jump, as one man, on poor Sandy.

"You see?"

"Crazy Scot—want to bust up the crew?"

"If I catch you doing that again, I'll lick you myself—"

"Pickles'll whale you if I can't—"

"Here, lay off me, you fellows!" cried Sandy. "They must have fallen out of my pocket. I didn't—"

"You'd no business with them in your pocket, and you know it! Think they make the rule for fun?"

Sandy said no more. But there was no more smoking that day, nor for several days thereafter.

Reddy was glad of it. He liked Sandy, and he knew the man for a capable engineer, brave to the point of foolhardiness and cool-headed. Too young himself to have had much experience of the world, Reddy couldn't understand why "an old man like Sandy" (Sandy must have been all of thirty-five!) couldn't appreciate the danger of matches in a tank. Even he knew that! Gasolene will leak sometimes, and shells have been known to puncture tanks; and matches and gasolene together in the inside of an iron box out of which you cannot get without being shot to small pieces do not make a happy combination. Every man of the crew, of course, would infinitely prefer being killed with Hun bullets to roasting to death inside their own tank, but that wasn't the last of the argument. If the tank was to be abandoned it might easily be captured by the gray-clad host across No-Man's-Land, and used against the Allied line.

"And all so you can have a forbidden smoke inside, off duty!" stormed Pickles, when he had heard of Captain Hammond's leniency. "Well, he didn't want to know, and, though I do know, I won't ask. But if I catch any one with matches inside again, I'll report him as sure as my name's Dill! Now that's flat and final, and you all hear me. And if I don't, then some of you report me for neglect of duty!"

And Pickles stalked away in wrath.

"You won't any more, will you, Sandy?" asked Reddy, after mess. "I—I don't want to be chief. I'd rather fight under you!"

"Humph! Listen to the kid!" mocked Sandy, puffing, puffing (it was not forbidden outside). But his eyes were not mocking.

But two days later the whole matter was forgotten. For in place of morning practice in the mud, came a messenger for Sandy to report at headquarters, and when he returned, his face told the news long before his joyous shout.

They were going into action!

It is a strange thing, but a true one, that even when soldiers know that their branch of the service is unusually dangerous, and that the thing they are going to do is as likely as not to result in painful wounds, death, capture, suffering, they hail with delight the chance to do it. No lad gets in a tank corps without knowing that while a tank *may* go through a battle unscathed, she may be disabled in the field and her entire crew wiped out. But there was none of that knowledge evident in the grins which all *Cutey's* crew wrapped round their faces, and which lasted during the journey to the lines, slow, tedious, interminable. Not even the sound of the guns, hourly clearer and clearer, the filling of the ammunition racks, the last inspection, the filling of the fuel- and oil-tanks, the final grooming of the machinery, could make other than joyous impress on these hardy sons of the service, the motto of which is, "Treat 'em rough!"

The attack was to be at daylight. "We're *all* going!" Sergeant Dill told them at the last mess—a difficult mess, for it was a dark one, eaten in the shelter of a little patch of woods too thin to permit a fire. "Yes, *Maud'll* be on our left an' *Peacemaker* to the right. Now boys, for heaven's sake, remember what we've been taught and don't go making any bulls. You, Ben, if I see you so much as raise your head to look out, I'll brain you! Sandy, for the love o' Bonny Scotland, have your oil hot and keep the old bus going. Reddy, don't forget to repeat every order whether Sandy gets it or not. Ellis—" and so on and so on to the point of weariness.

But they listened and liked it and nudged one another and grinned in the darkness, nor thought at all of the possible horrors of the day to come.

At the moment of going into battle there may have been some blanched faces. If there were, it was from excitement, not fear. They were wild to go. But the last hour of waiting is trying, and the guns were very loud and—no one knew what the day might bring forth.

But when they were actually over and into No Man's Land, then there was no fear. The battle sounds were dimmed by the rattle of the machinery—even the guns are muffled by the boiler-plate noise of a tank. Then the shells began to come, and they knew they were sighted. Their own machine-guns began to talk; *Maud* and *Peacemaker* rolled snare-drums to right and left—some grenades jarred on top of *Cutey,* and the noise became homogeneous —a mere blare of sound filling ears and brain, completely swallowing any extraneous impression. Literally deafened with din, *Cutey's* crew kept cool and calm, read arm-signals, did their duty, tended guns and engines as if in training and wallowing around in no danger. Such is discipline.

Reddy wondered at his own coolness. He even smiled a wry smile and shook his head as his eye lit on a box of the forbidden matches reposing on a ledge near the exit. How very far away it all seemed now— Sandy's besetting sin, Captain Hammond's threat, and Pickles's proposal to report! And what did it matter? They were in action! There—something hit! He could feel the blow—how he wished to look! Were *Maud* and *Peacemaker* and the rest still near? Or were they going on alone? Some craters under tread—it was hard to

keep one's feet—Sandy and his matches! He'd steal those matches and throw them out when they got back—save old Sandy a wigging. When they got back—if they got back—

And meanwhile, oil in an oil-cup, hand to a bearing, watchful eye on mechanism and on Sandy, just as if at practice—

"Ah!" One-Sixty-Seven toppled head first into a hole, crawled up, staggered, stopped. A burst from the machine-gun, then a motion from Pickles, and the engines stopped. Instantly, as if plugs of cotton had been pulled from their ears, came the sound of bullets on the iron tank, of explosions in the distance, of the machine-guns somewhere near. And through it all, Dill's voice, a whisper, though he shouted:

"Stalled! They've trapped us—run us up an incline! Treads off ground—"

It was true—too true! Sandy was for going out and tackling the obstruction with a crowbar or a grenade. But Dill wouldn't let him. It was simply suicide. And there might be a chance, after dark—

It was a long, long day. Crowding the slits, careless of stray bullets, they watched the tide of battle recede, watched the enemy in the distance, saw him surround them, saw there was no chance. "Of course, we can kill a few when they come to us —but they'll blow us to bits if we do—hear that 'plane overhead? Better surrender while we can, and hope for a new attack and escape later—"

It was a despondent crew which marched out of One-Sixty-Seven, hands over heads. Gray-clad captors crowded about, curious rather than hostile. Of course, their clothes were taken from them, their shoes, their arms—even Pickles had to smile at the appearance of his crew when it was dressed in German nondescript and worn-out clothing. But it was a wry smile.

Taken to a dugout and herded in like cattle, unfed, thirsty, their lot was not a happy one. Then came an officer, demanding in precise English, "Which of you is engineer?"

Sandy and Reddy stepped forward. "Both of us—why?"

The officer looked them both up and down. Sandy was tall, athletic, strong. Reddy small, wiry, compact. "You," said the officer to Reddy, "Come."

A guard put forth a hand and Reddy, wondering, followed. They led him to the tank—and Reddy saw with interest that the sand-bags on which they had stuck had been removed.

"Inside!" commanded the officer, and Reddy crawled obediently in.

"Now," began the officer, "we want to know how this thing works. Explain, please."

Reddy looked around. There were two other men besides the officer—strong-looking young fellows, each with a rifle in his hand. The officer had an automatic at his hip.

"You want me to show you how the tank works? So you can use it against us?" asked Reddy, slowly, "I'll see you—further first."

The officer smiled. "Oh, I guess you will!" he answered. "Of course, we can puzzle it out for ourselves. But that means getting engineers here, and we want to use this now—to-night. There are two methods I can use to make you talk. This is one," and he tapped his automatic, "that is the other," he pointed to the door. "Show us the whole thing, work it for us, make us its masters, and—you can go."

"I'll—" Reddy stopped. His eye fell on that box of matches. A wild scheme flashed through his head.

"I'll—I'll do it!" he stammered. "You must close the door."

"Do it!" was the command.

Reddy closed it, fastened it elaborately, showing just how the operation was accomplished. He picked up a handful of oily cotton-waste and wiped the handle, striving to do it casually. As casually, the oily-waste went into a pocket of the nondescript prisoner's clothing he wore. A sidelong look told him no one noted anything strange in the apparently natural action. Reddy sighed, internally. The first step in a hazardous plan was a success.

Then Reddy began. As if he liked the job, he told the story of *Cutey*. He took the officer from stem to stern, explaining the mechanism, told how it was run and started and steered. He showed one man where he stood to oil, the other how the machine-guns were operated, and answered their questions, asked in broken, but understandable, English, with perfect freedom. He smiled grimly to himself at the officer's look of contempt, and his resolution hardened. Finally, he started the engine and let it warm up.

"Better hold on when I start her," he yelled above the sound of the engine. "Tanking is right rough going—"

Would his scheme succeed? Could he do it? Would the men—ah! Reddy concealed his exultation. Both the guards laid down their rifles, the better to hold on. What had they to fear from an unarmed man—three to one?

Very slowly Reddy moved *Cutey* forward and demonstrated how she was steered.

The two guards, with their faces to slits, watched *Cutey's* slow progress over their own ground. And they didn't see, or, if they did, sensed no danger in, a careless hand which swept the box of matches from its resting-place to another pocket. The second step was taken.

Nor did the officer suspect when Reddy stopped One-Sixty-Seven and directed his attention to the gasolene tanks. "They're filled *here*," said Reddy, pointing; "wait, I'll show you."

He unscrewed the filling top, and held it while the officer looked. The men were still gazing from the slit.

"Now, I'll show you where they are drained," said Reddy, easily. But his heart was in his mouth. Would he have an instant—just one instant—unobserved?

The officer turned away. Two hands flashed rapidly for an instant—Reddy had put the top to the gasolene inlet back. But he had not screwed it home.

The third step had been taken.

"They are drained here," Reddy pulled open a pet cock. Gasolene spurted out in a stream.

"Yes, I see. Shut it off! It smells."

Reddy shut it off.

"Now, we'll go back," announced the officer.

"When do I go free?" asked Reddy.

"Why, when the war is over, of course!" laughed the officer. "Did you think I meant *now?*"

"I know darn well you didn't!" said Reddy, to himself. But he let his face fall as if disappointed.

"I forgot to tell you one thing," he went on, "you know if a match should light this gasolene, you'd burn to death, or it would blow up and kill you that way. I let out too much gasolene. And the tank is open. And—" Reddy drew the match-box from his pocket and struck a match as he spoke —"Hands up, *quick,* or I drop it."

He held the lighted match with one hand and lifted the cap with the other. And he shook inside, but the flame burned steadily in fingers that never trembled.

"Here—you—what—"

"Hands up!" commanded Reddy, and his voice was exultant. "See it? The tank's open! This match—" he waved it as he spoke. It blazed, potent of a terrible death, in hands which were steady. "I drop it in the tank—see?" The match was close to

the opening. "We'll all burn together! Back—*quick*—"

The officer's automatic was in his hand, but Reddy expected that. "Shoot, and the match drops in the gas on the floor!" he cried—"to kill me is to kill yourselves—"

The officer hesitated,—probably Reddy had never been closer to death,—but he might well hesitate; the prospect of being locked in an iron box full of burning and probably exploding gasolene is not a pleasant one. It was this that Reddy had calculated upon. Had all three been armed, he wouldn't have dared it. But the two guards had laid their rifles down the better to hold on. Had they possessed pistols, they would probably have shot. But the quicker intelligence of the officer saw that to shoot was to precipitate the result of Reddy's threat. As far as he was concerned, a lighted match dropping in gasolene from the hand of a dead prisoner was just as much to be feared as a live prisoner doing the same thing. Besides, it may have occurred to him that the flash of his pistol would be very likely to ignite the spilled gasolene.

"I'll give you five seconds—" Reddy calculated the length of the burning match. It all happened in half the time it needs to write it. "Three seconds, one, two—"

Horror shone on three pale faces. But, as if moved by a single spring, three pairs of hands rose in the air—one of them held an automatic; Reddy's courage flamed high, even as the match scorched his fingers.

But before he pinched it out he quickly lit another from it. "Now," he commanded. "*You*—drop that gun—"

It waved in the air.

"But—"

"I *mean* it!" Reddy cried. "One move, and we burn together. I give you another five seconds—one—two—three—four—" The gun fell with a sharp clang, at the same time the officer spat out a command in German.

"Stop it! You'll talk English! Kick that gun over here, you—"

"You'd—you'd never burn yourself—"

"Wouldn't I? Do you think your filthy German prison camps have such a reputation I want to go to one?" demanded Reddy. "If that gun isn't kicked over to me before I say 'five,' you can kiss yourself good night—one, two, three—"

But Reddy had won. In response to a shove of the foot, the gun slithered to Reddy's feet.

"Turn your backs!" was Reddy's next move. Again the match burned his fingers, again he lit another and pinched out the first.

Three gray-clad backs were presented to him.

Reddy stooped swiftly, picked up the gun, and heaved a sigh of relief. Then he picked up the rifles and felt better.

"Now we are more comfortable!" he remarked. "You with the shoulder-straps! Take off your belt and tie your friend's arms behind his back. See you tie him up tight! Don't make any mistake. I'll shoot a heap more readily than I'd have dropped the match!"

"But you can't escape! It will be very difficult for you. When they break in, you will be shot, you know!" The officer's protest lacked sincerity in Reddy's ears.

"There'll be four of us shot, then!" he grinned cheerfully. "And where do you get that 'can't escape' stuff? Get busy and tie him up!"

Well, it sounds absurd to think of one American lad bossing three German soldiers around that way, with their own guns, in their own lines. But believing, as most people do, that a match and gasolene *always* mean an explosion, what else could they do? Probably the danger was less

than the officer thought it, but a terrified man does not stop to reason.

And so the officer laced one guard's hands behind his back with a belt, and the other guard tied the officer's hands behind *his* back, and Reddy made the third lie down, after first taking off his belt, and attended to that job himself. After which he dragged them, with difficulty, to a little group in the center of the tank, just forward of the engine, set them back to back, and fastened them all together with wire from the pipe-cleaning coil!

Then Reddy started the engine again, *Little Cutey* moved off slowly, and ambled back over No-Man's-Land to her own lines! Not until she was half-way across did it occur to the Germans outside, apparently, that something was wrong. Then the rattle of rifle-bullets, the sound of a few grenades, but made Reddy smile. And by the time the distant artillery had been informed and had got into action, Reddy had climbed over his own front-line trench, waddled on and on and on until a fringe of wood hid him from possible visual gun-brackets—and the thing was done!

THERE was another attack that night. All the lost ground was recovered, and most of the prisoners the Germans had made were rescued. *Mischievous Maud* and *Peacemaker* played a heroic part in the rescue, and the latter was the better for an extra engineer, who was allowed to go, apparently, as a reward for bringing home his captured tank and three German prisoners. But the reward that pleased him most was not the special mention he received, but the look on the faces of the crew of *Little Cutey* when they were once more inside their own little inferno of steel plates, smelly oil and gasolene, and reverberatory noise.

"Reddy," asked Sandy McTodd, "if the

Germans had come at you when you threatened, would you have dropped the lighted match in the tank?"

"Don't ask me," laughed Reddy. "I *looked* as if I would, anyhow!"

"Reddy," asked Pickles, hearing the story in detail, while taking notes for the daily record, *"whose* were those matches?"

"Don't ask me, Sergeant," smiled Reddy. "If I tell, you'll have to can him. And suppose it was me?"

"Humph! Where is discipline going, I'd like to know? I think I'll have to have *Little Cutey* rechristened. How would *Matchless* do for a name?"

"Reddy," asked Captain Hammond, who heard him, "how did you dare hold a match so close to the open tank? Didn't you think you ran a hundred to one chance of an explosion from gasolene fumes?"

"No, sir!" answered Reddy, demurely. "You see, sir, that handful of oily waste— well, I *stuffed it down the filling neck when he wasn't looking*. He thought the match would drop into the tank. But—I didn't want to burn *Cutey* up if I could help it!"

"Certainly *not!*" agreed Captain Hammond, solemnly, and said never a word about the forbidden matches!

But under his breath he made the remark whicn did, indeed, rechristen *Little Cutey*. To the rest of the corps she is now known by the striking appellation of *"Some* Bluff!"

THE PATH OF THE SKY

by Samuel Scoville, Jr.

DEACON JIMMY WADSWORTH was probably the most upright man in Cornwall. It was he who drove five miles one bitter winter night and woke up Silas Smith, who kept the store at Cornwall Bridge, to give him back three cents over-change. Silas's language, as he went back to bed, almost brought on a thaw. The deacon lived on the tip top of the Cobble, one of the twenty-seven named hills of Cornwall, with Aunt Maria his wife, Hen Root his hired man, Nip Root, Hen's yellow dog, and—the Ducks. The deacon had rumpled white hair, a serene, clear-cut face, and, even when working, always wore a clean white shirt with a stiff bosom and no collar; while Aunt Maria was one of the salt of the earth. She was spry and short, with a little face all wrinkled with good-will and good works, and had twinkling eyes of horizon-blue. If any one was suddenly ill or had unexpected company or was getting married or buried, Aunt Maria was always on hand helping. As for Hen, he cared more for his dog than he did for any human. When a drive for the Liberty Loan was started in Cornwall, he bought a bond for himself and one for Nip, and had the latter wear a Liberty Loan button in his collar. Of course, the farm was cluttered up with horses, cows, chickens, and similar bric-à-brac, but the Ducks were part of the household. It came about in this way: Rashe Howe, who hunted everything except work, had given the deacon a tamed decoy-duck who

seemed to have passed her usefulness as a lure. It was evident, however, that she had been trifling with Rashe, for before she had been on the farm a month, somewhere in sky or stream she had found a mate. Later down by the ice-pond, she stole a nest, a beautiful basin made of leaves and edged with soft down from her black-and-buff breast. There she laid ten, blunt-ended, brown eggs which she brooded until she was carried off one night by a wandering fox. Her mate went back to the wilds, and Aunt Maria put the eggs under a big, clucking brahma hen, who hatched out four soft yellow ducklings. They had no more than come out of the shell when, with faint little quackings, they paddled out of the barnyard and started in single file for the pond. Although just hatched, each little duck knew its place in the line, and, from that day on, the order never changed. The old hen, clucking frantically, tried again and again to turn them back. Each time they scattered and, waddling past her, fell into line once more. When at last they reached the bank, their foster-mother scurried back and forth, squawking warnings at the top of her voice; but one after another, each disobedient duckling plunged in with a bob of its turned-up tail, and the procession swam around and around the pond as if it would never stop. This was too much for the old hen. She stood for a long minute watching the ungrateful brood, and then turned away and evidently disinherited them upon the spot. From that moment she gave up the duties of motherhood, stopped setting and clucking, and never again recognized her foster-children, as they found out to their sorrow after their swim. All the rest of that day they plopped sadly after her, only to be received with pecks whenever they came too near. She would neither feed nor brood them, and when night came, they had to huddle in their deserted coop in a soft little heap, shivering and quacking beseechingly until daylight. The next day Aunt Maria was moved by the sight of the four, weary, but still pursuing the indifferent hen, keeping up the while a chorus of soft, sorrowful little quackings which ought to have touched her heart—but didn't. By this time they were so weak that if Aunt Maria had not taken them into the kitchen and fed them and covered them up in a basket of flannel, they would never have lived through the second night. Thereafter, the old kitchen became a nursery. Four human babies could hardly have called for more attention or made more trouble or have been better loved than those four fuzzy, soft, yellow ducklings. In a few days the whole home-life on top of the Cobble centered around them. They needed so much nursing and petting and soothing that it almost seemed to Aunt Maria as if a half-century had rolled back and that she was once more looking after babies long, long lost to her. Even old Hen became attached to them enough to cuff Nip violently when that pampered animal growled at the newcomers and showed signs of abolishing them. From that moment, Nip joined the brahma hen in ignoring the ducklings completely. If any attention was shown them in his presence, he would stalk away majestically, as if overcome by astonishment that humans would spend their time over four yellow ducks instead of one yellow dog.

During the ducks' first days in the kitchen, some one had to be with them constantly. Otherwise, all four of them would go *"Yip! yip! yip!"* at the top of their voices. As soon as any one came to their cradle or even spoke to them, they would snuggle down contentedly under the flannel and sing like a lot of little tea-kettles, making the same kind of a sleepy hum that a flock of wild mallards gives when they are sleeping far out on the water. They liked the deacon and Hen, but they loved Aunt Maria. In a few days they followed her everywhere around the house and even out on the farm, paddling along just behind her in single file and quacking vigorously if she walked too fast. One day she tried to slip out and go down to the sewing circle at Mrs. Miner Rogers' at the foot of the hill, but they were on her trail before she had taken ten steps. They followed her all the way there and stood with their beaks pressed against the bay window, watching her as she sat in Mrs. Rogers' parlor. When they made up their minds that she had called long enough, they set up such a chorus of quackings and so embarrassed Aunt Maria that she had to come.

"Those pesky ducks will quack their heads off if I don't leave," she explained shamefacedly.

The road uphill was a long, long trail for the ducklings. Every now and then they would stop and cry, with their pathetic little yipping note, and lie down flat on their backs and hold their soft little paddles straight up in the air to show how sore they were. The last half of the journey they made in Aunt Maria's apron, singing away contentedly as she plodded up the hill. As they grew older they took an interest in every one who came, and, if they did not approve of the visitor, would quack deafeningly until he went. Once Aunt Maria happened to step suddenly around the corner of the house as a load of hay went past. Finding her gone, the ducks started solemnly down the road, following the hay-wagon, evidently convinced that she was hidden somewhere beneath the load. They were almost out of sight when Aunt Maria called to them. At the first sound of her voice they turned and hurried back, flapping their wings and paddling with all their might, quacking joyously as they came.

Aunt Maria and the flock had various little private games of their own. Whenever she sat down they would tug at the neatly tied bows of her shoe-laces until they had loosened them, whereupon she would jump up and rush at them, pretending great wrath, whereat they would scatter on all sides, quacking delightedly. When she turned back they would form a circle around her, snuggling their soft necks against her gown, until she scratched each uplifted head softly. If she wore button shoes, they would pry away at the loose buttons and pretend to swallow them. When she was working in her flower-garden they would bother her by swallowing some of the smallest bulbs and snatching up and running away with larger ones. At other times they would hide in dark corners and rush out at her with loud and terrifying quacks, at which Aunt Maria would pretend to be much frightened and scuttle away pursued by the whole flock.

All three of the family were forever grumbling about the flock. To hear them, one would suppose that their whole lives were embittered by the trouble and expense of caring for a lot of useless, greedy ducks. Yet when Hen suggested roast duck for Thanksgiving, Deacon Jimmy and Aunt Maria lectured him so severely for his cruelty that he was glad to explain that he was only joking. Once, when the ducks were sick, he dug angleworms for them all one winter afternoon in the corner of the pig-pen, where the ground still re-mained unfrozen, and Deacon Jimmy nearly bankrupted himself buying pickled oysters which he fed them as a tonic. It was not long before they outgrew their baby clothes and wore the mottled brown of the mallard duck, with a dark, steel-blue bar edged with white on either wing. Blackie, the leader, evidently had a strain of black duck in her blood. She was larger and lacked the trim bearing of the aristocratic mallard. On the other hand, she had all the wariness and sagacity of the black duck, than whom there is no wiser bird. As the winter came on a coop was fixed up for them not far from the kitchen, where they slept on warm straw in the coldest weather with their heads tucked under their soft, down-lined wings up to their round, bright eyes. The first November snow-storm covered their coop out of sight; but when Aunt Maria called, they quacked a cheery answer back from under the drift.

Then came the drake, a gorgeous mallard with a head of emerald-green and snow-white collar and with black-white-gray-and-violet wings, in all the pride and beauty of his prime. A few days and nights before he had been a part of the far North. Beyond the haunts of men, beyond the farthest forests where the sullen green of the pines gleamed against a silver sky, a great waste-land stretched clear to the tundras, beyond which is the ice of the arctic. In this wilderness, where long leagues of rushes hissed and whispered to the wind, the drake had dwelt. Here and there were pools of green-gray water, and beyond the rushes stretched the bleached brown reeds, deepening in the distance to a dark tan. In the summer, a heavy, sweet scent had hung over the marshland, like the breath of a herd of sleeping cattle. Here had lived uncounted multitudes of water-fowl.

As the summer passed, a bitter wind howled like a wolf from the north, with the hiss of snow in its wings. Sometimes by day, when little flurries of snow whirled over the waving rushes, sometimes by night, when a misty moon struggled through a gray rack of cloud, long lines and crowded masses of water-birds sprang into the air and started on the far journey southward. There were gaggles of wild geese flying in long wedges, with the strongest and the wisest gander leading the converging lines, wisps of snipe and badlings of duck of many kinds. The widgeons flew, with whistling wings, in long black streamers. The scaup came down the sky in dark masses, giving a rippling purr as they flew. Here and there, scattered couples of blue-winged teal shot past the groups of the slower ducks. Then down the sky, in a whizzing parallelogram, came a band of canvasbacks, with long red heads and necks and gray-white backs. Moving at the rate of a hundred and sixty feet a second, they passed pintails, black duck and mergansers as if they had been anchored, grunting as they flew. When the rest of his folk sprang into the air, the mallard drake had refused to leave the cold pools and the whispering rushes. Late that season he had lost his mate; and lonely without her and hoping still for her return, he lingered among the last to leave. As the nights went by, the marshes became more and more deserted. Then there dawned a cold, turquoise day. The winding streams showed sheets of sapphire and pools of molten silver. That afternoon the sun, a vast globe of molten red, sank through an old-rose sky which slowly changed to a faint golden-green. For a moment it hung on the knife-edge of the world and then dipped down and was gone. Through the violet twilight, five gleaming, misty-white birds of an unearthly beauty, glorious trumpeter swans, flew across the western sky in strong, swift,

majestic flight. As the shadows darkened like spilt ink, their clanging notes came down to the lonely drake. When the swans start south it is no time for lesser folk to linger. The night was aflame with its million candles as he sprang into the air, circled once and again, and followed southward the moon-path which lay like a long streamer of gold across the waste-lands. Night and day and day and night and night and day again, he flew, until, as he passed over the northwestern corner of Connecticut, that strange food sense which a migrating bird has brought him down from the upper sky into the one stretch of marshland that showed for miles around. It chanced to be close to the base of the Cobble.

All night long he fed full among the pools. Just as the first faint light showed in the eastern sky he climbed upon the top of an old muskrat house that showed above the reeds. At the first step, there was a sharp click, the fierce grip of steel, and he was fast in one of Hen's traps. There the old man found him at sunrise and brought him home wrapped up in his coat, quacking, flapping, and fighting every foot of the way. An examination showed his leg to be unbroken, and Hen held him while Aunt Maria, with a pair of long shears, clipped his beautiful wings. Then, all gleaming green and violet, he was set down among the four ducks, who had been watching him admiringly. The second he was loosed he gave his strong wings a flap that should have lifted him high above the hateful earth where tame folk set traps for wild folk. Instead of swooping toward the clouds, the clipped wings beat the air impotently and did not even raise his orange-webbed feet fom the ground. Again and again the drake tried in vain to fly, only to realize at last that he was clipped and shamed and earth-bound. Then for the first time he seemed to notice the four who stood by, watching him in silence. To them he fiercely quacked and quacked and quacked, and Aunt Maria had an uneasy feeling that she and her shears were the subject of his remarks. Suddenly he stopped, and all five started toward their winter quarters; and lo and behold, at the head of the procession marched the gleaming drake with the deposed Blackie trailing meekly in second place. From that day forth he was their leader, nor did he forget his wrongs. The sight of Aunt Maria was always a signal for a burst of impassioned quackings. Soon it became evident that the ducks were reluctantly convinced that the gentle little woman had been guilty of a great crime, and more and more they began to shun her. There were no more games and walks and caressings. Instead, the four followed the drake's lead in avoiding as far as possible humans who trapped and clipped the people of the air.

At first, the deacon put the whole flock in a great pen where the young calves were kept in spring, fearing lest the drake might wander away. This, of course, was no imprisonment to the ducks, who could fly over the highest fence. The first morning after they had been penned, they all sprang over the fence and started for the pond, quacking to the drake to follow. When he quacked back that he could not, the flock returned and showed him again and again how easy it was to fly over the fence. At last he evidently made them understand that for him flying was impossible. Several times they started for the pond, but each time at a quack from the drake they came back. It was Blackie who finally solved the difficulty. Flying back over the fence, she found a place where a box stood near one of the sides of the pen. Climbing up on top of this she fluttered to the top rail. The drake clambered up on the box and tried to follow. As he was scrambling up the fence, with desperate flappings of his disabled wings, Blackie and the others, who had joined her on the top rail, reached down and pulled him upward with tremendous tugs from their flat bills until he finally scrambled to the top and was safely over. For several days this went on, and the flock would help him out and into the pen every day as they went to and from the pond. When at last Aunt Maria saw this experiment in prison-breaking she threw open the gate wide, and thereafter the drake had the freedom of the farm with the others. As the days went by, he seemed to become more reconciled to his fate and at times would even take food from Aunt Maria's hands, yet certain reserves and withdrawings on the part of the whole flock were always apparent to vex her.

At last and at last, just when it seemed as if winter would never go, spring came. There were flocks of wild geese beating, beating, beating up the sky, never soaring, never resting, thrusting their way north in a great black-and-white wedge, outflying spring, and often finding lakes and marshes still locked against them. Then came the strange wild call from the sky of the killdeer, who wore two black rings around his white breast, and the air was full of robin notes and bluebird calls and the shrill high notes of the hylas. On the sides of the Cobble the bloodroot bloomed, with its snowy petals and heart of gold and root dripping with burning, bitter blood, frail flowers which the wind kisses and kills. Then the beech-trees turned all lavender-brown and silver, and the fields of April wheat made patches of brilliant velvet-green. At last there came a day blurred with glory, when the grass was a green blaze and the woods dripped green and the new leaves of the apple-trees were like tiny jets of green flame among the pink-and-white blossoms. The sky was full of water-fowl going north. All that day the drake had been uneasy. One by one he had molted his clipped wing-feathers, and the long curved quills which had been his glory had come back again. Late in the afternoon, as he was leading his flock toward the kitchen, a great hub-bub of calls and cries floated down from the afternoon sky. The whole upper air was black with ducks. There were teal, wood-ducks, bald-pates, black-duck, pin-tails, little blue-bills, whistlers, and suddenly a great mass of mallards, the green heads of the drakes gleaming against the sky. As they flew they quacked down to the little earth-bound group below. Suddenly the great drake seemed to realize that his power was upon him once more. With a great sweep of his lustrous wings, he launched himself forth into the air in a long, arrowy curve and shot up through the sky toward the disappearing company —and not alone. Even as he left the ground before Aunt Maria's astonished eyes, faithful, clumsy, wary Blackie sprang into the air after him, and with the strong awkward flight of the black-duck, which plows its way through the air by main strength, she overtook her leader, and the two were lost in the distant sky.

Aunt Maria took what comfort she could out of the three which remained, but only now they had gone did she realize how dear to her had been Greentop, the beautiful, wild, resentful drake, and Blackie, awkward, wise, resourceful Blackie. The flock, too, was lost without them, and took chances and overlooked dangers which they never would have been allowed to do under the reign of their lost king and queen. At last fate overtook them one dark night when they were sleeping out. That vampire of the darkness, a wandering mink, came upon them. With their passing

went something of love and hope, which left the Cobble a very lonely place for the three old people.

As the nights grew longer, Aunt Maria would often dream that she heard the happy little flock singing like tea-kettles in their basket or that she heard them quack from their coop and would call out to comfort them. Yet always it was only a dream. Then the cold came, and one night a great storm of snow and sleet broke over the Cobble and the wind howled as it did the night before the drake was found. Suddenly Aunt Maria started out of her warm bed and listened. When she was sure she was not dreaming, she awakened the deacon and through the darkness they hurried down to the door, from the other side of which sounded tumultuous and familiar quackings. With trembling hands she lighted the lamp, and, as they threw open the door, in marched a procession. It was headed by Greentop, resentful and reserved no more, but quacking joyously at the sight of light and shelter. Back of him, Blackie's soft, dark head rubbed lovingly against Aunt Maria's trembling knees with the little caressing, crooning note which Blackie always made when she wanted to be petted. Back of her, quacking embarrassedly, waddled four more ducks, who showed their youth by their size and the newness of their feathering. Greentop and Blackie had come back, bringing their family with them. The tumult and the shoutings aroused old Hen, who hurried down in his night-clothes. These, by the way, were the same as his day-clothes, except for the shoes, for, as Hen said, he could not be bothered with dressing and undressing except during the bathing season, which was long past.

"Durned if it ain't them pesky ducks again!" he said, grinning happily.

"That's what it be," responded Deacon Jimmy. "I don't suppose now we'll have a moment's peace."

"Yes, it's them good-for-nothin'—" began Aunt Maria, but she gulped and something warm and wet trickled down her wrinkled cheeks as she stooped and pulled two dear-loved heads, one green and the other black, into her arms.

THISTLEDOWN

WHEN the nights are long and the dust is deep,
  The shepherd's at the door;
Hillo, the little white woolly sheep
  That he drives on before!

Never a sound does the shepherd make;
  His flock is as still as he;
Under the boughs their road they take,
  Whatever that road may be.

And one may catch on a shriveling brier,
  And one drop down at the door,
And some may lag, and some may tire,
  But the rest go on before.

The wind is that shepherd so still and sweet,
  And his sheep are the thistledown;
All August long, by alley and street,
  He drives them through the town.

Lizette Woodworth Reese

The Runaway Dory

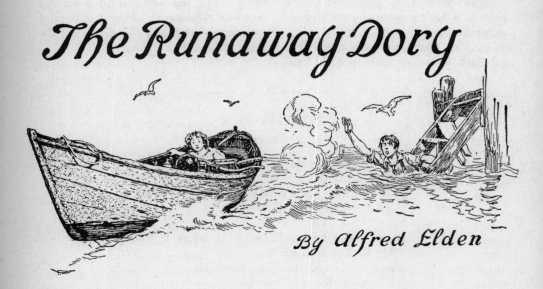

By Alfred Elden

"Now sit tight, kiddie, until I drop this bag of sand in," admonished Jack Maxon to his five-year-old sister Bess sitting in the little power-dory at the foot of the slimy steps.

"All right, Jackie," piped Bess, in her childish treble; "sister's waiting for you."

Jack Maxon was a strong youth for his age, having just turned his seventeenth birthday, but the big bag of white sea-sand he had obtained from the glistening beach at Crab Island was heavy, and he staggered under its weight as he picked his way down the rotting steps which led into the water from the old ramshackle wharf. The summer folks seldom came to this end of Crab Island, for the steamboat landing and the hotel were at the Western Point, and the crude wharf that had been built by the fishermen before the advent of the vacationists was now seldom used.

But Jack's mother knew that for scouring the kitchen floor nothing quite equaled the fine dry sand on the East Beach at Crab Island. And when the supply ran short, it was one of Jack's tasks, an agreeable one to be sure, to replenish it.

He took Bess with him everywhere in his power-dory, for she was an excellent sailor. She was never frightened, always sat where she was told to sit, and had the most implicit confidence in brother Jackie's ability to take her to and from any destination in the Big South Reach. Nor was it misplaced confidence, for the sons of Maine fishermen generally are as at home in a boat as the average farmer's boy is on a horse, and Jack Maxon was no exception to this rule.

During the school vacations he always went lobstering with his father, and Jacob Maxon soon taught his boy all the tricks of the trade. By the time he was twelve Jack could build a lobster-trap equal to any his father put together. He knew all about the proper kind of spruce saplings to cut for his end bows, and how to fashion his buoys and carve his name on them as the law required. He could even knit the heads and fasten them properly in place. So proficient did he become that Jacob bought him a dory when he was fourteen, and near Riggsport Jack had his own little gang of a dozen or so traps, which he baited and hauled as regularly as his father did the hundred or more he had set on a trawl farther off shore.

The motor was something new. Jack had saved every penny he could earn for it; but when the first of June came, he was still twenty-five dollars short of the required amount. Rather than have him lose the pleasure of another summer, Jacob Maxon had generously made up the deficiency, for he had learned, through the medium of his own big motor-Hampton, that the power-propelled craft is a business proposition,—a necessity, not a luxury, to the modern lobster-fisherman.

Jack left his motor running, with the clutch thrown into neutral, when he said good-bye to Bess and went after the sand. He would be absent only a few minutes, and he thought it hardly worth while to open the switch. He stopped on the third step from the water to rest a moment, and, looking off into the open Atlantic, noticed the white-winged coasters coming in, while the tang of the east wind was strong in his nostrils.

"Looks like a spell o' fog, kiddie," he grunted, as he lifted the bag preparatory to tossing it into the dory. "I'll just heave this old Crab Island sand in there and we'll send her over those three miles to Riggsport before any bad weather strikes us. Yo ho! Heave ho! Here she comes!" and he launched the bag at the stern of the dory.

As he gave the toss, there came a splintering sound, a splash, and Jack was struggling in the deep water under the wharf! The step had given way under his weight. Ordinarily a ducking would not have bothered him, for he could handle himself like a diving-loon in the water. But terrifying things were happening in the little power-dory. The breaking step had disconcerted Jack's aim, and the bag of sand, instead of falling in the stern, had landed squarely against the clutch, throwing it into the forward gear as truly as Jack's hand could have done it. As the water churned under her stern, the frail craft gave a plunge forward, snapped like a string the six-thread lobster-warp Jack had twisted around the old cleat, and chugged cheerily off— straight for the open ocean.

In a frenzy, Jack splashed around to the front of the steps, hauled himself out, and shouted at the top of his lungs: "Open the switch, Bess! Quick! Quick! Open the switch!"

But the wind was against Jack, and the smart little dory already was three or four hundred yards away. Moreover, the child did not know a switch from a carbureter. Beside himself with fear and excitement, Jack realized the gravity of the situation. The tank had been filled that morning, and, as the engine was lubricated by pouring the cylinder-oil directly into the gasoline rather than by feed cups, there was no possibility of the motor heating and refusing duty. For the first time in his life, he prayed that the engine might balk. But he knew its reliability only too well. Barring accidents, it would run for hours. Barring accidents! Jack turned pale at the thought. What perils might not be awaiting little Bess alone in the tiny dory with an open ocean and an increasing east wind confronting her?

Jack staggered up the shaky steps and quickly picked his way across the insecure planking. Wiping the blinding tears from his eyes, he looked once more at the rapidly receding dory. Already it was growing smaller, and he could just make out little Bess sitting bolt upright on the midship thwart, her flaxen hair showing plainly against the leaden background of the lowering sea and sky.

"She doesn't realize, she doesn't realize!" moaned the boy, and he started to run for help as fast as his water-soaked garments would permit.

It was full three miles to the western end of the island, where he would find the hotel, the cottages, and the boats which could give him assistance. And what might not happen to little Bess before he could cover the distance! Jack knew he must not keep up the mad pace he had struck, for already his breath was coming in short quick gasps, so he slowed down to a dog-trot, realizing that he would be better off in the end. Suddenly he stopped and looked down to the shore. There in little Gull Cove, bobbing easily at her moorings, was a handsome runabout. Jack gave an exultant shout and started like mad down over the bank for the only cottage in sight. It was owned by Mr. Derry, a Philadelphia merchant, who spent his vacations at Crab Island and had selected this out-of-the-way cove as an ideal place for rest. Jack had not thought of him. He seldom came until the latter part of July and it was now no more than mid-June. But there was the speedy runabout, and there was smoke curling from the cottage chimney.

Jack dashed up the cottage steps and pounded loudly on the door. As he did so, a white card fluttered to his feet. He picked it up and read: "Gone over to the city. Will be back on 5 o'clock boat." There could be no help from Mr. Derry then! Jack felt strangely weak as he hurried down the steps. The shock of falling overboard, the

excitement, and the strain of his unusual physical exertion were telling on him. But this would not do. He must continue his painful run.

Just then his eyes rested on the runabout again. Why could he not take it himself and go to Bess's rescue? He had never run the engine, but he had frequently been for a spin with Mr. Derry in summers past and felt sure he could manage it. It was a case of life and death. Surely there was no harm in it, there was nothing else for him to do, nothing else to be done. Mr. Derry would never call it stealing. So Jack argued with himself, but with Bess's life, perhaps, hanging in the balance, he already had his mind made up and with nervous fingers was untying the painter on the little landing-skiff. Dragging it to the water, he was soon alongside the runabout.

As Jack clambered aboard, his hand rested on one of the cylinders of the fourteen horse-power motor. It was noticeably warm. This was decidedly encouraging. It indicated that the craft was in running order and that Mr. Derry must have been trying out the motor that very morning. Seizing the starting lever, Jack pushed it into the ratchet as he had seen Mr. Derry do, closed the switch, and turned over the big fly-wheel. Nothing happened. Again and again the boy pulled and fumed at the lever, but the heavy fly-wheel ceased to move when he ceased his exertions. What could be the matter?

"I'm a fool!" exclaimed Jack, suddenly, as he scrambled forward. "Who could expect an engine to go without gas?" Opening the globe-valve under the forward deck he tried again, this time with better results. The motor picked up its cycles the first time Jack brought the wheel over the center. He soon had it adjusted and running smoothly. Then, giving the hard grease-cups a turn, he tossed off the mooring-painter, slowly threw in the clutch, and the runabout shot out of Gull Cove like a thing of life.

Rounding the Eastern Point, Jack headed for the open ocean and little Bess. Standing erect he peered ahead. There he made out a tiny dark object two or three miles distant which he knew to be the runaway dory and its precious human freight.

"A stern-chase ought not to be a long chase in this case," mused the lad. "I slowed the dory's motor down a little when I left it to go after the sand, so I don't believe it is making more than four or five miles an hour. This little flyer is doing twelve easily and I guess I could open her up to fourteen; but she's running so slick I won't take any chances of stopping her by monkeying around."

The runabout was fairly eating up the intervening gap between herself and the runaway and Jack began to breathe more easily. It was not going to be such a serious thing after all. He looked ahead again at the dark object which was rapidly assuming the outlines of his dory. Now he could make out a little upright figure on the seat and he knew it to be Bess. She was still all right, and he would soon have her safe in his arms.

But what was this? He strained his eyes ahead. The dory had vanished as if by magic! At the same time the hoarse drone of the fog siren on the Cape shore reached his ears. The fog was rolling in! Already it had enveloped the dory and Bess. So, too, was the wind increasing, and the slap of the waves against the bow of the runabout grew more vicious each moment, and frequent wisps of stinging spray struck him full in the face, half blinding him with the salty moisture.

Jack's heart sank within him. Then he thought of the compass. If he could keep the runabout headed about as she was he would probably come within sight of the dory again. It gave him a slight feeling of

encouragement as he remembered that he had left the steering-tiller in the center notch of the deck-comb. That meant the dory's rudder was straight fore-and-aft. And as the little craft carried but the very slightest port helm, she would not swerve much from a straight course. But it was getting nasty weather off shore, and the swells became higher and higher, longer and longer. The dory would ride them like a sheldrake, Jack reflected, but the runabout was built more for speed than for seaworthiness and was already beginning to act badly. He slid the cover back from the little brass-bound mahogany binnacle. There was no compass there! Jack then noticed for the first time that much of the regular equipment of the runabout was missing. Mr. Derry had not yet put it aboard. Jack bit his lips until the blood came.

"I must use my wits now. Darling Bess's life depends on me!" muttered the plucky boy, as he strove to keep back the tears. From all around there now came the usual Babel of noise that is synonymous with a foggy day. Hoarse blasts of ocean tugs, shriller alarms from harbor craft scurrying inshore, blatant squawkers and wheezy fish-horns from the coasters and trawlers hastening to reach port before the storm broke, now echoed across the water.

There was a possibility that some of these craft might sight the dory and rescue Bess. But Jack knew that in the thick atmosphere with no signal to make her whereabouts known the chances of this were indeed slight.

The runabout was equipped with an underwater exhaust, but the staccato clicking of the valves, as they seated and unseated, prevented Jack from hearing much of anything outside his own craft. He shut down the covers over the motor. That was better. He held his hand to his ears and listened. Faintly he could make out the rhythmic chug-chug-chug of the dory motor. He knew its tone as he knew a comrade's voice. It seemed to be off to the starboard a little. He shifted his wheel a trifle and opened the throttle another notch. The runabout leaped forward and nearly poked her nose through a big roller. Jack hastily slowed down.

"That won't do!" he ejaculated. "If she dives into one of those walls of water, she will keep right on to the bottom!"

But nearer and nearer sounded the exhaust and in another moment Jack made out the tiny craft no more than three or four hundred yards ahead. But where was Bess? There was no sign of her! In an agony of fear Jack clutched the spokes of the side steering wheel. Had she fallen overboard, or had she sunk exhausted to the wet floor-boards? He would soon know. Rapidly the runabout closed up the gap. In another minute it would shoot alongside the dory. Suddenly the motor began skipping and slowing! It would almost stop and then seem to pick up again for a moment, but its struggles became fainter and fainter, more frequent. Jack's heart sank. He was barely holding his own with the dory, and they were still a hundred yards apart.

Running forward he unscrewed the cap to the gasoline tank and peered in. It was too dark to see, but there was a piece of bamboo on the floor evidently used by Mr. Derry for just this purpose. Jack ran it to the bottom of the tank and quickly withdrew it. The end was barely wet half an inch. No gasoline! This settled it. There was nothing more he could do. Yes, there was—just one thing.

Like a madman Jack scrambled aft. Past his former seat, just forward of the motor, he crawled, and out on to the flat stern where his eye had fallen upon the brass steering quadrant to which the tiller ropes were fastened. He could steer by grasping

that, and his hundred and forty pounds weight might settle the stern enough to bring the bow a few inches higher. And this, in turn, might give the gasoline-piping from the tank sufficient pitch so that the last few cupfuls of precious fluid at the bottom would flow back to the carbureter and keep the rapidly dying motor alive until he came alongside the dory. It was a logical deduction, for instantly the motor picked up and ran again with its usual smoothness. But Jack knew it was only a temporary makeshift. However, he was now almost up to the dory. As he shot alongside, his heart gave a bound of joy, for he looked down on the form of little Bess. Tired out with fear and excitement of this strange kidnapping, unmindful of the buffetings of the sea, the child lay curled up on the dory's damp bottom, peacefully sleeping.

Just as Jack leaned out to open the dory's switch, the motor in the runabout stopped dead! Never could he tell just what emotions shot through him as the awful silence struck his ear. He gave one spring from the stern to the cock-pit, another tremendous one over the engine to the bow, and then, with a last, superhuman effort, jumped wildly into the air, both hands outstretched toward the dory. In that brief second it seemed to Jack the thoughts of a lifetime passed through his brain. If he missed, it probably would mean the end of them all, of everything; Bess, himself, and the two boats. And then his right hand closed over the very sternboard of the dory! He clawed his fingers into the unyielding wood as he was dragged along through the water like a huge fish at the end of a line, but in another second he relieved the awful strain by getting a reinforcing hold with his other hand.

He pulled himself forward until he got a good grasp on the starboard gunwale, and then it was a bit easier for him to hold on. But the dory careened frightfully as his weight drew it down. Once a pailful of water sloshed in, soaking little Bess, who awoke with a cry of fright at the strange apparition which, it seemed to her, emerged from the turbulent sea. With a word Jack reassured her, and by a supreme effort he drew himself through the water to the bow, where he reached the switch and opened it. The motor stopped for the first time since early that morning!

Jack allowed himself to slip back along the gunwale to the stern, over which, with a great deal of difficulty, he finally managed to climb. Soaked as he was, he clasped little Bess to his heart and sank exhausted on the dory's bottom. But this was no time for inaction. Quickly starting the motor again, Jack ran back to the runabout, which he could just make out through the fog, and after some difficulty succeeded in getting hold of her stout bow-painter. To this he bent his anchor-line and then paid off perhaps fifty feet, or a little better than eight fathoms. Again he sent his dory ahead and started off with his tow. But where should he steer? He had no compass in the dory, although he had planned to buy one as soon as he could afford it. The wind, he thought, was nearly due east, and he could run with the waves. This, at least, would be bringing him nearer the shore instead of carrying him out to sea. That is, unless the wind shifted!

Out of the mysterious shadows of the fog came a weird moaning. Louder and louder it sounded. It was the siren of some sort of steam craft which seemed to be approaching with terrifying swiftness. Frantically Jack blew back answering warnings with his little mouth chime-whistle. The thin tones were as impotent in carrying power against the rush of the waves and the roar of the wind as an infant's wail. Suddenly, cleaving through the wall of gray, came tearing a black monster. Scarce five hundred yards away it swept past, an ocean tramp bound up the coast to Portland, leaving in its wake a huge mountain of water that rolled on after the little dory and its tow, apparently bent upon engulfing them. But the dory has not been called "the broncho of the sea" for nothing, and gallantly it lifted itself to the very apex of the giant comber. Even more frightful was the dizzy slide down the sharply steep wall of water into the trough of the sea. But when the terror had passed, both tiny craft still floated.

"Whew!" muttered Jack, as he rubbed his hands across his eyes and peered after the monster, which was almost immediately swallowed in the fog, "that was a close shave! A few hundred yards this way, and it would have been all off with us. I don't believe those pilots even looked down at the water. Much they would care if they had crashed through us! I don't believe they would even stop her engines to see if they could help anybody. It is no wonder the poor fishermen on the banks in thick weather are frightened of their lives when they hear one of those ocean liners."

Soon Jack heard, off on his port bow, a low melodious whistle. One long and two short blasts it sounded. This was repeated every two or three minutes. "That's a towboat with some barges, Bess," he said. "Now, if I could get in that fellow's course, he would pick us up. He is moving slowly and there might be a chance." Nearer and nearer sounded the signal which indicated a steam craft with a tow was approaching. Then suddenly the black bow of the big railroad tug, *Antietam,* loomed through the mists. Frantically Jack blew four blasts.

He was now so near that, despite the roar of the elements, the tug captain heard him. He blew four more blasts. He was answered by a number of staccato toots. Down went a window in the pilot-house, and a man waved his hand reassuringly.

A big gong clanged in the engine room and the tug perceptibly slowed. The captain waved again at Jack, pointing ahead and beckoning as though for him to follow. "I know!" exclaimed the plucky boy; "he wants me to keep on until he loses headway, so his barges won't run over him. Keep a stiff upper lip, kiddie."

"I'm not 'fraid, now, Jackie. Brother's with me."

Soon the tow had slowed sufficiently for Jack to steer alongside. Willing hands caught the painter-rope he tossed them, and in a minute he and Bess were safe on board the staunch ocean-tug. The motor-boats were allowed to drop astern and the tow proceeded. Up in the steam-heated pilot-house, for it was cold and raw outside this June day, the captain saw to it that Jack and Bess were dried, given hot coffee, and made comfortable. When he heard the story of the day's adventure, he patted Jack on the back and stroked the little girl's flaxen curls. He also caused the lad to turn an uncomfortable red when he slowly remarked, "This old world seems to go right on turning out heroes, my boy. Somehow, it runs in the Yankee blood, I guess. I know I'd be mighty proud if I had a son like you."

It was the luckiest sort of thing for Jack and Bess that the *Antietam* was going in to Riggsport to drop one barge before proceeding to Portland with the other two. It meant that late that afternoon the boy and girl were clasped in the loving arms of their parents, while the people of Riggsport came from far and near to hear the modestly told story of the miraculous escape and of Jack Maxon's courageous pursuit and rescue.

As for Mr. Derry, he received his runabout back again the next day safe and sound. Angry? Well, if he was, he showed it in a most peculiar manner, for on his next trip to the city he brought back the finest dory spirit-compass he could buy and presented it to Jack with his compliments.

IN A FOREST AFLAME

by H. S. Canfield

On a late summer morning, in the North woods of Wisconsin, Sam Kawagasaga, of the Chippewas, said to his hunting-mates:

"Those coals amount to little; the Brule is fifty miles away, and there are many deer; let us go."

So in Indian file, their moccasined feet scarce stirring a dead leaf, they moved northward, and the coals smoldered and smoked a little. Sam had broken the white man's standing law of the woods: "All camp-fires must be extinguished." But he cared little for white man's law. The only one of the pale-faced tribes whose word was weighty was the agent who tried to govern the Chippewa reservation, and his word was weighty only when he had supplies to give out.

One of the coals fell a little apart from its comrades and scorched the edge of a red maple-leaf. The edge curled back from the contact, charred, and burst into tiny flame. The flame, not larger than that of a burning match, touched two fallen leaves of a red birch, and they threw up answering signals. A slow breeze, wandering through the forest, turned over the birch-leaves as if to look at them, then picked them up, carried them a yard or so, and tossed them upon a pile of pine needles and twigs as large as a boy's hat, and for the first time a thin column of smoke arose. It was still a fire that a child could have put out with a pitcher of water; but the pine needles lay next to a thick carpet of leaves, and the carpet ran to the bottom of a dead hemlock, clothed only in tindery bark to its top. "The dry-salt crackling of this," as Thoreau would say, "was like mustard to the ear." The flames spiraled up the trunk gleefully, climbing almost as speedily as squirrels climb, and in a little while the hemlock was a flaring torch from bottom to top, signaling "Danger!"

This tree had grown alone in a space of thirty feet square; and if one man had been there to watch, it would have burned out harmlessly; but it roared unheeded, a slender tower of blaze, and its great limbs fell with crashes, one by one, sending their embers far. Finally it swooned to its fall. One flying fiery branch pitched at the foot of a rotting oak. A small cloud passing swiftly overhead, the only cloud in all the bending vault of blue, shed some drops upon it in its flight, but vainly. The flame caught the brown interior of the oak, and rushed up its hollow shaft, which acted like a chimney. The oak went down, and its upper end caught in the fork of a Norway pine, a noble tree forty inches through at the butt, and its first fork sixty feet from earth. It had stood majestic and columnar for centuries, baring its dark green head bravely to storm and sun, and, when the blasting hand of the fire fell on it, writhed and shivered in protest. With all of its upper part one red waving furnace, black strands of smoke rising from its resin, and sparks pouring down from it in showers, a flashing cascade, it fought its last fight in despair; then, with a sound like the crack of a field-piece, split from fork to root, and fell widely. The conflagration was under headway then, and not any fire department of any city could have checked it for a moment. It was destined to spread havoc and death over a territory thirty miles wide by twenty deep. Looking back from afar, Kawagasaga saw the whirling pall of smoke against the blue of the sky, and hurried on.

It had been a dry summer. No rain had fallen for three months, and the woods were like tinder. So the great fire did not march. It leaped and ran, and old forest giants, green in their age, were withered before it touched them. The sound of it miles away was like the booming of distant thunder.

William Boyd, Jr., was eight years old. His mother called him "Willy," but he preferred to be known as plain "Bill." He always gave that name when asked. This was a North woods child, as different from a city boy as could be imagined—freckle-faced, snub-nosed, sturdy, with gnarled little hands, used to bruises and skin-scrapes in the timber, able to find his way through thickest forest, sound of wind, tireless of leg, and expert with a little ax which he valued above all things. One day, in shutting a new pocket-knife coaxed from his father, he cut a finger badly. Small June Lessard, a French orphan staying with the Boyds, turned pale and said:

"You had better go back to the kitchen, Willy, and wash your hand."

"No," he answered, gazing at the trickling crimson, and resenting both the "Willy" and the doubt of his stoicism; "the blood will wash it."

Through all of the densely shaded country lying along the north fork of the Flam-

beau River, William Boyd, Jr., was known to loggers, chainers, skidders, and drivers as a "sliver of the old stump," which was their way of saying that Boyd the elder was only such another child grown taller and stronger.

Father and mother left the shack on the homestead, three miles from the Flambeau, at daylight that morning, going to Pineville, fifteen miles away. They intended to return in the afternoon; but they had misgivings, not because the children would be left alone,—under ordinary conditions that would be safe enough,—but because the woods were dry.

Those people do not dread terrific winters, when the wolves come out of the timber. The horror of their lives is the forest fire: for they have seen its work. These two had to meet a lawyer, however, in the matter of the purchase of some wild land, and with them, as with all of their kind, a business engagement was paramount almost to life itself.

"Be good, Willy," said Mrs. Boyd, as she climbed into the wagon.

The boy, standing with his ax on his shoulder and a tuft of red hair sticking up through a hole in his hat, disdained to reply.

"Bill," said the father, genially, "take care of June, and split a lot of stove-wood by the time we're back."

That pleased him. "Look out for the bad log in the middle of the bridge over the slough," he advised. Then, as an afterthought: "Those horses will want water when you get to Pine Crick."

Boyd, Sr., laughed and drove off. Bill turned his attention to a large log in the rear of the house, using a wedge to rive stove-wood from it. June sat near him for company, drawing pictures with a charred stick on birch bark. Dinner had been cooked for them and left in the cupboard

—bread, venison, and a pan of milk. At ten o'clock Bill quit work, and said that it was dinner-time, or noon.

June dissented. There was a clock in the house, but it was a mystery to them both. Bill squinted critically at the sun, and declared with exactness.

"It wants ten minutes of dinner-time."

June, accustomed to obey, laid down the birch bark meekly. They dined, clearing up everything they could find. As befitted a man left in charge of the place, Bill strolled about, whistling shrilly and out of tune.

Everything seemed to be in order. The chickens, not realizing his importance, scratched busily and moved out of his way, clucking protests. The two cows and calves were in the four-acre pasture, browsing on brown grass, oblivious of his calls and orders. The black hound with a round tan spot above each eye refused wholly to notice him, lying half asleep on the porch floor, with his long ears spread upon the planking. Only June followed him about, patiently admiring, not daring to disturb his calm with questions.

Bill did not return to his ax and log, but sauntered jauntily, appraising the value of the timber which grew to the edge of the clearing, estimating the number of "feet" each tree would cut, and longing for the time when he could chop it all down and see it hauled to the mill. Desire to "fall" trees was in his blood.

Noon came, and the hound rose and threw up his muzzle and howled quaveringly. North and westward the sky was overspread by a dun cloud. The wind had freshened, and high up little glittering particles were floating past—ashes. There was a slight scent of burning wood in the air. Bill climbed a high stump, thinking he could see better from it, shaded his eyes with his hand, and said oracularly:

"There's a fire out yander."

"Yes," said June, indifferently.

"Fool Injuns, I guess," said Bill.

"Yes," said June.

"If I had my way with Injuns," said Bill, "I'd send 'em to Africa."

"Yes," said June.

Bill jumped eight feet down from the stump, and remarked, "Time f'r me to get at that log." He stopped half-way to it, however. The hound looked at him questioningly, then trotted into the woods, going east. Bill called and stormed, but the dog kept on. Across the back of the yard a rabbit scurried, its ears flat, its eyes bulging. It, too, was going east. A covey of ruffed grouse rose from the edge of the wood and whirred by, going east; then flocks of small birds twittered over, above them a gang of crows, above the crows a dozen hen-hawks, all going east. The river lay that way.

Bill went into the kitchen and locked the back door; though why he did so he could not have told. Passing through the house, he took a long drink of water, for the air was sultry. He saw June's sunbonnet lying on the floor, and picked it up. It was a characteristic of a North woods child that, before going out, he felt in his pocket and saw that knife and matches were safe. He kept the latter in a little glass bottle, tightly corked. He closed the front door behind him, locking that, too; then tied June's bonnet under her round chin. He was white under his freckles, but his brave gray eyes did not flicker as he looked at her.

"That fire's coming here, June," he said almost in a whisper; "we got ter hike."

Even then he ran swiftly back and snatched up his precious ax, patting the blade caressingly with his rough little hand and saying, "Come along, Betsy!"

The roar of the flames could be heard

plainly now—a steady, savage sound. Against the vast black background of smoke, deep crimson below, fading into rose above, sheets of burning bark and small limbs were whirled high. Its belly within a foot of the ground, its great antlers thrown back until the prongs touched its sides, a buck flashed past, distraught with terror. Grasping Jane's wrist firmly with his left hand, holding the ax in his right, Bill plunged into the woods, making for the river. He had no knowledge of the speed of forest fires, and believed that they were safe, but scurried on, determined to make the best time he could. The little girl went cheerfully, having utter confidence in him.

At first there was a trail nearly a yard wide, and along this they trotted comfortably, the boy slackening his pace to match hers, saying something now and then: wondering whether the house would be burned, whether the fire would reach Pineville, where the dog had gone, and so forth. Once, being struck strongly by the thought, he stopped long enough to pant, "It's a good thing we got that meat and milk," then started afresh. In the course of a half-mile, however, the trail narrowed to a foot in width. He placed June behind him and told her to take hold of the tail of his jacket. She did this, and, by leaning on him somewhat, found that she ran more lightly. She was almost as tireless as he, however. With them it was terribly a question of speed, not of endurance. The boy knew that the trail ran straight to the Flambeau,—he had been over it often,— and he headed for the stream because he hoped that its course would break the progress of the fire.

He could not help noticing, however, that, though they were doing their best, the roar of the flames grew louder and the heat more intense. Before they had gone a mile the perspiration was running into his eyes. He glanced back now and then, but the small orphan smiled at him cheerfully and seemed to be doing as well as he. They heard crashes and rustlings in the undergrowth on either hand, showing that many animals were fleeing for their lives. Most of these passed them easily. Some of them came into the path for a few steps, but when they saw the children behind them, turned again to the shelter of the woods.

They saw deer, does, bucks, and fawns half-grown, foxes and rabbits in numbers. The partridges thundered up around them, flying a quarter of a mile at a stretch, then dropping to the ground and running fiercely. Bill went silently over one deep indentation in the trail, and knew that a bear had gone by. They could beat the porcupines,—that was some satisfaction,—and they went past these lumbering creatures as if they had been standing still. It never occurred to them to feel fear of any of the animals. They seemed to know intuitively that at such a time there was universal truce. Once they stopped still for a second with beating hearts, for a great gray timber-wolf loped across the path not ten yards in front of them. Bill valiantly swung his ax high, with his throat thick; but the wolf only slung his head sidewise, glanced at them with a red eye, and went hurriedly on.

There was a half-mile yet to go, and the heat had become almost unbearable. June was sobbing in gasps that seemed to tear her little body. The wild voice of the conflagration was now so great that no other sound was audible. Great birds flapped along in sick fashion, or screamed in the smoke; but the children did not hear them. Looking up, they saw a mass of sparks rushing over them, darting along a hundred yards above the tallest trees, and above the sparks a solid curtain of pitch-black smoke. This smoke had descended to the ground and choked them. Often the wind seemed to bear down and drive the heat more strongly against them, and at such times their flesh smarted beneath their clothing; then it lifted and comparative coolness came.

The trail was barely visible now through the smoke, though all about them the trees still were green. They stumbled upon roots that crossed it, and its many holes; but the dogged fighting spirit of the boy— a spirit that came to him down a long line of woods-conquering folk—was awake, and he plowed on, not stopping to think whether or not he was beaten, possibly not caring, feeling only that his girl playmate was clinging to him, and the river was ahead, and he was going to get to it. He did not know it, but no finer, steadier courage burned in Richard Grenville when he strode the bloody deck of the "Revenge" and called to his sailors, "Fight on! Fight on!" while fifty Spanish sail ringed them around.

Then June fell—fell with a little sobbing cry, her arms helplessly spread out, her chubby face pressing the leaves, her red lips open, her shoulders heaving convulsively. Tired in her short legs was June, her fat knees bleeding from scratches, her cheeks tear-stained, her sunbonnet askew, her bright hair disordered. He turned instantly, and a terrified cry—his first and last—came from him as he saw, not three hundred yards behind them, that booming, sweeping, high-reaching wall of flame. Its breath, blown on him furiously, blistered one cheek even as he looked. The girl child's form was dim to him in the smoke, but he grasped her by both arms and dragged, calling frantically: "Come on, June! Come on!" dragged and tugged and strained, still facing the rushing furnace, then fell himself, down, down, and she with him. They had gone over the Flambeau's edge!

The rush of cold water revived him as he struggled to his feet, still holding to his comrade. The river came nearly to his shoulders, but like a muskrat he bored his way under the overhanging bank. The stream there had washed its way in deeply, and he had over him a roof of earth five feet thick and nearly as wide. Shivering, with the water eddying about his waist, both arms around June, he waited. The smoke swirled down to the surface of the river and far beyond; great brands fell in hissing and were extinguished; over all was the dominant roar of the fire itself. Upstream a great tree fell in and threw the drops high, lying across; fiery hazel-bushes seemed to be torn up by the roots and hurled blazing; the crashing was incessant. The Flambeau did not stop that fire. It was a hundred yards wide, but the flames leaped it as if it were a ditch, and went tearing on; they stopped only when the forest stopped, ten miles away.

The boy noted first the lessening of the noise; then a scorched porcupine, caught within six feet of the water, tumbled in and floated down, kicking feebly; then a wind blew down the river instead of across; fortunately it lifted the smoke a little, for he was almost choked.

There was a rocky ledge running two feet under the surface to a small island in the center of the river; he could mark its course by the water purling over it. They went along this, and clambered out. In the middle of the blackened bit of land a large log was burning, and they dried their clothing by this; the ground was not hot, as there had been little upon it to burn.

So they waited through the afternoon, not knowing what else to do. June snuggled to him, her young nerves still "twisted." Some men came down the river in a boat, looking for chance survivors. Luckily settlers were few, and they were about to turn back, after having hallooed lustily, when they were startled at hearing Bill's shrill "Whoopee!"

"Where's your dad and mam?" one of the men asked, as the children climbed in and squatted between the thwarts.

"Gone to town," said Bill. "He'll be back to-night. Seen our dorg?"

"No," said the man. "We'll put you off where the main tote-road crosses the river and your folks'll pick you up there. But you'll have to camp for a while, I guess. That fire ain't left any houses behind it. How you feeling?"

"Hungry," said Bill. "I think June's hungry, too; and—and I lost my ax."

JESSIE

By Bret Harte

Jessie is both young and fair,
Dewy eyes and sunny hair;
Sunny hair and dewy eyes
Are not where her beauty lies.

Jessie is both fond and true,
Heart of gold and will of yew;
Will of yew and heart of gold—
Still her charms are scarcely told.

If she yet remain unsung,
Pretty, constant, docile, young,
What remains not here compiled?
Jessie is a little child!

THE BLACK DUCK

by Virginia Woodward Cloud

YESTERDAY I found a delightful book, and of course it was in an attic. Our ancestors may not have stored things in attics expressly to have us discover them, but we continue to do so from time to time, and they are undoubtedly more interesting from being a bit cobwebby and mysterious. The attic in which I found the delicious book had in it hidden things which looked as if they might be the first patterns of everything we use now. Probably the most desirable trait about this attic was that it did not possess a place for anything or anything in its place.

For instance, I found a bonnet hanging on a pair of andirons.

But for the green silk strings no one would ever dream it was a bonnet. It looked much more like a coal-scuttle, and had as many enormous bones as a prehistoric skeleton. It must have belonged to a very-great-grandmother. No one without several greats before her name could have worn that bonnet! Behind the andirons was a cradle, and in the cradle was a long pole with a red silk arrangement which once meant a fire-screen. Beside it stood a clock with a moon face and long chains and weights. It looked so much like a Dutch doll, with just head and legs, that I laughed aloud. But an attic is not a place in which to laugh unless one has company. Everything was rebukingly still, and so was I immediately.

Near the clock was a table shaped like a long-legged spider. It looked as if just ready to walk off alone. I was quite sure it belonged to the bonnet and the firescreen, and that somewhere there were blue cups and saucers, which one might break by talking too loud, and that they belonged to the table.

In a far corner stood a picture with its face to the wall.

I drew it out and rested it against the table. Of course it was dusty. I never heard of the right sort of an attic which was kept dusted. It was the picture of a lady. I knew that at once, just as we always know a lady when we see one. The picture was rather dim, but I could easily discern that she was very young and slim, with a white throat and bright, dark eyes. Her hair, done very high, was of a ruddy brown, and she had on a short-waisted white satin frock, and held a half-open fan primly in her hands.

It was easy to see that she was just where she belonged—beside the spider-legged table. I had no doubt that she could have told the whereabouts of the blue cups and saucers! Thinking about this lady, my eyes encountered another pair of eyes staring straight at mine. My heart jumped once and stood still, until I recognized the eyes as my own.

I was gazing into a mirror. It was a dim, queer mirror with a crack like an enormous smile across its face, and pale enough to hold only the ghost of light which once shone in it. Two rods supported it. They held a brass candlestick

437

apiece, and rested on a little stand which had a drawer. I sat down on a hair-trunk before this little stand. The drawer had brass knobs and might have been locked once, but time or rust made it open easily, and then—such an assortment of odds and ends! Faded ribbons and flowers and beads, and a feather-fan which, when I opened it, filled the air with a musty dust that made me sneeze! Under these scraps was a box, and under the box was a book—*the* book.

The box first.

It held a silk bag, yellow with age—a bag which used to be called a reticule. In the reticule were a handkerchief, fine and lacy and also yellow; a tiny looking-glass set in shells; and a square of paper carefully pinned. The last contained only dry, yellow rose-leaves. Under the bag lay another fan. It had delicate sticks and a cord and tassel which once were rose-colored; and painted on one pale blue side was a young person in rose-colored panniers and enormous hoops, who was coyly accepting a bouquet from a young gentleman who wore crimson breeches and a white wig.

Where had I seen that fan? My eyes met those of the lady. Yes, the same fan was in her hand. I could just make out a glimpse of the rose-hued damsel and the bouquet. Inside the box-top was written one word, nearly faded out:

Lois

She was Lois, then, this young lady with the slim white throat and the dark eyes, and this was her fan; and Lois, I knew, had been my great-grandaunt. The book came next.

It had a square of paper pasted on its brown cover, and on it was written in unformed characters:

LOIS, HER BOOK

Underneath in the same childish letters:

"mother Says i shall Rite dayly in This book that Whitch doth impress Me most and Also that falt whitch needs Be coreckted."

She immediately adds:

"i need Care in My Riting and speling."

There begins from that date, on which she says she is eight years of age, a daily chronicle written with laborious care. It noted some occurrences which the child thought important, or some faults which she was trying to correct.

The second entry reads thus:

"the Ducks strayed to the Berynground [doubtless the churchyard] i Went to fetch them but Did not Want to."

The third entry:

"Father says i Can Hav Clovers Caf fore my Owne. i wud Hav it wen it Grows Bigger and Get More munny. Mother says Munny is A Root of Evle whitch I do not Understand We do Not plante munny."

These entries varied only according to the daily duties in the domestic régime, or the childish faults which were sometimes noted with a large black cross on certain days. On two occasions the pages were sadly smeared and blurred as if unwilling tears had been shed thereon. Once was when the Dominie made her turn her face to the wall for being late to school because she stopped to pick blackberries. Again was when her mother forced her to rip out a long seam twice and do it over. This last was evidently written in an outburst of childish rebellion, for the black cross was very heavy.

At a date two years later my Aunt Lois's handwriting and spelling had improved vastly. The steady, painstaking practice of writing daily in her book showed its results. In the time which followed she grew older rapidly, doubtless from hearing and experiencing the excitement shed around her by the expected War of the Revolution. The Day Book soon ceased to be a daily duty. When she wrote, it was with the grave fears and hopes which she heard uttered by her elders, yet, withal, a note here and there of her own vivacious spirit which she admits "doth cause my mother ofttimes to shake her head and rebuke me for having many words."

At the bursting of the war-cloud of American Revolution she goes on to tell of busy hours filled by herself and her mother in preparing food and supplies. Then comes the day when her father left home to enter the army, and again the page is blurred.

There is little of importance thereafter until the longest entry of all, which I will copy from my Aunt Lois's book, beginning under the date of January 10, 1777.

She writes:

When I awakened New Year's night and beheld my mother over me with a candle, I thought it was a dream, but she laid her hand on me and spake aloud:

"Lois! Lois! Awake quickly; I have need of thee!"

[The mother of my great-grandaunt being raised a Friend, both she and Aunt Lois had acquired their mode of speech. She continues:]

"It is not dawn," said I; for not having a man to help us, I must even go out to the barn at dawn and make ready for the day.

"No, God be thanked, it is not dawn," quoth my mother. "Thou must be up and away before break of dawn, my child; so hasten!"

I sprang up and quickly put on my clothing, knowing that my mother would explain it in her own time, for at best she hath few words. Coming nearer, she said, "Breathe it not, Lois, but thy father is here,—shot!"

"My father!—here—shot?" I began in fear. But she urged me to hasten and pause not. My mother then made known to me how that my father had been given a most perilous errand,—namely, to gather some information, and bear it or send it by means of a paper to our Commander-in-chief, General Washington, he then being, as my father surmised, on his way from Trenton to Princeton, but nobody knew by what road. My father, in making a wide circuit around for better concealment, was shot; but not so "General," his horse, who rushed for the woods, and in so doing concealed my father the better. My mother went on to tell me that inasmuch as my father did lose several hours from unconsciousness and weakness, though still clinging to General's neck, he found himself when he roused all but home, whereto General had brought him straight.

"'T is wonderful he did not fall off!" spake my mother; "and, Lois, see to 't no one learns from thee of thy father's coming."

"Nay," quoth I; "there is no other gossip to prattle with saving thyself and Clover."

Then marked I my mother's face as she laid her hand upon her heart and let her eyes rest upon me, and some way I understood.

"Lois," quoth she, "thy father's errand must be finished for him. I dare not leave him to go."

"Nay," said I; "I will go, mother."

She spake not, but turned away, and I saw she was sorely troubled.

"Mother," spake I, hastening the more, "let it not fright thee. I know not wha the errand be, but my father is wise and good, and I will but do as he saith. I have no fear!"

"Nay, hadst thou more I would fret less," spake my mother. "Thou art thy father again, Lois,—ever venturesome and knowing not of fear!"

While speaking she laid by me my heavy quilted petticoat and pelisse, for the snow which came after was already in the air. Then by the lantern's light, at my mother's bidding, I put my own saddle on General George, adding my father's saddle-pockets. For General, whom I have named after good General Washington, hath tremendous strength, and was already, having had a meal, fit to be off again. I then straightway ate a hasty bit which my mother had prepared, placing the remainder in the saddle-pockets. My mother then put on me her own quilted bonnet, and over it tied a heavy comforter: I still not knowing what it was I should undertake, but knowing I should hear in good time. I strove to push back the comforter, but my mother adjusted it, saying:

"Nay; let be! 'T were better to have thy face covered when a lass like thee goes about at such an hour."

Then in the dim light I sought my father's couch, where he had fallen an hour before.

"My daughter, are you there?" spake my father.

I answered, and drew nigh as he said:

"You are going an errand for me, daughter?"

"Yes, father," quoth I.

"Do you know its nature, Lois?" said he, weakly.

"No, father," said I.

"It is to bear that which is of value and intrusted to me. It must go to the first officer of the American army you can find this side of the town."

"The town!" quoth I, in wonderment; for that is full thirty miles away.

"And I would not have you go thinking it a safe or wise thing for a maid to do," quoth he. "There are dangers which I cannot even warn you against, not knowing them. Only this: you may be arrested and searched, Lois; hence you must bear

naught about your person. You must also feign some reason for going toward the town at this time; hence, your mother will put in the saddle-pockets two ducks she hath already killed. You are going to bear them to Mistress Van Tyne, who dwells this side of the town; they are a New Year's dinner from thy mother—" His voice failed from weakness, and my mother held a hot drink to his lips before he went on.

"One thing, my daughter: should you be halted on the way, and should they strive to take the ducks, give up the white one with a show of resistance, but hold to the black one with life and wit—"

"And why the black one, father?" I asked.

"The papers are in its craw."

I being too amazed at this to speak, he went on.

"Should you find no trouble, and should you meet with one of our own commanders, give him the paper or the duck, and tell him straightway what I have told you. Should no one meet or molest you, ride on to Mistress Van Tyne's, near by the town. Tell her all, and that 't is pressing needful that the black duck be sent on to General Washington. I know not where you may find any of our men six hours hence. Keep but your eye keen, your wit clear, and your trust in God. Go, now!" I kissed my father and went, as he bade me.

"The pass, which may be of use to thee, is stitched in the crown of thy hood, lest wind blow it away," said my mother, kissing me. She followed me with a lantern, as I went out and mounted General George.

It was very dark and cold; and my mother held my hand closely for an instant, and then went in and shut the door. There was no sound as General cantered down the lane, saving here and there the faint bark of a dog, and always the echo of the horse's hoofs on the frozen ground. I knew that he must not go too hard at the first; for both he and I would need the speed and exercise when it grew colder, as it soon did. I felt it but little for some time, so muffled was I by the comforter. Indeed, at cock's crow I marked two women going toward their barns with lanterns; but they would not have known me, and remembering I was about business of moment, I made no sign. Now and then I felt the saddle-pockets to be certain of the safety of the ducks, and of the bag of feed which mother had tied on for General.

Of the long, lonely ride in the darkness my Aunt Lois says but little. I think she must have been bent too seriously on her errand to feel actual fear, although once she speaks of being startled for an instant by a scarecrow in a field "which did come upon me suddenly." She continues:

The way was all alike save that as I rode I became more and more stiff and tired; but I feared to get down lest some one should come suddenly from ambush and steal the ducks. Mile after mile did General and I travel before the first summons to halt, which was about daybreak. The sudden stopping brought my heart into my mouth. I had turned a corner and come upon a clearing against a bit of woods. There was a small fire, and some men around it. Another did walk sentry-like to and fro. 'T was he who bade me halt. He scanned me most curiously, and then laid his hand on General's bridle.

"You are my prisoner, mother; so dismount!" quoth he, very superior-like.

"Nay, nay, good sir," said I, ducking a courtesy as well as one may on horseback. "I have often heard tell how that the brave British would fight only their equals or superiors in strength, whereas old women and children are by right left unmolested."

"Truly said, mother," quoth he, laughing. "You bear at least a ready tongue, but you may be bearing more than your tongue, for aught I know. Whither would you ride at this hour, and alone?"

"I go alone because I know each stick and stone of the way, good sir; and I go for that I bear a pair of ducks for Mistress Van Tyne as a New Year's gift from our own farm."

He shook his head, and the men near by began to gather around, while my heart did sink lower than the ground on which General was pawing. But at the instant two horsemen appeared out of the woods. One rode rapidly up and drew rein before me, and I marked that he was fair and well-built, with honest blue eyes and fearless of mien.

"Whom have we here?" he asked.

"A prisoner, sir," said the man at General's head.

"Nay," quoth the young officer, "'t is an old lady! What will you, mother? You had better turn about and go back home before you meet others."

"Nay, good sir," quoth I; "for I have a pass permitting my family to go to and from the town with supplies. But 't is stitched in the crown of my hood. So I would I might remove my hood, good sir, and prove it thee!"

At this the young officer laughed, and said he, "I am sorry, mother, to have you remove your hood in the cold; but it needs must be unless you become my prisoner before instead of afterward!"

"Nay, nay," quoth I; "I would fain remove my hood, then; for I have had that off before, but I have never yet been prisoner of war!" So dropping the reins on General's neck, I unwound the comforter. The air felt most grateful to my head, which was warm, and my face flushed; and as I pushed the hood back my hair did tumble all about my neck in troublesome confusion, and the soldier who had cried "Halt!" exclaimed aloud:

"By my sword, 't is a lass!"

The officer made a sign toward him, and as I looked up he bowed, his own face being quite flushed, and said:

I was fumbling at the saddle-pockets, meanwhile, with a show of courage which I did not feel, for my heart was thumping because of the black duck.

I drew it out,—for I saw he was waiting to see what I might carry,—and laid it

Lois delivers the black duck to General Mercer

"You will pardon me, fair Mistress, for mistaking your age!"

"Surely, sir, 't was the fault of the hood and comforter," quoth I, meeting his frank, blue eyes as I handed him the pass from out the hood.

"This allows no luggage, Mistress," he spake hesitatingly.

"Oh, I bear no luggage," said I, "save a New Year's dinner which I did raise myself."

across General's neck, meanwhile stroking its glossy plumage.

"And wilt thou help me lift the other one out, good sir," said I, "that thou mayest examine the saddle-pockets and the bag of feed for my horse?" So, holding the white duck in one hand, he examined the saddle-pockets with the other.

"Following my own will, Mistress," said he, "I would fain let you go on; but know you not that Lord Cornwallis hath already crossed the Assanpink, and hath his forces stationed in the town? Hence you will surely be arrested and searched this side of it. Therefore, Mistress, my duty is—" He paused, and in a second I saw that I had to do as my father had enjoined, and use my wit.

Taking up the black duck, I held it outward, saying, "Good sir, please hold this, too, for me an instant"; which he did; and I slipped from General's back, nearly falling from stiffness as I reached the ground. I shook out my petticoat, and showed the empty saddle; then I laid my hand upon his horse's neck, looking up in his face, and said I:

"Thou hast my word, sir, that thou dost hold in thy hands my sole reason for going up to town. I bear naught else about my person, and that I may prove the ducks quite good to eat, I pray thee keep one of them, and so share our New Year's dinner."

"Go to, little Mistress!" quoth he, looking down on me, with a laugh. "A skilful pleader for one so young! Thinkest to bribe the British army?"

"Nay," said I, meeting his honest blue eyes as I leaped back on General. "I think not, good sir, indeed; but I would fain thou shouldst keep one, for it is like as not thou art far from home." As I spoke, I took the black duck, and left the white one in his hand.

"Thank you kindly, sweet Mistress," said he; "but despite my will, I must do my duty, and I fear me thou must come with us."

Even as he spake there was a burst of musketry from the woods behind them, which made him wheel around, and every man spring to his feet. In a trice I had given General such a cut as he never had before, and darting ahead, dashed down the road to the left, whither I galloped like mad, pausing not to look behind until I knew there was a mile or more between us, and that I was not being overtaken. Then, halting, I fastened the duck again in the saddle-pocket, and let General take it slowly while I wondered what next to do.

My Aunt Lois then tells of her quandary on learning the town to be full of British. "I did not fret to think of being a prisoner," she writes; "for at worst I knew they would not shoot a defenseless maid. But I feared me lest they should seize the black duck."

She then made up her mind to go straight ahead, and to hold until the last to the black duck—"which," she says, "they should not take from me unless by force of arms, and then I was determined to go likewise!"

She had no further stoppings until she found herself six miles from the town, riding by a piece of woods. She heard there the sounds of horses and of tramping.

"And then it was," she writes, "that I felt somewhat of fright, and straightway wheeled · General into the woods, and waited. It was a body of men coming very rapidly and, methought, quietly, and my heart thumped loudly until—what was my joy to see the uniforms of our own American army! Knowing this, perhaps, to be my only chance, I rode out in the road straight before them, whereat they halted in much surprise."

Then Aunt Lois tells of her interview with their leader, General Mercer, who got his mortal wounds shortly after at Stony Bridge.

"He was in great haste," she writes, "and I said I did but bear a black duck of which I must tell him, whereupon he ordered his men to march on, and straightway said he, in some surprise:

"'Now, Mistress, what is it?'

"'It is my father's—John Bradley's—errand,' quoth I, 'to bear this black duck to one who would send it or its contents to General Washington this morn, immediately.'

"'So!' said he, drawing a long breath. 'And thy father?'

"'Was shot while making his way with the papers.'

"'And the papers?'

"'Are in the duck's craw, sir,' said I, drawing the bird from out my saddle-pocket.

"'And at what time didst start, little Mistress?'

"'At two o'clock this morn, sir.'

"'Well, well!' He took the duck and slung it across his saddle before him. 'I must hasten. I shall see General Washington within an hour, God willing, and he shall get the papers—if not by me, by some one else. Good day, Mistress Bradley.' He bowed. 'The American army has done well to count you in it!'

"'In truth, sir,' said I, 'if they count by hearts, and not by muskets, their biggest following is left behind!'

"Which, when I did tell my mother today, she shook her head at me from the buttery door, saying, 'Lois! Lois!' But my father, from his couch where he lieth weak, saith, 'Tut! Let the lass be, so that she doth but speak the truth!'—which from my heart I did."

My Aunt Lois's ride home was uneventful. As every step took her further from the approaching armies, she was unmolested, and feared naught save that General might give out. It was snowing hard for the greater part of her journey, and the horse stumbled homeward, stiff with cold and lame with fatigue. She writes:

"Twice after night-time I fell asleep on General's neck; and when I spied the candle-light from the kitchen window, from sheer joy I could have wept. But I called to mind what the officer had said about being in the American army, so bore up until my mother did open the door and fly outward. I could not stand alone, and fell forward when I slipped from General's back. They raised me and bore me into the house.

"But once in the light of the fire, I marked, for the first time in my life, the tears running down my mother's face as she held a hot posset to my lips.

"'Tell father it went safely,' said I,— 'the black duck'; and then I must have fallen dead asleep at once, on the settle Whereunto my mother drew me."

My Aunt Lois must have slept for many hours after that ride, of the hardship of which she says so little, though she owns, the second day after, to "a sorely stiff and cramped feeling."

I think, though, that she was fully repaid even before her father showed her a letter, long afterward, signed "G. Washington," which among other things expressed the writer's thanks "for an important service rendered his country."

"I went a dangerous errand," said Aunt Lois's father; "but 't would have been naught save for thee, my daughter; so yours was the service!"

A year later my Aunt Lois writes light-heartedly of a short trip southward with her father, who was quite recovered "but for a slight lameness," when she attended a grand ball "with my hair done high, and wearing a new sleeveless white satin gown —the same which father hath had done in the portrait." On which occasion she had the honor of a presentation to General and Lady Washington; whereupon General Washington, who knew her father, said:

"And is this the Mistress Bradley who carried the duck?"

"Yes, your Excellency," said Aunt Lois, laughing,—"a *pair* of ducks; but I bethought me that thou wert sharing naught else with the British, hence I gave them one!"

"At which," she writes, "my mother doth shake her head, and say, 'Oh, Lois! Lois! Thou wilt ever have the last word!'"

Sweet, bright, brave Aunt Lois!

I closed the book, smiling at its blithe pages, and knowing that some time sad ones must follow. But, if they do, they belong solely to the dim, ghostly attic and the dead rose-leaves, whereas I know she would gladly have us read about the black duck!

MORNING

By Emily Dickinson

Will there really be a morning?
  Is there such a thing as day?
Could I see it from the mountains
  If I were as tall as they?

Has it feet like water-lilies?
  Has it feathers like a bird?
Is it brought from famous countries
  Of which I have never heard?

Oh, some scholar! Oh, some sailor!
  Oh, some wise man from the skies!
Please to tell a little pilgrim
  Where the place called morning lies!

ON A MOUNTAIN TRAIL

by Harry Perry Robinson

We had no warning. It was as if they had deliberately lain in ambush for us at the turn in the trail. They seemed suddenly and silently to rise on all sides of the sleigh at once.

It is not often that the gray timber-wolves, or "black wolves," as the mountaineers call them, are seen hunting in packs, though the animal is plentiful enough among the foot-hills of the Rockies. As a general rule they are met with singly or in pairs. At the end of a long and severe winter, however, they sometimes come together in bands of fifteen or twenty; and every old mountaineer has a tale to tell,—perhaps of his own narrow escape from one of their fierce packs, perhaps of some friend of his who started one day in winter to travel alone from camp to camp, and whose clean-picked bones were found beside the trail long afterward.

It was in February, and we, Gates and myself, were driving from Livingston, Montana, to Gulch City, fifty miles away, with a load of camp supplies—a barrel of flour and some bacon, coffee, and beans; a blanket or two, and some dynamite (or "giant powder," as the miners call it) for blasting; a few picks and shovels, and other odds and ends. We had started at daybreak. By five o'clock in the evening, with some ten miles more to travel, the worst of the trail was passed. There had been little snow that winter, so that even

in the gulches and on the bottoms the exposed ground was barely covered; while, on the steep slopes, snow had almost entirely disappeared, leaving only ragged patches of white under overhanging boughs, and a thin coating of ice in the inequalities of the hard, frost-bound trail, making a treacherous footing for the horses' hoofs.

The first forty miles of the road had lain entirely over hills,—zigzagging up one side of a mountain only to zigzag down the other,—with the dense growth of pine and tamarack and cedar on both sides, wreathed here and there in mist. But at last we were clear of the foot-hills and reached the level. The tall forest trees gave place to a wilderness of thick underbrush, lying black in the evening air, and the horses swung contentedly from the steep grade into the level trail, where at last they could let their legs move freely in a trot.

Hardly had they settled into their stride, however, when both animals shied violently to the left side of the trail. A moment later they plunged back to the right side so suddenly as almost to throw me off into the brush.

Then, out of the earth and the shadow of the bushes, the grim, dark forms seemed to rise on all sides of us. There was not a sound,—not a snap nor a snarl; but in the gathering twilight of the February evening, we saw them moving noiselessly over the thin coat of snow which covered the ground. In the uncertain light, and moving as rapidly as we did, it was impossible to guess how many they were. An animal which was one moment in plain sight, running abreast of the horses, would, the next moment, be lost in the shadow of the bushes, while two more dark, silent forms would edge up to take its place. So, on both sides of us, they kept appearing and disappearing. In the rear, half a dozen jostled one another to push up nearer to the flying sleigh,—a black mass that filled the whole width of the trail. Behind those again, others, less clearly visible, crossed and recrossed the roadway from side to side. They might be twenty in all—or thirty—or forty. It was impossible to tell.

For a minute I did not think of danger. The individual wolf is the most skulking and cowardly of animals, and only by some such experience as we had that night does a hunter learn that wolves can be dangerous. But soon the stories of the old mountaineers came crowding into my mind, as the horses, terrified and snorting, plunged wildly along the narrow trail, while the ghost-like forms glided patiently alongside—appearing, disappearing, and reappearing. The silent pertinacity with which, apparently making no effort, they kept pace beside the flying horses was horrible. Even a howl or a yelp or a growl would have been a relief. But not so much as the sound of their footfalls on the snow was to be heard.

At the first sight of the wolves, I had drawn my revolver from the leather case in which it hung suspended from my belt. Gates, handling the reins, was entirely occupied with the horses; but I knew, without need of words, that he saw our pursuers and understood the peril as well as I. "Have you your gun?" I shouted in his ear.

A negative shake of the head was all the answer. So we must trust to the six cartridges in my revolver.

"How many wolves are there, do you suppose?" again I called.

Again he shook his head, as if to say that he could not guess.

So the minutes passed and we swept on, rising and falling and swaying with the inequalities in the trail. The dark forms, growing more indistinct each minute, were hanging doggedly to the sleigh.

Suddenly I became aware that a wolf was almost at my elbow; its head was on a level with my waist as I sat in the low sleigh. In the darkness I could plainly see the white teeth, and the dim circle of the eyes. I hardly had to lean over at all to place the muzzle of the revolver within a foot of the great round head before I fired. I saw the black form roll over and over in the snow as we went by. Simultaneously, two other shadowy shapes that had been running abreast of the horses, in advance of the animal that was shot, dropped back; and looking over my shoulder I could see them throw themselves upon their wounded fellow. As the sea-gulls, following in the wake of a vessel in mid-ocean, swoop from all directions upon some floating scrap that has been thrown overboard, so from both sides of the trail the dark figures rushed together into one struggling mass behind the sleigh; and for the first time we heard them snapping and snarling at one another, as they tore their comrade to pieces.

The horses appeared to know that in some way a gleam of hope had come. They ceased plunging and seemed to throw all their energies into putting as wide a space as possible between them and the yelping pack behind.

How long would the respite be? Seconds passed until half a minute had gone. Then a minute. Could it be that they had left us —that the horrible race was over?

But even as the hope was forming itself in my mind, I became aware of a dim, gray thing moving beside me. A moment later another appeared, close by the horses' heads, and behind us the trail was again full of the jostling pack.

It was terrible beyond expression, the utter noiselessness with which they resumed their places,—apparently tireless; keeping pace with the racing horses without a sign of effort; patient as fate itself. Have you ever been on a fast steamship— say a "P. and O." boat in Indian waters where the sea is transparent—and, leaning over the stern, watched a shark following the vessel? If so, you remember how, hour after hour and day after day, the dark, vaguely outlined body, not more distinct than the shadow of a cloud upon the waves, stayed, motionless to all appearance, just so many feet aft in the ship's wake, no matter how fast she moved. To me, and I think to every one who has seen it, that silent, persistent, haunting presence is the very embodiment of ruthlessness and untiring cruelty. There, in the twilight and shadow, was the same silence, the same indistinctness, the same awing impression of motionless speed, the same horror of the inevitable, in that pursuit by the wolves.

But soon their tactics changed. Either they had grown bolder, or the wolf they had eaten among them had put a keener edge upon their appetites. There were now four or five of the ghostlike forms moving abreast of the horses on my side of the sleigh alone. On the other side more were visible. They were now closing in upon us, with determination. Suddenly I saw one make a spring at the throat of the off horse, and, missing his aim, fall back. The horses had been terrified before; from that moment they lost all control of themselves. Neither the driver's voice nor his hands

upon the reins had any influence upon them as they tore wildly down the narrow path between the bushes, snorting, throwing their heads from side to side, and breaking now and again into short, shrill neighs of terror. The breath from their nostrils and the steam from their bodies made a white cloud in the wintry night air, almost enveloping them and us, and at times blotting out of sight the wolves beneath.

But the pack was again closing in. In front of all, I could see one running under the very noses of the horses, keeping just beyond the reach of their hoofs, and evidently waiting for the right moment to make a final leap at their throats. Leaning forward, and steadying my aim as well as I could in the rocking sleigh, I fired full at the whole dark mass in front. Apparently the ball passed harmlessly through them, but in an instant all had vanished—behind and into the bushes—as a swarm of flies vanish at the waving of a handkerchief. Only for a second, however, and one after another they were back again.

A second shot, fired again at random into the mass, was more successful; and once more we saw them drop back and crowd together in the trail behind us while the snapping and snarling grew fainter as the horses plunged on.

Half of the last ten miles had now been traveled, and five miles more would bring us to Gulch City and security. The excitement of that race was unspeakable: the narrow lane of the trail lying white ahead of us and behind us between the dark borders of the brush, seen fitfully through the steam from the maddened horses.

But the respite this time was shorter than before. Once more our relentless foes gathered round us, silently, one by one. The wolves seemed to know as well as we, that time was short and escape lay not far away; for hardly had the pack settled in their places round us before I saw one animal throw himself recklessly at the horses' throats. There was a sudden mad rearing up of both the horses, a wild, despairing neigh, a short yelp from the wolf's throat, and the dark form that had seemed to hang for a moment, leech-like, to the chest of one of our brave beasts was beaten down under the hoofs.

The others did not wait even for the sleigh to pass, but leaped upon the struggling form even as the runners were upon it. In my excitement I did a foolish thing. Leaning over, and thrusting my revolver almost against the skins of the fierce brutes, I fired two shots in quick succession. They had their effect, I know, for I saw one of the dark figures throw itself convulsively out of the mass into the brush, where others sprang upon it, and a death-cry went up in the night air. But we could ill spare the ammunition.

This idea evidently occurred to Gates. Leaning suddenly toward me, but with his eyes fixed on the horses and the road ahead, he called:

"How many shots have you left?"

"Only one."

"Not even one apiece for us?"

And I knew that he was in earnest. I knew also that he was right; that it would be better to die so, than to be torn to pieces by that snarling, hungry crew.

But it was too late now. Five shots out of the six were spent, and twenty minutes yet must pass before we could reach the camp. And even while these few words were being said the pack was close upon us again. Fiercer now, and more determined than ever to make an end of it, they crowded around. One even flung himself at the low side of the sleigh to snap at me, and his teeth caught for a moment in the sleeve of my coat as I struck him on the head with the clenched hand holding the pistol. On both sides, too, they jostled each other, to reach the flying horses, and I knew that in

a few seconds more I must sacrifice the last cartridge in my revolver.

As a forlorn hope I snatched the buffalo-robe which lay on Gates' knees, and threw it to them. But they hardly stopped to tear it to pieces. There was more satisfying food in the sleigh. And they closed around the horses again.

For the first time Gates turned to look at me.

"Jack!" he called excitedly, "the giant powder!"

For a moment I did not grasp his meaning. Seeing my indecision he shouted again:

"The giant powder, Jack!"

Then it came to me. Thrusting the pistol into its case, I scrambled over into the rear part of the sleigh, and as I did so the wolves that were following behind fell back a few feet. Hastily fumbling among the various supplies, I found the old sack in which the sticks of dynamite were wrapped, and with them the small package of caps and fuse. Taking three of the sticks, I tied them tightly together with my handkerchief and, quickly fitting the end of an inch of fuse— for, in this case, the shorter the piece the better—into a cap, I thrust the latter into the center of the three sticks. I was still at work, when a sudden swing of the sleigh and a cry from Gates warned me that something was the matter. The horses were plunging violently, and as the near horse reared I saw that a wolf had leaped upon its withers and was clinging, with its teeth apparently in the side of the horse's neck. In their terror, the horses had stopped, and were actually backing us into the brush. Something had to be done, and with some vague hope, I fired the last shot from the revolver into the dark circle which already surrounded the plunging horses. The shot had its effect, for one of the brutes leaped into the air with a yelp and fell backward into the bushes. The horse, too, sprang sud-

denly forward, and the wolf that was clinging to it fell to the ground and was trampled under the hoofs. In an instant, those of
the pack that had not already flung themselves upon the wounded animal in the
bushes, rushed upon this one that was lying
lifeless or stunned from the horses' feet;
and once more, for a few seconds, we had
breathing space, and the sleigh sped along
through the keen air, our enemies snarling
and quarreling behind us.

But the last shot was spent!

Turning my attention again to the giant
powder, I fixed the cap and fuse more
firmly in their place, and taking off my belt
wound that tightly round the whole.
Round that again I wrapped one of the old
sacks, and tearing off my coat made an
extra covering of that, knotting the sleeves
tightly on the outside, that the ravenous
teeth might be delayed in tearing the bundle apart. Crouching down in the sleigh, I
lighted a match, and, as I did so, I saw
that the wolves were upon us again, apparently as numerous and as tireless as
ever. The match went out; and a second.
Crouching lower still, I made a barricade
against the wind with anything I could lay
my hands on in the sleigh, and at last a
dull red spark caught the end of the fuse.

The pack was already crowding round
the terrified horses, which, it seemed to
me, were almost worn out, and moved
more heavily than heretofore. And how
slowly the fuse burned! Nursing it carefully with my hands, I blew upon the
spark and kept it glowing as it ate its way
slowly into the cotton. Why had I not
made it shorter? Every moment I expected
to feel the sudden jolt which told that the
wolves had pulled down one of the horses
and that the end had come!

At last the dull red glow had almost
reached the end of the cap. A few seconds
more and it would explode. Thrusting the
bundle hastily into another sack, forgetting

even the wolves in my terror lest it should
explode in my hands, I threw it with all
my force into the midst of the moving
forms abreast of the horses.

The beasts flung themselves upon it, and
as we swept by, the whole pack was again
collected into a struggling, snarling heap
beside the trail. We were sweeping round
a curve in the road, and before the horses
had taken a dozen strides, the brush shut
out the path behind us and the wolves.

A moment later and the air and the
earth shook around us. I was still half
standing, clutching the low side of the
sleigh, and the concussion threw me upon
my face. The report was not the crash of
a cannon nor the sharp noise of gunpow-
der, but a dull, heavy roar like an instantaneous clap of distant thunder. The stillness that followed was intense, but I
thought that I heard, from the direction
where the wolves had been, one broken,
muffled howl.

What had been the effect of it? Both
Gates and myself leaned forward and with
voice and hand urged the horses on. When
would those grim, gray, ruthless forms re-
appear? The seconds passed; minute followed minute, and the horses, breathing
painfully, labored on over the level trail.
With every yard traveled, hope grew
stronger, until leaning over again I said
to Gates:

"I don't believe they're coming, Char-
lie."

But his only reply was a shake of the
reins and another word to the horses.

Then suddenly there came a twinkle of
light in the distance. The brush fell away
from the trail and the white expanse of
the clearing of Gulch City was before us.

For a distance of fifty yards, at a point
about a mile and a half north of Gulch
City, the old Livingston trail had to be
abandoned. It would have been more labor

to repair it than to clear a new pathway through the brush. And when I left that part of the country two years afterward, the packers would still turn out of their way for a minute to look at "Giant Hole," and to kick up out of the weeds and brush that had grown around it the skull or part of the skeleton of a wolf.

SKATING

By Odell Shepard

We are off in a trice on the glittering ice
  Where the cold is as keen as a knife,
Where the winds at our back are a galloping pack
  Of wolves on the warm scent of life,
And the frost-laden air is a blustering dare,
  A wager and challenge to strife.

Then, swifter than arrows, we speed through the narrows,
  We circle and quarter and reel,
We dodge and we race, play at prisoners' base,
  Snap-the-whip, figure-eight, and cartwheel;
While the river-banks ring to the songs that we sing
  And the hiss of the glistening steel.

But the wind gathers might at the coming of night,
  And we ride on the wings of the gale
Down the river again o'er the glimmering plain
  Where the light is beginning to fail,
On the strength of the blast spinning dizzily past
  The trees in the twilight pale.

Forgetful of care as the birds of the air,
  Or as boats on a breeze-bright sea,
We are wafted along with our laughter and song
  While the valleys reëcho our glee;
And our hearts are in tune with the cloud-driven moon
  And the boughs of the wind-blown tree.

Over the level ice, joining our revel,
  The snow, a dim flurry of white,
Drives drifting and rollicking by in a frolicking
  Dance through the halls of the night.
The stars are a-quiver with glee, and the river
  Rings with our shouts of delight
As we race on together before the keen weather,
  Borne by the wild wind's might.

HALF A MAN

by Walter Archer Frost

OFF outside the harbor the wind still lashed the smashing seas to a lather. The gale had blown the worst of itself out, but everything was loose yet and the sky looked dirty.

In the harbor, though, all was snug, and *The Charming Lass,* comfortable at her moorings, courtesied daintily, bow into the wind, her long, keen cut-water slitting the in-swaying seas.

She was a sixty-five-ton schooner, fitting out now for the cod-grounds, as everyone in Trinity Bay, Newfoundland, knew. But no one in all the bay knew it any better than Murdock Fraser.

The schooner had wintered at Trinity Bay. She'd shot her big anchor down in the lee of the island and slept soundly there, frozen in, comfortable as an eel in the mud. And all through the long cold weeks Murdock had looked at her with admiration and longing.

For he came of a long line of fishermen. The sea and the lure of the rigors of a fisherman's life—they were what he dreamed of; he hungered to be about the work which had summoned his father and his grandfather and those of his kin before them; he burned to be off on the banks, fishing for cod in one of the dories of a trim schooner that never took in a sail for anything.

That was why he watched *The Charming Lass* with such longing: he wanted to ship on her not as a cabin boy, but as a member of her crew. And word had gone about through Trinity Bay that the trig schooner was short-handed.

"It's my chance," Murdock said to his mother. "I'm only fourteen, but," he stretched himself, "I'm bigger'n one or two o' th' men on her. I'm goin' down an' try."

His mother smiled. He was good to her eyes: she knew that he was going to be big and brawny and powerful like his father. Murdock was her only son. She knew, too well, the dangers of a fisherman's life; and she winced at the thought of the boy's going. But she knew the call of the blue water. It was in her blood as in his. So she did not try to dissuade him.

"Try your luck, Murdock," she said, and touched his big-boned shoulder in veiled caress.

The boy laughed in his quiet way, and turned and walked down the path which led to the wharf. A dory was just putting out to the schooner, and Murdock jumped in, saying to the two men at the oars, "I want to see yer captain."

"Don't know's he'll want to see *you,*" said one of the men. But Murdock paid no attention.

A few moments later the dory made fast astern of the schooner, Murdock clambered over the rail, and stood on the deck. He was so dazed at finding himself here, where he'd dreamed of being, that he hardly felt, for the first second, the heavy hand which fell on his shoulder.

"I'm Cap'n Peter Johnson," a big voice rumbled above him. "You want to see me?"

"Yes," said the boy, "I hear you're short-handed," and he looked up confidently.

"Meanin'," the big voice rumbled with the laugh in it, "you want to help me out? I got a cabin-boy already."

"That's good," Murdock said, giving the captain a straight look from a pair of frank blue eyes. "It's fillin' out yer *crew* I'm thinking of."

Captain Peter Johnson smiled more than ever. "But you're only half a man. You could cut bait, mebby, but—"

"Yes, I kin cut bait as good as th' next," Murdock said, "but what I want is to do my trick at th' wheel, an' take my turn with th' oars in the dories, an' handle my lines *after* they've been baited. Then when I'm through, I want my *lay* like the other men."

Captain Johnson stopped smiling. "How old are you?" He liked the boy's confidence in himself, but half a man wasn't a whole one, and no captain that ever sailed blue water was more painstaking than Captain Johnson in picking men for his crew.

"I'm fourteen," said Murdock, honestly, "but my name's Murdock Fraser."

Captain Johnson nodded. He knew the Frasers of Trinity Bay. "You'll be a good man for me in four or five years, but now you couldn't even haul up the jumbo."

The "jumbo" was the big jib. Murdock knew this, and looked forward eagerly. "Lemme have a try at her! No," he corrected, like the sailor he said he was, "you don't want her set while you're fast to th' bottom."

Maybe Captain Johnson felt himself weakening; or it may be that he thought of the toll the sea already had taken of the Frasers. Be that as it may, he said sharply,

"Into th' dory, boy! I'll have two o' th' men take you back to shore!" Murdock said nothing. A lump had risen unexpectedly in his throat. He walked slowly astern, the captain following him.

Then, when the men started clambering over the side, the boy made one last appeal to Captain Johnson. "Mebby I am only half a man, like you say; but if you'd let me ship, you'd find I'd work like a whole one."

"Cast off that line!" was the captain's only answer. The boy leaped into the stern of the dory. Then, humiliated, and heavy with disappointment, Murdock was rowed ashore.

"But I'll ship on her yet!" he told his mother that evening at supper. "She'll take me 'long with 'er when she clears," he said, as the night came down. "I'll work like a man and get my lay like the rest, and the money'll help us here."

The *lay* meant the individual share of each member of the crew of the catch of cod. He was trying to reassure his mother and, understanding this, she nodded and said, "Yes, Murdock, it'd help." But, like him, she knew he was answering the irresistible summons of the sea.

So she was not surprised when he kissed her and his sisters good night, and, instead of going to his room, walked forth into the darkness which had held the harbor like a cloud of ink.

But through this seemingly impenetrable gloom the boy walked swiftly with sure tread; off, out there in the harbor, he could see the riding-lights of *The Charming Lass* as she swung: a red lantern to port and a green to starboard.

Half-way to the wharf he left the deeper path for one of his own making. A few moments later he was at the beach, where his own boat was moored. Easily she slid into the water, down the "slip" he'd made of spruce sticks. The oars found the locks apparently of their own instinct. Then he headed the boat for the stern of *The Charming Lass.*

In the rush of the waves he might have rowed without regard to the sound he made, for the click of his oarlocks was drowned by the breakers. But he rowed with his nicest pains. He pulled carefully, too, taking the larger seas bow on, and shipping not a cup of water.

On through the thick blackness he rowed, now sinking deep between towering black cliffs of water, now riding high on their snowy crests. Elated and confident, he rowed on. His spirits mounted even as he mounted the waves, but, unlike the waves, they suffered no depression.

He felt like shouting aloud in his ecstasy. Last night he would have so shouted. But he set his lips grimly now—as he thought a man would do—as he believed a sailor would do, a fisherman who was joining his mates aboard the schooner.

"Half a man?" Murdock said to himself. "I'll show 'em I'm a whole one!"

But there was that immediately ahead of him which was to tax severely this new manhood of his, and he knew it; once he reached the schooner's side, he could make her rail easily, but his own boat he must say good-by to.

Now was the ordeal, for he came suddenly on the schooner; checked the momentum of his rowboat by thrusting his hand against the schooner's side; in another moment was over her rail; for a long heart-beat tried to catch once more the clean lines of the boat he loved—then he let go her line and saw her drift astern into the blackness.

"I hope Rory McAuley remembers and watches out for her," Murdock said to himself. He had outlined his plans to Rory, his playmate.

Then the half a man, who was going to prove that he was a whole man on this cruise of *The Charming Lass,* stole noiselessly along the deck to the port stack of dories. The instant his hands found them, he undid the rope which made fast their canvas covering, crawled into the top dory, fastened the cover over the top again, and re-tied the rope as best he could.

Then he stretched himself comfortably on the dirty bottom of the dory. And when *The Charming Lass* got her hook up, just before dawn the next morning, and her sails sang up, and she sprang happily before the thrust of the fair wind, she carried forth on her over the blue water a half-a-man whose presence none of her crew was aware of, but whose heart was singing.

It was not until the schooner had raced over many miles of tumbling seas that Murdock slipped the rope and slid out to the deck from the dory. He had breakfasted on what his mother had put up for him. He had slept happily. He held his sturdy body well erect; the roll of the schooner was joy to him—but, for the moment, his heart was somewhere below his boot-tops.

Drawn by some power he could not explain, he turned, and met the keen eyes of the man at the wheel. A roll, as of thunder, seemed suddenly to envelop the boy. But it was only the roar of the helmsman. "Get below, an' tell th' old man we got a stow-'way!"

"Yes, sir," said Murdock. He obeyed, and he did it proudly: no matter what the result, he was being sent, as a member of the crew, with a message to the captain.

Knowing his way about a schooner as well as if he'd never been off her in his life, Murdock went swiftly to the captain's state-room, knocked, then, at the brusque command, opened the door and touched his thick hair:

"Man at th' wheel says we got a stow-

'way aboard, Cap'n," said Murdock Fraser. "W— w— what're we goin' to do with 'im, Cap'n?"

Captain Peter Johnson reflected, or seemed to. He was angry, and he was not one to forgive easily an infringement of his orders; he was on the high-seas now. On *The Charming Lass* Peter Johnson was a despot. That is to say, he was the captain of the schooner, and what he said *went*. On the other hand, this "stow'way's" obstinate perseverance appealed to him.

But Captain Johnson had selected his course and would not diverge from it, for he was obstinate himself. Fixing the boy with penetrating glance, the captain said. "Seen this stow'way, have you, Fraser?"

Murdock's heart leaped. "Yes, s-sir."

"Is he the Cape Bretoner that come aboard us in Trinity Bay, afternoon 'fore we cleared, Fraser?"

Murdock's brain reeled. "N-no, sir."

"What sort o' looking man *is* he, then?" asked Captain Johnson.

Murdock looked down, then up, straight into the captain's eyes. "He ain't very big, Cap'n, this man ain't, but he says he can do th' work—" Murdock gulped.

Peter Johnson leaned slightly toward Murdock. "Say, Fraser," he began, "you don't mean that kid I sent ashore in a dory's stowed away onto us?"

And poor Murdock could answer only, "Yes—sir."

The captain nailed the boy with a stern stare. "Then, Fraser, you tell this here stow'way to jump to the galley an' ask th' cook for a job peelin' potatoes. I remember that kid, he wasn't even half a man. Tell 'im if he touches a line or a dory or speaks to any man aboard but th' cook, I'll know what to do to 'im."

"He can do a man's work," Murdock cried desperately. "He'll *prove* it."

Captain Johnson was at the boy's side in one bound. "He'll learn obedience first!" roared the captain. "Get to the galley!"

"Yes, sir," Murdock cried once, then fled —as ordered.

"You'll peel potatoes, an' you'll wash dishes an' wipe 'em, an' you'll scrub decks, an' you'll clean bunks, an' you'll clean lamps, an' you'll sweep this galley, an' you'll sew on buttons, an' you'll mend clothes, an' you'll wait on th' table, an' you'll be cabin-boy's helper, an' you won't have time to be a fisherman," said the cook, grimly, having his orders from the captain.

And that, Murdock sorrowfully found, was what he'd won by stowing-away on *The Charming Lass*. On she flew, seeming to skim the blue water like a gull, on, on to the cod-grounds, the paradise of deep-sea fishermen.

Her decks were alive with the eager energy of the crew; the bait was of the best; the lines were sure; the hooks filed painstakingly; the dories tight; the oars and oar-locks ready for the water.

But Murdock, bending over his scrubbing, or spending himself on any one of his other monotonous duties, felt as far removed from the life of the flying schooner as if he'd been buried in the bottom of the Sydney mines.

More than that, the captain had forbidden him so much as to speak to any member of the crew. As a result, he was thrown for companionship on the cook and the cabin-boy. The former was taciturn. The latter, two years older than Murdock, was a blundering bully, who welcomed Murdock as one he could domineer over.

"Half-a-man," the cabin-boy would say, "get more elbow-grease into yer sweepin' this galley. Huh, you ain't even *half* a man; you're only a *quarter!*"

The cabin-boy's name was Herbert, and he threw his jeer at the boy who had been working since five in the morning like a Trojan. Then, as Murdock didn't so much as look up, Herbert began again: "You ain't even a quarter of a man. You're only a—"

"I'll show you what I am, if you want me to," Murdock said abruptly.

Herbert snatched the broom out of the other's hand, and stood over him. "Now show me!" Then, because he mistook Murdock's calmness for cowardice, Herbert sent his open hand to Murdock's face.

At the same instant, Herbert felt a solid fist crash against his side. He struck out with all his power, and Murdock slid across the narrow galley to the ladder. But Herbert's rush to pin the boy in the corner was met and broken before it was fairly started. All the larger boy knew was that something caught him with the clutch of a cable about his knees; he was lifted, swung clear off the floor, and slammed down with a force which dazed him. Then he was jerked to his feet and flung, big as he was, on the cook's bunk.

"You lie there!" a deep voice said quietly. And Herbert obeyed that quiet voice, for he'd found what was behind it. And when Herbert got up, some twenty minutes later, he'd lost all his bully and brag. He walked over to the other side of the little room and held out his hand.

"I was wrong: you're *more*'n half a man: you're blame near a whole man," said Herbert to Murdock Fraser.

After that, the two boys worked side by side and came to be good friends. But, though gratified, Murdock was not satisfied. He had convinced Herbert, but he wanted to convince the captain.

Murdock longed for some chance to show that, though he was only a boy in years, he could do a man's work on a fishing schooner. Hour after hour, while Herbert slept soundy in his bunk, Murdock wrestled with his problem. Every morning

he rose determined, that day, if any opportunity came, to prove the truth of his boast to the captain.

But it seemed that no chance would come. *The Charming Lass* made the fishing-grounds; the covers were snatched impatiently from the dories; the boats were shot to the water; in leaped the crew, two men to a dory, and off the boats raced to see which should make the first trip back laden down with cod.

There were nine men, counting the captain and crew, and Murdock hoped that he'd be allowed to make the tenth when the time came; but the fifth dory went out with only one man in her, and the boy watched her disconsolately. What wouldn't he have given to have pulled an oar and handled a line with the rest of them! What were tumbling mountains of water and floating ice to him? He yearned to be fighting them.

So it went, day after day. There was a wealth of cod running; the dories came back and back to the clean sides of *The Charming Lass,* emptied their loads, and went back to the fishing. Indeed, the cod were so keen in their biting that when the schooner was nearly full Captain Johnson ordered Herbert, the cabin-boy, to take a line with the ninth man in the fifth dory.

"Too bad, Murdock!" Herbert said honestly. "Wish t' you were comin', too."

But Murdock said nothing: by his promotion Herbert had been converted, for the time, to a member of the schooner's crew so Murdock could not speak to him.

The boy went back to his work in the galley, heavy-hearted. For he told himself that his last chance to prove himself in the big captain's eyes was gone now. In the morning would be begun the cruise home; on *The Charming Lass* he'd have showed his worth only in the galley.

There he seated himself listlessly on the cook's bunk. What was the use of hoping?

No use! He wasn't good for anything. If he had been, he'd have found a way of proving it. Over in the corner, between the foot of the bunk and the stove bolted to the floor, the cook dozed. All the work was done. Murdock set his teeth. How he hated this opportunity for idleness! How he sorrowed that no chance had come!

An hour passed, two, three.

Then something, instinct surely, roused him, sent him swiftly up the ladder, and turned his keen eyes over the schooner's rail. None too soon, either. For down from the Straits of Belle Isle had come a gigantic ice-floe. Now, silent as death, it was closing in grimly, inexorably, on *The Charming Lass;* once those two yawning jaws of ice closed up the blue water, nothing could save the schooner.

No time to cry out to the sleeping cook, Murdock knew. He sprang to the wheel, spun it over, and lashed it, having caught in a twinkling the narrow path of safe water that led to the open sea beyond. Like lightning, he had lashed the wheel, then he dashed forward to the "jumbo," the big jib, broke out the frozen rings, then flew to the sheet-line and began to haul.

"I got to get her up!" he cried aloud between his clenched teeth, as he hauled desperately. "I got to get her up, for we got to get steerageway!" Would the rope never start? He flung his weight on it again, but still it was not starting.

Then, as he'd seen men do, he made the rope fast on the cleat, and, catching the up-haul at shoulder-height, he hurled himself on it, then outward toward the rail, and the sheet sang free with a suddenness which almost sent him and the released line overboard. Then he hauled, hauled, hauled, felt *The Charming Lass* heel, hauled once more with all his strength, made fast and sure the line on the cleat, then dashed aft to the wheel, released its lashing with one hand, then spun the wheel until the schooner came in line with the safe lane of blue water and ploughed gaily ahead through it.

And that was the sight which gladdened the desperate eyes of Captain Peter Johnson, who, rowing hopelessly for the schooner on which he had seen, too late, the ice closing in, now sank back in his seat, his hand gripping on the thwart to steady himself.

"Who done *that?*" Captain Johnson demanded of the man in the bow seat. "Who knew enough to do th' only thing that could've saved her?"

"Not th' cook, he didn't," said the other man. "No, sir. He couldn't 've brung 'er out like that in a thousan' years. See 'er come! Look at 'er!"

The Charming Lass, though she had only the jumbo set, was dancing daintily along the blue lane as if she were laughing at the on-creeping ice each side of her. She had half a mile yet to go, but she didn't seem worried. Her jumbo filling until it stood rigid as sheet-iron, the schooner danced onward. Each instant the ice closed in more, but she continued on her way as if the whole thing were a joke, or as if she knew that, let the ice threaten as it would, she was safe in the capable hands of one who understood her and loved her.

"Bring 'er more to starb'rd," yelled Captain Johnson, though he knew his voice couldn't carry that far.

Simultaneously he saw the schooner's clean bow swing just the right degree to starboard; and while he watched, spellbound, *The Charming Lass* slid through the last fifty feet of the blue lane into the safe open water.

Then, as if that were not enough, she swung still farther around, though not enough to spill the wind out of the jumbo, and bore gracefully down to where the dories, now clustered, were watching her.

"I'm coming up into th' wind," called a voice from the wheel. "Then I'll stand by for you!"

And Captain Peter Johnson, good man that he was, sprang up in answer to that hail. He leaped up until he towered on the thwart, and he roared through his big hands, "Ay, ay, sir!"

The cook, white-faced, said: "He done it! I was below. Look here where the ice started piling over! It'd carried away the anchor, snapped th' chain, an' got a lot o' th' gear. Two minutes more, an' it'd got *us!*"

"Yes, of course," said Captain Peter Johnson. He looked about him. "Where's he gone to, that boy—I mean that *man?* Fraser," he said, when two of the crew dragged the boy up from where he had retreated to the galley, "where'd you have headed th' schooner for if we hadn't rowed for you?"

And Murdock said: "I'd 've took 'er to Lark Tickle Cove, sir," jerking his head over his right shoulder. "They's another schooner layin' there, an' I figured they might be able to spare us an anchor."

Captain Johnson looked down at the boy, then put a big hand on his shoulder. "Take the wheel again, Fraser," he said, "an' head where you was goin' to—Lark Tickle Cove. We need that anchor. In a little while I'll have *another* member of the crew relieve you at th' wheel. I want to see y'u."

And what Captain Peter Johnson said to Fraser, the new member of his crew, is best shown by the fact that when *The Charming Lass* danced back into Trinity Bay and shot her mud-hook down through the blue water, a sturdy boy went ashore with his mates in the dories. He'd signed articles for the next cruise; he had two hundred and fifty dollars in his pocket, representing his *lay* of *The Charming Lass's* record catch—nine hundred quintals of cod. His head was held well back, his chest swelled full, wide, and deep, he whistled a sea song as he faced off up the dock; and with a deep-sea roll, he strode up the path to his mother's cottage. For the half a man was a whole man, and he'd proved it!

THE "ARRIVAL" OF JIMPSON

BY RICHARD STILLMAN POWELL

I.—THE DEPARTURE

THE rain fell in a steady, remorseless drizzle upon the rain-coats and umbrellas of the throng that blocked the sidewalks and overflowed on to the cartracks; but the fires of patriotism were unquenchable, and a thousand voices arose to the leaden sky in a fierce clamor of intense enthusiasm. It had rained all night. The streets ran water, and the spouts emptied their tides between the feet of the cheerers. The lumbering cars, their crimson sides glistening, clanged their way carefully through the crowds, and lent a dash of color to the scene. The back of Gray's loomed cheerless and bleak through the drizzle, and beyond, the college yard lay deserted. In store windows the placards were hidden behind the blurred and misty panes, and farther up the avenue, the tattered red flag above Foster's hung limp and dripping.

Under the leafless elm, the barge, filled to overflowing with departing heroes, stood ready for its start to Boston. On the steps, bareheaded and umbrella-less, stood Benham, '95, who, with outstretched and waving arms, was tempting the throng into ever greater vocal excesses.

"Now, then, fellows! Three times three for Meredith."

"'Rah, 'rah, 'rah! 'rah, 'rah, 'rah! 'rah, 'rah, 'rah! Meredith!" A thousand throats raised the cry; umbrellas clashed wildly in mid-air; the crowd surged to and fro; horses curveted nervously; and the rain poured down impartially upon the reverend senior and the clamorous freshman.

459

"Fellows, you're not *half* cheering!" cried the relentless Benham. "Now, three times three, three long Harvards, ànd three times three for the eleven."

"'Rah, 'rah, 'rah! 'rah, 'rah, 'rah! 'rah, 'rah, 'rah! Har-vard, Har-vard, Har-vard! 'Rah, 'rah, 'rah! 'rah, 'rah, 'rah! 'rah, 'rah, 'rah! 'Leven!"

Inside the coach there was a babel of voices. Members of the eleven leaned out and conversed jerkily with friends on the sidewalk. Valises and suit-cases were piled high in the aisle and held in the owners' laps. The manager was checking off his list.

"Cowper?"

"Here."

"Turner?"

"All right."

"Truesdale?"

"Hey? Oh, yes; I'm here." The manager folded the list. Then a penciled line on the margin caught his eye.

"Who's Jameson? Jameson here?"

"Should be Jimpson," corrected the man next to him; and a low voice called from the far end of the barge:

"Here, sir." It sounded so much like the response of a school-boy to the teacher that the hearers laughed with the mirth begot of tight-stretched nerves. A youth wearing a faded brown ulster, who was between Gates, the big center, and the corner of the coach, grew painfully red in the face, and went into retirement behind the big man's shoulder.

"Who is this fellow Jimpson?" queried a man in a yellow mackintosh.

"Jimpson? He's a freshie. Trying for right half-back all fall. I suppose Brattle took him along, now that Ward's given up, to substitute Sills. They say he's an A 1 runner, and plucky. He's played some on the second eleven. Taunton told me, the other day, that he played great ball at Exeter, last year."

The strident strains of the "Washington Post" burst out on the air, urging the cheerers to even greater efforts. They were cheering · indiscriminately now. The trainer, the rubbers, the coaches, even the bulldog "mascot," had received their shares of the ovation. But Benham, '95, with his coat soaked through, was still unsatisfied, and sought for further tests. Two professors, half hidden under umbrellas, had emerged from the yard, and were standing at a little ·distance, watching the scene.

"Three times three for Professor Dablee!" The cheers that followed were mixed with laughter, and the two professors moved off, but not until the identity of the second had been revealed, and the air had filled with the refrain of "Rah, 'rah, 'rah! Pollock!"

"They look as though they ought to win; don't you think so?" asked one of them.

The other professor frowned.

"Yes, they look like that; every eleven does. You'd think, to see them before a game, that nothing short of a pile-driver or dynamite could drive them an inch. And a few days later they return, heart-broken and defeated."

Across the square floated a husky bellow:

"Now, then, fellows! Once more! All together! Three times three for Harvard!"

The band played wildly, frenziedly, out of time and tune; the crowd strained its tired throats for one last farewell slogan; the men in the barge waved their hands; the horses jumped forward; a belated riser in Holyoke threw open a front window, and drowsily yelled, "Shut up"; and the Harvard eleven sped on its way up the avenue, and soon became a blur in the gray vista.

"Say, Bob, you forgot to cheer Jimpson."

The wearied youth faced his accuser, struck an attitude indicative of intense despair, and then joyfully seized the opportunity.

"Fellows! Fellows! Hold on! Three times three for Jim—Jim—who'd you say?"

"Jimpson," prompted the friend.

"Three times three for Jimpson! Now, then, all together!"

"Say—who *is* Jimpson?" shouted a dozen voices at once.

"Don't know. Don't care. Three times three for Jimpson!"

And so that youth, had he but known it, received a cheer, after all. But he didn't know it—at least, not until long afterward, when cheers meant so much less to him.

II.—A LETTER

New Haven, Conn., November 19.

Dear Mother: I can imagine your surprise upon receiving a letter from this place, when your dutiful son is supposed to be "grinding" in No. 30 College House, Cambridge. And the truth is that the dutiful son is surprised himself. Here am I, with some thirty-five other chaps, making ready for the big football game with Yale tomorrow. Here is how it happened:

Yesterday morning, Brattle—he's our captain—came to my room, routed me out of bed, and told me to report to the coaches for morning practise. You know, I've been trying for substitute right half-back. Ward, the regular, sprained his knee in the Dartmouth game, and a few days ago it went lame again. So now Sills has Ward's place, and I'm to substitute Sills. And if he gets laid out—and maybe I ought to hope he won't—I go in and play. What do you think of that? Of course Sills may last the entire game; but they say he has a weak back, only he won't own up to it, and may

have to give up after the first half. Gates told me this on the train. Gates is the big center, and weighs 196. He is very kind, and we chummed all the way from Boston. I didn't know any of the fellows, except a few by sight—just enough to nod to, you know.

We left Cambridge in a driving rain, and a big crowd stood out in it all, and cheered the eleven, and the captain, and the college, and everything they could think of. Every fellow on the first and second elevens, and every "sub" was cheered—all except Mr. Jimpson. They didn't know of his existence! But I didn't feel bad—not very, anyhow. I hope the rest of the fellows didn't notice the omission, however. But I made up my mind that if I get half a show, I'll make 'em cheer Jimpson, too. Just let me get on the field. I feel to-night as though I could go through the whole Yale team. Perhaps if I get out there, facing a big Yale man, I'll not feel so strong.

You know, you've always thought I was big. Well, to-day I overheard a fellow asking one of the men, "Who is that little chap with the red cheeks?" I'm a midget beside most of the other fellows. If I play tomorrow, I'll be the lightest man on the team, with the exception of Turner, our quarter-back, who weighs 158. I beat him by three pounds.

Such a hubbub as there is in this town to-night! Everybody seems crazy with excitement. Of course I haven't the slightest idea who is going to win, but to look at our fellows, you'd think they would have things their own way. I haven't seen any of the Yale players. We practised on their field for an hour or so this afternoon, but they didn't show up. There was a big crowd of Yale students looking on. Of course every fellow of us did his very worst; but the spectators didn't say anything—just looked wise.

Most of the fellows are terribly nervous to-night. They go around as though they were looking for something, and would cry if they didn't find it soon. And the trainer is the worst of all. Brattle, the captain, is fine, though. He isn't any more nervous than an alligator, and has been *sitting still all the evening,* talking with a lot of the old graduates about the game. Once he came in the writing-room, where I was sitting, and asked whom I was writing to. When I told him, he smiled, and said to tell you that if anything happened he'd look after my *remains* himself! Maybe he thought I was nervous. But if I am, I'm not the only one. Gates is writing to his mother, too, at the other table.

Give my love to Will and Bess. Tell Will to send my old skates to me. I shall want them. There is fine skating on Fresh Pond, which, by the way, is a lake.

We're ordered off to bed. I guess some of us won't sleep very well. I'm rather excited myself, but I guess I'm tired enough to sleep. I'll write again when I get back to college. With bushels of love to all,

Yours affectionately, TOM.

III.—THE "ARRIVAL"

JIMPSON sat on the ground and watched with breathless interest two charging, tattered, writhing lines of men. Jimpson felt a good deal like an outcast, and looked like a North American Indian. Only legs and face were visible; the rest of Jimpson was enveloped in a big gray blanket with barbaric red borders. Some two dozen counterparts of Jimpson sat or lay near by, stretching along the side-line in front of the Harvard section of the grand stand. Behind them a thousand en-thusiastic mortals were shouting pæans to the goddess of victory, and, unless that lady was deaf, she must have heard the pæans, however little she approved of them. The most popular one was sung to a well-known air.

"As we're strolling through Fifth
  Avenue
With an independent air,
The ladies turn and stare,
The chappies shout, 'Ah, there!'
And the population cries aloud,
'Now, aren't they just the swell-
  est crowd,
The men that broke Old Eli at
  New Haven!'"

And a mighty response swept across the field from where a bank of blue rose from the green of the field to the lighter blue of the sky. It was a martial air, with a prophecy of victory:

"Shout aloud the battle-cry
  Of Yale, Yale, Yale!
Wave her standard far and high
  For Yale, Yale, Yale!
See the foe retreat before us,
Sons of Eli, shout the chorus,
  Yale, Yale, Yale, Yale, Yale!"

Harvard and Yale were doing battle once more, and thirty thousand people were looking on. The score-board announced: "Harvard, 4; Yale, 0; Yale's ball. 15 minutes to play."

The story of twenty minutes of the first half is soon told. It had been Yale's kick-off. Haag had sent the ball down the field to Harvard's 20-yard line, and Van Brandt had gathered it in his long arms, and, with Meredith ahead, had landed it back in the middle of the field. But the fourth down gave it to their opponents after a loss of two yards, and the pigskin went down again to Harvard's territory, coming to a stop at the white line that marked thirty-five yards. Here Harvard's new half-back kick had been tried, and the ball went high in air, and the field went after it; and when the Yale full-back got his hands on it, he was content with a bare five yards, and it was Yale's ball on her 40-yard line. Then happened a piece of ill luck for the wearers of the blue. On the second down, Kurtz fumbled the pass, the ball rolled toward Yale's goal, and Brattle broke through the opposing left-tackle and fell on it.

And while a thunderous roar of joy floated across the field from the followers of the Crimson, the teams lined up on Yale's thirty yards. Twice Meredith tried to go through between center and left guard, and a bare yard was the reward. Then Van Brandt had run back as for a kick; the ball was snapped, passed to Sills, Harvard's right half-back, and, with it safely under his arm, he had skirted the Yale left, and fallen and wriggled and squirmed across the goal-line for the first touch-down.

Then ensued five minutes of bedlam, and after the victorious seats had settled into excited complacency, Van Brandt had tried for goal. But success was too much to hope for, and the two teams trotted back to the middle of the field, with the score 4 to 0. Then had the sons of Eli shown of what they were made, and in the next ten minutes the ball had progressed with fatal steadiness from the center of the field to the region of the Crimson's twenty yards. And now it was Yale's ball on the second down, and the silence was so intense that the signal was heard as plainly by the watchers at the far end of the field as by the twenty-two stern-faced warriors who faced each other almost under the shadow of the goal-posts.

"Twelve, six, twelve, fifty—two!"

And the backs, led by the guards, hurled their weight against Harvard's right tackle; and when the ball was found, Baker held it within a few inches of the 10-yard line.

The cheers of Yale had now grown continuous; section after section passed the slogan along. The stand across the field looked to Jimpson like a field of waving blue gentians. On the Harvard seats the uproar was less intense, and seemed a trifle forced; and the men near by were breathing heavily, and restively creeping down the line.

Again the lines were formed. Jimpson could see the tall form of the gallant Gates settle down into a hunchback, toad-like position to receive the coming onslaught. Billings, the right tackle, was evidently expecting another experience like the last. He looked nervous, and Gates turned his head and spoke to him under cover of the first numbers of the signal.

The guards were back of the line again, and their elbows almost brushed as they stood between the half-backs. Silence reigned. The referee skipped nimbly out of the way.

"Seven, seventeen, eighty-one, thirty."

Again the weakening tackle was thrust aside, and although the Crimson line held better, the ball was three yards nearer home when the whistle blew, and Billings, somewhat dazed, had to call for a short delay.

"First down again," muttered a brawny sub, at Jimpson's elbow. "Why doesn't he take Billings out?"

Again the signal came. Again a jumbled mass of arms and legs for a moment hid the result. Then the men on the stand overlooking the goal-line arose *en masse,* and a mighty cheer traveled up the field, growing in volume until Jimpson could not hear his own groans nor the loud groans of a big sub. Back of the line, and almost equidistant from the posts, lay the

Yale full-back; and the ball was held tightly to earth between outstretched hands. The prostrate players were slowly gaining their feet; but Billings and Sills lay where they had fallen. Then Brattle stepped toward the side-line, holding up his hand. With a leap Jimpson was on his feet. But the big chap beside him had already pulled off his sweater, and now, tossing it into Jimpson's face, he sped gleefully toward the captain.

Jimpson sat down again in deep disappointment; and a moment later, Billings, supported on either side, limped from the gridiron, amidst the cheers of the Harvard supporters. Sills was on his feet again, and the trainer was talking to him. Jimpson could see the plucky fellow shaking his head. Then, after a moment of indecision, the trainer left him, the whistle sounded, the Crimson team lined up back of the line, and Kurtz was poising the ball for a try at a goal. The result was scarcely in doubt, and the ball sailed cleanly between the posts, a good two feet above the crossbar; and the scoreboard said, "Harvard, 4; Yale, 6"; and there were three minutes more of the half.

Back went the ball to the 55-yard line, and loud arose the cheers of the triumphant friends of Yale. Gates kicked off, and Warner sent the ball back again, with a gain of ten yards. Sills caught it and ran, but was downed well inside Harvard territory, and the half ended with the ball in Yale's hands. Jimpson seized his blanket, and trotted after the eleven to the quarters. He found Gates stripping for a rub-down.

"Well, my lad," panted the latter, "could you discern from where you were just what kind of a cyclone struck us?" But Jimpson was too much interested for such levity.

"Do you think I'll get in this half, Gates?"

"Can't say. Take a look at Sills, and judge for yourself."

That gentleman was having his lame back rubbed by a trainer, but he appeared to Jimpson good for at least another quarter of an hour.

It seemed but a moment after they had reached the rooms that the word of "Time's up, fellows," was passed, and renewed cheering from without indorsed the fact. But a moment or two still remained, and that moment belonged to Brattle. He stood on a bench and addressed the hearers very quietly:

"We're going to kick, this half, fellows. I want every man to get down the field on the instant, without stopping to hold. I don't think they can keep us from scoring at least once more; but every man has got to *work*. When the time comes to put the ball over the line, I expect it to go over with a rush. Let every man play the best game he knows, but *play together*. Remember that lack of team work has often defeated Harvard. And now, fellows, three times three for Harvard!"

And what a yell that was! Jimpson went purple in the face, and the head coach cheered his spectacles off. And then out they all went on a trot, big Gates doing a coltish hand-spring in mid-field, to the great delight of the Crimson's wearers. The college band played; thirty thousand people said something all together; and then the great quadrangle was silent, the whistle piped merrily, and the ball soared into air again.

Jimpson took up his position on the side-line once more, and watched with envious heart the lucky players. For the great, overwhelming desire of Jimpson's soul was to be out there on the torn turf, doing great deeds, and being trampled under foot. He watched the redoubtable Sills as a cat watches a mouse. Every falter of that player brought fresh hope to Jimpson. He would have liked to rise and make an impassioned speech in the interests of humanity, protesting against allowing a man in Sills' condition to remain in the game. Jimpson's heart revolted at the cruelty of it.

Some such idea as this he had expressed to Gates, that morning; and the big center had giggled in deep amusement; in fact he had refused to recognize the disinterested character of Jimpson's protest.

"Don't you think," Jimpson had pleaded, "that I might ask Brattle to give me a show in the second half?"

"No, I don't," Gates had answered bluntly. "You're an unknown quantity, my boy; as the Frenchies say, you haven't 'arrived.' For a player who hasn't 'arrived' to try to give the captain points would be shocking bad taste. That's how it is. Sills is a good player. As long as he can hold his head up, he'll be allowed to play. When he's laid out, Brattle will give you a show. He can't help himself; you're the only chap that he can trust in the position. And look here; when that time comes, just you remember the signals, and *keep your eye on the ball*. That's all you'll have to do. Don't take your eyes off the leather, even if the sky falls!"

Jimpson remembered the conversation, and thought ruefully that it was easy enough for a fellow who has everything that heart can desire to spout good advice to chaps on the side-lines. Perhaps if Gates were in his (Jimpson's) place he'd not be any too patient himself. The scoreboard said fifteen minutes to play. Sills still held up his stubborn head, and Jimpson's chances grew dimmer and dimmer as moments sped.

Harvard's kicking tactics had netted her long gains time and again, and twice had she reached Yale's 10-yard line, only to be grimly held and hurled back. Yale, on the other hand, had only once reached scoring-distance of their opponent's goal, and had been successfully held for downs. Veterans of the game declared enthusiastically, be-

tween bets, that it was "the snappiest game of the decade!" and supporters of Harvard said among themselves that it was beautifully conducive to heart-disease. Perhaps never had the two colleges turned out teams so evenly balanced in both offense and defense. The bets had become "one to two that Harvard doesn't score again."

Harvard's quarter had given place to a substitute, and her left guard had retired injured. Yale had fared no better, possibly worse, since her crack full-back had been forced to yield to a somewhat inferior sub. And now the hands on the score-board turned again, and only ten minutes remained.

The ball was down near Harvard's 40-yard line, and when it was snapped back Sills took it for a "round-the-end run." But Yale's big left half-back was waiting for him, and the two went to earth together near the side-line and almost at Jimpson's feet. And then it was that that youth's heart did queer feats inside him, and seemed trying to get out. For Sills lay awhile where he had fallen, and when he could walk the doctor had sent him from the field. Brattle beckoned to Jimpson. With trembling fingers Jimpson struggled with his sweater; but had not a neighbor come to his assistance, he would never have wriggled out of it before the game was called.

Brattle met him, and, laying an arm over his shoulder, walked him a few paces apart. Jimpson's heart, which had become more normal in action, threatened another invasion of his throat, and he wondered if everybody was looking on. Then he stopped speculating, and listened to what the captain was saying.

"We've only eight minutes to play. The ball has *got* to go over, Jimpson. I've seen you run, and I believe you can make it if you try. The ball is yours on the second down. Try the right end; don't be afraid of swinging out into the field. Whatever you do, don't let go of the ball. If Turner puts you through the line, keep your head down, but jump high. Now, go in, lad, and let's see what you can do." He gave Jimpson an encouraging slap on the back that almost precipitated that youth into the quarter, and Jimpson saw the broad backs before him settling down, and heard the labored breathing of the men.

"*Ninety-one, twenty-eight, seventy-three, sixty-four—six!*"

Jimpson suddenly found himself pushing the left half-back against a surging wall of tattered blue. Then some one seized him about the waist, and he picked himself up from the ground eight feet away from the scene of battle.

"That's what comes of being so small and light," he growled to himself, as he trotted back. But the thirst of battle was in Jimpson's soul, and he marked the Yale end who had treated him so contemptuously.

The try between right-tackle and end had netted a bare yard, and Jimpson tried to look self-possessed while his back was running with little chills and his throat was dry as dust. The next chance was his, and he waited the signal anxiously, to learn whether the pass was direct or double. The other half-back imperceptibly dropped back a foot. The quarter looked around. The lines swayed and heaved.

"*Twenty-seven, sixty-three, forty-five, seventy-two—five!*"

Jimpson leaped forward; the left half-back darted across him, the quarter passed neatly, and, with the Harvard left-end beside him, he was sweeping down to the right and into the field. The Yale end went down before the mighty Cowper; and Jimpson, sighting a clear space, sped through. He could feel the field trailing after him, and could hear the sounds of the falling men. Before him in the distance, a

little to the left, came the Yale full-back. Almost upon him was the Yale left-half, looking big and ugly. But, with a final spurt, Van Zandt ran even, and gave the shoulder to the enemy; and as they went down together, Jimpson leaped free, and, running on, knew that at last he was left to shift for himself. Of the foes behind he had no fear; of the full-back running cautiously down on him he feared everything. But he clutched the ball tighter, and raced on straight as an arrow toward the only player between him and the goal that loomed so far down the field.

He heard now the mighty sound of voices cheering him on, saw without looking the crowded stands to the right; and then something whispered of danger from behind, and, scarcely daring to do so, lest he trip and fall, glanced hurriedly over his shoulder into the staring eyes of a runner. And now he could hear the other's short, labored gasps. Before him but a scant ten yards was the full-back. Jimpson's mind was made up on the instant. Easing his pace the least bit, he swung abruptly to the left. He well knew the risk he ran, but he judged himself capable of making up the lost ground. As he had thought, the pursuer was little expecting such a deliberate divergence from the course, and, as a result, he overran, and then turned clumsily, striking for a point between Jimpson and the left goal-post. The full-back had noted the change of course on the instant, and was now running for about the same intersecting point as the other. The three runners formed a triangle. For the moment the pursuer was out of reckoning, and Jimpson could give all his skill to eluding the full-back, who faced him, ready for a tackle.

And here Jimpson's lighter weight stood him in good stead. Clutching the ball tightly, he made a feint to the left, and then flung himself quickly to the right. As he did so he spun around. The full-back's hand reached his canvas jacket, slipped, and found a slight hold upon his trousers; and Jimpson, scarcely recovered from his turn, fell on one knee, the full-back also falling in his effort to hold. At that moment the pursuer reached the spot, and sprang toward Jimpson.

The shouts had ceased, and thirty thousand persons were holding their breath. The next moment a shout of triumph went up, and Jimpson was speeding on toward the Yale goal. For as the last man had thrown himself forward, Jimpson had struggled to his feet, the full-back following, and the two Yale men had crashed together with a shock that left the full-back prostrate upon the turf. The other had regained himself quickly, and taken up the pursuit; but Jimpson was already almost ten yards to the good, and, although his breath was coming in short, painful gasps, and the white lines seemed rods apart, the goal became nearer and nearer. But the blue-stockinged runner was not done, and the cries of the Crimson well-wishers were stilled as the little space between the two runners grew perceptibly less.

Jimpson, with his eyes fixed in agony upon the last white line under the goal-posts, struggled on. One ankle had been wrenched in his rapid turn, and it pained frightfully as it took the ground. He could hear the steps of the pursuing foe almost at his heels, and, try as he might, he could not cover the ground any faster. His brain reeled, and he thought each moment that he must fall.

But the thought of what that touch-down meant, and the recollection of the captain's words, nerved him afresh. The goal-line was plain before him now; ten yards only remained. The air was filled with cheers; but to Jimpson everything save that little white line and the sound of the pounding steps behind him was obliterated.

Success seemed assured, when a touch on his shoulder made the landscape reel before his eyes. It was not a clutch—just fingers grasping at his smooth jacket, unable as yet to find a hold.

The last white line but one passed haltingly, slowly, under his feet. The fingers traveled upward, and suddenly a firm grasp settled upon his shoulder. He tried to swing free, faltered, stumbled, recovered himself with a last supreme effort, and, holding the ball at arm's length, threw himself forward, face down. And as the enemy crashed upon him, Jimpson tried hard to gasp "Down!" but found he couldn't, and then—didn't care at all.

When he came to he found a crowd of players about him. Faces almost strange to him were smiling, and the captain was holding his head. His right foot pained frantically, and the doctor and rubbers were busy over him.

"Was it—was it over?" he asked weakly.

"Easy, old chap—with an inch to spare," replied the lips above. "Listen!"

Jimpson tried to raise his head, but it felt so funny that he gave up the effort. But, despite the woolen sweater bunched up for a pillow, he heard a deep roar that sounded like the breakers on the beach at home. Then he smiled, and fainted once more.

But the score-board had changed its figures again: "Harvard, 8; Yale, 6. Touchdown. Harvard's ball. 3 minutes to play."

And the deep, exultant roar went on, resolving itself into "H-a-r-vard! H-a-r-vard!"

The band was playing "Washington Post." Harvard Square was bright under a lurid glow of red fire. Cheering humanity was packed tight from the street to the balustrade of Matthews, and from there up and across the yard. Cannon crackers punctuated the blare of noise with sharp detonations. The college was out in full force to welcome home the football heroes, and staid and prim old Cambridge lent her quota to the throng. From the back of Gray's the cheering grew louder, and the crowd surged toward the avenue. The band broke ranks and skeltered after. A four-horse barge drew up slowly at the curb, and, one after another, the men dropped out, tightly clutching their bags, and strove to slip away through the throng. But each was eventually captured, his luggage confiscated, and himself raised to the shoulders of riotous admirers. When all were out and up, the band started the strains of "Fair Harvard," and thousands of voices joined in. The procession moved. Jimpson, proud and happy and somewhat embarrassed, was well up in the line. When the corner was turned and the yard reached the roar increased in volume. Cheers for the eleven, for Harvard, for Brattle, were filling the air. And then suddenly Jimpson's heart leaped at sound

of his own name from thousands of throats.

"Now, fellows, three long Harvards, and three times three for Jimpson!" In the roar that followed Jimpson addressed his bearers.

"Won't you please let me go now? I—I'm not feeling very well, and—and I'm only a sub, you know."

The plea of illness moved his captors, and Jimpson was dropped to earth, and his valise restored. There was no notice taken of him as he slipped stealthily through the outskirts of the throng, and as he reached the corner of Holden Chapel he paused and listened.

To the dark heavens arose a prolonged, impatient demand from thousands of Harvard throats. The listener heard, and then fled toward the dark building across the street, and, reaching his room, locked the door behind him. But still he could hear the cries, loudly and impatiently repeated: "We—want—Jimpson! We—want—Jimpson! Jimp-son!"

THE BEARER OF GOOD TIDINGS

by Charles N. Lurie

IT was not by chance that Billy Briggs was loitering about the door of the church on Orange Street, in the town of Nantucket, on a warm, clear, sunny spring morning. His mother had sent him down to Marm Hopkins's for a spool of thread, and, returning to his home, diagonally opposite the church, he had seen Obed Macy enter the door of the church.

Only one thing could have brought Obed there on a week-day morning; he was going to climb into the gilded tower, and scan the water with his far-seeing eyes —trained by long gazing at ocean horizons —for a sign of a home-coming vessel. In all Nantucket there was no place like the tower of the Second Congregational Church for keeping watch for the return of the whaling ships from their long voyages in search of oil and bone. Sometimes four or even five years passed between the going forth of a whaler and her return.

While Obed mounted to his lookout, Billy waited, with the spool of thread in his pocket, and watched for the return of the one-armed sailorman. Of course, if his mother called him in, he would have had his trouble in vain. But Billy hoped that his mother would keep busy with her housework until Obed came down. When he did—well, it *might* mean a dollar or two in Billy's pocket. Dollars were mighty scarce in boys' pockets eighty years ago.

"I'm lucky," said Billy to himself. "None of the other boys are around to ask me why I'm waiting and watching the church."

It seemed to him a very long time before Obed reappeared at the door of the church, although it was only about ten minutes. The sailorman's eye fell on Billy, waiting impatiently. He did not need to ask why the boy waited; he was a Nantucket native himself, and he knew the customs of the island.

"All right, son," Obed said. "It's the *Minerva,* sure enough, back from her three years' trip to the Horn. I know her well; I was one of her crew last voyage when that 'bow-head' stove her boat and I lost my arm. Light out now for Captain Coffin's and see what you get."

"I'm going to Bicknells', too, to tell the mate's wife," shouted Billy, but Obed caught only the first part of the words, since Billy was running up the street as he spoke.

Captain Coffin and his wife lived on the road to Wannacomett, about half a mile from the outskirts of Nantucket town. It seemed to Billy that he did not run that half mile; he flew it.

There were only a few houses along that road then, and in one of them lived Bob Hussey, who was Billy's schoolmate, playfellow, and rival in all kinds of sports. He could run well, but not as fast as Billy; at the island "squantum" (picnic), the summer before, Billy had proved himself Bob's master, both in the sprints and longer races.

Bob was not at home when Billy, going like the winds that blow forever around Great Point, ran past the Husseys'. But Mrs. Hussey saw Billy flying down the road.

"The *Minerva's* in," she said to herself. "There's Billy Briggs going down to Mrs. Coffin's to tell her the news, and he'll get a dollar from her, sure. I wish Bob was home; I'd send him to Mrs. Bicknell's. Of all mornings to be away! I'm sorry I sent him to the cobbler's; his shoes could have waited another day; they weren't so bad; there's no reason why Billy Briggs should get *all* the money for bringing the good news."

In the meantime, Billy, out of breath, had reached Mrs. Coffin's. Without waiting to knock at the door, he lifted the latch, dashed through the hall, and to the kitchen.

"Oh, Mrs. Coffin!" he gasped. "The *Minerva's* coming in! Obed Macy saw her, rounding Sconset, from the church tower, and he sent me here to tell you!"

Mrs. Coffin was a true Nantucket woman. It took more than the news of her husband's safe return from a perilous three-year whaling voyage to upset her. She was a kinswoman—in spirit, at least— of the good wife of the island, who saw her husband coming up the street from a four years' voyage around the Horn, and, taking an empty water-pail from its place on her dresser, greeted him with, "Hullo, John, got back, have you? Here, go get me a bucket of water."

So the wife of Captain Coffin said quietly, to Billy:

"Well, I'll be glad to have Josiah back home. Thank you for coming to tell me. Wait a moment—here's a little gift for you." And she went to the old sea-chest

that served her for a bureau, and handed Billy a silver dollar.

"Thank you, thank you, Mrs. Coffin," he said. "But excuse me—I'm off to Mrs. Bicknell's."

In a jiffy, Billy, his wind fully restored by his stop at the captain's house, was off again, at top speed, down the road along which he had come. "Perhaps I'll get to Mrs. Bicknell's before any one else brings the good news," he said to himself. In his mind, he had already spent the dollar which Mrs. Coffin had given him, and the one he hoped to get at the home of the mate.

But when he got almost to the Husseys' front gate, he saw Bob flinging it open, and starting to run in the same direction as himself. While Billy had been covering the short distance that lay between the Husseys' home and the Coffins', Bob had returned from the cobbler's, and had been told by his mother what was in the wind.

"He's gone to tell her of the *Minerva's* arrival," said she. "With a start, you can beat him to Mrs. Bicknell's, even if he can run faster than you."

It was a close race between the two boys, in the quarter of a mile that lay between the Husseys' and the Bicknells'. Despite Bob's start and Billy's weariness frim his run to the captain's house, the latter was right on the heels of Bob at the house of Mrs. Bicknell. When Bob rushed through the front door, Billy was close behind him, and they tumbled into the entry together, scaring Mrs. Bicknell half to death. No housewife can be expected to keep her composure when two boys of thirteen rush in on her like that, and fall through her doorway without even stopping to knock.

"Land's sake!" she said. "What's the matter?"

But when she understood what their

errand was, she laughed and cried all at once, and handed out a dollar, saying Billy and Bob might divide it. But Billy would no do that; by all the laws and rules of Nantucket's boys, and by the customs of the island, the money belonged rightfully to Bob, for he was the first one to cross Mrs. Bicknell's threshold with the good tidings of her husband's return.

"Anyway," said Billy, "I've got the dollar from Mrs. Coffin, and that makes it a pretty good morning's work for me. Besides, I think I'd better get that spool of thread home to Mother."

A NORSE LULLABY

By M. L. van Vorst

Over the crust of the hard white snow
The little feet of the reindeer go
(*Hush, hush, the winds are low*),
   And the fine little bells are ringing!
Nothing can reach thee of woe or harm—
Safe is the shelter of mother's arm
(*Hush, hush, the wind 's a charm*),
   And mother's voice is singing.

Father is coming—he rides apace;
Fleet are the steeds with the winds that race
(*Hush, hush, for a little space*);
   The snow to his mantle's clinging.

His flying steed with the wind 's abreast—
Here by the fire are warmth and rest
(*Hush, hush, in your little nest*),
   And mother's voice is singing.

Over the crust of the snow, hard by,
The little feet of the reindeer fly
(*Hush, hush, the wind is high*),
   And the fine little bells are ringing!
Nothing can reach us of woe or harm—
Safe is the shelter of father's arm
(*Hush, hush, the wind 's a charm*),
   And mother's voice is singing.

"ONE MINUTE LONGER"

by Albert Payson Terhune

WOLF was a collie, red-gold and white of coat, with a shape more like his long-ago wolf ancestors' than like a domesticated dog's. It was from this ancestral throw-back that he was named Wolf.

He looked not at all like his great sire, Lad, nor like his dainty, thoroughbred mother, Lady. Nor was he like them in any other way, except that he inherited old Lad's stanchly gallant spirit and loyalty. No, in traits as well as in looks, he was more wolf than dog. He almost never barked, his snarl supplying all vocal needs.

The Mistress or the Master or the Boy —any of these three could romp with him, roll him over, tickle him, or subject him to all sorts of playful indignities. And Wolf entered gleefully into the fun of the romp. But let any human besides these three lay a hand on his slender body, and a snarling plunge for the offender's throat was Wolf's invariable reply to the caress.

It had been so since his puppyhood. He did not fly at accredited guests, nor, indeed, pay any heed to their presence, so long as they kept their hands off him. But to all of these the Boy was forced to say at the very outset of the visit:

"Pat Lad and Bruce all you want to, but leave Wolf alone. He doesn't care for people."

Then, to prove his own immunity, the Boy would proceed to tumble Wolf about, to the delight of them both.

In romping with humans whom they love, most dogs will bite more or less gently, —or pretend to bite,—as a part of the game. Wolf never did. In his wildest and roughest romps with the Boy or with the Boy's parents, Wolf did not so much as open his mighty jaws. Perhaps because he dared not trust himself to bite gently. Perhaps because he realized that a bite was not a joke, but an effort to kill.

There had been only one exception to Wolf's hatred for mauling at strangers' hands. A man came to The Place on a business call, bringing along a two-year-old daughter. The Master warned the baby that she must not go near Wolf, although she might pet any of the other collies. Then he became so much interested in the business talk that he and his guest forgot all about the child.

Ten minutes later, the Master chanced to shift his gaze to the far end of the room, and he broke off, with a gasp, in the very middle of a sentence.

The baby was seated astride Wolf's back, her tiny heels digging into the .dog's sensitive ribs, and each of her chubby fists gripping one of his ears. Wolf was lying there, with an idiotically happy grin on his face and wagging his tail in ecstasy.

No one knew why he had submitted to the baby's tugging hands, except because she *was* a baby, and because the gallant heart of the dog had gone out to her helplessness.

Wolf was the official watch-dog of The Place, and his name carried dread to the loafers and tramps of the region. Also, he was the Boy's own special dog. He had been born on the Boy's tenth birthday, five years before this story of ours begins, and ever since then the two had been inseparable chums.

One sloppy afternoon in late winter, Wolf and the boy were sprawled, side by side, on the fur rug in front of the library fire. The Mistress and the Master had gone to town for the day. The house was lonely, and the two chums were left to entertain each other.

The boy was reading a magazine. The dog beside him was blinking in drowsy comfort at the fire. Presently, finishing the story he had been reading, the Boy looked across at the sleepy dog.

"Wolf," he said, "here's a story about a dog. I think he must have been something like you. Maybe he was your great-great-great-great-grandfather, because he lived an awfully long time ago—in Pompeii. Ever hear of Pompeii?"

Now, the Boy was fifteen years old, and he had too much sense to imagine that Wolf could possibly understand the story he was about to tell him; but long since he had fallen into a way of talking to his dog, sometimes, as if to another human. It was fun for him to note the almost pathetic eagerness wherewith Wolf listened and tried to grasp the meaning of what he was saying. Again and again, at sound of some familiar word or voice inflection, the collie would prick up his ears or wag his tail, as if in the joyous hope that he had at last found a clue to his owner's meaning.

"You see," went on the Boy, "this dog lived in Pompeii, as I told you. You've never been there, Wolf."

Wolf was looking up at the Boy in wistful excitement, seeking vainly to guess what was expected of him.

"And," continued the Boy, "the kid who owned him seems to have had a regular knack for getting into trouble all the time. And his dog was always on hand to get him out of it. It's a true story, the magazine says. The kid's father was so grateful to the dog that he bought him a solid silver collar. Solid silver! Get that, Wolfie?"

Wolf did not "get it." But he wagged his tail hopefully, his eyes alight with bewildered interest.

"And," said the Boy, "what do you suppose was engraved on the collar? Well, I'll tell you: *'This dog has thrice saved his little master from death. Once by fire, once by flood, and once at the hands of robbers!'* How's that for a record, Wolf? For one dog, too!"

At the words "Wolf" and "dog," the collie's tail smote the floor in glad comprehension. Then he edged closer to the Boy as the narrator's voice presently took on a sadder note.

"But at last," resumed the Boy, "there came a time when the dog couldn't save the kid. Mount Vesuvius erupted. All the sky was pitch-dark, as black as midnight, and Pompeii was buried under lava and ashes. The dog might have got away by himself—dogs can see in the dark, can't they, Wolf?—but he couldn't get the kid away. And he wouldn't go without him. You wouldn't have gone without me, either, would you, Wolf? Pretty nearly two thousand years later, some people dug through the lava that covered Pompeii. What do you suppose they found? Of course they found a whole lot of things. One of them was that dog—silver collar and inscription and all. He was lying at the feet of a child. It must have been the child he couldn't save. He was one grand dog—hey, Wolf?"

The continued strain of trying to understand began to get on the collie's highstrung nerves. He rose to his feet, quivering, and sought to lick the Boy's face, thrusting one upraised white fore paw at him in appeal for a handshake. The Boy slammed shut the magazine.

"It's slow in the house, here, with nothing to do," he said to his chum. "I'm going up the lake with my gun to see if any wild ducks have landed in the marshes yet. It's almost time for them. Want to come along?"

The last sentence Wolf understood perfectly. On the instant, he was dancing with excitement at the prospect of a walk. Being a collie, he was of no earthly help in a hunting-trip; but on such tramps, as everywhere else, he was the Boy's inseparable companion.

Out over the slushy snow the two started, the boy with his light single-barreled shotgun slung over one shoulder, the dog trotting close at his heels. The March thaw was changing to a sharp freeze. The deep and soggy snow was crusted over, just thick enough to make walking a genuine difficulty for both dog and boy.

The Place was a promontory that ran out into the lake, on the opposite bank from the mile-distant village. Behind, across the high-road, lay the winter-choked forest. At the lake's northerly end, two miles beyond The Place, were the reedy marshes where a month hence wild duck would congregate. Thither, with Wolf, the Boy plowed his way through the biting cold.

The going was heavy and heavier. A quarter-mile below the marshes the Boy struck out across the upper corner of the lake. Here the ice was rotten at the top, where the thaw had nibbled at it, but beneath it was still a full eight inches thick, easily strong enough to bear the Boy's weight.

Along the gray ice-field the two plodded. The skim of water, which the thaw had spread an inch thick over the ice, had frozen in the day's cold spell. It crackled like broken glass as the chums walked over it. The Boy had on big hunting-boots, so, apart from the extra effort, the glass-like ice did not bother him. To Wolf it gave acute pain. The sharp particles were forever getting between the callous black pads of his feet, pricking and cutting him acutely.

Little smears of blood began to mark the dog's course; but it never occurred to Wolf to turn back, or to betray by any sign that he was suffering. It was all a part of the day's work—a cheap price to pay for the joy of tramping with his adored young master.

Then, forty yards or so on the hither side of the marshes, Wolf beheld a right amazing phenomenon. The Boy had been walking directly in front of him, gun over shoulder. With no warning at all, the youthful hunter fell, feet foremost, out of sight through the ice.

The light shell of new-frozen water that covered the lake's thicker ice also masked an air-hole nearly three feet wide. Into this, as he strode carelessly along, the Boy had stepped. Straight down he had gone, with all the force of his hundred-and-ten pounds and with all the impetus of his forward stride.

Instinctively, he threw out his hands to restore his balance. The only effect of this was to send the gun flying ten feet away.

Down went the Boy through less than three feet of water (for the bottom of the lake at this point had started to slope upward toward the marshes) and through nearly two feet more of sticky marsh mud that underlay the lake-bed.

His outflung hands struck against the ice on the edges of the air-hole, and clung there. Sputtering and gurgling, the Boy brought his head above the surface and tried to raise himself, by his hands, high enough to wriggle out upon the surface of the ice. Ordinarily, this would have been simple enough for so strong a lad, but the glue-like mud had imprisoned his feet and the lower part of his legs and held them powerless.

Try as he would, the Boy could not wrench himself free of the slough. The water, as he stood upright, was on a level with his mouth. The air-hole was too wide for him, at such a depth, to get a good purchase on its edges and lift himself bodily to safety.

Gathering such a finger-hold as he could, he heaved with all his might, throwing every muscle of his body into the struggle. One leg was pulled almost free of the mud, but the other was driven deeper into it. And as the Boy's fingers slipped from the smoothly wet ice-edge, the attempt to restore his balance drove the free leg back, knee-deep into the mire.

Ten minutes of this hopeless fighting left the Boy panting and tired out. The icy water was numbing his nerves and chilling his blood into torpidity. His hands were without sense of feeling as far up as the wrists. Even if he could have shaken free his legs from the mud, now he had not strength enough left to crawl out of the hole.

He ceased his uselessly frantic battle and stood dazed. Then he came sharply to himself. For, as he stood, the water crept upward from his lips to his nostrils. He knew why the water seemed to be rising. It was not rising. It was he who was sinking. As soon as he stopped moving the mud began very slowly, but very steadily, to suck him downward.

This was not a quicksand, but it was a deep mud-bed, and only by constant motion could he avoid sinking farther and farther down into it. He had less than two inches to spare at best before the water should fill his nostrils; less than two inches of life, even if he could keep the water down to the level of his lips.

There was a moment of utter panic. Then the Boy's brain cleared. His only hope was to keep on fighting—to rest when he must for a moment or so, and then to renew his numbed grip on the ice-edge and try to pull his feet a few inches higher out of the mud. He must do this as long as his chilled body could be scourged into obeying his will.

He struggled again, but with virtually no result in raising himself. A second struggle, however, brought him chin-high above the water. He remembered confusedly that some of these earlier struggles had scarce budged him, while others had gained him two or three inches. Vaguely, he wondered why. Then turning his head, he realized.

Wolf, as he turned, was just loosing his hold on the wide collar of the Boy's mackinaw. His cut forepaws were still braced against a flaw of ragged ice on the air-hole's edge, and all his tawny body was tense.

His body was dripping wet, too. The Boy noted that; and he realized that the repeated effort to draw his master to safety must have resulted, at least once, in pulling the dog down into the water with the floundering Boy.

"Once more, Wolfie! Once more!" chattered the Boy through teeth that clicked together like castanets.

The dog darted forward, caught his grip afresh on the edge of the Boy's collar, and tugged with all his fierce strength, growling and whining ferociously the while.

The boy seconded the collie's tuggings by a supreme struggle that lifted him higher than before. He was able to get one arm and shoulder clear above the ice. His numb fingers closed about an upthrust tree-limb which had been washed down stream in the autumn freshets and had been frozen into the lake ice.

With this new purchase, and aided by the dog, the Boy tried to drag himself out of the hole. But the chill of the water had done its work. He had not the strength to move farther. The mud still sucked at his calves and ankles. The big hunting boots were full of water that seemed to weigh a ton.

He lay there, gasping and chattering. Then, through the gathering twilight, his eyes fell on the gun, lying ten feet away.

"Wolf!" he ordered, nodding toward the weapon, "Get it! *Get* it!"

Not in vain had the Boy talked to Wolf for years as if the dog were human. At the words and the nod, the collie trotted over to the gun, lifted it by the stock, and hauled it awkwardly along over the bumpy ice to his master, where he laid it down at the edge of the air-hole.

The dog's eyes were cloudy with trouble, and he shivered and whined as with ague. The water on his thick coat was freezing to a mass of ice. But it was from anxiety that he shivered, and not from cold.

Still keeping his numb grasp on the tree-branch, the boy balanced himself as best he could and thrust two fingers of his free hand into his mouth to warm them into sensation again.

When this was done, he reached out to where the gun lay, and pulled its trigger. The shot boomed deafeningly through the twilight winter silences. The recoil sent the weapon sliding sharply back along the ice, spraining the Boy's trigger finger and cutting it to the bone.

"That's all I can do," said the Boy to himself. "If any one hears it, well and good. I can't get at another cartridge. I couldn't put it into the breech if I had it. My hands are too numb."

For several endless minutes he clung there, listening. But this was a desolate part of the lake, far from any road, and the season was too early for other hunters

to be abroad. The bitter cold, in any case, tended to make sane folk hug the fireside rather than to venture so far into the open. Nor was the single report of a gun uncommon enough to call for investigation in such weather.

All this the Boy told himself as the minutes dragged by. Then he looked again at Wolf. The dog, head on one side, still stood protectingly above him. The dog was cold and in pain, but, being only a dog, it did not occur to him to trot off home to the comfort of the library fire and leave his master to fend for himself.

Presently, with a little sigh, Wolf lay down on the ice, his nose across the Boy's arm. Even if he lacked strength to save his beloved master, he could stay and share the Boy's sufferings.

But the Boy himself thought otherwise. He was not at all minded to freeze to death, nor was he willing to let Wolf imitate the dog of Pompeii by dying helplessly at his master's side. Controlling for an instant the chattering of his teeth, he called: "Wolf!"

The dog was on his feet again at the word, alert, eager.

"Wolf!" repeated the Boy. *"Go!* Hear me? *Go!"*

He pointed homeward.

Wolf stared at him, hesitant. Again the Boy called in vehement command, *"Go!"*

The collie lifted his head to the twilight sky in a wolf-howl, hideous in its grief and appeal—a howl as wild and discordant as that of any of his savage ancestors. Then, stooping first to lick the numb hand that clung to the branch, Wolf turned and fled.

Across the cruelly sharp film of ice he tore at top speed, head down, whirling through the deepening dusk like a flash of tawny light.

Wolf understood what was wanted of him. Wolf always understood. The pain in his feet was as nothing. The stiffness of his numbed body was forgotten in the urgency of speed.

The Boy looked drearily after the swift-vanishing figure which the dusk was swallowing. He knew the dog would try to bring help, as has many another and lesser dog in times of need. Whether or not that help could arrive in time, or at all, was a point on which the Boy would not let himself dwell. Into his benumbed brain crept the memory of an old Norse proverb he had read in school:

"Heroism consists in hanging on one minute longer."

Unconsciously he tightened his feeble hold on the tree-branch and braced himself.

FROM the marshes to The Place was a full two miles. Despite the deep and sticky snow, Wolf covered the distance in less than six minutes. He paused in front of the gate-lodge, at the highway entrance to the drive. But the gardener and his wife had gone to Paterson, shopping, that afternoon.

Down the drive to the house he dashed. The maids had taken advantage of their employers' day in New York to walk across the lake to the village to a motion-picture show.

Wise men claim that dogs have not the power to think or to reason things out in a logical way. So perhaps it was mere chance that next sent Wolf's flying feet across the lake to the village. Perhaps it was chance, and not the knowledge that where there is a village there are people.

Again and again, in the car, he had sat upon the front seat alongside the Mistress when she drove to the station to meet guests. There were always people at the station, and to the station Wolf now raced.

The usual group of platform idlers had been dispersed by the cold. A solitary baggageman was hauling a trunk and some boxes out of the express-coop on to the plat-form to be put aboard the five o'clock train from New York.

As the baggageman passed under the clump of station lights, he came to a sudden halt, for out of the darkness dashed a dog. Full tilt, the animal rushed up to him and seized him by the skirt of his overcoat.

The man cried out in scared surprise. He dropped the box he was carrying and struck at the dog to ward off the seemingly murderous attack. He recognized Wolf, and he knew the collie's repute.

But Wolf was not attacking. Holding tight to the coat-skirt, he backed away, trying to draw the man with him, and all the while whimpering aloud like a nervous puppy.

A kick from the man's heavy-shod boot broke the dog's hold on the coat-skirt, even as a second yell from the man brought four or five other people running out from the station waiting-room.

One of these, the telegraph operator, took in the scene at a single glance. With great presence of mind he bawled loudly: "MAD DOG!"

This, as Wolf, reeling from the kick, sought to gain another grip on the coat-skirt. A second kick sent him rolling over and over on the tracks, while other voices took up the panic cry of "Mad dog!"

Now, a mad dog is supposed to be a dog afflicted by rabies. Once in ten thousand times, at the very most, a mad-dog hue-and-cry is justified. Certainly not oftener. A harmless and friendly dog loses his Master on the street. He runs about, confused and frightened, looking for the owner he has lost. A boy throws a stone at him. Other boys chase him. His tongue hangs out, and his eyes glaze with terror. Then some fool bellows:

"Mad dog!"

And the cruel chase is on—a chase that ends in the pitiful victim's death. Yet in every crowd there is a voice ready to raise that asinine and murderously cruel shout.

So it was with the men who witnessed Wolf's frenzied effort to take aid to the imperiled Boy.

Voice after voice repeated the cry. Men groped along the platform edge for stones to throw. The village policeman ran puffing upon the scene, drawing his revolver.

Finding it useless to make a further attempt to drag the baggageman to the rescue, Wolf leaped back, facing the ever larger group. Back went his head again in that hideous wolf-howl. Then he galloped away a few yards, trotted back, howled once more, and again galloped lakeward.

All of which only confirmed the panicky crowd in the belief that they were threatened by a mad dog. A shower of stones hurtled about Wolf as he came back a third time to lure these dull humans into following him.

One pointed rock smote the collie's shoulder, glancing, cutting it to the bone. A shot from the policeman's revolver fanned the fur of his ruff as it whizzed past.

Knowing that he faced death, he nevertheless stood his ground, not troubling to dodge the fusillade of stones, but continuing to run lakeward and then trot back, whining with excitement.

A second pistol-shot flew wide. A third grazed the dog's hip. From all directions people were running toward the station. A man darted into a house next door, and emerged, carrying a shotgun. This he steadied on a veranda-rail not forty feet away from the leaping dog, and made ready to fire.

It was then the train from New York came in, and momentarily the sport of "mad-dog" killing was abandoned, while the crowd scattered to each side of the track.

From a front car of the train the Mistress and the Master emerged into a bedlam of noise and confusion.

"Best hide in the station, Ma'am!" shouted the telegraph operator, at sight of the Mistress. "There is a mad dog loose out here! He's chasing folks around, and—"

"Mad dog!" repeated the Mistress in high contempt. "If you knew anything about dogs, you'd know mad ones never 'chase folks around' any more than typhoid patients do. Then—"

A flash of tawny light beneath the station lamp, a scurrying of frightened idlers, a final wasted shot from the policeman's pistol, as Wolf dived headlong through the frightened crowd toward the voice he heard and recognized.

Up to the Mistress and the Master galloped Wolf. He was bleeding, his eyes were bloodshot, his fur was rumpled. He seized the astounded Master's gloved hand lightly between his teeth and sought to pull him across the tracks and toward the lake.

The Master knew dogs, especially he knew Wolf, and without a word he suffered himself to be led. The Mistress and one or two inquisitive men followed.

Presently, Wolf loosed his hold on the Master's hand and ran on ahead, darting back every few moments to make certain he was followed.

"*Heroism — consists — in — hanging — on — one minute — longer,*" the Boy was whispering deliriously to himself for the hundredth time as Wolf pattered up to him in triumph across the ice, with the human rescuers a scant ten yards behind!

THE BUFFALO DANCE

by Cornelia Meigs

I n the cool silence and in the level light of the late afternoon, Chanuka's canoe seemed to be the only moving thing in the wide expanse of marshy lake country. There was so little breeze that the tall reeds stood motionless, knee-deep in the still water. The Indian boy was not hunting to-day, nor was he watching for any enemy, that he moved so silently. It was only his unwillingness to break that spell of utter quiet that made him guide his light craft so noiselessly across the narrow stretches of open water, over the shallows where the water grasses brushed softly along the birch bark bottom and between those tufts of green, where rocks, brush, and poplars or pines rose from the water here and there in a myriad of tiny green islands. Everywhere the tall rushes stood stiffly erect, so that he could not see, in any direction, more than a few yards beyond the high painted bow of his boat. Yet he moved forward steadily, threading his way without hesitation through that maze of concealing reeds and winding water lanes.

He liked to feel that he was the only human being within twenty, fifty or perhaps a hundred miles, that he and the fish and the water-fowl had all to themselves this stretch of lake and marsh and river which lay to the southward of the hunting grounds of his tribe. Somewhere beyond that watery domain lay the grassy open country where dwelt the Dacotahs, the unforgetting enemies of his tribe.

The older warriors still talked beside the camp-fire of the long wars which had raged intermittently and furiously between nation and nation for a hundred years. Neither tribe could ever call itself actually victorious; but fighting would cease at times from sheer exhaustion on both sides. For some years now there had been uneasy truce, with the smoldering hatred ready to break out into fierce flame again at any moment.

Once Chanuka had said to one of the old braves, "The Dacotahs live on the prairies and hunt the buffalo, and we dwell in the forest and get our meat from the deer and the moose. We do not need to quarrel over hunting grounds. Why should we be always at war with the prairie men?"

To which the scarred and wrinkled fighter had replied, "We hate them; so did our fathers, so will our sons. That is cause enough. And you will understand, when you grow older, that when spring comes, then the young warriors are ever restless and eager to be on the war-path. And for us the war-path must always lead southward."

Chanuka could understand the second explanation better than the first, for he knew that stirring of the spirit and the body in the spring, which might lead one anywhere.

Through those last years when there had been no fighting between Ojibway and Dacotah, both sides had avoided this special stretch of lake and swamp which lay between their two domains, so that it had long been left empty even of hunters. Now, moved by that same restlessness, which comes with the bursting loose of ice-imprisoned streams and the stir of life in the vast green wood, Chanuka had turned aside from his hunting to explore this unknown land and these unfamiliar waters. In spite of the knowledge that such journeying was forbidden by his chief, he could not forbear going farther and farther southward into the empty waste.

The last lake through which he had passed was wooded only on three sides, while the grassy prairie swept all the way up to its southern banks. This was proof indeed that he was coming close to the lands of the enemy. But the dense forest was still massed behind and immediately about him, and the sharp hoof-prints of deer and the big splay-footed tracks of moose had trampled the grass and mud of the shores where the wild creatures had come down to the water to drink or to feed on the lily-pads.

A blot of dense green, showing through the pale stems of the rushes, told him finally that he was approaching an island, solid ground in this empty wilderness of ripples and swaying reeds. He came near, dipping his blade easily and lightly, and then suddenly paused, with his paddle half lifted, frozen into an immovable statue of wary listening. He had heard a voice issuing from the dense undergrowth of the island, a voice which muttered, dropped into silence, then fell to muttering again or rose to a curious half-choked cry.

With a motion as soundless as that of a fish's quivering fin, Chanuka paddled nearer, yard by yard, until he was stealing under the drooping boughs of overhanging trees, until he was peering out at a bit of gravel beach and a narrow grassy clearing.

That which he saw first was a canoe, or rather had once been a canoe. It was not a trim birch-bark vessel such as was bearing Chanuka on his voyaging, but the clumsier dugout craft of the sort that the Indians dwelling on the southern rivers fashioned from tree trunks. It was battered and trampled now into hopeless ruin, stamped halfway into the soft ground, with the snapped blade of the paddle lying beside it along with a broken bow and a spilled quiver of arrows. After one long, silent survey, Chanuka stepped ashore and walked, without attempt at concealment, across the slope where the turf was plowed and torn by the stamping hoofs of some great animal.

The master of that broken vessel was extended at full length, half hidden below a thicket of brambles. One arm was crumpled under him; the other was flung before his face. Long, lean, and red-skinned, he lay inert and helpless, muttering and whispering to himself, taking no notice, even when Chanuka finally knelt down beside him on the grass. The arm under him was undoubtedly broken; his whole body was bruised and torn with a dozen jagged gashes, while the hot fever of untended wounds was evidently running like fire through his whole being. Chanuka laid his firm brown fingers against that burning skin and nodded.

"No one but a plains-dwelling Dacotah," he commented within himself, "would know so little as to stand against the charge of a wounded moose."

All up and down upon the grass was written the record of that encounter when the great ugly-tempered beast, wounded and furious, had turned upon the unwary hunter. Here were wounds of lashing, goring horns, here was the broken bow from which the arrow had sped too late.

"He thought he was hunting a creature like one of his stupid buffalo," the Ojibway boy reflected in scorn.

The Dacotah had evidently followed the animal through the marsh, not knowing that the moment it felt firm ground under its feet the moose would turn upon him in deadly attack. Canoe, weapons, the limp, helpless body under its feet—all alike were objects of the huge beast's blind onslaught. One final charge had carried it clean over the fallen quarry, and it had gone, plunging and splashing across the marsh, leaving the silent glade far behind. The keen eyes of the Indian boy could read plainly the whole tale.

Chanuka's eyes glinted with a sudden spark as he stooped over the wounded stranger. He had thought, more than once, as he paddled through the reeds and the rapids, of the black disfavor with which the chief of his village would greet him upon his return. The year before in the same foolhardy curiosity he had journeyed down into the prairie region and on his return had been met with severe reprimand and punishment as well.

"If a warrior seeks out the enemy's country, he must not come home empty-handed," the hard-faced old Indian had said and had set the boy to do squaw's work for the waxing and waning of the first snow-moon. The memory of that penalty had often burned hotly in Chanuka's heart; but it had not kept him back when the spring unrest set him once more to roving. And this time he would not come home empty-handed; he would bring a captive from the tribe of their foes, a Dacotah warrior, helpless in the bottom of his canoe.

He stooped and half lifted, half dragged the limp figure out from among the brambles to lie upon the open grass. As he did so the glittering light in his eyes died suddenly. For a long minute he stood frowning down upon that truth which a better view had revealed. Long of limb though the Dacotah might be, he was evidently

not yet a grown warrior. His age must be much the same as Chanuka's own.

A boy, a boy taken with the same sudden impulse to wander into hostile country for no better reason than that it was forbidden! It would have been glorious triumph to carry home a captured brave. But would the triumph be quite the same, when the captive was a headlong, blundering lad, who had dared the same dangers as himself and had fallen into unexpected misfortune?

Hardly admitting, even in his own mind, just what was his final purpose, Chanuka stooped once more and began, as best he could, to tend the other's hurts. Every warrior knew a little of how bleeding wounds could be bound up with leaves and bark. Darkness fell while he was still at work; he kindled a fire, brought from his canoe a wild duck which he had shot earlier in the day and set it to broiling before the coals.

When the savory fowl was ready he attempted to feed the wounded Dacotah, but that burning throat would swallow nothing but water. After the first long cool draught from the bark cup which Chanuka set to his lips, the long lad's tossing and mumbling eased a little. He kept repeating a single word thereafter, which Chanuka began to understand stood for water—ever more water. In the end the Ojibway boy forgot to eat and bent all his absorbed effort upon bringing sufficient water, and moving the sufferer from time to time when one position became unbearable and he stirred and struggled feebly to shift to another.

The moon rose and stood high above the trees; the dark ripples lapped softly on the shore, and that muttering voice went on and on. There was never a groan, never a querulous note of complaint. Even with his mind and spirit wandering somewhere in that land of shadows which borders upon death, the young Dacotah's instinct held true. Not once did he cry out with the pain which was consuming him.

All night Chanuka toiled over him. It was only when the moon was dropping and the sky growing white to the eastward, that the fever seemed to abate and the Dacotah lay more quietly. When the morning broke over the silent marsh, the two Indian boys lay together upon the grass, side by side, both fast asleep.

There followed some days of strange comradeship. On the second morning the Dacotah tried to stand, but could not; on the third he made determined effort to walk, and by the fourth could move about, although but slowly and painfully. His wounds would give him pain for a long time still, and the scars would be with him throughout his life; but the iron strength of an Indian would not yield to weakness and fever for more than the briefest stretch of days.

The two could not talk together; nor did they make any real effort to communicate by that language of signs with which all red men are familiar. That they were enemies, brought together in surprising and accidental truce, was a thing which neither of them seemed able to forget. Yet they caught fish and cooked them together, snared rabbits and ate them in company, and, as on that first night, slept side by side upon the grass.

It was the Dacotah who made the only effort at further acquaintance. His name, it seemed, was Neosho. He offered this information and once or twice seemed to be trying, further, to give his rescuer some knowledge of the country in which he dwelt and the life of his people in their buffalo-skin lodges beside the big southward-flowing river. But Chanuka did not offer much attention to what the other was attempting to tell, and, after a little, the Dacotah ceased any efforts at a semblance

of talk. Had not Chanuka, on that foolhardy journey of seven moons ago, seen those same lodges of Neosho's people in the open country near that same river? He had stolen so close, under cover of the darkness, that he had actually lain hidden on one side of a small creek, while, upon the flat open ground of the opposite bank, the people of that Dacotah village had built their circle of fires and had danced the Buffalo Dance. He could see and hear them still, the red flames, the strangely moving dancers, the chanting voices and the thumping of the drums coming out of the darkness.

The Buffalo Dance celebrates the festival when the Dacotah braves have come home from their summer hunting, laden with the meat which is to be their provision against the winter. Only three dancers take part in it. First comes the warrior who represents the buffalo, wrapped in a brown, hairy robe and bearing the shaggy horned head pulled down over his own like a mask. He crouches and dances forward, tossing the head from side to side, imitating the lumbering gait of the buffalo. Next comes the horse, a man wrapped in a pony's hide and covering his face with the rude effigy of the animal's head. He moves it up and down, imitating the jogging motion of a horse loping along the buffalo trail. Last comes the hunter with his bow and arrows, rehearsing in pantomime all the adventures of the summer's chase.

Much as Chanuka would have liked to know more of the Dacotahs and their ways, he fought against paying heed to what Neosho was trying to tell him. He would sit beside the fire moody and brooding, or would go silently about his work of bringing food and caring for his comrade's wounds. There had been some idea in his mind, at first, of letting the Dacotah boy recover somewhat, and then of challenging him to mortal combat, as was fitting between enemies. But as he watched the other limping back and forth across the glade, slowly coming again to his former strength, the Ojibway's determination failed. The days passed, and no challenge came.

Even through their long silences, there was something growing up between them. Could it be called friendship between two mortal enemies? One had fallen into dire misfortune; the other had scorned to take advantage of his helplessness. Does such a thing make friends? Neither would betray by word or sign whether such were possible.

It was on the fifth day that they finally parted. The sun was rising red above the marsh when Chanuka signed to the other to take his place in the bow of the bark canoe. Neosho could not have known whether he was to be carried to freedom or back into the forest to fall into the hands of his deadly foes. He cast one glance at his broken bow still lying upon the ground and then with unchanging face stepped into the light craft which was already lifting to the ripples. Chanuka dipped his paddle and they slipped away through the rushes.

The unseen hand of a slight current bore them away southwestward, carried them at gathering speed through a narrow stream, then out upon the broad silver of a quiet lake. The forest was behind them; from the opposite shore the prairie lands, dotted with groves of trees, stretched away in green and rolling ridges. Chanuka brought the bow of the boat to land, and sat waiting without a word while his companion stepped out upon the grassy bank and strode away up the green rise. As he crossed the shoulder of the ridge, Neosho looked back and raised his hand. Chanuka lifted his paddle. That was the whole of their leave-taking before the Dacotah disappeared beyond the grassy summit. The Ojibway pushed off his vessel into deep water, swung the bow and set himself to paddling steadily northward.

If Chanuka wondered, on his homeward journey, what was to be the end of that forbidden adventure, he wondered still more when he arrived at his journey's end. He had been made to do sharp penance for that earlier expedition into the plains country; but this time, when he returned after an unexplained absence of eleven days and with nothing to show but a few wild ducks and a string of fish, no word was said. He was conscious that the eyes of the wrinkled old chief followed him as he went to and fro in the village. But if there was to be punishment for his disobeying, it was slow in coming.

The months of the summer passed with all the braves occupied by the season's hunting. Then the autumn began to draw on. The wild rice was ripening along the edges of the marshes, the swamp maples were turning red, and the dry rustle of the wind in the poplars foretold the coming of the winter tempests.

It was after a long day of hunting in the rice swamps that Chanuka was summoned at evening to the lodge of his chief. The great man sat alone before the smoldering fire and looked at the young brave with hard, narrow eyes. The moment of reckoning for that stolen expedition had come.

"You who have a heart so set upon voyages to the southward, are now to take a new journey," the chief said at last.

As a proper brave should, Chanuka waited in silence for the whole substance of his leader's commands.

"It may be that the time is coming close for us to do battle once more against our age-long enemies, the Dacotahs," the other went on. "The signs of sky and forest point to a hard winter; but our hunting has been good, so that our tribe will not have lost in strength before the spring. We must discover whether our foes are to fare as well through the season of the snows. That is to be your task."

He paused, seeming to search the boy's face for any sign of dismay. Yet Chanuka's countenance was as unmoving as his own, as the chief continued:

"You are to seek out that largest village of the Dacotahs which lies in a great grove of walnut-trees where one big river forks into three; and you are to go in haste so that you may see their braves come home from the buffalo hunt. If their store of dried meat for the winter is scanty, they will hunger and weaken when the snows begin and sickness will go from lodge to lodge. And then, when spring comes the Ojibway will fall upon them. It is of this matter that you are to bring news, whether the Dacotah hunters come home heavily or lightly laden. By the word which you carry we will determine whether there is to be war again, or longer peace."

A journey is apt to seem shorter each time that it is repeated. Chanuka, traveling over the now familiar waterways, seemed to approach his journey's end more swiftly than either time before. It almost seemed that his paddle lagged; but brisk autumn winds and streams brimming from autumn rains carried him relentlessly onward. It was not until he had passed over half the distance that a strange question began to form itself within his mind. Was it possible that he did not wish to go so quickly? Was he a reluctant messenger; had those days upon the island in the marsh so weakened the resolution of a proper warrior that he, the first one chosen for the war-path, was going forward unwillingly? The thought stung him as though it were one of the wild black bees who were gathering their final store of honey in the sheets of yellow flowers which bordered all the streams. He dipped his blade and sped southward with all the haste which his paddle could add to the breezes and currents behind him. Yet as he journeyed his face darkened; for ply his paddle as he would, he could not seem to leave that haunting question behind. He did not know that he was offering vain battle against a natural force far stronger than even the relentless will of an Indian warrior. Wars may last a hundred years, or a thousand; but the spirit of fellowship which can grow up between one growing youth and another is older and more powerful than tribal hatreds.

He came to that green shore where he had left Neosho; and from there hastened forward on foot until he came in sight of the forks of the big river and saw the Dacotah lodges scattered through the grove of walnut-trees. From daybreak until evening he lay in hiding on the opposite side of the stream, watching all those who went back and forth amongst the lodges or came down to the bank for water. At first it was plain that only squaws and children and old men inhabited the place, that all the young and able-bodied braves were still away hunting the buffalo. Chanuka's chief had timed well the sending of his messenger; for the boy had waited only a night and a day before he witnessed the return of the hunters.

They advanced across the plain in a cloud of dust, a long line of laden ponies and weary huntsmen. From the shouts and from the delight with which they were greeted by those who ran out to meet them and escort them to their own lodges, it seemed that the chase had been crowned with success. Of that, however, Chanuka could not be certain until he stole nearer. This it was his plan to do on the night when the Dacotahs lit their ceremonial fires on the flat bank just across from him and made ready to dance the Buffalo Dance.

Another warrior, so Chanuka reflected,

might be content to watch and spy and carry home his news gathered only by observing from a distance. But he was determined to steal through the whole village, to peer into every lodge, and to carry away, perhaps from the dwelling of the chief, some token of actual proof that he had walked among the very camp-fires of the enemy. A beaded pouch, a bow or a carved pipe, something he must surely have to bear away. Had not his chief said that he who seeks out the country of the enemy must not come home empty-handed? The darkness of the chosen night had fallen and the women were preparing the heaps of wood for the circle of fire, when he slipped into the river to swim silently across.

He came out dripping, and crouched under the low bank to listen. All the voices and movement were on the flat ground to the right of him, where the whole village seemed to be gathering. He found his way to a break in the slope of the shore and, under the scanty cover of wild blackberries and hickory brush, he crept unnoticed to the very edge of the camp. The lodges stood tenantless, with the embers of spent fires dying before every door. He peered into one empty dwelling, then another and another. It was even as he had guessed from afar, the stores were plenty; the hunt had been successful. The Dacotahs were rich indeed this season with dried meat and buffalo robes; there would be no starving when the winter came.

He had reached the very center of the camp and was looking about him to determine which was the chief's lodge, the most worthy dwelling to be plundered. It would be easy to bear away anything that he wished; for every living soul, it seemed, was on the open ground beside the river. A sudden tumult of voices almost at his elbow startled him into the knowledge that he was mistaken.

From the Medicine Lodge below the biggest walnut-tree there came forth a group of laughing, shouting warriors. The dull fire behind them and the light of the stars above showed him that here was the Medicine Man himself, with an escort of young braves, walking down through the lodges, to appear the last of all beside the river, and to give the signal for the dance to begin.

The young men spread their line out through the camp, perhaps to see whether every person had gone. There was nothing for Chanuka to do but to give way before them, slipping from one shadow to another, taking advantage of any possible cover, but still being driven steadily down toward that space of light and tumult where the whole village was gathered. In absolute desperation he took refuge at last under the edge of a great pile of firewood.

The shouting warriors passed close beside him. One of them even stopped, seemed to hesitate a moment, and then went on with the others. An old brave came hobbling up to the opposite side of the heap of fuel and gathered an armful to fling upon the fire just kindled not ten yards away. The flare of red light showed the crowding women and children, the warriors in their feathered head-dresses, and the fringed branches of the walnut-trees moving softly in the rush of hot air. It would be impossible now to slip from that hiding-place and reach the river unseen. From time to time more wood was thrown upon the fire, keeping the light ablaze and steadily lessening Chanuka's only cover. The drums thumped under the trees; the Medicine Man's voice rose in slow chant. The dance was about to begin.

Of a sudden, Chanuka, tense as a whipcord, felt a touch upon his arm. He started; in the pressure of his excitement he might have cried out. Some one was stooping over him, a queer misshapen figure quite unrecognizable in the firelight. But the voice which spoke Chanuka's name in a whisper was Neosho's.

At such highly wrought moments minds move quickly, and understanding comes without need of words. Neosho, it seemed; was to take the part of the horse, in the coming dance. Crouching low at the edge of the heap of wood, he wrapped about his former comrade the sheltering garments of horse-hide and thrust into his hands the wooden, skin-covered likeness of a horse's head. Already the brave who was to take the part of the buffalo was dancing and stamping his slow way around the circle inside the ring of fires. Every eye was upon that moving figure with its tossing horns and lashing tail. One round the buffalo was to make alone, then was to be followed by the horse, then by the hunter. So intent were all the spectators about the fires that no one noted the brief pause before the horse came out from the shadows and the second dancer joined the first.

As has been said, Chanuka had seen the dance before, watching from afar across the stream. It was well for him that an Indian's mind is trained to notice and to store up every detail which his eye has once seen. With his heart hammering against his ribs, and with his eyes peering desperately through the holes in the clumsy head, Chanuka set himself to imitate the stamping dance step of the man before him, while he moved the horse's head, up and down, up and down, just as he had seen the dancer, a year ago, imitate the jogging motion of a loping pony. In that breathless moment during which Dacotah and Ojibway had changed places, Neosho's quick eye had noted one detail which might have betrayed them both. He had kicked off his beaded moccasins, and had pointed to Chanuka's, cut and embroidered in a different fashion and proclaiming his tribe to any watchful eye. The long limbed plainsman was larger than the lad of the forest, so that now Chanuka, dancing for his life, found the moccasins awkwardly big as he jerked and shuffled forward in the wake of the shuffling buffalo.

He had circled the ring of flickering red light, and now, from a shout behind him, knew that the hunter had joined the other two and that all interest and every glance was centered upon the final dancer alone. Once more they made the circuit, the three together. It seemed to the panting boy wrapped in the heavy horse-hide that the round of fire-lit grass had stretched to the compass of a mile. But at last he saw the buffalo stop, look backward over his shoulder and then step aside to mingle with the crowd. A few more steps he danced; then, where the spectators had dwindled to a broken line on the rough footing just above the river bank, the horse also slipped out of the circle and disappeared beyond the curtain of darkness that hung beyond the fire.

There was a soft splash in the water, as though a great fish had jumped. It attracted the attention of a single lean young warrior who alone turned to listen, and who, presently, edged his way to the brink of the river and there gathered up an abandoned horse-hide and the rudely fashioned model of a horse's head. Although he stood, silent and hearkening, for long minutes, there was no sound to be heard above the drums, no hint of a wet, supple figure clambering out of the stream on the opposite bank, and setting forth to bear a message northward.

It was three days later that Chanuka stood before his chief again and gave the news that the Dacotah tribe had had good hunting and that this was no time to prepare for renewing the war. The other heard him, frowning.

"And how do I know that you really traveled so far, that you speak the truth when you say that you actually peered into the Dacotah lodges beside the river?" he asked.

"By these," returned Chanuka briefly. He held up a pair of buffalo-hide moccasins, beaded and ornamented after a pattern never used by an Ojibway. And from the lodge pole of a certain dwelling of the Dacotahs, there swung at that same moment a pair of smaller moccasins, embroidered with bright porcupine quills, such as are worn by the forest hunters. For long years they hung there, the silent witness of a friendship of which no word had ever been spoken aloud.

THE BLACKBIRDS: A QUEER STORY

by Robert Emmet Ward

WHEN my Uncle Henry was about twelve years old, he had been "up to the Big Woods" one summer afternoon, and was coming home carrying a large watermelon. In that part of Kentucky, when forest land is cleared for growing tobacco, a portion is usually planted in melons the first summer, the ground being so rich that the yield is remarkably fine. The melon that Uncle Henry was "toting" home that afternoon, from the patch only that spring cut off the Big Woods, was so heavy and so ripe that when he happened to stub his bare toe against a projecting root and drop his burden, it burst wide open as it struck the ground.

Uncle Henry, even at that early stage of his history, had two marked characteristics —kindliness of disposition, and an impenetrable reticence. He stood looking at the ruin before him, nursing his stubbed toe, and saying nothing.

Presently the curious sense that one is being watched, which we all have experienced at times, caused him to glance around. On the rock-fence, not ten feet away, sat another boy, no older than himself, gazing at him in silence as unbroken as his own. He was, Uncle Henry thought, without exception, the thinnest, the most sunburnt, and most ragged boy he had ever seen.

"Howdy; want to help me to eat it?" Uncle Henry asked, hospitably, sitting down beside the melon's remains.

The boy nodded, joined him in the middle of the lane, and without further words, they both fell to.

There was little left, even of the fragments, except green rind and black seeds, when Uncle Henry's guest had finished. He drew the back of his thin hand across his mouth, and observed,

"That tas'e mighty good."

Uncle Henry looked at him, and reflected that he had never seen him before— he who knew everybody in several counties. Boys of twelve, however thin, do not blow along with the wind. It was no part of Uncle Henry's code to ask questions which might prove embarrassing, so he hesitated. But further reflection convinced him that here a question or two might prove justifiable.

"Going on a piece?" he ventured, politely.

"I reckon," answered the other boy, forlornly. "I dunno whereabouts I *am* goin'. Me and my father started out las' month from Buncombe County, No'th Caliny, after he done sold the farm; and he 'lowed we was goin' to Missoury. But I reckon he got tarred o' me taggin' along, fer he's done lef' me. I been lingerin' 'round lookin' fer 'im, but hit's three days now, and I ain't never seen 'im, so I reckon he's done lef' me fer good. So I'm jus' goin' along anywheres."

Uncle Henry made no display of the effect of this simple recital upon his warm, boyish heart. He only said cordially,

"Better come to my house for supper, and stay all night. My father'll be glad to see you. I live right near here. My name's Henry."

"Mine's Sam." No further acquiescence seemed, to either boy, necessary.

The two went along in amicable silence, occasionally exchanging ideas by means of a nod, a gesture, a half-articulated word, as some object of interest by the wayside attracted the attention of either. Once a flock of blackbirds flew up out of a field, and Sam, who had a crooked stick in his hand, threw it up to his shoulder, took careful aim at the birds, ejaculated *"Bing!"* with much fervor, and, after deliberately blowing down an imaginary barrel, let his weapon fall with evident satisfaction. Uncle Henry looked on with entire approval.

"Like shooting?" he asked, presently.

"I *kin*—but I ain't got no real sure-enough gun," returned Sam.

"You can shoot mine," responded Uncle Henry, promptly. "My father'll take us both out with him. That is, if you think you'd like to stay with us a while."

Sam made no reply. He may have been speechless; he may have thought reply superfluous. At any rate, welcomed with considerate courtesy by his new friend's father and mother, he stayed the night, and all the next day. His visit lengthened to a week, a month, and by the end of that month the whole family had forgotten that Sam was not by right of birth a member of the household.

The two boys grew up together, in much the same amity with which their acquaintance had begun over the watermelon. Both remained boys of few words. Sam's most marked peculiarity was one which seldom failed to strike the casual observer with surprise, although the family soon grew so accustomed to it that it excited no comment. In summer, the big old black locust-trees on the lawn in front of the Hall are much frequented by blackbirds: and whenever a noisy flock would fly up into the boughs, Sam would dart into Uncle Henry's room, which was on the first floor, snatch his gun from the rack, dart out again on the porch, and fire. Whether he brought down several birds or none, the one shot seemed to content him; he would invariably blow down the barrel—thus ornamenting his countenance, around the mouth, with a black circle of powder, of which he never seemed aware—and then somewhat sheepishly replace the gun and go about his affairs without further concern. But that one shot he seemed obliged to have, just as surely as a flock of blackbirds came in sight; and he was never known to omit the ceremony of blowing down the barrel of the gun before he put it away.

He stayed on until Uncle Henry and he were a little over twenty-one years old: then he seemed to grow restless, and one day announced he wanted to "go West." Uncle Henry made no attempt to dissuade him. The whole family wished him God-speed, and, as suddenly as he had come, Sam went. Uncle Henry did not say that he missed him; but sometimes, when the blackbirds were especially noisy in the big locust-trees, he would glance up at them reminiscently, with what, from a less cheery, pleasant-hearted young fellow, would have been a sigh. Years passed, and it was as if there had never been a Sam.

Uncle Henry was a more than middle-aged man when, late one summer afternoon, as he was smoking on the porch, a stranger rode up the drive and stopped at the gate. A hearty hail brought him up to the house, where he and Uncle Henry fell into conversation that soon led to a cordial invitation to stay to supper. The stranger told Uncle Henry that he had heard a great deal of old Hurricane Hall—the first brick house to be built in that part of Kentucky—and had stopped to ask permission to see it. He was a well-dressed, prosperous-looking man, tall, spare, and gray-haired, and of much quiet dignity of manner; Uncle Henry fancied that they had met before, although he could not recall where. The guest, however, said nothing of himself or his affairs, and it still was no part of Uncle Henry's code to ask questions.

While they sat on the porch waiting to be summoned to supper, a flock of loud blackbirds swept across the lawn and up into the trees. Without a word Uncle Henry's visitor sprang from his seat, dashed into the house, and, returning with Uncle Henry's shot-gun, blazed away. Hardly noticing, it seemed, whether any birds fell, he carefully blew down the gunbarrel, and, oblivious of the powder mark around his mouth, walked back into the house to replace the gun on the rack in Uncle Henry's room, after which he returned composedly to his chair in the porch. The two men smoked in silence for several moments.

"Blackbirds," observed Uncle Henry then, "are unusually plentiful this year."

"I've noticed that," said the other.

No further remark was made, and an instant later, supper was announced. Open-hearted Southern hospitality gave the stranger welcome from all the family: it was enough that Uncle Henry brought him in. If any eye were arrested by the unusual decoration around the guest's grave mouth, none could detect the most fleeting glance of curiosity or surprise.

After supper the two men walked about the old place a little; but very soon the stranger, whose manner began to show a faint trace of constraint, declared he must be getting on, thanked his host briefly, shook hands with a hearty grip, and, mounting his horse, rode away into the gathering twilight.

Uncle Henry's eyes followed him for a little distance; then, turning back toward the house, he looked up into the trees where the blackbirds were now at rest for the night.

"Good old Sam!" he mused. "I doubt if we ever see him again."

And they never did.

THIS PLEASANT WORLD

by Rachel Field

CRANBERRY ROAD

I'D like to be walking the cranberry road,
  Where the sea shines blue through the
    bristling firs,
And the rocky pastures are overgrown
  With bayberry bushes and junipers;
Where orchards of bent old appletrees
  Go trooping down to the pebbly shore,
And the clapboard houses are seaward
    turned,
  With larkspur clumps at every door;
Where there's plenty of time to say good-
    day
  When friendly eyes from a window
    peer—
Oh, I'd like to be back on the cranberry
    road;
  I wish I were there instead of here!

IF ONCE YOU HAVE SLEPT ON AN ISLAND

If once you have slept on an island,
  You'll never be quite the same;
You may look as you did the day before
And go by the same old name;

You may bustle about in street and shop,
  You may sit at home and sew,
But you'll see blue water and wheeling
    gulls
  Wherever your feet may go.

You may chat with the neighbors of this
    and that,
  Or close to your fire keep,
But you'll hear ship-whistle and lighthouse
    bell
  And tides beat through your sleep.

Oh, you won't know why, and you can't
    say how
  Such change upon you came,
But—once you have slept on an island,
  You'll never be quite the same!

GENERAL STORE

Some day I mean to keep a store,
With a tinkly bell hung over the door,
With real glass cases and counters wide
And drawers all spilly with things inside.

There'll be a little of everything—
Bolts of calico, balls of string,
Jars of peppermint, tins of tea,
Pots and kettles and crockery,
Seeds in packets, scissors bright,
Kegs of sugar brown and white,
Sarsaparilla for picnic lunches,
Bananas and rubber boots in bunches.
I'll fix the window and dust each shelf,
And take the money in all myself.
It will be my store and I will say:
"What can I do for *you* to-day?"

HOUSES

I LIKE old houses best, don't you?
They never go cluttering up a view
With roofs too red and paint too new,
With doors too green and blinds too blue.
The old ones look as if they *grew;*

Their bricks may be dingy, their clapboards
    askew
From sitting so many seasons through;
But they've learned, in a hundred years
    or two,
Not to go cluttering up a view!

TWO BIDDICUT BOYS

(AND THEIR ADVENTURES WITH A WONDERFUL TRICK DOG)

by J. T. Trowbridge

I

ON THE LAKE-SHORE

THE boys were putting on their clothes in the shadow of the ice-house, when a young man, walking along the edge of the railroad embankment, sauntered down to the shore, followed by a dog. The man had on a narrow-brimmed, speckled straw hat, and a loose sackcoat, and he carried a short stick jauntily in his hand.

He didn't seem to observe the boys, but the boys observed him.

"Looks like a lightning-rod man off on a vacation," said Cliff Chantry. "The one that rodded our new barn had just such a free and easy, I-own-the-earth sort of swagger."

"Bright-looking cur he's got," said Ike Ingalls, tugging at a stocking half-way on his wet foot.

"It's an Irish terrier," said Dick Swan, hopping on one foot to jar the water out of his ear.

"That's no terrier," said the tallest of the boys, as he stood buttoning his shirt-collar, with his elbows spread, his chin up, and a prominent nose high in the air. "It's some sort of a spaniel; don't you see the ears?"—lowering his chin and glancing in the direction of the dog and his master. "His legs are too long for any Irish terrier's."

"A spaniel it is, then; when Quint Whistler says a thing, that makes it so!"

Having uttered this sarcasm, Dick hopped on the other foot, to jounce the water out of his other ear.

Quint paid no attention to the taunt, but pulled down his wristbands under his coat-cuffs, and remarked dryly:

"What's that he has in his hand?—I mean the man, not the dog. It's too big for a toothpick, but not big enough for a walking-stick."

"I'll tell you," suggested Cliff Chantry. "He's the leader of a band, and that's his band-stick. Don't you know?"—and he stopped combing his wet hair with his fingers to make fantastic motions with an imaginary baton. "He's waving it now. See?"

"The dog's his band. He's waving it for him," said Quint. "There!"

The stick went splashing into the water a few rods from shore, and the dog went plunging and paddling after it.

"I knew he was a water-dog," said Quint.

"That's no sign," Cliff replied. "A terrier could do that. I'll ask him. I say, mister, what sort of a whelp is that?"

The young man waited until the dog brought him the stick, then turned to the boys coming down the slope and buttoning their last buttons.

"What sort of a whelp?" he repeated. "He's a sparkler. Didn't you ever see a sparkler?"

493

"Can't say I ever did," Cliff replied. "Never heard of one. What's a sparkler like?"

"As much like the animal you see here as your two thumbs are like each other. See him, and you see a sparkler. Hear him,"—at a motion of the stick the dog barked,—"and you hear a sparkler. Did you ever read Shakspere?"

"I know the dialogue between Brutus and Cassius, in the 'Advanced Speaker,'" Cliff replied. "I acted Cassius once, at a school exhibition, to this fellow's Brutus." He turned, and with a smile looked up at Quint Whistler, who was the last to come down to the shore, buttoning his vest by the way.

"Brutus—Marcus Brutus—this slab-sided chap with the gambrel-roof nose?" cried the dog's owner, with a laugh which infected the whole crowd of boys, except Quint himself.

He had, as has been suggested, an exceptionally bold nasal protuberance; and there was a break in the high slope of it, somewhat suggestive of the roof in question. Cliff's nose, on the contrary, was short, but shapely, belonging to a frank, freckled, mirthful face—the face of a farmer's boy about sixteen years old. He was of medium height, and rather stocky. Quint was perhaps a year older, fully a head taller, lank of face and bony of frame. His countenance was grave almost to sternness at this moment, as if he did not altogether relish the personal nature of the young man's remarks.

The young man confronted the two, looking from one to the other, with an air of lively satisfaction at having made their acquaintance. The boys' companions, half a dozen or more, gathered about them in a group, to listen to the conversation.

"Brutus has got the most nose, but Cassius knows the most," the stranger rattled on gaily. "Though it's easier to decide about the nose than about the knowledge. If I could see you two act Brutus and Cassius, that might help settle the question."

Quint kept his frowning countenance, but Cliff answered laughingly:

"He's great as Brutus! You should see him once! He used to step up on the teacher's platform to spout, 'When Marcus Brutus grows so covetous'; then when he got to,—'Be ready, gods, with all your thunderbolts! dash him to pieces!'—he would jump down on the floor with a jar that made the old school-house shake. Cassius was nowhere! But what have Shakspere, and Brutus and Cassius, to do with your pup?"

"That's what I was coming to," replied the pup's master, holding the stick again, ready to throw. "In one of the plays is a heroine, 'created,' as her lover says, 'of every creature's best.' That can't always be true. But it applies exactly to my dog. He is *multum in parvo, e pluribus unum, ne plus ultra*. He's a land-dog and a water-dog, a sheep-dog and a watch-dog; as honest a dog as ever you saw steal a sausage, and the cunningest trick-dog in the wide world; as sly as a fox, and as amusing as a monkey. Sparkler's his name, and Sparkler's his nature. Young gentlemen, that paragon is for sale, and I invite you to make an offer for him."

He threw the stick, and as the "paragon" went splashing after it, he added:

"What'll you give, Brutus? Name a figure, Cassius? Don't be bashful because I happen to be a stranger."

"I shouldn't think you would want to sell such a perfect creature as that," remarked Cliff Chantry.

"My young friend, you're right. Nothing but dire necessity could ever induce me to part with him. Necessity is a hard mistress; she'll part a good boy and his gran'ma, often a man and his money, sometimes a man and his dog. Have you a silver dollar, Brutus? You, Cassius, a quarter? I'd like to flip it into the lake, for you to see him paddle out and find it —dive to the bottom for it, and bring it ashore. Anybody got a piece of bright money?"

Brutus lifted his eyebrows at Cassius with a droll expression. Cassius drew down one side of his face with a sagacious wink. The other boys likewise winked and smiled, and two or three of them might have been observed to press their hands prudently on their pockets. Bright pieces with which to strew the bottom of the lake were not forthcoming.

"I am pained to perceive an air of incredulity among some of you," said the stranger. "But to convince you—" He put his hand into his own pocket, and asked, "How deep is it out where he is now?"

"About up to your neck," said Cliff.

"That's all right. This is the last quarter that remains to me out of a small fortune; but to show you the confidence I have in the sagacity of my four-footed friend— Here, Sparkler!"

Sparkler dropped the stick on the sand, put his nose to the coin, and yelped wishfully.

"Watch carefully!" his owner said to the boys. "Look alive, Sparkler!" And he tossed the coin boldly out into the lake, where it sank in a circle of ripples.

The dog swam swiftly after it, put down his head into the clear water two or three times as he neared the spot, and finally went down altogether. He seemed to be gone a long while; a few seconds seem a long while when you are watching a feat of that sort.

"I bet you he doesn't bring up any silver quarter," said Cliff Chantry.

"How much will you bet?" cried the dog's owner eagerly. "Any fellow here wants to make a bet? You, Brutus? Put up some money, some of you!"

"But you've no money to put up," said Quint Whistler.

"I've that quarter—"

"At the bottom of the lake!" Cliff laughed excitedly.

"I'll bet the dog! The dog against a dollar! That's a hundred to one! Quick!" cried the young man. "There he comes! Will you take the wager, on what he's got in his mouth?"

"I'm not in the habit of backing up my opinions with bets," remarked Quint Whistler. "All I can say is, I'm glad 't wasn't my quarter you flung."

"He's got his mouth shut," said Ike Ingalls. "It was open when he swam out."

"He's got a pebble in it! He's got his mouth full of sand! Ho, ho!" The boys clamored and jeered, at the same time watching with eager curiosity the dog paddling shoreward.

"Boys," said the young man, gaily, "you are a squad of young Solomons! You'll sprout wisdom when you get free from your mothers' apron-strings! Isn't that so, Sparkler?"—as the dog came dripping out of the lake, and dropped into his master's open palm, along with some gravel, before the eyes of the intensely interested spectators, the recovered piece of money!

II

A ROMANTIC STORY

"THAT'S nothing to what he can do," said the young man, dipping the coin in the water and then wiping it with his handkerchief before returning it to his pocket. "Shake yourself, Sparkler!"

Sparkler shook himself, sending a

shower of spray into the faces of the recoiling and backward tumbling boys. Quint Whistler alone stood his ground, receiving the drops on his nose with an equanimity that amused the stranger.

"Now I see what that gambrel-roof is for—to shed water! My object, young gentlemen, was not to get the water on to you, as you may perhaps imagine, but to get it off from Sparkler, and reduce his weight by so much liquid; for now I am going to show you how he can jump. Sparkler!"

The young man held out the stick horizontally, about eighteen inches from the ground, and the dog leaped over it. He raised it six inches, and the dog went over it again. So he kept raising it, and the dog continued to jump over it, until it was finally placed across the top of Ike Ingall's head.

Ike shut his eyes, giggling nervously, and holding himself still, while the dog, just touching his shoulder lightly, went over the stick, and came down on the grass beyond.

"He's a regular trick-dog," said the stranger. "Now let me suggest a scheme. Brutus and Cassius will buy him for twenty-five dollars, and star the country with him. See? Play Shakspere and exhibit the dog! Can Mr. Whistler whistle?" He had heard the boys call Quint by his full name. "Can either of you sing a comic song? If you can, your fortune is made!"

"I can whistle," said Quint, "like an empty jug. And we can both sing like a couple of cats on a back shed at two o'clock in the morning. But I'm afraid that sort of whistling and singing wouldn't be popular, let alone our Shakspere!" Everybody laughed, except Quint himself, who looked up with an appearance of mild surprise, as if to see where the fun came in.

"The dog alone will be attraction enough," said the stranger. "See what else he can do." He took off his coat and laid it on the grass. "Watch it, Sparkler!"

The dog lay down beside it, with his paws on the collar.

"Now, would any of you young gentlemen like to earn a quarter? If so, bring away that coat, and the lucre is yours."

"I don't care for the quarter, but I can get that coat," said Dick Swan, stepping carefully toward it, undeterred by the growls of Sparkler.

All watched with excited interest till he made a sudden snatch at it. But before his hand grasped the garment, Sparkler's teeth were fast in his sleeve—so fast, indeed, that as he sprang back he left a piece of his cuff in the dog's mouth, amidst the loud laughter of his companions.

"He can do a hundred things," said the stranger. "Here's one."

Beside his coat on the grass he placed his handkerchief; beside that he laid his stick, and near that the silver quarter; then over the quarter he turned his hat.

"Now, boys," he said stepping back a few paces, "which of those articles shall he bring to me?"

"The handkerchief," said Cliff.

"You hear, Sparkler," said the master; "the handkerchief."

And without hesitation the dog picked it up and brought it to him.

"Now, Brutus, what will you have?"

"I say the thing that's under the hat," Quint replied.

"Very well, the money that's under the hat," said the master. Whereupon Sparkler tipped the hat over with his nose, nipped daintily at the coin, which, together with some grass, he took up and dropped into the young man's extended hand.

"That's judgmatical!" said Quint.

And Cliff exclaimed, "He's great! Why don't you exhibit him yourself?"

"That's what I am doing at this moment," said the dog's owner; "and that's what I've done to hundreds of delighted spectators. Sparkler never fails to sparkle. But to pass around the hat—that's another question. If I've a weak point, it's my modesty."

"Your modesty is as plain as a gambrel-roof nose," said Quint Whistler solemnly.

"Brutus," said the young man, laughing good-naturedly with the rest, "we're even. You owed me one, and you have paid it." He put on his coat, and proceeded: "I am the son of a distinguished lawyer, lately deceased; and I am now on my way to the bedside of a sick mother in Michigan, who has sent for me, without knowing that I have no money for the journey."

Cliff fondled the dog's wet head, and inquired: "How do you happen to be out of money so far from home?"

The young man pulled down his cuffs under his coat-sleeves, and smilingly answered:

"That's a long story; but it can be briefly told. I was employed as clerk in the big hotel in Bennington—the Stark Hotel, which was burnt two weeks ago. What? you didn't hear of that big fire? Well, you *would* have heard of it if you had been in town that night. 'Twas a clean sweep! The guests lost about everything —barely escaped with their lives. I was so busy getting out the hotel books, and helping the women and children, that I could not give any time to my own personal effects; so I lost all my clothing, except what I had on my back, and all my books and private papers. I had some money in my pocket, but I've spent that waiting to get my back salary from the proprietor. He owes me seven hundred dollars; but I couldn't get it, because he hadn't settled with the insurance companies. I was lucky in one thing—I saved my dog. I threw him from a three-story window."

"Seems to me that's a three-story kind of a story," observed Quint.

"Wait till I tell you," said the young man, not at all disconcerted. "That was twelve o'clock at night. Think of it! He saw I was in danger—would stick to my heels, you know, while I was rousing the guests; he really helped me, by barking up and down the corridors, till I tumbled a feather-bed out of a window, and dropped him on it."

"I don't see how you *can* part with him!" Cliff exclaimed, caressing the wonderful quadruped.

"Necessity—sheer necessity," answered the young man. "To be perfectly frank with you, I shall sell him conditionally, if at all,—with the privilege of buying him back, at double the price, any time within three months. Give me twenty-five dollars for him, and if I don't pay you fifty within ninety days, the dog is yours. I'm willing to put that in writing."

"I haven't got twenty-five dollars in the world," said Cliff, his eyes glistening with excitement as he looked appealingly at his companions. "And I know I couldn't raise so much."

"How much can you raise?"

"I don't know."

Cliff walked aside with Quint, two or three others following.

"You don't really think of buying him, do you?" said Ike Ingalls.

"I would, in a minute, if I could," said Cliff. "He's just wonderful! Say, Quint! what do you say to going in with me?"

"I'm afraid 't wouldn't work well for two boys to own one dog," replied Quint. "But I should like to see you own him; and I'll lend you a little money, if you like."

"Will you?" said Cliff eagerly.

"Yes, but let me give you something else first; that's advice. You are worked up now. You are more excitable than I am. You'd better wait till you've had time to think it over and ask your folks. You want to do a thing like this when your head is cool."

"My head is cool enough," said Cliff. "But, cool or not, I want that dog! As for my folks, I know they wouldn't consent if I should ask them. But if I take him home, show his tricks, and let out by degrees that I've bought him conditionally, to double my money when the owner comes for him,—if he ever does come: I shall hope he won't!—I don't think they'll say much."

"Well, you know best about it," said Quint. "I've got four or five dollars at home I can let you have."

"I can lend you three dollars," Ike Ingalls whispered, eager to see the sale go on.

Dick Swan, likewise interested in seeing so wonderful a dog brought into the neighborhood, offered to advance two more.

"Now, don't you appear too anxious!" Quint warned his enthusiastic friend.

"Oh, no!" said Cliff, with flushed cheeks and suffused eyes. "I'm as cool as a cucumber in an ice-house!"

III

THE STRANGER AND HIS DOG PART COMPANY

WHEN the friends went back to where the dog was, they found him sitting up in a comical attitude, with his fore paws pointing at the handkerchief thrown over the top of the stick, which was stuck in the turf.

"He feels a little chilly after his bath, and he is warming his hands," his master explained. "You may think it's rather a cold fire; but that's nothing to a dog that has a little imagination. Don't burn your fingers, Sparkler!"

The dog actually drew his paws back a little, showing his teeth and winking with his pleasant brown eyes, as if he enjoyed the humor of the situation.

"That will do. Now put out the fire."

The dog pulled the handkerchief from the stick, and put his paws upon it.

"You see what he is," cried the owner, turning to Cliff. "What do you say?"

Cliff was more than ever determined to possess so marvelous a creature. But keeping in mind his friend's caution, and remembering how he had seen shrewd jockeys swap horses, he assumed an indifferent air, and answered diplomatically:

"I can't raise the money; I told you before."

"How did you come by the dog?" Quint inquired.

"That's a part of the story I believe I didn't tell you," replied the young man. "He was a puppy one of the hostlers had in the hotel stables. I saw there was good stuff in him, bought him for a six-bladed jack-knife with a corkscrew and a gimlet, and gave my leisure time to training him."

Quint stooped to look at the dog's collar, and remarked that it bore no name or number.

"Has he ever been licensed?" he inquired.

"Licensed? yes," said the young man, with a smile of amusement at the simplicity of the question. "But in country places, where every dog is known, the law requiring names and license numbers on dogs' collars is apt to be a dead letter." He turned to Cliff. "How much can you raise?"

"I can raise five dollars; I'll give that for the dog," said Cliff, with a composed expression, such as he had noticed on the faces of horse-traders, but with a wildly throbbing heart.

The owner regarded him with a sad and pitying smile.

"I gave you credit for being a well-intentioned young man," he said; "and I supposed any one who had ever taken the great part of Cassius would have too high an appreciation of good acting to make such an offer for such a performer as my dog Sparkler. Why, sir, it would make him blush, it would make him hang his head for shame, to be sold for a paltry sum like that!"

It certainly made Cliff ashamed to have the pettiness of his offer held up to contempt in this way, and he would have blushed if his face had not been so very red before. He murmured something about having no more money.

"But your friends will lend you some; I see it in their eyes. Now, I'll tell you what I'll do. I believe you'll be a kind master; and I saw when you were stroking him that he had taken a liking to you. He knows a good dog-lover when he sees one, and he picked you out of the crowd. Give me twenty dollars, and the privilege of buying him back at forty, and he's yours."

"I'll give you ten," said Cliff quickly. "That's all I will give."

The other boys looked eagerly from his face to that of the young man, in which they saw signs of relenting. As Cliff couldn't be moved to raise his offer, the owner finally said:

"And I hold the right to buy him back?"

"Yes," replied Cliff, "at double the price."

The young man laughed, and shrugged. "On the whole," he said, "I think that will be as well for me. I shall save money when I come to reclaim him; and the ten dollars will take me as far as Buffalo, where I have friends who will help me over the rest of the journey. I wouldn't have sold him outright if you had offered a hundred."

He took a small cord from his pocket, which he made fast to the dog's collar.

"This is hardly necessary," he observed; "for if I tell him to go with you he will go. But it will be safer to place him under some restraint until I get well out of the way. I shall hurry down to the Junction, and take the first west-bound train." He stood ready to put the loose end of the cord into Cliff's hand. "Now where is your ten dollars, young man?"

"These boys are going to get it for me," said Cliff; "they live nearer here than I do. You'll give me a bill of sale?"

"Certainly, if you require it. Hurry up, and I'll wait here."

Some of the boys went off with Cliff and Quint, while the rest remained in the delightful company of the performing dog and his master. In a short time those who had departed came running back, Cliff at their head and Quint lagging in the rear; and Cliff, out of breath, paid with trembling hands his borrowed money. He received in return the end of the cord, and a leaf torn from the stranger's notebook. On this was penciled a memorandum of the transaction, signed "A. K. Winslow."

"My usual signature," said the dog's late owner. "Though I may as well tell you that the A. stands for Algernon, and the K. for Knight, and that my address will be Battle Creek, Michigan, till further notice. That is your receipted bill, with the redemption clause inserted. Now here is something for you to sign for my protection."

He held out his open note-book, in which Cliff read, on a penciled page:

"Purchased of A. K. Winslow, for ten dollars ($10), his trick-dog Sparkler, which I agree to re-deliver to him, or to his order, on the payment of twice that sum ($20), any time within three months."

This, like the bill of sale, was duly dated; and Cliff, after consulting with Quint, who thought it "judgmatical," attached his signature.

"I keep this, you keep that, and these friends of yours are our witnesses," said Algernon Knight Winslow, in the best of spirits, notwithstanding the present necessity of parting from his four-footed companion. "Sparkler! look alive!"

The dog sat up, with fore legs lifted and paws drooping, while his late master addressed him, with one forefinger pointed impressively:

"Sparkler, sharer of my fortunes, will you go with this young gentleman who holds you by the cord, stay with him faithfully, serve him obediently, and perform tricks for him as you would for me, till I send or come myself to claim you? Answer!"

Sparkler regarded him with half-closed, sleepy-looking eyes, and dropped one paw.

"That means 'yes,'" said Algernon K. Winslow. And now you have him."

"You don't mean to say he takes in all you've been saying?" Cliff queried wonderingly.

"He takes in the gist of it as well as any of you. Now, with regard to his tricks." And Mr. Winslow went on to give Cliff some useful hints on that all-important subject.

The dog was never to be whipped under any circumstances, but always to be treated kindly, and rewarded with nice bits from the table after each performance.

"And I advise you to feed him as soon as you get home; for he has been on rather short allowance lately. Now, good-by. Farewell! Adieu! Au revoir! Till we meet again!" cried A. K. Winslow gaily.

Cliff had still some questions to ask regarding the tricks, which being obligingly answered, he said, "Come, Sparkler!" and set off, cord in hand, accompanied by the dog, who went as readily as if he had been acting one of his well-understood parts. Cliff was overjoyed; and his friends, running beside him and the leashed animal, were almost as jubilant as he. Next to owning a trick-dog is the pleasure of having a friend own one.

"By-by!" Algernon K. Winslow called after them, waving his hand, as he turned and walked smilingly away.

IV

CLIFF BRINGS HOME HIS PURCHASE

"LAND's sake alive! What's up?" exclaimed Mrs. Chantry, looking from the window of the old Chantry farm-house, and seeing a rabble of boys, headed by her son Clifford leading a strange dog, turn in at the gate.

On their way through the village the original party of six or seven had been joined by other boys eager to hear about the dog; and now two more, younger brothers of Cliff, ran out from the barn to meet the astonishing procession.

"What you got there? Where'd you get that dog?" cried the younger brothers, aged twelve and ten, almost with one voice.

"Bought him!" replied Cliff, walking proudly in, followed by his rabble.

"Where? What did you give? What's

he good for?" clamored the younger brothers, falling into the ranks.

"He's a trick-dog, and he's worth a hundred dollars!" replied Sparkler's new owner. "Say, just keep quiet, and let me get him tied up in the wood-house, before you scare him to death. I'll tell you all about it in a minute, ma!" he cried, passing on to the rear of the house, regardless of his mother's expostulations.

She intercepted him at the back door.

"Tell me now! Stop right where you are!" she commanded him. "Have you been buying a dog without permission from your father or me?"

"I didn't have time to get permission; 't wouldn't do to let such a chance slip. He's just the knowingest dog you ever saw or heard of! You and pa will both say it's all right when I tell you," said Cliff, leading his prize and his mob of boys into the wood-shed, a barn-like addition to the house, with one large door opening into the back yard, and a smaller one within, communicating with the kitchen.

"The boy's out of his head!" Mrs. Chantry exclaimed. "I should think they had all broken out of bedlam! Amos and Trafton have run wild with the rest. Where are *you* going, Susie?"

"I want to see the dog," said Susie, a fourteen-year-old sister of Cliff's.

"I declare, you're crazy too! Didn't anybody ever see a dog before?" cried the mother impatiently, but not ill-naturedly, for she was one of the indulgent sort. "Run and find your father, and tell him if he doesn't want his wood-house turned into a pandemonium, he'd better come quick!"

Having got Sparkler into the wood-shed and fastened him by his cord to the leg of a grindstone, Cliff told his brothers they might "just stroke his ears a little," but not to "fool with him," and charged Quint Whistler to look out for the other boys, who were crowding around; then he went bustling into the kitchen, calling out, "What can I feed him? Say, ma, what can I give my dog to eat?"

"That's a strange how-d'e-do!" Mrs. Chantry exclaimed; "before you've told me what dog it is, or how you came by him! As if I was your servant, to feed any stray creetur' you choose to bring into the house!"

"He isn't a stray creetur'!" cried Cliff, "and I don't ask you to feed him; I'll do that myself. The man I had him of said cold chicken was particularly nice for him."

He was already on his way to the cellar, where the cold victuals were kept.

Having relieved her feelings by scolding him for his folly, his mother helped him prepare a bountiful repast for Sparkler. She even showed her interest in his strange purchase so far as to go and stand in the doorway that opened from the kitchen into the wood-shed, and see the "stray creetur'" fed.

There she was found by Susie, returning from the errand to her father.

"You are not going to be crazy too, are you, ma?" said the girl mischievously.

The good woman's countenance, which she endeavored to keep severe, beamed with kindness and curiosity.

"Law, no, child!" she said; "but I want to see that good victuals ain't wasted. I don't wonder you are surprised, father!"

"Father" was the father of the children, a sturdy, red-faced farmer, with a shaven chin hedged by long side-whiskers, who had just appeared at the outer door of the wood-shed. This door had been shut to prevent the possible escape of the dog; but he opened it to the width of his broad shoulders, and looked in with a scowl of humorous amazement.

"What's all this?" he demanded. "I

should think Barnum's 'Greatest Show on Earth' had settled itself on my premises!" Over the heads of the smaller boys he saw tall Quint Whistler standing by the grindstone, keeping back the crowd while the dog ate. "That your dog, Quint?"

"No; I don't own so much as a wag of his tail! Wish I did!" said Quint.

"He's got a mortgage on him; so have I," said Ike Ingalls. "He's a trick-dog, and a wonder!"

Just then Cliff got up from the floor.

"He's my dog," he said, turning only the side of his flushed face toward the outer door, without venturing to look at his father. "He's been trained to do almost anything. There's no end to the tricks that he can perform. And he's a good watch-dog, —look at Dick's coat-sleeve! He got that trying to pull a coat away from him after he had been told to guard it."

The mouth between the long sidewhiskers worked with grim humor, and said sarcastically:

"There seems to be another thing he can do pretty well—dispose of a plate of victuals! Did you pick him up in the street?"

"No, I didn't; you can't pick up such dogs as this in the street, nor anywhere else," Cliff replied with spirit.

"He bought him," spoke up his younger brother Amos, his face in a broad grin.

All eyes turned again to the father in the doorway, who gave a pull at the fleece of his left whisker, and exclaimed:

"You didn't pay money for a mangy cur like that, I hope!"

"He isn't a mangy cur!" Cliff declared indignantly. He didn't know just what "mangy" meant, but inferred that it must be something discreditable. "He's just as nice as he can be. Here, ma, take the plate. He has licked it clean of everything but the cold potato. Now stand a little further off, boys, and I'll show you his tricks."

V

THE ORIGIN OF THE WORD "DOGGED"

A SPACE was cleared for the first exhibition of Cliff's wonderful trick-dog. Some of the spectators climbed upon the piled wood; one stood on the frame of the grindstone, another on the chopping-block, two or three sat on a board placed across the tops of empty barrels, and the rest of the boys filled up the ring.

In the midst stood Quint Whistler and Ike Ingalls, in the distinguished capacity of Cliff's counselors and assistants: thus favored because they had advanced money for the purchase. Dick Swan's mother had refused to let him lend his money, greatly to his disappointment; but he had the next place, on account of the good-will he had shown.

In the kitchen-door stood smiling Mrs. Chantry, with Susie clinging excitedly to her elbow. Amos and Trafton were on the steps below. The father's broad shoulders and straight-brimmed straw hat were defined against the afternoon light in the partly opened wood-shed door, the sarcastic smile still playing about his mouth.

Cliff held in one hand the end of the cord, which he had detached from the leg of the grindstone, and in the other a thin stick of pine kindling. At his feet was the dog, couched on his paws, with his tongue out, looking complacent after his meal.

"Make him jump the first thing," said Ike Ingalls, proud of his part in the show. Then, turning to Mr. Chantry, Ike added: "He can jump over my head. He did it down on the shore."

"Get up, Sparkler!" Cliff commanded.

Sparkler lolled, without any apparent thought of stirring from his comfortable position.

"Say 'Look alive,'" Quint suggested, in a low voice.

"Look alive!" Cliff repeated, in a tone of authority.

As the trick-dog showed no disposition to obey, he gave the cord a jerk, which brought him to his feet.

"Now jump!" he said, holding his stick about eighteen inches from the floor, while Ike Ingalls made the nearest boys take a step or two backward, to give ample room for the leap.

But it was a useless trouble. Sparkler never moved.

"You hold it too high to begin with," said Quint.

So Cliff lowered the stick a few inches, and again commanded: "Jump now!" with no better result.

"Lower yet!" whispered Quint.

Cliff did so, and repeated his commands, at the same time jerking the cord, to rouse the wonderful trick-dog from his indifference. But Sparkler only lolled and looked stupid.

"Lay the stick on the floor," came from the whiskered face in the doorway. "Maybe he'll walk over it."

The spectators began to titter. Cliff, confused, covered with perspiration and blushes, pulled the cord and knocked the dog's paws with the stick, repeating sharply, "Jump, I say!" But Sparkler hung back.

The mother's face wore a look of disappointment and of pity for her son's humiliation; but the whiskered visage in the doorway was wreathed with ironic smiles.

"He *can* jump, but he won't," said Ike Ingalls. "He's balky."

"He's showing us the origin of the word *dogged,*" said the amused father.

"He didn't like it because you yanked him by the cord," Quint Whistler argued. "Don't you remember his owner said you must never be rough with him?"

"I didn't think I was rough," Cliff replied.

He found a handkerchief somewhere in his pockets, and wiped his forehead, still looking down, with a face of perplexity and disgust, at the disobedient beast.

"Another thing he said, too, which I'd forgotten," Quint proceeded—"he said he must be fed after a performance, not before. You couldn't expect him to jump after a full meal."

"That's so!" Cliff assented, with a long breath.

"Try making him sit up," said Dick Swan.

Cliff was averse to the attempt, in the present state of the canine appetite; but as Dick's suggestion was clamorously backed up by the crowd of boys, and there was still a possibility of the dog's redeeming his reputation, he stroked and coaxed him; and finally, remembering the late owner's word and gesture, threw up the hand that held the stick, and cried out cheerily:

"Look alive now! look alive, Sparkler!"

Sparkler looked anything but alive; on the contrary, he looked quite asleep, as he stretched himself out, closing his languid eyes, by the leg of the grindstone.

"What a wonderful dog! Oh, Cliff!" jeered the boys who had previously been most envious of his purchase. "Why don't you brag some more about him?"

"There, there, boys! don't make fun," said Mrs. Chantry. "And don't feel bad, my son. The best of us are liable to be deceived in a bargain."

"Say, Cliff! How much did you give?" asked his brother Amos.

The father laughed pitilessly.

"If he gave ten cents, he got swindled," was his cruel comment. "Now quit your nonsense, and come and help me mend the pig-pen. When I said you could go in swimming, I didn't expect you to bring home a beggarly pup to fool with all the afternoon."

Cliff stood for some moments with bent brows, eying the "dogged" dog with extreme discontent. When he raised his head, his father's unwelcome face had disappeared, and his mother had drawn Susie back into the kitchen. The crowd was beginning to disperse, some laughing as they went, others lingering to hear what Cliff would have to say.

One lingered from a different motive: that was Ike Ingalls.

"If you'd just as lieves pay me the three dollars and a half I lent you,"—he began, in a low voice, at Cliff's ear.

Cliff turned upon him a scornful scowl. "I'll pay you so quick it'll make your head swim!" he exclaimed, loud enough for all to hear. "You were glad enough to lend it, and help me buy the dog, and you felt easy enough about it till you began to think I'd been cheated. Ame, go up to my room and get my money-pouch out of the till of my chest; and say nothing to anybody."

"Don't mind about paying me," said Quint. "I wouldn't ask for my money even if I knew you'd bought a worthless dog; but I don't believe you have. You couldn't expect him to perform tricks in a crowd of strangers, before he'd got well acquainted with you."

"No, he hasn't got used to his new master," said Dick Swan, encouragingly. "I wouldn't come down on you for *my* money, would I? I'm sorrier'n I was before, ma wouldn't let me lend it to you."

"*You*'re all right, Dick; so is Quint," Cliff replied, his brows clearing. "So am I! I don't give him up as a bad job—not yet! His dinner made him logy; that's what's the matter. Then again, father looking on the way he did, made me nervous. I knew he was just waiting to laugh at me. Ten

cents!" the boy repeated, with a dismal laugh.

"You never must be nervous when you are training an animal," Quint remarked. "That's so with horses, and it must be so with dogs. He'll come out all right, I know! If he don't, you needn't pay me back more than half my money; for it was partly my fault, your buying him."

"By jingo, Quint!" Cliff exclaimed, with a burst of grateful feeling, "you are a whole load of bricks! But I shall pay you every cent, all the same; some time, if not to-day. Give it here, Ame";—to the boy bringing the pouch of money.

Cliff untied the string, and began to count out silver half-dollars.

Ike, meanwhile, feeling that his eagerness to receive back his loan contrasted unfavorably with Quint's more generous conduct, and with what Dick would likewise have done in his place, looked furtively around for evidences of his own waning popularity on the faces of his companions.

"Here, Ike!" said Cliff, jingling seven half-dollars in his extended palm.

Ike was conscious of a chilly social atmosphere surrounding him; but he was nevertheless glad to see his money again.

"I didn't want you to think I was in any hurry for my pay," he said, as he reached out his hand for it. "I thought—"

"That's all right, Ike," said Cliff, without any show of resentment. "I can give you a part of yours, Quint,—"

"No, leave it now," replied Quint. "Or—just as you say." And Cliff insisting, he took the last of the silver which Cliff withdrew from the pouch. "And don't worry about the rest; let it go till—what's his name?—A. K. Winslow buys back his dog," he added, with a droll smile.

"Not a word, boys, about this money," Cliff cautioned his brothers. "I prefer to tell father myself. Now, fellows, I've got to shut up here; sorry to turn you out, but—" tying the dog's cord again firmly to the leg of the grindstone—"father wants me, and I'm going to leave Master Sparkler to meditate upon his disgraceful conduct."

Having got the last of the boys out of the wood-shed, and shut the large outer door, he beckoned Quint to remain, and said to him confidentially:

"Can't you come around this evening? When everything is quiet, and he has digested his dinner, I am going to try him again, and see if he'll do his tricks any better on an empty stomach."

Quint readily agreed to come.

VI

"DIDN'T I TELL YOU SO?"

WHILE the two were at work repairing the pig-pen, Mr. Chantry forbore to ask any questions regarding the "beggarly pup" his son had brought home.

"What he has to say about that will keep," Cliff reflected ruefully, remembering that the paternal remarks never lost any of their sharpness by being well thought over. That they were in preparation he could see by an occasional quiet smile in which his father indulged; but he was glad to have them kept in for the present.

"After I've had another chance to try Sparkler," the boy said to himself, "then he may ask questions and have his joke."

Mr. Chantry was particularly fond of a joke at his children's expense. He never struck them, but his stinging ridicule was often worse than a whip.

"If Sparkler doesn't sparkle next time, and I have to tell what I paid for him, won't I get it!" thought Cliff, watching the satirical quirk of the mouth in its parenthesis of long, fine whiskers.

The afternoon waned, they finished their work, and the subject uppermost in one mind, if not in both, was not once mentioned. At the supper-table Susie and the younger boys could talk of nothing but the dog in the wood-shed; and the mother scolded about it in her mild way, alternately blaming Cliff for bringing the creetur' home, and blaming the creetur' for ungratefully refusing to perform his tricks after he had been fed so bountifully.

"He's been asleep almost ever since you left him," said Amos. "I shouldn't think he'd had any more sleep than victuals lately. He wouldn't even open his eyes for me."

"I told you not to go near him," said Cliff, severely.

"I had to go there for an armful of wood," was the younger brother's excuse. "You'll have to put him into a bandbox, if he's too precious to be looked at or spoken to; or hang him in the well, as we do butter in hot weather, when we are out of ice."

The youngster's grin was a very good reduced copy of the father's amused, ironic smile. Father and son were much alike, but for the paternal whiskers, and a difference of some thirty years in their ages.

After supper the cows were to be milked, and other evening chores to be done; and all the while the dog was left to his dreams and reflections in the darkening wood-shed. It was deep dusk when Quint Whistler strolled in at the front gate, and Cliff went out to meet him.

"How's your ten-cent pup?" Quint inquired.

"He's humble, and I hope penitent,"

said Cliff. "Now, if we can have him by ourselves, we'll see whether he can perform tricks, or whether we've dreamed it."

He let Quint into the wood-shed, and went to the kitchen for a lamp. This he brought, followed by the younger boys, whom he cautioned to "keep quiet and hold their tongues," if they wanted to see the show.

"Now, Sparkler," he said, proceeding to remove the cord from the collar, "remember what you promised Mr. Winslow, and be a good dog. Treat me well, and I'll treat you well."

"I believe he understands," said Quint. "See how knowing he looks! I believe he's laughing!"

"We'll all laugh soon," Cliff exclaimed hopefully, looking for a suitable stick in the pile of kindling-wood. "Shut that door, Susie!"

"Father says bring the dog in," replied the girl, looking down from the kitchen doorway.

"Jehu! I can't do that," Cliff muttered. "It'll spoil everything. Tell him I don't want to—just yet."

Susie disappeared, but returned with a peremptory message.

"He says bring him in, whether you want to or not. If there's a show, he wants to see it."

"There won't be any show if I have him looking on and making fun," Cliff growled. "I suppose I shall have to, though. When he says a thing like that, he means it. You come too, Quint, and back me up. I know Sparkler won't do a thing!" And he threw down the stick in bitter discouragement.

To his surprise, Sparkler picked it up, and stood, with wagging tail, ready to follow him.

"See that! See that!" cried Amos and Trafton together. "He's going to perform!"

"It looks more like it—sure!" said Cliff, thrilled with joyous expectation. "Out of the way, boys!" Then to Susie: "Have all the doors shut in there, for it's a strange place, and there's no knowing what he may do."

Preceded by the boys, and followed by Sparkler bearing the stick, Cliff entered the large, old-fashioned, lamp-lighted kitchen, Quint lagging awkwardly behind.

Mrs. Chantry at the same time came in from a room beyond, with a half-knitted stocking in her hand. The bright needles shone in the lamp-light, and a dark thread of yarn meandered down across her white apron to a pocket, a bulge in which showed where the ball was lodged. The kindly face was crinkled with smiles of anticipation, as she saw Sparkler trotting along with the stick in his teeth.

Backed up toward a corner under the clock sat Mr. Chantry in a splint-bottomed rocker, parting his long, fleecy side-whiskers away from his shaven mouth and chin with the fingers of both hands, as his frequent habit was when preparing for a little pleasantry at the expense of the youngsters. Cliff, without looking at him, perceived the motion, and knew that his father's lips were twitching and his eyes twinkling in a manner that boded mischief. But he determined not to be disconcerted.

"Come along, Quint!" he cried, with an air of confidence. "Ame, give him a chair."

"I'm all right," said Quint, placing a flat stick across a corner of the wood-box, and sitting on it.

With his hat removed, exposing a high, robust forehead, he was a good-looking fellow, notwithstanding his disproportionate nose. He held his hat on his knee, and put an arm around Trafton, the youngest boy, who was standing at his side.

Cliff made his mother sit down, and

placed a chair for himself beside the table. There was a hush of suspense, in which the old clock was heard ticking loudly, and the farmer's chair squeaking, as he rocked gently.

Cliff sat down, with the dog at his feet, and looking up inquiringly into his face.

"Sparkler," said he, "what are you going to do with that stick?"

Immediately Sparkler got on his hind legs, holding up the stick before his new master. The youngsters shrieked with delight.

"I declare, that's complete!" said the mother, staying her hands, which had begun to ply the knitting-needles vigorously.

Mr. Chantry stopped rocking; he even stopped stroking his whiskers.

Trembling with joy, yet almost afraid to ask anything else of the dog, Cliff took the stick. Sparkler sat erect, with his fore paws at his breast, his bright, soft eyes wistfully studying his young master's face.

"Are you going to jump for me?" Cliff asked, in a tone of affectionate comradeship.

The dog's whole body gave an eager start, his tail wagged, and one paw dropped.

"That means 'yes,'" Quint interpreted, from his seat on the wood-box.

Cliff could hardly keep from hugging the animal, so intense was his delight.

"Jump, then!" he said, holding out the stick. Sparkler leaped over it. "Higher!" he cried, suiting the action to the word. "Higher yet! Higher!" At each command, with its accompanying upward movement of the stick, the dog leaped to and fro with extraordinary liveliness, describing at each rebound a loftier curve.

"Didn't I tell you so?" cried Cliff, triumphantly, with tears of pride and joy shining in his eyes. "He could jump over Ame's head, but I won't have him try on this hard floor."

"Oh, yes, let him," said Amos. "I never had a dog jump over my head."

"Well, bring a rug for him to come down on," said Cliff.

But, seeing that Sparkler was panting, Quint suggested that he should be allowed to rest a minute.

"Winslow," he said, "always let him rest between his tricks. He's a beauty, isn't he, boys!"

Mrs. Chantry joined with the children in praising Sparkler's nimbleness and docility. Her husband forgot his whiskers, forgot his sarcasms, and leaned forward, with his arms on the arms of the chair, hardly less interested than the rest, although still wary of committing himself by any word of approval. The dog might yet make a failure, and give him an opportunity to get in some of his cutting remarks.

VII

CLIFF TRIUMPHANT

THE rug being put in place, and Sparkler having recovered his breath, he made the leap over Ame's head, in a manner that elicited applause from everybody but the non-committal farmer.

"Now roll over!" said Cliff; which Sparkler promptly did, choosing the rug for his performance. Then Cliff cried, "Look alive!" and Sparkler was erect before him in a moment. "Give me a handkerchief, somebody!"

Susie gave him hers, and he wrapped it around the end of the stick, which he set up between his feet.

"That's supposed to be a fire, and he's going to warm his hands. Warm your hands, Sparkler!"—which the dog did, sitting erect before the handkerchief, and holding up his paws before it, with amusing mimicry.

"How's that for a ten-cent pup?" Quint asked in his dry way, as soon as the tumult of admiring exclamations had subsided.

"Ten cents!" exclaimed Mrs. Chantry. "You don't mean to say that's what you paid?"

Cliff said nothing, but sat patting Sparkler's head, and breathing fast with excitement.

"That's the price father guessed, and he told Cliff he got cheated if he paid it," tittered Amos, while the father smiled, and watched the dog.

"Now I'll try his great trick, though I'm by no means sure it will succeed," said Cliff. "How is it, Sparkler?" Sparkler sat up. "Will you do your best?"

He dropped one of his fore paws affirmatively; and the children cried out in jubilant chorus: "He will! He says he will!"

Then Cliff laid in a row on the floor, before the kitchen sink, the handkerchief, the stick, and one of the boy's hats, calling each article by name as he placed it.

"Now, father," he said, when all was arranged, "which shall he fetch?"

Before Mr. Chantry could speak—the boys clamored for the hat; and Mrs. Chantry said: "Yes, Cliff, I'd like to see him fetch the hat."

Sparkler looked up inquiringly at Cliff.

"Fetch the hat," said Cliff; and the dog brought the hat and put it into his hands.

"It is past belief!" Mrs. Chantry exclaimed. "There's witchery in it!"

"The witchery is in his superior knowingness," said Cliff proudly. "You've no idea how bright he is. Fetch the stick, Sparkler!"

Sparkler brought the stick. Then Cliff replaced all the articles, and asked his father for a piece of money. Mr. Chantry hesitated, lifting his brows quizzically; but finally produced a half-dollar. Cliff took it and placed it under the hat.

"He'll go for that, of course," said Amos.

"You'll see," Cliff answered. "Ask for anything else."

So Amos named the handkerchief, which Sparkler brought, after waiting for his master to repeat the order. Then Cliff said, "Fetch the money"—which the dog did, after some trouble in getting the coin between his teeth.

The Mr. Chantry for the first time opened his lips; not, however, to utter sarcasms.

"How did you say you came by that dog?"

"A man named Winslow sold him to me, this afternoon, down by Gibson's ice-house."

"I can't conceive of the owner selling a dog like that for any such price as a boy like you is likely to give," said Mr. Chantry gravely. "There must be some hidden reason."

"Oh, he told us the reason," Cliff replied. "He was out of money; and he was on his way to his mother in Michigan. He was clerk in the big hotel in Bennington when it was burned, two weeks ago; he lost everything by the fire, and was obliged to part with the dog."

"Big hotel in Bennington?"

"Yes; the Stark Hotel, wasn't it, Quint?"

"Stark Hotel in Bennington?" pondered the farmer. "There may be a Stark Hotel there, for General Stark was in the battle of Bennington. Yet that's a small town, and I don't know what they should want of a big hotel there."

"Maybe for summer boarders," Mrs. Chantry suggested.

"Possibly. But if any such great hotel has

been burned lately, we should have seen something of it in the papers. And if he was on his way to Michigan, what brought him here?" Mr. Chantry argued. "This is out of his way."

"He didn't explain that," said Cliff. "Oh, I remember!—he was going to stop in Buffalo, where he has friends."

"That doesn't better the matter. I'm afraid there's some crookedness in the business. Ah!" Mr. Chantry had taken hold of the dog's collar, and was examining it. "No name, but here's a place for one."

The strap was of maroon-colored leather, ornamented with a row of nickel studs set about an inch and a half apart. There were, however, two vacancies in this row: one where the collar buckled at the throat, the other where, instead of the studs, there were two rivet-holes in the leather.

"I noticed those holes," said Quint; "and I supposed two of the studs had been lost out."

"It looks to me," said the farmer, "as if there had been a name-plate here, and as if it had been picked off. I'll wager something, the fellow stole the dog!"

"I can't think that," exclaimed Cliff. "He was very particular to put it into the bargain that he was to have the privilege of buying him back. He made me give that to him in writing."

"And did he give you any writing?"

"Yes; a regular bill of sale."

"Let me see it."

The paper was produced. Mr. Chantry read the writing carefully, and mused.

"So you gave ten dollars in cash?" he said, lifting his eyes, and looking straight at Cliff.

"Isn't he worth it?"

"I should say he was, and a good deal more. I don't at all approve of you buying him without my advice and consent; but 't was a temptation, and I shan't whale you for it." All the children laughed at what

appealed to them as a good joke,—Mr. Chantry not being in the habit of "whaling" his boys. "Did you have money enough to pay for him?"

"I still owe a little that I borrowed of Quint," Cliff answered.

"Pay it up," said his father, taking out his pocket-book.

But Cliff declined the proffered assistance.

"Quint is willing to wait," he said. "And I don't want anybody to have a claim on the dog except me—and Mr. Winslow. All I'm afraid of is that he'll come to get him back."

"I guess you'd better feed him a little now, hadn't you?" said his mother. "He can have some bread and milk as well as not."

"Let's have some more tricks first!" pleaded the youngsters.

"Well, just one or two, to please the children," she assented.

"Oh, ma!" Susie laughed, "you want to see the tricks just as much as we do!"

Cliff was glad to put Sparkler again through some of his performances. Then the dog was petted and fed, and taken back to the wood-shed. Cliff gave him the rug to lie on, and patted him, and talked to him, as he slipped the cord once more through his collar, and made him fast to the frame of the grindstone.

"I shan't have to do this many times more," he said to his friend Quint, standing by. "But for a while it's best to be on the safe side. Forgive me, Sparkler."

Taking affectionate leave of the dog, who licked his hand, he went out with Quint, and walked home with him, and they talked for half an hour longer, standing at Quint's gate.

"Well, good-night, Quint!" Cliff said at parting. "Hasn't it been a great day? I owe ever so much to you!"

Then he returned home. He took a last

peep at his prize curled up on the rug in the wood-shed; saw that everything was quiet, and all doors fast; said "Good-night" to his mother in a voice thrilling with happiness, received from her hand a candle she had lighted for him, and went up-stairs to bed. He was soon asleep, and dreaming of dogs that could swim in the air and balance poles on their noses.

VIII

ONE OF SPARKLER'S TRICKS

WHEN Cliff awoke in the morning, Sparkler was the first thing in his thoughts. He hurriedly put on his clothes, and hastened downstairs, eager to learn how his pet had passed the night; also to assure himself that the wonderful creature was a reality, and not a part of his vanished dreams.

He was astonished to meet Amos at the foot of the stairs. The boy was frightened, and hardly able to speak.

"What's the matter?" Cliff demanded.

"Gone!" Amos whimpered.

"Who's gone? What's gone?"

"The dog!"

"Not my trick-dog—not Sparkler?" Cliff exclaimed, in wild consternation.

"Yes! skedaddled!" said Amos. "I was hurrying to tell you."

"Who let him go?" Cliff asked fiercely, rushing past him.

"I didn't mean to," whined Amos. "I thought he was tied. I just opened the door to look at him, and he ran into the kitchen. That door was open, and he ran out."

"He *was* tied! Who untied him? Where is he?"

Cliff was already out of the house. At the corner of the wood-shed he met his mother, pale with excitement.

"Which way did he go?" he demanded, hardly pausing for her reply as he ran past her.

"Down the road—toward the village," she answered, catching her breath. "He had a piece of the cord tied to his collar."

"A piece of it?" cried Cliff, turning back.

"Yes; just a few inches. I was standing by the stove when he went by me like a flash; in at one door and out of the other, in an instant. I had just time to follow and get another glimpse of him before he was out of sight."

Cliff hurried to the wood-shed to examine the cord. He found one end tied to the grindstone, as he had left it; but Sparkler was off with the end fastened to his collar.

"He has gnawed it in two!" Cliff moaned.

Much the longer piece remained attached to the grindstone. With sudden resolution he untied it, twisted it into a loose ball, and thrust it into his pocket.

"What are you going to do?" his mother asked, as he was hurrying from the wood-shed.

"Follow him! Find him and bring him back!"

"Eat your breakfast first," she entreated.

"I haven't a minute's time!" he declared.

"You may be away longer than you think. I'll give you something to put in your pocket."

"Hurry up, then!"

He went with her into the kitchen, and came out presently with a piece of berry-pie in his hand, and his pockets bulging. He met his father approaching from the barn.

"What's the trouble?" cried the farmer. "What's the matter now?"

"My dog!" said Cliff. "He has gnawed off his cord and got away. Ame opened the door."

"Bah!" exclaimed his father. "That's one of his tricks his owner didn't tell you of. You never'll see him again."

"Yes, I will. He won't go farther than the Junction, where Winslow was to take the train. Or, if he does, I can trace him."

"Let me go too!" Amos entreated. "I can leg it as fast as Cliff can."

"No, no!" said Mr. Chantry. "It's bad enough to have one boy start off on such a wild-goose chase. You'd better not go far, Cliff." But Cliff was out of hearing, past the gate. "I wouldn't have had it happen for a good deal; I took quite a notion to that dog. Come, Amos. You must help about the chores."

"I let him out, and I ought to go and help find him," said Amos, making a merit of his share in the accident.

Just then the youngest son appeared, with hair uncombed, staring wildly, and highly incensed because he had been allowed to sleep at a time of such excitement.

"Any other morning I'd have been called six times!" he complained. "Why didn't you ketch him, ma, when he shot by you?"

"I might as well have tried to ketch a streak of lightning by the tail," replied his mother. "I just heard a pattering sound, and he was out in a jiffy. He's a mile away by this time, I warrant!"

IX

CLIFF IN PURSUIT

CLIFF ran fast until he came in sight of Quint Whistler's home, on the outskirts of the village, and saw Quint himself standing in the open barn door. Quint's father, a mason and contractor, had just driven away to look after some business in an adjoining town, leaving Quint to shut up the barn and take care of the premises.

"Quint! Quint!" called Cliff from the street. "My dog has got away!"

"Got away!" Quint called back, beginning to walk fast toward the gate. "Which way did he go?"

"Right past your place here; at least he started this way. He'll most likely go straight to the shore where he saw his master last, and then try to track him." Cliff stopped to gather breath, and added, "I'm so glad I've found you. Come along, won't you, and help me hunt him?"

"I don't know," said Quint doubtfully. "As I was off yesterday afternoon, I'm expected to do some hoeing in the garden this morning. That's the order, and it seems only reasonable."

"So was I expected to work to-day," said Cliff. "But I can make it up; and I'll help you for all the time you lose. We may overhaul him in an hour."

"And it may take all day. Besides, I haven't had my breakfast," was Quint's objection.

"Neither have I! Take a bite in your hand and something in your pocket, as I have," said Cliff.

As he spoke, Cliff seemed to remember the wedge of pie he carried, which he hadn't yet thought of eating. He took a deep mouthful, staining his lips with the juice of the berries with which it was filled; while Quint, as deliberate in thought and action as his friend was impetuous, balanced considerations.

"Of course I must help you out of this," he said at length. "I'll be with you in a minute."

He entered the house, and presently came out, stuffing the side pockets of his coat with doughnuts.

"Whether it's to be a long or a short chase," he said, "you can count me in. I helped you buy him, and I'll stick by you as long as there's a chance of running him down."

And the chase began.

X

THE BEGINNING OF THE CHASE

THE boys walked fast through the village, and broke into a run as they approached the lake-shore, where they hoped to find Sparkler looking for his master. But no dog was anywhere in sight.

Two men were loading ice into a wagon backed up against the ice-house. Cliff called out to them.

"Yes!" one called back, in reply to his inquiries. "We saw a dog come down to the pond just a little while ago. He snuffed around, and capered up and down for a while, then started off down the railroad track as fast as he could clip it."

"He seemed to have a little piece of rope, or something, dangling from his neck," said the other man.

"That's my dog! He's gone straight to the Junction!" Cliff said confidently to his companion, as they hurried on.

It was nearly a mile to the Junction; they kept the railroad track all the way, but saw nothing of the fugitive. On the platform they found the station-master checking a trunk; and Cliff accosted him breathlessly.

"No," he said; "I haven't noticed any such dog."

"That is strange," said Cliff. "Did you sell a ticket yesterday afternoon, at about four o'clock, to a young man—who had on a narrow-brimmed hat, kind of a checkered straw?"

The station-master remembered him very well; he had sold him a ticket, and noticed that he had no baggage, not even a gripsack, when he stepped aboard the train.

"That's all right," cried Cliff. "That man sold me a dog yesterday; he was a trick-dog, and he got away this morning."

The station-master called a switch-tender, who said:

"Yes, I saw that very dog, half or three quarters of an hour ago. He snuffed about the platform, then all of a sudden he seemed to remember a previous engagement, and put out toward Tressel, with a full head of steam on!"

Tressel was a station a mile or more beyond.

"Come on," cried Cliff eagerly. "He's going the wrong direction to find Winslow. He'll fetch up somewhere."

But Quint was deliberating. "Wait a minute! I want to be sure of a thing or two. You say that man bought a ticket. Was it to go West?"

"No; he bought a ticket for Kilbird." Kilbird was the first station beyond Tressel.

"He said he was going West!"

"No matter what he said, he boarded the east-bound accommodation train, here!"

It took Cliff a moment to recover from his bewilderment; then he turned to Quint and said:

"I'd like your company ever so much, and I don't know what I shall do without you; you think of more things than I do, and look further ahead. But I'm afraid this is going to be a long pull; and I know I ought not to drag you along."

"If you call it dragging, why, I'll turn back," said Quint. "I know I'm slow."

"I don't mean that!" cried Cliff. "But I've no right to ask so much of you; that's what I meant to say."

"Then don't say it again!" Quint replied, starting off resolutely on the road to Tressel and Kilbird. "Come along!"

The boys now settled down to a fast walk, discussing by the way Sparkler's chances of rejoining his late master. On reaching Tressel, they met three boys who gave them some interesting information. They had seen the dog with the dangling piece of cord pass through the village in the direction of Kilbird; and one of them reported having seen, the day before, a man offering to sell just such a dog to a teamster who had stopped to water his horses at the wayside trough.

Quint thought a moment, then observed: "It's all plain to me. Winslow came from Kilbird, or some place around there, yesterday; he took the train to Kilbird after selling you the dog, and now the dog has gone back there to meet him. See?"

Cliff did see, greatly to his chagrin and vexation. Just then a locomotive whistled.

"Here comes the down-train," he exclaimed. "How would it do for one of us to board it for Kilbird, and try heading him off that way, while the other keeps the road?"

"That's judgmatical," said Quint. "We've just time to buy a ticket. Have you got any money?"

"Jehu! I forgot all about money," cried Cliff.

"Never mind," said Quint, consolingly. "The dog will be in Kilbird before the train will, if he isn't there already. It will be better for us to keep together."

The dangling cord was a fortunate circumstance; for it attracted attention to the runaway, and rendered the pursuit for a while comparatively easy.

They had been walking some time on a lonely country road, without meeting any one of whom they could make inquiries, when Cliff said: "There comes a team. We'll ask the driver."

Quint stopped suddenly, and stood staring straight before him down the turnpike. "By hokey, Cliff," he exclaimed, "I know that horse, for I harnessed him this morning! The wagon is our carryall, and the driver is my father."

Mr. Whistler was much surprised to meet his own boy and a neighbor's traveling that dusty road, so far from home. He listened with amused interest to Quint's story of the runaway dog.

"Did he bite you both, and give you the running-away distemper?" he asked. "Get into the wagon, and ride back with me, both of you. That's the wisest thing you can do."

"Quint can. I guess it's the wisest thing for him," said Cliff; "but I shall keep on till I find the dog, or drop down in my tracks."

"Get up here, Quint! No more nonsense!" the elder Whistler commanded. "Cliff can do as he likes."

"He would like to borrow a little money of you, anyway," said Quint. "We have both come away without any."

Mr. Whistler demurred. "I don't know what his father'll say to my lending him money for such a tom-fool expedition."

"My father knows what I am doing, and he'll be obliged to you for giving me a little help," Cliff put in.

"Well, about how much do you want?" said the mason and contractor, putting his hand in his pocket.

"Enough to take me home from Kilbird by the train, anyway," said Cliff, "and maybe a little over."

"Enough to take us both home," Quint added, "if I go with him."

"It's a foolish business," Mr. Whistler commented; "but if Cliff's father approves, I don't know why I should stand out." Leaning over the wagon side, he reached down a handful of small change. "Will this do?"

"Oh, yes; ever so much obliged!" cried

Cliff delightedly, pocketing the money. "If you see any of my folks, please tell 'em—"

"I'll tell 'em that I saw you going off in company with another lunatic," said the elder Whistler, driving on.

XI

ANOTHER DOG-HUNTER

THE boys resumed their tramp, keeping up their inquiries for Sparkler. Nobody on that part of the highway had seen a dog with a cord dangling from his collar, nor, indeed, any stray dog.

"He may have turned off on some other road, or taken to the fields," said Cliff at length. "What shall we do?"

"I believe our best way is to keep straight on to Kilbird," said Quint. "If we don't strike his trail there, we may at least hear from Winslow."

"There comes some one we can ask," said Cliff; for a man on horseback was approaching along a by-road. The horse was a heavy, hard-trotting animal, and the rider a stout little man, who at every jolt went up and down like a bouncing ball. The boys stopped to speak with him.

Before they could accost him he called out, with the jolts in his voice, as the animal's ponderous trot broke to a walk:

"Say — have — you — seen — a — stray — dog — along — here — anywheres?"

It seemed almost as if he must have known their business, and that he was a joker, who took this means of heading off their expected inquiries.

Quint gave Cliff a nudge, and said, with a droll twist of his mouth:

"It seems to be a pretty good day for stray dogs!"

"A rather small dog," said the man. "Kind of curly brown hair; a sort of spani'l. Had on a collar fastened with a buckle; sort of reddish-brown leather with bright studs in it."

The boys listened with astonishment, the description fitted Sparkler so exactly.

"What do you want of that dog?" Cliff demanded. "Does he belong to you?"

"He ought ter belong to me, for I bought him. Day before yes'day. A man brought him along and offered him for sale. I give a five-dollar bill for him! He wanted twenty-five, but I beat him down to five. My name is Miller; I live over in Wormwood."

Cliff's throat had become so dry that he couldn't utter another word. Quint took up the colloquy.

"How did he get away from you?"

Mr. Miller eased his position by leaning sidewise on his horse, and explained.

"The man advised me to keep him shet up for a day or two, and I put him in the barn. I fed him well, and he seemed as contented as if I'd always owned him. A couple of hours later I went to look at him. It was kind o' dusky in the barn,—I couldn't see him nowheres; so I spoke to him, and opened the door jest a crack wider—swish! he zipped past my legs, and out o' that door like a kicked foot-ball! That's the last I've seen of him. But half an hour ago a neighbor come over to say he'd seen that dog this morning, over by the Lippitt place, this side of Tressel. He tried to head him off, but he took to the woods, and he lost sight of him. So I jest throws a blanket on old Bob, and jogs off to hunt him up. You hain't seen no such animal around anywheres?" Mr. Miller continued, talking down to the boys.

"Not to-day," Quint replied; "but I saw that very dog yesterday afternoon. A man offered him for sale, over in Biddicut, and a neighbor of mine bought him for ten dollars. He got cheated more than you did."

"Yes, he did, for he bought my dog! Where is he?"

"The boy or the dog?" Quint inquired.

"Both," said Mr. Miller.

"The boy is right here before you," said Quint, laying his hand on Cliff's shoulder. "But where the dog is, we're as anxious to know as you are. He got away this morning, and we tracked him a good piece this side of Tressel village,—to about where your neighbor saw him, I should say."

Mr. Miller thereupon kicked his clumsy heels into the horse's ribs, slapped him with the looped end of the reins, clucked like a hen, threw up his arms like wings, and started off on his hard-trotting beast.

"Well, Cliff!" Quint said, with a strange smile.

Cliff was so astounded by the proof of Winslow's bad faith, that he made two or three attempts to speak before he finally replied:

"Quint, it's no use! We may as well turn around and go home."

"How do you work that out?" Quint inquired.

"Don't you see? I've no claim on that dog, anyway! If Winslow had a right to sell him, he belongs to Miller, who bought him before I did."

"I can't help laughing!" Quint suddenly broke forth. "Algernon K. Winslow is a man of genius. He has invented a new business—selling a dog! Who knows how many times he had sold him, before he sold him to Miller? Your title is probably as good as Miller's."

"It may be, and yet not be worth taking this tramp for."

"I beg to differ with you. If we get that dog," Quint continued, "we can hold him till somebody shows a better claim; and if the rightful owner turns up, I'm sure he'll be willing to pay your ten-dollar

mortgage on him, and other expenses. There's no discount on that dog, Cliff; the discount is all on Winslow."

Cliff's face brightened. "There's a good deal in what you say, Quint."

"It's judgmatical," said Quint.

He gave a last look at the disappearing horseman, and said smilingly:

"Mr. Miller is welcome to all the satisfaction he will get from his trip to the Lippitt place; we'll hunt for both man and dog at Kilbird. And it's my humble opinion that the man will be about as well worth catching as the dog. I'll squeeze your ten dollars out of him!" he concluded, clenching his fist, while his strong features settled into an expression of grim resolution.

XII

THE VILLAGE LANDLADY

AT Kilbird the boys traced their man to a hotel where he had been staying, and put their question to the landlady, who came out on the porch to speak with them.

"Why, yes," she said; "you mean Mr. Knight?—a very nice man! And the wonderfullest dog I ever did see! He spent the night here last night, and the night before. He hasn't been gone much more than half an hour."

"Gone?" Cliff gasped out, standing with one foot on the porch step. "And the dog—did he have the dog?"

"I'll tell you about that," replied the landlady. "He lost the dog some way, yesterday, and came back last evening without him. The dog didn't come till this morning; Mr. Knight seemed to be waiting for him. He said the dog had a bad trick of straying off, but that he always turned up again."

Cliff stepped up on the porch floor, and said earnestly:

"The man you call Mr. Knight told me his name was Algernon Knight Winslow; and he sold me that very same dog yesterday for ten dollars."

The landlady expressed a great deal of surprise and sympathy, and invited the boys to sit down and rest on a bench inside the cool porch.

"You look kind of beat out," she said, noticing that they were flushed and covered with dust.

But Cliff said they were not tired; they couldn't stop; they were bound to follow Winslow. And he asked:

"Did he take a train?"

"No; he hired my husband to drive him over to Corliss in his buggy."

Quint inquired, "Did he have any baggage?"

"Only a small linen bag, which he left here when he was off on excursions. But he took it with him this morning, saying he didn't expect to come back."

The landlady became exceedingly friendly and sympathetic, and insisted on opening a bottle of spruce beer for the wayfarers, while they rested on the shaded bench. It was a welcome refreshment, and Cliff offered to pay for it, but she laughingly told him to "put up his money." Then perceiving that they nibbled furtively at something they brought out from their pockets, between sips, she entered the house, and presently reappeared with two generous sandwiches, consisting of slices of excellent buttered bread, lined with cold sliced ham.

"You are taking too much trouble!" Cliff exclaimed, with hearty gratitude.

"You seem to be proper nice boys," she replied; "and I'm very glad to give you a little treat, after you have been so imposed upon. I shall want you to write your names in our book. I'll bring it right out here, with a pen, so you can be eating all the while."

"Cliff," said Quint, glancing over his shoulder, to see that she was out of hearing,—he held his glass in one hand and his bitten sandwich in the other,—"if I wasn't already fitted out with a tolerably good mother, I know where I'd go to adopt one!"

Cliff nodded and winked, and whispered, as he lifted his glass to his lips, "She's coming back."

She brought the hotel register, which was not a large one, and laying it open on Cliff's knee, offered him a freshly dipped pen.

"You write for both," said Quint.

Cliff wrote in a fair round hand, "J.Q.A. Whistler," saying as he raised the pen, "That small regiment of initials stands for John Quincy Adams; I was afraid there wouldn't be ink enough to write out the name in full, and I didn't want to keep you running to the inkstand."

Then Cliff wrote his own name, "Clifford P. Chantry," made a flourish against both names, and at the right of it put the address—"Biddicut."

"I declare!" exclaimed the landlady, looking down over the end of the bench. "I know your mother! She was Lucinda Clifford, and she married Jonathan Chantry. We were school-girls together, and I was at her wedding. Tell her you have made the acquaintance of Emmeline Small that was, now Mrs. Robert Grover; and that my husband keeps the Grover House, here in Kilbird."

"She'll be pleased enough," said Cliff. "And when I tell her how you treated two strange boys, it isn't going to make her sorry she ever knew you."

She offered to remove the hotel book, but Quint asked to look at it.

"Just a second," he said. "Here's our friend's name, Cliff; did you notice it? A little twisted,—'A. W. Knight,'—with a flourish as long as the cord he gave you to lead the dog by!"

"Burlington!" Cliff exclaimed, reading the address. "He told us Bennington; and here it is as plain as print,"—slapping the register,—"Burlington, Vermont!"

"The trouble with that man is, he forgets," said Quint. "He'll forget us, if we don't hurry along and overhaul him."

XIII

A NICE PET FOR AN OLD COUPLE

FROM Mrs. Grover's husband, whom they soon met, and from other persons of whom they made inquiries, they gained all needful information regarding the movements of Winslow and the dog. They followed fast, and in a little more than an hour, hot with haste, but high in hope, they entered a small village, to which they had traced the fugitives.

It was a village of scattered houses, in front of one of which they found a bareheaded man leaning over a gate. His back was toward them, and he seemed to be gazing very intently up the street. Farther on were other people in doorways or front yards, or standing in the street, all gazing in the same direction. By his leather apron and the sign over his door, the boys perceived that the man leaning on the gate was a shoemaker.

"What's the show?" Quint asked.

"Show!" said the man, turning upon them a look of disgust. "There's no show! And I've been fooled out of five dollars! Clean as a whistle!"

Cliff asked how that had come about, and the man told his story to an intensely interested audience of two.

"A man come along here about an hour ago, and stepped into my shop, to git me to rasp a nail out of his boot. He had a dog he bragged about, and made him do some tricks. We hain't got no children, and we'd been wishin' for some kind of a pet; and when my wife heard the man say he had got out of money, and would have to part with his dog, she looked at me, and I nodded, and then she says, 'How much do you ask for him?' she says. When he said, 'Twenty dollars,' I thought of course 't wa'n't no use for us to think of buyin' him; but as he wanted me to make him an offer, I looked at my wife, and she nodded to me, and I says, 'I'll give three,' I says, without the least idea he'd take me up. He didn't, exactly, but he come down to ten dollars, then to seven, then he said he'd split the difference; and I looked at my wife and she winked to me, and I says, 'All right,' I says, 'I'll give ye five, though I wish to gracious now I'd stuck to my first bid."

"Where's the dog now?" Cliff asked, although he knew well enough already.

The man pointed with his thumb over his shoulder, in the direction in which he and the other villagers had been gazing.

"Skipped!" he said. "Skipped like a hopper! We fed him in the shop, with the doors closed; and he was so nice and quiet, my wife wanted to have him a little while in the kitchen; and I said, 'Yes, but keep him shet in for the present,' I said; for the owner advised us to do that till he'd had time to get well out of the way. There was just a window open, over the kitchen sink; but we didn't think nothin' about that, and he didn't seem to, neither; till all to once—whish!—he was up on that sink and out o' that winder 'fore the scream was out of her mouth. I've got the rheumatiz, and can't run; but she rushed out. There she comes now!"

"Without the dog," said Cliff, gazing eagerly.

The shoemaker's wife had to run the gauntlet of questions from all her neigh-

XIV

AN UNPLEASANT SURPRISE

THE chase became exciting, and our Biddicut boys gave little heed to the circumstance that it was taking them farther and farther from home.

"Winslow will be waiting somewhere

bors, as she returned with excited looks and panting breath to her husband.

"I never see the beat on 't!" she said. "He went off like a sky-rocket, and it's my belief that we never shall see him again."

The boys asked for water, which she brought in a tin dipper, with a trembling hand. It was cold from the pump, and having drunk and condoled with the worthy couple for their loss, they resumed their tramp, without deeming it necessary to proclaim their own personal and peculiar interest in the many-times-sold dog.

for Sparkler to come up with him," Quint observed. "Then he'll be trying to sell him again; so we shall be gaining on him all the while."

Soon a team overtook them—a real "team" this time, consisting of a span of horses harnessed to an empty and clattering farm-wagon. The wayfarers turned up sweaty and appealing faces to the driver; and, pulling reins, he invited them to "hop in." It was a welcome change to the boys, enabling them not only to rest their limbs, but also to get over the road faster than they could have done on foot.

They told their story, while the driver, a farmer of the neighborhood, drove them on a mile or more farther to his own house. There a boy came out, and met them with the exciting news that a man with a thin linen bag had stopped at the door, a little while before, to ask for a glass of milk.

"Yes," he said, in answer to Cliff's eager questions; "the man hadn't been gone long when a dog came. We shouldn't have noticed him, only he ran into the yard and out again, and snuffed around, as if he was following the man."

"That's great news!" Quint exclaimed. " 'T was a judgmatical idea of Winslow's, that glass of milk!" he said aside to Cliff. "I shouldn't object to sampling the pan myself."

"By the way," the farmer called to them as they were hurrying on, "wouldn't *you* like a glass of milk, or a bowl of milk, or a bowl of bread-and-milk? I'm just sitting down to my dinner, and I guess we can give you a plate of boiled victuals too, if you have time to eat it."

"We shouldn't have time for that," Quint replied. "But bread-and-milk and I are good friends. What do you say, Cliff?"

"We are in an awful hurry," said Cliff; "but—such an offer as that!"

They did, however, take time to give their hands and faces a much-needed washing, and to brush their dusty clothes on the back porch. Meanwhile, the farmer's daughters—two merry young girls, whose bright eyes made our Biddicut boys feel untidy and awkward—placed bread-and-milk on the table opposite the single plate set for their father's late dinner; his family having dined in his absence.

They were profuse in their thanks at parting. But the farmer said:

"You are quite welcome. If you come back this way, stop in. My name is Mills. You may want another bite by that time; and I shall want to hear how you make out dog-hunting."

"Wasn't that bread-and-milk a god-send!" said Cliff, when they were once more on the road. "That meal may have to last us till we get home to supper."

"Home to supper!" Quint replied, with a laugh. "I gave that up hours ago. We shall be lucky if our folks see us at breakfast-time tomorrow—or dinner! We're in for it, Cliff!—did you know it?"

"The worst of it is," said Cliff, "we're beginning to look like a couple of tramps; anyhow, that's the way I feel."

"Was it the pretty girls back there that made you feel so?" Quint queried.

"I couldn't help looking at myself with their eyes, and wishing I had better clothes on," Cliff blushingly acknowledged. "And I wish we had more money. I'm afraid we shan't have enough to get home with."

"Winslow is our bank," replied Quint. "The farther we go, the more need there is of our catching him. We can't turn back."

They walked fast again, being sure of their trail, and soon got news of Winslow and the dog traveling together. It was easy to trace them; for as he went on through the well-settled but open country, Winslow offered the dog to almost everybody he met, stopping to talk often; so that our Biddicut boys felt at length that they had the trick-dog merchant almost within view.

They were unaccustomed to such journeys; their legs were beginning to ache. Cliff suffered from a pain in his side, Quint was unpleasantly reminded that his shoe hurt him, and both discovered that bread-and-milk, and the few berries they picked by the wayside, were a diet deficient in staying qualities. But now, inspired by the certain nearness of their game, they forgot soreness and fatigue; and Quint, whose breath held out better than Cliff's, proposed that they should try a trot.

"A *dog*-trot," he said, with a laugh. "Think you can stand it?"

"Yes, if my confounded side-ache doesn't take me again," replied Cliff.

They set their hands to their hips, each with his coat hooked on one arm, and jogged on in silence, Quint always a pace or two ahead.

"I'm getting my second wind," he said presently. "I feel more like running than I did two or three hours ago. Don't you?"

"Y-e-s!" said Cliff, admiring his companion's easy and steady lope. "We ought to get sight of 'em—from the top—of that knoll!" speaking with difficulty.

"Hello!" said Quint, "there's a crossing that's going to bother us."

Crossings and forks were their chief source of delay and vexation, but for which they must have overtaken the fugitives long before. This one, however, hindered them hardly long enough to enable Cliff to recover breath. Fresh dog-tracks were discovered, and a little further on they saw a man mowing briers by the roadside fence.

Yes, he had seen a man and a dog pass ten or fifteen minutes before.

"Did he want to sell his dog?"

"No; he just asked how far it was to the Snelling farm. That's a great stock-farm, where they have all sorts of live critters. You can see it from the top of the hill above here, a spread of buildings, with a tall windmill and a red-painted water-tank."

Wild roses in bloom, and raspberry bushes in full bearing, were the briers the man was cutting. The boys hurriedly picked and ate the berries while they talked.

"It seems too bad to cut them," said Quint.

"They spread into the fields," replied the man. "Wild roses don't do no good, and I never git none of the berries."

He slashed away at the briers, while the boys hastened on.

"Wild roses don't do no good!" Quint repeated disdainfully. "And he cuts the raspberries because he never gets none! A good man enough, I guess, but not exactly my style."

He had cut off a spray of the wild roses, which he stuck in his hat-band. Cliff carried a raspberry branch, plucking and eating the berries as they pushed on.

They were soon at the summit of the hill, gazing down upon a long stretch of open road; and near by, on the left, the orchards and buildings and windmill of the great Snelling farm.

"No such need of hurrying now," said Quint, wiping his forehead. "We must save our wind for emergencies. If he's there, he'll stay till we come. Then there's no knowing what will happen!" He laughed grimly.

They put on their coats, and talked in low tones, as they walked, still at a brisk pace, under the shelter of some orchard trees growing near the street.

"You look out for the dog; get hold of him the first thing, and leave me to deal with Winslow," said Quint. "Keep cool!" for he saw that Cliff was excited.

They came in sight of the great granite posts of the Snelling gateway, before entering which they stopped to wait for a carriage coming toward them along the road beyond. The driver answered their concise inquiries without drawing rein. He had met no man and dog.

"Then he's here!" Quint said to his companion, as with all their senses alert they turned in at the open gate.

One branch of a broad driveway curved in toward the front of the house; the other led to the rear, and to the farm-buildings beyond. This the boys followed, keeping close to a thick border of Norway spruces that thrust out heavy boughs above their heads. So they came to an open coach-house in the doorway of which an old coachman in overalls was polishing the brass mountings of a handsome harness.

"Have you seen a man and a dog come into the place lately?" Cliff asked, in a low voice, which he couldn't keep from trembling.

"I have, not many minutes ago," replied the old coachman. "He inquired for Mr. Snelling, and they have just gone into the yards together."

"The yards?—where are they?"

The old coachman dropped his polishing-brush on a chair, dusted his fingers on his overalls, and said, "Come along." The boys were careful to keep a little behind him, and partially concealed by his broad shoulders, as he passed the gate toward an open shed between two barns. There was a sound of voices in that direction, and presently the old man said:

"There's Mr. Snelling, patting the cow's neck, and there's your man with his dog."

The little group was in an angle of the shed, not twenty yards away. The boys peered over the shoulders of their guide, eager to command the situation, yet cautious of exposing themselves to view. He had stopped; they stopped too, in sudden amazement.

The man in the shed with Mr. Snelling was putting a rope on the cow's horns. He was an Irish laborer, and his dog was an ugly bull-terrier!

"Wasn't there another man?" Cliff gasped.

The old coachman had seen no other, and no other dog. Quint was utterly dismayed. But he soon recovered his equanimity, and questioned the Irish laborer.

The man had been sent for the cow from a farm about two miles away; and it appeared that he had come by the cross-road at the corner of which the boys had last stopped to look for tracks, and found them, although they were probably those of the wrong dog.

"Well, Quint, what now?" said Cliff, almost ready to cry with disappointment and vexation.

"What time is it?" Quint asked, turning to the coachman, who pulled out a big silver watch, and obligingly turned the full moon of its rimmed face toward the boys. "Thank you," said Quint. "Only half-past two. Earlier than I thought."

"We might get home to-night, if we start now," said Cliff. "We've lost the trail."

"But we may pick it up again," replied Quint. "If you are tuckered out and discouraged, you can rest here, while I start out alone to make discoveries."

"If you keep on, I shall," said Cliff. "It was partly on your account I felt we ought to take the shortest cut home."

Quint answered with a droll smile: "As for me, I'm just finding out what my gambrel-roof nose is for; it's to follow through thick and thin the man who named it. Come on!"

XV

"AN ENGLISH LORD WITH SIX TRUNKS"

THE cook of the Star Grove Hotel was old and lame and cross, and she was put into specially ill humor that afternoon by being called upon to broil a beefsteak for a late-arriving traveler.

"He's just as pleasant as he can be," said light-footed Jenny Ray, a college girl turned waitress for the summer, coming from the dining-room, after serving the traveler. "He told me to give this to the only cook he has found since he has been in the States who knows how to broil a beefsteak."

The old woman had seated herself in the broad-roofed, open passage connecting the dining-room and the summer kitchen, and was cooling her flushed face and heated temper in the breeze that blew freshly through.

"Huh!" she said, looking at the coin which Jenny dropped into her hand. "Since he has been in the States? He's an English gentleman, I'll be bound. Is there anything else he would like? There's a little of that sherbet left in the freezer."

The English gentleman *would* like the sherbet, and it was served accordingly.

"I hope he has come for the rest of the season," the old cook muttered to herself. "Well, what do *you* want?"

Two tired, dusty, forlorn-looking boys came around a corner of the hotel, and stood waiting to have a word with her.

"We don't find anybody in the office," said the younger of the two.

"The office generally runs itself from now till the five-o'clock coach arrives," she replied. "What might you be wanting in the office?"

"We are looking for an acquaintance," said the older boy, who was also the taller, and had a well-developed nose on a strong, honest face.

"We thought he might have come to this hotel."

"He had on a loose-fitting brown coat, and he had a dog with him, the last we heard," said the younger boy—Cliff Chantry, in short.

"There's been no such person here, with or without a dog," said the old woman sourly. "There's been no arrival this afternoon, but an English gentleman, about an hour ago."

Cliff's face wore a hopeless expression; it seemed useless to pursue the inquiry. But Quint queried:

"An English gentleman?"

"An English gentleman," she repeated haughtily. "He isn't the first one that's honored this house, and I hope he won't be the last. We had an English lord here once, and I'm thinking this is another."

That she was not to prove a treasury of obliging information was evident enough. But Quint said:

"Did he—your English lord—come afoot, and carry a linen grip-sack; was his shirt-collar just the least mite frayed about the edges?"

With her other excellent qualities the old cook possessed a bold imagination, to which she now gave free rein.

"He came in a carriage from the station, and he has six trunks coming this evening. He engaged the two best rooms in the house by letter, and ordered a beefsteak by telegraph. Not at all the sort of gentleman you claim as an acquaintance. Frayed shirt-collar, indeed!"

The glowering look with which she said this discouraged further questions. The boys stepped aside for a brief consultation.

It was now two hours since they had lost Winslow's trail; and they had worn out their strength and patience in the vain endeavor to pick it up again. Since the bread-and-milk they had had at the Mills farm-house, they had tasted nothing but cold water and wayside berries, and they were faint with hunger. At the close of their whispered consultation, Quint said:

"Beefsteaks are not exactly in our line; but if you can give us a couple of sandwiches, we'll be glad to pay you for your trouble."

The old cook answered tartly, "The Star Grove Hotel ain't a sandwich-shop, I'd have you know. There's a grocery in the village."

"I gave them a string of yarns as long as a kite-tail!" the old woman chuckled with malicious glee, as they disappeared around the corner of the hotel.

"But why did you?" said Jenny. "They seemed to be honest boys."

"Claiming any guest of this house as a friend of theirs, and asking for sandwiches!" scoffed the cook. "Of course they never expected to pay for 'em. An English lord—he, he! And six trunks!"

Meanwhile the possible British nobleman strolled into the reading-room, where he glanced at the newspapers for a few minutes; then he took a turn or two on the long hotel piazza, and finally came around to the roofed passage where the cook still sat at her ease cooling her round face in the refreshing breeze.

She was rather unpleasantly reminded of the two boys' description of their "friend," when she noticed the singular coincidence that this foreign tourist also had on a loosely fitting brown coat, and a standing shirt-collar frayed about the edges.

In suavity of manner, however, he was all that Jenny's words and her own fancy had painted him. With an ingratiating smile he inquired:

"Have you, madam, seen a stray dog about here anywhere, while I have been in the dining-room?"

This was another remarkable coincidence. Without waiting for a reply, he went on glibly:

"Mine chased a squirrel into some woods back here, and I left him barking up a tree. He'll turn up before long, and if he doesn't find me the first thing, he'll make for the kitchen door. That's a rule of his: a moral principle." He laughed and looked about him. "Your hotel is delightfully situated. That shady retreat is very inviting."

He walked back into the hotel, and presently reappearing with a light duster on, strolled out into the grove.

The old cook watched him with a curiously puzzled expression.

"An English lord with six trunks!" she repeated to herself with a derisive titter. "I suppose I ought to have told him his friends are looking for him; but that's none of my business. See the cheek of him now," she suddenly exclaimed; "stretching himself in Mrs. Mayhew's hammock, that she's so awful particular about. But that's not my affair either. I've something else to think of, from now till supper-time."

XVI

THE HOT BOX

ON their way to the grocery the boys noticed three or four wagons halted on a side street, and a group of men and boys standing near one of them. After they had provided themselves with a luncheon of crackers and cheese, Quint left Cliff sitting on the grocery steps, and went to speak with the teamsters.

An axle-box of a heavy draft-wagon loaded with wood had become heated by friction, and the wheel had ceased to revolve. It was a rear wheel, and three men were lifting that corner of the load by means of a plank used as a lever. Two others were swinging upon the wheel thus raised a few inches from the ground, while the one they were aiding gripped the spokes opposite the hub. One of the bystanders was holding a stick and a pot of grease, ready to give the axle the necessary oiling as soon as it was exposed.

Seeing the wheel loosening a little, Quint also laid hold of the spokes, and forgetting how weary he was from his all-day tramp, helped pull it off.

"You've a pretty good grip, young man!" the teamster said to him. "I'm much obliged to everybody."

Then, while the grease was being applied, Quint introduced his own business to a remarkably well-disposed audience. The driver of a light carryall remarked:

"Your man was a slim-waisted party, not above three or four and twenty?—and the dog looked like some kind of a spaniel? —had on a collar with nickel-headed studs on it?"

"The very same!" cried Quint.

"That party," said the driver of the light carryall, "begged a ride of me this afternoon, and took his dog with him into the wagon."

From the information he proceeded to give, Quint concluded that Winslow and Sparkler had been taken up not far from the crossing where he and Cliff lost track of them. The driver of the light carryall had come from that direction, and was now on his way back.

"How far did you carry them?" Quint inquired.

"May be a couple of miles in this direction, and then half a mile off on the Fulton road, where I had business with a man by the name of Ames. I left your chap there trying to sell his dog. I am driving right back in that direction. I can take you along and show you the house."

"I jump at that!" Quint exclaimed. "Only please wait till I can speak to my chum."

Cliff, as he confessed afterward, was feeling that he could never get up from those grocery steps, when Quint came hurrying toward him with the exciting news. He was off the steps in an instant, quite forgetting that he had ever known fatigue; and in three minutes they were riding away with their new friend. He was

sociable and had a good deal to say about Winslow; among other things this:

"Before he got into my wagon, he took a long, glossy duster out of a bag, whipped the dust from his shoulders with it, and then put it on over his coat. There didn't seem to be much left in the bag; so he just made a roll of it, which he held in his lap, or under his arm. His dog lay in the bottom of the wagon, where he wouldn't be much noticed."

"That accounts for our losing trace of them so suddenly," said Cliff. "For we made inquiries all along that road."

They related their adventures, and Quint asked the driver if he knew the Mills farm-house, where they were treated to bread and milk, and were laughed at by two bright girls.

"I rather think I do!" the man replied, with a broadening smile. "My name is Putney. If you had mentioned it, those girls might have told you I won my wife in that house. She is their eldest sister."

The boys were delighted to hear this, and went on praising the hospitality of the Mills household in a way that caused their new friend to take to them more and more.

"It isn't over three quarters of a mile from my house to theirs, across country," he said. "Now, I'll tell you what I'll do. I'll drive you to Ames's; then if you find you've missed your man again, and don't see much chance of catching him or the dog, I'll put you on the way to my father-in-law's, where I advise you to pass the night; or I'll keep you over myself. Then you can start out fresh in the morning."

The boys were touched by the kindness of this proposal, and impressed by the wisdom of the advice. To Cliff particularly it seemed as if it would be the most blissful thing imaginable to settle down in some quiet farm-house for the night, talk over their adventures after a good supper, and then go to bed. He felt, as he told Quint afterward, as if he would like to sleep about forty hours out of the next twenty-four. He almost hoped that, if they didn't come upon Winslow or Sparkler, they might not get any encouraging news of them, so that they would not feel obliged to bestir themselves further in the thankless business.

The road was smooth, the country pleasant, the sun low, and the air cool; and the boys were enjoying greatly their restful mode of travel, when Quint suddenly threw up his hands, and uttered a startling cry.

"There! Look! Hold on!"—at the same time making an instinctive clutch at the reins.

Cliff looked, and saw before them, coming on the roadside, running fast, a dog—the dog they sought—there could be no doubt of it—the trick-dog Sparkler!

XVII

A MEETING AND A PARTING

"OH, jingo!" Cliff exclaimed. "Stop him! Stop him!" Whether he meant to "stop the horse," or "stop the dog," he himself could not have told. Before the wagon came to a halt, the boys tumbled themselves down over the wheel and foot-board, and rushed with outstretched hands to head off the fugitive. Sparkler was running directly toward them; and Cliff almost hoped for a moment that his pet was hastening to meet him, equally eager for their reunion.

But the dog's conduct quickly dispelled that fond fancy. There dangled from his collar just such a piece of cord as he started

with in the morning, as if he had been running with it all day. He passed so near that Cliff actually reached down to clutch it, at the same time calling and coaxing, "Sparkler! Come, Sparkler!" when the animal turned suddenly aside, darted between the horse's legs, escaped under the wagon, and was rods away before the boys were fully aware what had happened.

"That's the dog," sair Mr. Putney.

"Of course it is!" cried Cliff, wildly excited. "He has been sold again!"

"And has gnawed his rope," said Quint.

"What will you do?" their new friend asked—"follow him, or drive on with me, and see if you can find his master?"

"His master has gone in the direction the dog took," said Quint. "Following one, we follow both."

"We can trace the dog more easily now, as we did in the morning, with the flying piece of cord to attract attention," cried Cliff, once more full of the ardor of pursuit.

"Sorry to bid you and your carryall good-by, Mr. Putney," said Quint; "but you see how it is." And the boys shouted back their thanks and good-bys as they ran.

The tide of human life, which had been at its lowest ebb when the Biddicut boys first touched at the Star Grove Hotel, was by this time rising again, in and about that favorite summer resort.

"Where's my maid?" cried a bustling and important woman, coming out upon the piazza. "Where's Betsy? Betsy!" as the maid appeared, trundling a baby-carriage. "Who is that man lounging in my new hammock? Go at once!—say you have orders to take the hammock in, as its owner thinks it will rain. Dear me, what dog is that? How strangely he acts! Don't dare to touch him, Philip! He may be mad."

The dog, just arrived, had a short piece of cord attached to his collar, and he was acting strangely indeed. There wasn't the slightest danger of Philip Mayhew or any other boy touching him, although two or three were soon trying to lay hold of the cord.

He ran in at the door and out again, darted between two of his pursuers, who bumped heads as he slipped through their fingers, capered around the corner of the hotel toward the kitchen, occasionally dropping his nose to the ground, and finally ran into the grove, where he jumped joyously upon the trousers of the stranger, who, at Betsy's request, was just then rolling out of the hammock.

"That your dog, mister?" cried Philip.

"He is mine—he is everybody's; at least, everybody seems to think so. What were you boys chasing him for?" said the stranger.

"I thought he had got away from somebody; I saw the rope on his neck," replied Philip.

"That cord is very useful in the performance of one of his favorite tricks," said the owner, with a peculiar laugh—stooping, however, and quickly removing the cord from the dog's collar. "He can do things that will astonish you. If enough of the boarders were interested, I could show you, right here in the grove, or on the hotel piazza, what a wonderful dog he is."

"Show us his tricks! Oh, mister, show us some of his tricks!" clamored the boys.

"Get some men—some ladies—somebody that can appreciate the most intelligent canine creature in the world," said the owner, looking around on his not very satisfactory audience of nurses and children. Just then the hotel gong sounded. "It's of no use now. Perhaps after supper—" He stooped again and caressed the dog. "Look alive now!"

The animal sat up immediately, raising his fore paws, to the delight of the boys and nurses.

"What do you want? Food?"

The dog made no motion, but watched his master with bright, intelligent eyes.

"No; he has been fed, and so have I. Walk? take a walk?" The dog dropped one of his lifted paws. "That means 'yes'; he would like to take a walk and see something of the beautiful country around here. I approve of his judgment. You see what sort of a prodigy he is, and you'll know what to expect if I am back in time to show you some of his tricks this evening."

About half an hour after this our two Biddicut boys came panting up the Star Grove driveway. They had had more trouble than they expected in following Sparkler, having lost track of him in consequence of an unexpected turn he had made; and had learned to their bewilderment, that such a dog had been seen going toward the very hotel they had so lately visited.

Eager to verify this report, they hastened up the piazza steps and met the office-clerk in the doorway. Yes, he said, a dog with a cord hanging from his collar had been dodging about there a little while ago, and he had last seen him running around the corner of the hotel pursued by some boys.

Where were the boys? At supper. Which corner of the hotel? He told them; and a minute later Quint and Cliff were standing on the spot where they had interviewed the crusty-tempered old cook.

The cook was no longer there, but presently Jenny Ray appeared, with some dishes on a tray, between the dining-room and the kitchen. She recognized them, and smiled at their question.

"The dog was here only a little while ago," she told them, "and I believe that the man himself was in the dining-room at the very time you were inquiring for him."

"The English lord!" exclaimed Cliff.

Jenny laughed. "The cook told me how she fooled you. It was too bad!"

"I'd like to fan her with her own gridiron!" said Quint indignantly. "Where is he now—the man who was in the dining-room?"

"I don't know; he was in the grove till his dog came and found him. But I can't stop longer!" And Jenny went on into the kitchen.

The boys hastened to the grove, where they found a nurse with two small children, and learned from her that Winslow had gone off with his dog shortly after the supper-gong sounded.

She showed the way he had taken through the grove, and they started in pursuit.

XVIII

THE WAYSIDE SHED

A DRIVEWAY skirting the grove in the rear of the hotel led to an open road not far beyond. This the boys soon reached, and they were fortunate in hearing of Winslow and the dog before much time was lost in looking for tracks along the road.

They found themselves in a beautiful upland, with the grove on their left, a rolling farm region on the other side, and before them a pleasant road stretching away to the westward, across a cool valley, toward distant wooded hills. The sun was not yet setting, but masses of black cloud with wondrously illuminated edges surging up in a wild sky cast a strange gloom over all the landscape.

"There's rain-water in that cloud," said Quint, "and thunder and lightning. I've felt a storm brewing all the afternoon."

"Do you believe it will come here?" Cliff asked.

"If it keeps on the way it is moving, we shall get it," Quint replied. "The lightning is having a circus!" as the black face of the cloud crinkled with sudden flashes.

At no time during the day had they felt more certain hope of coming up with their game. If Winslow did not turn back on his course, or lose time by offering Sparkler for sale, and so allow them to gain upon him, he must soon, they reasoned, seek shelter from the coming storm; and they determined not to pass a wayside house without stopping to make inquiries.

These stops caused some delay; but they succeeded in keeping his trail, and came at length to a gloomy hollow, where there was a solitary farm-house a little back from the street, and an open wagon-shed on the roadside. A short distance beyond this the road made a fork, arrived at which they were again puzzled, as they had been similarly so many times in the course of that day's adventure. Although it was not yet night, the shadow of the advancing storm was gathering so fast that they would hardly have been able to detect footprints, even if any had been impressed in the hard, gravelly road-bed.

"Well! what now, Quint?" said Cliff, his face showing pale and anxious in a gleam of lightning which just then lit up the landscape.

"I'll go ahead on this left-hand road, which shows most travel," Quint replied, "while you wait here, or perhaps go as far as the first farm-house on the other branch. Whether we find out anything or not, we'll both come back here; and the one who comes first will wait for the other under the shed. That will be as good a shelter as any when the storm breaks."

A feeling of dread came over Cliff at the

thought of parting from his friend, even for a brief interval, at such a crisis. The increasing darkness, the dazzling lightning, the far-off thunder rolling ever nearer, and the utter loneliness of their strange surroundings, filled him with vague forebodings. But without breathing a syllable of his shuddering fears, he agreed to Quint's plan. So they separated at the fork, and hurried on their separate ways, bushy and hilly fields soon hiding each from the other's view.

Cliff had not gone far before he came to a farm-house, where he was assured no such man as he inquired for had been seen. A little farther on he met a wagon, the driver of which pulled up his horses reluctantly, shook his head sullenly, and with an anxious look at the sky, whipped his horses on again.

Cliff did not stop long to consider what he should do. A dazzling zigzag rift running across the blackness of the heavens, followed by an appalling crash of thunder and splashes of rain, put an end to all irresolution.

"By jingo!" he exclaimed aloud, with thrills of fear crawling all over him, "I am going back!"

He hoped to find Quint in the shed before him; but it was empty. It was a most desolate place, but he was glad to have a roof between him and the lightning-riven sky and echoing thunder. He stood at the great opening and looked out, straining his eyes in the obscurity, or blinking at the glare, and listening for footsteps, caring little now for Winslow, but longing for Quint to come. He seemed to think that, whatever happened, it wouldn't be half so bad if his friend were present; such comfort is companionship in times of trouble.

He explored the shed. At one end was an old tip-cart, while nearer the center was a farm wagon, run in diagonally with the neap pushed into the vacant corner above a manger at the rear. He discovered, to his satisfaction, that the manger contained bundles of straw. This he gathered up, and made a bed of it on the ground against the end of the shed. Then again he stood in the opening, looking, listening, longing for his friend. A wind was rising, and the gusts blew whiffs of rain into his face, causing him to draw farther back beneath the roof.

"Wishing won't fetch him, and worrying won't do any good," he said; and yielding to a sense of overpowering weariness, he lay down upon his bed of straw.

He remembered how often, under the attic roof at home, he had been lulled to rest by the mild music of the wind and rain. Something like the same influence stole over him now, and he thought what comfort it would be to cuddle down there, forgetting Winslow and Sparkler and all anxiety and care, and sink into blissful slumber!

But where all the while was Quint?

It was darker again, but still light enough for him to perceive anybody who might be passing on the road. He still thought of Winslow, but his chief solicitude was to see the tall lank form of his friend appear at the opening. Had some accident happened to him? What could keep him so long? It had not rained hard at first, but now the torrents came down with a rushing sound.

He tried to console himself with the reflection that Quint had sought shelter in some farm-house; but that wouldn't be like Quint. All at once the tired boy stopped thinking altogether. A whole procession of dogs and Winslows might have passed; Quint's mysterious absence, his own pains and fatigues and disappointments, thunder and lightning and wind and rain—he was sweetly oblivious of all, fast asleep on his bed of straw.

XIV

"WHAT DO YOU WANT OF ME?"

QUINT proceeded some distance, making fruitless inquiries at farm-houses, and meeting no travelers. At length he came to a cross-road presenting the usual difficulties, and he saw the uselessness of keeping on.

"Cross-roads, I should say!" he muttered, as he stood and gazed off in the three directions, any one of which Winslow might have taken. "They make *me* cross enough. Well! that's rather sharp!"

It was a frightful flash of lightning, with its quickly following peal. Still he stood deliberating, holding out his hand to catch the raindrops.

It was a lonely situation, surrounded by barren and bushy fields, except on one side, where a clump of dark woods straggled down to the very corner of the cross-roads. He stood among the scattered trees,—stunted oaks and hard pines,—and strained his every nerve to watch and listen.

He was on the point of turning reluctantly back, when he heard quick footsteps, and presently perceived, a little way before him, the figure of a man walking fast in the middle of the road. Quint stepped out from the wayside to accost him.

"Good evening, stranger," he began, and stopped.

No need to put the inquiry that was on his lips. A lightning flash just then flooded heaven and earth, and poured its white instantaneous glare on the two human figures facing each other in that terrible solitude.

"Hullo!" said the dog-seller, skipping aside with an exceedingly alert movement, very much as if he had been stopped by a highwayman. "What do you want of me?"

Quint also took a step, so that he still confronted him. "You know pretty well what I want! I see you remember me."

"Remember you?" cried Winslow with a light laugh. "Brutus—or Cassius?—which is it? Brutus, I believe. Well, Marcus Brutus, what can I do for you? This is really like meeting an old friend!"

Quint had many times rehearsed to himself what he would do and say upon the chance of falling in with Winslow; but the present occasion was so different from any he had foreseen, that he hardly knew how he alone was to deal with the swindler. But his wits did not desert him. Cliff was too far away to be called to his assistance; he must then try to take Winslow to Cliff.

"If you don't object," he said, "I'll walk along with you."

"All right!" said Winslow. "But you seemed to be going in the opposite direction."

"You were going in that direction too, a short time ago," said Quint, falling in by his side.

"I was out for a little walk," said Winslow. "Now I am going back."

"Just my case," said Quint. "I was out for a walk, and now I am going back."

"And I've got to hurry, for I don't care to get wet," said Winslow, quickening his step.

"Just my case every time," said Quint, keeping at his side. "I don't fancy a wetting."

"I shall be drenched before I get back to the Star Grove Hotel, if I don't run for it!" And Winslow broke into a light trot.

"That's a nice house—worth running for," observed Quint, always within easy clutching distance of the dog-seller's right arm. And he calculated, with secret glee, that their present rate of speed would in

five minutes bring them to the shed where
Cliff would soon be, if he wasn't there
already.

It seemed as if Winslow must have read
his mind. He was certainly suspicious of
Quint's too evident willingness to accompany him in that direction. All at once he
stopped.

"It is too far," he said. "It will pour before I get half-way there. I am going back
to a house I passed just before I saw you."

"There's a house only a little farther
on," replied Quint; "and just beyond the
forks of the road is a shed we can wait
under till the shower is over."

Winslow turned and faced him with a
sarcastic grin.

"The shed wouldn't be big enough for
us both. I am going back."

"I'm afraid it will be lonesome there
without you; guess I'll go back, too"; and
turning as Winslow turned, Quint still
kept close by his side.

"Now, look here, young man!" cried
Winslow. "This is a great country—big as
all outdoors! It almost seems as if there
was room in it for me and you and your
gambrel-roof nose without crowding."

"I'll try not to crowd you," Quint answered; "but the fact is, poor company is
better than none on such a night as this."

"My amiable friend," cried Winslow, his
tones growing hard and sharp and menacing, "doesn't it appeal to your common
sense that a person has a right to choose
his own company in this land of the free
and home of the brave?"

"That's just what I think," said Quint;
"and I choose yours."

For a moment Winslow made no response as he walked fast back toward the
crossing, Quint's elbow constantly close
to his own.

Quint would have yelled for Cliff, but
he wasn't sure Cliff was within hearing;
and he hoped Winslow would yet conclude

to return to the Star Grove Hotel. Upon
one thing the boy from Biddicut was fully
determined—to stick to him until, with or
without Cliff's assistance, he had got back
Cliff's money. The dog was not with his
master; but Quint cared little for that
often-sold animal.

Their hurried footsteps were the only
sounds on that lonely road; but now and
then the thunder tumbled down the cloudy
crags of heaven, and the leaping lightning
severed the gloom of the storm and night.
On reaching the wooded corner, Winslow
turned sharply on his unwelcome companion.

"I'm inclined to the opinion," he said,
"that it's about time for you and me to
come to some sort of an understanding."

"This seems to be a good place for it,"
Quint replied, sternly regarding him. "We
needn't be afraid of an interruption."

"Then have the kindness to inform me
just why you dog my footsteps in this
way," said Winslow threateningly.

"Because I can't *dog* them in any other,"
Quint replied. "I'm not a Sparkler."

"I see the point," remarked Winslow.
"State your case, and we'll settle it on the
spot. If not in one way, then in another.
A very good spot, as you say!"

"You know the case perfectly well,"
said Quint, without heeding the threat.
"You go about the country selling that
dog. You have sold him once too often.
That's my case, Mr. Algernon Knight
Winslow!"

"I never sold him to you!" Winslow retorted, insolent and defiant. "You are not
Cassius."

"Cassius and I are solid in this business," said Quint. "You have got back
your dog; now we want our money."

"How much?" Winslow asked, as coolly
as if he had been prepared to fork out
millions.

All the while the rain was slowly pat-

tering, and the lightning was winking at them as they confronted each other on the edge of the lonely woods.

For a moment Quint had hope of bringing the dog-seller to an easy settlement.

"You remember the agreement you put your name to. We gave you ten dollars. I want the twenty you promised." And he held out his hand.

"Was that the bargain? Show me the paper you say I signed. Business is business," said Winslow.

"Come with me," Quint replied, "and I'll show you the paper in the presence of witnesses."

"Bring on your witnesses. I'll wait here," said Winslow, stepping under the trees on the dreary roadside, and placing his back against one of the largest trunks.

A DESPERATE ENCOUNTER

XX

QUINT also stepped aside under the trees and stood facing him.

The dark woodland beyond looked impenetrably dense until lighted up by a vivid flash that showed each silent trunk distinct in its space, and quiet saplings ranged on each side of a broken and ruined wayside wall. The utter solitude, the surrounding desolation, the fitful gleams and peals, the on-coming night and storm, might well have tried the nerves of one older and more experienced than Quint, but no one could have been more determined.

"I can wait here as long as you can," he said; coolly adding, "I don't think there's going to be much of a shower."

Winslow moved to a fallen tree-trunk and sat down upon it. Quint guessed there was room for two, and sat down beside him.

"How long have you been following me?" The dog-seller's tone was quite friendly now.

"All day," Quint replied. "Cassius and I have been on the war-path ever since the dog got away this morning."

"Seems to me you are giving yourselves a deal of trouble for a small matter," Winslow remarked sarcastically.

"It's no small matter to us, let me tell you," Quint replied. "Ten dollars is a big sum to a poor country boy. It's more than my chum had saved up in all his life; that's why he borrowed of me. Now we are bound to have it back, with something for our trouble."

"You are a precious pair of country bumpkins!" said Winslow laughing. "But I rather like your pluck. Come now, be reasonable. What will you settle for?"

"Twenty dollars," Quint responded in a direct and quiet tone.

"That's absurd! I haven't got so much money as that."

"You've got more than that, Mr. Winslow. Before you sold that dog to us you sold him to Mr. Miller in the town of Wormwood. To-day you sold him first to an old shoemaker, then again to somebody else, just before you went to the Star Grove Hotel, and you've sold him again this evening. How many more times you have sold him," Quint went on, "you know better than I do. You certainly have money, and the best thing in the world for you to do, Mr. Winslow, is to hand out mine." And he looked squarely at the dog-seller over four feet of pine log between them.

"And what if I decline to give up to you my hard-earned profits?" sneered Winslow.

"Then I'll see that you don't earn any more in that way; I'll see that you are put where even your dog can't find you! That's the size of it, Mr. Winslow."

The dog-seller laughed derisively.

"You imagine you can make people believe your absurd story? I deny every word of it. I never sold you and Cassius a dog. Never sold anybody a dog. My dog is not for sale; he is with my mother in Michigan. Besides, I never had a dog. If you have a paper signed with my name it's a forgery. I don't sign my name to papers. More than all that, my name is not Winslow."

He rattled this off with bewildering volubility, and taking a knife from his pocket, opened it with a peculiar motion, and began to stick the blade into the log they sat on—merely to display his weapon, Quint thought. It was not so dark but that Quint could see that the blade was long and bright. He also took out his knife and began to stab the log.

"It's funny, then," said he, "what we have hunted you all day for!"

"I know what for," cried Winslow. "You have trumped up false charges against me, and think you'll force me to buy you off. That's what I say and what I'll maintain."

"And the other people you've swindled, —I know just where to find some of them, —how will it be when they come to tell their stories?" Quint demanded.

"Brutus!" said the dog-seller, snapping his knife shut and putting it into his pocket, "I'll give you five dollars, and you shall go your way and I'll go mine."

Quint quietly closed and pocketed his own knife, and asked dryly:

"You will submit, then, to our 'false charges' as you call them?"

"I'll submit to anything for a dry skin. We're a couple of fools to sit here and palaver when our little affair can be compromised so easily."

"So I think. But five dollars won't compromise it," said Quint.

"Very well, then!" exclaimed Winslow, a blaze of lightning showing a sinister resolution on his keen face; "we'll sit it out. I've got on a waterproof; I think I can stand it, if you can!"

"I've got a better waterproof than that," said Quint, with ominously set lips. "I'm going to get mad by and by; that will keep me from caring about the weather. You'd better not put off settling too long."

The thunder was terrific. Then, between the peals, a rushing and roaring sound could be heard, distant and faint at first, then nearer and louder, and they knew that the storm, with tempest and down-pouring and fracas of tossing boughs, was sweeping toward them over the woods and fields. The lightning shot through fringes of the coming rain, and shone in the large, near, slant-streaking drops.

Winslow turned up the collar of his duster, or waterproof, and pulled the flaps over his exposed knees. Quint likewise turned up his coat-collar, and buttoned the top button, remarking coolly:

"When this tree gets wet through, we can move under another."

The pleasantry did not appeal to Winslow's sense of humor. He sprang to his feet with an outburst of unquotable adjectives, threw down his head against the gusts, and exclaiming," I'm going to get out of this!" started to run.

Quint started at the same time, catching him by the arm.

"Hands off!" Winslow yelled, in the turmoil of rain and wind and thrashing boughs. "Don't stop me! or I'll—. Take that—on your gambrel-roof nose!" with which half-stifled ejaculation, he whirled and aimed a furious blow at Quint's head.

Quint ducked in time to receive only a glancing stroke on his crown. Then throwing up an elbow to parry a second blow, he made a headlong dive at Winslow's waist; he closed with him, and in a minute the two were engaged in a desperate struggle.

They were about equally matched as to weight; but the lank Biddicut boy was the taller and longer-limbed of the two. He had had some school-boy practice at scuffling and wrestling; and his mates had usually found him what they termed a "tough customer" in their rough-and-tumble contests. If one attempted to lift him from the ground, his feet seemed to stick to it, as if they had glue on them, and his sinewy legs to stretch out like legs of india-rubber.

He gripped Winslow firmly about the waist, at first with the sole idea of holding him, and of shielding his own head and face from the blows. With his right arm he managed to secure his favorite under-hold, while his left fought, and finally grappled, Winslow's right.

Though slight of build, Winslow was lithe and athletic, and a more formidable adversary than he appeared. Forced to desist from his blows, he cried in a lull of the scuffle:

"Will you let go now and go your way, while I go mine?"

"Your way will be mine till you give me my money!" Quint replied.

"I'll give you a broken back over that log!" Winslow snarled. And the struggle recommenced, both settling down to business.

They tugged, and wrenched, and lifted, Winslow trying to throw Quint over the log; Quint avoiding it, and at the same time doing his utmost to get Winslow on his hip, fling him, and fall upon him.

Suddenly Winslow, freeing one hand, got it inside his waterproof, and into his trousers' pocket. But before he could fairly grasp the knife he was evidently reaching for, his arm was clutched again, he was forced violently backward; in another moment he was tripped over the log, and falling, both went down together.

XXI

CLIFF'S AMAZING DISCOVERIES

THROUGH all the tumult of the storm Cliff slumbered on his heap of straw, to be at last awakened by something like a blow grazing his cheek and striking him full upon the breast. He started from his dreams and put out his hand.

He thought he was in his bed at home, and that he had been hit by his brother Amos tumbling about in his sleep. Then it seemed as if something was moving in the room; he heard a rustling sound, and the hand he put out for his brother touched straw.

It was not so dark but that he could see the great open front of the shed, the overhanging roof, and the dim shape of the farm-wagon under it. Recollection returned with a shock, and he was terrified to find that he had fallen asleep while waiting for his friend; he couldn't imagine how long ago. It might have been hours.

"Hullo!" he cried out, in the wild hope that the movements he had heard were those of Quint, who might perhaps have returned.

No answer. But the movements continued. There was some live creature close behind him. The straw rustled at his very side. He started up, thrilled through and through with horrid fear.

Suddenly the blow on his breast was repeated, and a dark object came between him and the light. Something wet touched his hands; something warm and moist flashed, so to speak, across his face.

His companion in the shed was a dog. The wagging tail thumped his arm; the caressing tongue lapped his face. He uttered a sudden cry—something between a gasp of astonishment and a cry of joy.

"Sparkler! Oh, my gracious Jehu! Sparkler! Quint! Quint!" he called; "I've got him!"—as if Quint were near.

Securing a hold of the collar, he hugged the wet creature to his heart.

"You don't get away from me again, you rogue!" he said, in a tremor of excitement, as he pulled from his pocket the cord he had carried all day, slipped one end of it about the dog's collar, and fastened it with a firm knot. "Now this never goes out of my hand!"

Sparkler did not even try to get away; he seemed, on the contrary, to recognize Cliff with pleasure, to which his smiting tail gave vivacious expression.

"Why did you run away from me? Why did you come back? How did you find me here?" said the boy, talking as if his dumb companion could comprehend. "Oh, Sparkler, I wish you could speak! What a story you could tell!"

The exciting occurrence diverted his mind for a minute from its anxieties about Quint. But now he thought of him again with growing amazement and alarm at his mysterious absence. He stilled the dog's movements, and knelt upon the straw, listening and wondering; then advanced to the opening of the shed.

The storm was over; the few drops that fell upon his hand and shoulder came from the still dripping eaves. He went out upon the wet roadside, the dog capering at the end of his cord, and gazed up and down,

feeling sure that some dreadful thing had befallen his friend.

"Oh, Sparkler!" he exclaimed in his misery, "can't you tell me what to do?"

The dog had at first seemed averse to quitting the dark corner of the shed, even bounding back toward the manger when Cliff pulled him away. But now, on the open road, as if he had understood the boy's appeal, he began to tug at the cord in the direction in which Cliff was himself inclined to go.

"Go ahead!" cried Cliff, with sudden hope and confidence. "I'll trust you!"

He was still full of imaginary fears; but he was comforted by the companionship of the dog; and occasionally, through all his troubles, would break a gleam of pure joy at the thought of Sparkler once more in his possession.

At the same time the world was growing lighter and still lighter; and he perceived that the western sky was clearing. A bright star appeared beneath the edge of broken and low-hanging clouds, and shone with inexpressible beauty and purity in the opening rift. Then all at once a flood of white radiance filled the night. Cliff looked up, and there, almost overhead in the wild sky, was the moon. It peered over the edge of a great black rampart of cloud, as if to reassure the storm-buffeted sphere with its cold, placid smile.

Cliff kept on, often pausing, and taxing every sense to discern signs of his lost comrade, until suddenly Sparkler jumped up on the roadside, jerking at the cord. They were on the outskirts of a wood-lot, and a passing gust of wind shook down pattering drops from the branches overhead. The moonlight slanting through the boughs and silvering the undergrowth showed a dark log on the ground, toward which Sparkler led the way.

Near the log was a dark-gray object at

which Sparkler was presently sniffing. Cliff ran to it, stooped over it, caught it up and examined it with astonishment which quickly became consternation. It was a hat —a common felt hat, of a well-worn appearance, with a narrow rim and shapeless crown, crushed as if it had been trampled on, yet just such a hat as his friend had worn; and there, as if more certainly to identify it, was a spray of wild roses, such as Quint had stuck under the band that afternoon.

Cliff's fears were thus confirmed. Quint had certainly had an encounter with the desperate character they were pursuing; and that he had not had the best of it seemed proved by the fact that his hat, and not Winslow's, was left on the field.

But what had happened to him since? In continuing the struggle, he might have met with some terrible mishap, and Cliff's excited imagination pictured his friend lying on the ground, somewhere in the woods, disabled—possibly worse.

He stood in the edge of the moonlit woodland, and called with all his force of throat and lungs.

"Hello-o-o, Quint! Hello-o-o!"

His voice died away in the depths of the forest, and not even an echo came back. A curdling terror crept through his veins.

Sparkler meanwhile tugged at his leash, and sniffed along the ground. The drenching shower must have carried away, for the most part, such evidences of his master's presence as his delicate canine scent would otherwise have been quick to detect and follow; but he was strangely uneasy.

"Oh, Sparkler!" Cliff pleaded, "seek— seek him!"—in the fond belief that, by pursuing Winslow, the dog might help him find his friend.

Sparkler's nose stopped at something half-buried in a clump of moss. It was a bright object, with a shining edge turned up in the moonlight. Cliff darted to pick it up.

"Only a piece of knife-handle!" he exclaimed. "Have they been breaking knives?" he wondered. It appeared to have been trodden into the moss.

He would have thrown it away as something worthless, but for the possibility of its affording some clue to the harrowing mystery.

It was about the size and shape of the thing he took it for; but unlike any knife he had ever seen in Quint's hands. He was carefully scrutinizing it, holding it up in the moonlight with one hand,—the end of the cord in the other, along with Quint's hat,—wholly forgetting Sparkler in that moment of intense thought, when he was reminded of the dog in an unpleasantly surprising manner.

Sparkler, who had been sniffing again about his feet, gave a sudden bounce, the cord was jerked from Cliff's relaxed hold, and in an instant the dog darted away in the checkered moonshine, with the cord flying like a faint streak at his heels.

"He's gone!" said Cliff, in rage and despair. "Let him go! I don't care if I never see him again! I wish I had never seen him!"

XXII

CAPTOR OR CAPTIVE?

QUINT's hat had been knocked off by the first glancing blow from Winslow's fist; and when, in the final struggle, he plunged after Winslow over the log, he struck his unprotected head against the root of a tree. Though partially stunnned, he was on his feet again almost immediately, but only in time to see a dim figure dart away in the rain, in the direction of the cross-road.

Without waiting to recover his hat or to search for the knife, which he thought flew from Winslow's pocket when he seized his arm, he started at once in pursuit, stumblingly at first, then with more certain steps as he rallied from the effect of his fall.

It was a strange race, in the midst of the mad storm, gusts of wind, rain that came down in veiling sheets, lightning gleams and crashes of thunder. A flash at a critical instant showed the fugitive taking the southern branch of the cross-road; and from that time Quint had little difficulty in following him.

At first the distance between them seemed to increase, then for a while to continue about the same. Each had started out with breath spent by the scuffle, and Quint was put to a still further disadvantage by his dive against the tree. Then gradually his forces returned; he drew deep breaths as he ran, and with the sense of restored power, the fury of his resolution came back.

So, though a fair match for him in a wresttling bout, the dog-seller soon found that he couldn't compete with the tall Biddicut boy in a foot-race. His breath was utterly gone, when, hearing Quint close at his heels, he turned and faced him.

"Aren't we a couple of fools!" he articulated pantingly.

"If you are speaking for yourself, I don't know of anybody that will dispute you," Quint replied, in much better breath and voice.

He didn't offer to lay hands on Winslow; but, bareheaded, his hair disordered, his features dripping in the rain, and showing a ghastly streak caused by the blow upon the left temple, he confronted the swindler.

"What do you intend to do now?" said the dog-seller.

"Stick by you," said Quint grimly.

"Hadn't you better go back and pick up your hat? You seem to have come off in a hurry," said Winslow, walking on.

His own duster, or waterproof, had been torn open in the scuffle, and he was holding it together over his breast.

"I've more important business just now," Quint answered, again keeping close to his side.

How extremely anxious he was to go back, he was careful not to betray. Not for his hat, indeed; but in following Winslow he was going farther and farther away from Cliff, of whose assistance he was in desperate need. But he would not go back without his captive, and he could not devise any means of taking his captive with him.

It was a singular dilemma—the captive leading away the captor! But there seemed to be no help for it, unless he abandoned his purpose; and this he had no thought of doing, although far more apprehensive than he appeared as to the outcome of the amazing adventure.

Winslow would no doubt have offered more liberal terms of settlement if he had known what sort of a boy was behind the "gambrel-roof nose." But a rogue may have pride as well as an honest man; and he was not one to give up his ill-gotten "profits" at the demand of a seventeen-year-old "country bumpkin." He knew no more than Quint did how the affair was to end; but he would trust to luck and his sharp wits to carry him through. While Quint was "sticking" to him, he was watching for an opportunity to get rid of Quint.

The thunder and lightning ceased, or became distant, but it rained steadily, and the darkness was increasing.

The road ran at right angles with the one to which Quint would gladly have returned. But he shrewdly guessed that it would soon strike one parallel to that, perhaps the main thoroughfare that traversed the village where he had bought crackers and cheese with Cliff, and had helped the teamsters with their hot box.

The two walked on without speaking, and before many minutes came to the very street of Quint's conjecture. The cross-road ended there, and a broader highway stretched away in the darkness to the right and left. To the right it led into an unknown region; to the left, it led back to the village Quint knew. There were no lights visible, except in the windows of a few scattered houses.

"Here's a lamp-post," said Winslow, stopping on a corner. "Why is there no light?"

"Because there is supposed to be a moon," replied Quint. "That's the way it is in Biddicut; no matter how dark and stormy the nights are, the street lamps are never lighted, if there happens to be a moon in the almanac."

"Do you know where we are?" Winslow inquired.

"We are about a mile and a half from the Star Grove Hotel, which lies in this direction," Quint answered, pointing.

"That's according to my calculation," Winslow remarked, as he turned the corner in the direction of the village, to the immense but secret satisfaction of his captor.

Another long silence. They were rapidly approaching the village.

"Are we going to keep this up all night?" the dog-seller inquired.

"That's for you to say," Quint replied.

"If you walk, I walk. After the shower is over, exercise will dry us."

Another silence. Then Winslow asked:
"Where's Cassius all this time?"

"He's getting rested, so he'll be fresh for hooking on to you, if I find the thing growing monotonous."

"Well," said Winslow, decisively, "I'm going to the Star Grove Hotel!"—the lights of which were now visible, over the village roofs and trees. "I've engaged a room there."

"I'm with you," Quint remarked cheerfully. "The hotel will be a good place to call a convention of the people you've sold your dog to."

"That's what you're after, is it?" Winslow retorted.

"I'm not after anything. What I do will depend on you. I've only one plan—to get my money back, or to see you locked up. That's the kind of country bumpkin I am."

"You want to try that game?" cried Winslow defiantly. "Here's your chance!"

It was a chance Quint had been eagerly looking for, with but little hope, however, that he would be allowed to take advantage of it.

They had reached the center of the village, which he recognized, although its aspect was changed from what it had been when he and Cliff passed and repassed through its principal streets that afternoon. They were now plashy and deserted, and doors were closed against the storm. A little off from the corner, not far ahead, was the broadly lighted front window of the grocery, on the steps of which Cliff had rested and munched his crackers and cheese while Quint went to join the teamsters around the hot box.

On another corner, still nearer, was an establishment in which Quint was more intensely interested just now. This was the police station. Here he had stopped with

Cliff to make inquiries, while following Sparkler back through the village, and had told enough of their story to insure him a ready hearing, he believed, if he could now succeed in taking Winslow to the door.

He had hardly expected to bring him even within sight of it; for Winslow probably knew the town as well as he did, and that was one of the places which persons of his character are usually solicitous to avoid. Perhaps he had not been so quick as Quint, to recognize the situation; but he certainly recognized it now. For there, right across the way, on a broad transparency lighted from within, were the conspicuous letters—POLICE.

Winslow perceived the sign as soon as Quint did; but instead of retreating or hurrying by, he put on a bold front and repeated:

"Here's your chance! Think I'm afraid of that?"

Fearing some trick, but holding himself ready to fling himself upon Winslow the instant he should attempt any suspicious action, Quint answered promptly:

"All right! Cross over with me!"

"I'll do that," said Winslow, "and we'll soon see what your trumped-up charges will amount to."

So saying, he crossed over with Quint to the door of the station. It was closed, but the light from the window shone mistily upon them as they stood there a moment in the rain, alert, suspicious, each eager to fathom the other's intentions.

"Why don't you go ahead?" said Winslow, with an ironic smile.

"The elder first; age before beauty," Quint replied.

"Come along, then!" said the dog-seller, with an air of bravado, mounting the two steps that led to the door.

Quint was so intent upon getting him into the station and cutting off his retreat

in case he should turn back at the last moment, that he was wholly unprepared for what followed.

"Come along!" Winslow repeated, raising his voice as he threw open the door, at the same time clutching the astonished Biddicut boy by the collar and dragging him forward over the threshold. "Police!" he cried, "I've brought you a highway robber!"

Captor and captive had all at once changed places.

XXIII

"A PRODIGIOUS BLUNDER"

THERE was but one person in the room — a sturdy Americanized Irishman. Unfortunately he was not the officer of whom the boys had made inquiries that afternoon. He was writing at a desk, in a little railed-off space, with his broad back toward the door, when it was burst open in this extraordinary manner.

He stepped promptly outside the rail, and seized hold of Quint, who was struggling with Winslow.

"Be quiet, will you!" Then to the pretended captor: "What has he done?"

"Stopped me on the street!" Winslow exclaimed, showing his thin outer garment torn open at the breast. "Snatched my watch and ran! I caught him, and he flung it away—a few rods back here."

Quint meanwhile was holding fast to Winslow and trying to speak. His bare head, his drenched hair and garments, his rain-streaked features, showing the effects of his wearisome all-day tramp and of the present excitement, — rendered ghastly, moreover, by an ugly bruise on the temple, —all combined to give him the aspect of a desperate and disreputable character.

"Be quiet, or I'll quiet you!" said the officer roughly. "Take away your hand!"

Quint relaxed his hold upon Winslow.

"I'll be quiet," he said; "only allow me to tell my story."

"You'll have time for that," said the officer, quickly slipping a pair of handcuffs on the astounded prisoner.

"Wait till I pick up my watch; I know just where he dropped it," said Winslow.

"Keep him! keep him! Don't let him go!" Quint fairly howled.

But Winslow, without awaiting an answer, was already out of the station.

Even with the handcuffs on his wrists Quint would have rushed out in pursuit if the officer had not detained him.

"*He* is the robber! Let me go!" he cried, trying to get away.

"Will you quit?" demanded the officer, holding him firmly by one manacled wrist.

"I'll quit if I must," Quint replied fiercely. "But I never thought it was the business of the police to help the rogues instead of the honest men."

"We'll see who is the rogue in this case," said the officer, slightly disconcerted by Winslow's sudden disappearance, and by the prisoner's vehement protest; "when he comes back with the watch."

"There was no watch!" Quint declared. "He won't come back! If he does, you may believe I am the robber, and not that *he* has got *my* money."

It is not probable that the deliberate Biddicut boy had ever before spoken so volubly and vehemently. Fully roused, furiously indignant, he turned from gazing after the vanished figure, and glared upon the officer.

Only the pouring rain was heard outside the open door. The sound of fleeing footsteps had died away. No figure groping along the ground in search of a watch, nor any other moving object, was visible in the rainy street. After looking out and listening a moment, the officer addressed his prisoner:

"What were you resisting for?"

"I wasn't resisting. I was only trying to hold on to him, while you were letting him go. Couldn't you see what he was up to?" said Quint, his grim face wrathfully glowering. "*I* had brought *him* in, instead of his having brought me!"

"It didn't look so," said the officer, incredulous, but evidently disturbed. "He was dragging you after him."

"I'll tell you how that was," said Quint. "The minute I got him to the door, and was making him come in first, he grabbed me by the collar and snaked me over the top step so suddenly I stumbled; then you thought I was fighting to get away, when I was only keeping *him* from getting away."

The officer was all the while looking out for the returning watch-hunter, and frowning dubiously. Again he turned and looked Quint carefully over.

"It's an improbable story you tell," he declared. "You couldn't capture and bring in a man like him. Impossible!"

"Would it be any more possible for him to bring me in?" Quint retorted, standing at his full height, and looking sternly into the eyes of the officer, who, though a good-sized man, was hardly taller than he.

"You are bigger than I thought, when you came sprawling in."

"You thought then I was big enough to play the highway-robber. I own I couldn't have brought him here, if he hadn't been willing, any more than he could have brought me. I had been following him all day—I had just caught him—

and then to have the *police* help him get away!"

Quint crushed some angry word in his teeth, and his ghastly features worked with repressed emotion.

"How had he robbed you?" the officer demanded.

Quint told something of the dog-seller's operations, and went on:

"We followed him all the way from Biddicut through I don't know how many towns. I was alone when I fell in with him this evening. He tried to shake me off, and we had a squabble. But I stuck to him till we came in sight of your station. Then I should have called for help, if he hadn't himself proposed to come in. He must have had this rascally trick of his already planned."

"Did he give you that blow on the forehead?" the officer inquired.

Quint put up his hand. "I didn't know I had one! He struck me three or four times. But I must have got this when we fell over a log together, and my head tried to occupy the same place with the butt of a tree!" he explained solemnly.

The officer, evidently no longer expectant of Winslow, kept glancing up at the clock. He had told Quint he could sit down, but Quint remained standing.

"The chief will be here in a few minutes," the man said. "Then if we find you are telling a straight story, we'll see what we can do for you."

"You can't do anything now," Quint answered sullenly. "Unless you take off these bracelets. They aren't comfortable, and they aren't ornamental, and they happen to be on the wrong pair of wrists. The other pair is far enough out of your reach by this time. After all the trouble we'd had!" He choked a little. "Nobody is going to follow him again as we followed him!"

Footsteps were heard approaching along the wooden sidewalk. They had a heavier sound than would have been made by the tread of the light-heeled young dog-seller.

Another officer stepped up on the threshold. Quint recognized him as the one of whom he and Cliff had made inquiries that afternoon, but he at first said nothing.

The newcomer regarded the Biddicut boy with astonishment, recognizing him only after an effort of puzzled reflection.

"Hello!" he said, "what has happened to you?"

"Ask him!" Quint replied, with morose wrath.

"What is it, Terry?" the chief demanded, turning to the officer.

Terry told his story. Then Quint related all that was necessary of his. An expression of disgust settled upon the face of the chief —a much more refined and intelligent face than that of the subordinate.

"Terry," he said, "it's a prodigious blun der. This boy's story corresponds with what he and his chum told me this afternoon. That fellow won't find any watch; 'tisn't a good night for finding watches. Take off that pair of rings!"

Terry quickly removed the handcuffs.

"Now go out and see if you can find anything of the other party to this affair," said his superior. "I'll give you fifteen minutes to produce him, with or without the watch. If he doesn't put in an appearance by that time, we shall know he's a fraud."

With a sarcastic smile he watched Terry's departure on his ridiculous errand; then looked at Quint, silent, surly, his pale face rain-streaked and blood-stained, his wet clothes beginning to steam as they were dried in the warm air of the station.

"You may as well sit down, and take it easy," the chief said kindly, pushing a stool toward him.

"I'm too mad to sit down," said Quint. "Besides, my partner is waiting for me in that cart-shed, if he hasn't already started hunting for me. I must put out and find him, so soon as you make up your minds that I'm not a highwayman."

He seated himself on the stool, nevertheless, with a strangely haggard aspect.

"You've had a pretty hard time," observed the chief, regarding him curiously.

"I haven't had leisure to think of that," Quint replied. "If I had kept the fellow, that would have rested me for all my life! I shouldn't mind anything,—lost hat, empty stomach, broken head, wet skin! As it is—" he could say no more, for he choked up again with rage and grief.

"I'll dry you off," said the chief, stooping to open the door of an air-tight stove.

There were kindlings laid in it ready for lighting. He touched a match to them; and in a few seconds it was roaring and crackling close behind the boy's wet back.

"I wish—Cliff—was here!" Quint murmured, with a long-drawn sigh. Even he was breaking down at last.

Considerably within the allotted fifteen minutes, Terry returned, disconsolate, and obliged to confess that his watch-hunter was still missing.

"But he looked so respectable compared with—" he glanced at poor Quint as he spoke—"anybody might have made the mistake."

"Anyhow, it has been made," said the chief; "and now we must see what can be done to rectify it. We can't catch the scamp —not to-night, anyway; but we may do something for this boy. It's high time that we were thinking of that."

It was time indeed. His weariness and discouragement, the reaction from his late terrible excitement, his want of substantial food, and now the stifling heat of the stove and the odor of his own steaming garments, were producing an alarming effect upon the boy from Biddicut. He turned sick and dizzy, and the chief had but just time to spring to his support, when he reeled sidewise, tumbling limply from the stool into the officer's outstretched arms.

XXIV

WHAT WAS HIDDEN IN THE MANGER

THE last trick of the trick-dog had surprised Cliff at a moment when he was so full of trouble that in his despair he had exclaimed, "Let him go!" and cared little if he never beheld Sparkler again. What disappointments, what fatigues, that wily and treacherous animal had caused him!—and now had come this acme of the boy's woes, this horrible uncertainty as to what had befallen his faithful friend Quint. Nevertheless, even in his wretched state of mind, it was a matter of interest that Sparkler had gone back in the direction from which they had come —the way Cliff must now return.

He called again; he explored the ground all about, under the trees and on the corners of the intersecting roads; he looked in every direction in the vain hope of seeing a human figure start out from the shadows; then with a heavy heart he turned back toward the shed.

He had but a flickering hope of finding that Quint had reached there, and it died within him before he had fairly passed beneath the roof. He called Quint's name and kicked the heap of straw; for although Cliff's friend was foremost in his thoughts, he also remembered the bare possibility of Sparkler's having gone back again to that comfortable bed. But then neither the dog nor his friend made sound or sign in that solitary shelter.

He stood gazing up and down the road, when he perceived a light. It was evidently in motion; it was approaching in the middle of the highway. The moon's beams reduced its rays to a feeble glimmer and soon revealed a man carrying it; a stocky man, in a buttoned frock coat, and wearing a round-topped hat.

Cliff watched his approach and drew back into the shed to wait, filled with a fearful hope that the coming of the man with the lantern somehow concerned him and Quint.

Arrived at the shed, the man turned into it, and holding up the lantern where Cliff stood in the shadow, cast its light upon both their faces. His own was that of a ruddy, Americanized Irishman—our friend Terry, in short.

"Are you the boy from Biddicut?" he inquired, peering at Cliff curiously.

Cliff had already noticed that the stocky man wore the uniform of a police officer.

"The other Biddicut boy sent you?" he answered eagerly. "Where is he?"

"Down at the police station," the officer replied. "He has had a rough time. He was troubled about you, and so I offered to come and find out about you."

Cliff anxiously inquired of the officer what had happened to the other boy from Biddicut.

"Nothing very serious," Terry answered. "Only he caught your dog-seller, and had a set-to with him. But he stuck to him, and brought him to the station."

"Oh, Quint!—he's great!" cried Cliff, rejoicing too quickly.

" 'T was a fine piece of strategy," Terry admitted. "But at the last moment the rogue turned the tables on him by a cunning trick and got away."

"Oh!—how could he?" Cliff wailed.

"I'll tell you on the way back. We've made your friend pretty comfortable, and he wants you to join him. You have his hat? I was to look for that, as well as for you."

"To think," exclaimed Cliff, "that he should have caught Winslow and I should have caught the dog, and that both should have got away!"

He was explaining how Sparkler had found him on the straw there, when he paused in amazement at sight of an object revealed by the rays of Terry's lantern. It was a piece of most familiar-looking cord, hanging over the side of the manger. He sprang to seize it.

"The lantern! hold the lantern!" he cried, slipping his hand carefully along the cord toward some object to which it was attached.

Terry lifted the lantern, and exposed to view, curled up in the bottom of the manger and pretending to be fast asleep, but doubtless as wide-awake as any four-footed creature could be, the thrice-lost Sparkler! —Sparkler, wisest of dogs, yet not wise enough to know it was a short-sighted and ostrich-like policy, in hiding, to leave the piece of cord trailing at length behind him!

"I'll hold you this time, if I live!" Cliff exclaimed jubilantly. He fastened the cord about his wrist.

Sparkler seemed reluctant to leave the manger, but Cliff forced him to take the leap.

"What's this, do you believe? He was guarding something," said Terry, lowering his lantern so as to shed its light into the vacated manger.

Sparkler, seizing the officer's coat-tail, tugged at it with a menacing snarl.

"Sparkler!—behave!" Cliff commanded. "See what it is. I'll hold him."

Terry thereupon fished up a curiously-shaped roll, which fell open in his hand, and assumed the shape of a flat, empty bag; Sparkler growling, and springing to get at him.

"That's Winslow's!" cried Cliff, in high excitement. "It's his gray linen grip-sack! I understand the whole business now!"

As the officer was mystified, the boy briefly explained.

"He followed Winslow as long as he carried that. It might be a roll he could put into his pocket, or it might be a bag with his duster in it. But if he left it anywhere, then the dog knew he was to meet Winslow at that place, or wait for him there. He had come back to stay with the bag when he found me here."

"If that was the scheme," observed Terry, "then your man will return here. Leave the bag just as we found it."

"It must have been covered with straw; I got all of this litter out of the manger," said Cliff. "Now let's have it all back, and put out the light, and leave everything till my partner and I can come in the morning and waylay the crafty Mr. Winslow."

XXV

WHAT CLIFF CARRIED IN HIS POCKET

SPARKLER had become quiet after the bag was returned to its place; and he followed readily when Cliff led him from the shed and set off, guided by Terry, down the road.

"What time is it?" Cliff inquired.

The officer pulled out his watch and turned its white countenance up to the moon.

"Twenty minutes to nine."

"No later?" exclaimed Cliff. "Will any stores be open in the village?"

He explained his purpose, and on entering the village Terry took him to a store where small articles of hardware were re-tailed. He laid Quint's hat on the counter and inquired:

"Have you any copper wire?" Some samples being shown, he selected one that was sufficiently light and flexible, and said, "Cut me off three yards of this."

The piece obtained, he made one end fast to the dog's collar; then passed the rest in a long spiral around the entire cord, including the loop at his wrist. The two men watched him with interest, giving him such assistance as he required; but Sparkler looked sleepy and indifferent.

"He may gnaw the cord, but I defy him to bite off the wire! How much is to pay?"

As he said this he thrust his free hand into his pocket, and drew it out again with something that might have been silver or nickel, but wasn't money.

"What's this?" he muttered; and it was a moment before he recognized the shining object he had picked up near the spot where he found Quint's hat. He had not since given it a thought; indeed, he had hardly been conscious of slipping it into his pocket in the moment of surprise when Sparkler got away from him. Examined in the lamplight, it resembled less the part of a knife-handle, which he had at first taken it for. It was in shape a long oval, about three inches in length by nearly three quarters of an inch in width; thin and slightly curved; on the innermost surface were two short rivets. The outer surface was brightly polished, with rounded edges, and it bore an engraved inscription.

Cliff held it up to the light and read the lettering, with a face betraying the utmost astonishment, his eyes staring and his lips forming an inaudible exclamation. Then he flung himself upon Sparkler, as if with intent to throttle that unconcerned and impassive quadruped.

His immediate business, however, was not so much with the dog as with the dog's collar, a strap of maroon-colored leather, starred with nickel studs about an inch and a half apart, except in one place where two studs seemed to be missing.

With hands trembling in their eagerness, Cliff applied his metal plate to the space thus left, and found that it not only fitted, but that the rivets corresponded exactly with the two rivet holes in the collar.

He sprang to his feet, unwilling to tell any one of his discovery until he had imparted the tremendous secret to his friend. "What will Quint say," was the thought uppermost in his mind, as he accompanied Terry to the station.

The door was wide open, and within sat Quint with his back to the stove, and his coat and vest hanging near it on the office railing. On the stove were two bowls containing hot chocolate, and on a stool beside him was a tray containing a comfortable repast for two,—boiled eggs, as white as the saucer that held them, a loaf of bread, butter and salt, knives and spoons and plates. The air of the room was warm, despite the open door, and humid from the vapor of steaming garments.

This banquet set before him must have been tempting to the tired and hungry boy, now quite recovered from his faintness. But Quint was unwilling to taste food until his friend could partake of it with him.

The appearance of Cliff at the door, with Sparkler capering before him, very nearly proved disastrous to the contents of the tray, which Quint's knee knocked in his sudden attempt to rise. Fortunately he caught it, and steadied it on the stool.

"The dog?" he cried, his face lighting up joyfully. "Cliff, you've beaten me! I'm glad *one* of us has had some luck!"

"Don't say luck till I tell you," replied Cliff, in gleeful agitation. "Whether it's luck or not, I don't know. But it's great!" And he held out the metal plate.

No common adjective seemed strong enough to express Quint's astonishment as he read the inscription; but the famous words of Brutus, which he had so often spouted, broke from his lips with a force of feeling he had never put into them before:

"'Be ready, gods, with all your thunderbolts!' How did you come by that?"

"See how it fits," said Cliff, pulling Sparkler forward, parting his curls, and showing the place in the collar, which the plate and the rivets fitted. "I found it near your hat, up there in the woods. I feel certain Winslow must have lost it."

"And I know just how he lost it," exclaimed Quint.

"May I see?" asked the Chief.

"Yes, you can see it," said Cliff, passing the name-plate over to the chief, who read the inscription with delighted curiosity. "'P. T. Barnum!'" he exclaimed. "'Bridgeport, Conn. License 373.' Thunderation, young fellows, that's Barnum's celebrated circus dog! He's worth a thousand dollars!"

Cliff stroked the spaniel's head affectionately.

"If he belongs to Barnum, Barnum must have him back again, I suppose. I only wish he was mine! Now tell about your tussle with Winslow, Quint."

"Begin your supper, boys," counseled the chief, "and tell your stories over your eggs and chocolate."

"That's judgmatical," observed Quint.

XXVI

HOW THE BOYS FOUND SUPPER AND LODGING

"SUPPER? our supper?" said Cliff, eyeing the contents of the bowl and tray with an interest which the more exciting question of the moment could not wholly eclipse. "How is that?"

"We sometimes have to feed a prisoner, and your friend here came so near to being one, that I thought we owed him a treat. He'll tell you about it; or perhaps Terry would prefer to. Eh, Terry? Well, lay to, boys, before the supper gets any colder."

He placed a second chair for Cliff opposite Quint's, with the tray on the stool between them, and handed them the chocolate. Hungry, happy, grateful, they cracked their eggs and told their stories, while Terry, kneeling before the open stove-door, toasted slices of bread for them on a fork.

Quint in his narrative cast no blame upon the officer, but called it a "very natural mistake," and took his slice of crisp toast from the friendly hands that prepared it, ate it with immense relish, declaring they "would have Winslow yet."

"He will certainly go back to the shed for the dog and his bag," he said; "and we must be there to nab him, very early in the morning, if we don't go to-night. I am getting dry, and rested. How is it with you, partner?"

"My little nap in the shed was almost as good as a night's sleep," Cliff replied. "Then there was a good deal of the right kind of medicine in catching the dog, finding you all right—and such a supper as this! I could start for home, if there was any hope of reaching it in three or four hours."

As that was out of the question, the chief offered to find lodgings for them in a house near by, where their supper had been ordered.

"You are kindness itself!" said Cliff. "But we can turn in for only a little while; and I mustn't be parted from this dog."

"Then allow me to make a suggestion," said the chief, between puffs of his cigar. "We've got a couple of cells downstairs, and they open into an airy room. Unoc-cupied—no bedding—straw mattresses—rather thin, but clean. You won't find 'em bad to sleep on; and you can keep the dog with you."

Cliff shrugged and lifted his eyebrows at Quint. Quint smiled his drollest smile and looked quizzically at Cliff over the devastated tray.

"It will be enough for me to brag that I've had on a pair of iron wristbands," he remarked. "If it should get to the boys in Biddicut that I'd slept in a police-station I wouldn't answer for the result. I'm afraid some of 'em would die of envy."

The chief laughed as he knocked the ashes off his cigar, while Terry stood by and grinned.

"If we could get into a barn somewhere and put in three or four hours' sleep on the hay," said Cliff, "that would be better than going back to the shed before daylight."

"That would suit me," said Quint. "I've more than once slept in a barn in summer, just for fun. I'm getting dry enough."

He put on his vest, but held his coat to the fire for a turn or two, while Cliff offered the fragments of their repast to Sparkler. At first the dog had declined food, and he now winked at it somewhat contemptuously as he lay curled up by the stove.

"If you had spoken about the barn a little earlier I might have managed it," said Terry. "Deacon Payson's barn," with a consulting glance at the chief. "Maybe I can now. The deacon is usually up later than this."

As the boys welcomed this suggestion, Terry, with the chief's approval, went out to see what arrangements could be made. In his absence the boys talked over their affairs with the chief and got his advice as to what they should do if they found Winslow, and what if they didn't, and as to their best course in regard to the dog that had in so strange a manner come into their possession.

Then Terry returned and said, "It's all right. Deacon Payson's haymow will accommodate you."

He relighted his lantern, Quint put on his coat and shoes, and Cliff, with a pull of the wire-wound cord, woke up Sparkler, who had been dozing by the stove. Then the boys shook hands with the chief, who wished them luck, and promised them further assistance, if they should require it; and they departed, preceded by Terry carrying his lantern, and followed by the dispirited spaniel.

A little way up the street, Terry knocked at a door, which was opened by an old gentleman in shirt sleeves.

"I've brought my young chaps, Mr. Payson," said the officer, stepping aside and holding his lantern so that his "young chaps" could be seen.

The old gentleman looked them over and fixed his eyes on Quint.

"I thought so," he remarked. "I've seen one of 'em before. Haven't I?"

"You were in the crowd around the hot box this afternoon when I was inquiring for a man and a dog," Quint replied, glad to recognize the kindly face.

"Terry tells me that you want to sleep in my barn," said the old gentleman. "I'll be with you in a second."

He stepped back into the room, and reappeared putting on his coat, then he led the way along a path lighted by the mingled rays of the moon and of Terry's lantern. Having unlocked a stable door, he took the lantern from Terry's hand and preceded the others, past a stall in which there was a horse lying down, into a well-filled barn beyond.

"Here's hay right here on the floor," he said, "and I can get you blankets."

"If it was my case," said Terry, "I should get up on this load of hay. Here's a ladder a-purpose. Then you'll be out of the way of rats."

Quint surveyed the premises with satisfaction, and said he wasn't afraid of rats.

"Particularly with the dog to watch us," Cliff added, laughing. "He's good for almost everything else; he ought to be death on rats; I believe he smells 'em now."

Sparkler was, in fact, sniffing about excitedly, putting his nose in the littered hay, whining, and finally setting his forefeet on a round of the ladder, with a wistful upward look, as if he understood and approved Terry's suggestion.

"The dog votes for the top of the load," said Quint; "and I'm not so sure but that will be the best place for us. It may be the safest for him, if he is going to try any more of his tricks."

"You mean, if he gets away from me!" said Cliff. "He isn't going to do that, I tell you! But if he should, he'd find his way down from that load quicker than you or I could!"

"I guess the best place is right here on the floor," Quint concluded. " 'Twon't do any harm to pull down a little more hay, will it?"

"None at all," Mr. Payson replied. "And here are some carriage cushions."

"Quint, this is luxury!" said Cliff.

"Cliff, this is judgmatical!" replied Quint. "We wouldn't ask anything more comfortable, if we had our choice of lodgings."

"I wish our folks could know!" said Cliff. "How are we to get out in the morning?"

"I shall have to lock you in," Mr. Payson answered; "but if you are stirring before my man comes round, you can open this big front door from the inside; I'll show you how the swivel-bar works. Or you can unbolt the door in the rear. Unless you start too early in the morning, my folks can give you some breakfast."

"If you want any help from us, you'll find the station open," said Terry. "I'll post the night officer, so there'll be no more mistakes at our end of the line."

The boys had made their bed between the side of the load and the front door, and were preparing to lie down in their clothes after kicking off their shoes.

"Come here now!" Cliff commanded, making Sparkler lie down by his side. "He heard us talk of rats, and can't forget it." He took the precaution to make a couple of turns with the leash about his arm in addition to the loop at his wrist. "Even if he should get loose, I don't suppose he can get out of the barn."

"Not before the doors are opened," Mr. Payson replied, regarding his guests with amused satisfaction. "I should say that you are pretty cozy."

With an exchange of good-nights, the men went out with the lantern; and the boys found themselves alone on the floor of the great, shadowy, moon-visited barn.

"I don't know how to thank folks," said Cliff. "Somehow, when anybody has been good to you, any words about it sound foolish."

"We have had more kindness shown to us than anything else on this trip," Quint replied, "even putting Winslow and the old cook into the opposite scale."

"I'm thinking," said Cliff, "we'd better let Winslow slide. Now that we have the dog, we can make enough out of him to pay for the trouble."

"I'm rather surprised at you, Cliff," Quint answered, after a moment's silence. "Just after we started on this expedition, and it was growing a little mite interesting, you'd have given it up two or three times, if it hadn't been for me."

"I've wished we had given it up more times than that," Cliff confessed. "Think of what you have gone through! Such a wetting as you got, and the trouble the rascal gave you, up there in the woods—let alone his turning you over to the police! It makes me laugh, though, to think of that!"

"We'll laugh at the whole thing when we're safe through it," said Quint. "Maybe we sha'n't get much satisfaction out of Algernon, in one way, even if we catch him. But as I owe him for the wetting, *and* the broken head, *and* the cold wristbands, not to mention other small items, I want to pay him in a lump, and get his receipt in full. In short, I mean to get even with Algernon K. if it takes another day to do it."

Cliff made no reply to this declaration, which suggested such possibilities of still further hardships and disappointments. Quint waited a minute, then went on in a tone which betrayed how deeply hurt he was by his friend's silence:

"You have the dog, and now you naturally want to hurry away with him. That's all right, Cliff; that's the important thing to you. The important thing to me is the bear-hug I am saving up for Winslow. This may be a weakness on my part; and I've no doubt the course you propose is the wisest. But if I don't get in that squeeze, I shall feel a want, as if I had missed something useful and agreeable, all the rest of my life."

"I feel just so too," Cliff replied. "Although we've secured the dog, I never shall feel quite happy about it unless we get Winslow. But I'm doubting whether the chance of catching him is worth what it will cost."

"We can find that out only by making the trial. Just give me a little help in the morning," said Quint; "then if we don't scoop him in, and if I should feel like sticking to his trail a little longer, I'll go ahead on my own account, and let you start for home without me."

Cliff reached over and gave Quint's arm an affectionate grip.

"See here, Quint," he said; "don't misunderstand me. Remember what Cassius says—'A friend should bear a friend's infirmities.' I've played that part to your Brutus too many times, to have a disagreement with you in earnest."

"Oh, it's no disagreement!" Quint protested.

"The fact is," said Cliff, "I was used up too soon on this tramp. I haven't anything of your tremendous 'stick-to-it-iveness'; and I—but no matter!" choking a little. "You've been such a friend to me—you've helped me to get the dog, which is your dog now just as much as he is mine; and now I'm going to help you overhaul Winslow again, no matter how long it takes; and you won't hear me say another word about turning back as long as you want to follow him."

"Cliff! you're the pluckiest fellow I ever saw!" Quint exclaimed; and the boys' two hands were clasped in a hearty pressure. "Pluckier than I am!"

"Don't be absurd!" Cliff remonstrated.

"I mean it!" said Quint. "You have stuck to this business when you've seen it would be wiser to give it up. I am a little more obstinate than you are, that's all. And now you offer to give up your wisdom to my obstinacy. Well, I think we've a good chance of trapping Winslow in the morning. We must stop talking now and get some sleep."

"I forgot you didn't have a nap, as I had," said Cliff. "I feel as if I could talk all night. Isn't it pleasant in here!—the moonlight slanting in at that window, and striking down over the stalls! Sparkler is sleeping, as quiet and contented as the most honest dog in the world."

Quint made no reply, and his heavy breathing soon showed that he was asleep. Nor was it long before Cliff succumbed to blissful drowsiness, and slept soundly on their bed of hay, between his friend and the dog.

The moonbeams mounted higher and higher over the stalls, and sent their radiance through the racks, as the great, slow, solemn, starry wheel of night rolled on. The last fading yesterday joined the countless yesterdays of the past, and another untried morrow was at hand.

Then a dark figure crept to the edge of the load of hay, put one foot after the other on the rounds of the ladder, and slowly and with the utmost caution began to descend.

The dog gave a whine and a start, tightening the cord about the arm at his side. Cliff roused instantly, put out his hand, felt the dog's head, and patting it, told him to lie still. His eyes opened enough to see that only a few feeble flecks of moonlight rested high up on the partition, and that all was quiet in the deepening gloom of the barn. Then he slept again.

During this slight disturbance, and for some minutes afterward, the figure on the ladder remained perfectly motionless against the side of the load. Then it put out a hand in the direction of the dog and waved it with an expressive downward gesture. From that time Sparkler made neither sound nor movement; the wary feet felt their way down the ladder, and Algernon K. Winslow stood upon the barn floor.

XXVII

"WHAT MAN-TRAP IS THAT?"

STANDING so close to the load of hay that he might have been taken for a part of it, the dog-seller contemplated the situation. He had slipped into the barn when the owner was bedding down his horses the evening before, found a lodging on top of the load, and had been, no doubt, highly edified by the conversation of the two boys on the floor below. Now the time had come for him to anticipate their well-laid plans by some shrewd action.

Quint's prominent features were distinctly visible in the dim, diffused light. His face was pale, and the shut eyelids with the discolored bruise on his temple gave it a sad and stern expression even in sleep. He lay on his back, with one relaxed arm on his breast, the other outstretched on the blanket, and with his shoes and hat beside him on the floor.

Nearer the silent standing figure lay Cliff, turned over on the arm to which the cord was attached, with his face toward Sparkler, curled up close by on the hay. Cliff's hat and shoes were under the corner of the load, at Winslow's very feet. All this the keen eye of the observer took in, even to the slender, serpent-like coil of gray cord about the dark sleeve.

He looked at the great door, then down at the legs in his way, and the eyes that would open, if they opened at all, upon any object moving in that direction. Thanks to overhearing Mr. Payson's explanations, he had knowledge of another door in the rear of the barn. He stooped to give Sparkler a quieting caress, and to look into his slyly blinking eyes, then glided away to make discoveries.

With movements so furtive that if they had been heard, nothing more than the presence of mice on the littered floor would have been suspected, he passed the load of hay, groped his way around the carriage beyond, and found the door he sought. He had no difficulty in slipping the bolt without noise, and in opening the door a little space, to see that his way of

escape was clear. It was bright starlight without; the moon was near its setting, if not already set.

Leaving the door open a good arm's breadth, he stole back toward the front of the barn, observing every turn, and every obstacle to be avoided in any precipitate retreat. Within half a yard of Cliff's head, he got down upon his hands and knees, under the corner of the load of hay. It was darker now, and the faces of the sleepers were indistinct in shadow, but their steady breathing reassured him. He advanced his hand until he felt the cord.

He took out his knife intending to cut it, but something harder than hemp stayed his blade. Wire!—a long flexible piece encircling the cord, and extending from a small loop at the dog's collar to a larger one at the boy's wrist.

Upon making this discovery he was minded to cut the collar, but the boy was sleeping so heavily that he decided to unbuckle it. This he did without difficulty, and having freed it from both cord and wire he put it into his pocket.

He was now ready to depart and to take the dog with him; but he must first devise some means of delaying pursuit. He crept by the cushions that pillowed the boys' heads, and reached until his groping hand touched Quint's shoes. These he took, with the hat, and creeping back, placed them beside Cliff's hat and shoes. He was now ready for his last, most ingenious device, which he couldn't think of, even at that critical moment, without a chuckle of delight.

"Since he's determined to hold something, I'll oblige him," he whispered facetiously to himself, as he carried the released end of the cord toward one of the wagon-wheels, meaning to make it fast to the rim. "He sha'n't wake up and feel he has been wasting his time!"

But that very large substitute for the

dog's collar was too far away to permit a turn of the cord to be taken about it, without a coil or two from Cliff's arm; which could be had only at the risk of disturbing his slumber. Winslow thereupon produced from his pocket another piece of cord, which he had not found it necessary to part with, and was about to cut off enough for his purpose, when another happy thought struck him.

"No use being mean about a little string." His position, kneeling on the barn-floor, was becoming irksome; and having knotted his cord to the end of Cliff's, he rose to his feet. Then, instead of tying it to the wagon-wheel, he put it through the wheel, and made the end fast to the ladder, quite at his leisure. "To make things lively for 'em, if they start off in a hurry!" was his amiable intention.

So far all was well, from his own point of view; although our boys, if they had been awake to the situation, might have regarded it differently. He was prepared to resume his career in a gullible world, and only one other slight precaution remained to be taken.

He would have stolen their clothes if that had been possible. As it was, he could make free only with their hats and shoes.

The hats, one after another, he tossed up on the load of hay, where they lodged noiselessly. All this time the dog had lain as still as the sleeping boys; but now, at a signal from his master, he crouched on his paws, alert and intelligent, awaiting orders. Then in one hand Winslow gathered all the shoes except one; this he gave to Sparkler to carry, and with that too faithful accomplice, stole away, as silent as the shadows amid which they passed.

And still the tired Biddicut boys slept on.

At this juncture an astonishing thing occurred.

As Winslow approached the door, which he had left unlatched and slightly ajar, he was startled to see it swing all at once wide open, as if moved by an unseen hand. He stopped, half expecting a human form to appear in the square of star-lit space suddenly confronting him. But all was strangely quiet, and it seemed for a moment as if the door had opened magically, of its own accord, to let him pass.

The mystery was quickly solved; a wind was rising, and it had carried the outward-swinging door around on its hinges. He foresaw what might happen next, and hastened forward to prevent it. But he was too late. A counter-gust swung the door again, shutting it with a loud, rattling bang.

An indescribable hubbub ensued. The boys started up with cries of amazement, demanding of each other what had happened.

"It was a door that slammed!" exclaimed Quint.

"Somebody has been in the barn!" cried Cliff, feeling hurriedly for the dog.

"Where in thunder are my shoes?" Quint roared.

"The dog! the dog is gone!" said Cliff, in wild consternation. "He's here, though!"

He was on his feet, following up the cord, which was certainly attached to something, but which seemed to be miraculously lengthened, as if it had grown in the night.

"Jehu!—what's all this?"

His hand encountered the wired knot that had clasped Sparkler's collar; but instead of the collar he found more cord— more cord!

"The old Harry has been here!" he wailed, in mad bewilderment.

"It's the old Winslow!" said Quint. In springing up he had struck his head a stunning blow against the projecting frame of the hay-wagon. But without heeding the hurt, or waiting to find his shoes, he started for the door that had made the bang, and which was now slowly swinging open again.

In his headlong rush he passed between his friend and the load of hay.

"Look out!" Cliff implored. But Quint kept on, plunging over the cord, dragging Cliff after him, and bringing the ladder down upon both their shoulders. If Winslow had remained to witness the unqualified success of his scheme for "making things lively" in the deacon's barn, he would have had no cause to complain of the result.

"What man-trap is that?" murmured Quint, as he scrambled off, freeing his legs from the cord and his back from the encumbrance of the ladder, and made for the open door.

XXVIII

ANOTHER MYSTERIOUS MAN-TRAP

It had taken the dazed Cliff some moments to assure himself that there was no dog at the other end of the cord. But he was thoroughly satisfied of the fact by this time. His shoulder had received a staggering blow from the tumbling ladder, and his wrist a tremendous wrench from the sharply drawn wire-wound loop; but he quickly disengaged himself from both, and forgot his hurts in the fury that possessed him to rush out in pursuit of the author of his woes.

Outside the barn he found night and silence, the dim earth outspread, and the starry firmament—nothing else. Not a footstep was heard, not a human figure was seen—not even Quint's.

"Quint! where are you?" Cliff called out in a thrilled voice, standing bareheaded amid the great mystery into which he had rushed. Then something which might have been a post detached itself from a fence near by and moved toward him. It was the shoeless Quint.

"Which way did he go?" Cliff demanded.

"That's more than I know," Quint replied. "He was out of sight and hearing before I pitched out of the door."

"I can't understand it!" said Cliff. "I'm sure somebody went out of the barn, not ten seconds before you did!"

"Ten seconds is a good while when you are racing with slippery Winslow!" Quint said.

"I believe he has dropped into a hiding-place somewhere," said Cliff. "Or he is half a mile away by this time. That dog! that dog!" he moaned in angry despair. "Just after we had found out about him, and I was so sure of holding fast to him this time!"

"The ground will be wet and soft, and we can track 'em by daylight," said Quint. "I don't see what else we can do. He must have been in the barn when Mr. Payson locked us in."

"That's what the dog's strange actions meant," replied Cliff. "You remember how he tried to bounce up the ladder? Winslow must have heard all our talk."

"Did he take your shoes too?" Quint inquired.

"I guess so; I didn't stop to hunt."

They were searching for some sign to guide them, when Cliff's unshod foot hit some dark object lying loose among the sparse weeds and stunted grass by the yard fence. It was so much like a shoe that he stooped and picked it up. And a shoe it was.

"Mine, I do believe!" he declared.

"Look for mine," said Quint. "We may track 'em by our own shoes!"

"Here's another!—and another!" said Cliff. "All right here by the fence!"

"This is the way he went; he dropped the shoes as he jumped over."

Beyond the fence was an open space lying between Mr. Payson's house and an apple orchard not far off. The boys concluded that Winslow had vanished among the trees. Cliff sprang upon the fence; Quint stood looking over it.

"What's that?" Cliff whispered, intently gazing and listening—"I hear something coming toward us."

"A dog?" Quint suggested.

"A dog, as sure as I am crazy!" said Cliff, in wild excitement; for what he saw appeared too marvelous to be true. He jumped down from the fence to meet the returning truant.

"Sparkler!—it's Sparkler!" he cried, darting forward to seize him.

But Sparkler had no intention of allowing himself to be so easily recaptured. As Cliff advanced, he retreated, turning and capering, as if to lead him on; and when Quint came up, he ran away toward some dark object lying on the ground. Just then, from that direction came a horrible groan.

"Jehu! What's that?" said Cliff, his imagination conjuring up appalling mysteries, in the strange night-scene they were exploring.

"I'll see what it is!" exclaimed Quint, striding eagerly forward over the wet turf.

The dark object became a man, and rose to a sitting posture. The dog leaped upon him, then ran back toward the boys, who were now within a few paces of the spot.

The ground was level, with no visible impediment anywhere; and yet here was a human being struggling up with pain and difficulty from the ground, upon which he had evidently fallen from no discernible cause—the human being they sought!

Even Quint was startled by the strangeness of the chance that had so suddenly and mysteriously interrupted Winslow's hasty flight. What could have happened to him? Why that dreadful groan? And why had he permitted his presence to be betrayed by the very dog he had been hurrying away?

The shadowy orchard was on the left. On the right were the kitchen porch and rear gable of the Payson house, only two or three rods distant. The boys slackened their speed, very fortunately, as it proved, and advanced cautiously, peeringly, along the open space, toward the man, who was by this time struggling to get upon his feet.

"No hurry! We've got him, sure!" said Quint.

Seeing the boys close upon him, Winslow sank down again, resting upon his knees.

"My young friends," he said, in a badly shaken tone of voice, "the luck is against me."

"What are you saying your prayers here for?" Quint demanded.

"That's what I'm trying to find out," Winslow answered, feeling his head and shoulders with both hands in a dazed sort of way. "I was running, just skipping along about as fast as I could go—it seemed to be a clear course—when all at once—"

He paused, turning his head tentatively, as if to make sure that the joints were still in working condition.

"What happened?" Quint inquired, bending over him.

"I've had my throat cut, and my neck broken. I was caught by a lasso, and jerked back and over and whirled in the air, and dropped on my back, which is another part of me that's badly damaged. I feel as if I had had a tussle with a cyclone."

Uttering these words disconnectedly, the dog-seller looked up and around, and felt his neck again, as if trying to realize the kind of calamity that had befallen him.

"Shall I tell you what did it?" said Quint.

"You'll oblige me," said Winslow, his eye following the motion of the boy's lifted hand.

"You tried to cut off your useless head with this galvanized-wire clothes-line. Do you see it running between these two posts?"

"The posts I see. I'll take your word for the wire clothes-line." It seemed painful for the injured man to look upward. "I've proof enough that it's there."

"It's a wonder it didn't kill you!" Quint exclaimed.

"Where's this dog's collar?" cried Cliff, who had succeeded in catching Sparkler.

"In my waterproof's pocket, I suppose; at least I put it there." It was produced, and Cliff replaced it on the dog's neck. "Did he bring you to me?" Winslow inquired.

"Sparkler? Yes," said Cliff. "He seemed to know you were in trouble, and needed help."

"I was in trouble, fast enough!" said Winslow. "But still, I could have dispensed with the help. Now what do you propose to do?"

"Bring a doctor, if you need one," replied Quint.

"No doctor for me!"

"Then a policeman."

"Worse yet! Of the two, I prefer the doctor every time," said Winslow. "But this isn't a case for either. Boys, can't we go back into the barn there, and talk this little business over, in an amicable sort of way? You needn't try to hold him"—to Cliff, who was attaching his handkerchief to the dog's collar. "You've got him; and with the help of a slamming door and a wire clothes-line, you've got me. That's the mournful truth, my young friends. I am yours to command. All I ask is, be reasonable. Oh, yes! I can walk; thanks!" as Quint handed him his hat, which he picked up from the ground.

"Perhaps you can tell us where *our* hats are," Quint said. "And the other half of my pair of shoes? I found only one of them."

"I'll square the shoe account, and the hat account, and all the other accounts, to your entire satisfaction," Winslow replied; "only give me a chance."

"And how about the tumble you gave me in the woods?" Quint inquired.

"I've had a worse tumble! Such a jar, and a wrench, and a shaking-up generally, as I never had before, in all the ups and downs of my varied career," said Winslow, who had risen to his feet, and was clasping the tightly drawn wire that had come so near to cutting the said career tragically short. "I believe that you're about even with me, boys!"

"We mean to be quite even," said Quint, "before we get through with you."

XXIX

IN DEACON PAYSON'S BARN

THEY were walking back toward the barn, Winslow assisted by an arm Quint had passed through one of his; Cliff leading Sparkler by his handkerchief tied to the dog's collar.

The way was clear before them, surrounding objects being more distinct. The darkness that precedes the dawn was dissolving by such delicate degrees that the change from minute to minute was not noticeable; the east was brightening behind the orchard trees. Then, in the orchard's edge, as they passed, a robin piped suddenly his familiar note among the boughs overhead. Another answered near by; then a song-sparrow trilled ecstatically; other tuneful throats joined in; and soon the whole choir of field and orchard birds burst into song.

The boys were not so absorbed in the sordid business of the moment as not to feel the beauty and freshness and melody that ushered in the daily miracle of the dawn. All the doubts of the night-time passed away; their sense of the morning was one with the hope and joy that filled their hearts. The object of their journey was accomplished, or nearly so; and soon they would be on their triumphant homeward way.

When they reached the fence, Winslow got over into the yard, still carefully guarded by Quint. As Sparkler couldn't leap back while confined by the handkerchief, Cliff handed him over to his friend, then got over himself.

"The missing shoe, the first thing," said Quint, finding the other three where he and Cliff had left them.

"If you'll give the dog a chance, he'll find it," said Winslow. "He had the handling of that one. You needn't be afraid to let him go; he'll come back, while you have me."

"I won't risk it," Cliff replied. "He and you are up to too many tricks."

"To convince you of my good will— here, Sparkler!" said Winslow, directing the dog's attention to the shoe in Quint's hand. "Find!"

As the dog began to pull the handkerchief in the direction of the barn, Cliff followed him to the plank-way that sloped up to the rear door. Under its edge Sparkler thrust his nose and brought out the missing shoe.

"You wouldn't have found it without

his help and mine," said Winslow, eager to gain credit with his captors.

"No; and I shouldn't have lost it without his help and yours!" Quint replied dryly.

The boys didn't stop to put on their shoes, but made Winslow carry back into the barn the three which he had carried out of it, while Sparkler likewise did penance by transporting the other in his teeth.

"Now, here's a kind of string puzzle which you can amuse yourself by undoing," said Quint, "if you are feeling well enough."

"Oh, that!" replied the dog-seller, with a feeble attempt at jocoseness. "When I took the cord from Sparkler's collar I wanted to put it where it would do the most good, so I pieced it out and tied it to the ladder. It seems to have got into a tangle."

"Untangle it!" commanded Quint.

Obeying with cheerful docility, Winslow began loosening the knots from the fallen ladder. As soon as he had freed the end of the cord, Quint made a noose in it, which he immediately slipped over the dog-seller's wrist and drew tight.

"You are not going to do such an ungentlemanly thing as that!" Winslow remonstrated, taken unawares.

"If that's what you call ungentlemanly, you set the example," Quint replied. "A while ago I had iron on my wrists, thanks to you; and you are going to have hemp on yours, thanks to me."

"Before going any further," said the dog-seller, "allow me to make a proposition."

"We'll hear that by and by," said Quint. "Just now, please, help my chum about those other knots."

The broadening daylight, coming in through the wide-open door, shone upon a strange group, there in Deacon Payson's barn. Quint held the cord, one end of which was fast to his captive's wrist, while his captor undid the knots of his own tying which united the two cords. Then Cliff, on his knees, turned Sparkler's head toward the door, and held him while Winslow unbuckled the collar, slipped it through the small wire-wound loop, and buckled it again; both boys looking on, to see that the thing was honestly done.

"You see, young gentlemen," said the dog-seller, never once losing his assurance, or betraying any sense of his humiliation, "I am doing everything I can to oblige you, trusting you will reciprocate. Now, I sha'n't even wait for you to ask me where your hats are. I'm still pretty stiff, but if my cracked joints are equal to the effort, please give me a little freedom of the cord, and I'll restore the missing articles."

He took the ladder from the floor, and replacing it against the load of hay, put one hand on his back and the other on his neck and begged that he might be allowed to breathe a moment.

"I was deucedly shaken up by that lasso business!" he remarked with a dreary grimace.

"You are getting over it faster than I thought you would," said Quint. "Take your time. You must have been in the barn when we came into it."

"That's a natural and just conclusion"; and the dog-seller frankly explained how he had got in. "I overheard all your talk, and I was pleased with the ingenuity of your plans. If it hadn't been for the dog, I should have left you undisturbed, to waylay me in the shed. As it was, I thought you would appreciate the means I took to let you know who had been your roommate. Now a little rope, Brutus!"

So saying, he mounted the ladder, drawing after him the cord still attached to his wrist, Quint paying it out through his fingers, as he looked up, with a humorous smile, to observe the dog-seller proceeding on his extraordinary errand. Cliff too stood watching the movement; and Sparkler's soft, bright eyes were also upturned with an expression of intelligence almost human.

From the top of the ladder Winslow stepped upon the load of hay, Quint mounting a round or two at his request, to "give him more rope." Having picked up both hats, he descended the ladder, holding them by the rims.

"It has cost me a pang," he remarked; "for I feel as though every bone in my body had been run through a stone-crusher! But anything to oblige! The fact is, Brutus and Cassius, I am not the unconscionable scamp my conduct may have led you to suppose; and I am bound to do what I can to atone for the errors I have been betrayed into by the stress of circumstances. So allow me the pleasure—this is yours, I believe, Brutus. Cassius, with my compliments!" handing the hats with the airy politeness which not even the "lasso business" had jerked out of him.

As Quint put on his hat, he was reminded of the ugly bruise he had received in the tumble the man now in his power had given him. He gathered up the cord, and laid hold of his captor's unbound wrist. Winslow remonstrated.

"Have I done nothing to earn your confidence, but you still contemplate so—excuse me for saying it—so brutal a thing as that? I was just going to make my proposition."

"We'll hear your proposition," said Quint very coolly.

"Thanks, ever so much! And will you kindly allow me to recline against this ladder?" The dog-seller practically answered his own question by settling himself against the rungs. "My accident has left me as loose-jointed as a jumping-jack."

Quint suspected some crafty pretense in this. But he was willing his captive should play the jumping-jack as long as he himself held the string.

XXX

SETTLING WITH THE DOG-SELLER

"My proposition is to pay you the twenty dollars I agreed to pay, and to take back the dog," said the smiling Winslow.

"You had a fair chance to make that settlement," replied Quint. "Now it's too late. We are going to have our money, but you are not going to have the dog."

"We know whose dog it is," spoke up Cliff, sitting on a box and putting on his shoes.

The captive persisted in his smile, though it showed rather ghastly in the morning light, and asked with mock politeness:

"Will you have the kindness to inform me how you came by that interesting information?"

"You dropped it from your pocket when you reached for your knife to use on me," replied Quint.

"And I picked it up!" said Cliff, showing the engraved plate that had so evidently been removed from the dog's collar.

"You are giving it to me pretty straight, boys," the captive admitted, grinning at the piece of metal, while his free hand pressed his pocket.

"It's a good deal straighter than what you gave us about the burnt hotel and your sick mother in Michigan," Cliff said, returning the polished piece of nickel to his pocket.

"The burnt hotel was, I acknowledge, a myth," the captive answered. "But the sick mother, boys," he went on, with a change of tone; "she—well, I can't talk about her! Only—I'll tell you this. I've as good a mother as ever a bad son had!"

Quint, too, sat on the box preparing to put on his shoes.

"Then how happens it—?" he began.

"I know what you are about to ask," said Winslow, nursing with his free hand the cord-encircled wrist, and speaking in the deeper tone into which his feeling had surprised him. "How does any son of a good mother ever go wrong? I'll tell you what the trouble was in my case. I wanted to have the earth without paying for it. See?"

"No; I don't see," replied Cliff, with a growing interest which he was afraid might degenerate into pity. He was determined not to be guilty of that weakness.

"I'll explain. My mother was indulgent —too indulgent. But she was poor. It was all she could do to give me a fair education, but she did that. I think you'll allow that I have the language and breeding of a gentleman." And a smile of pride came back into the dog-seller's pale face.

"People's ideas of a gentleman differ," said Quint. "You've the 'gift of the gab' as folks hereabout call it; I won't dispute that."

"I suppose I deserve that sarcastic cut," said the captive, with a sad expression. "But it shuts off the gift, if I have it."

"Let him tell his story," Cliff interrupted, resolved beforehand not to believe half of it.

"Of course," Quint assented. "Though when he talks of the breeding of a gentleman after playing us such low-down tricks —but never mind!"

"Is your mother really sick?" Cliff inquired.

"Yes—sick with the bad-son affliction!" Winslow exclaimed. "And she'll have it worse than ever if she hears what I've been up to lately. The truth is just here, boys. I got into extravagant habits; I wanted more money than she could afford me; I wouldn't work for it, and the result was, I left home under what you may call a cloud. I have been a hotel clerk, and I have been many other things, but nothing very long at a time. I've been an actor—light comedy, and I've been in the show business—employed in Barnum's Circus, boys!" he added boastfully.

"I'll believe *that,*" said Cliff.

"That was my last situation, and I ought to have kept it," the captive continued; "but I was foolish. I got the idea that I was a bigger man than P. T. Barnum himself. Unfortunately, Barnum didn't see it in that light; and when I tried to run my end of the show in a way that didn't suit P. T., there was a little rumpus, and I found myself on the wrong side of the canvas. The trick-dog was one of my specialties, and it didn't require much of a trick to take him with me."

He looked down at Sparkler, who was looking up wistfully at him, wagging a sympathetic tail.

"Whatever you may think of *me,* boys, *he* is genuine all through! The best friend I ever had!" Winslow actually sniffed a little as he said this. "I had no thought of selling him when I started out. But necessity was the mother of that scheme. I had to raise money, and that was the way I raised it. I found it worked well, and I worked it for all it was worth. I could have made it more profitable but for one thing. Men who had money, and brains, too, and knew what such a dog was really worth, were—in short—suspicious. Then I couldn't sell him in the big towns without too much danger of losing him, so I played him off on the rustic population."

"My father knew he was stolen!" Cliff exclaimed.

"That's a mistake," the captive remonstrated. "I had the care of the dog, and when I left he left, too. I kept clear of the law in that."

"But not in selling him over and over again!" Quint averred sternly, seizing his unbound wrist.

"Now, see here!" said the captive. "If you march me to the police station and enter a complaint, what do you gain?"

"We're going to stop your little business of swindling the rustic population," Quint declared. "We'll gain so much!"

"Don't be too hard on me, boys," Winslow entreated. "I've made a clean breast of it." And he really seemed to think his confidences entitled him to their favorable consideration. "Put yourselves in my place. *You've* got good mothers, both of you, and one of *you* may be in a bad fix some time."

"He's trying the sentimental game," Quint said, with a frowning look at Cliff. "Are we going to be humbugged by him with our eyes open?"

"No," Cliff replied; "but I don't see the good of giving him over to the police. He can't sell the dog any more. And he'll give us back our money."

"Here it is waiting for you," Winslow exclaimed, producing his pocket-book with alacrity. "Here's your twenty dollars,"—putting a roll of bills into Cliff's hand. "And I promise to return the dog to Barnum's Circus just as soon as I can."

"We ought to have as much as this, after all our trouble," said Cliff, looking at the money. "But *you* are not going to return him to Barnum's Circus. I'm not going to give up Sparkler to you for one minute, am I, Quint?"

"That's judgmatical!" said Quint, with stern satisfaction. "If we want Barnum to have his property again, we should be fools to trust *him* to restore it."

XXXI

WINSLOW'S POCKET-KNIFE

Winslow besought them to stick to the bargain and give him the dog; then, finding they would not do this, he insisted upon Cliff's handing back to him ten dollars of the money.

"What do you think, Quint?" asked Cliff. "We are not robbers, though he tried to make you out one last evening. Our ten dollars we are bound to have, anyway; but we don't want any of the money he has swindled other people out of."

"No, sir!" exclaimed Quint; "but those other people want it, and we will see they have it, as far as the extra ten dollars will go. We'll begin with the old shoemaker and his wife. Won't they be glad? No, Cliff; don't give him back a dollar of it."

"You are right, as you are every time," said Cliff after a moment.

As Winslow strongly objected to this manner of settlement, Quint said: "What right have you to complain? You are getting off what you may call dog-cheap. I'm thinking we ought to hand you over to the police, after all, for the sake of those other people; and it's only the idea of our paying some of them that quiets my conscience in letting you off."

Winslow reflected a moment, then stooped from his seat on the ladder, and patted Sparkler affectionately.

"We part for good, Sparkler, this time! Boys," he said pathetically, "are you aware that I am not much more than a boy myself? I'm not twenty-two yet, and sha'n't be till next September."

"You look older than that," said Cliff.

"So will you at twenty-two, if you live the kind of life I've lived. 'Tisn't the right kind of life, boys, and I'm going to quit it. Live easy and pay to-morrow—the kind of to-morrow that never comes—that's been my style. That's what has brought me to this humiliation."

The captive didn't seem to take the humiliation very much to heart, however, for he added cheerfully:

"We part friends, I trust? And now I suppose I can dispense with this!" And he recommended loosening the cord that was about his wrist.

"Not yet!" cried Quint. "I want to see the knife you tried to draw on me last night. Your knife!" he thundered, as Winslow answered evasively. "We have had enough of delay and palaver!"

The captive brought out reluctantly what seemed to be an ordinary but rather long pocket-knife, with a single blade. As it did not open in the ordinary way, Quint examined the handle and found in it a suspicious-looking rivet, which he pressed with a surprising result. A slender dirk-shaped blade flew out like a flash in the morning light, and he held in his hand a deadly weapon.

"Jehu! that's dangerous!" Cliff ejaculated, with a horrified backward start. "Think what he would have done to you last night!"

Quint gave a cruel laugh, as he turned upon the owner of the knife. "That's the sort of lady-bird you are!" he said with grim irony.

"I declare to you I never used it, and never meant to!" said Winslow earnestly.

"And I declare you never shall!"

So saying Quint drove the blade into the partition behind him, and snapped it short off. The stub that was left he pressed into a crack, where it stuck.

"None of that!"—as the captive was again at work loosening the cord. At the same time Quint seized his other wrist.

"It serves him right!" said Cliff, shuddering at the thought of what his friend had escaped the night before.

Quint drew the bound wrist behind the ladder, and drew its fellow around the other way to meet it.

"No nonsense!" he cried, as his captive resisted. "If you prefer the police-station, all right! But do you think I'm going to leave you to follow on our track, and keep the dog in sight till you can contrive some plot for getting him back again? Stop that!" he roared out; "if you don't stop working your wrists we'll march you to the station instanter! You tied my partner to the ladder; now it's your turn."

"I hoped," said the prisoner, yielding because he must—"I hoped I had gained your confidence, and I expected more honorable treatment."

"It will take something besides your cheap talk to gain much confidence with us; and it's droll to hear *you* preach about honorable treatment! How's this, Cliff?"

Quint showed the prisoner's hands bound behind him, and lashed to the ladder in knots above the utmost reach of his fingers, wriggle how they might. Then taking a turn with the remainder of the cord about the captive's wrist and back again, he made another knot in it, and tied the end to the ladder in a cluster of knots, which Cliff regarded with satisfaction.

"I've heard of jugglers getting out of such tangles," he said; "but they didn't have John Quincy Adams Whistler to tie the knots!"

"If I had known what you really meant to do with me, you never would have got me into this shape!" muttered the prisoner.

"Think so?" said Quint, good-humoredly. "One of us was enough for you last night; and you have had us both to deal with this morning. Besides, you had been monkeying with a galvanized-wire clothes-line."

"For my part, I feel as if we had been almost too easy with him," said Cliff; "though we might have been easier still if it hadn't been for the knife. I never can forgive that!"

"But we are doing this chiefly in self-defense," said Quint, giving a final tug at his hard knots. "Now if he follows us very soon, it will be with the ladder on his back."

The captive continued to protest and entreat, but Quint only said: "My partner was very near being taken in by your humble confessions and fine promises; but they won't hurt anybody now, and they won't do you any good. Talk away, if it will amuse you; try to console yourself for our absence. I know it will be a sad thing for you to see the last of my gambrel-roof nose!"

He was fastening the rear door; this done, the two Biddicut boys, accompanied by Sparkler, went out by the great front door, which they closed after them, leaving Winslow lashed to the ladder in the lonesome barn.

XXXII

HOMEWARD BOUND

As they were passing near Deacon Payson's kitchen porch, they were delighted to see the deacon himself coming out of the door.

"Starting so early?" said the good man. "I'd been hearing voices, and I thought I'd come out and see how you had got through the night."

Then if ever there was an amazed old gentleman at four o'clock on a fine summer morning, it was the worthy deacon, standing beside his kitchen porch and listening to the story of the strange happenings in his barn and orchard.

"My wife said she heard the voices outdoors first, but she didn't wake me. That wire clothes-line must have been a savage thing to run afoul of. No wonder it floored him! And he's in the barn there now? I never heard anything so surprising!"

"We think he had better stay there an hour or so until we get a good start," said Cliff; "then do what you please with the fellow."

"We make you a present of him," said Quint; "only hoping he won't give you much trouble."

"I'll leave him till my man comes; then I suppose we'd better cut him loose. Though I'm inclined to think," said the deacon, "that he ought to be put in pickle for all his misdemeanors. Come into the house," he went on; "you can't start off this way with nothing to eat."

He made the boys go in, which they did very willingly, and talked over with them their homeward trip, while his wife set before them butter and bread and cold sliced ham, and glasses of milk, and golden honey dripping from the comb; Sparkler also receiving a share. Then they took leave of these kind people; listened for sounds in the barn as they went out, but heard none; and set off in the cool morning air, on the clean-washed country roads, with the light of the new-risen sun on their glad faces.

Winslow did not follow them, with or without the ladder on his back, and they never saw him again.

The boys were minded to make directly for the nearest way-station, on the railroad connecting with the Biddicut branch. But it was early for trains; and remembering their promise to Mr. Mills, they determined to take his house on their way, and report to him the success of their expedition. Perhaps they also wished to enjoy their triumph in the merry eyes of the two girls who had been so mischievously inclined to laugh at them.

They found a shorter course than the one by which they had hunted Winslow; and reached the farm-house just as the family were sitting down at table. They were heartily welcomed, treated to a second breakfast, which they accepted with frank good-will, and paid well for the hospitality in the entertainment the tale of their adventures afforded. There was open admiration as well as merriment in the bright eyes of the girls opposite them, as the boys took turns in the narrative, Cliff reciting the more dramatic portions in his impulsive way; and Quint setting off the whole with his droll commentary.

The meal over, Cliff would have had Sparkler perform some of his tricks. But the dog had also had a second breakfast; or his last parting with his late master had sobered him too much; or he resented the restraint of the cord, of which Cliff would on no account relieve him. Whatever the cause, he was in one of his sullen moods, and would do nothing.

Then Cliff took from his pocket five dollars of the money received from Winslow, and handed them to Mr. Mills for the old shoemaker, whom he knew, and whom he promised to see and reimburse for his loss within a few days.

"Now I have five dollars which I must manage to get to Mr. Miller of Wormwood," said Cliff. "Plenty more dog-purchasers may turn up, and there won't be money enough to go around; so first come, first served."

Having kept the boys as long as he could, the farmer offered to harness a horse and drive them over to a station on the connecting road. This offer they gratefully accepted, and the wagon was brought to the door.

Then adieus were said and smiles exchanged, the girls waved their handkerchiefs, and the boys their hats, the farmer touched up his nag, and our Biddicut adventurers felt that they were indeed on their way home.

They drove along the green-bordered country roads, where every wayside bush and tree glistened in the early sunshine.

"No stop now till we see Biddicut!" Cliff said exultantly; "only as we may have to wait for trains."

"I wouldn't stop now," observed Quint, "even to make a friendly call on Winslow working his passage in Deacon Payson's barn."

Yet it wasn't long before both boys called out simultaneously for a halt, as they were passing another barn, on their way through a small town.

It was a weather-worn structure, all of a dreary brown hue, except for one end, which was conspicuously and garishly red with enormous posters advertising the incomparable attractions of Barnum's combined circus and menagerie—"the Greatest Show on Earth." There were pictures of monkeys at their tricks; a big-muscled man grappling with a lion; a tiger pouncing upon a sleeping Arab; elephants playing at see-saw, or balancing themselves on rolling balls; and athletes in all sorts of startling and impossible positions, linked together, or leaping, or falling head-foremost through the air.

"They ought to have Sparkler here somewhere," said Cliff. But the boys searched in vain among the flaming marvels for a performing dog.

"Here's what we want to know!" exclaimed Quint, standing up in the wagon, in front of the red-gabled barn, and studying the dates and names of places advertised for appearances of "the Greatest Show on Earth."

XXXIII

BACK IN BIDDICUT

"HE's coming! Cliff's coming! And he's got the dog! He's bringing the dog!"

Trafton Chantry, who had been watching at the gate for his absent brother, shrieked out this welcome news at about nine o'clock that morning.

Susie took up the cry: "Cliff is coming! Cliff is coming with the dog!" She flew through the kitchen, calling, "Amos! he's come! Tell pa, quick! He's come with the dog!"

The mother hastened to the door, to behold with her own amazed and happy eyes the return of the wanderer, of whom no word had been received since Quint's father brought news of the two boys the day before.

"I declare," she exclaimed, "wonders will never cease! My son!—and he has got the prize!" For to her, also, the appearance of the dog led captive was the crowning triumph of her boy's return.

Trafton had rushed out again to meet his brother, and they came into the yard together, walking fast and talking fast, with Sparkler trotting demurely between them. Amos came running and shouting, and Mr. Chantry appeared, his amused face quirking between his fleecy sidewhiskers; and soon a jubilant group was gathered, of which Cliff was the central figure and flushed hero.

He stood holding Sparkler by the cord, and with gleeful excitement answering, or attempting to answer, the volleys of questions of which he was the target.

"Pa said he'd bet a thousand dollars you wouldn't bring home any dog," cried Amos, glorying in his brother's glory.

"I wish I could have taken that bet!" Cliff retorted, while the father stood parting his whiskers with both hands, and smiling again with good-humored sarcasm.

"I didn't think you would get him," he said; "and I didn't see much use in it, even if you should. 'T would take a good many dogs to pay for the anxiety your mother suffered sitting up for you last night."

"I thought of that," Cliff replied, "and I would have helped it, if I could!"

"That's nothing now," said his mother. "Your father was just as anxious as I was. But we both had faith that you and Quint would be able to take care of yourselves. Do sit down, Cliff! You must be tired. And we'll all try to keep still and let you tell your story."

"I'm not a bit tired," Cliff protested, sitting down, nevertheless; "and I don't know what to tell first. Only this I'll say, first and last and all the time: I owe everything to Quint. He's great! You never saw such a fellow! And now—!"

He couldn't help telling the most surprising part of his story at the beginning.

"If you want to know who is the real owner of the dog, see here!" He held something clasped in his hand, which he opened under his father's peering gray eyes. "See how it fits the place on the collar! And the fellow himself owned up that he stole him from the circus. He's Barnum's famous performing spaniel!"

Any disappointment Cliff may have felt in consequence of his father's seeming lack of enthusiasm was amply compensated by the exclamations of wonder with which the others regarded the engraved plate and heard his account of how he came by it.

"P. T. Barnum" was a famous name in those days, known in every household in the land. In the minds of all, it added immensely to the importance of the dog lolling at their feet, and to the fact of Cliff's possession of him, to know that he belonged to the great traveling circus and menagerie they had read about.

Nor was Mr. Chantry's enthusiasm as unmoved as it appeared. There was a glistening brightness in his eyes as he held the plate in his hand and glanced at it occasionally while Cliff told his story; and finally, when he heard how the boys had followed Winslow through hardships and discouragements, and captured him at last, he no longer attempted to disguise his satisfaction.

"I always knew Quint Whistler had good stuff in him," he remarked; "and I don't see that the other Biddicut boy's conduct was anything to be very much ashamed of. Yes, Cliff; I think you did right to take the twenty dollars. But I'm glad you intend to keep only the ten you had been tricked out of. I've heard of your Mr. Miller in Wormwood, and I'm pretty sure Quint's father knows him; we'll get his five dollars to him in some way. And now"—Mr. Chantry glanced at the engraved name again—"now about the real owner of this dog with too many owners."

The younger boys were on their knees, patting and hugging the object of so much solicitude and excited discussion.

"Can't we buy him of Barnum?" was Trafton's pathetic appeal.

"That isn't likely," said the father. "Such a dog as that is worth too much money. Barnum must be notified the first thing."

"I wouldn't give him up!" said Susie.

"Nor I!" "Nor I!" chimed in the younger boys, while Cliff looked thoughtfully down at the pet crouched lazily between his feet.

"It isn't a question of what you would or you wouldn't do," said the father; "it's a question of what is right. Stolen property belongs to the owner, no matter what innocent hands it has fallen into. You said you looked up the names of the places where his show is to be the next few days?"

"It's in Lowell to-day," Cliff replied. "Next Monday it is to be in Worcester, and the day after in Springfield. I tell you, it was a temptation for Quint and me to go as straight to Lowell as we could, and have the business settled before there was a chance for any more accidents. But we concluded to come home and tell the news and consult our folks."

"A wise conclusion," said Mr. Chantry, who commonly put so much pepper in his praises of his children that any commendation of his that was free from such ironic condiment gave them all the greater satisfaction. "I don't see but you have acted, all through, about as discreetly as two boys could. Now we'll consult Quint's folks, and decide what's best to do."

"That's my idea," said Cliff; "for of course he has just as much interest in the dog now as I have. He stopped to see his folks, but he promised to come by and by, and talk the matter over."

"To-day is Saturday," Mr. Chantry mused aloud. "I believe Mr. Barnum generally travels with his show, but he may be going home to Bridgeport to spend Sunday. I'll write to Bridgeport. If he isn't there, the letter will be forwarded. A little delay may be unavoidable, but it won't do any harm."

"It seems to me," said Mrs. Chantry, "it would be a good idea for Cliff himself to write the letter; why not?"

"That's so! To be sure!" said her husband.

"Oh, I can't write a letter to Mr. Barnum!" Cliff exclaimed, looking up with frightened eyes.

"Do the best you can," said his father.

"Make it as brief and businesslike as possible, without trying to tell anything more than is necessary. You never wrote a letter to a great man, and very likely you never will have another chance."

And Mr. Chantry went out, laughing and stroking his whiskers, leaving the boy to face the formidable difficulty of the letter.

XXXIV

CLIFF WRITES A LETTER AND RECEIVES A TELEGRAM

HOWEVER, his father's hint had set the boy's mind to working, and while putting Sparkler into the shed, and afterward when he was refreshing himself with soap and water and clean clothing, he thought out the substance of what he would write.

"If I just say in plain words that I've found the dog, and would like to know what to do with him, won't that be enough?" Cliff asked his mother, as he seated himself at the sitting-room secretary.

"Why, that's just what you want to say," replied his mother. "Write just as you would talk. Now, boys, don't bother him; keep away till he has his letter written."

Cliff, nevertheless, chewed his penhandle a good deal, and started two or three letters, before he found just the "plain words" he wanted, and put them together in this way:

DEAR SIR: Two days ago a man calling himself Algernon K. Winslow came to this town and sold me a dog for ten dollars. The dog is a small spaniel of mixed breed, and he has been trained to perform tricks. The dog got away the next morning, and another boy and I followed him through five towns, and caught him last night, and brought him home to our house this forenoon. We found the dog had been sold to several different persons, and he had got away from everybody. There was no name on the dog's collar, but we think we have proof that he belongs to you. I like the dog, and would be glad to keep him; but if he is yours, and you want him, please let me know what you wish to have done with him.

This letter he signed in formal fashion and showed to his mother.

"Why, Clifford!" she said. "I think it is a very creditable letter, and I'm sure your father will say so, too!"

"I had no idea of writing so much, but it all came in," said Cliff, well pleased with his composition, now that she had commended it. "But I want to correct and copy it before father has a chance to make fun of it. I've got too many *dogs* in it, for one thing; I want to take out five or six."

He had the letter corrected and neatly copied (for Cliff wrote a very good hand), with the word *dog* occurring in only two places, by the time his father came in.

"Did you do all that without help from anybody?" said Mr. Chantry—the very question Cliff knew he would ask.

"Of course," said Cliff, carelessly. "I found there wasn't much to say. If it isn't all right, I can try again." The evidence of his previous trials had disappeared in the kitchen fire.

His father gave a nod of decided approval.

"Well, Clifford! I don't mind telling you I couldn't have done better myself."

"Isn't there too much of it?" said Cliff, trying to conceal his gratification.

"I don't see that there is. You tell how you came by the dog, and it's right to say something of the trouble you had in hunting him, and to let Mr. Barnum know that

you would like to keep him. No!" said Mr. Chantry, emphatically; "I don't find anything in it to alter; and now we'll see to posting it in time for the noon mail."

"I think I'd better not seal it till Quint sees it," pursued Cliff, "since it's his affair as much as mine."

"You are right, my boy—right in every particular!" said his father, quite forgetting that jeering habit of his by which, without ever seriously intending it, he had embittered for his children so many occasions when a single kindly word would have made them happy.

Quint came in soon after, and, being shown the letter, remarked:

"That's judgmatical! I don't see how it could be better—unless I had written it myself."

The two boys went together to mail it in the village; which done, Cliff drew a long breath, exclaiming:

"Now to wait for an answer! We are pretty sure none will come to-day or to-morrow, but after that Sparkler may be sent for at any time. It makes me feel blue to think of it."

"You ought to show off his tricks once more," Quint suggested. "I'd like to have my folks see him. And why not ask in a few friends?"

"I'll do it! I'll do it this very evening!" Cliff exclaimed. "Come over early, and bring along as many as you like. I'll try to have him in good condition—only a little hungry, so he sha'n't go back on us."

The entertainment took place in the Chantry sitting-room, with doors closed, and only screened windows open, and it proved delightfully successful. Quint's father and mother and sister were present, and there were, besides, a few boys of the neighborhood (Dick Swan and Ike Ingalls among them), who regarded the invitations as precious favors.

Sparkler performed his tricks, some of

them over and over again, with a charming alertness that won all hearts, and made the children more than ever unwilling to part with him. During the rests between, and afterward, Cliff and Quint, in response to many questions, gave a most diverting account of their adventures, with many details which Cliff had omitted from his previous narrative.

To Mr. Chantry, who sat quietly rocking and stroking his whiskers, what was most gratifying in this part of the entertainment was the generous forwardness each boy showed in attributing the chief credit of their exploit to his companion. For of what value, after all, are victories won and prizes gained, unless the character be at the same time enriched?

Sunday was a day of delicious rest to both our Biddicut boys; and Monday, fortunately, found them ready to renew their adventure.

No letter came from Mr. Barnum, but early in the forenoon a messenger-boy from the village brought a yellowish-brown envelope, which he displayed as, with pretended ignorance, he inquired for Clifford Chantry.

"What is it?" cried Cliff, running to receive it.

"It's a telegram," replied the boy, holding it behind him. "Who is Mr. Clifford Chantry, anyway, and where can I find the gentleman?"

"No fooling, Bob Elden!" said Cliff, pouncing upon the messenger, capturing the envelope, and tearing it open.

It contained a telegraphic blank, dated at Bridgeport, and filled out thus:

Deliver dog to Barnum's Circus, at Worcester to-day, or at Springfield to-morrow. Reward and expenses will be paid.
P. T. Barnum.

Cliff was reading this message in a highly excited state of mind when Quint arrived, having immediately followed the messenger-boy, who, as he passed the Whistler premises, had yelled out the startling news that he carried a despatch for Cliff.

All the Chantry household quickly gathered to hear and to discuss the momentous intelligence, and Mr. Chantry observed:

"The dog should go to-day, for you'll have so much farther to take him to-morrow. Now, which of you boys will go? Or shall I go in your place?" he asked quizzically.

"We'll both go!" said Cliff and Quint, speaking together.

"That's just the answer I expected," Mr. Chantry replied, laughing humorously. "And it's my opinion the sooner you start the better, for I don't know about the railroad connections."

Quint hastened home to put on suitable clothes, and to be rejoined by Cliff on his way with Sparkler to the station. Cliff also prepared himself for a possible interview with the great showman, and led Sparkler out from the shed by the cord, from which he had ventured to remove the wire. All the family followed him to the gate, the parents to give him good advice, and the children to pat and hug for the last time the wonderful quadruped.

"Let me go and see him off! Can't I?" pleaded Trafton.

"Me too!" cried Amos.

The granting of the request made Susie wish she was a boy, that she might claim the same privilege.

The three Chantry boys were joined by Quint as they passed the Whistler house; and as they went on, other village boys ran out to swell the procession, the surprising report having spread that Cliff had received a despatch from the great Barnum, and that he and Quint were on their way to return the dog to the circus at Worcester—an event that made the envious youngsters wish Winslow would come along with more trick-dogs, of which they might become the purchasers.

The two partners, with their captive, did not have long to wait for the train, which relieved them of their too noisy and officious host of friends, and soon set them down at the Junction. There they had to wait for another train; and they had still one more change of cars to make, and then a ride which seemed interminable to their impatience, before they alighted at the station in Worcester.

XXXV

HOW THE BOYS WENT TO THE CIRCUS

MANY people were getting out of the cars, evidently bound for the same destination as the two boys from Biddicut. Some climbed into omnibuses and wagons in waiting; others set off rapidly on foot.

"Shall we walk?" said Cliff. "We've only to follow the crowd."

"Since our expenses are to be paid, I rather think we can afford to ride," replied Quint, as they approached a wagon bearing a placard inscribed:

CIRCUS GROUNDS—10 CENTS.

They had already discussed the question, whether the word in the despatch meant that expenses would be paid for as many as might come with the dog, and had decided that it couldn't be strictly so construed. But they felt that their business was important, and that a little lavishness of expenditure would therefore be justifiable. Cliff took Sparkler in his arms, and, climbing to a seat in the wagon, made him lie down between his knees; Quint took the only other vacant place; and they were soon passing the throngs of pedestrians in their rapid course to the circus grounds.

Cliff's bosom swelled mightily at sight of the great white tents, the swaying flags, and the converging crowds, with the blue dome of a perfect summer sky arching over all. He turned to see if Quint's face betrayed any unusual emotion, and Quint answered his look with a beaming smile.

They were out of the wagon almost as soon as it stopped, and found themselves in a stream of people before rows of small tents or booths containing side-shows, the venders of which were noisily advertised by hand-organs, drums, and shouting men.

Avoiding the stand of the ticket-sellers, the boys made directly to the main entrance of the circus tents. Two men were taking tickets from the throng passing between them. They hardly noticed anybody, and observed neither our Biddicut boys nor the dog until, as one held out his hand for Cliff's ticket, he received this extraordinary greeting:

"We've come to see Mr. Barnum—if he is here."

"He is here, or will be," replied the man. "You'll see him when he makes his speech. Your ticket!"

"We haven't any. I—"

"Don't come here without tickets!" exclaimed the ticket-taker sharply. "Stand aside and let the people pass!"

Cliff held his ground, with Quint close behind.

"I have this telegram from Mr. Barnum," he cried out, to the surprise of the entering spectators, and of the ticket-taker himself especially, "and we have brought the dog."

The man regarded Cliff more carefully, and cast his eye down at the poor little animal shrinking from the legs of the entering crowd.

"It's 'King Francis!'" he said to his fellow ticket-taker. "I never expected to see him again!"

He would have taken the telegram as if it had been a ticket; but Cliff kept tight hold of it, allowing him merely to glance at it.

"You should have gone to the private entrance. But all right! Dick," the man called to somebody within the tent, "here's King Francis back again! Go with that man," he said to Cliff, and went on with his ticket-taking, which had hardly been interrupted.

Cliff passed into the tent, but Quint was stopped in attempting to follow him.

"He's my partner!" Cliff called back, standing aside to let the crowd pass.

"He can't go in without a ticket," the man declared. "One of you is enough to go with the dog. Pass along! pass along!"

At the same time the attendant named Dick offered to take the cord from Cliff's hand; but Cliff exclaimed:

"The dog doesn't go without me, and I don't go without my partner! We are here on Mr. Barnum's business, and if we can't—"

"Go in! go in!" said the ticket-taker, nodding at Quint; and Quint, laughing at the effect of Cliff's defiant words, quickly rejoined him in the tent.

It was a sort of vestibule to the great wild-beast show and the greater amphitheater beyond. In it were a number of living curiosities, among which the boys noticed a very tame giant stalking about, and a human mite, placed, in effective contrast with him, on a low platform from which he shouted up at every spectator who passed: "How's the weather up where you are?"—his invariable salutation,—in a squeaking mite of a voice.

They passed in through a large circular tent redolent of wild beasts, with great iron-barred cages on either side, and a group of elephants chained, each by one foot, in the central space. There was the monarch of elephants, the mighty "Jumbo," rocking himself on his hips, and dusting himself with wisps of hay, which his huge, elastic, swinging trunk swept over his shoulders and back. Beyond were other trunks, like writhing and twisting anacondas, with open, upturned mouths, which they passed around like contribution-boxes, begging peanuts and bonbons of the spectators. In the cages were mischievous monkeys, restless hyenas walking to and fro, sleepy-looking lions, and beautiful pards and panthers, only glimpses of which could be had through the human groups pressing against the ropes, but which the boys promised themselves they would see more of before they left the show.

The attendant Dick looked down occasionally at the dog Cliff persisted in leading, and made a single remark as they passed the last of the cages:

"The old man will smile to see his pet back again!"—the "old man" being, as the boys understood, the great showman himself.

The next tent was vastly larger still; it was the "mammoth tent" of the circus performances, supported by tall masts, and hung, high overhead, with all the apparatus used by acrobats in their daring aërial feats. The benches, rising one above another from the ample ring, were rapidly filling with spectators; attendants were arranging spring-boards and laying mats for the tumblers; and the members of the band, wearing shining uniforms, and bearing shining instruments, some of prodigious size, were filing to their places. To the boys, who had never seen a great circus, there was in all this preparation an inspiring suggestiveness which filled them with wonder and joy.

Dick lifted the flap of a curtain, and

ushered them into a side-tent, where a troop of athletes in costume, and two or three fantastic clowns, were gossiping together, or walking about, as if waiting for their work to begin, now and then one stepping aside to turn a handspring or a backward somersault on the grass, in mere exuberance of spirits, hardly ceasing from his talk and laughter while whirling in the air.

Past this picturesque and interesting group Dick led the boys toward a part of the tent where a full-proportioned man in a black hat and a swallow-tailed coat, standing with his back toward them, was talking with two other men, one of whom had a ring-master's whip in his hand.

The large man was speaking earnestly, and did not look around until the ring-master, seeing the boys approaching with the dog and their guide, broke out jovially:

"Ho, ho! There's his Majesty, Mr. Barnum! King Francis has arrived!"

Thereupon the man in the swallow-tailed coat turned a full, genial face smilingly toward the boys, and snapped his thumb and finger at the dog. Sparkler had so far shown but little interest in anything he saw; but at this signal he darted forward the length of his leash, leaping up and manifesting the most joyous emotion under his real owner's caresses.

XXXVI

AN INTERVIEW WITH THE GREAT SHOWMAN

"You have got along earlier than I expected," Mr. Barnum then said, looking pleasantly at Cliff.

Cliff stood with his hat off, flushed and panting; but the showman's genial manner quickly relieved him of the embarrassment the boy felt on finding himself in his presence.

"I started as soon as I got your message," he replied. "This is my partner, Quincy Whistler. I never could have got the dog back if it hadn't been for him; so I thought we'd better both come and fetch him."

Quint also stood with his hat off, gravely smiling—a youth without blemish, except for the bruised spot on his left temple. Cliff noticed that the showman's comprehensive glance rested for a moment on that discoloration, and hastened to explain:

"He got that in a tussle with Winslow —the man who sold me the dog. He might have got worse, for Winslow tried to draw a knife on him."

"Winslow?" queried the showman.

"That's one of the names he goes by," said Cliff, "though I don't suppose it is his real name. I've brought the bill of sale he signed when he sold me the dog"— producing the paper from his pocket.

The showman glanced his eye over it with a smile that struggled with a frown.

"I know the handwriting," he said, "and I know the man. A scapegrace, if ever there was one! You are quite right; his name is not Winslow."

"He told us—not when he sold me the dog, but after we had followed him up and caught him—he told us," said Cliff, "that he had been connected with your show."

"He told you the truth, for once," replied the showman. "I know his family— respectable Bridgeport people; for their sakes I set the fellow on his feet, when he was down, and gave him employment. He is smart enough,—he could make himself useful if he chose,—and I engaged him at a fair salary. But it wasn't safe to trust him with money; so I made him sign an agreement that all but a small part of his earnings should be reserved for the payment of his debts,—chiefly debts to his own father, who has ruined himself by helping him out of scrapes. Yes,"—in answer to a question from Cliff,—"he has a good mother, a refined, intelligent woman. From his boyhood, he has given them no end of trouble."

"He told us he was hardly more than a boy even now,—not yet twenty-two," said Cliff.

"He is twenty-four years old," said the showman. "I'd like to retain this,"—taking the bill of sale and putting it into his pocket. "He might have kept his place in my show, but he became dissatisfied with the arrangement, and demanded his wages, cash in hand. Knowing he would squander every dollar I gave him, I refused—for his own good and his family's, as he knew very well. He was intolerably conceited; he imagined 'the Greatest Show on Earth' couldn't be run without his assistance. I promptly dispelled that illusion; he became impertinent and disappeared with the dog."

"He gave us that part of the story pretty straight," observed Quint.

The showman regarded him with friendly interest, remarking:

"He's a reckless fellow; but I should hardly have supposed he would attempt to draw a knife on you."

"I was a little too quick for him; but his intentions were good," said Quint, with a smile.

"Instead of getting out his knife, my partner tripped him so suddenly he pulled out this, and dropped it," said Cliff, exhibiting the name-plate. "I picked it up afterward, and that's the way I came to know who was the real owner of the dog."

"That certainly resembles my name!" laughed the showman. After a little further talk with the boys, mainly about the frequent selling of the dog, he asked: "Have you seen any of his tricks?"

"Winslow showed us some of them," replied Cliff, "and I made him perform them afterward."

"Did he show you this? Take hold of that end of the cord."

It was the cord which another attendant (Dick had disappeared) took from Sparkler's collar. Cliff held an end of it, the showman swung it by the other end, and at a word the dog, running in, began to jump the rope with surprising ease and gracefulness.

"I wish I had known he could do that!" Cliff exclaimed admiringly. "Wouldn't it have pleased our folks!"—turning to Quint, who smiled amused assent.

"Here's another very pretty performance."

The showman tossed aside the cord, and reached for a drum brought by the attendant. He requested Cliff to hold one side of it, while he held the other, facing him, and raising the drum about three feet from the ground. At a word Sparkler made a swift dash and leaped straight through it, bursting both drumheads, with a double explosion, and landing on the turf beyond. The drumheads, as the boys perceived, were of paper.

Mr. Barnum then asked the boys a few questions about their adventure, and laughed heartily at the amusing parts of it.

"Have you seen a notice of the reward offered? I am having it posted now with the show-bills, and I've had it sent to a few country papers."

"I haven't seen it," Cliff replied; "I don't know anything about any reward, except what you said in your telegram."

Mr. Barnum was opening a long, well-filled pocket-book.

"I offered a moderate sum—forty dollars. Then, there are your expenses. Of course I meant your expenses bringing the dog from Biddicut; but I think, with all the trouble you've had, I ought to allow ten dollars on the expense account. Then, there's the money you paid for the dog—ten dollars more. Besides, there are two of you, and I am glad to get King Francis back at any price. How's this? Satisfactory?"

And he put into Cliff's hand six ten-dollar bank-notes.

"Oh, Mr. Barnum!" Cliff exclaimed, completely overcome by such unexpected munificence. "Forty dollars is enough—more than we expected! You needn't say anything about the expenses. And I forgot—I meant to tell you—Winslow gave me back *that* ten dollars."

"So much the better!" said the showman, smiling in hearty enjoyment of the surprise and pleasure he was able to afford two such honest-minded youths. "It is thirty dollars apiece. I think you have earned it; and if you are the sort of boys I take you for, a little nest-egg like that isn't going to do you any harm."

"It's a small fortune to us!" said Cliff, with glistening eyes. "Here, Quint! you must take charge of your share,"—dividing the money on the spot. "I am afraid to have so much money about me!"

"Well, thanks! and good fortune to you!" said the showman, holding out both hands to the boys.

"Oh! *we* thank *you,* Mr. Barnum!" replied Cliff. "I suppose I must say good-by to Sparkler, too; that's the only thing I am sorry for now. Sparkler isn't his name?" he said, looking up, as he gave the dog a parting caress.

"King Francis is the only name we know him by." Mr. Barnum then said: "Did you ever see my show?"

"Never; but we have always wanted to," said Cliff, with shining eyes.

The attendant who had carried away the drum now returned with two packages looking like books in wrappers. Mr. Barnum said, as he took them:

"Show these young men to the best reserved seats there are left." Then, presenting a package to each of the boys: "This is the story of my life. I hope you will find it instructive, and that your interest in it will not be lessened by the fact that you have seen and talked with the writer."

Cliff was stammering his thanks, when Quint in a low voice said something in his ear which the showman overheard.

"Write my autograph in the books? Certainly, if you wish it. Go to your places now, and I will send them around to you before the show is over."

The proud parade of the Roman hippodrome, with its horses and chariots and solemn elephants, glorious banners glittering and trumpets braying, was making its stately circuit of the triple-winged arena when the boys reëntered the great tent. Then, as they mounted to the places to which the attendant guided them, with opulence in their pockets and exultation in their hearts, the sonorous, brazen measures of the band burst forth, rivaling in sound the majestic movement and gorgeous colors of the pompous procession of the performers.

"Isn't this grand?" said Cliff, his face beaming as with the light of victory.

"It's judgmatical!" replied Quint, with a high and haughty smile.

WEEDS IN MY LANE

By Lucius A. Bigelow (age 8)

(GOLD BADGE)

I LIKE to live in nature's glory. I love
the sunny silence of my lane, where
everything grows with all its might.
Why do people call weeds common?
They are frequent, but very wonderful,
and I have spent my happiest summer days
among them. First, I find yellow dandelions peeping from the green grass. Because they are the first to appear, they seem
dearest, for in winter only the faithful fir-
trees bear us company. The dandelions
have long, narrow petals, and French boys
call them *dent de lion*. They soon pass into
little balls of down, which scatter in the
breeze. They sow early; therefore they are
thrifty. Next arrive a multitude of buttercups. They also have a French name—
bouton d'or. They are happy, and nod to
each other in the wind. Soon I gather
white and buff daisies. Sometimes I make
a nosegay of several hundreds. I hunt for
clover, not with my eyes, but with my
nose and also my ears; for where I find
fragrant clover, there hums the big bee,
looking for a honey breakfast, and never
disappointed. Butter-and-egg grows in my
lane, but I do not approve the name. I
have christened it "orange-and-lemon,"
after its cousin fruit. Have you ever noticed
how gracefully this blossom sits in its
calyx chair? The silver yarrow and the

gold tansy grow abundantly. I love the
strong smell of tansy, because it means
midsummer, when everything splendid is
in sight. Burdock has a cool, shady leaf,
a pretty pink blossom, and little burs,
which I use to make baskets for amusement. There are many other weeds in my
lane. They are my intimate friends. I have
noticed that yellow is the color often
chosen by weeds—I suppose because yellow
is so cheerful.

The nature studies in ST. NICHOLAS explain reasons. They interest me. I think
about them a great deal. Last comes the
tall goldenrod. It closes in my lane on each
side, waving good-by; for with its arrival
summer makes preparation to leave us.

THE LOST POCKET-BOOK

By Margaret E. Scott (age 13)

(HONOR MEMBER)

THE great ocean liner was just steaming out of the dock, and last fare-
wells were being waved, when suddenly a wail of despair came from an elderly lady on the deck. "Oh, I've gone and
lost my pocket-book! What shall I do!
What shall I do?"

"Tell the captain," suggested a sympathetic passenger. "Maybe he can help you."

She rushed into the cabin and grasped
the captain's hand. "Oh, captain!" she
cried, "my pocket-book is gone! I must
have dropped it on the pier. It was imi-

tation black seal, with a strap across the back. Can't you stop the boat?"

"Madam," said the captain soothingly, "I can't do that, but I'll send a wireless back to port, asking if such a purse has been found. If it has, I'll have a tug sent after us with it."

"Oh, thank you, thank you!" said the old lady.

The captain hurried out and soon returned, beaming though breathless. "It's been found, Madam," he panted, "and the tug has started!"

Ten minutes later the tug came chugging to the side of the vessel. A man climbed over the rail and handed the pocket-book to the lady.

"Well, I *am* thankful," sighed she, "and so relieved."

"Was all your money in it?" asked the sympathetic passenger.

"No money was in it," said the old lady calmly, "I keep all that in my bag. But I value the purse so much! I bought it at a bargain-sale, when I was shopping with cousin Mehitabel. Now she's gone out west to live, and I may never see her again. The purse was so cheap, too. Only thirty-nine cents! I should have hated to lose it!"

The captain rubbed the perspiration off his forehead, and stood for some minutes gazing steadily out to sea.

"A Study from Life," by Frances Leone Robinson, age 12. (*Gold badge*)

TELL-TALE TONGUES

By Janet Denton (age 9)
(HONOR MEMBER. MERIT ENTRY)

ANIMALS cannot talk, yet their tongues can tell tales. If we will study the members of the animal kingdom, we will find that their tongues tell many tales—tales of how they live, and what they live on.

Our friend, Mr. Frog, has a long, slender tongue, with a little knob at the end, much like a pop-gun cork tied to a string. When a bug or fly alights near Mr. Frog's long, sticky tongue, it darts out like a streak of lightning, and the poor fly has been swallowed before he knows what has happened to him.

The humming-bird has an interesting tongue. It is long and slender, and it is hollow like a soda-water straw. The humming-bird poises over a flower, pushes his long tongue down the flower's throat, and sips the nectar that he finds there. The whole thing is as simple as drinking a chocolate soda through a straw.

The woodpecker has a cruel sort of tongue. It is long and needle-like, and it has pointed barbs on its tip, just as a fish-hook has. After boring into the tree and finding the worm he has been seeking, he darts his needle-like tongue into the hole and spears the worm on its barbs. Then he draws the worm out and eats it.

The ant-eater has an unusual tongue. It is slender and flexible, and is eight or nine inches long. The ant-eater plows up an ant hill with his nose, and then, as the startled ants dash about, he sweeps his long tongue back and forth over the ground, and gathers in the ants by the hundreds.

All the members of the cat family have tongues with a very rough surface. Let your cat lick your hand, and you will find that her tongue is as rough as sandpaper. This sort of tongue helps the cat in her method of drinking, lapping up the milk with her tongue. Her rough tongue also helps her in cleaning the meat of the bones that are given her.

Her larger cousins, the lion and the tiger, have tongues much rougher than hers. If a lion or a tiger should lick your hand, he would scrape the skin right off. Tame lions and tigers have sometimes turned savage by scraping the skin off their trainer's hands, and getting their first taste of human blood.

The prize tongue of all belongs to the whale, who has an enormous flabby tongue which weighs from one to two tons. Mr. Whale cannot stick out his tongue, because it is so securely attached that he cannot extend it.

When we study the way in which the whale feeds, we can understand why he needs such a tongue. The arctic waters in which he lives are swarming with millions of tiny sea animals. As the whale swims along, he scoops in a mouthful of water, and strains it out through the thick fringe of whalebone which hangs from the roof of his mouth, and this catches his food. It is his great tongue which enables him to force the water through this sieve.

"A Heading for May," by *D. M. Shaw, age 14.* (*Gold badge*)

WAVES

By Isadore Douglas (age 17)

(HONOR MEMBER)

From somewhere out of the woods by the
 lane
  An idle wind wanders and touches the
  wheat;
And where was but now a field of grain,
  A shimmering sea ripples out at my feet,
Whose waves go eddying up the hill,
  Stray over the field—now here, now
  there,
Then quicken, swayed by the mad wind's
 will,
  Race on to the fence where two fields
  meet,
To break in a swirling of daisy-heads
  And the tossing spray of bittersweet.

BE BRAVE, MY SOUL

By Robert Friend (age 17)

(HONOR MEMBER. CASH AWARD)

Be brave, my soul, though flesh be weak;
Be brave before the truths you seek.
 Though aching to the heart you find
 The truth compatible to mind,
Be faithful to the mind and speak.
I know the heart gives to the meek
The consolation that they seek
 When truth is hard to bear defined.
      Be brave, my soul.
But I have climbed the barren peak
Of truth and found the prospect bleak—
 And oh, how easy to be blind
 And to one's heart be false—but kind;
Yet say I like the stoic Greek:
      Be brave, my soul.

"A Heading for August," by Florence Mason, age 13. (Silver badge)

SPINACIA OLERACEA

By Sturges D. Dorrance, Jr. (age 14)

(HONOR MEMBER. CASH AWARD)

The family was in turmoil;
 Racked in civil strife.
The father stamped and tore his hair
 And shouted to his wife.

"See here, see here," he roared aloud,
 "Is there nothing which
Will make our little Benny eat
 His nice, fresh green spinach?"
His wife, she frowned a dreadful frown,
 And shed a salty tear.
Up little Benny piped at last,
 With voice so shrill and clear:
"Oh! Father, would you have me eat,

Assimilate, osmose
A plant, which like the spinach
  (As every wise man knows),
Is formed of protoplasm
  With chlorophyllous grains
In upper epidermis,
  And deliquescent veins
Which carbohydrates circulate
  And chromosome connects
With photosynthetic bast
  And plumuled green cortex?
The vasculary bundles
  With turgescence swell away
While hydrotropic elements
  Cross every small pith ray.
And Father, dear, remember,
  The lenticel's small slit,
And that the lowly spinach
  Has other things than grit."

The father's angry cries are stilled;
  Son's cruel words will harry
Till he doth find a solace
  In Cent'ry dictionary.

"What I Love Best." By William
H. Savin, age 15. (Honor member.)

SNOWY DAY

By Elizabeth Lehman (age 17)

(HONOR MEMBER)

Morning—

When snow first falls, the pines possess
  A new coquettish sort of grace—
Born of the trust of womankind
  In powder and bit of lace.

Afternoon—

Now they have lost the first delight.
  They seem a little sad and old;
Each clutching close a ragged shawl,
  Seeming to shiver with the cold.

Evening—

Like ladies at the opera
  How elegant and debonair!
Each tree in spotless ermine cloak,
  A star tiara in her hair.

A MIDSUMMER SONG

By Elizabeth H. Parsons (age 12)

The sun shines through the wind-swept,
  straggling clouds
That wander far across the summer sky;
O'er hills and valleys, over plains and seas,
The clouds will always wander, on and on.
Like ships that sail across an endless sea
To meet the golden sunsets of the West,
The clouds go onward, ever farther on,
As if in search of something that is lost.

SUMMER FAIRIES

By Lewis S. Combes
(age 8)

(GOLD BADGE)

Airy little fairies
   Dancing in the sun;
Playing all the daytime,
   Having lots of fun.

Hungry little fairies,
   Eating honey sweet
Hidden in the blossoms,
   Think it is a treat.

Thirsty little fairies,
   Sipping drops of dew
Sparkling on the roses
   And the grasses too.

Tired little fairies,
   Resting all the night;
Sleeping in the flowers,
   Cuddled up so tight.

A SONG OF THE WOODS

By Nellie Adams (age 13)

(SILVER BADGE)

Oh what so gay, on a summer day,
   When sultry and hot the hours,
As a forest scene, with its pine-trees green,
   And carpet of fairy flowers?
When the zephyrs sigh in the tree limbs
   high,
   And temper the sullen heat;
With the leaves aloft, and the mosses soft
   Spread smoothly for elfin feet?

Oh what so rare as the forest fair
   When autumn brings frosty cold;
The pine-trees green, with a bush between
   Aflame with crimson and gold?

But a winter night, when the snow is
   white,
   Is lovelier yet, by far;
When every flake the snow-clouds make
   Is a dazzling, diamond star.

But, oh! and it's spring when the glad
   hearts sing,
   And the shy white violets peep;
When the herald's mouth calls the birds
   from the South,
   And the wood-mice from their sleep.
And the wood folk sing, "From the fall 'til
   spring,
   And from spring again to fall,
You may seek and roam, but the pine-trees'
   home
   Is the loveliest spot of all."

IN VACATION

By Myra Bradwell Helmer
(age 11)

I'm tired of the world and its pleasures,
And gold coming in by the measures.
Give me something new, something else
   to do;
Give to me the sweet, still country town,
Where every one is met by a smile, not a
   frown;
Give to me the simple country church, with
   people dressed in modest style,
Not the city church, where oft they dress to
   show off in the aisle.
Let me be awakened by the crowing of the
   cock
Instead of the tones of a much-used silver
   clock;
Let me hear the little calves and the little
   lambs say "Baa!"
For this will do me much more good than
   a trip to Panama.

Oh, take the hothouse city flowers away
from my sight,
And give to me the country ones that have
God's rain and light;
Give to me the hearty farmer, with his
merry, laughing jokes,
And the rickety old wagon with hardly any
spokes;
I'd rather have that than the dude with the
automobile,
With perfumed handkerchief, stupid head,
and military heel.
My ears are full and ringing
Of the songs the birds are singing;

And my only sorrow is,
And a very sad one 'tis,
That the farmer will not let me pile up his
golden hay,
Like the lads and lassies round here, chant-
ing all a merry lay.
Oh, what fun to catch the russet apples as
they fall!
But one must haste away to the farmer's
wife's dinner-call.
Give to me the boiled dinner, with bread
and preserves.
If I stay here so very long I shall soon
regain my nerves.

"A Heading for November," by Anna Zucker, age 16. (Silver badge)

SPRING

By Elizabeth Connolly (age 9)

(SILVER BADGE)

Little snowdrop, lift your head
From the brown earth's wintry bed;
Blue-eyed violet, come up, too,
Blue-eyed violet, shy and true.
Spring has come to call you all.
Hark! I hear the bluebird's call!

THE DAY AFTER THANKSGIVING
By Aileen Hyland
(age 12)

"Our community's diminished," said the
turkey with a sigh.
"Indeed it is," the duck replied, tears stand-
ing in his eye.
"Alas, I am a widow!" cried poor young
Mrs. Hen,
"And so am I," sobbed Mrs. Goose, "My
husband's left the pen."

So they set up such a wailing that the
    farmer was quite scared.
And his knees knocked on each other, for
    he thought they had not cared.
But the day had been Thanksgiving and
    the poultry had been caught,
And the farmer's wife had cooked them,
    and to the table brought.

So within himself he whispered, "I will
    take my things and go.
For one never kept an awful farm like this
    I'm sure you know."
Then he got up, and he scuttled, and he's
    not been heard of since.
And the feathered folk now rule there, and
    the turkey cock is prince.

AN OFFERING

By Lucius A. Bigelow (age 8)

(A WINNER OF SILVER AND GOLD BADGES)

To St. Nicholas—this valentine:
A spray of spruce, with a branch of pine.

When the leaves fall, the doors into Tree-land open wide. I can hear the cheerful thud, thud of the dropping nuts and cones as I enter in.

There is brightness everywhere, for summer has gathered up her garments of green and glided away, leaving space for winter's sun-gift. I like to look at the shapes of trees; they make me think of strength. In cold weather I can feel color more than in summer days. The blue is brighter and the evergreen seems darker, and there are not so many other things to occupy my mind.

The brown mat that arranges itself underneath the pines is composed of fine needles.

Hemlock glistens in a breeze. Everything that nature uncovers has silver or gold somewhere, if we carefully look. The story of Socrates makes the name hemlock solemn; but there is silver under that sadness also.

I love the pine-tree. Its breath makes everything around seem perfectly clean. The spruce is not so loving in fragrance. Often I shut my eyes; then I hear music. It comes from the tree-tops as the wind sweeps along.

Arbutus is the only flower that forces its way up through the needles to the companionship of the pine. On cold winter days, sitting by the open fire, I like to talk of these happy things.

Pines persevere. They are our steadfast friends. They do not go away to the south, or hide in the earth, but remain brave and glad the whole winter through; nor in the summer do they leave us.

THE EBBING TIDE

(REFLECTIONS OF A SIX-YEAR-OLD)

By Betty Humphreys (age 14)

(HONOR MEMBER)

I love to stand upon the shore
    When lower grows the tide,
And watch the many things it leaves
    Upon the beach's side.

It always leaves a starfish
    Half buried in the sand,
And pretty shells, and sea-weed,
    Are thrown upon the land.

And once I found a funny thing—
    An "urchin of the sea";
I thought it was a chestnut-bur—
    It looked like that to me.

My mother thinks I'm careless
    When I neglect my pets;
What would she say at all the things
    The ebbing tide forgets?

GALATEA, AN ENGLISH SONNET

By Judith F. Mar (age 14)

(GOLD BADGE)

PYGMALION before his statue knelt.
He prayed high Aphrodite that his love,
By right of its own heat and aid divine,
    might melt
Cold marble. He sacrificed a dove
To please the goddess and propitiate
His cause. She heard and granted his desire
For Galatea as his living mate.
Through all her marble veins ran living
    fire.
Pygmalion cried out, "She lives!" but she
Stared straight ahead, was silent and stirred
    not.
In one brief flash she saw life's agony,
The pain that all too soon would be her lot.
For this her marble peace, that was so dear,
Was lost. In either eye there shone a tear.

"The Object Before Me," by Laura Gardin, age 14. (Silver badge)

CHARADE

My *first,* an unknown quantity,
Yet represents my *second;*
If from it *third* should take my *fourth,*
But two could then be reckoned.

My *fourth* and *second* numbers are,
My *first* and *third* are letters;
To *whole* themselves before the law
Is often tried by debtors.

A. W. CLARK.

WORD-SQUARE

1. A violent gust of wind. 2. A weapon of war. 3. To join or attach. 4. Odor. 5. Passages of Scripture.
EDNA MASON CHAPMAN (League Member).

CONCEALED DIAGONAL

(Silver Badge,
St. Nicholas League Competition.)

ONE word is concealed in each sentence. When these have been rightly guessed and written one below another, the diagonal (beginning with the upper left-hand letter and ending with the lower right-hand letter) will spell something that comes in November.

1. The messenger she sent ran certainly very fast, but failed to reach here in time.
2. Should you slip, persons of all ranks would run to assist you.
3. Peleg, ancestor of Abraham, died at a very great age indeed.
4. Have you ever seen pitch in great quantities? I saw a barrel of it which had been buried by thieves.
5. The troops in action fought bravely, but were soon defeated.
6. In Paris I announced the coming of the great general to a large crowd.
7. She did not throw the bag over, nor did she push it through the fence.
8. That the recently captured fox is much tamer I can plainly see.

L. ARNOLD POST.

TWO ZIGZAGS

I. 1. A grain. 2. A gentle bird. 3. A large stone. 4. Soon. 5. A bag. 6. Solitary. 7. Part of a teapot. 8. A chill.
From 1 to 2, a harvest poem.
II. 1. A blemish. 2. A pain. 3. A Biblical name. 4. A small particle. 5. An outer garment. 6. A den. 7. A story. 8. To peel.
From 3 to 4, the author of the harvest poem.
KATHARINE H. WEAD (League Member).

580

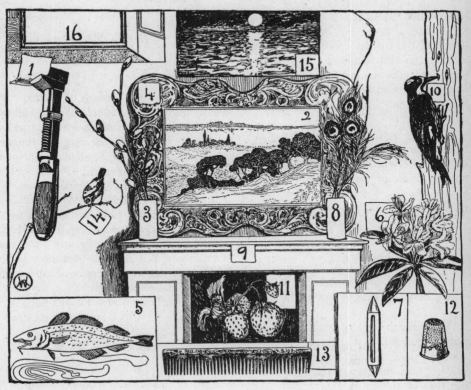

This differs from the ordinary numerical enigma in that the words forming it are pictured instead of described. When the sixteen objects have been rightly guessed, and the letters set down in the order given, the hundred and twenty-one letters will form a quotation appropriate to the season, from one of our best-loved poets.

Picture No. 1: 5-11-61-67-44-39-103-19-17-76-43-63.

No. 2: 91-83-57-96-33-10-66-24-9.

No. 3: 24-36-74-7-34-110-25-107-82-20-59-93.

No. 4: 88-119-75-31-6.

No. 5: 10-102-117-48-46-84-8.

No. 6: 26-45-50-73-30-87-54-95-92-115-120-76-21.

No. 7: 47-1-36-51-112-82-99.

No. 8: 18-2-94-40-98-86-41-23.

No. 9: 12-42-104-85-108-13-55-89-80-3-32.

No. 10: 121-60-35-69-55-116-3-67-80-101.

No. 11: 52-22-115-38-70-118-90-26-101-111-6-56.

No. 12: 97-79-89-5-100-82-68.

No. 13: 29-71-31-81.

No. 14: 15-49-12-78-27-62.

No. 15: 37-72-58-95-109-16-106-65-114.

No. 16: 53-113-119-64-14-105-4-91-77.

No. 28: is served at five o'clock.

A. R. W. and F. H. W.

ENDLESS CHAIN

(Gold Badge,
St. Nicholas League Competition.)

ALL of the words described contain the same number of letters. To form the second word take the last two letters of the first word, to form the third word take the last two letters of the second word, and so on.

1. A juicy fruit. 2. Mild. 3. Extent of anything from end to end. 4. To beat soundly. 5. To shake with cold. 6. A valuable fur. 7. The drink of the gods. 8. A fleet of armed ships. 9. A girl. 10. To pass away. 11. To look for. 12. To alter.

MARGARET ABBOTT.

ZIGZAG

(Silver Badge,
St. Nicholas League Competition.)

WHEN the following words have been rightly guessed, and written one below another, take the first letter of the first word, the second letter of the second word, the first of the third, the second of the fourth, and so on. These letters will spell a familiar word.

CROSS-WORDS: 1. An inn. 2. To flourish. 3. A season. 4. Yearly. 5. To light. 6. Mien. 7. The sound made by a turkey. 8. A ring. 9. A modest flower. 10. To separate. 11. Heed. 12. Terrified.

MARJORIE HOLMES.

MATHEMATICAL PUZZLE

(Gold Badge,
St. Nicholas League Competition.)

ADD together: one fourth of four, one, five hundred, five hundred, fifty, one third of ten, one seventh of billion, zero, and ten,

and you will find the sum in the ST. NICHOLAS Magazine.

SAMUEL WOHLGEMUTH.

DIAGONAL

(Gold Badge,
St. Nicholas League Competition.)

ALL the words described contain the same number of letters. When rightly guessed and written one below another in the order here given, the diagonal (beginning with the upper left-hand letter and ending with the lower right-hand letter) will spell a December festival.

CROSS-WORDS: 1. An assembly. 2. Tending to promote health. 3. A beautiful blue mineral. 4. Withdraws definitely from a high office. 5. Additional. 6. To find out for a certainty. 7. A plum-like fruit, very harsh and astringent until it has been exposed to frost. 8. The principal church in a diocese. 9. A full collection of implements.

MARJORIE HOLMES.

TRIPLE CROSS-WORD ENIGMA

(Gold Badge,
St. Nicholas League Competition.)

MY *firsts* are in butcher, but not in kill;
My *seconds,* in note, but not in bill;
My *thirds* are in gallon, but not in quart;
My *fourths* are in long, but not in short;
My *fifths* are in rain, and also in hail;
My *sixths* are in thunder, but not in gale;
My *sevenths,* in almond, but not in nut;
My *wholes,* three countries of Europe.

DAISY JAMES.

NUMERICAL ENIGMA

(Silver Badge,
St. Nicholas League Competition.)

I AM composed of eighty-one letters, and I form a quotation from one of Scott's poems.

My 76-61-54-73-47-19-21-58 is an old name for Christmas. My 59-42-30-69-77 are juicy fruits. My 72-66-67-15-80-10-31-60-57 is an ancient heathen emblem used at Christmas. My 24-44-9-12-81-71 are songs of joy. My 52-70-40-23-3-22-50 is a beverage formerly much used in England at Christmas. My 7-79-65-34-16 is merriment. My 5-14-35-20 is an ancient Norse deity. My 37-26-6-36-2-75 is the coldest season of the year. My 56-17-43-28 is part of a ship. My 25-13-4-33 is expectancy. My 64-49-32-68 is the handle of a sword. My 18-46-27-55 is to determine. My 11 is a point of the compass. My 29-8-41-1 mean a couple. My 63-74-53-45-78 is the summit. My 48-38-39-62-51 is to swing in a circle. ETHEL PAINE.

CONNECTED DIAMONDS

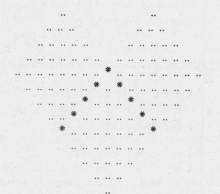

THESE diamonds are only to be read *across*. The long middle word, however, may be read either across or up and down.

I. UPPER LEFT-HAND DIAMOND: 1. In strong. 2. A cooking utensil. 3. A poet. 4. To associate with. 5. A flower named for a beautiful youth who became enamoured of his own image. 6. A vegetable. 7. A bowl. 8. The whole amount. 9. In strong.

II. UPPER RIGHT-HAND DIAMOND: 1. In strong. 2. A weapon of war. 3. A musical instrument. 4. A masculine name. 5. A large, showy flower. 6. A feminine name. 7. Birds of prey. 8. A large body of water. 9. In strong.

III. LOWER DIAMOND: 1. In strong. 2. To stuff. 3. The next after the eighth. 4. Pastures. 5. A small shore game-bird. 6. A fruit. 7. A scholar. 8. To perceive. 9. In strong.

DAISY JAMES (League Member).

CHARADE

MY first proclaims the peep of day;
  My *second*'s filled with sweetness;
My *second* smooths life's tangled snarls
  And aids the maiden's neatness.
My *whole* adorns my pompous *first;*
  My *whole* in pride is basking;
My *whole* believes that every maid
  Would wed him for the asking.

AUGUSTA L. HANCHETT.

CONCEALED PRIMAL ACROSTIC

One word is concealed in each sentence. When these have been rightly guessed and written one below another, the initials will spell the name of a famous cardinal.

1. If you fear a certain animal, avoid it.
2. He slid each time he passed the slippery path.
3. Tragic as the ending was, it made no great impression.
4. Hannah and I will join you soon.
5. Henry says the moon will disappear late to-night.
6. The animal ate all the food I offered.
7. I risked my life in climbing the steep cliff.
8. Grace picked a large bouquet this afternoon.
9. The house, repainted, looked as good as new.

MADGE OAKLEY (League Member).

SWORD PUZZLE

```
          . .
        .   . .
  1 * * * * * * * * * * * * * * * * 2
    . . . . . . . . . . . . .
    .       .       .
    . . . . .
    .       .           .
```

READING DOWNWARD: 1. A feminine name. 2. A book for autographs. 3. An organ of the body. 4. In addition. 5. A waterfall. 6. To endure. 7. A poem. 8. A swamp. 9. Skill. 10. An article. 11. Useful in a small boat. 12. A feminine name. 13. To lubricate. 14. Entire. 15. Consumed. 16. A measure of weight. 17. In cardinal.

From 1 to 2, a famous man who perished by the sword.   ANGUS M. BERRY.

ZIGZAG

(Silver Badge,
St. Nicholas League Competition.)

ALL the words described contain the same number of letters. When these have been rightly guessed and written one below another, the zigzag (beginning with the upper left-hand letter and ending with the lower left-hand letter) will spell the first and last names of a President of the United States.

CROSS-WORDS: 1. To tell over again. 2. Good sense. 3. Posture. 4. A cap worn in bed to protect the head. 5. A brief statement of facts concerning the health of some distinguished personage. 6. An absolute sovereign. 7. To establish the identity of. 8. One of the United States. 9. A severe snow-storm. 10. Faint-hearted. 11. Aloft. 12. The universe. 13. A pointed instrument of the dagger kind fitted on the muzzle of a rifle. 14. A formal method of performing acts of civility. 15. Approbation.

JEAN C. FREEMAN.

DIAGONAL

ALL of the words described contain the same number of letters. When rightly guessed and written one below another, the diagonal, beginning with the upper left-hand letter and ending with the lower right-hand letter, will spell the name of a famous musician.

CROSS-WORDS: 1. Method. 2. An engine of war. 3. A nose. 4. To conduct. 5. Showy clothes. 6. A sudden alarm.

RICHARD BLUCHER (age 9).

BEHEADINGS

1. DOUBLY behead to chide sharply, and leave aged. 2. Doubly behead high estimation, and leave a conjunction. 3. Doubly behead a kind of small type, and leave devoured. 4. Doubly behead the Mohammedan Bible, and leave raced. 5. Doubly behead passages out of a place, and leave a possessive pronoun. 6. Doubly behead a fish, and leave a place of refuge. 7. Doubly behead value, and leave a form of water. 8. Doubly behead the after-song, and leave a lyric poem. 9. Doubly behead to dress, and leave a line of light. 10. Doubly behead an inhabitant of Rome, and leave a human being. 11. Doubly behead a masculine name, and leave to conquer.

The initial letters of the words before beheading will spell the name of a very famous personage.

SAMUEL P. HALDENSTEIN
(League Member)

CONCEALED CENTRAL ACROSTIC

WE hold the merry Christmas cheer
And greetings of the glad new year.

CROSS-WORDS

(One word is concealed in each sentence.)

1. Minerva pinned, with perfect taste,
   A chestnut bur upon her waist.

2. A band of coral one inch wide
Adorned her hat-brim's under-side.
3. And, as she walked, she swung with grace
A parasol around her face.
4. Across the lawn she swiftly moved,
But high-heeled boots her downfall proved.
5. For when the bordering walk she jumped,

She hurt her pride—her nose was bumped.
6. She tried to run because it rained,
And found her foot was badly sprained.
7. She simply said: "I jumped too soon;
One should not jump in May or June.
8. I've hurt my instep some—it feels
As if I needed higher heels."

ANNA M. PRATT.

ANSWERS TO RIDDLE BOX PUZZLES

CHARADE. Extenuate (x-ten-u-8).

WORD-SQUARE. 1. Blast. 2. Lance. 3. Annex. 4. Scent. 5. Texas.

CONCEALED DIAGONAL. Election. CROSS-WORDS: 1. Entrance. 2. Slippers. 3. Elegance. 4. Pitching. 5. Inaction. 6. Parisian. 7. Governor. 8. American.

TWO ZIGZAGS. I. 1. Corn. 2. Dove. 3. Rock. 4. Anon. 5. Sack. 6. Lone. 7. Nose. 8. Ague. From 1 to 2, Corn-song. II. 1. Flaw. 2. Ache. 3. Levi. 4. Mite. 5. Coat. 6. Lair. 7. Tale. 8. Pare. From 3 to 4, Whittier.

ILLUSTRATED NUMERICAL ENIGMA.
He comes! He comes! The Frost Spirit comes!
You may trace his footsteps now
On the naked woods and the blasted fields
And the brown hill's withered brow.

J. G. WHITTIER.

ENDLESS CHAIN. 1. Orange. 2. Gentle. 3. Length. 4. Thrash. 5. Shiver. 6. Ermine. 7. Nectar. 8. Armada. 9. Damsel. 10. Elapse. 11. Search. 12. Change.

ZIGZAG. Thanksgiving. Cross-words: 1. Tavern. 2. Thrive. 3. Autumn. 4. Annual. 5. Kindle. 6. Aspect. 7. Gobble. 8. Circle. 9. Violet. 10. Divide. 11. Notice. 12. Aghast.

MATHEMATICAL PUZZLE. R-I-D-D-L-E B-O-X.

DIAGONAL. Christmas. Cross-words: 1. Concourse. 2. Wholesome. 3. Turquoise. 4. Abdicates. 5. Accessory. 6. Ascertain. 7. Persimmon. 8. Cathedral. 9. Apparatus.

TRIPLE CROSS-WORD ENIGMA. England, Holland, Belgium.

NUMERICAL ENIGMA.

Heap on more wood! The wind is chill,
But let it whistle as it will,
We'll keep our Christmas merry still.
"Marmion," Introduction to Canto VI.

CONNECTED DIAMONDS. I. 1. N. 2. Pan. 3. Byron. 4. Consort. 5. Narcissus. 6. Parsnip. 7. Basin. 8. Sum. 9. S. II. 1. S. 2. Gun. 3. Banjo. 4. Wilfred. 5. Sunflower. 6. Dorothy. 7. Hawks. 8. Sea. 9. R. III. 1. S. 2. Pad. 3. Ninth. 4. Meadows. 5. Sandpiper. 6. Apricot. 7. Pupil. 8. See. 9. R.—CHARADE. Coxcomb.

CONCEALED PRIMAL ACROSTIC. Richelieu. 1. Race. 2. Idea. 3. Cast. 4. Hand. 5. Earl. 6. Late. 7. Iris. 8. Epic. 9. User.

SWORD PUZZLE. From 1 to 2, Alexander Hamilton. Downward: 1. Frances. 2. Album. 3. Heart. 4. Extra. 5. Cataract. 6.

Stand. 7. Ode. 8. Fen. 9. Art. 10. The. 11. Oar. 12. Amy. 13. Oil. 14. All. 15. Ate. 16. Ton. 17. N.

Zigzag. Rutherford Hayes. Cross-words: 1. Rehearse. 2. Judgment. 3. Attitude. 4. Nightcap. 5. Bulletin. 6. Autocrat. 7. Identify. 8. Colorado. 9. Blizzard. 10. Cowardly. 11. Overhead. 12. Creation. 13. Bayonets. 14. Ceremony. 15. Sanction.

Diagonal. Mozart. Cross-words: 1. Man-ner. 2. Mortar. 3. Nozzle. 4. Manage. 5. Finery. 6. Fright.

Beheadings. Shakespeare. 1. Sc-old. 2. Ho-nor. 3. Ag-ate. 4. Ko-ran. 5. Ex-its. 6. Sh-ark. 7. Pr-ice. 8. Ep-ode. 9. Ar-ray. 10. Ro-man. 11. Ed-win.

Concealed Central Acrostic. Holidays. Cross-words: 1. Aches. 2. Alone. 3. Solar. 4. Thigh. 5. Order. 6. Train. 7. Mayor. 8. Epsom.